David Grossman was born in 1954 in Jerusalem, where he now lives with his family. He has written two novels, a collection of short stories and three children's books, and has won seven awards including the 1985 Israel Publishers Association's Prize for the best novel in Hebrew. His most recent book was *The Yellow Wind*, also available in Picador.

DAVID GROSSMAN

See Under:
LOVE

Translated from the Hebrew
by Betsy Rosenberg

published by Pan Books
in association with Jonathan Cape

First published in Great Britain 1990 by Jonathan Cape Ltd
This Picador edition published 1991 by Pan Books Ltd,
Cavaye Place, London SW10 9PG
in association with Jonathan Cape

9 8 7 6 5 4 3 2 1

© David Grossman 1989

English translation © Betsy Rosenberg 1989
from the Hebrew *'Ayen 'erekh: ahavah*

ISBN 0 330 31669 9

Printed in England by Clays Ltd, St Ives plc

Contents

MOMIK

IT WAS LIKE THIS, a few months after Grandma Henny was buried in her grave, Momik got a new grandfather. This grandfather arrived in the Hebrew month of Shebat in the year 5317 of the Creation, which is 1959 by the other calendar, not through the special radio program *Greetings from New Immigrants* which Momik had to listen to every day at lunch between 1:20 and 1:30, keeping his ears open in case they called out one of the names on the list Papa wrote down for him on a piece of paper; no, Grandfather arrived in a blue Mogen David ambulance that pulled up in front of Bella Marcus's café–grocery store in the middle of a rainstorm, and this big fat man, dark but like us, not a shvartzer, stepped out and asked Bella if she knew anyone around here called Neuman, and Bella got scared and wiped her hands on her apron and said, Yes, yes, did something happen, God forbid? And the man said, Don't get excited, lady, nothing happened, what can happen. No, I bring them a relative, see, and he thumbed backward over his shoulder at the ambulance in the street which seemed empty and quiet, and Bella suddenly turned as white as this wall and everybody knows she isn't scared of anything, but she wouldn't go anywhere near the ambulance, she only edged closer to Momik, who was doing Bible homework at one of the little tables, and said, "Vay iz mir," a relative now? And the man said, "Nu, lady we don't got all day, so if you know these people maybe you can tell me where they are, because is nobody home." He talked broken Hebrew like that even though he didn't look so much like a newcomer, and Bella said to him, Sure, what did you expect, sure nobody's home, because these people are not parasites, these people work plenty hard for their bread, morning to night they're working in the lottery booth two streets down, and this little boy here, he's theirs, so just you wait a minute, mister, I'm going to run get them. And she ran out with her apron still on and then the man winked at Momik, and when Momik didn't do anything because he knows how you're supposed to behave around strangers, the man shrugged his shoulders and started reading the newspaper Bella left there and he said to the air, Even with this rain we're having, seems like it's going to be a drought year, yeah, that's all we need. And Momik who is usually well-mannered didn't hang around for more but ran outside to the ambulance and climbed up on the back step, wiped the rain from the little round window, and peered inside where the oldest man in the world was swimming like maybe a fish in an aquarium. He wore blue-striped pajamas and was all wrinkled like Grandma before she died. His skin was yellowish-brown, like a turtle's, sagging down around his skinny neck and arms, his head was bald, and his eyes were blank and blue. He was swimming hard through the ambulance air, and Momik remembered the sad Swiss farmer from Aunt Idka and Uncle Shimmik in the little glass ball with the snowflakes which he had accidentally broken once, and he opened the door without a second thought, but then he jumped back when he heard the old man talking to himself in a weird voice that went up and down excitedly, and then sounded almost like crying, as if he were in some play or telling a tall tale, but at the same time, and this is what's so hard to understand, Momik was one thousand percent sure that this old man was Anshel, Grandma Henny's little brother, Mama's uncle, the one everybody said Momik looked like, especially around the chin and forehead and nose, the one who wrote children's stories for magazines in Europe, but didn't Anshel die by the Nazis, may-their-name-be-blotted-out, and this one is alive all right and Momik hoped his parents would agree to keep him in the house because after Grandma Henny died Mama said that all she wanted now was to live out her life in peace, and suddenly there was Mama with Bella hobbling after her on ailing legs, lucky break for Marilyn Monroe, and she yelled at Mama in Yiddish to calm down, you shouldn't upset the child, and behind them trudged the great giant his papa, panting and red in the face, and Momik thought it really must be serious for both of them to leave the booth together. Anyway, the ambulance driver calmly folded the newspaper and asked if they were the Neumans, the family from the late Henny Wasserman, rest her soul, and Mama said, Yes she was my mother, what happened? and the fat driver smiled a big fat smile and said, Nothing happened, why are always people expecting something happened; no we came to deliver just the grand-father to you, a mazel tov. And they all went around to the back of the ambulance and the driver opened the door and climbed in and lifted the old man lightly in his arms and Mama cried, Oy, no, it can't be, it's Anshel, and first she sort of swayed and Bella ran to the café and brought a chair back just in time and the driver said, There, there, we didn't bring to you bad news, God forbid, and after setting the old man down on his feet he gave him a friendly slap on the back which was bony and crooked and he said, Nu, Mr. Wasserman, so here's the mishpocheh, and to Mama and Papa he said, Ten years he's been with us at the insane house in Bat Yam, and you never know what he's talking to himself like now, maybe praying or who knows, and he doesn't hear what you say like a deaf man nebuch, so here's the mish-pocheh! he screamed in Grandfather's ear to prove to everyone that he really was deaf, ach, like a stone, who knows what they did to him there, may-their-name-be-blotted-out! and nu, we don't even know which camp he was by or what, there came out people in a worse condition, you should see, no, better you shouldn't see, but now one month ago he all of a sudden opens his mouth and says the names of people, like Mrs. Henny Mintz, and our boss, he made like a detective and so he found out that those names he says are the names of people dead, may-they-rest-in-peace, and the list shows Mrs. Mintz here in this house, but she's dead too now, may-she-rest-in-peace, so you are the only family left, and it doesn't look like Mr. Wasserman will be getting any healthier and he can eat by himself already and, you should pardon the expression, make his duty by himself, and this country nebuch isn't so rich, and the doctors say in his condition he can be looked after in the home, family is family right? So here are his clothes and his papers and things and his prescriptions too for medicines that he takes, he's a sweet old man, and quiet too, except for the noises and all the moving around, but not too bad, nothing serious, everybody likes him, they call him the Malevsky family, because he all the time sings, that's a joke, see, now say hello to the children! he shouted in the old man's ear. Ach nothing, like a stone, here, Mr. Neuman, you sign here and here that

I bring him to you, maybe you got an ID or something with you? No? Never mind, I believe you anyway. Nu, shoin, well, a mazel tov, this is a happy day like a new baby coming to you, oh sure, you get used to him, so now we better be heading back to Bat Yam, plenty of work waiting there, so goodbye, Mr. Wasserman, don't forget us! And he smiled cheerfully in the old man's face, though Grandfather didn't seem to notice, and got into the ambulance and drove away, fast.

Bella ran to fetch Mama a piece of lemon to give her some strength. Papa stood still and stared at the rain running into the empty gully where the city was supposed to have planted a pine tree. The rain trickled down Mama's face as she sat on the chair with her eyes shut. She was so short her feet didn't touch the ground. Momik took the old man by his bony hand and gently led him under the awning of Bella's grocery store. Momik and the old man were about the same height because the old man was all hunched over and had a little hump at the back of his neck. And then all of a sudden Momik noticed there was a number on the new grandfather's arm, like Papa's and Aunt Idka's and Bella's, although Momik could see right away it was a different kind of number and he tried to memorize it but Bella came back with the lemon meanwhile and started rubbing Mama's temples with it and the air smelled good but Momik kept waiting because he knew Mama wouldn't wake up so soon.

And who should come walking down the street just then but Max and Moritz, whose real names were Ginzburg and Zeidman, though nobody remembers that anymore except for Momik who remembers everything. They were inseparable, those two. They lived together in the storeroom at Building Number 12, where they kept the rags and all the junk they collected. Once when city inspectors came to kick them out of the storeroom, Bella screamed so loud they beat it out of there. Max and Moritz never talked to anyone outside of each other. Ginzburg who was filthy and smelly always walked around saying, Who am I who am I, but that's because he lost his memories on account of those Nazis, may-their-name-be-blotted-out, and the small one, Zeidman, just smiled at everyone all the time and they said he was empty inside. They never went anywhere without each other, Ginzburg the dark one leading, Zeidman behind him carrying the old black briefcase you could smell a mile away, grinning at the air. Whenever Mama used to see them coming she would mutter, Oif alle poste palder, oif alle viste valder, a calamity in the empty fields and the empty woods, and of course she told Momik never to go anywhere near the two of them, but he knew they were all right, because Bella didn't let the city inspectors kick them out of the storeroom, although she did call them funny names like Mupim and Chupim and Pat and Patashon, who were these cartoon characters back where they all came from.

So it was pretty weird how this time the two of them walked slowly by and didn't seem to be afraid of anyone and they stepped right up to Grandfather and looked him over and as Momik watched Grandfather he noticed his nose twitching as though he could smell them, which doesn't mean a whole lot since Ginzburg you could smell even without a nose, but this was something else because all of a sudden Grandfather stopped singing his tune and stared at the two dodos, which is another name Mama called them, and Momik saw the three of them stiffening as if they all had the same feeling, and then the new grandfather suddenly swerved around like he was angry he'd wasted his time which he had no business wasting and he sang that stupid tune again as if he couldn't see anything and paddled through the air like he was swimming or talking to someone who wasn't there, and Max and Moritz stared at him, and the small one, Zeidman, started making noises and moving around the way Grandfather does, he's always copying people, and Ginzburg growled and started to walk away, with Zeidman following in his trail. And you also always see them together on the stamps Momik draws for the royal kingdom.

So anyway, meanwhile Mama stood up white as this wall, all weak and wobbly and Bella braced her and said, Lean on me, Gisella, and Mama wouldn't even look at the new grandfather and she said to Bella, This will kill me, mark my words, why doesn't God just leave us in peace and let us live a little, and Bella said, Tfu, tfu, Gisella, what are you saying, this is not a cat, this is a live human being, you shouldn't talk that way, and Mama said, It's not enough I'm an orphan, not enough we had so much suffering from my mother, now this, now everything all over again, look at him, look how he looks, he's coming here to die, that's what, and Bella said, Sha sha, and held her hand and they huddled together next to Grandfather but Mama wouldn't look at him and then Papa coughed, Nu, why are you standing there, and he bravely put his hand on the old man's shoulder and looked at Momik with a shy expression and led the old man away, and Momik, who already knew he would call the old man Grandfather even though he wasn't his real grandfather, told himself that if the old man didn't die when Papa touched him, that must mean a person from Over There is safe from harm.

The same day, Momik went to search in the cellar. He'd always been afraid to go down to the cellar because of the dark and the dirt, but this time he had to. There, together with the big brass beds and the mattresses with straw sticking out and the bundles of clothes and the piles of shoes was Grandma Henny's kifat, a kind of box you tie up, with all the clothes and stuff she brought from Over There and this book called a *Teitsh Chumash* and also the *Tzena u-Rena*, and the bread board Grandma Henny used there for making pastry dough and three bags full of goose feathers she had dragged halfway around the world in boats and trains braving terrible dangers just so she could make herself a feather quilt in Eretz Yisrael to keep her feet warm, but when she arrived it turned out that Aunt Idka and Uncle Shimmik, who got here first and quickly made a lot of money, had already bought a double feather quilt, so the feathers stayed in the cellar where pretty soon they caught mildew and other cholerias, but you don't throw out a thing like that around here. So anyway, the point is that at the bottom of the kifat was a notebook with Grandma's Yiddish notes, all her memories like from the days when she still had a memory, but then Momik remembered that a long time ago before he could even read, before he'd turned into an alter kopf, which means the head of a smart old man, Grandma showed him a page from an old, old magazine, and in it was a story by Grandma Henny's brother, this Anshel, written one hundred years ago, but Mama got mad at Grandma for upsetting the boy with things that are no more and shouldn't be mentioned, and sure enough the magazine page was still in the notebook but when Momik picked it up it started to crumble, so he carried it between the pages of the notebook with a fluttering heart and sat down on the kifat to tie it back up with the ropes but he was too light so he left it open because he wanted to get out fast but suddenly he had an idea that was so strange he just stood still and forgot what he wanted to do next, but his thingy knew and he made it out just in time to piss under the stairwell, which is what always happens to him when he goes down to the cellar.

So anyway, he sneaked the notebook into the house without anyone noticing, and ran to his room and opened it and saw that the page had crumbled a little more on the way and the top corner was torn off. The page was yellow and cracked like the earth after a long time without rain and Momik knew right away he'd have to copy what it said on another piece of paper, otherwise, kaput. He found his spy notebook under the mattress and, wild with excitement, he wrote out the story on the torn page, word for word.

THE CHILDREN OF THE HEART *Rescue the Red Sk*
A story in fifty chapters by the popular auth
Anshel Wasserman-Scheheraz
Chapter the Twenty-seventh

O Constant Reader! In our previous episode, we saw the Children of the Heart swiftly borne upon the wings of the "Leap in Time" machine: destination—the lesser luminary called the moon. This machine was the product of the craft and intelligence of the wise Sergei, whose mastery of technics and the currents of electricality in the case of the magnificent machine we did so fully elucidate in our foregoing chapter, whither we refer our Constant Reader for the sundry particulars effaced from memory. And so, aboard the machine, arm in arm with the Children of the Order, were Red Men of the Navajo tribe and their proud king, who rejoiced in the name: Red Slipper (mayhap our Amiable Reader knows of the Red Skin's predilection for suchlike names fantastical, though we may smile to hear them!). And together they fled the truculence of the martial men who would drive them from the land of their fathers, chief among these the sanguineous native of the country of England, John Lee Stewart. Thus they betook themselves to the moon for shelter and succor in their distress, in the hope likewise of turning a new leaf in the copybook of their wretched lives. Lo! The wondrous machine traverses the stars, and breaches the rings of Saturn, streaked with gossamer, swift as light! And on they venture while the amiable Otto Brig, first and foremost among the Children of the Heart, to soothe the spirits of the Red Skins (so lately delivered from the hands of their enemies, and whisked aloft in the chariot of fire) rehearsed for them the glorious deeds of the Children of the Heart, anent our Faithful Reader is informed to the last letter and with which we shall not tire him at this time. And Otto's young sister, blithe Paula of the golden hair, prepared a repast for the company to refresh their troubled minds and flagging spirits. And Albert Fried, the silent boy, was just then sitting privily at the helm, nobly pondering whether humankind should ever set foot upon the moon, since as the Amiable Reader knows so well, Albert Fried was conversant with every sort of creature, from lice eggs to horned buffaloes, and likewise the language of each, as was King Solomon of yore, and he hastened to find his small copybook in which to record the scientific facts he would observe in short order, for our friend Albert Fried is a lover of order, and it well behooves the younger readers amongst us to follow his example in this and other matters. And as he was writing, the dulcet murmur of a flute fell upon his ears, and this so astonished him that he rose to his feet and approached the hall of passage. In the doorway he stood, bewildered by the sight which met his eyes: for there stood Harotian, the small Armenian fellow, a wizard skilled in every work of wonder and of sorcery, piping for the company, whilst the melody he played so nimbly upon his flute becalmed the anxious hearts of the Red Skins and allayed their fears. The piping was balm to them, and small wonder: for little Harotian himself had long ago been rescued by the Children of the Heart when the Turks of Turkestan plundered a village in the hills of Armenia, and Harotian alone was spared, as fully recounted in the adventuresome tale entitled "The Children of the Heart Rescue the People of Armenia," and the young Harotian was touched to the heart by the sadness of these voyagers. And meanwhile, as Sergei was standing watch on deck, a heavy cloud descended, for he grasped in his hand the horn of vision that magnifies two-hundred-fold, and screamed: "Woe is he who faces such calamity! Flee! To the moon!" And they beheld it, and were filled with horror. Otto their leader looked through the horn of vision, and his heart stopped, his face turned ashen, while Paula clasped his hand, screaming: "For God's sake, Otto, what is it that you saw?" But Otto's tongue was pinched and doughlike, and no reply could he make, though his face bore testimony to the evil which had befallen them all, and horror, perhaps Death, lurked at the window.

Continued in next week's issue of
LITTLE LIGHTS***

This was the story Momik found in the magazine, and as soon as he started copying it down in his spy notebook he knew it was the most exciting story ever written, and the paper smelled about a thousand years old and seemed to come out of a Bible with all those biblical-looking words Momik knew he would never understand no matter how

many thousands of times he read the page over, because to get the
meaning of a story like this you need a commentary by Rashi or somebody because people don't talk that way anymore except maybe Grandfather Anshel, though even without understanding every word in it you
could tell this story was the origin of every book and work of literature
ever written, and the books that came later were merely imitations of
this page Momik had been lucky enough to find like a hidden treasure,
and he felt that once he knew this he would know just about everything,
and then he wouldn't have to go to school anymore, so right away he
started to memorize it because brains he's got, bless him, and it only
took him a week to learn it all by heart, and he would recite while
getting ready for bed: "Harotian, the small Armenian fellow, a wizard
skilled in every work of wonder and of sorcery, piping for the company,"
etc., or on his way to school the next morning, till he got so caught
up in the story he couldn't stop wondering what that awful thing they
saw on the moon through the horn of vision was, and sometimes he
would try to guess how the story ended, though he knew a real Bible
ending was something only Grandfather Anshel could invent, but
Grandfather Anshel hadn't.

Mama and Papa decided Grandfather should have the small room
Grandma Henny used to live in, but he wasn't anything like Grandma
Henny. He couldn't sit still for one minute and even in his sleep he
twitched and gabbled and flapped his arms around. Whenever they
locked him in the house he would cry and make such a scene they had
to let him out. In the morning after Mama and Papa left for the lottery
booth and Momik had gone off to school, Grandfather Anshel would
walk up and down the street till he was tired and then he would go sit
on the green bench outside Bella's grocery-café and talk to himself.
Grandfather stayed with Momik and his parents for a total of five
months before he disappeared. The first week of his stay, Momik started
drawing pictures of him on the imperial stamps, with the legend "Anshel
Wasserman: Hebrew Writer Who Perished in the Holocaust." Bella
brought a weak glass of tea out for Grandfather. She reminded him
gently, "Mendarf pishen, Mr. Wasserman," and led him to her toilet
like a child. Bella is a real angel from heaven. Her husband, Hezkel
Marcus, died a very long time ago and left her all alone with Joshua,
a difficult child and a bit meshuggeneh, and with these ten fingers here
Bella made an army officer out of him and a college graduate too.

Besides Joshua, Hezkel left her his own father, old Mr. Aaron Marcus—zal er zein gezunt und shtark, may he be healthy and strong—who was sick and weak and feebleminded and hardly ever left his bed anymore, and Bella, whom Hezkel used to treat like a real queen—and he wouldn't even let her move a glass from here to here—did not sit around the house with her feet up all day long after Hezkel died but went to work in the little grocery store so as not to lose the regular customers at least, and she even expanded and brought in three more tables and a soda fountain and an espresso machine, and Bella was on her feet from dawn till dusk spitting blood, only her pillow knows how many tears she cried, but Joshua never went hungry, and nobody ever died of hard work.

Bella's café served breakfast specials and home-cooked meals for people of taste. Momik remembered the words "people of taste" because he was the one who wrote the menus three times (for Bella's three tables), and decorated them with drawings of people looking all fat and smily after eating such a good meal at Bella's. And she served home-baked cookies too, fresher than Bella, as she would tell anyone who asked her, though not too many people asked these days, because hardly anyone ever came in besides the Moroccan construction workers from the new housing developments at Beit Mazmil who showed up around ten in the morning for a quart of milk, a loaf of bread, and a cup of yogurt, or the few neighborhood customers and then of course Momik. Only Momik didn't pay. The other regulars stopped shopping there when the new modern supermarket opened at the shopping center where they gave a free set of cork coasters for buying thirty pounds worth of groceries, as if people always had a glass of tea on a coaster with the princess, and now they rush over like maybe they're going to find gold there instead of smoked fish and radishes, and also because everyone gets to push a solid-steel shopping cart around, says Bella, not really angry, and whenever she mentions the supermarket, Momik blushes and looks the other way, because he goes there too sometimes to see the lights and all the stuff they sell and the cash registers that ring, and how they kill the carp in the fish tank, but she doesn't mind so much about her regular customers leaving (says Bella), or that rich she'll never be, tell me, does Rockefeller eat two dinners, does Rothschild sleep on two beds, no, what bothers her most is the tedium, the boredom, and if things go on like this much longer she'll go out and scrub floors rather than sit around here all day, because to Hollywood she won't be going, not this year, because of her legs maybe, so Marilyn Monroe can relax with that new Jewish husband of hers. Bella sits at one of the empty tables all day long reading *Woman's Own*, and *Evening News*, smoking one Savyon cigarette after another. Bella isn't afraid of anything, and she always says exactly what she thinks, which is why when the city inspectors came to throw Max and Moritz out of the storeroom, she gave them such a piece of her mind they had a conscience for the rest of their lives, and she wasn't even afraid of Ben-Gurion and called him "The Little Dictator from Plonsk," but she didn't always talk that way, because don't forget that like all the grownups Momik knew Bella came from Over There, a place you weren't supposed to talk about too much, only think about in your heart and sigh with a drawn-out krechtz, oyyyy, the way they always do, but Bella is different from the others somehow and Momik heard some really important things from her about it, and even though she wasn't supposed to reveal any secrets, she did drop hints about her parents' home Over There, and it was from her that Momik first heard about the Nazi Beast.

The truth is, in the beginning Momik thought Bella meant some imaginary monster or a huge dinosaur that once lived in the world which everyone was afraid of now. But he didn't dare ask anyone who or what. And then when the new grandfather showed up and Momik's mama and papa screamed and suffered at night worse than ever, and things were getting impossible, Momik decided to ask Bella again, and Bella snapped back that there are some things, thank God, a nine-year-old boy doesn't have to know yet, and she undid his collar button with a frown, saying it choked her just to see him buttoned up like that, but Momik decided to persist this time and he asked her straight out what kind of animal is the Nazi Beast (since he knew there weren't any imaginary animals in the world and surely no dinosaurs either), and Bella took a long puff on her cigarette and stubbed it out in the ashtray and gave a krechtz, and looked at him, and screwed her mouth up and didn't want to say, but she let it slip out that the Nazi Beast could come out of any kind of animal if it got the right care and nourishment, and then she quickly lit another cigarette, and her fingers shook a little, and Momik saw he wasn't going to get any more from her this time, and he went out to the street, thoughtfully dragging his schoolbag along the wet pavement, buttoning his collar absentmindedly, and then he stood contemplating that Grandfather Anshel of his, sitting on the green bench across the street as usual, lost in his own world, waving his hands while he argued with the invisible somebody who never gave him a moment's rest, but the interesting thing is that Grandfather wasn't alone on the bench anymore.

It seems that in the past few days, without his noticing, Grandfather had started to collect all kinds of people around him. In fact they were these very old people nobody had noticed in the neighborhood before, or if anyone did notice them, they tried not to talk about them, people like Ginzburg and Zeidman for example, who'd walk up and stare in his face, and Zeidman would start making signs like Grandfather right away, because he always does what other people do, and then came Yedidya Munin who sleeps in the empty synagogue with all the martyred saints. Yedidya Munin is the one who walks bowlegged because of his hernia, and wears two pairs of glasses one on top of the other, one for the sun and the other not, and children are absolutely forbidden to go anywhere near him because he's obscene, but Momik knows Munin is really a good person, that all he wants in life is to love someone from a fine, distinguished family, and to make children with her in his own special way, which is why every Friday Momik secretly takes Bella's newspapers and clips out the personal ads of the famous Mrs. Esther Levine, modern matchmaker and leading expert in arranging contacts with visitors from overseas, but no one is allowed to know this, God forbid. And then came Mr. Aaron Marcus, father of Bella's Hezkel, whom nobody had seen for ten years and all the neighbors said Kaddish over him already, and here he was, alive, looking nice and all dressed up (well, Bella wasn't about to let him go out to the street looking like a shlumper), only his face, God help him, was twitching and cracking into a thousand and one faces you wouldn't want to see. And then came Mrs. Hannah Zeitrin, whose husband the tailor deserted her, may-his-name-be-blotted-out, and now she is a living widow, that's what she's always hollering and screaming and it was lucky the compensation money came in, because otherwise she would have died of starvation, God forbid, because the tailor, pshakrev, didn't even leave her the dirt under his fingernails, everything he took with him choleria, and Mrs. Zeitrin is a very good woman, but she's also a whore and she mates with shvartzers, a shvartz yar oif ir, a black year on her, as Mama says whenever she walks by, and Mrs. Zeitrin really does do that with

Sasson Sasson, a fullback on the Jerusalem Ha Poel soccer team, and
with Victor Arussi, who's a taxi driver, and also with Azura, the butcher
from the shopping center whose hair is full of feathers, and who looks
like a nice guy actually, the kind that wouldn't mate, but everyone
knows he does. At first Momik hated Hannah with a black hatred, and
he swore he would only marry somebody from a fine, distinguished
family, like the women in the ads of Esther Levine the matchmaker,
somebody who would love him for his handsomeness and intelligence
and shyness, and who would never mate with others, but once when
he said something about Hannah Zeitrin to Bella, Bella got angry with
him and said what a poor woman Hannah Zeitrin is, and you should
pity her, the way you should pity everyone, and you don't know everything about what happened to Hannah Over There, she never dreamed
when she was born that this is how she would end up, sure everyone
has hopes and dreams in the beginning, that's what Bella said, so then
Momik started to understand Hannah a little differently, and he saw
that she was very beautiful kind of, with her big blond wig like Marilyn
Monroe, and her big red face with the nice little mustache, and her
swollen legs all bandaged up; she's pretty in a way, only she hates her
body and she scratches herself with her fingernails, and calls her body
my furnace, my tragedy, and it was Munin who explained to him that
she screams like that because she needs to mate all the time, because
otherwise she'll go out somewhere or something, and that's the reason
the tailor ran away from her, because he isn't made of steel you know,
and also he had some kind of problem with horns, and that was something Momik would have to find out about from Bella, and these stories
began to worry him a little, because what if someday none of her maters
showed up and she happened to see Momik walking up the street? But
thank God it didn't happen, and another thing is that Mrs. Zeitrin is
also angry with God, and she shakes her fists at Him and makes all
kinds of not-so-nice gestures, and she screams and curses at Him in
Polish, which is bad enough, but then she starts swearing in Yiddish
too, which you can be sure He understands. And all she wants is for
Him to dare show His face, just once, to a simple woman from Dinov,
but anyway, He hasn't dared so far, and every time she starts screaming
that way and running up and down the street Momik dashes to the
window for a view of the meeting, because how long will God be able
to control Himself with all her insults, and everyone listening yet; what,

is He made of steel? And now Mrs. Zeitrin has also been turning up at the bench and sitting next to Grandfather, but nicely, like a good little girl, still scratching herself all over, but quietly, without screaming or fighting with anyone, because even she could see that, deep inside, Grandfather is a very gentle man.

Momik is too shy to walk up to them, so instead he kind of moseys by, dragging his schoolbag along the sidewalk, till all of a sudden there he is, casually standing beside the bench where he can hear what they're saying in Yiddish, which is a slightly different Yiddish from the kind Mama and Papa speak, though in fact he understands every word: Our rabbi, whispers little Zeidman, was such a smart man even the top doctors declared he had two brains! And Yedidya Munin says, Eht! (a noise they all make). Our rebbeleh in Neustadt, the "yanukeh," they called him, he met his end There too, nebuch, he didn't want to write his commentaries in a book, nu, sure, the greatest Hasidim didn't always want to, so what happens? I tell you what happens: three things the little rebbe of blessed memory had to realize were signs from Above! You hear me, Mr. Wasserman? From Above! And in Dinov, says Mrs. Zeitrin to no one in particular, in Dinov where I come from, Jagiello's monument in the square was fifty meters high maybe and all marble! Imported marble!

Momik is so excited he forgets to shut his mouth! Because they're talking freely about Over There! It's almost dangerous the way they let themselves talk about it, but he has to make the most of this opportunity and remember everything, everything, and then run home and write it down in his notebook, and draw pictures too, because some things it's better to draw. So that when they talk about certain places Over There, for instance, he can sketch them in the secret atlas he's preparing. Like that mountain Mr. Marcus talks about, he can draw it in now, that huge mountain the goyim Over There call Jew Mountain, which is a magic mountain, so help us both, Mr. Wasserman, if you happened to find something up there, it disappeared before you got it home, a terrible sight! *Schrecklich!* And wood you gathered on the mountain, it wouldn't catch fire! It burned but was not consumed! That's what Mr. Marcus said, changing faces at incredible speed, God help us, but Mr. Munin tugs Grandfather's coat sleeve like a child and says, Another thing, Mr. Wasserman, in Neustadt where I come from there was a man called Weintraub, Shaya Weintraub, they called him. A young fellow. A boy.

But such a genius! Even in Warsaw they heard of him! He received a special award from the Minister of Education himself! Imagine that, the Pole gave him an award! Now listen to this, says Mr. Munin, digging deeper than usual in his pocket (searching for a treasure any beggar can find, says Bella), this Weintraub, if you asked him in the month of Tammuz, Tammuz shall we say, Please, Shaya, tell me how many minutes to go, God willing, before next Passover, you hear that, minutes, not days, not weeks, and then, just like that, may we both live to see our children married, Mr. Wasserman, he gives you the exact answer, like a regular robot. And Mrs. Hannah Zeitrin stops scratching and hitching her skirt up to scratch the top of her legs, and she looks at Munin and asks with a sneer, Would this Weintraub be the one with a head like an ear of corn by any chance, God forbid, the one that moved to Krakov? And Mr. Munin who seems kind of annoyed suddenly says in a quieter voice, Yes, that's the fellow, a genius like no other . . . and Hannah Zeitrin throws her head back, with a screechy-sounding laugh and says, And what became of him? Shaya Weintraub played the stock market and sank down down down. A genius, ha!

And they talk on and on this way, never stopping or listening to each other, to a singsong Momik has heard before somewhere, though he can't remember where exactly, speaking the language of Over There, the top-secret codes and passwords, recklessly, brashly saying: District of Lubov, Bzjozov Province, and the old cattle market, the big fire at the Klauiz, army work, protection, apostate out of spite, Red Feige Lea and Black Feige Lea, and the Goldeneh Bergel, the golden hill outside Zeidman's town where the King of Sweden buried caskets filled with gold when he fled the Russian Army, ach, and Momik swallows hard and remembers it all, for this kind of thing he has an excellent mind, a real alter kopf head, okay, so a Shaya Weintraub, a regular robot, he isn't yet, but Momik too can tell you on the spot how many gym classes to go before summer vacation, and how many hours of school (minutes too), not to mention some of the other things he knows, like his prophecies, because Momik is practically a prophet, a kind of Merlin the Magician, why he can guess when the next surprise quiz in arithmetic is going to be, and Miss Aliza, the teacher, actually did walk in and say, Please put away your notebooks, boys and girls, and take out paper and pencil. And the children stared at Momik in amazement, but that prophecy was a cinch because three months earlier

when Papa went to have his heart checked at Bikkur Cholim Hospital
they had a quiz, and Momik gets a bit nervous whenever Papa goes
for his heart checkup, which is why he remembered, and next time
Papa went they had another surprise quiz, so after that Momik guessed
that four weeks from Monday Miss Aliza would give another quiz, but
the other children don't understand this type of thing, for them four
weeks is too long a time to measure, so they think Momik is a magician,
but anyone who has a spy notebook and writes down everything that
happens can tell that things that happen once will happen again, so
Momik drives the children crazy with his accurate, spylike prediction
about the tank column crossing the Malcha road once every twenty-
one days at ten o'clock in the morning, and he can also tell (it spooks
him too) the next time those ugly pimples are going to pop out all
over Netta the science teacher's face, but these are silly prophecies,
hocus-pocus stuff to make the kids respect him and stop teasing him,
because the really big prophecies are for Momik alone, there's no one
he can tell them to, like spying on his parents, and all the spy work to
put together the vanished land of Over There like a jigsaw puzzle,
there's still a lot of work left on this, and he's the only one in the whole
wide world who can do it, because who else can save Mama and Papa
from their fears and silences and krechtzes, and the curse, which was
even worse after Grandfather Anshel turned up and made them remember all the things they were trying so hard to forget and not tell
anyone.

Momik intends to rescue Grandfather Anshel too of course, only he
doesn't quite know how yet. He's tried one or two methods already,
but so far, nothing works. First, when Momik used to sit with Grandfather and give him his lunch, he would accidentally knock on the table
sometimes the way Raphael Blitz and Nachman Farkash the convicts
did when they were planning their prison break. He couldn't tell
whether the knocking meant anything or not, but he had this hunch,
this hope actually, that someone inside Grandfather would knock back.
But nothing happened. Then Momik tried to figure out the secret code
on Grandfather's arm. He'd tried this before with Papa's and Bella's
and Aunt Idka's code numbers, but he didn't get anywhere that time
either. The numbers drove him crazy because they weren't written in
ink and they couldn't be washed off with water or spit. Momik tried
everything to wash Grandfather's arm, but the number stayed fixed,

which gave Momik an idea that maybe the number wasn't written from
the outside but from the inside, and that convinced him more than
ever that there was somebody there inside Grandfather, and the others
too maybe, which is how they call out for help, and Momik racked his
brains to understand what it could be, and he wrote down Grandfather's
number in his spy notebook next to Papa's and Bella's and Idka's, and
did all kinds of calculations, and then luckily in school they learned
about gematria and the numerical values of the alphabet which naturally
Momik was the first in his class to understand, and when he got home
he tried to turn the numbers into letters in different ways, but all he
got was a bunch of strange words he didn't understand, and still Momik
would not give up, and once in the middle of the night he had an
Einsteiny idea, he remembered there are things called safes where rich
people hide their money and diamonds, and these safe things will only
open if you turn seven dials in a certain secret way, and you can bet
Momik spent half the night experimenting, and the next day, as soon
as he picked Grandfather up at the bench on his way home from school
and gave him his lunch and sat down across the table from him, he
called out various combinations of the numbers from Grandfather's arm
in a slow, solemn voice. He sounded kind of like the guy on the radio
who announces the numbers that won the thirty-thousand-pound prize
in the lottery, and he had a peculiar feeling that any minute now his
grandfather would split down the middle like a yellow string bean, and
a smily little chick of a grandfather who loves children would pop out,
only it didn't happen, and suddenly Momik felt strangely sad, and he
got up and went over to old Grandfather, and hugged him tight, and
felt how warm he was, like an oven, and Grandfather stopped talking
to himself, and for maybe half a minute he was quiet, and kept his face
and hands still, and sort of listened to what was going on inside, but
he could never stop talking for very long.

Then Momik used his systematic approach, the kind he's really good
at. Whenever he and Grandfather were left alone in the house together,
Momik would start following him around with a notebook and pen,
recording Grandfather's gibberish in Hebrew letters. Okay, he didn't
write down every single word he said, not every single word, that would
be too dumb, but he did write down what he thought were the most
important sounds Grandfather made, and it only took a couple of days
for Momik to notice that what Grandfather was saying wasn't all gib-

berish, in fact he was telling somebody a story, just as Momik had thought all along. Momik tried hard to remember what Grandma Henny used to tell him about Anshel (that was a long, long time ago, before Momik understood things like an alter kopf, before he ever heard about Over There), but all he could remember was that she said Grandfather wrote poems for grownups too, and that he had a wife and daughter who were killed Over There, and he also tried to find hints in the story from the old magazine, but he didn't come up with anything. Then Momik went to the school library and asked Mrs. Govrin the librarian if she had any books by a writer called Anshel Wasserman, and Mrs. Govrin peered at him over her glasses and said she never heard of him, and she knows everyone. Okay, so Momik didn't say anything, he just smiled to himself inside.

He went over to Bella's to share his discovery (that Grandfather was telling a story), but she only looked at him with that expression he doesn't like, pitying him and shaking her head from side to side and unbuttoning his top button, and she said, Sport, yingaleh, you're going to have to start pulling yourself together now, you're pale and scrawny, a real little fertel, how will they ever take you into the army, tell me, but Momik was stubborn and he explained that Grandfather Anshel was telling a story. Grandma Henny also used to like to tell stories when she still had her mind, and Momik remembered her special story voice and the way she stretched the words out and how her stomach filled with the words, and the peculiar way his palms would start sweating and the back of his knees, which is just how it felt when Grandfather talked now. And then he explained to Bella that he understood now that his poor grandfather was locked up in the story like the farmer with the sad face and the mouth open to scream that Aunt Idka and Uncle Shimmik brought from Switzerland, and this farmer lived his whole life in a glass ball where the snow fell if you shook it, and Mama and Papa put it on the living-room buffet, and Momik couldn't stand that mouth so one day he accidentally broke the glass and freed the farmer, and meanwhile Momik continues to record Grandfather's gibberish in the spy notebook slyly labeled *Geography*, and little by little he makes out a word here and there like Herrneigel, for instance, or Scheherazade, for instance, which he doesn't find in the *Hebrew Encyclopedia*, so he asks Bella for no particular reason what does Scheherazade mean, and Bella's just glad to hear he's stopped thinking about Over

There, and she says she'll ask her son Joshua, the major, and two days later she answers Momik that Scheherazade was an Arab princess who lived in Baghdad, which is a little strange since if you read the papers you know there isn't any princess in Baghdad, there's a prince, Prince Kassem, pshakrev, who hates us like all the goyim, may-their-memory-be-blotted-out, but Momik doesn't know the meaning of the word "surrender," he has the patience of an elephant, and he understands that a thing may seem mysterious and scary and confused today, but it will clear up by tomorrow, because it's just a question of logic, there's always an explanation, that's how it is in arithmetic, and that's how it is in everything else, but till the truth comes out, you just do things normally as if nothing happened, you go to school every morning and sit there for hours, and you don't let it hurt your feelings when the children say you walk like a camel, the way you slouch, oh, what do they know, and you don't feel bad when they call you Helen Keller because you wear glasses and have braces which is why he tries not to talk, and you don't give in when they try to butter you up so you'll tell them when the next surprise quiz in arithmetic will be, and on top of this Momik has to worry about the deal he made with Laizer the Crook who swipes his sandwich every morning and then there's the distance home from school every day which you use arithmetic to figure out, seven hundred and seventy-seven steps, no more, no less, from the school gate to the lottery booth where Mama and Papa sit squeezed together all day long not saying one word, and they see him turn the corner, all the way up the street, for this they possess animal instincts, and when he gets there Mama comes out with the house keys. Mama is very squatty, and looks something like a kilo bag of flour, and she wets her fingers with spit to comb the hair of Motl Ben Paisee the Chazzan, he should look tidy, and she wipes a speck of dirt off his cheek and his sleeve too, though Momik knows very well there isn't any dirt there, she just likes to touch him, and he, poor orphan, patiently faces her fingernails, gazing anxiously into her eyes, because if there's anything wrong with her eyes they won't grant us papers to get into America, and Mama, who doesn't know she's Motl's mother just now, says quickly under her breath, Your papa is becoming impossible, and she can't stand those krechtzes one more minute, like an old man ninety years old he sounds, and she swings around to look at Papa who just stares up in the air like there's nothing there and doesn't budge, and

Mama tells Momik Papa hasn't washed in a week, it's the way he stinks that keeps the customers away, no one's stopped at the booth for two days now except the three regulars, why should the lottery people let us keep the booth with no customers and where are we supposed to get money to eat I'd like to know, and the only reason she stays here with him all day long like a sardine is because you can't trust him with money, he might go off and sell the tickets at a discount, or he could get a heart attack from the hooligans, God forbid, why is God punishing me like this, let Him kill me right now instead of a little at a time, she says, and her face falls exhausted, but then she suddenly gazes at him, and for just a minute her eyes are pretty and young-looking, not frightened or angry, the opposite, you might say she seems to be trying out some new chendelach on Momik to make him smile, to make him special to her, and her eyes light up, but it only lasts about a half a minute and she changes back into the way she was before, and Momik sees her eyes change, and Motl whispers softly to her, in the voice of My Brother Elijah, Hush, nu, hush, Mama, weep no more, the doctor said it isn't good for you to cry, please, Mama, for our sake, and Momik makes a vow, tfu, may he die in Hitler's black tomb unless he finds a green stone that cures diseases of the eye and other cholerias, and this is what Momik is thinking so hard to help him not hear the seventh-grade hooligans shouting a safe distance away from big fat Papa: "Lottery little, lottery big, turns a pauper into a pig," a kind of ditty they made up, but Momik and Mama hear nothing, and Momik sees Papa, the sad giant of an Emperor, staring down at his enormous hands, no, all three of them are deaf to the hooligans, because they hear only their own secret language which is Yiddish, which soon the beautiful Marilyn Monroe will understand because she married Mr. Miller, a Jew, and every day she learns three new words, and these hooligans, let them drop dead, amen, and Mama touches Momik here and there while he says the magic word "Chaimova" seven times to himself, which is what you're supposed to say to infidels at the border tavern in the Motl Ben Paisee book, because when you say "Chaimova," they drop everything and obey you, especially if you ask them to help you cross the border to America, not to mention a simpler thing like handling a gang of seventh-graders whom Momik will only refrain from throwing to the infidels out of the goodness of his heart.

"There's a drumstick in the refrigerator for you and one for him," says Mama, "and be careful with the small bones, you shouldn't swallow any, God forbid, and he shouldn't either. Be careful." "Okay." "And be careful with the gas too, Shleimeleh, and blow the match out right away, so there won't be a fire, God forbid." "Okay." "And don't forget to make sure you turn off the gas knob when you're done, and the little tap behind the stove too. The one behind is the most important." "Yes." "And don't drink soda water out of the refrigerator. Yesterday I noticed at least one glass less in the bottle. You drank it, and it's winter now. And as soon as you're inside lock the door twice. The top lock and the bottom lock. Just once is no good." "Okay." "And make sure he goes to sleep as soon as lunch is over. Don't let him go out like a shlumper." "Okay." She carries on talking to herself a little longer, making sure with her tongue that there are no words left over, because if she's left out a single word, then everything she said will be wasted, but it's all right, there's nothing left out, nothing bad will happen to Momik, God forbid, so Mama can make her last speech, like this: "Don't open the door to anyone. We're not expecting company. And Papa and I will be home at seven as usual, don't worry. Do your homework. Don't turn the heater on even if it gets cold. You can play after you do your homework, but no wildness, and don't read too much, you'll ruin your eyes. And don't get into any fights. If anyone hits you, you come here to us right away." Her voice sounded weaker and farther away. "Goodbye, Shleimeleh, say goodbye to Papa. Goodbye, Shleimeleh. You be careful."

This must be how she bade him goodbye when he was a baby in the royal nursery. His father, who was still the Emperor and a commando fighter in those days, summoned the royal hunter and, with tear-choked voice, ordered him to take this infant deep into the forest and leave him there, prey to the birds of the sky, as they say. It was a kind of curse on children they had in those days. Momik didn't quite understand it yet. But anyway, luckily the royal hunter took pity on him and raised him secretly as his own, and many years later Momik returned to the castle as an unknown youth and became secret advisor to the Emperor and Empress, and that way, unbeknownst to anyone, he protected the poor Emperor and Empress who had banished him from their kingdom, and of course this is all imaginary, Momik is a truly scientific, arithmetically gifted boy, there's no one like him in fourth grade, but meanwhile, till the truth will out, Momik has to use imaginary things and hints and hunches and the talking that stops the minute he walks into the room, that's how it was when Mama and Papa sat talking with Idka and Shimmik about the compensation money from Germany, and Papa said angrily, Take a man like me, for instance, who lost a child Over There, which is why Momik isn't so sure it's only imaginary, and sometimes when he's really feeling low, it makes him so happy just to think how glad they'll be the day he can finally tell Mama and Papa that he's the boy they gave away to the hunter, it will be exactly like Joseph and his brothers. But sometimes he imagines it a different way, that he's the boy who lost his twin brother, because Momik has this feeling that he used to have a Siamese twin, and when they were born, they were cut in two like in *Believe It or Not*: "300 astonishing cases that shook the world," and maybe someday they'll meet and be joined together again (if they want).

And from the lottery booth he makes his way home at a precise and scientific pace, they call it the camel walk because they don't understand that he's directing his footsteps through the secret passages and shortcuts only he knows, and there are some trees you have to brush against accidentally, because he has this feeling maybe there's somebody inside and you have to show him he hasn't been forgotten, and then he crosses the dump behind the deserted synagogue where old Munin lives all by himself and you have to hurry past on account of Munin but also on account of the saintly martyrs waiting there impatiently for someone to release them from holy extermination, and from here it's just ten steps to the gate of Momik's yard, and you can see the house already, a kind of concrete block perched on four wobbly legs, under which is a small cellar, they should have gotten only one apartment in the house actually, not two, but they signed Grandma Henny up as a separate family, like Uncle Shimmik told them to, and that's how they got the whole building to themselves, so even though nobody lives in the other half of the house or ever goes in there, it's theirs, they suffered enough Over There, and it's a mitzvah to cheat this government, choleria, and in the yard there's a big old pine tree that keeps out the sun and twice Papa went out with an ax to chop it down, but he scared himself each time and came back quietly, and Mama stormed at him because he had mercy on a tree but not on this child who was going to grow up in the dark without the vitamins you get from the sun, and Momik has a room all to himself, with a portrait of Prime Minister David Ben-

Gurion and a picture of Vultures with their wings spread like steel birds boldly defending our nation's skies, and it's too bad Mama and Papa won't let him hang any more pictures on the wall because it ruins the plaster, but except for the pictures, which really do ruin the plaster a little, his room is neat and tidy, everything in its place, and this room could definitely be a model for other children, if they would ever come over, that is.

It's a very quiet street, more like a lane really. There are only six houses on it, and it's always quiet, except when Hannah Zeitrin insults Our Lord. Momik's house is pretty quiet too. His mama and papa don't have many friends. In fact they don't have any friends at all except for Bella naturally, whom Mama goes to see on Saturday afternoons when Papa sits by the window in his undershirt and stares out, and except for Aunt Idka and Uncle Shimmik, who come twice a year for a whole week, and then everything changes. They're different from Mama and Papa. More like Bella really. And even though Idka has a number on her arm, they go to restaurants and to the theater and to Gigan and Schumacher, the comedians, and they laugh so hard, Mama glances sideways and kisses her fingertips and touches her forehead, and Idka says, What harm is there in a little laughter, Gisella, and Mama smiles a foolish smile like she's been caught and says, Don't mind me, laugh, laugh, there's no harm, I do it just to be safe. Idka and Shimmik play cards too and go to the seashore, and Shimmik even knows how to swim. Once they sailed on a luxury ship, *The Jerusalem*, for a whole month because Shimmik owns a big garage in Natanya, and also he knows how to cheat on his income tax really well, pshakrev, and there's only one small problem, which is that they don't have any children, because Idka did all sorts of scientific experiments Over There.

Momik's mama and papa never go away on trips, not even out of town, except once a year, a few days after Passover when they spend three days at a small pensione in Tiberias. This is sort of strange because they even take Momik out of school for the three days. In Tiberias they're different. Not so different, but a little different somehow. For instance, they sit at a café and order sodas and cake for three. One morning of the vacation they all go to the beach and sit under Mama's yellow umbrella which you could call a parasol, with everybody dressed very lightly. Then they rub Vaseline on their legs so they won't burn, and on their noses all three of them wear little white plastic shades.

Momik doesn't have a swimming suit, because it'd be silly to spend all that money on something you use only once a year and shorts are good enough. They allow him to run on the beach then as far as the water, and you can bet he knows things like the exact depth, length, and breadth of the Sea of Galilee, and what kinds of fish live in it better than any of those hooligans swimming out there. In the past when Momik and his parents went to Tiberias, Aunt Idka would come up to Jerusalem alone to take care of Grandma Henny. She always brought a stack of Polish newspapers with her from Natanya which she left with Bella when she went home. Momik used to clip out pictures of Polish soccer players from the newspapers (especially *Pshegelond*) like Shimkoviak, the fantastic goalkeeper with the catlike leaps, but the year Grandfather Anshel arrived, Idka didn't want to stay with him on her own because he's so difficult, so Mama and Papa went by themselves, and Momik stayed with his aunt and with Grandfather, because only Momik knows how to handle him.

That was the year he discovered his parents were running away from home and the city on account of Holocaust Day. He was already nine and a quarter by then. Bella used to call him the neighborhood mizinik, but actually he was the only kid around. It had been that way since the day he arrived in his baby carriage, and the neighborhood women leaned over him and cooed, "Oy, Mrs. Neuman, vas far ein mieskeit," what an ugly thing, and the ones who knew better looked away and spat three times to save him from what they carry inside them like a disease, and for nine and a quarter years after that, every time he walked down the street he heard the same greeting and spitting, and Momik is always nice and well-mannered, because he knows what they think of the other children in the neighborhood, they're rude and wild and shvartzers, all of them, so you can see Momik has a lot of responsibility for the grownups on the street.

His full name, it should be mentioned, was Shlomo Efraim Neuman, in So-and-so's and So-and-so's memory. They'd have liked to give him a hundred names. Grandma Henny did it all the time. She would call him Mordechai Leibeleh, and Shepseleh and Mendel and Anshel and Shulam and Chumak, and Shlomo Haim, and that's how Momik got to know who they all were, Mendel who ran off to Russia to be a Communist nebuch, and disappeared, and Shulam the Yiddishist who sailed for America and the ship sank, and Isser who played the violin

and died with the Nazis, may-their-name-be-blotted-out, and tiny Leibeleh and Shepseleh there was no more room for at the table, the family
was so big by then, and Grandma Henny's father told them to eat like
the gentry, and they believed him and ate on the floor under the table,
and Shlomo Haim grew up to be a sports champion and Anshel Efraim
wrote the saddest, loveliest poems and then he went to live in Warsaw
and became a Hebrew writer nebuch, and they all met their end with
the Nazis, may-their-name-be-blotted-out, one fine day they closed in
on the shtetl and gathered everyone together by the river—aiii, little
Leibeleh and Shepseleh, forever laughing under the table, and Shlomo
Haim who was half paralyzed and recovered by a miracle and became
a Samson the Hero, forever flexing his muscles at the Jewish Olympics
with the Prut River in the background, and little Anshel, the delicate
one, they wondered how he would ever get through the winter, and
they put hot bricks under his bed at night so he wouldn't freeze, there
he sits in his sailor suit with his hair parted in the middle looking so
serious with his big eyeglasses; Goodness me, Grandma clapped her
hands, you look just like him. She told him all about them long long
ago, in the days when she could still remember, and they thought he
was too young to understand, but once when Mama saw that his eyes
weren't staring blankly anymore, she told Grandma Henny to stop right
away, and she also hid the book with the amazing pictures (she probably
sent it to Aunt Idka). And now Momik is trying as hard as he can to
remember what was in the pictures and the stories. He writes down
every new thing he remembers, even the little things that don't seem
important, because this is war, and in war we use everything we have.
That's what the State of Israel does when it fights against the Arabs,
pshakrev.

Bella helps him sometimes too, of course, but not so willingly, and
the main part he has to do for himself. He isn't angry with her or
anything, no, of course not, obviously anyone from Over There can't
give him real clues, and they also can't ask him to help in a simple,
straightforward way. It seems they have all these laws of secrecy in the
kingdom. But hardships like these don't worry Momik, who has no
choice, because he's got to take charge once and for all. And over the
past few weeks an awful lot of crooked lines have gone into his spy
notebook which he now writes in under the covers where he can't see.
He isn't always exactly sure how you're supposed to write those words

in Hebrew that Papa screams out in his sleep every night. Anyway, Papa seemed to have calmed down a little and he'd stopped with the nightmares for a while till Grandfather arrived and then everything started up again. The screaming is certainly weird, but what do we have logic and brains and Bella for? When we examine the screaming in the light of day, it turns out to be quite simple. It was like this, there was a war in that kingdom, and Papa was the Emperor and also the chief warrior, a commando fighter. One of his friends (his lieutenant?) was called Sondar. This strange name may have been his name in the underground, like in the days of the Etzel and Lehi. They all lived in a big camp with a complicated name. There they were trained to go on daring missions, which were so secret even today you have to keep mum about them. Also there were some trains around, but that part isn't so clear. Maybe those trains are like the ones his secret brother Bill tells him about, the trains attacked by savage Indians. Everything is so mixed up. And there were also these big campaigns in Papa's kingdom called Aktions, and sometimes (probably to make the people feel proud) they would have really incredible parades, like we have on Independence Day. Left, right, left, right, Papa screams in his sleep, Links recht, he screams in the German language Bella will positively not translate for Momik, till he practically shouts at her and she gets angry and tells him it means left, right, to the left, to the right. Is that it, Momik wonders, then why didn't she want to translate it? Mama wakes up at night from Papa's screaming and she pokes him and shakes him, and cries, Nu, Tuvia, sha, be still, the child can hear you, Over There is gone, it's the middle of the night, a klag zal im trefin, you'll wake the boy, Tuvia! And then Papa wakes up scared and starts with the big krechtzes that sound like a frying pan sizzling under the faucet, and Momik in his room meanwhile has shut the notebook under the covers, but he still hears Papa sort of sighing into his hands, and now he thinks carefully, the way Amos Chacham does before answering a very interesting question, Supposing Papa touched his eyes and went on seeing as usual, would that mean that the death in his hands is gone?

Well, he must touch Mama sometimes when they're jammed together in the lottery booth. And he always used to lift Grandma Henny in his arms and carry her to the table and back to bed again. And every Thursday he bathes Grandfather Anshel with a washrag and a little basin, because Mama is disgusted.

Okay, okay, they're from Over There, so maybe that's why he can't hurt them. But here's one important thing to think about: when he's selling tickets in the lottery booth he wears little rubber thimble things on each finger!

Not to mention the most conclusive scientific evidence of all, the thing that happened with the leeches the time Madame Miranda Bardugo came to cure Papa when he had eczema all over his hands. Momik has worked out various theories like a serious investigator: a boiling kettle? To look at them, if you didn't know, you'd think they were just ordinary hands. Or sandpaper maybe? Porcupine quills? Momik was having a hard time falling asleep. For a long time now, ever since Grandfather Anshel showed up, he hadn't been able to fall asleep at night. Dry ice? A needle?

In the morning, before breakfast (Mama and Papa always leave first), he quickly jots down another guess: "Boldly charging from the camp, our valiant heroes surprised the savage Indians with Red Slipper, who had attacked the mail train. The Emperor galloped ahead on his faithful steed, bursting with splendor, also shooting his rifle in every direction. Sondar of the Commandos covered him from behind. The mighty Emperor shouted to me, his bold roar resounding through the frozen kingdom." Momik paused to read what he had written so far. This was definitely an improvement over what usually came out. But it still wasn't good enough. So much was missing. The main thing was missing, he felt sometimes. But what was this main thing? No, the writing should have more power, more biblical splendor, like Grandfather Anshel's writing. Only how? He would have to be bolder. Because whatever it was that happened Over There must have really been something for everyone to try so hard not to talk about it. Momik also started including some things they were learning about in school just then, like Orde Wingate and the Night Platoons, and also the Super Mystère jets we'll soon have, God willing, from our friends and eternal allies the French, and he even used the first Israeli nuclear reactor currently under construction in the sands of Nahal Rubin, and in next week's issue, a sensation-something article with exclusive photographs of the pool where they actually do the atomic thing! Momik felt he was getting closer to solving the riddle. (Momik always remembered what Sherlock Holmes said in "The Adventure of the Dancing Men," that what one man invents another can discover, so he's sure he will succeed.) It's a fight for his parents and for the others too. Of course they know nothing about it, why should they know. He's fighting like a partisan. Undercover. All alone. So that they'll finally be able to forget and relax a little, and stop being so scared for once in their lives. He's found a way. It is dangerous, to tell the truth, but Momik isn't scared. That is, he's scared, but there's just no other way. Bella unknowingly gave him the biggest clue of all when she mentioned the Nazi Beast. That was a very long time ago though, and he hadn't quite understood it then, but the day Grandfather arrived and Momik went down to the cellar to look for the sacred old magazine with his story in it, he understood exactly. And in a way that was when Momik made up his mind to find the Beast and tame it and make it good, and persuade it to change its ways and stop torturing people and get it to tell him what happened Over There and what it did to those people, and it's been about a month now, almost a whole month since Grandfather Anshel arrived that Momik has been busy up to his ears, in complete secrecy, down in the small dark cellar under the house, raising the Nazi Beast.

That was a winter they would remember for years. Not because of the rain, it didn't rain in the beginning, but because of the wind. The winter of '59, said the old people of Beit Mazmil, and no one had to say any more. Momik's father walked around the house at night with yellow gatkes showing under his trousers, and a big wad of cotton in each ear, and he would stuff pieces of torn-up newspaper into the keyholes to stop the wind from getting in (which could get in even through there). At night Mama worked on the sewing machine Shimmik and Idka gave her. Bella fixed it so lots of ladies would bring Mama their quilt covers to mend and their old sheets to patch up and she could earn a little extra for the house. It was a secondhand Singer sewing machine, and when Mama sat working at it and the wheel turned and creaked, Momik felt as if she were controlling the weather outside. The noise from the machine made Papa jumpy, but he didn't say anything, because he also needed the little extra, and besides he didn't want to get into trouble with Mama and her mouth, so he would pace around the house, krechtzing and switching the radio on and off, saying, This wind and all the other troubles are from the government, choleria. He always voted for the Orthodox Party, not because he was Orthodox, he wasn't one bit, but because he hated Ben-Gurion for being in power, and the General Zionists for being in the Opposition, and Ya'ari for being a Communist, pshakrev. And the winter with the winds and the drought began when the Orthodox Party left the Coalition, which is a sign from God that He is not pleased with the way things are going around here, Papa said, with a brave and careful look at Mama, who just kept sewing and said to herself out loud, Oich mir a politikacker— Dag Hammarskjöld.

But Momik was pretty worried, because he noticed that the whistling winds were confusing the people he'd become friendly with lately, and he had this feeling, not that he believed it could actually happen, but things were sure weird and a little scary too. Mrs. Hannah Zeitrin for instance. She got another installment of her compensation for the tailor shop her family used to own in Danzig, but instead of spending it on food or stuffing it into an old shoe in the storeroom, she went out and bought herself new clothes, aza yar oif mir, may such a year befall me, and the wardrobe of that woman, says Mama to Bella, her eyes burning with rage, the way she wiggles like a boat, the slut, what did she lose out in the street? And Bella, who is pure gold, and who gives even Hannah a free glass of tea, just laughs and says, What do you care, Gisella, tell me, did you give birth to her at the age of seventy that you should worry so much about her? You know why a woman buys herself a fur coat, don't you, she wants to keep herself warm and the neighbors boiling. And Momik listens and sees that Bella and Mama don't understand, Hannah just wants to look beautiful, that's all, not to make Mama mad, and not even for mating, but because she has a new idea which only Momik knows about from listening to her when she talks to herself and scratches on the bench with the old people. But Hannah Zeitrin isn't the only one around here who's overdoing it lately. Mr. Munin is acting stranger than ever. Actually, with Munin it started even before Grandfather arrived, but now he's really gone too far. Sometime around the beginning of the year, Mr. Munin heard that the Russians sent Lunik 1 to the moon, and he started to be very interested in space things and became so impatient he made Momik come and tell him anything new he heard about Sputniks, right away, and even promised to pay Momik two piasters for listening to New World of Science on the radio Saturday mornings, and for bringing him a report on everything they say about Our Friend, that's what he calls Lunik 1, as if they know each other. So on Saturday morning after the program Momik runs outside and crawls through the hole in the fence to the back yard of the deserted synagogue where Mr. Munin lives as caretaker. Straight-away he tells him everything they said on the program, and Munin gives him a note on which he wrote in advance on Friday: "In exchange for this note I will pay bearer the sum of 2 (two) piasters after the Holy Sabbath." The deal has been working out pretty well for a couple of weeks now. When Momik brings really good news about space and the latest discoveries, Munin is very happy. He bends down and draws the moon like a round ball in the dirt with a stick, and beside it all nine planets whose names he knows by heart, and next to that, proud as a baleboos, he draws a picture of his friend, Lunik 1, who didn't quite make it to the moon and so became, nebuch, planet number ten. Munin is very knowledgeable, and he explains all about rockets and jet propulsion, and about an inventor called Zaliukov Munin wrote to once about an idea that could get him the Nobel Prize, but then the war broke out and everything went kaput, and the time is not yet ripe to discuss this but someday the whole world will understand who Munin is, and then they'll envy him, oh yes, that's all they'll be able to do, because they will never know what the good life is, the true life, true happiness, yes, he isn't ashamed to say it, the word is happiness, Momo, happiness, it must exist somewhere, right? Ah, nu, here I go, talking your head off. He drew in the dust as he talked, and Momik stood by, not understanding any of this, facing the bald spot with the dirty black yarmulke on it, and the two pairs of glasses tied together with a yellow rubber band, and the long white whiskers on his cheeks. Munin almost always had an unlit cigarette dangling from his lips that had a strange, sharp smell, not like anything he'd ever smelled before, kind of like the smell of carobs on a tree, and in a way Momik does enjoy standing close to Munin and smelling that smell, and Munin doesn't mind too much either. And once when the Americans launched Pioneer 4 and Momik went over before school to tell Munin, he found him sitting in the sun as usual, on an old car seat, warming himself like a cat, and beside him, on an old newspaper, were pieces of wet bread for the birds he always feeds, and the birds know him now and they fly around with him wherever he goes, and Mr. Munin had just been reading a holy book with a picture of a naked prophetess on the cover, and it seemed to Momik he'd seen that book somewhere before maybe at Lipschitz's in the shopping center, but how could that be, Mr. Munin wouldn't be interested in things like that, Momik knows the kind of ladies he looks for in the ads. Munin quickly hid the book away and said, Nu,

Momo, what news dost thou bring? (he always talks like that, in the language of Our Sages of Blessed Memory), and Momik tells him about Pioneer 4 and Munin jumps up from the car seat and lifts Momik high in the air, and hugs him with all his might, to his prickly whiskers, and his coat and the stink, and he dances wildly all around the yard, a strange and frightening dance under the sky and the treetops and the sun, and Momik is afraid that someone passing by will see him like this, and Munin's two black coattails fly up in the air behind him, and he doesn't let Momik down until he's all worn out, and then he takes a crumpled piece of paper out of his pocket and looks around to see if anyone's watching, and then he crooks his finger for Momik to come closer, and Momik who's still pretty dizzy comes closer and sees it's a kind of map with names written on it in a language he doesn't understand and a lot of little Mogen Davids everywhere, and Munin whispers in his face, "The Lord redeemeth in the twinkling of an eye, and the sons of light soar high," and then he imitates a flying leap with his big hand and says, "Feeeiiiww!!" so loud and furiously that Momik who is still dizzy trips over a stone and falls down, and that's when Momik with his very own eyes saw stinky black hilarious Munin taking off diagonally in a strong wind to the sky like the Prophet Elijah in his chariot maybe, and at that moment, a moment he would never-ever-black-and-blue forget, he understood at long last that Munin was actually a kind of secret magician like the Lamed Vavim, the way Hannah Zeitrin isn't just a woman but a witch too, and Grandfather Anshel is a kind of prophet in reverse who tells what used to be, and maybe Max and Moritz and Mr. Marcus are also playing secret roles and they aren't just here by chance, they're here to help Momik, because before he started fighting for his parents and raising the Nazi Beast, he rarely even noticed them. Okay, maybe he noticed them, but he never used to talk to any of them before except Munin, and he always tried to keep as far away from them as possible, and now he hangs around with them all the time, and when he isn't hanging around with them he's thinking about them and what they say about Over There, and what a dope he was not to understand it before, and the truth is, he did use to sort of make fun of them sometimes because of how they look and stink and things like that, but now Momik hopes for one thing only, that they'll pass him all their secret clues so he'll be able to figure them out before this crazy wind gets them.

And at noon when Momik and Grandfather walk home together they have to lean so far against the wind they can hardly see the way, and they're afraid because they hear weird noises that sound like many tongues and Momik is sure there's something hiding inside the tree and in the pavement cracks, that it was probably there for ages till the wind blew it out, and Momik digs deeper in his pockets, and he's sorry now he didn't eat more last summer and put on a little weight, and Grandfather uses his crazy movements to cut through the wind, only suddenly he forgets where he's going, and he stops and looks around, and holds his hands up like a baby waiting for someone to pick him up, and this could turn into something dangerous because what if the wind grabbed him just then, but thank goodness Momik has Chodorov instincts and he always gets there just in time to catch Grandfather and to squeeze his hand, which is so soft on the inside, and they walk on together, and by then you can tell the wind is absolutely furious and it pounces on them out of the Ein Kerem Valley and the Malcha Valley, and sails wet newspapers at their faces and old campaign posters from the walls, and the wind howls like a jackal, and the cypress trees go stark raving mad from the howling, and they bow and writhe as if somebody were tickling their bellies, and it takes Momik and Grandfather forever to get home, and Momik finally unlocks the two locks and locks the bottom lock again right away, and only then does the wind stop howling in their ears, and they can start to hear something.

Now Momik can throw his schoolbag down and help Grandfather off with Papa's big, old overcoat, and sniff him quickly and sit him down at the table, and warm up the food for both of them. Grandma Henny used to have lunch in her room because she couldn't get out of bed without help, but Grandfather keeps him company, which is nice, like having a real grandfather you can talk to and all that.

Momik loved Grandma Henny very much. To this day it makes his heart ache to think of her. And all the suffering she suffered when she died too. But anyway, Grandma Henny had a special language she used when she was seventy-nine after she forgot her Polish and Yiddish and the little bit of Hebrew she learned here. When Momik came home from school he used to run in to see how she was, and she would get all excited and turn red and talk in that language of hers. Momik would bring her food in and sit down to look at her. She pecked at her plate like a bird. She had a permanent smile on her little face, a kind of faraway smile, and she talked to him through her smile. It usually started

with her getting angry at him, Mendel, for leaving the family like that
and going to do poor people's work in a place called Borislav, and from
there he wandered off to Russia where he vanished, how could you do
such a thing and break our mother's heart, and then she begs him,
Sholem, never, ever, even when he reaches America where the streets
are paved with gold, to forget that he's a Jew, and to wear tefillin and
pray in the synagogue, and then she would ask him, Isser, to play
"Sheraleh" on the violin, and she would close her eyes and you could
tell she actually heard that violin, yes, and Momik watched not daring
to disturb her. This was better and more exciting than any movie or
book, and sometimes he had real tears in his eyes, and Mama and Papa
asked what he liked about sitting with Grandma Henny in her room
so long, listening to her talk that language no one understands, and
Momik said he understood everything. That was a fact. Because Momik
has this gift, a gift for all kinds of languages no one understands, he
can even understand the silent kind that people who say maybe three
words in their whole life talk, like Ginzburg who says, Who am I who
am I, and Momik understands that he's lost his memory and that now
he's looking for who he is everywhere even in the garbage cans, and
Momik has decided to suggest (they've been spending a lot of time on
the bench together lately) that he should send a letter to the radio
program *Greetings from New Immigrants*, and maybe someone would
recognize him and remind him who he is and where he got lost, oh
yes, Momik can translate just about anything. He is the translator of
the royal realm. He can even translate nothing into something. Okay,
that's because he knows there's no such thing as nothing, there must
be something, nu, that's exactly how it is with Grandfather Anshel,
who also eats like a bird, peck and gulp, only slightly more frightenedly
than Grandma Henny, probably because they had to eat very very fast
Over There like the Jews in Egypt on the eve of Passover. And Momik
has also finally managed to crack Grandfather's code, and he knows
now that Grandfather is telling the story to a man or boy by the name
of Herrneigel, and he calls his name in different ways, sometimes angrily,
sometimes flatteringly, or sometimes a little sadly, but three days ago
while Momik was listening to Grandfather talk to himself in his room,
he distinctly heard him say "Fried," and Momik had come across that
name before in the sacred magazine, and his hands started to tremble
with excitement, but he told himself, Look, those are old stories, why

would Grandfather tell the same stories over and over and get all excited like that? But naturally he had to check it out now, so when he brought Grandfather home from the green bench and sat him down at the table, he blurted out, "Fried! Paula! Otto! Harotian!" Okay, that was pretty risky, and suddenly he had a feeling Grandfather might do something bad to him. He did give him a very spooky look as a matter of fact, but he didn't do anything, and after sitting still for almost a whole minute, Grandfather said softly and very clearly, "Herrneigel," pointing back over his shoulder with his crooked thumb, as if there were some big or little Herrneigel standing behind him, and then he whispered, "Nazikaput!" but suddenly he smiled a real smile at Momik, the smile of a person who understands, and he leaned over his plate till his face was very close to Momik's and said, "Kazik," kind of gently, as if he had a present to give him, and he formed a little man with his hands, a dwarf or baby or something, and rocked it to his heart the way you rock a baby, and the whole time he kept smiling that sweet smile at Momik, and suddenly Momik saw that Grandfather did resemble Grandma Henny, which is no wonder since they were brother and sister, but then Grandfather's face closed up again, as if someone inside ordered him to stop everything on the outside and come back as quickly as possible because there's no time, and then the mumbling started again with the stupid tunes and the jerky movements and the white spit squirting out of the sides of his mouth, and Momik leaned back, very proud of his commando invasion into the heart of Grandfather's story, like a real Captain Meir Har-Zion alter kopf, and although maybe he didn't know a whole lot just yet, he was absolutely positive that Grandfather Anshel and this Herrneigel had something to do with the war Momik had been waging for a while against the Nazi Beast, and that even though Grandfather came from Over There, maybe he refused to stop fighting, maybe he was the only one from Over There who wouldn't surrender, and that's why he and Momik have a secret pact.

And Momik just sat there looking at Grandfather, his eyes filled with admiration, and now Grandfather seemed to him exactly like an ancient prophet, Isaiah or Moses, and suddenly he realized that all his past plans about what to be when he grew up had been one big mistake, that there was only one thing worth being in life and that's a writer, like Grandfather Anshel, and the thought puffed him up so much that he almost started flying around the room like a balloon, which is why he had to dash to the toilet, but this time it was different, he didn't have to pee after all, and in bewilderment he ran to his room and pulled out his secret notebook, which is also his diary and a truly scientific catalogue of things from Over There, the emperors and kings, the soldiers and the Yiddishists and the athletes from the Jewish Olympics, and the stamps and currency, and precise drawings of all plants and animals, and across the page in great big letters he wrote IMPORTANT DECISION!!!, and under this heading he wrote the important deci- sion, which was to become a writer like Grandfather, and then he looked at the writing and saw how good it looked, much better than it usually came out, and now he wanted to find a really terrific finish to match his great decision, and thought of writing "Chazak Chazak Venitcha- zek" like it says when you come to the end of a book in the Holy Bible, but his hand took over and boldly scrawled sportscaster Nechemia Ben- Avraham's heroic battle cry, "Our boys will do or die!" and no sooner had he written these words than he was filled with a sense of duty and maturity too, and he walked back to the kitchen, slowly and responsibly, and gently wiped the drumstick grease from Grandfather's chin, and led him by the hand to his room, and helped him undress, and caught a peek of his thingy though he tried to look away, and then he went back to the kitchen muttering, No time, no time.

First he switched on the big radio with the glass panel showing the names of capital cities around the world, and he waited for the green eye to warm up; it looked as if he had already missed the beginning of *Greetings from New Immigrants and Locating Lost Relations*, and he did hope none of his names had been called out meanwhile. He picked up the list Papa wrote in big letters like a first-grader, and lip-read together with the radio announcing that Rochaleh, daughter of Paula and Avra- ham Seligson from Phashmishul, is trying to locate her little sister Lealeh who lived in Warsaw between the years . . . Eliahu Frumkin, son of Yocheved and Herschel Frumkin from Stri, is trying to locate his wife Elisheva née Eichler and his two sons Jacob and Meir . . . Momik doesn't even have to glance at the paper to check, he knows his names by heart. Mrs. Esther Neuman née Shapira, and the child, Mordechai Neuman, and Zvi Hirsch Neuman, and Sarah-Bella Neuman, a lot of lost Neumans wandering around Over There, and Momik is only half listening now, pronouncing the names like the woman on the radio, in a sad singsong that sort of sinks into despair which he has been listening to every lunchtime since he first learned how to read and they gave him the list with the names, Yizhak son of Avraham Neuman, and Arieh Leib Neuman, and Gitel daughter of Hirschel Neuman, all the Neumans, Papa's family, very, very distantly related, he's been told so many times, and he traces circles on the paper which is stained with the grease of a thousand lunches, and in each circle there's a name, but suddenly Momik notices that this is like the singsong of the old people telling their stories about Over There.

It's 1:30 now, time to get going. He wipes the table meticulously, and washes the dishes in his own special way (soap, rinse, soap and rinse again) till the forks and plates glisten and give him naches, because he can't stand dirty silverware lying in the sink, as they very well know, and then he puts the quarter of a chicken he didn't touch into a brown paper bag and looks through the refrigerator to see what he can take for the Beast. He pokes around the bottles of medicines old and new, and the jars of red horseradish and the plate of jellied calf's leg left over from the Sabbath among the pots full of food for the big supper that lies ahead, and for the thousandth time he peers behind the bottle of rosé wine they got as a present a few years ago from the anonymous person who bought a lottery ticket from their booth and won a thousand pounds, the biggest prize anyone ever won from them, and Momik printed on a piece of cardboard: *From this booth, ticket number such and such won 1,000 pounds*, and the man was a mensh and came around to say thank you and brought the bottle of wine with him, that was really nice, but nobody around here drinks crap like that, still it isn't nice to throw it away, and Momik took out the jar of yogurt (he could always tell Mama he ate it), and a cucumber and an egg, and after listening behind Grandfather's door to make sure he was asleep or talking to himself as usual, Momik went outside and locked the door behind him, the bottom lock too, and he ran down the steps under the wobbly concrete pillars, right into the wind, and forced the creaky cellar door open with all his might, and breathing hard, now or never, he walked in, and his face and back broke out in a cold sweat, and he stood there leaning heavily against the wall with his fist between his teeth to keep from screaming, but inwardly he was screaming, Get out get out get out or it will eat you up, but he doesn't, he mustn't, this is war, and it's stuffy and it stinks in there, like must and mildew, and animals and animal doo-doo, and there are weird noises in the dark, rasping and sputtering and cooing, and a big claw scraping the cage, and a wing spreading slowly, and a beak snapping open and shut somewhere, Get out get out, but he doesn't, and one spot of light breaks through the tiny window also covered with cardboard, and this light helps his eyes get used to the dark little by little, and even then he can hardly see the wooden crates lined up against the wall; not all of them are full yet actually, because the hunt is still on.

So far so good though. He's had some great catches. A big hedgehog he found in the back yard with a pointy black face, sad-looking like a little person, and there's a turtle he found down in Ein Kerem that's still in hibernation, and there's a toad that wanted to cross the road but Momik saved its life and brought it down here, and a lizard that unhitched its tail the instant Momik caught it, but Momik couldn't resist so he scooped up the tail with a piece of paper (it was pretty disgusting) and put the tail in a separate cage with a sign saying: *An as yet unfamiliar animal. May be venomous*. But then he had a scientific conscience about it and added a correction that looked more honest: *Tail may be venomous*, because you never can tell. And there was also a kitten that most likely went crazy in the dark cage, and then—this is what you could call the crowning touch of the collection—there was the young raven that fell out of its nest in the pine tree kerplunk onto the little balcony. The young raven's parents are very suspicious of Momik, and they swoop down at him whenever they see him in the yard; a few weeks ago they even pecked his back and his arm and there was blood and a big commotion, but they can't prove anything, and the young raven gets the drumstick every day and tears it to pieces with its claws and crooked beak, and Momik watches it and thinks, How cruel, maybe this is the Beast, but you can't really tell who it's going to come out of in the end, and we won't know till they all get the right kind of nourishment and care.

A few days ago he saw a gazelle. He saw her on his way down the Ein Kerem path, a light brown patch on the rocks sweeping by suddenly. She stopped in her tracks and turned toward him looking beautiful and frightened and wild. A gazelle. She stretched forward to sniff him, and Momik held his breath. He wanted a good smell to come out of him, a friendly smell. She raised one hoof off the ground and checked the smell. Then she jumped back and stared at him with wide-open eyes, not lovingly, she was afraid of him and she ran away. Momik searched the rocks for about an hour, but he didn't find her. He was angry and he couldn't understand why. He asked himself if she might have the Beast in her too, because Bella said it could come out of any animal. Any animal? He'd better check with Bella again.

Momik took crates labeled TNUVA PRODUCE and REFRESHING TEMPO SODA from behind Bella's grocery store. He padded them with rags and old newspapers, and made little locks for them out of wire. He lugged all the stuff in the cellar off to one side, Grandma Henny's kifat, the big Jewish Agency beds, the straw mattresses that stank of pee, and the suitcases practically bursting with shmattes that were tied up with rope to keep them from springing open, and two big sacks full of shoes, because you never throw out old shoes, as anyone who's ever walked barefoot for twenty kilometers in the snow can tell you, Papa said, which was about the only clue he ever got from Papa, and he wrote it down right away. The snow did pretty much fit in with that business about the Snow Queen who freezes everybody. And from the kitchen cupboard he stole a couple of old plates and half-broken cups for the food in the cages, and Mama noticed right away of course, and he screamed that he didn't do it, and he saw she didn't believe him, and he threw himself on the floor, kicking and pounding, and he even said something mean—that she should leave him alone already and stop butting into his business, which he never said before he started fighting the Beast, not to her or to anyone, and Mama was really frightened, and she shut up, and her hand trembled over her mouth, and her eyes popped open so wide he was afraid they would burst, okay, so what could he do, the words came out. He never guessed he had words like that inside him. But she shouldn't have made such a big fuss about it. Maybe they can't help because they aren't allowed to, okay, but do they have to butt in?

After that he stopped taking things from the house. It's risky to take anything because Mama has eyes in the back of her head, and she even sleeps with her eyes open, and she can always tell what he's thinking, that's happened several times. She knows about everything in the house. When she's drying the forks and soup spoons and knives after supper, she counts them quietly, humming a kind of tune. She knows how many tassels there are on the living-room carpet, and she always but always knows exactly what time it is, even when she doesn't have her watch on. Prophecy must run in the family, because it seems to have started with Grandfather Anshel and passed down to Mama and now Momik. The way diseases pass down.

And another thing worth mentioning is that Momik never slouches on the prophecy job, and he always tries to be a genius like Shaya Weintraub who calculated the minutes till Passover, and for the past few days Momik has been experimenting with numbers, not something really big, but fairly interesting all the same—it goes like this: he counts the number of letters in words people say on his fingers, and it could be that Momik Neuman of Beit Mazmil, Jerusalem, is the inventor of a spectacular new method of counting on your fingers, faster than a robot, and no one could ever guess how it works, because it looks as if Momik is just listening to what the person is saying, his teacher for instance, or Mama for instance, but in his head and on his fingers something else is going on. Not every word though, every word, what, is he crazy? Only words with a certain ring to them, if he hears that kind of word, his fingers start running up and down as if they were playing the piano, and they count at Super Mystère speed as if they were jet-propelled and could break the sound barrier. For instance, if someone says the word "infiltrators" on the radio, right away his fingers start running automatically, and he makes a fist which means five fingers and another fist which means five fingers and another two fingers which makes twelve letters all together. Or "national league coach," and the fingers calculate it right away, nineteen letters, or how about the magic word "uranium" which is the most important element in the atomic reactor, bzzz! One fist, two fingers, that's seven letters altogether. And Momik's had so much practice now that he can calculate whole sentences on his fingers, especially juicy ones like "Our forces returned safely," four fists, three fingers; it's really fun too, a very interesting, quiet game, and it also strengthens your hand and finger muscles, which is important because Momik's a little on the short side, and even skinnier than he is short, but—(1) short people can be strong, look at Ernie Tyler who's a dwarf (a midget, that is) and he saved Manchester United, and this year they traded him off again to save Sunderland, and (2) with the help of finger exercises and willpower like Raphael Halperin, Momik may soon become stronger, God willing, than the famous Jewish wrestler Over There, the one and only Zisha Breitbart, feared even by the goyim, may-their-name-be-blotted-out, which must be what they call a deterrent, one fist, four fingers, and by the way, according to the rules of Momik's new game, a word that ends with the middle finger is a word that brings good luck, and that's why he sometimes adds on a "the" to a word to make it come out on the middle finger. Why not? You're allowed to use strategy. In war you have to use strategy.

He waits in the cellar a little while longer. Maybe it's not long enough for the Beast, but it's still pretty hard to stay down there the way you really have to if you want to make it come out. But then he has to go so bad he wets his pants like a baby, and runs home to change. He still hasn't found a way to keep it from happening. The raven flutters its black wings—and before you know it, his pants are wet. And his undershirt is damp too, and it stinks like sweat after two hours of gym class, and meanwhile the cat is yowling, and Momik's eyes are half closed. The first night they could hear the cat all the way up in the house, and Papa wanted to go look for it down there and throw it to the devil, but Mama wouldn't let him go out by himself in the dark, and they just got used to it eventually and didn't even hear it anymore, and pretty soon the yowling got softer, as if it was coming from the cat's stomach. Momik does feel kind of bad about that cat, and he even considered setting it free, only the trouble is, Momik is scared of opening the cage door because the cat might spring at him, so the cat stays, but Momik feels more like the cat's prisoner than the other way around.

So he forces himself to stand there with his eyes shut, his body tense with battle alert, two fists, one finger, in case, God forbid, something happens, and the raven and the cat are watching and all of a sudden the raven opens its beak and makes a terrible croaking sound, and in less than no time Momik finds himself outside with his leg wet all the way down.

And then he runs upstairs and opens the door and locks the bottom lock too and shouts, "Grandfather, I'm here," and changes his pants and washes the disgusting pee from his leg, and sits down to do his homework, but first he has to wait till his hands stop shaking. Okay. Now he can draw an equilateral triangle and answer the who-said-what-to-whom questions in the Bible homework, and things like that. This he finishes pretty fast, because homework is never a problem for Momik, and he also hates to put off doing homework so he does it the same day, because why should he let it burden his mind? Then he sits down and times his breathing with his watch (a real watch that used to belong to Shimmik), and he practices so that someday he'll be able to enter a contest and sing in one breath against Lee Gaines, the Negro singer from the Delta Rhythm Boys, who are currently performing in our country bringing us their new kind of music called jazz, and just then he remembers that he forgot as usual to ask Bella for a recipe for sugar cubes to give to Blacky, the horse that belongs to his secret brother Bill, and he decides to do the homework his science teacher is going to assign three lessons from now, the questions are at the back of each chapter and he likes to be three chapters ahead, too bad he can't do that in the other subjects, and he finishes his homework now and wanders around the house, has he forgotten anything, yes: what do you feed baby hedgehogs, because the hedgehog seems to be getting fatter so maybe it's a female and you have to be prepared, because the Beast can come from anywhere.

He ran his fingers over the large volumes of the *Hebrew Encyclopedia* Papa subscribed to with the special discount offer and installment payments for employees of the National Lottery. These were the only books they bought, you can always find books to read in the library. Momik wants to save up his money to buy some books, but books are very expensive and Mama won't allow him to buy any, even with his own money. She says books attract dust. But Momik simply must have books, and when there's enough money saved up in his hiding place from presents and what he gets from Mr. Munin sometimes, he hurries down to Lipschitz's to buy a book, and on the way home he writes in the jacket in deliberately crooked handwriting: *To my good friend Momik, from Uri*, or in big, grown-up-looking letters like Mrs. Govrin's he writes: *Property of Beit Mazmil Elementary School*. This way, if Mama should ever happen to notice a new book with his school things, Momik has a cover. But the *Encyclopedia* was no use this time, because they weren't up to P for pregnancy yet, and there was nothing under Cubs either. There seemed to be an awful lot of things the *Encyclopedia* was trying to ignore, as if they didn't exist, some of the most interesting things of all in fact, like the thing Mr. Munin has been talking about more and more lately, "Happiness," the *Encyclopedia* doesn't even mention it, or maybe there's some good reason for this because usually it's very very smart. Momik loves to hold the big books in his hands, and it makes him feel good all over to run his fingers down the smooth pages that seem to have a protective covering that keeps your fingers away, so you won't get too close, because who are you, what are you compared to the *Encyclopedia*, with all the little letters crowded in long, straight columns and mysterious abbreviations like secret signals for a big, strong, silent army boldly marching out to conquer the world, all-knowing, all-righteous, and a couple of months ago Momik vowed he would read an entry a day in alphabetical order, because he's a very methodical little boy, and so far he hasn't missed once, except for the time Grandfather Anshel arrived, so the next day to make up for it he read two entries, and even though he doesn't always understand what they're talking about, he likes to touch the pages and feel deep in his stomach and his heart all the power and the silence, and the seriousness, and the scientificness that makes everything so clear and simple, and best of all he likes Volume VI, which is all about Israel, and from the cover you might think it was an ordinary volume like the others, because it looks serious and smart and scientific, but in this volume, right before the end, you suddenly see a burst of fantastic colors, two fantastic whole pages of pictures of all the stamps issued by the State of Israel, and Momik gasps when he turns the pages in this volume slowly and all the beautiful colors leap out at him and take him completely by surprise like huge bouquets of flowers or a peacock's tail fanning out in his face and all those pictures and colors and the wildness of it, and the one thing that reminds him a little of this is the red lining that looks like fire in Mama's black evening bag.

And another secret which can be told now is that those were the stamps that gave Momik the idea of drawing his stamps from Over There. In the past few days, thanks to everything the old people have been teaching him about Over There, he managed to fill nearly a whole album. Once, he had to make do with what he knew already, which wasn't that much, and which wasn't that interesting either, why not admit it; for instance, he used to draw Papa the way they draw Chaim Weizmann our first President on a blue three-piaster stamp, and he drew Mama holding a peace dove, one fist, four fingers, wearing a white dress as in the 1952 Holiday Greetings stamp, and Bella as Baron Edmond de Rothschild, she's a famous philanthropist too, with a bunch of grapes on one side, just like the real stamp. There didn't use to be that much to draw before, but now everything has changed. Momik draws lots of stamps with Grandfather Anshel as Dr. Herzl, Seer of the Nation at the Twenty-third Zionist Congress (because Grandfather Wasserman is a seer and a prophet like that), and little Aaron Marcus as Maimonides with the beads and the funny hat on the brown stamp, and Max and Moritz like the two people carrying the pole of grapes on their shoulders, Ginzburg in front, with his head bowed, and a little balloon coming out of his mouth with his three words, and behind him, Zeidman, small and pink and polite, carrying a tiny briefcase in one hand, with Ginzburg's words coming out of his mouth too in a balloon, because he always does what he sees someone else doing. But the best idea of all is the one with Munin. It's like this: on the Holiday Greetings stamp for 1953 there's a picture of a white dove flying nobly in the air and it says on the stamp, *My dove in the mountain clefts*, and for three days Momik sat down and drew maybe twenty sketches till it came out the way he wanted, a picture of Mr. Munin flying in the air with a bunch of other little birds that always fly around with him because of the bread he crumbles, and Momik drew Munin just like he is in real life, with his black hat and his big red nose like a kartofeleh, only in the picture Momik gave him white wings too like a dove, and in the corner he drew a little white star and wrote *Happiness*, because that's where Munin wants to go so much, isn't it? And there were a lot of other pretty and interesting stamps in his collection, like Marilyn Monroe with her blond hair, as pretty as Hannah Zeitrin's wig, and in the margin he wrote (Bella helped him translate), *Marilyn Monroe redst Yiddish*, because she did promise, but the one with Marilyn is just for fun, and the important stamps in the collection were the new ones from Over There and all the places and historical things like the Old Klauiz (he drew it like the new Cultural Center), and the annual fair at Neustadt which the Prophet Elijah in person used to attend, they said, disguised as a poor farmer, and the hanging pole in Plonsk with the terrible criminal Bobo hanging from it, and he also drew the Jewish Olympics, and even Elijah Leib the miser from Hannah Zeitrin's shtetl who they said wouldn't give his wife any lunch to eat (he was such a miser), and in the stamp you could see where the miser drew a Mogen David with his knife on a loaf of bread so no one would take any while he was out, and then Momik made another series, very well drawn, with all the animals from Over There. He was pretty lucky with that series because by chance he found statues of all the animals on the glass buffet in Bella's living room. He'd been there a thousand times and he never understood what they were till Grandfather Anshel arrived and Momik started to fight and then suddenly he realized that those tiny colored-glass figures were obviously the kind of animals they used to have Over There, because that's where Bella brought them from! On Bella's buffet there were blue gazelles, green elephants, purple eagles, and fish with long, bright, delicate fins, and a kangaroo, and lions, all dainty and tiny and transparent, trapped inside the glass, and you're not allowed to touch them because they're breakable, and they look as if they froze in motion, which is just what happened to everyone from Over There.

Anyway, that afternoon Momik drew a picture of Shaya Weintraub with a head like an ear of corn, with a wrinkled forehead from thinking so much, and over him he drew a bottle of Passover wine and matzo, and then he drew good old Motl as the parachutist on the Tenth Anniversary of Hebrew Parachuting stamp, and he cut out little teeth on the new stamps and pasted them in his stamp notebook, and looked at his watch and saw that it was six already, and then he turned the radio on because it was time for *Children's Corner*, and they told the story of King Matt I, and Momik listened, but he jumped up every other minute because he remembered something or other he'd forgotten to do, like sharpening his pencils till they were sharp as a pin, or shining Mama's and Papa's shoes and his own shoes too on a piece of newspaper till they glistened and gave him naches, or making a note in his geography notebook, the secret one, about what he read in the paper yesterday, that the first two mares at the Hebrew Agricultural Exhibit at Beit Dagan are already pregnant, and everyone's waiting, and after the program was over he turned the radio off and picked up *Emil and the Detectives* which he likes to read because of the suspense but also because of the five printing errors he enjoys finding and then he can check to see if he's entered them in his notebook of printing errors from books and newspapers (he's collected almost a hundred and seventy errors already), and even though he knows those mistakes from *Emil and the Detectives* have been in his notebook for a long time, it's 6:33 already, and now Momik goes over to the living-room couch and lies down under the picture his parents got from Idka and Shimmik, a big oil painting of a forest and snow and a stream and a bridge, which must be what Neustadt looked like or Dinov where his old friend once lived, and if you lie down in a certain way, kind of curled up on the couch, you can see when you look up through the branches of the tree in the corner there's a face almost like a child's face which only Momik knows about, and maybe that's his Siamese twin, but you can't tell for

sure, and Momik looks at it very hard but the truth is that today he
can't concentrate because his head's been hurting badly for a few days
now, his eyes too, but don't get tired yet, because today's war has not
even begun.

And then Momik suddenly remembered that it was a couple of hours
already since he'd decided to become a writer and so far he hadn't
written anything, and the reason was that he hadn't found anything to
write about. What did he know about dangerous criminals like in *Emil
and the Detectives*, or about submarines like in Jules Verne, and his own
life seemed so ordinary and boring, all he was was a nine-year-old kid,
what's there to tell about that, and he checked his big yellow watch
again, and slid off the couch and walked around in circles saying com-
ically, It makes my head ache to watch you krechtzing and spinning
like a top, Tuvia, as a certain person we know says to another person,
but it wasn't really so comical, though at least when he looked at his
watch again it was twenty-one minutes to seven already, and in his head
he started broadcasting the final minutes of the big game soon to take
place in Yaroslav, Poland, between us and the Polish team, and he let
them win by four goals, and then with only five minutes to go and the
situation looking kaput, our coach, Giula Mandy, raised his sad eyes
to the bleachers full of cheering Poles, when who should he see there
but a boy! And one look is enough to tell him that this boy is a born
soccer player, the player who will save the day, and if only they had let
the boy play at school he would have shown them too, oh well, and
Giula Mandy stops the game and whispers something to the referee,
and the referee agrees, and a hush falls over the crowd, and Momik
wends his way down the stairs to the playing field where he plans a
really spectacular defense and offense (he had some experience training
Alex Tochner), and in less than four minutes Momik has turned the
tide, as they say, and our team wins 5–4, please God, amen, and the
time was now fourteen minutes to seven, nu, pretty soon now, and
Momik went to the bathroom and washed his face with warm water
and held his head exactly where the long crack runs down the middle
of the mirror, and he heard the rain start falling outside and the police
car that went around the block warning people to drive slowly, and all
of a sudden Momik remembered he forgot to give Grandfather his tea
and laxative at four o'clock, and he felt a sting of conscience, you could
do just about anything to Grandfather and he wouldn't even notice,

like a baby, and lucky for him Momik was so goodhearted, because other children might take advantage of a dodo like Grandfather and do mean things to him, and Momik stuck his head out the bathroom door and heard Grandfather waking up and talking to himself as usual, and with nine minutes to go, Momik removes his braces and brushes his teeth with ivory toothpaste which is made from special elephants they grow at the Health Clinic, and meanwhile he practices saying words that have the letter *S* because when they put braces on you, it ruins your *S* and you have to make sure you don't lose it, and then finally the living-room clock strikes seven, and in the distance, from Bella's house maybe, comes the sound of news beeps, and Momik's heart races and he counts the steps from the lottery booth to the house but more slowly because they have trouble walking, and the sweat behind his knees and elbows itches, and exactly when he predicted it (almost), he heard the gate creaking in the yard and Papa's cough, and a moment later the door opened and there stood Mama and Papa who quietly said hello, and with their coats still on, and their gloves and the boots lined with nylon bags, their eyes devoured him, and even though Momik could actually feel himself being devoured, he just stood there quietly and let them do it because he knew that was what they needed, and then Grandfather Anshel came out of his room all confused in the big coat and Papa's old shoes on backward, and he tried to go outside in his pajamas but Papa stopped him gently and said, We're going to eat now, Papa; he's always gentle with poor things like him and Max and Moritz, he's nice to them and he feels sorry for them, and Grandfather doesn't understand what's holding him back and he puts up a fight, but in the end he just gives in and lets himself be seated at the table, but he doesn't let them take his coat away.

Supper:
It goes like this: first Mama and Momik set the table very fast, and Mama warms up the big pots from the refrigerator, and then she brings supper in. This is when it starts getting dangerous. Mama and Papa chew with all their might. They sweat and their eyes bulge out of their heads and Momik pretends to be eating while he watches them carefully, wondering how a woman as fat as Mama could come out of Grandma Henny, and how the two of them could have had a scarecrow boy like him. He only tastes what's on the tip of his fork, but it sticks in his

throat because he's so nervous. This is just how it is—his parents have
to eat a lot of food every night to make them strong. Once they escaped
from death, but it isn't going to let them get away a second time, that's
for sure. Momik crumbles his bread into little wads which he arranges
in squares. Then he makes an even bigger ball of dough, and breaks it
exactly in half, and then in half again. And again. You need the hands
of a heart surgeon for this kind of precision. And again in half. They
won't get angry with him for doing things like this at supper, he knows,
because they're not paying any attention to him. Grandfather, in his
big woolly overcoat, tells himself the Herrneigel story, sucking on a
piece of bread. Mama is all red now and puffing with effort. She chews
so hard you can't see her neck. The sweat runs down Papa's forehead.
They mop the pots with big chunks of bread and gobble them up.
Momik swallows spit and his glasses steam. Mama and Papa vanish
then and return behind the pots and frying pans. Their shadows dance
on the wall behind them. Suddenly they seem to be floating away on
the warm steam from the soup pot and he almost shrieks in fear; God
help them, he says in Hebrew in his heart, and translates it into Yiddish
so God will understand, Mir zal zein far deine beindelach, Do something
to me instead and have mercy on their little bones, as Mama always
says about him.

And then comes the big moment when Papa lays his fork aside and
gives a long krechtz, and looks around as if he only just noticed he was
home, and that he has a son, and that there's a grandfather sitting there.
The battle is over. They've earned another day. Momik jumps up and
runs to the kitchen faucet and drinks and drinks. Now comes the talking
and the annoying questions, but how can you get angry with someone
whose life has just been saved by a miracle? Then Momik tells them
that he did his homework and that tomorrow he'll start preparing for
the Bible test, and that his teacher asked again why his parents won't
let him go on the class trip to Mt. Tabor with everybody else (a new
teacher who doesn't know), and meanwhile Papa stands up and goes
over to the coffee table in the living room, and unbuckles his belt, and
his body floods over like a river that fills the room and just about pushes
Momik into the kitchen, and Papa sticks his hand out and starts fiddling
with the radio. He always does it like that. He waits for the radio to
warm up and then starts turning the dial. Warsaw Berlin Prague London
Moscow, not really listening, he hears a word or two and turns it some

more, Paris Bucharest Budapest, no patience at all, from country to country he moves like that, from city to city, he never stops moving and only Momik guesses that he's waiting for a message from Over There, a message calling him back from exile so that he can be the Emperor he really is again, not like he is here, but so far they haven't called.

And then Papa just gives up and turns the dial back to the Voice of Israel, and listens to the program about Knesset committees, and closes his eyes and you might think he was sleeping, but he hears every single word, and to whatever they say there he makes nasty remarks, and anyway, politics is something that makes him furious and dangerous, and Momik stands in the doorway to the kitchen, and hears Mama counting the forks and knives in her singsong as she dries them, secretly watching Papa's arms falling limply on both sides of the chair. His fingers are puffy, with gray hair on the joints, and you can't tell how they feel when they touch you because they don't.

In bed at night, Momik lies awake thinking. Over There must have been a lovely land with forests everywhere and shiny railroad tracks, and bright, pretty trains, and military parades, and the brave Emperor and the royal hunter, and the Klauiz and the animal fair, and transparent jewel-like animals that shine in the mountains like raisins on a cake. The only trouble is, there's a curse on Over There. And this is where it starts getting kind of blurry. There's this spell that was put on all the children and grownups and animals, and it made them freeze. The Nazi Beast did it. It roamed the country, freezing everything with its icy breath like the Snow Queen in the story Momik read. Momik lies in bed imagining, while Mama works at her machine in the hallway. Her foot goes up and down. Shimmik adjusted the pedal a little higher up because otherwise her foot wouldn't reach it. Over There everyone is covered in a very thin layer of glass that keeps them motionless, and you can't touch them, and they're sort of alive but sort of not, and there's only one person in the whole world who can save them and that's Momik. Momik is almost like Dr. Herzl, only different. He made a blue and white flag for Over There, and between the two blue stripes he drew an enormous drumstick tied to the back of a Super Mystère, and below it he wrote the words *If so you will, it is no fairy tale*, but he knows he doesn't have the least idea yet about what he's supposed to do, and that kind of worries him.

Sometimes they come into his room at night and stand next to his bed. They just want to take one last look at him before they start with the nightmares. That's when Momik strains every muscle to look as if he's asleep, to look like a healthy, happy boy, just as cheerful as he can be, always smiling, even in his sleep, ai-li-luli-luli, we have the most hilarious dreams around here, and sometimes he has a really Einsteiny idea, like when he pretends to be talking in his sleep and says, Kick it to me, Joe, we're going to win this game, Danny, and things like that to make them happy, and once on a really horrible day when Grandfather wanted to go outside after supper and they had to lock him up in his room and he started hollering and Mama cried, well, that horrible day Momik pretended to be asleep and he sang them the national anthem and got so carried away he wet his bed, and all to make them understand they didn't have to get so upset, they didn't have to waste their fears on him or anything, they ought to be saving their strength for the really important things, like supper and their dreams and all the silences, and then just as he was finally falling asleep he heard as if in the distance, or maybe he was dreaming already, Hannah Zeitrin calling God to come already, and also the quiet yowling of the cat who was going crazy in the cellar, and Momik promised to try even harder from now on.

He had two brothers.

Or put it this way, once he had a friend.

The friend's name was Alex Tochner. Alex came from Rumania last year and he knew only a little Hebrew. Netta the teacher sat him next to Momik, because Momik would be a good example, and also because he knows Hebrew best in the whole class, and also maybe because she knew Momik wouldn't make fun of Alex. And when Alex sat down next to Momik, the whole class started laughing at them because they were two four-eyes.

Alex Tochner was short but very strong. Whenever he wrote something his arm muscles popped out. He had bristly yellow hair, and even though he wore glasses, they didn't look as if they were for reading. He was always fidgeting and he didn't talk much. When he did talk though he rolled his *r*'s, like the old people. The children called them "the two Polacks," and Momik and Alex hardly spoke a word to each other. But then Momik decided to do something, and one day during

General Science he passed Alex a note asking if maybe he could come over after school tomorrow. Alex shrugged his shoulders and said yeah, he guessed so. Momik could hardly sit still for the rest of the day. After supper he asked Mama and Papa if it would be all right to bring home a friend, and Mama and Papa gave each other a look and started asking him a bunch of questions like Who is this friend, what does he want from Momik, and is he one of us or one of them, and is he the kind that steals things and would he go snooping around the house, and what do his parents do? Momik told them everything and in the end they said it was all right if he wanted to bring him over, but to keep an eye on him. That night Momik was too excited to sleep. He thought about how he and Alex would get along together, and how they would be a two-man team, how this, and how that, and the next morning he was at school by 7:30.

After school Alex came over and they went out for a falafel at the shopping center; Alex liked falafel, Momik didn't, but it was exciting to pay and eat out for once, and in the end he gave his half to Alex; Alex used so much hot sauce the falafel man said he'd have to charge him double. Then they went home and did their homework and then they played checkers. It was definitely more fun to play with another person. Momik made up his mind that night to be a man from now on and keep his mouth shut like Alex, but he couldn't not talk, because what are friends for? What, were they supposed to just keep quiet like a couple of blockheads? And he went on asking Alex questions about Alex and Alex's homework and about where Alex came from, and Alex gave him short answers and Momik was afraid Alex was getting bored and that he'd leave, and he ran to the kitchen and climbed up on a chair and reached into Mama's hiding place and took out the bar of chocolate which isn't for company, but this was an emergency, as they say, and when he offered it to Alex he told him that Grandma Henny died not long ago and Alex took one square of chocolate and then another square and said his father died too, and Momik was excited because he knows about things like that, and he asked if his father was killed by Them, and Alex didn't understand what he meant by Them and said that his father was killed in an accident, he was a boxer and he was knocked out, and now Alex was the man of the house. Momik was silent thinking, What an interesting life this Alex has, and Alex said, "Over There I was the best runner in my class."

Momik, who knew the record times of all Olympic runners and class champions by heart, said that to be on the team here you had to run sixty meters in 8.5, and Alex said maybe he wasn't in condition right now, but if he started working out he'd make the team for sure. He liked to talk big, and he never smiled at Momik, and he ate up square after square of the chocolate bar that would normally have lasted a month. "They called me an Ashkenazi Bech Bech," said Alex woodenly, "and that's why I'm gonna make the team." Momik said, "They're Ashkenazim too, you know, not all of them, but the ones who called you that." "Nobody calls Alex a Bech Bech."

Alex had so much confidence that Momik was sure he would win, but at the same time he felt kind of glum and he didn't know why. Alex hung around for a little while longer, shamelessly touching everything in sight. He twirled the sewing machine wheel roughly, asked questions guests aren't supposed to ask, and then he said he was sick of being in the house, so Momik jumped up and asked if maybe he wanted a nice cup of tea, because that's what you say when the guests (like Bella or Idka and Shimmik) say they'd better be going now, but Alex made a face and said, There's nothing to do around here, and Momik thought a minute and said maybe they could go hang out at Bella's café because she always had very interesting things to tell, and Alex made another face and asked Momik was he always like this, and Momik didn't understand and asked, Like what? and Alex asked, Aren't there any kids on this street? and Momik said, No, it's not a very big street. He was surprised because he'd thought that Alex, since he was a new immigrant, wouldn't want to play with the other children, that's why Momik hoped he and Alex could be buddies, because Momik is well behaved and nice and he doesn't make fun of people or cuss and things like that, but Momik thought, Well, Alex is still a new immigrant and he doesn't know what's what yet exactly, and it might take a little while for him to catch on that Momik has more in his little finger than all those hooligans and ruffians who laugh and run the sixty at 8.5. So anyway, they walked down the street together, and it was autumn, and the old pear tree in Bella's yard was full of half-rotten fruit, and Alex looked up and said, What?! You've gotta be crazy to let this go! and he sneaked into the yard and swiped a couple of pears and gave one to Momik, and Momik, whose heart was pounding, took a bite and chewed but didn't swallow, because that's stealing, and look who from, too. They walked in the direction of Mt. Herzl, and Alex again said that he was going to make the team, and suddenly Momik had a really brainy idea, and he told Alex that he would be his coach, and Alex said, "You?! You don't know noth . . ." but Momik quickly explained that he would be an excellent coach, that he'd read things about all the coaches in the world, that at home he had sports pictures and clippings from the newspapers ("And I mean newspapers from all over the world," he said, which wasn't exactly a lie because of *Pshegelond*), and that he could draw up an Olympic training schedule, and that his watch had a second hand, which is the main thing a running coach needs. Alex wanted to see the watch, and Momik showed it to him, and Alex said, Let's try it out, I'll run over to that pole and you time me, and Momik said, Ready Set Go, and Alex ran and Momik timed him and said 10.9, and maybe we shouldn't wave our hands around like that because it wastes energy, and Alex said maybe he wouldn't mind a little coaching, but he didn't feel like coming over to Momik's house anymore. That's how the great friendship began, but Momik doesn't like to think about it anymore.

And he has a pair of brothers too.

The older one's name is Bill. Every month the magazine with the latest adventure comes in at Lipschitz's in the shopping center. Momik stands in the corner and reads and Lipschitz doesn't say anything, because he and Mama come from the same shtetl. And the stories are suspenseful and educational too. His brother Bill is pretty tough. He's so tough he's not allowed to stick up for Momik if someone in Momik's class bothers him, because one blow from Bill and you're dead, and that's why Momik made Bill promise never ever to stick up for him, not even when that business with Laizer the Crook started, and at least twice a week Momik picks himself up off the schoolyard full of blood and dirt but smiling a mysterious smile, because he has mastered his impulses once again, as they say, and held Bill in check.

Bill calls him Johnny, and when they talk together they use short sentences with a lot of exclamation marks, like Punch him in the jaw, Bill!! Good work, Johnny!! etc. Bill has a silver star on his chest which means he's a sheriff. Momik doesn't have a star yet. Together they own a horse called Blacky. Blacky understands every word you say, and he loves to gallop wildly through the countryside, but in the end he always comes back and nuzzles Momik's chest with his head, and it's great, and just then Netta the teacher asks, Just what are we smiling about, Shlomo Neuman? and Momik hides Blacky away. He steals sugar from the kitchen and experiments with different ways of making sugar cubes which is what Blacky likes best, but so far no luck, and the *Hebrew Encyclopedia* isn't up to Sugar yet, and meanwhile he'll just have to find some way to feed this horse of his, won't he. At least three times a week they go galloping through the Ein Kerem Valley in search of missing children or children whose parents lost them, and they set Orde Wingate ambushes for train robbers. Sometimes as Momik lies on his stomach in ambush, he sees the tall smokestack of the new building they just finished over on Mt. Herzl, which they call Yad Vashem, a funny sort of name, and he pretends it's a ship sailing by, full of illegal immigrants from Over There that nobody wants to take in, like in the days of the British Mandate pshakrev, and he's going to have to rescue that ship somehow, with Blacky or Bill or with mindpower or with his animals or the atomic reactor or with Grandfather Anshel's story and the Children of the Heart, anything, and when he asked his old people what the smokestack is for, they looked at each other, and finally Munin told him that there's a museum there, and Aaron Marcus, who hadn't been out of his house for a couple of years, asked, Is it an art museum? and Hannah Zeitrin smiled crookedly and said, Oh sure it is, a museum of human art, that's what kind of art.

And the whole time they're there in ambush Momik has to keep making sure Bill's star isn't flashing light, so that the criminals won't spot them, but anyway Bill gets killed at least twenty times a day by the bullets and knives of the villains, and in the end he always comes back to life, thanks to Momik who gets really scared when Bill dies, and maybe it's the fear, his very hopelessness, you might say, that brings Bill back to life, and he sits up and smiles and says, "Thanks, Johnny, you saved my life!!" And meanwhile Blacky gorges himself on sugar cubes stuck together with mud and spit, and sugar cubes made out of plastic glue, and sugar cubes Momik freezes between the ice blocks in Eizer the milkman's ice chest, and Bill died and came back to life and died and came back to life again and again, and that was the best part of the game, only it wasn't really a game at all, a game, ha! Momik didn't enjoy it one bit, but he could never dream of stopping it because he has to practice, because there are so many people waiting for him to become a leading world expert, just as everyone waited for Professor

Jonas Salk to invent the polio vaccine, and Momik knows someone's got to be the first to volunteer to enter the frozen kingdom and fight the Beast and rescue all the people and take them away, and you just have to have a plan, that's all, something that hero Captain Meir Har-Zion would do if he were fighting it, a bold, daring stunt maybe only Giula Mandy the coach we brought here all the way from Hungary could devise to make his parents better both now and backward in time, only the Beast doesn't seem to want to take off its disguises yet, and there hasn't been that much progress with the animals lately either, and it made him feel bad to think maybe he was keeping all those poor animals in the dark for nothing, but then he would tell himself, In war there's suffering and sometimes the innocent suffer too (these are the words that came to him), like Laika the dog who sacrificed herself on the scientific altar of Sputnik 2, so he was just going to have to try harder and sleep less, never forgetting the example of Grandfather Anshel, who tells his story in the hope of someday beating Herrneigel once and for all, and sometimes Momik has a feeling Grandfather is getting so mixed up in his story that Herrneigel must be losing patience too.

And one time at lunch there was a terrible rumpus. Grandfather started screaming at the top of his lungs, and then he cupped his hand over his ear and listened, and his face turned red and his lips were trembling, and Momik jumped up and went over to the door because suddenly he understood all the things he hadn't understood before, stupid him, that Herrneigel himself was the Nazikaput, because kaput means finished, as Momik knew from Hebrew, and a Nazi is a beast and now it was clear to him that Herrneigel was angry with Grandfather because of the story, because he didn't want to be kaput and so he was trying to force Grandfather to change the story the way he wanted it, but Grandfather is no weakling, that's for sure, you touch his story and he turns into a different man! Yes, Grandfather grabbed a drumstick and waved it wildly, hollering in old-fashioned Hebrew that he would not let Herrneigel interfere with his story because his story was his whole life, and Momik, whose heart sank all the way down to his underpants, saw by the look on Grandfather's face that Nazikaput was getting a little worried now and he must have decided to give in to Grandfather because Grandfather was so convincingly in the right, but suddenly Grandfather turned away from the wall and stared blankly at

Momik, and Momik knew that if Grandfather wanted to, he could pull him right into his story just the way he did Herrneigel, and Momik would have run away only he couldn't move, and he tried to scream but no sound came out, and then Grandfather motioned with his finger for Momik to come closer, and it was like a magic spell, Momik moved toward him thinking, This is it, he would get into Grandfather's story now and nobody would ever find him, and he was just lucky Grandfather didn't want to do that to him, he wouldn't do a thing like that to Momik, Momik was such a good little boy; okay, maybe he tortures the animals in the cellar a little but that's because of the war, and then when he got up close to Grandfather, Grandfather said in a low, clear voice, like a completely normal person, Nu, did you see that goy? Oich mir a chucham, and Grandfather smiled a normal smile at Momik, like a smart and ancient man, and he put his hand on Momik's shoulder like a real grandfather and whispered in his ear that he was going to turn this goy around and send him back to Chelm, and Momik didn't want to miss his big chance to ask Grandfather what the story was about, and find out if he was right that the Children of the Heart were after Herrneigel, and by the way, what did they need that baby for (Momik does know something about suspense stories and when there's danger, babies are big trouble), but then the usual thing happened: Grandfather stepped back and stared at Momik as though he'd never seen him before in his life, and he started talking very fast, saying those things he always says in that tune, and Momik was all alone again.

Then as he slipped his untouched lunch into a brown paper bag for the animals, he started thinking that maybe it would be a good idea to consult this expert he read about in the newspaper, the expert who's in the same profession as Momik. Wiesenthal, they call him, and he lives in Vienna, which is where he sets off from to hunt them. Momik hoped that if he wrote him a letter, the hunter would give him some information about important matters, like where they hide and what their habits are in food and prey, and also if they run in herds, and how can it be that out of one single beast comes a whole army of people, and whether there's some magic word (Momik thinks there isn't) like "Chaimova" or "uranium" that if you say it to them makes them obey you and follow you everywhere, and maybe the hunter has a picture of them, alive or dead, so that Momik will be able to see what he's looking for. Momik was pretty busy for a few days planning what to write to him. He tried to imagine the hunter's house, with big rugs made from the fur of the Beast, and a special shelf for rifles and bows and pipes, and heads of Nazi Beasts hunted down in the jungles hanging from the wall, with glassy eyes, and Momik tried to write the letter, but it didn't come out right, he tried maybe twenty times but it still didn't come out right, and that week it said in Bella's newspaper that the hunter was setting off on another trip to South America, and they showed a picture, a man with nice, sad eyes, with a bald forehead, not at all as Momik imagined, so Momik was left alone again with no one to help him, and now he was getting a little nervous.

But he told himself that the hunter wouldn't be able to help him anyway, because the weird thing about this war against the Beast is that each person has to fight it alone, and even people who really need his help can't ask straight out, because of this secret oath it seems they've taken, and Momik keeps telling himself that he isn't trying hard enough and that he isn't concentrating hard enough, and it was also around this time that he had a couple of hunting accidents, starting when an abandoned jackal cub bit him under the knee and he had to have twelve agonizing rabies shots. And after that he accidentally fell on top of a little porcupine that was hiding under a bush in the valley, and his knee began to look like a sieve. Momik had always liked reading about animals, but it wasn't until he started fighting the Beast that he'd ever had to actually touch one, and the truth is, it kind of disgusted him, though in a way it didn't. He had a real instinct for animals, he guessed, and maybe when it was all over, he would get himself a pet dog. A regular dog. Not for the war, for fun. But meanwhile the injured pigeon he found in the back yard practically pecked his eye out, and another cat he tried to catch by the garbage cans as a replacement for his crazy cat scratched his arm all over. Momik was certainly being brave in this war. He never knew he could be so brave, but it was bravery out of fear, and he knew it. Because he was afraid. And what about the ravens, the parents of the raven that was his prisoner, who now knew for sure that Momik was the one who snatched their kid, and every time he went out of the house they swooped down on him like a pair of Egyptian MiGs, and the first time it happened, by the way, one of the ravens actually jabbed his neck and arm and he almost had a fit, as they say, and he ran all the way to the lottery booth and told Mama and Papa about the attack, but he didn't explain it too well, and also he didn't know the word for raven in Yiddish, and Mama didn't quite understand seeing the blood and the rip in his shirt, and she rushed him over to the health clinic and shrieked and fainted as she tried to explain to Dr. Erdreich that something terrible happened, an eagle tried to take my child away, and some people in Beit Mazmil remember Momik to this day as the child the eagle tried to snatch.

But it was no use. The cellar was turning blacker and more suffocating every day, and Momik didn't dare make a move. The animals grew wild and voracious, and flung themselves against the walls of their cages, and hurt themselves and howled and shrieked. The injured pigeon died, and it was too sickening to take the body out, and it started to stink and the ants came in, choleria. Momik always had this feeling that the cellar was full of big, sticky old cobwebs just waiting to grab him if he made a move. He'd never felt so dirty and smelly in his whole life. These little animals were a lot stronger than he was, he could see that now, because they hated him and they knew what it meant to be wild and to fling themselves and shriek in their cages, and he thought maybe that was a sign that the war had begun and the Beast wasn't kidding around anymore, that it was sneaking up on him now, paralyzing him with a polio Jonas Salk had never dreamed of, and this was serious, because Momik couldn't tell where the Beast was going to pounce from, he didn't know what to do if it decided to show itself, maybe it would pounce out of two animals at the same time, how would he be able to say something like "Chaimova" before it tore him to shreds?

He rubbed some kerosene from the heater all over his arms and legs so that maybe the smell would make it sick, and he also put a mothball in each pocket of his shirt and trousers, but that still didn't seem like enough, so then he decided to write a welcoming address. It took him at least a week to write it, and he knew that it would have to be the best speech in the whole world to have an effect on the Beast the split second before it attacked. First he wrote how you should always be good and think of the other person, and that you have to learn how to forgive like on Yom Kippur, but when he read it out loud, he knew the Beast would never believe this kind of thing. It had to be stronger. He tried to figure out how the Beast feels things, what affects it. He tried to draw a picture of it, but it came out looking like a lonely little polar bear, full of anger and hating the whole world, and he understood now that the speech was going to have to wipe out all the hatred and loneliness in one stroke, because there are things even a frozen polar bear longs for in its heart, so then Momik wrote a long speech about friendship between two friends who love each other, and about nice, simple conversations between a mother and father and a father and son. And he told the Beast about how sweet little brothers and sisters are, and how much fun it is to pick them up and put them in their strollers and show them off at the shopping center, and other silly things; he had a feeling this was the kind of thing that would really get the Beast, like a soccer tournament when you score and everyone cheers and no one calls you names, or like a Saturday morning walk with Mama and Papa when they both hold him by the hand and say, "Little bird, little bird, fly a-wayyy!" and toss him in the air, or like the school trip to Mt. Tabor, when the whole class goes hiking and they sing songs, and at night they whoop it up in the hostel, but when he saw it written down, he knew it was a stupid speech, a sickening speech, it was a crummy stinking speech, and he tore it to pieces and burned it in the kitchen sink, and decided to give up on the speech idea and just sit and wait and see what it would do when it turned up, and it was clear to Momik now that the Beast was only stalling like this to get him mad and bring him down even more, and he made up his mind to show the Beast it could never-ever-black-and-blue do that to him.

And for two weeks it did look as if there was going to be a chance for a surprise victory, because a third brother had now joined the other two: Motl Ben Paisee, the Chazzan. Momik would never forget those days. In school they read this story by Sholem Aleichem, and Momik had a strong feeling about it and decided to say something sort of casually after supper. Nu, Papa opened his mouth and started to talk! He talked in complete sentences, and Momik listened and almost cried for joy. Papa's eyes, which are blue with red rims, turned a little brighter, as if the Beast had left them for a second. Momik was as sly as a young fox! Like the fox in the story about the cheese and the raven! He told Papa (casually) about My Brother Elijah, and Manny the calf, and the river they poured barrels of kvass into, and with your own eyes you could see the Beast open its mouth a little, to let Papa tumble right out to Momik.

Little by little Papa told him all about his tiny village and the muddy lanes and the chestnut trees we don't have in this country, and the old fishmonger and the water drawer and the lilac blossoms, and the heavenly taste of bread Over There, and the cheder, which was the schoolroom, and the rebbe, who earned a little extra money mending broken pottery with the help of a wire he would wind around the pots, and how at the age of three he used to walk home from cheder all by himself on snowy nights, lighting his way with a special lamp made out of a radish with a candle stuck inside it, and then Mama said, There was a kind of bread there they don't have in this country, now when you mention it, yes I remember: we used to bake it at home, where else, and it lasted the week, if I could taste that taste once more in my life, and Papa said, Where we used to live, between our village and Chodorov, there was a big forest. A real forest, not like these toothless combs the National Smashional Fund plants around here, in that forest we had big pojomkes they don't have in this country, like great big cherries, and Momik was amazed to hear that there was a village called Chodorov just like the name of the goalkeeper on the Tel Aviv Ha Poel team, but he didn't want to interrupt so he kept quiet, and Mama gave a little krechtz full of memories and said, Yes, but where I come from we called them yagedes, and Papa said, No, yagedes is something else, yagedes is smaller. Ach, the fruit there, a mechayeh, and the grass, you remember the grass? And Mama said, Remember, what do you mean remember, oy, how can I forget, zal ich azoy haben koach tzu leben, may I have the strength to live, how I remember all those things, such green you never saw, and strong, not like the grass in this country that looks half dead, you call that grass, it's a leprosy of the earth, and Over There when they mowed the wheat and stacked it in the fields, remember, Tuvia? Ach! says Papa inhaling, and the way it smelled! Where we lived people used to be afraid to fall asleep on a fresh bale, God forbid they shouldn't be able to wake up again . . .

They talked like this to each other and they both talked to Momik. This was why Momik read some other stories by Sholem Aleichem (what a funny name for a writer!), which they didn't even tell you to read in school. He borrowed the stories about Menachem Mendel and Tevye the Dairyman from the school library, and read them chapter by chapter, quickly and thoroughly the way he does. The village was becoming very familiar to him. In the first place, he realized that there were a lot of things he knew about already from his friends on the bench, and whatever he didn't understand Papa was glad to explain, words like gabai, galach, melamed dardakai, and things like that. And each time Papa would start explaining, he thought of something else and would tell a little more, and Momik remembered everything, and afterward he would run to his room and write it down in his geography notebook (he was up to notebook 3 by now!), and on the last pages of the notebook he made a little dictionary with the translation of the words in the language of Over There into our language Hebrew, and so far he had eighty-five words. In geography class at school, with the atlas open on his desk, Momik carried out experiments, substituting Boibrik for Tel Aviv, and Haifa for Katrielibka with Mt. Carmel for the Hill of the Jews, the hill where miracles happen, and Jerusalem is Yahoupitz, and Momik made little pencil marks like an army commander makes on a battle map: Menachem Mendel goes from here to there, from Odessa to Yahoupitz and Zamrinka, and the Menashe Forest is where Tevye rides his old horse, and the Jordan is the San River which demanded a fresh victim every year, they believed, till one day the rabbi's son drowned and the rabbi cursed the river and it shrank to the size of a little creek, and on Mt. Tabor Momik writes Goldeneh Bergel, and pencils in the little barrels of gold that the King of Sweden left there when he was running away from the Russians, and on Mt. Arbel he draws a small cave, like the one Dobush the terrible robber dug in the mountain near Mama's town, Bolichov, to hide in and plot his crimes. Momik has no end of ideas.

And down in Ein Kerem, three brothers galloped their horse Blacky, wildly and fiercely, holding each other by the waist. Bill the strong one sat in front, Momik the responsible one sat in the middle, and Motl sat in the rear, his payes curled behind his ears, his eyes gleaming, and his muscles getting stronger by the day, and soon they would be able to take him out on a real mission.

Okay, so there were a lot of things you had to explain to him that he never knew before like what the sound barrier is, which is broken by the jets given to us by our Eternal Allies the French, and who Nathaniel Balsberg the religious runner on the Elizur track team is, who beat the five-kilometer record, with-the-help-of-God, and what the Suleiman Fire Gang is, and what exactly they use the swimming pool at the new atomic reactor in Nahal Soreq for, and how you should always have a piece of cardboard folded in your shirt pocket wherever you go, to stop bullets aimed at your heart, and what a reprisal is, one

fist three fingers, and Motl nearly botched things up because he just
didn't know how to sit still in an ambush and wait quietly, or what an
Uzi is, and a Super Mystère and an EMX, because in his shtetl they
probably had different names for guns and airplanes.

One time Momik dawdled in the school library waiting for it to get
dark outside, and Mrs. Govrin told him to go home, so he hung around
a little while longer in the playground, and when the coast was clear,
he took the big surprise out of his schoolbag, the radish he had cut in
two and scooped out with his jackknife, and he stuck a candle into the
radish and lit it, and walked all the way home like this in a very gentle
rain that didn't blow the candle out, through the snowdrifts of the
chestnut forest and the lilac groves and the big pojomkes which might
in fact be yagedes, but who cares, and the good smell of the bread they
baked at home, and the big river with the tadpoles and the tiny leeches,
and the animal fair where they sold the good horse they loved dearly
because they didn't have enough money for food, and so the three-
year-old child made his way home from Rabbi Itzla's cheder to a house
full of boys and girls, brothers and sisters, where he would sit and eat
under the table like the gentry, and Mama and Papa came out to meet
him because they were worried sick and they saw him walking through
the streets of Borochov, slowly and carefully, shielding the candle with
his hand to make sure it wouldn't blow out, striding responsibly with
the emotion of the torch runner at the Maccabean Games, all the way
here from a foreign land, and Mama and Papa huddled together not
knowing what to do, and he looked up at them and wanted to say
something beautiful, but all of a sudden Papa's face changed and shrank
as if he were disgusted or something, and he raised his enormous hand
and smacked the candle with all his might (his fingers didn't touch
Momik), and the candle fell into a little puddle and was extinguished,
and Papa said in a choked voice, Enough of this nonsense. You pull
yourself together now, and be normal, and never again did he tell
Momik about his village and how he was a boy there, and Motl never
returned again either, maybe he didn't want to, or maybe Momik felt
funny because of what had happened, and so, Momik was left alone
once more to face the Beast, but the Beast wasn't ready to appear yet.

At night Mama leans over his bed and sniffs his feet which smell of
kerosene and then suddenly she says something really hilarious in Yiddish, she says, God, maybe you could play with some other family?

And don't forget there were other things besides the search and the hunter and the sweat to think about, there were regular things too, and no one was allowed to suspect anything was wrong so they wouldn't start asking questions and butting in, and he had tests to study for and there was school every day from eight to one, which is pretty unbearable unless you keep telling yourself that all the kids around you go to a secret school we established in the underground, and whenever you hear footsteps outside you have to get your guns and prepare to die, and there was Grandfather who was becoming grouchier and jumpier than ever to look after, his Nazi must have really been upsetting him, and Momik had strategies and special oaths to think about every time Nasser pshakrev says he's going to stop one of our ships in the Suez Canal, and what about those stupid postcards somebody stuck Momik's name on, and he had to send off more and more postcards with names of people he didn't even know, you erase the top name on the list and add the name of another boy at the bottom, or God forbid something terrible will happen to him, like the banker from Venezuela who didn't take it seriously and lost all his money and his wife died, poor man, and don't even ask how much those postcards cost him, though luckily Mama didn't skimp on this and gave him whatever he needed to mail them all, so anyway besides all the regular things there was that kid Laizer from seventh grade, who'd been snatching Momik's sandwich every day now for three months. At first it really scared him, because how could a boy only three years older than him be such a crook and a shvartzer and desperate enough maybe to commit a terrible crime like extortion which you can go to jail for. But Momik realized that since this was how things stood, he'd better not think about it too much because he had to save his energy for more important things, and since Laizer was stronger than him anyhow, what good would it do to think about it all the time and feel insulted and want to die and start crying, right? And since Momik is a scientific boy who is very good at making decisions, he walked right up to Laizer and explained to him in a logical way that if the other children saw him give his sandwich away, they'd tell the teacher on him, and therefore he had a more spylike method to propose. The extortionist criminal who lived in a hut and had a big scar on his forehead was about to get angry and say something, but then he thought over what Momik told him and just kept quiet. Momik took a piece of paper from his right pocket with a list of the six safest places in school where you could hide a sandwich which someone else could pick up later without getting into trouble. Momik detected as he read the list out that Laizer was beginning to regret the whole thing, but he was just beginning to develop a little confidence now. From his left pocket he took out a second list he'd made for Laizer. This was a list of all the days of our first trial month (he told Laizer), noting where the sandwich would be on each particular day. Laizer was clearly sorry about the whole thing now. He started to say, Cut the crap, Helen Keller, I was only fooling, who needs your stinkin' sandwich anyway, but Momik wouldn't hear of it, he felt stronger than the criminal now, and though he could have just said okay then, no more extortion, he didn't want to stop, and he practically shoved the papers at Laizer, telling him, We start tomorrow, and the next day he put the sandwich in the appointed place and sat waiting in ambush according to plan, and watched as Laizer walked up, glanced at the paper, looked both ways, and picked up the goods, though he didn't look very happy about it to Momik; in fact, when he peered into the little bag Momik had packed so nicely, he looked thoroughly revolted but there was no choice, like it or lump it, he had to do what Momik said so as not to spoil this devious plan which was more than he and maybe Momik too could handle. And to top it off, Momik had the Beast to fight in various ways he thought up from day to day, because it was clearer than ever now that he must not fail, this was really serious, too many people and things were involved and everything depended on him, and if the Beast wouldn't take off its disguise, it was just being trickier than him, that's all, it had more combat experience than he had, but if it ever did decide to show itself, it would show itself to Momik and no one else, because who else but Momik would challenge it like this, with so much daring, chutzpah, and the devotion of soldiers who charge ahead and fling themselves on the barbed-wire fence so the others can climb over them. And by the end of winter, when the wind was having one last fling at wrecking Beit Mazmil, Momik reversed his tactics, figuring that what he needed in order to fight the Beast was the very thing that most scared it, the thing he'd been avoiding all along, which was to get to know more about the Beast and its crimes, because otherwise he'd just be wasting energy no matter what he did, because the fact of the matter is, he didn't have a clue about how to fight it. And that's the truth. Which is how he got involved with the Holocaust and all that. In total secrecy, Momik joined the public library (his parents wouldn't allow him to be a member of two libraries) and he would take the Number 18 bus to town some afternoons and read everything the library had on it. The library had a big shelf with a sign saying LIBRARY OF THE HOLOCAUST AND VALOR, and Momik started going through it book by book. He read incredibly fast because he was afraid that time was running out, and though he didn't understand most of it, he knew that someday he would. He read *Mysteries of Fate* and *The Diary of Anne Frank; Let Me Stay the Night, Feifel; The Doll House; The Cigarette Vendors of Three-Cross Square*; and many other books. The children he met in the library were kind of like him, like he'd always felt deep inside all these years. They spoke Yiddish at home with their parents and didn't have to hide it, and they were also fighting the Beast, which is the main thing.

On the days Momik didn't go to the library, he would spend hours in the gloomy cellar. From a quarter to two in the afternoon till it got dark, and even a few minutes after sometimes, he would sit on the cold floor in front of the animals with their shiny eyes and nasty noises, and the way they tried to act as if they didn't care when he was around, but he knew it could happen any minute, because obviously even the Beast would crack up if you made it nervous enough by studying its crimes in a scientific way, and by sitting and staring at it so maddeningly day after day, and it took all Momik's effort to sit there one minute more, two minutes more, with his feet firmly planted to keep him from beating it out of there, and he started making weird noises like wheezing or like a kitten squealing, he was beginning to remind himself of Grandfather with all these noises, but he stayed put even after the light coming through the tiny slit in the window faded and it was pitch-dark, and he was doing this because of what seemed to be a very important clue which he found tucked slyly away in *Mysteries of Fate* where it said distinctly, "From utter 'darkness' sprang the Nazi beast."

Day after day. In the adult reading room at the public library Momik sat on a high-backed chair, with his feet dangling down. He told Hillel the librarian that he was working on a special report for school about the Holocaust, and no one asked any questions. He read history books with tiny print about what the Nazis did, and stumbled over a lot of words and expressions that weren't used anymore. He puzzled over some peculiar photographs, he couldn't figure out what was going on and what went where, but deep down inside he began to sense that these photographs might reveal the first part of the secret everyone had tried to keep from him. There were pictures of a mother and father forced to choose between two children, to choose which one would stay with them and which one would go away forever, and he tried to figure out how they would choose, according to what, and he saw a picture of a soldier forcing an old man to ride another old man like a horse, and he saw pictures of executions in ways he never knew existed, and he saw pictures of graves where a lot of dead people lay in the strangest positions, on top of each other, with somebody's foot stuck in somebody else's face, and somebody's head on so crooked Momik couldn't twist his head around like that, and so little by little Momik started to understand new things, like how weak the human body is, for instance, and how it can break in so many shapes and directions if you want to break it, and how weak a thing a family is if you want to break it, just like that it happens and it's all over. At six in the evening Momik would leave the library, tired and quiet. On the bus home, he didn't see or hear anything.

Almost every day at recess he would sneak out of school and detour around the street where the lottery booth is to Bella's grocery store. He would get there all out of breath, pull her by the hand to the corner (if there happened to be a customer in the store just then), and start firing questions at her in a whisper that was more like a roar: What was the death train, Bella? Why did they kill little children? What do people feel when they have to dig their own graves? Did Hitler have a mother? Did they really use the soap they made out of human beings? Where do they kill people nowadays? What's a Jude? What are experiments with human beings? What and how and why and why and how and what? Bella, who could see for herself by now how important and serious it was, answered his every question and didn't cover anything up, only her face looked miserable and grim. Momik was also a little worried. Not nervous, just very worried. It was getting harder all the time, the Beast was winning, that much was certain, and though he knew everything about it now and wasn't a little nine-and-a-quarter-year-old ninny anymore who believed the Beast would come out of a hedgehog or some poor cat or even a raven, he was still in one terrible mess; he'd found out where the Beast actually was, though he couldn't tell how it happened, or how it could appear from just thinking and imagining it, but this much was clear, the Beast did exist, he could feel it in his bones the way Bella could tell when it was going to rain, and it was also clear that Momik had been the one who stupidly woke it out of its long sleep, the one who challenged it to come out, the way Judah Ken-Dor challenged the Egyptians at the Mitla Pass to shoot at him, so they'd give themselves away; only Judah Ken-Dor had his buddies covering him from behind, while Momik was all alone, and now he had to fight to the finish, though nobody cared whether he wanted to or not, and he knew only too well that if he ever tried to run away, the Beast would chase him to the ends of the earth (it has spies and supporters everywhere), and little by little, it would do to him what it did to all the others, only this time in an even slyer, more diabolical way, and who could say how many years it would torture him like that and what would happen in the end.

But then singlehandedly Momik discovered how to bring the Beast out of the animals in the cellar, and it was so simple really, it was amazing he hadn't thought of it sooner, since even the sleepy turtle knows it's a turtle when it catches a whiff of cucumber peels, and the raven ruffles its feathers when Momik comes with the drumstick, so quite simply, all Momik had to do now was show the Beast the food it liked best—a Jew.

So then he started to put a plan together, cleverly and very carefully. First he copied out pictures from the library books into his notebook, and made notes to remind him what a Jew looks like, how a Jew looks at a soldier, how a Jew looks when he's frightened, how he looks in a convoy, and how he digs a grave. He also made notes from his own store of experience with Jews, like how a Jew krechtzes, how he screams out in his sleep, and how he chews on a drumstick, etc. Momik worked like a combination scientist and detective. Take the boy in this picture, for instance, the one with the visor cap and his hands up. Momik tried to figure things from the boy's eyes, like what the beast in front of him looked like just then, and whether he knew how to whistle with two fingers, and whether he'd ever heard that Chodorov isn't just the name of a town but the name of a great goalie, and what his parents had done to make him have to stick his hands up like that, and where they were when they ought to have been taking care of him, and whether he was religious or not and had a collection of real stamps from Over There, and whether he'd ever imagined that someday in the State of

Israel, in Beit Mazmil in Jerusalem, there would be a boy called Momik
Neuman. There were so many things to find out about how to be a
real Jew, about how to have the kind of expression a Jew has, and to
give off the exact same smell, like Grandfather, for instance, and Munin,
and Max and Moritz, a smell that's known to drive the Beast insane,
so that day after day as Momik sits in the dark cellar facing the cages
not doing anything much, just staring blindly ahead, trying not to fall
asleep, because lately, he doesn't know why, he's sort of exhausted all
the time, he can hardly move or concentrate, and sometimes he has
these not very nice thoughts, like what does he need this for, and why
does he have to do all the fighting himself, and why does no one step
in to help him or take notice of what's going on around here, not Mama
or Papa, not Bella or the children in his class or his teacher Netta who
only screams at him that his grades are going down down down, and
not Dag Hammarskjöld from the United Nations who today arrived
in Israel and went all the way to Sedeh Boker just to eat supper with
Ben-Gurion, this Dag Hammarskjöld who founded UNICEF for the
children of the world and worries about saving the children of Africa
and India from malaria and other cholerias, the only thing he doesn't
have time for is the war on the Beast. And to tell the truth, there are
days when Momik sits in the cellar half awake and half asleep and he
envies the Beast. Yes, he envies it for being so strong that it never
suffers from pity, and that it can sleep soundly at night even after all
those things it did, and that it even seems to enjoy being cruel, the way
Uncle Shimmik enjoys it when you scratch his back, and maybe the
Beast is right and it isn't so terrible to be cruel, but really cruel, and to
tell the truth, Momik has also been kind of enjoying it lately when he
does something really bad, it happens mostly after dark, when he starts
being more afraid and hating the Beast more than ever and hating the
whole world, it suddenly happens, he gets this feeling as if he has fever
all over but especially in his head and his heart, and he almost explodes
with power and cruelty, and that's when he could almost fling himself
against the cages and shatter them and smash every head on the Beast
without mercy, and could even let it wound him with its claws and
teeth and all its beaks, before jamming into it as hard as he can so the
Beast will know once and for all what Momik feels, or maybe not,
maybe it would be better to kill it without jamming into it, just to
smash it and bash it and kick it and stomp on it and torture it and

blow it to bits, and you could even throw an atom bomb in its face now because that article finally came out about our atomic reactor which is huge and awesome rising out of the golden sand dunes of Nahal Rubin near Rishon Le-Zion, towering proudly over the shore and the roaring blue waves, the builders' hammers gaily tapping its splendid dome, that's what it said in the newspaper, and even though the newspaper says "for peaceful purposes," Momik can read between the lines, as they say, and he catches the meaning behind those smiles of Bella's, whose son is a very high-ranking major in the army, peaceful purposes, yeah sure, sure, let them blast the Arabs away pshakrev, but he had to admit the Beast didn't seem too worried by his threats, and sometimes Momik even suspected that whenever he started feeling this way, wild and hateful that is, the Beast was smiling slyly to itself in the dark, and then he would get even more frightened and not know what to do and tell himself, Calm down, but how much longer would he have the strength to calm down all by himself, and he would get frightened like this and wake up from his dream and look around and smell the stench of the animals which clings to him so strongly he sometimes feels as if it's coming out of his mouth, and he doesn't get up even though it's pitch-dark now and his parents are probably worried to death about where he is, and please don't let them think of coming down here to look for him, no they wouldn't come down here, they better not, and he sits a while longer, dozing on the cold stone floor, wrapped in Papa's big old overcoat to which Momik had pinned a lot of yellow cardboard stars, and sometimes when he wakes up and remembers, he reaches out to show the animals what he's glued on his arms with plastic glue, numbers cut out of old lottery tickets he collected by the lottery booth, and if that wasn't enough, he would sit up and pause for a refreshing cough or krechtz, and before he stood to leave, he would challenge the Beast one last time in a really disgusting way, by turning his back on it in the pitch-dark and copying a few passages from the diary of Anne Frank, who also hid from it, into his Geography Notebook #4, and whenever he finished copying out a really sad line from the book (which he stole from the public library), his pen would tremble a little, and then he would have to add a few words of his own about a boy called Momik Neuman who's also hiding like that and fighting and afraid, and the amazing thing is that what he wrote came out sounding just like her, like Anne that is.

And sometimes after lunch, when Momik wants to get Grandfather out of the way and put him to sleep so he can go down to the cellar right away, Grandfather stares at him strangely and begs with his eyes to let him go out for a while, and even though sometimes it's raining and cold outside, Momik can feel how much Grandfather is suffering in the house, and he takes him along, they put their coats on and go out, and lock the bottom lock too, and Momik holds Grandfather's hand and feels the warm currents of Grandfather's story flow into his own hand and up to his head, and he draws strength from Grandfather, unbeknownst to him, and squeezes and squeezes the strength out for himself till finally Grandfather lets out a kind of howl and pulls his hand away and looks at Momik as if he understands something.

They sit down on the wet green bench and watch the gray street that seems slanted on account of the rain, and the fog changes the shapes of things, and everything looks so different, everything is so sad, and out of the wind and the whirling leaves comes a black coat with two tails, or a blond wig, or the two dodos hand in hand, scrounging through the garbage pails, and so Grandfather's friends gather at the bench, though no one told them he was there, and then the door at Bella's opens and cute little Aaron Marcus steps out even though Bella begs him not to, and when she sees that Momik is there too, boy does she ever open her mouth and tell him to take Grandfather home this minute, but Momik just stares at her and doesn't answer, and in the end she slams the door.

Mr. Aaron Marcus walked over and sat down with a krechtz, and they all made room for him and gave a krechtz, and Momik gave one too and it felt good. Momik wasn't afraid anymore of Marcus's twitches which made his face look a hundred years old, may-he-live-to-be-a-hundred-and-twenty. Once he asked Bella whether Marcus made faces on account of some disease, God forbid, or something like that, and Bella said, The father of my Hezkel, may-he-rest-in-peace, deserves more than the inquisitiveness of rude little children who must know every-thing and what will there be left to learn when they're ten years old, but of course Momik didn't give up—we know Momik and the type of person he is—he went off to think it over, and returned to Bella a little while later and told her he knew the answer. That was funny because meanwhile Bella had forgotten the question, but Momik re-minded her and said probably Mr. Marcus makes those faces because he escaped from a certain place (Momik did not want to spell out that it was Over There) and he wants to keep people from recognizing his real face and capturing him, and Bella pursed her lips as if she was getting angry, but you could see that she was holding back a smile, and she said, Maybe it's the other way around, smarty, maybe Mr. Marcus is trying to keep alive the faces of all the people who were with him in a certain place, and it isn't at all that he wants to run away from them, he wants to stay with them, nu, what do you say to that, Einstein? And this answer knocked Momik for a loop, as they say, and he looked at Mr. Marcus in a completely different way after that, in fact he discovered the faces of a lot of people he never met before in Mr. Marcus's face, old people, men, women, and children and even babies, not to mention the fact that everyone around here made faces all the time, which was a sure sign that Marcus like the others was fighting a secret war.

The rain fell and the old people talked. You could never tell exactly when the noises and the krechtzes turned into real talking all of a sudden. They told their usual stories which Momik knew by heart already but loved to hear over and over. Red Sonya and Black Sonya, and Chaim Eche the cripple who played "Sheraleh" at weddings, and that meshuggeneh they called Job who sucked lavender candy and the children dragged him around everywhere like a dog and made him do whatever they wanted by promising him candy, and the big, beautiful mikva they built, and how everyone put the cholent in the bakery on Thursday to cook overnight, and the whole shtetl smelled of it, and this way you could rest from the war and the Beast and the stink in the cellar, you could forget everything and sort of not exist, and just then, for some reason, oftzeluchus as they said around here, he thinks of something annoying and troubling, the memory of a big fat palm slapping the candle, and the candle fell and the flame went *tsss* in the puddle, and Papa's face, and the word he said, and suddenly Momik sits up and moves his head away from Hannah Zeitrin's shoulder where he was leaning a little without noticing, and he said in a hard, loud voice that in the big game coming up in Yaroslav we're going to beat those Poles 10 to 0, Stelmach alone will score five, and at once the old ones grew quiet and looked at him blankly, and Hannah Zeitrin said sadly and clearly, Alter kopf, and Yedidya Munin on his other side reached his skinny hand with the black hairs out to him, and for once he wasn't going to pinch his cheek but gently cup his chin and draw it closer very slowly, who would have believed Momik would let Munin do such a thing to him, and in public too, but now Momik is a little tired and he doesn't mind feeling his face against the black coat with the strange smell, and he thinks it's a good thing he isn't alone and that he has these secret warriors with him here, they're like a band of partisans who fought together for a long long time, and the big battle is about to begin and they've sat down to rest a while in the forest, and though to look at them you'd think they were just a bunch of meshuggeners, who cares, it's so nice to lie here on Munin's coat beside his friends and hear the wool rustling and the quiet ticking of the pocket watch and the heartbeats that seem to come from far away, it's nice like this.

That night something terrible happened, which started like this: they heard terrible screams coming from the street, and it was fourteen minutes past eleven o'clock at night by Momik's watch, and the shutters rolled open and the lights went on, and in his heart Momik felt uh-oh now the Beast is coming out of the cellar, and he hid under the covers, but it was a woman screaming, not a Beast, so he jumped out of bed, ran to the window, and raised the shutters, and Mama and Papa called from the other room to close the shutters, but he'd stopped listening to them a long time ago, and he looked out the window and saw a real live naked woman running up and down the street screaming terrible screams, and you couldn't understand her, and even though the moon was almost full, it took Momik a couple of minutes to see that it was Hannah Zeitrin, because her pretty blond wig had fallen, and her hair was bald underneath and she had great big breasts that were flopping all over, and it was a good thing she had on a kind of small, triangle thing, like black fur down below, and Hannah Zeitrin who only this afternoon had been sitting on the bench next to him like a good friend raised her arms and screamed in Yiddish: God, God, how long must I wait for you, God, and people started screaming, Quiet, go home and sleep, you're crazy, it's the middle of the night, and somebody on the second floor where the uppity young couple live threw a whole bucketful of cold water down and drenched her, but she didn't stop running and tearing out her hair, and when she ran under the streetlamp, you could see the makeup she always smears on her face dripping, and suddenly the lights went on at Bella's and wouldn't you know it, Bella ran down the stairs and hugged Hannah with a big blanket, and Hannah stood still at first, trembling a little from the cold with her head drooping and Bella led her very slowly, but suddenly she stopped and shrieked, "Brutes!" and when she passed the house of the uppity couple she shrieked, "You're worse than they are! God will pay you double for this!" and then she and Hannah disappeared between the black cypress trees next to Hannah's house, and one by one the lights went out in all the houses, and Momik rolled down the shutters and went back to bed. But he had seen something no one else noticed, that while Hannah was running naked, Mr. Munin came out of the synagogue next door to Momik's and stood there, in the shadows but also a little in the moonlight. He wasn't wearing his glasses and his whole body jerked back and forth, and his eyes looked at Hannah and shone, and his hands were down in the darkness, and Momik saw his shoulders shake and his lips move, but he couldn't tell what he was saying though he had the feeling it was probably something very important, that Munin may have been revealing a great secret about the Beast and how to fight it, and Momik wanted to scream out the window, I can't hear you, but Munin's eyes suddenly popped open, and his mouth opened together with his eyes, and his body fell forward and backward as if somebody were shaking him with all his might, and then he raised his arms like a big black bird and started jumping and screaming, but without a voice, as if somebody above were pulling him up by a string, and suddenly the string broke and Munin fell down in a heap and lay there for a long time, and Momik could still hear him krechtzing quietly to himself like the crazy cat for a long time after it was over, and in the morning Munin wasn't lying there anymore.

But the Beast knew it was a trick and it wouldn't come out. None of Momik's tricks was any use. The Beast could probably tell the difference between a real Jew and Momik suddenly trying to act like a Jew, and if Momik could tell the difference he'd do the right thing, but he doesn't. He's become like his own shadow lately, dragging his feet when he walks, and he has this new chendeleh, as Bella called it, krechtzing like an old person, even at school, and everybody made fun of him, and the only good thing that happened around that time is that he came in fifth in his class in the sixty-meter dash, which never happened before, why now all of a sudden when he didn't have the strength to do anything, and everyone said he ran like Zatopek the Czech Locomotive, and they only laughed because he ran the whole race with his eyes shut tight and made faces as if a monster were after him, but at least now they saw he could do it if he really wanted to, and even Alex Tochner who was a friend of his once for two weeks and Momik coached him every day in the Ein Kerem Valley till Alex broke the class record and made the team like nothing, even Alex came up to him and said, Nice going, Helen Keller, but even these words of praise made no difference to Momik.

Bill and Motl had disappeared long ago, and he couldn't bring them back. It was as if the Beast had frozen his brains, and everyone noticed now. Bella wouldn't answer his questions anymore, and when he pleaded with her she told him she could eat herself for the harm she'd done by telling him what she'd told him already, and that she'd had it up to here with his investigations, that he should go play with children his own age please, and she didn't say it in an angry way but pityingly, which is worse. His parents had also been giving him funny looks lately, and you could see that they were just waiting for a chance to explode because of him. They'd started acting really strange: first they cleaned the house like crazy, washing and scrubbing everything each day (including windows and panels), and there wasn't a speck of dust anywhere, but they just kept cleaning and cleaning, and one night when Momik got up to pee he saw that all the lights in the house were on and Mama and Papa were down on their knees scraping the cracks between the tiles with kitchen knives, and when they saw him they smiled like children caught red-handed, and Momik didn't say anything, and in the morning he pretended he'd forgotten. A few days later, on Saturday, Bella said something to Mama, and Mama turned white as this wall, and early Sunday morning Mama took Momik to the health clinic to see Dr. Erdreich who examined him thoroughly from head to toe and told Mama no no it wasn't the Disease, that's how they talk about polio, which in our country is contracted by several children each year even after vaccinations and shots, and the doctor prescribed vitamins and cod-liver oil twice a day, but nothing helped, how could it, and though Mama and Papa started eating bigger suppers than ever and forced Momik to swallow more and more food, they knew the child was breaking down before their very eyes, and that there was nothing they could do about it, they tried everything, you have to admit, they brought over a little bearded rabbi from Mea Shearim who rolled a hard-boiled egg all over Momik and whispered, and they even went to see Madame Miranda Bardugo who was practically the queen of Beit Mazmil, and she used leeches on people and cured everything, but she refused to come on account of what happened to her leeches the time she used them on Papa's hands, and Mama and Bella sat in the kitchen together drinking tea, and Bella said crying tears of pity for the boy, Something must be done, look at him, there's nothing left but his eyes, and as usual Mama started to cry with her saying, If only we knew what to do, if you tell me the name of a doctor we'll take him to that doctor, but I don't need a doctor to see what this is, Bella, I should be a doctor, a doctor of tsuris, and what Shlomo has, no doctor can help, I tell you, we brought it with us from Over There, and it sits on us here and here and here, and only God can help, and Bella gave a krechtz and blew her nose and said, Oy, God help us till God helps us.

These were very bad days. Everyone around Momik was scared and didn't know what to do. They were waiting for him to get better, and meanwhile they wouldn't move or breathe. It all depended on him. When he moved they moved, and when he screamed they screamed. And it felt like the street was different too, as if you were hearing the voices of people who were already dead and stories that only people around here remembered and names and words that only people around here understood and hungered for, and Hannah Zeitrin came out naked almost every night now and shouted at God, and people just waited patiently for Bella to come and take her away, and sometimes when you looked up you could see, between the treetops and the clouds, a fast-moving shadow, something that resembled black coattails flying, and the glint of glasses, and a minute later Munin landed next to Momik who couldn't drag himself any farther, and glanced cautiously around (because he isn't allowed to come close to children for some reason) and put his hand on Momik's shoulder and walked that strange walk of his (because of the hernia) and whispered things in his ear about the stars and God and thrust and where the happy life awaits us, not here not here, and the burned-out cigarette danced from his upper lip, while he muttered words from the Bible and synagogue prayers, and he laughed and laughed the weird laughter of someone who's about to hoodwink the world, and Momik didn't have the patience for him anymore.

All day long Momik's head burned, but the thermometer showed nothing. He felt as if his mind were doing an oftzeluchus on him and

making him think thoughts that weren't good. Momik had been starting
with the nightmares himself lately and crying out in his sleep at night,
and Mama and Papa would come running, and beg him with their eyes
to stop this please, to go back to being what he was before only a few
short months ago, but enough, he hasn't got the strength to pretend
to be happy in his sleep for them anymore, aililuliii, what's happening
to him, what's happening, everything is breaking down, the Beast is
beating him, beating him before ever coming out of its disguise, and
he punched his pillow which was wet all over and saw that his fingers
were cramped and crooked with fear or whatever, and again and again
he punched his pillow and screamed at his parents who huddled together
and cried, and then he fell asleep but he woke up right away with a
new nightmare: Motl was walking down the street of a city Momik
didn't know, Motl was small and scrawny and he walked funny, and
Momik was glad to see him and screamed, Motl! But Motl didn't hear
him or pretended not to, and Momik saw a booth in the corner like
the lottery booth, and in it sat Mama and Papa crowded together and
sad, right in the corner where the Golden Ray of Fortune is painted
on the lottery sign, and then he saw that it wasn't a street at all, it was
a river, maybe the San, and maybe not, and the lottery booth was
floating in it like a little boat, and Motl was walking toward this boat,
he was walking in the water but he wasn't getting wet and he never
reached the boat, because the closer he came, the farther away it moved,
and suddenly a couple of boys were there, and a grown-up man was
walking with them, and they were walking in circles around Motl, and
suddenly for no reason at all one of them boxed him in the face, and
they all jumped on him and started kicking him and punching him
and yelling at each other, Bash him in the teeth, Emil, Punch him in
the belly, Gustav, and Momik almost fainted when he realized it was
Emil and the detectives, grown up now in Germany, and the man
watching them and laughing to himself must have been Yashkeh the
policeman who sometimes went to Emil's mother's house for a cup of
tea, and Motl lay there bloody and half dead, and Momik looked up
and saw Mama and Papa in the booth rowing their boat away, and
Mama looked at Momik and said, God will help him, there's nothing
I can do to help him now, and Bella suddenly slipped out of her window
(how did she get there anyway?) and screamed at his parents, Brutes,
at least someone should stay home with him in the afternoon, if you

knew the company he keeps, and Mama shrugged her shoulders and said, We don't have the strength anymore, Mrs. Bella, we ran out a long time ago, that's life, and everyone is alone in the end, and on they rowed till finally they were gone, and when Momik looked at Motl again, he saw that the river wasn't really a river but a crowd of people streaming in from the side streets, and when he looked again he saw some people and children he recognized, from the famous Fives and secret Sixes, and Captain Nemo's children, and Sherlock Holmes was there with Watson, and they were all yelling and laughing and rolling these strange little bundles, and when they came close to him he saw that all the bundles were his good friends, Yotam the Sorcerer, and My Brother Elijah, and Anne Frank, and the Children of the Heart from Grandfather's story, and even baby Kazik was there, and Momik started to scream and he woke up, and this kept happening all night long, and next morning as Momik lay more dead than alive in his bed which stank of sweat, he realized he'd been making a huge mistake, that he'd been wasting his efforts, because obviously the Beast knew he wasn't Jewish enough, so all he had to do now was to get hold of a real Jew, someone who actually came from Over There who'd be able to taunt the Beast till it showed itself, and then we'll see, and Momik knew of just the person.

Grandfather Anshel wasn't at all surprised when Momik shared his secret and asked him to help. Momik of course knew Grandfather didn't understand any of this, but he wanted to be completely fair so he frankly explained the pitfalls and dangers, while also pointing out that his parents had to be rescued from their fears once and for all, and when he said this, he didn't quite believe it himself anymore because it wasn't his parents he had to save, and who needs that Beast anyhow, let it go to sleep and leave us alone, but there was no choice, and he had to keep talking and arguing. At the end of the speech Momik told Grandfather that for such a major decision Grandfather was entitled to have three days to think it over, but he was only saying that of course.

Grandfather didn't need three days, he made his mind up there and then. He shook his head so hard Momik was afraid his neck would snap, God forbid, and you'd have thought he understood something after all, that the whole time he'd only been waiting for Momik to ask him, and maybe this was the real reason he came to them in the first place, and Momik started to feel a little better.

As he was getting the cellar ready for Grandfather's first visit, he felt
almost cheerful. First he brought down the little duster with the colored
feathers Mama had for dusting, and he used it to sweep the filthy floor.
Then under a pile of junk he found the little bench they called a benkaleh
and he put it in the middle of the room and decided this would be
Grandfather's benkaleh. He also hung Papa's overcoat with the yellow
stars from the nails that stuck out of the wall, and he ripped the empty
sleeves, and then he tore out all the pictures he'd copied from library
books into his fake Geography Notebook #3 and taped them to the
wall, and when he looked around he said twice in Yiddish, Zer shoin,
very pretty, and rubbed his palms together and said Whew over them
as if he were blowing on a little fire, and then he went up to the house,
and inside he locked the bottom lock too, and saw that Grandfather
had fallen asleep after lunch with his head resting on the table next to
the plate with the drumstick on it, and a fine thread of spit dribbling
from his mouth. Momik woke him gently and they went outside and
Momik locked the bottom lock too and they walked carefully down
the stairs and Momik opened the cellar door and went in first to make
sure everything was all right, and quickly, quietly he said, Here, I
brought him to you, and then he stepped aside (his heart was pounding)
and let Grandfather in, and only then did he dare open his eyes because
nothing was happening as far as he could tell, and he led Grandfather
to the middle of the room and turned him a little to the right and to
the left so his smell would spread in all directions, and the whole time
he kept watching the animals, thinking they seemed a little more alert
than usual but nothing else, and Grandfather didn't even notice the
animals, he just wandered around muttering like a dodo.

Okay, Momik reminded himself that he couldn't really expect any-
thing to happen so fast. Maybe the Beast forgot what a real Jew smells
like and Momik would just have to wait patiently for it to remember.
He sat Grandfather down on the benkaleh in the middle of the floor.
Grandfather did try to resist a little, to tell the truth, but Momik had
lost patience with this kind of nonsense, so he put his hands around
Grandfather's neck and pressed slowly till he gave in and sat down.
Momik sat before him on the floor and said, Now start talking, and
Grandfather gave him a funny look as if he was afraid of him or some-
thing, and why should he be afraid now, all he had to do was to obey
Momik with no nonsense, there was nothing to be afraid of, and sud-

denly Momik shouted as loud as he could, Talk, you hear? Start talking or else, but he didn't know why he was shouting or what he meant by "or else," and Grandfather started talking very fast, and that disgusting spit squirted out of his mouth, which is exactly what Momik had hoped would happen, and he said, Wave your hands too! And Grandfather waved his hands the way he does, and Momik watched him closely to make sure he was really trying hard and doing what he was supposed to do, and he also glanced at the cages and the suitcases and the torn mattresses and silently cried, Jude! Jude! Here, I brought you the kind you like, a real Jude that looks like a Jude and talks like a Jude and smells like a Jude, a Jude grandfather with a Jude grandson, so come on out . . .

In the days that followed, Momik did some pretty desperate things. They would sit on the floor together, eating pieces of dry bread, as Momik softly sang partisan songs, in both Hebrew and Yiddish, and recited prayers from Papa's High Holiday prayer book. He even covered the far wall of the cellar with pages torn out of Anne's book, but the Beast would not come out. It simply would not come out.

The poor animals howled and shrieked and scratched, and the cat was dying now, but Momik wasn't afraid of the animals, he was afraid of the Beast which was here in the cellar, you could really feel it flexing its huge muscles, ready to pounce, only how could you tell where it was going to pounce from, darn it, and Momik sat looking at Grandfather Anshel and didn't know what to do. He was fed up with this stupid grandfather who did nothing but drawl out his crummy story in a whiny voice. Sometimes Momik felt like going over to him and snapping his mouth shut. Once when Grandfather made a sign that he had to pee, Momik didn't get up to take him out but sat staring into his eyes instead, and he saw how confused Grandfather was, howling like some crazy cat and grabbing himself there and writhing desperately and then he wet his pants and they smelled revolting, but Momik wasn't the least bit sorry for him anymore, on the contrary, when Grandfather looked up at him with a dazed and pitiful expression on his face, Momik just got up and walked out, leaving Grandfather all alone in the dark, and he went back to the house and locked himself in and listened to the radio and heard how our team lost the game against the Poles in Yaroslav 7 to 2, while the Poles jeered at our boys, and Nechemia Ben-

Avraham the sportscaster described how Yanush Achurak and Liberda
and Shershinsky are walking all over our boys Goldstein and Stelmach,
so Momik could see he was losing right down the line, as they say,
though on the other hand, as everyone knows, Momik isn't the kind
of boy who cares about losing or jeering or harassment or extortion,
but there is one thing he will never allow himself to lose at, because
there is no other way, and that's why he had a new plan, more daring
than anything up to now, which he worked out because Grandfather
Anshel was apparently too small to bring out the Beast wherever it was,
and as always, Momik had to think this through like a good shopkeeper
(Bella was the one who taught him this even though she herself was a
regular shlimazel when it comes to business things), and get some more
Jews in, enough to make the Beast think it was worth coming out, and
this seemed so funny to him that he laughed a weird laugh which startled
him and he shut up and listened to the game on the radio, and thought
about Grandfather who might be gobbled up any moment down there,
and in his mind, which he could no longer control, Momik planned to
ask his classmates to lend him their grandmothers and grandfathers for
a little while and bring them down to the Beast in a big group, and he
let out another laugh like a high-pitched squeak on the radio, and then
stifled it and looked around to see if anyone had heard.

And he didn't even wait to hear the end of the game because he
stopped believing a miracle would happen and some wonder boy of a
soccer player would leap down from the stands past the jeering crowds
and join our eleven-man team on the field and show those Poles a thing
or two, and run circles around them and save the day and clobber them
8 to 7 (the last goal with the final whistle), and he stomped out of the
house and locked the bottom lock and went down the stairs and waited
at the door for a second, listening for the victim's screams, but all he
heard was Grandfather's tune, and then Momik went in and sat down
facing Grandfather, feeling all tired out; he must really have been tired
out because sometime later he found himself stretched out at Grandfather's feet, and decided that maybe it wouldn't be such a good idea
to bring any more Jewish grandfathers in, because it sure was getting
harder to put up with people lately, they were simply impossible, with
their secrets and ideas and the craziness darting out of their eyes, and
how come there's the other type of people, like the kids in his class,
everything seems so simple to, only Momik knows how not simple it

is, because once is enough; once you know how not simple it is and
how frightening it is, you can never believe in anything again, oh what
an act it is, but even though he was asleep now he couldn't stop fighting,
and he heard someone calling, Get up, get up, if you fall asleep now,
you're done for, and maybe it was this voice that kept him from falling
asleep, no, it was something else too, hard to remember what exactly,
maybe he got up, yes, and he walked out of the cellar, and wandered
around in a fog, dragging his feet, till he got to the green bench where
he stopped a while; he just sat there and waited, thinking of nothing,
watching a big brown autumn leaf that had fallen from some tree long
ago, and he saw the veins sticking out of the leaf like the veins on
Mama's legs, and down the middle there was a long line that split the
leaf in two, and he thought what would happen now if he tore the leaf
in two and threw each half in a different direction, would they miss
each other or what, and as he sat there his old people approached, and
they didn't have to ask any questions, they knew, they looked at his
face and saw it was time to do what they'd planned all along, and
Momik waited another minute till they all had the same smell, and then
he said, Ah well, nu, and they all followed him, Hannah and Munin
and Marcus and Ginzburg and Zeidman, like sheep they followed wherever he led, they traipsed down the street forever along the paths with
the snowdrifts and the black forests and the churches and haystacks
with the fresh smell, and someone who saw them on their way asked
Momik, Where to? but Momik didn't look up to see who it was, and
he didn't answer, he led his Jews onward to the cellar, and heard
Grandfather talking to himself inside, and Momik opened the door for
them and beckoned them in and shut the door.

They waited patiently inside for their eyes to get used to the dark,
till gradually they could make Grandfather out on his benkaleh, and
the white pages on the walls, and Mr. Munin was the first who had
enough nerve to go to the wall and look at one of the pictures up close,
and it took him a while to figure out what he was looking at but when
he did understand he stiffened and backed away and he must have been
frightened because you could feel his fear run through them like an
electric current, and they huddled together, but then slowly they spread
out through the cellar and started to file past the walls, looking at the
pictures as if they were at an exhibition, and the more they looked at
the pictures like that, the more they gave off the sharp, old smell which

nearly suffocated Momik, but he knew this smell was probably his last
chance, and inwardly he screamed, Show it, show it, go on, be Jews
and show it, and he crouched down with his hands on his knees as if
he were coaching the players on the soccer field and inwardly shouted,
Now, now, go on, be wizards and prophets and witches and let's give
it one more battle, one last fight, be so Jewish it won't know what to
do with itself, and even if the Beast was never here before, now it's got
to come out, but nothing happened, except that his poor animals were
getting even jumpier; the raven flapped its wings and made swooshing
sounds, and the cat yowled horribly, and Momik went down on his
hands and knees and drew his head in and thought what an idiot he'd
been to believe in wizards and witches and all that, a nechtiger tog, as
Bella would say, there's no such thing, look at them, this poor bunch
of crazy Jews who stuck to him and ruined everything, his whole life
they ruined, and what made him think they could ever help him, huh,
he could teach them a few things, come to think of it, every single one
of them, what you do in an emergency, one fist four fingers, how to
run circles around the world, but what do they care anyway, they seem
to like it even when you hurt them and when you laugh at them and
they're miserable, they've never done anything in their whole lives to
fight back, they just sit there bickering about those stories no one gives
a darn about, what the rabbi said to the widow and how a piece of
meat fell into the milk soup, and meanwhile more and more of them
were killed, and they always have to get the last word in too, as if the
one who gets the last word in stays alive, and all those stupid exag-
gerations which are a pack of lies, the genius in Warsaw everyone
supposedly knew, and the nobleman Munin claims kissed him and
hugged him like a brother! and the Polish government minister who
bowed to Mr. Marcus once, oh yeah, sure, sure! And even Bella, believing she's prettier than Marilyn Monroe, really! And even when they
talk about what the goyim put them through, the pogroms and ex-
pulsions and tortures, they talk about it with a kind of krechtz, forgiving
it all, like someone who makes fun of himself for being weak and a
nebuch, and anyone who laughs at himself gets laughed at by others,
everyone knows that, and slowly Momik raised his head from the floor
and felt himself fill with hatred and rage and revenge, and his head was
on fire and the room danced before his eyes, and these Jews were
scurrying along the walls and pictures so fast he could hardly tell what

was real and what was a picture and he wanted to stop them but he didn't know how, once he had a magic word but he couldn't remember it, and he raised his arms and begged, Enough, stop it now, he raised his arms as if to surrender, like a boy he saw in a picture once, but a terrible scream escaped him, the cry of a Beast, and it was so frightening that everything stood still and the room stopped dancing and the Jews fell down and lay panting on the floor, and then he got up and stood over them, and his legs wobbled and everything was fuzzy, and then he heard Grandfather humming his tune in the silence like an electric pole, only this time the story sounded clear and he told it nicely with biblical expression, and Momik held his breath and listened to the story from start to finish, and swore he would never-ever-black-and-blue forget a single word of the story, but he instantly forgot because it was the kind of story you always forget and have to keep going back to the beginning to remember, it was that kind of story, and when Grandfather finished telling it, the others started telling their stories, and they were all talking at once and they said things no one would ever believe, and Momik remembered them forever and ever and instantly forgot them, and sometimes they fell asleep in the middle of a word and their heads drooped down on their chest and when they woke up they started where they left off and Momik went over the pictures he'd copied in pencil once out of those books, and he remembered that each time he'd copied a picture he felt he had to draw it a little differently, like the one with the child they forced to scrub the street with a toothbrush, well Momik drew the toothbrush bigger than it was in the photograph, and the old man they forced to ride on the other old man, Momik drew him half standing so he wouldn't be so heavy, yes, he felt he had to make these changes, but now he couldn't remember why exactly, and he was kind of angry with himself for not being precise and scientific enough, because if he had been, maybe his latest problems would be over by now, and he leaned against the wall, because he couldn't stand up anymore, and his Jews were still talking and bobbing around as if they were praying, and sometimes it seemed to him that he was imagining all this, and his eyes kept darting around in search of where it would pounce from, and then Grandfather Anshel started telling his story from the beginning again, and Momik squeezed his head because he didn't think he could stand it anymore, he wanted to vomit everything, everything he'd eaten for lunch and everything he'd learned about

lately, including himself, and now these stinky Jews here too, the kind
the goyim called Jude, before he thought that was just an insult, but
now he saw it suited them perfectly, and he whispered, Jude, and felt
a warm thrill in his stomach and felt his muscles filling out all over,
and he said it again out loud, Jude, and it made him feel strong, and
he shook himself and stood over Grandfather Wasserman, sneering,
Shut up already, enough already, we're sick of your story, you can't kill
the Nazikaput with a story, you have to beat him to death, and for that
you need a naval commando unit to break into the room and take him
hostage till Hitler comes to save him, and then they catch Hitler and
kill him too with terrible tortures, they yank his nails out one by one,
shrieks Momik, leaving Grandfather and approaching the cages, and
you gouge his eyes out without an anaesthetic, and then you bomb
Germany and wipe out every trace of Over There, every good trace and
every evil trace, and you liberate the six million with a spy mission the
likes of which have never been seen, you turn back the clock like a time
machine, sure, there must be someone at the Weizmann Institute who
could invent something like that, and they'll bring the whole world
down on their knees, pshakrev, and spit in their faces, and we'll fly
overhead in our jet planes, war is what we need, screamed Momik, and
his eyes were like the eyes of his cat, and his hands ran down the cages
and opened the metal latches, and once again he turned and saw his
little shtetl, and he stood there motionless, watching the raven and the
cat and the lizard and the others slowly leave their cages; they didn't
understand what was going on, they didn't believe this was it, that it
was over now, but the Jews understood all right, and got up from the
floor and huddled together with their backs to the animals and whispered fearfully, and the animals made noises at each other and wouldn't
let each other move, when anyone moved even the teensiest bit, there
was shrieking and howling and feathers standing on end, and the cellar
was filled with the sounds of danger and fear, and it seemed incredible
that only half a minute from here there was a city and people and books,
and Momik who thought he might be dead or something, closed his
eyes, and, risking his life, passed the raven and the cat and didn't feel
them scratching and pecking him, what was that to him after all he'd
been through, and he went over to his Jews, and they looked at him
with sad, worried faces, but they moved over all the same and made
way for him, and he was still laughing at them in his heart for their

willingness to forgive him so soon after what he'd done to them, but it felt good when they closed in around him and he was standing in the ring, and he thought the Beast would never be able to get him in the ring, it would never try to get in, because it knows it wouldn't stand a chance, but when he opened his eyes and saw them all around him, tall and ancient, gazing at him with pity, he knew with all his nine-and-a-half-year-old alter kopf intelligence that it was too late now.

There are just a few things more worth mentioning here in the interest of scientific accuracy: Momik couldn't say goodbye to his cellar just like that, and though he never brought Grandfather or any of the others with him, he still went in sometimes to be alone in the days that followed. The animals he let go, but their smell lingered on and the smell of the Jews did too. His teacher Netta came over to talk to Mama and Papa, and they agreed about certain things. Momik didn't care. He didn't even ask. He didn't make a note that Yair Pantilat broke the record for the 800-meter dash, or that Flora and Alinka, the two mares at the Beit Dagan Agricultural Fair foaled, and the foals were given Hebrew names, Dan and Dagan. At the end of the school year Momik's report card said *Promoted*, but not at our school, and Mama told him that the following year he would attend a special school near Natanya, and he wouldn't be living at home, but this was for his own good, because there would be fresh air and healthy food there, and once a week he could visit Idka and Shimmik who lived nearby. Momik said nothing. That summer, when he went away to visit his new school, Grandfather walked out of the house and never returned. This happened exactly five months after he arrived in the ambulance. The police searched a while but they never found him. Momik used to lie in bed at night in boarding school, wondering where Grandfather was now and who he was telling his story to. At home Grandfather was never mentioned again, except one time when Mama thought of him and said to Idka angrily, "If there was at least a grave to visit, but to disappear like that?"

BRUNO

AT THE DEEP-WATER PORT OF DANZIG he jumped into the sea.
It was a drizzly evening, and the handful of people on the dock were
too busy to notice him. Stevedores had built a fire under a tin lean-to,
and he could smell the coffee brewing: real coffee! He walked briskly
through the rain. He had been forced to leave his hat behind in the
gallery cloakroom, as well as his black briefcase with the manuscript of
The Messiah inside. Four years of thinking and writing. It was a mistake
that spread malignantly before he realized the Messiah would never
come in writing, would never be invoked in a language suffering from
elephantiasis. A new grammar and a new calligraphy had first to be
invented. He glanced anxiously at the Port Authority buildings. Two
soldiers stood talking in the alleyway nearby. Bruno clenched his fists
unconsciously, as he had been training himself to do ever since it became
illegal for a Jew to put his hands in his pockets in the presence of a
uniformed German. He walked quickly, making himself small: the gait
of an unattractive man. Rain dripped down his tight-skinned, sallow
face—

How well I know that face: I often find it peering at me from his
grotesque drawings, surrounded by other dwarfed and miserable men
under the patent-leather heel of Adela, the beautiful servant girl, or
some other disdainful female. (But notice the sea, Bruno: the gray sea
shaking out its bedding for the night, popping clumps of kelp that bob
up to the light for an instant and sink back into the foam again.)

They displayed Munch's painting in the farthermost corner of the gallery (so disturbing was it to them), in the midst of his milder, more colorful works. It was cordoned off, with a sign in Polish and German saying: DO NOT TOUCH.

Idiots. They should have protected the public from the painting, not the other way around. That figure on the wooden bridge, mouth open in a scream, had deeply touched him. Kissing it there in the gallery, Bruno felt infected. Or perhaps the kiss had brought a latent infection to life. Now Bruno walks past the heavy boats, rolling his eyes and twisting his lips as the scream from the painting makes its way from heart to mouth, like a fetus whose time has come. He shivers: Bruno is the weak link in the chain. Take care of him. The great Zofia Nalkowska once beseeched her friends, "Look after Bruno, for his sake and for ours."

Now he fell down. He tripped over a coil of algae-covered rope and almost dropped into the water. For a moment he lay on the dock, doubled over with pain. The rips under his arms and elbows were exposed. He scrambled to his feet. Get up. Mustn't be a sitting duck. They're after him. The SS and Polish police are after him for leaving the ghetto in Drohobycz and taking the train, strictly forbidden to Jews, and then daring to attend the Munch exhibit in Danzig, where he did what he did before they threw him out. But Bruno fears neither the SS nor the Polish police, his latest persecutors. He fears only the great searchlights that converge inside and chastise him to be-like-everybody-else, to live the gray life he can never redeem with a touch of his pen.

The moment Bruno saw *The Scream* at the Artus Hopf Gallery, he knew: the artist's hand must have slipped on the canvas. Munch could not have planned such perfection. He would not have dared to. He may have had intimations of it, he may have had aspirations, but he could never have achieved it intentionally. Bruno recognized this with a grieving heart: all his life he had been longing for—as he called it— *"the day the world would shed its scales like a fabulous lizard."* "The Age of Genius," he called that day, and till that day he cautioned us never to forget that the words we use are but fragments of primeval stories; that we have built our homes—like barbarians—out of shattered idols, the graven images of archaic gods, snatched from mighty mythologies." The question remains, however, Will the Age of Genius ever dawn? This is difficult to answer. Bruno is not certain either. *"Because some things never happen to the full. They are too immense to be contained in the turn of events. They try to happen, they try the groundwork of reality out to see if it will hold, but they retreat, afraid to lose their integrity through a faulty materialization, leaving behind those pale marks in our biographies, the fragrant tokens or faded silver footprints of barefoot angels, sporadic giant steps across our days and nights . . ."* So he wrote in *Sanitorium under the Sign of the Hourglass*. I know the book by heart.

A little yolk of a sun was blotted up by leaden clouds, and the light faded. Slowly God put his toys away. Bruno knew: the kind of perfection Munch discovered was either a mistake or a case of serendipity. Because someone had bungled it. Someone somewhere distracted momentarily had leaked the truth out in the wrong quarters. Bruno wondered how many pictures Munch had dashed off in a panic to blur the strong impression of his intrusion into that forbidden zone. Munch himself, thought Bruno (stepping into an oily puddle and shattering a series of iridescent arabesques with the heel of his shoe), must have been staggered by his catch.

Atoms of indivisible truth. An ultimate, crystalline truth. Bruno sought this high and low: in the people he met, in snatches of conversation that drifted to his ears, in cases of synchronicity, in himself; in the books he read he sought the one phrase, the pearl, which launched the writer on a voyage hundreds of pages long. The bite of truth. He rarely found it. A masterpiece sometimes yielded two, three such phrases to record in his notebook: bits of solid evidence, collected with the greatest of effort and care, out of which one day to piece together the original mosaic. The truth. Coming across these passages later, he often mistook the writing for his own. And no wonder, he told himself, it's all from the same source.

Bruno had perceived that Munch was a weak link, too. He'd guessed as much long before, on finding reproductions of *The Scream* in art books back in Drohobycz. But seeing the original with his own eyes convinced him: Munch was a weak link, too. Like Kafka and Mann and Dürer and Hogarth and Goya and the others gracing his notebook. A fragile network of weak links across the world. Look after Munch. Look after Bruno for his sake, for ours. Cherish thine artist, but guard him well. Ring him round with love, join hands and circle him. Study his paintings. Cheer him. Rejoice in his stories, but remember to be shocked on occasion, and thank him for his beautiful expression of blah-blah-blah, and join hands around him to let him feel your sympathy and your toughness, too, and your iron-door-like impenetrability.

Spread your fingers while you clap, suggesting prison bars, and always love him, because that is the bargain: your love for his prudence. His loyalty for your aplomb.

Munch turned traitor. He allowed himself to be unraveled, and the scream burst rudely into your midst. And now it is here, so quickly patch the hole. And they loved Munch all the more! Gather round him and let him feel your breath on his face: he who failed once may fail again. Join hands and cordon him off with a red sign warning: DO NOT TOUCH.

Bruno is still running. Hewing the wind with his sharp features, rounding his lips in an effort to ease the pain; oh, the fullness in Bruno, and his fear of that fullness. Look after him, for his sake, and for ours. Don't let his dangerous passions tempt him to forgo your trusty, thread-bare words. Do not allow him to write in body code, to a rhythm unmeasured by clock or metronome. And for heaven's sake, don't let him talk to himself in that unintelligible language he had to invent because of "*those sly merchants we know who are only too eager to lead him by the hand to their filthy stalls of human speech, so they can open up their odious display cases and offer him their wares with a truckling smile; oh, no, sir, it's absolutely free of charge, yes yes, a brand-new language, and it's all yours. Still in its cellophane wrapping complete with your very own, very private dictionary, the pages of which appear to be blank but are covered in fact with invisible writing you have to smear with bile, your own pungent essence, in order to read and, no sir, no sir, we will not take a single penny from you! It isn't often a customer stumbles—happens by, so we would be daft to scare him away with vulgar talk of costs and spending, rather let us say, dear sir, that we consider you a kind of modest investment, a down payment, as it were, ha-ha, a foot in the door of markets at present closed to us, and would you be kind enough to sign here and here and here.*"

Munch signed, Kafka signed, Proust signed, and Bruno signed too, it seems. He can't remember when exactly, but it seems that something was signed. Because his sense of loss grew deeper. And then the war came, and he began to think he'd made a mistake: people were turning treacherous, and the stalls of the sly merchants concealed "*untrod markets, dark and deep, corrupt streets curbed with the debris of crumbling walls like rows of crocodile teeth . . .*"

So Bruno ran away.

From the Drohobycz he loved. From the house on the corner of Samburska and Market Streets, Olympus of his private mythology, dwelling place of gods and angels in human form, or—forms less than human . . . ah, Bruno's house! What pleasure pervades him at the thought of this ordinary-looking house, so utterly insignificant, yet transformed by the architectural wonders of Bruno's imagination into a fabulous mansion with halls and labyrinthine corridors and gardens filled with life and color. On the ground floor was the family dry-goods store, Henrietta, named after his mother and bunglingly mismanaged by Bruno's father, Yacob Schulz, *"the secret poet, singlehandedly parrying the mighty forces of boredom, his father, brave explorer of mutable existence, who used his will and vision to transform himself into a bird, an insect, a crab, his father, forever dead-and-alive . . ."*

And over the store—the living quarters. And Mother Henrietta. Plump, soft, devoted to Yacob the seer who was suffering from cancer, and whose business deteriorated before his wandering, unseeing eyes; and Mother is especially attuned to Bruno, this tender shoot of their declining years. This hypersensitive child, struggling against foes she can't begin to imagine . . .

(One hazy, melancholy evening, she entered his room to find him feeding sugar crystals to the last flies of a chilly autumn.

"Bruno?"

"To give them strength for winter.")

He has no friends. Not that he isn't a gifted pupil, our Bruno. In fact, his teachers are quite astounded. Particularly the drawing master, Adolf Arendt. Bruno has been drawing in this mature fashion since the age of six. How puzzling he is. First he went through his coach phase, drew nothing but coaches, or *drushkas*. A fast coach with a folding top. Again and again he drew the coach with a *"team of black horses sallying forth from the woods at midnight, its passengers unclad, their eyes dusted silver with sylvan reveries."* Then later he started to draw automobiles. Like most children, but not like children draw them. He drew horses, and he drew runners, too. Always motion. Yet the drawings are suffused with age and death and bitterness.

And he has no friends. "Nyedoenga," the boys call him. A shlimazel. And at home Adela the servant girl.

Her legs. Her body. Her female smell. Her combs. And the combings all over the house. Adela dispelling father Yacob's chimeras with threats of a sound tickling, and Adela provocatively strutting on dainty heels; notice the shoes, Bruno!

The rhythmical movement of his lips and his slight, swift-moving body give Bruno the appearance of a fish. He walks along the pier, with eyes shut, reviewing his actions back at the gallery: a quick hop over the chain with the warning sign, and a kiss on the picture. An old woman in one of the boats stands looking out at the ocean. Her long, brittle hair flies around her face in the fierce wind. The sleepy gallery guard jumped up in alarm and blew the whistle. Another guard joined him and they dragged Bruno out of the painting zone and into their own. There they thrashed him silently, dispassionately, it seemed. A spot of dribble remained on the picture. Bruno had missed the mouth on the screaming figure and kissed one of the wooden posts on the bridge instead. But it was enough for him. First aid: mouth-to-mouth respiration. And Bruno was saved.

He opens his eyes now and sees that his feet are leading him to the bow-shaped jetty curving out to sea. With a sinewy tongue the sea probes the driftwood stuck between its rocky teeth. The many eyes of the sea follow Bruno from the holes in a reef.

Bruno reflected on the unfinished manuscript in his briefcase. After his forcible removal from the gallery, the trams and automobiles on Langasse had splashed him with puddle water. Surreptitiously he reached out to touch the tall wooden lampposts, then licked his fingertips. He seemed to be savoring the taste of the bridge posts. Every time he did so, a tortured muscle inside him contracted. He thought about his life, a life which had never been his. Not really his. Because force of habit had always deprived him of it. People lived by robbing each other's lives. Before the war, they had at least shown some tact, taking care not to inflict more pain than necessary, with a sense of humor, in fact, but nowadays nobody even made an effort to pretend. He had come to understand lately that his first two books, and this third one, *The Messiah*, in which he had been drowning and floundering for the past four years, were merely the clumsy scaffold he had built with his own two hands around a creature unknown. As yet unknown. He realized he had spent most of his life as a daring trapeze artist on that high scaffold, and that he had always been careful not to look down, because looking downward and inward would have frightened him and made him recognize, much to his sorrow, that he wasn't a trapeze artist after all but a jailor. That somewhere along the line force of habit, fatigue, and negligence had turned him into the accomplice of the people with their hands joined around him.

And so he was making his last escape. He was not afraid of the

Germans or the Poles, nor was this a protest against the war. No. At
last he was running away to meet something new, not the tenses and
verbs by the dozen he had served as junction for till now.

Bruno already knows he's going to die. An hour from now, a day
from now. So many are dying. There is an air of silent resignation in
the streets of the Drohobycz Ghetto. Bruno has succumbed to it: perhaps he really is guilty of something. Of looking as he does. Of being
the Jew he is. Of writing as he does. The question of justice lapsed
long ago, of course, but there is a different question now, Bruno thinks,
walking faster, to which I must address myself, the question of life; the
life I have lived and the life I have failed to live because of my short-
comings and my fears. And I have neither the strength left nor the time
to wait for a miracle. Bruno smiles inwardly, a wry, impassioned smile.
His bruised face lights up for an instant. Was it Lenin who said that
one death is a tragedy, a million are statistics; yes, it must have been
Lenin who said that, and now Bruno wishes to salvage the one tragedy
of his life out of the million, to comprehend, however briefly, what he
has been inscribing in the big book of life. And in his heart he cherishes
the even deeper hope that by being split off from that final, crystallized
truth, he may yet learn what sent the Supreme Creator coursing through
an infinity of pages.

Bruno removes his tattered overcoat and throws it on the concrete.
His eyes are blank. What is he thinking? I don't know. I've lost his
train of thought. Maybe he's thinking about Mirabeau, the revolution-
ary poet turned thief, or Thoreau, the recluse of Walden Pond?

Bruno shudders. No. Such protests will not do: the thief robs people.
The recluse is reclusive from people. He gauges his solitude in proportion to their fellowship. But more than this is needed: an uprising
that will banish your inner self. He trembles, hypnotized by the rich,
dark waves rolling by, the waves that can sense in him the tension of
one who has reached the brink, and whose extremities are even now
in the process of being transformed into another substance, midway
between flesh and longing.

The old woman in the boat looks on motionlessly. She guesses what
is about to happen. But this is the way of the world, and death is more
than the opposite of life. Death has dominion over all our schemes.
Two stevedores catch sight of him in the distance and start to scream.

Bruno throws off his shirt and trousers. With moist, airy fingers the
sea probes the emaciation and fatigue that rack his body. The sea doesn't

care: an eager merchant spits at the submissive customer. The sea buys everything. Who knows when all the junk in the cellar will come in handy. Bruno opens his anguished eyes. Someone inside him is still trying to save the frail body: the writer in him must be quailing at the thought that he, too, will be lost if his host is drowned. Then suddenly he realizes that it was the prisoner in him who planned the escape. The jailor–trapeze artist is now the hostage. And in his terror he tries this last pitiful ploy: why not at least leave your shoes on the pile of clothes so you'll have something to wear when you get back; just a minute, not so fast, let's talk this over rationally. (The writer can see what Bruno himself cannot: that from the far end of the dock people are running toward the pier: two stevedores and a third man, an officer.)

He kicks the pile of clothes and they drop into the water, float for a moment, swell briefly, and sink down. The sea smiles. It slides a wave Bruno's way, an experienced croupier dealing out a lucky card to a regular customer. The writer clenches his teeth in horror. How well I understand him! He spits with disgust at the moldering culture of humanity, his insane and unexpected former abode and writing hand. And he is the frightened, pampered, rational one, who lays two delicate fingers on Bruno's nose and melts away as Bruno sinks into the cold water and floats up to the surface again, happiness inflating him like a sail. Then there was a long, muffled sound: perhaps a ship blaring in the distance, or the sea itself blaring as this new bastard landed on its bosom.

Bruno swam with long strokes, drawing curtain after curtain before him. He detected a first crack in the distant horizon, where the muted slates of sea and sky collide. Through this crack he tried to escape, but his strength was fading too quickly, and when his feet hit a reef, he stopped to rest a while.

He looked back. He saw the gray docks, the rotting shingles and wind-worn harbor buildings. He saw the ships rocking and creaking sadly, round ships, pregnant with the faraway, and the figure of a gorgon on one of the dinghies, and people crowding and calling to him from the pier. Or cheering him? In any case, they could no longer join hands around him in a ring. He laughed and shivered with waves of heat and cold. He noticed that his wristwatch was still on, but his fingers were trembling so, he couldn't remove it.

Someone out by the pier was working on the motor of a small boat but the motor would not respond. Bruno leaned back to look at the sky and take a deep breath. For the first time in years he did not feel hunted. Even if he were captured now, he would never be recognized as the man they were pursuing. They would catch an empty vessel. No police interrogator would be able to make sense of what Bruno was saying now. No writer would ever be able to record it accurately. At best they might try to reconstruct it with the aid of superficial evidence. How sad the fate of those Bruno abandoned on the shore. The whole world must have felt a pang as Bruno lowered himself into the water. Indians along the Orinoco stopped chopping rubber trees for a moment to listen. The shepherds of the Australian Fire Tribe stood suddenly still, and cocked their heads when they heard that distant sound. I did, too, and I wasn't even born yet.

And not far from Bruno the waters parted. Something flickered and fluttered there. A greenish glare or a frozen eye, and furrows plowed in a flurry, foaming with the soft pit-a-pat of many fins. Tiny mouths surrounded him, stung him on the belly and the knees, nibbled at his buttocks and chest. Bruno froze in astonishment as he read the code tattooed upon his body. The credentials of a one-man delegation setting off on a journey. The fish wondered at his tough, skimpy flesh, investigated the veins protruding on his white feet. Silently they followed the flashing object that dropped into the depths to tell the time that was already past. The ranks broke before him, and the fish let Laprik through to regard Bruno with his piercing eyes. He was a big salmon, more developed than the rest, with a body as big as Bruno's. For a moment he swam around him circumspectly, his tail lightly aquiver, or perhaps the ripples came from the motorboat approaching with two stevedores and a Port Authority official, all yelling at him angrily, but Laprik quickly returned to his place, the shoal folded slowly like an enormous, limp accordion, and Bruno sailed away.

[2]

THREE YEARS HAVE GONE BY since we broke up. I am healing. Just as you predicted. Sometimes, when the tension is unbearable, I take the bus to Tel Aviv. To you. I walk along the beach, stepping over shells and seaweed and dead fish, and if there aren't too many people around, I actually speak to you out loud. I tell you that the book is coming along, that for three years the *torag* has been on, a relentless war between me and Bruno the fish. Meanwhile, I've made some headway. Here's the list. I love lists: I did it! I finished writing Grandfather Anshel's story, the one he told Neigel, the German; and I also finished the story of baby Kazik, that mistake Ayala was pleased to call my "crime against humanity," bless her little heart.

But the important thing is Bruno's story, and it's on his account that I return to you almost every week: to shout the latest installment into your cockleshell ears, and also, of course, to pump you for the moist information in your bottomless depths, to charm you into making disclosures, into letting me sniff you till I catch the scent of Bruno, because for me the two of you are indissoluble, which is why I put you in my story in the first place, and why I'm telling you about it now, though I know it makes you furious. Oh sure, you never admit you notice me when I show up at the beach—but I know you: I hear you snarling the moment my foot touches the breakwater. I see you arch your back to snatch me away.

But I am careful. You said so yourself.

People hear I'm interested in Bruno and send me all kinds of material. You'd be surprised how much has been written about him. Mostly in Polish. And I've come across a number of theories concerning his lost novel, *The Messiah*: that it's about how Bruno lures the Messiah into the Drohobycz Ghetto with his spellbinding prose, or that it's about the Holocaust and Bruno's last years under the Nazi Occupation. But you and I know better, don't we? Life is what interested Bruno. Simple, everyday life; for him the Holocaust was a laboratory gone mad, accelerating and intensifying human processes a hundredfold . . .

In any case, they all praise him. They say he's one of the greatest writers of the century; they compare him to Kafka, Proust, and Rilke. They disapprove of my writing about him. They tactfully suggest that to write about him one would have to be a writer of comparable stature at least. Well, I don't care. It's not their Bruno I'm writing about. I read their letters politely, and tear the papers to bits, and then, as of course you know, when I come to see you in Tel Aviv, I climb the breakwater, ho-hum, just taking a little stroll up here on the rocks, when suddenly I shake my pockets out and a heap of shredded paper hits the water, plumpety-plump, anyone notice anything? Those letters mean more to you than they do to me, anyway. Maybe you detest academic harangues, but if I know you, you'll paste the pieces together and file them below in your benthic archives. You're not about to part with documents like these.

And I also wanted to tell you that I'm back to my old self again. That is, I'm back to my old style. The style my poems were written in. And Bruno is slowly letting go of my pen. He's peeling off. I have only a few notebooks left now which nobody would ever be able to identify positively as either his or mine. And of course you and I both know I was merely the vessel, the writing hand, the weak link through which his stifled energy could flow.

I can't stop coming back to you. I come back to tell you the real story, the story I can't put down in writing as it really happened, as it should be told: not sensibly, but ardently. From start to finish. For once you're going to listen to something that isn't directly about you, and you will listen patiently and quietly (I wouldn't dream of asking you to listen eagerly) to everything that happened to me when I returned from Narvia, damn you, listen. That is, let the Bruno in you listen.

On May 25, 1980 (I remember the exact date), I received a parting gift from Ayala: *The Street of Crocodiles* by Bruno Schulz. I'd never heard of the book before, and I was even put off by the German ring of the author's name. Anyway, I started reading it immediately, mainly because of the bitter circumstances in which it had been given to me, and because of the giver.

And then suddenly, ten pages into the book, I forgot everything and read in breathless excitement, the way you might read a letter smuggled to you over the back roads and byways, a terse communication from the brother you had assumed was dead all these years. It was the first time I ever began to reread a book as soon as I finished it. And I've read it a good many times since. For months it was the only book I needed. It was The Book for me in the sense Bruno had yearned for *that great tome, sighing, a stormy Bible, its pages fluttering in the wind like an overblown rose*—and I believe I read it as such a letter deserves to be read: knowing that what is written on the page is less significant than the pages torn out and lost; pages so explicit they were expunged for fear that they would fall into the wrong hands . . .

And I did something I haven't done since I was a child: I transcribed entire paragraphs in my notebook. To help me remember, and to feel the words streaming out of my pen and collecting on the page. On the first page I copied his indirect testimony that *God's hand had passed over his face while he slept, and transformed him into one who knows what he knows not and whose drooping eyes are filled with sublime intimations of distant worlds* . . .

Then one night, a few weeks later, I woke out of a sound sleep and knew for certain that Bruno had not been murdered in the Drohobycz Ghetto in 1942. He had escaped. When I say "escaped," I don't mean it in the usual sense of the word but, in the special sense Bruno might have given a word like "pensioner," signifying *someone who crosses the prescribed and generally accepted borders and brings himself into the magnetic field of a different dimension of existence, traveling light* . . . Whenever I finished copying some passage, my pen would jiggle around a few more times and litter the page with a line or two of my own—though how shall I put it—in Bruno's voice, by straining to hear him, having clearly perceived his desperate need to express himself, now that he was deprived of his writing hand. How well I understand the agony, the affliction of a writer in exile like him. I mean "exile" in a very broad sense, and I, as you know, proffered my hand and my pen.

How strange it is. And frightening.

Because just think, here I was—a Hebrew poet with four books out in a highly distinctive style, a style one paragon of literary criticism who crooks his little finger when he writes described as "thin-lipped," and which Ayala called "mean and niggardly"—experiencing a veritable stampede of panting, perspiring words in my notebook *like the mating dance of the peacock, or a vivid cloud of hummingbirds*, as Bruno once wrote.

(Or did I write that?)

Bruno Schulz. A Jew. Possibly the most important Polish writer between the two world wars. Son of the eccentric owner of a dry-goods store. Taught drawing and technical drafting at the Drohobycz Gymnasium. A lonely man.

And in 1941, when the Germans entered the city of Drohobycz, Bruno was forced to leave his home and move to a house on Stolareska Street. Under orders from the authorities, he painted giant murals at the riding academy and catalogued libraries commandeered by the Germans. To earn a living, he also worked as a "House Jew" (light carpentry, sign painting, family portraits, etc.) at the residence of SS Officer Felix Landau.

Felix Landau had an enemy—another SS officer by the name of Karl Gunther. On November 19, 1942, on the corner of Czeczky and Miz-kewitz Streets, Karl Gunther shot Bruno and, as the story goes, went to Landau and said, "I killed your Jew." To which Landau replied, "In that case, I will now kill your Jew."

You're with me, I know it: for a minute the water turned to stone. Two gulls collided with a screech. You're here.

I killed your Jew. In that case, I will now kill—

Just like that.

I've hurt you, I know. It hurts me, too.

But listen. We have other things to talk about. Shall we change the subject? I don't want to hurt anyone. There's something I have to tell you. Listen.

For many years after Grandfather Anshel's disappearance I used to hum his story to the German. I tried to write it down a couple of times before I went to Poland, with no success. And I grew more and more frustrated and angry with myself, filled with self-reproach mixed with wistful visions of the old man locked inside the story for so long, a ghostly ship turned away at every port, while I, his only hope of lib-eration, of salvaging his story, deserted him.

So I began to hunt for Grandfather's writings. I went through old archives and the dusty libraries of remote kibbutzim. I read crumbly magazines that reminded me of prehistoric cave drawings that disin-tegrate under the explorer's torch. Among the literary remains of a Yiddish writer who died in an old-age home in Haifa, I found a real trove: four yellow issues of *Little Lights*, the children's magazine (Shi-mon Zalmanson, editor) published in Warsaw in 1912. There were four complete chapters of an adventure where the Children of the Heart rescue a Roman gladiator ("Anton the Luder") from the lion pit. I read eagerly: by now I had begun to detect certain limitations in the narrative skills of Anshel Wasserman, but this in no way hampered my enjoyment or my nostalgic feelings for him and his archaic prose, the awe-inspiring language of a prophet of yore, and the war it seems he waged through-out his life, the "only war there is," to quote Otto Brig, the hero of the serial.

So I did some piecing together: a few episodes from a children's magazine called *Sapling* (Krakow, 1920; I wonder if Grandfather Anshel ever received royalties for the stories that were reprinted), one in which the Children of the Heart help Louis Pasteur fight rabies, one Polish translation of a story about rescuing young flood and famine victims in turn-of-the-century India, and other fragments of adventures from around the world. I traveled everywhere, combing the musty attics of persons deceased in the hopes of finding something. It was so important to me, I spent all my spare time at it.

Incidentally, around this time I came across an article about early-twentieth-century children's magazines in Poland that mentions him: "Anshel Wasserman, Yiddish storyteller." According to this article, "opinion is divided" on the quality and importance of his writing, "the influence of contemporaneous authors is strongly in evidence—often embarrassingly so—" and, then with the peremptoriness so typical of literary criticism, the article pronounced "the literary value of his work . . . scant indeed, its main aim being to acquaint the youthful reader with historical events and personages," though the author of this article acknowledged, albeit grudgingly, that "these simple adventures called 'The Children of the Heart' achieved a surprising popularity among young readers, and were translated into Polish, Czech, and German, and published in a number of European illustrated children's magazines."

The critic further remarks—not without a hint of reproach—that my grandfather was one of the few Hebrew authors "writing at a time of national and linguistic revival (the early part of the twentieth century) to deal chiefly with universal themes, scarcely touching on the issue of Jewish nationalism, indeed, ignoring it altogether. This may account for his favor with the children of the world and his attainment of a popular success beyond the reach of more masterful Hebrew writers imbued with a sense of Zionist mission."

I was furious at this pompous ass of a "critic": you don't judge a man like Anshel Wasserman according to the commonplaces of literary analysis. Couldn't he see that?

But I didn't write the story, the unique story of Grandfather and Herr Neigel.

When I returned from Narvia, I was eager to write again. Because of Bruno. Because of what he told me. Or rather, in spite of what he told me. I had reached an impasse with the story of Grandfather and Herr Neigel, so I decided to go after documentary material, quotations from books about the Holocaust, excerpts of the victims' testimony, psychological profiles of the murderers, case notes, etc. Ruth said, But none of this is really necessary, is it? Why do you insist on making things so difficult? You're just swamping yourself under a lot of details. Look at it this way, you have two people, your grandfather and Neigel, two human beings, and one tells the other a story. That's it. She was only trying to help, of course, as usual, but we had reached a point in our marriage, Ruth and I, where the most innocent remark could start a fight.

Are you with me?

You shake your head at my awkward attempts to tell the story. I can just hear you muttering, If that's how he writes, he'd better not write about me. He'd better not dry me out on his pages or plaster me all over his notebooks. Because with me, dearie, you're going to have to write with wild abandon, in rarest ink made of pungent male and female secretions and the passions of life, not like this, sweetie pie . . .

But listen, will you, please?

As I tried to write the story of Anshel Wasserman, my own life became more and more circumscribed. The Greek philosopher Zeno argued that motion is impossible because a moving object has to reach the halfway point before it can reach the end, and therefore a body that traverses a finite distance must traverse an infinite number of halves in a finite time, i.e., the time it actually takes to traverse the finite distance in question. Which is exactly what happened to me: I wrote, but could not progress from one word to the next. From one idea to the next. My pen scored the page with a kind of terrible stammer. I had a regular desk at the Yad Vashem Holocaust Library by this time, and the librarians all knew me. Every morning at around ten I used to shut my books and go to the cafeteria for a snack. A roll with hard-boiled egg and tomato. Followed by coffee and the excellent yeast cake they serve there. I would sit around listening to the employees talk about their children and their paychecks, and think to myself dejectedly, Somewhere inside this edifice is an empty white room with thin, membranous walls, if only I could find it.

Ruth would pick me up at five on her way home from work in our beat-up Mini Minor. One look at me as I climbed into the car and she bit her lip to keep from saying anything that might start a fight. We had no children at the time. Yariv wasn't born yet. Ruth was undergoing horrid, expensive gynecological treatments I didn't want to know about. I was prepared to pay for them, sure. Have sex with her every morning at 6:30 on the dot—yes, I was prepared to do that, too. But listen to the gory details—no, thank you. And anyway, what right had she to complain? Before she married me, I warned her that when you really need me, I'm useless. That's how it is. Nobody's perfect. I consider this fair, though, because I don't expect help from anyone, including her. Of course, my talking this way used to infuriate her. Coming home from her latest gynecological idol, she would attack me with a vehemence that amazed even her. I had never seen her let go of her inhibitions and lose control like that. Her broad, coarse face, poised between prettiness and raw peasant health, would suddenly turn ugly and brutal. I, of course, would remain perfectly cool and levelheaded, my only worry being that she might do herself harm in this hysterical state. And all else failing, I was sometimes forced to give her a swift slap in the face to calm her down, after which she would throw herself on the bed and fall asleep sobbing. All this nastiness spewing out when she screamed at me made me sick, though I did remark that these outbursts often had the effect of purging her rather quickly so she could go on loving me unperturbed. There are some things I will never understand about women. Ruth would say, I know you don't believe your own words. It's a kind of inner conflict you're taking out on me, and it isn't fair, Momik.

Maybe she's right, I don't know. Sometimes I want to make it up to her. I could cry when I think about the day she'll be lying there in critical condition and I walk in to donate a kidney that saves her life. It's hard to imagine a nobler sacrifice. Sometimes I actually look forward to it. Then she'll see: her whole life with me will take on a different meaning. She will understand the truth and her heart will bleed. Oh, my darling, the hell you must have lived through.

I tried another tack. The trial of Rudolf Hoess, commander of Auschwitz, in the winter of 1946. For a few weeks I considered reconstructing the trial: Anshel Wasserman vs. Rudolf Hoess. I'd worked out some fairly good segments of the case. Would Anshel Wasserman send Hoess "back to Chelm"? Grandfather rises in the witness stand and hurls a curse at Hoess, may his face take on a striking resemblance to the anti-Semitic cartoons in *Die Stürmer*. "And now, Herr Hoess," says Grandfather Anshel, pronouncing his verdict, "you are free to wander the earth, and may God have mercy on your evil soul." I worked on this story for the better part of two months. I wrote in a fever. The humming inside me grew louder. It was unmistakably the old, monotonous story-tune Grandfather used twenty-five years ago, though it was still a tune without any words. I sometimes wondered if anyone else could hear it.

But this story, too, ground to a halt. I could not bring Anshel Wasserman to look Hoess in the face. I suppose there are certain things you shouldn't demand of your own characters. This had never occurred to me when I was writing poetry, maybe because I never brought two people together in a poem. Maybe, said Ruth, but your grandfather and the German are just that, two people, so let something happen between them. If only I knew what, I said. I'll have to go back to the facts. People I'll never understand. Nobody's perfect, okay?

I searched through back issues of the *Times*. Our Warsaw correspondent reports on the trial of the decade: "Spectators at the trial were seated two to a desk. Rudolf Hoess, the accused, with sad, intelligent eyes, wore a light green uniform." Snowflakes fell on the windows of the Praga School in Warsaw. Incidentally, the snow in the concentration camps had a peculiar smell on account of the ash. I can't think what will happen to me someday when I explode with all these facts. I want to write, but I can't get rid of my blocks and inhibitions. Every step becomes impossible because of the half step that must precede it. I'm trapped in Zeno's paradox. The prosecutor said to Hoess, "It will not be possible at this time to read all the charges against you, because they fill twenty-one volumes, three hundred printed pages in each, with the descriptions of your crimes. Therefore we open this trial with a simple question: You are charged with the murder of four million human beings. Do you plead guilty?" The accused reflected a moment, wrinkled his forehead, raised his eyes to the judge, and said, "Yes, your Honor. I plead guilty. Though according to my calculations, I murdered only two and a half million."

"Damn it," cried Ayala, flushing the way she does when she gets excited. "Think how many times that man must have murdered himself to come out with a statement like that."

"He must have been dead inside," cried Ruth, appalled, "a million and a half—the difference—the man must have been dead."

"I can't go on like this," I sobbed to each in turn. "I just can't take it anymore. It's so horrifying. How can you go on living and believing in humanity once you know?"

"Ask your grandfather," said Ayala in exasperation. "He's the one to ask, can't you see that now?"

"But I don't know anything about him, or the story."

"He was an old man, he told a story to a Nazi. He survived. Nazi kaput. If you want to stick to the facts, these are your facts. From now on, write ardently. Not sensibly."

She was referring to the White Room, the one she told me about the first time we met. I had said, "When you're writing about things that happened Over There, you have to stick to the facts. Otherwise, what right do I have to touch the sore?"

"Write in human terms, Shlomik," said Ayala. "Which is enough. Almost like poetry."

I was still sidestepping, I recall. "Adorno says after Auschwitz, poetry is no longer possible."

"But there were human beings at Auschwitz," said Ruth in her heavy, deliberate way, "and that's exactly what makes poetry possible, I mean—"

"I mean"—Ayala beamed, her round cheeks shining red—"not poetry with rhyme and meter and all that, just two people trying to connect in a faltering, self-conscious way. You don't need much."

But you need courage, which I, of course—

Oh, bravo!

For the past few moments I have been trying to work out my exact location on the breakwater. I felt you tensing in the dark, and I made the mistake of hoping my story had touched your heart at last. And then I saw you throw a basin of briny water from your cool, cool cellars at the fishermen on either side of me, and I heard them curse in amazement, and call out to each other, Bitch of a sea tonight! And I couldn't understand what was happening to you.

How puny your weapons seem to the people on the shore! Oh well, I'm soaking wet anyway, what have I got to lose, so as a token of my generosity, of my largesse as opposed to your pettiness, I will now tell you about Bruno, and—more particularly—about you. I know you'll love that.

And I'll skip the parts that don't concern you—like the letters I sent to Warsaw, my credentials and references, the many appeals, the strings my publisher pulled, and the list of instructions from my mother, who was so anxious about my trip Over There she furnished me with twenty-

one self-addressed envelopes to make sure I would send her a sign of
life every day; and the ten pairs of nylon stockings to sell on the black
market ("in case you run out of money") she smuggled into my suitcase
with ancient cunning; and my sad leave-taking from Ruthy ("I hope
you find what you're looking for so we can start living again"), and the
flight to Poland, the suitcase "lost" in customs and returned two days
later (minus the nylon stockings).

The necessary permits took four days to arrive. Meanwhile, I wandered around Warsaw alone in the big, silent city: it was as if somebody
had turned off the sound. I saw a long queue in front of a store dis-
playing a lone tomato. In a café I found the Franzuski pastries Papa
once mentioned nostalgically, so I ate them in his memory, not that
they were any good. I saw pictures of clowns with scarves and colorful
butterflies on the houses, symbols of the Solidarity movement, and I
had an exciting meeting with Julian Strikowsky, the Polish Jewish
writer, who told me stories about the shtetl in fluent Hebrew and—
yes! Yes! All right! I'll get to the point! And then after the permits
arrived—the train ride to Danzig, the scenery, Motl's villages, forests
of linden trees and slender birches, barns and silos—and all the while
I had the strongest impression "he" was moving toward me from the
opposite direction, from Drohobycz, now under Russian rule. Just as
I had felt while transcribing passages into my notebook: as though I
could hear him rapping out answers from the opposite side of the page;
as though we were two miners tunneling from opposite sides of a
mountain . . .

And finally to the edge of the pier.

Facing the waves I knew I was right: Bruno hadn't been murdered.
He had escaped. And I use "escape" here not in the ordinary sense but
as Bruno and I might have used it, to mean *one who has pulled himself
relentlessly toward the magnetic field* of—you recite with me like a little
girl finishing a sentence. I hear you whisper before I can even say, "A
man who defected to a form of existence largely given to vague guesses,
demanding great effort and goodwill from his neighbors. A man who
travels light . . ."

And I took a broken-down bus to Narvia, and rented a room in the
cottage of the widow Dombursky, who dressed in black and had three
hairy warts on her cheek. She cleared out a room for me, with a picture
of Mary and baby Jesus on the wall above the bed, and a photograph

of Mr. Dombursky in his postman's uniform and mustache on the wall facing it. The afternoon of my arrival in the village, I changed into my gray bathing trunks and sat down on a derelict chair on the empty beach, in the keen wind of an unusually cool July day, feeling lonely and tense—and I waited.

Little by little, things began to change. All day long, I waited on the beach. I watched the fishermen set off in the morning, and I was still there when they returned in the evening and called their families out to the quay to help them pull in the boats with a primitive kind of crane and divide the day's catch on a long, wooden table; only then would I head back to eat the "Cyclops fish," or sole, the widow Dombursky cooked—the way all village women cooked it in the evenings— and then I would sit down to write or, rather, to erase. I had by now brought Bruno as far as Danzig; I had smuggled him there by train, past the police and literary authorities. Now I was obliged to wait patiently. To vacate myself and serve as his writing hand, or even more than that: who could say what he would demand of me in return for re-creating his lost work, *The Messiah*? I toned down, and listened. In nearby Gdansk, the Solidarity people were rioting, and here in the village there were frequent power failures. At times I had to write by the light of a smoky oil lamp. Some mornings there was no bread on the table. I wrote not a single word to Ruth or Ayala, nor did I send my mother any letters. For the first time since my brief affair with Ayala, I felt I was in love. I didn't quite know with whom yet, but at any rate, I was ready for love. Maybe that was why things turned out so well . . . Ah, now we're getting there. You're flouncing impatiently, you're gushing all over me. Listen: my fourth morning in Narvia I went in the water. The smooth waves bore me gently. Already you seemed to know. The story made it necessary for me to go to the sea and wait. Ever since I first read Bruno and began to transcribe those passages of his works, I had attached a special significance to what my hand would write. I constantly expected an important message.

But the sea in my story was a cunning old giant, kindly and gruff, with a wet beard like Neptune's, and I could not understand why I didn't feel right about him. I floated patiently in the water all day, my back turning lobster-red, till at around five o'clock in the afternoon I discovered that my old man of the sea was actually—a woman. A woman's psyche in a body of water. An immense blue mollusc, asleep most of the time because it can't satisfy its own immense demands for energy, enveloped by the runny, medusa-like essence of her infinitesimal soul, surging, billowing, a thousand petticoats in green, white, and blue; and she sleeps, deep in one of a thousand lunar basins, her face upturned like a giant sunflower and her liquid body softly sustaining the reflexive motion in wavy contractions, foamy shivers, surrealistic reveries, fashioning fantastical creatures out of her depths; but beware, make no mistake about her serene and dignified appearance, because underneath it all she's nothing but a cheap little slut, utterly shameless, not to say primitive in her wanton cravings, a typical specimen of paleontological times, with hardly the education one might expect in view of her advanced age and experience and her travels over the globe, no, rather, like certain women—one of whom I encountered several years ago and came to know intimately—she has learned a way of blithely combining little bits of knowledge with a thousand-and-one amusing stories and "piquant" anecdotes to win her listener over, though on the whole I would say she is equipped with keen intuition and the instincts of a hunter, all of which tends to mislead certain people, yes, you see you can't hide anything from me anymore, I know you now, down to the last cranny in your blackest depths, and it seems I have succeeded where other men failed, other less daring men or, rather, men who were not "obliged" to be so daring; because (not that you'd ever admit it) I succeeded in catching something elusive about you and compressing it into a single iridescent gleam of endless forms and colors and fields of blue light in a delirium of flickering expanses whose greatest magic is that they never exist enough to be recalled, to be recorded—

These and other things I whispered to you there, on the beach in Narvia. My lips touched the water and my body was very hot. It's about "him," I said, but it's also about me. It's about my family and what the Beast did to us. And I spoke about fear. And about Grandfather, whom I can't seem to bring back to life, not even in the story. And about being unable to understand my life until I learn about my unlived life Over There. And I told you that, for me, Bruno is the key: an invitation and a warning. And I quoted his stories from memory . . .

"Hey, you there"—an eerie, nasal voice addressed me crossly. I raised my head but saw no one. The sand was white and bare except for my beach chair with the torn canvas flapping in the wind. But then an unusually warm, slick viscosity enveloped me, only to vanish, and returned a moment later. "Listen," you said tentatively, coolly, "you talk like somebody I used to know." My heart nearly burst with joy in the water, but I went on floating as if nothing had happened.

"Oh yes?—and who would that be?"

You studied me briefly, raised a sudden blue screen between me and the shore, and licked me all over, smacking your lips, and then you lowered the screen again, peering over your shoulder at the shore.

"I'm certainly not going to tell you about it here."

"In my room, then?" I asked politely.

"Ha!!"

It was there, for the first time, that I heard your snort of contempt, a wave snuffed into a maelstrom which has been your derisive greeting to me ever since. I don't suppose you'll ever give it up. Although you're sound asleep when I arrive at the beach in Tel Aviv, you terrify bathers and fishermen for miles around with that irritating sound. They don't realize, of course.

"I'll take you there, far away," you said, indicating the horizon with an arching of the waves.

"And will you bring me back again?"

"Come hell or high water."

"I've heard about people who never return."

"Scared?"

"That's interesting. You talk like somebody *I* know, too."

"Shut up, will you? Do you always talk so much? Okay, let's go."

Again you licked me, with obvious reluctance, and howled in rage and amazement. "Couldn't be! So different! Just the opposite, in fact! Still, he does know things nobody else . . . hmm, we'll soon find out." And you retreated into your inmost self, and vanished with a whistle and a gurgle, leaving me disappointed and dazed.

But only for a moment.

Because an angry breaker came along, whinnied, and knelt at my feet while I climbed on its sinewy back and grabbed its ears—and away we went.

[3]

I'LL NEVER FORGET IT, BRUNO, the burning sensation when you jumped off the pier and the warmth flowing out of you, but there was something else then, I didn't know quite what, and at first I thought

it was the rutting smell you creaturelings give off; later, though, I
realized it was only the scent of despair, that you have this gland, I still
hadn't figured where yet, and there was this awful awful burning and
a slash down my middle, like a birth pang maybe, and then I coiled
around you, I rolled into you on every side, and galloped furiously on
the strongest waves I could catch just then, from Madagascar, which
is where I happened to be sleeping at the time (snoozing, really, I don't
sleep much), and by the shortest route to the Cape of Good Hope,
where the Malagasy waves crashed under me, so I picked up some new
ones, fresh ones, and went on through a squall to the gulf of Guinea,
and from there to the Strait of Gibraltar, a mistake of course, because
I should have turned right at the English Channel instead, I always do
that, and before I realized it and made the turn, my waves had fainted
on me, the little weaklings, and I could barely tow them back to the
Atlantic, where they broke down completely, crying and begging for
mercy, and I went on alone to Biscay, where I found the kind of waves
I really like, seventeen-meter breakers roaring and spuming with ne'er
a whiff of land, and I picked a garland of long morays and brandished
them over the waves, crying, Faster, faster, and the morays squirmed
furiously in my hand and butted each other with their mighty snake
heads, and everywhere we went the water heaved and vomited fantastical
creatures out of my blackest depths; it overflowed and flooded entire
beach colonies of cormorants, the poor darlings, and caused the most
ter-ri-ble *torag* in a gam of blue whales, and stole the color from a vast
shoal of red mullets. What a trip, Bruno, what a trip! A million years
from now I will still be amazed, I will still laugh at myself for not
recognizing the pain of you inside me, for how I whisked over thousands
of miles propelled by rage at my rude awakening and on my way to
you, no less, somewhere off the island of Bornholm, I'd sent my scouts
out, the little Baltic runners, my sprightly wavelings, and they galloped
ahead and touched you and hurried back to me, gasping and choking
on the carcasses of fish they'd hit and the planking of the ships they'd
sunk, and they raced out to my chariot and offered themselves to me
for a lick, and phewww! I tasted them, and spat in a giant arc because
my little wavelings were bitter as puffers, and now I was rip-roaring
mad and I galloped ahead, spitting foam and fish and curses I learned
from sailors, and I could feel myself heaving this nuisance the way a
sea cucumber spits its guts out together with the pearl fish inside it.

And I drew nearer and nearer, but cautiously, because you have to be ready for anything with a being even my successful sister has trouble with, and I have to admit, especially now that I know him better, I'm not at all surprised she threw him out, poor thing, because a creature like that is more than she can bear, the little darling, she can't stand anything more complicated than a volcano or more spectacular than snow, because—and by the way, this is a well-known fact, and I would tell her so to her face—she loves simplicity. She really, I mean *really*, appreciates order and reason and everything in its place. I'm sure she'd slam the door on most of my creaturelings on grounds of "reason" and "aesthetics," as if a sea horse were any less beautiful than a land horse, though it's true that those who became dissatisfied with the topsy-turvy life I had to offer got out and went to her, and it's also true that the solid, civilized ones live with her, and the adventurers and sailors and crazy romantics come to me, and we sort of divided things up between us like that without a plan or anything and now we have this curious problem all of a sudden, this human creature comes along, a speck, a crumb, who starts making more trouble for her than a volcanic ulcer. So what do you do with him? Right: send him to me. Oh, she won't mind, she tells herself, my kindhearted sister, she probably won't even notice, and if she ever does, she'll be thrilled to pieces because he's exactly her type, this Bruno, perfect for her romantic temperament, and though she's about four million years old, deep down inside she's just a girl, isn't it marvelous—says my sister—how young at heart and playful she is and uh—well, adventurous, ye-es . . . (You've got to hear the way she says "adventurous." It's so adorable she starts sprouting warty lemon groves in India.)

What can I tell you—she's right. She's right, she's right, she's right. That's how I am. And the same evening, I flew in breathless to the Danzig coast from Madagascar and saw this little man here for the first time, slapping the water like an old manatee that spreads its wings, flies out of the water, and lands with a terrible thud (that's how they calve), and when I saw how desperately he was trying to swim deeper and deeper into me to get away from her, I suddenly felt something, I could swear I was dancing inside, I'm like that sometimes, and then my island chains clattered in the Pacific, icebergs creaked in Antarctica, and I said to myself, Come now, don't lose your head, remember how it ended with Odysseus and Marco Polo and Francis Drake, you know they always leave you in the end and go back where they came from, they only need you when they're beyond despair, but once you've patched them up, they leave without a word of gratitude, icy and insensible, never to discover who and what you are beneath all that water . . .

And then I said, Hell, I said, what's the sense of living if I have to be hemmed in and choked by continents and coasts and isthmuses, when all I know about the world is what the rivers tell me with their cloying tongues, or what the gulls shriek at each other overhead, or what the silly little raindrops get so flustered about, and what's the sense of living if I can't get a little loving and a heartache once in a while, yes that's right, a heartache, by all the easterlies, and, oh, how sweet it is, like the time I held the Red Sea in for an eternity and a half to let the Jews pass through and I thought I'd go crazy (it's unbelievably hard to hold it in like that, and between two banks, no less), and I took one look at the small, strong, concentrated man, at his slightly triangular head, his thin white physique, and I knew there and then that I would be his, that I would give myself to him in wild abandon, from my heights down to my blackest depths, and without a moment's thought about where this was leading, and how he would go back to her when he finished poisoning me and stirring me up, once he unburdened himself inside me and crumbled into the many components which I—and only I—can offer him, all the shimmers and colors and loops of longing and madcap waves, and suddenly I was hot and cold and flushed all over, because that's how I am in these situations, everything shows, and you might have thought I brought the whole Red Sea to Danzig by mistake, but I managed somehow to remember the errands and things I had to attend to, but where was I going to find the patience for any of that now—temperature maintenance and fixing a precise arc for the Gulf Stream, and a steady rate for the glaciers to drift, and all that bureaucratic stuff about high tide and low tide I could never get straight though the bitter truth is that I just didn't care anymore, I only knew I would follow that man of mine forever, *che sarà sarà*, as the Italians say (I simply adore Venice, which in my opinion is the most brilliant idea my sister ever had), and believe it or not, it was only then that I noticed my man was not alone, in fact he was surrounded by about a million salmon on the way back to their river, and I must confess I couldn't remember exactly what kind of life cycle the salmon have; that is, I used to know, but I forgot.

That's the kind of thing that goes in one ear in Panama and out the other in the Bosphorus, because how are you supposed to remember all the details about fish and seaweed and sponges and shrimps and corals and monsters and sirens, a million stories, a million troubles, though in this particular instance I decided not to indulge in ignorance, and I dispatched my speedy cubs, my quick, pliable wavelings, my boon companions, my bond slaves, who promptly circled the salmon and touched their fins, brushing past them as if by chance, and then headed for the beach, because . . . how shall I explain it . . . it's so silly really . . . you see, I have this minor health problem, temporarily of course, on account of which I can only understand what my wavelings tell me after they've touched the shore, or a reef or an island or any other land object like a ship, it's nothing really, just a flaw in the plan I know will be corrected before long, after which I'll be able to do it alone, but who cares about that now, the important thing is that my sweet little wavelings had finished rendering the feel of salmon skin, the roughness of fins and the rings embroidered there, ye-es, how easy to understand fish compared to human creatures, and they returned to me directly, my swift, secret fish, and I read the cruel story of those salmon in a single lick, their birth in a sweetwater river in Scotland or Australia (these particular salmon happened to be from the river Spey in Scotland), and their wanderings to me, the salty sea, and then, roughly three years later, the return voyage spanning tens of thousands of my miles, in giant shoals, fifty knots per day, seldom resting, with fishermen and predators and storms in pursuit, and finally the return to their native river, swimming against the current, leaping the falls, higher and higher, with all their remaining strength, and I hear there are places where human creatures build special locks for them like passages around the falls to ease the journey, but no, they have to leap against the mighty current, till finally they reach their birthplace, I mean their *exact* birthplace, and at last their strength gives out and they spawn and die, leaving one or two survivors from each shoal to lead the newborn to me for another round, and the others—

But there was no time to drown myself in misery, because "he" was there, swimming and spurting bitterness, giving me the shivers wherever he went, and I sent my wavelings back to learn everything they could about him, but I hate to wait, so I dived down to my blackest depths where the fish have eyes like saucers, and the corals glow with a pale light, and the floor is cluttered with petrified yet living fish and petrified forests and huge loamy swamps under a constant rain of fish scurf and clouds of plankton from the upper zones, and I felt as if I was suffocating there and shot up to the zone I love the best, the chiaroscuro near the surface, but not too near, where I grow those ra-vi-shing coral reefs, and fish you have to see to believe, and where would you find a gorgeous creature like the blue, green, and red cichlid on *her* I'd like to know, I mean does *she* have anything to offer as majestic as the mature emperor angelfish decked out with arabesques of purple, yellow, and black?

And with these annoying thoughts running through me I spent the next eternity and a half drumming on the rocks and taunting every passing fish, till my wavelings returned a second time, but they still couldn't tell me anything about him, and they threw themselves down, wriggling and trembling before me like seal puppies, saying, We doodint understid what goed on, O Lady, the creature had a yuck-yuck tasty like a hornfish and a speeching we doodint anyvus understid, and so hot 's scare us to touch and burnier than actinias, O Lady, and then I bellowed, Back to him, I bellowed, Fly to the man and learn him inside out, be reckless and cruel, drag him, roll him, tickle him, taste his excrement and the bile flowing out of him, render his saliva and lick his urine, and copy the wrinkles around his eyes and the tiny follicles where his hair fell out; run now, fly now, a-way!!!

Ye-es, that was a fab-u-lous show of me in a rage, though I seldom get really angry, but this time I was very curious and eager and alert, and I was also a little frightened and, as usually happens in such cases, I blew myself into giant waves, and gushed high in the air out of the spout of a blue whale, and squirted out of a squid in an inky cloud, till my wavelings came back to me, tired and worn and buffeting each other, crying, All's well, O Lady, we founded out the story, and 's no wonder, O Lady, we doodint understid right away 'cause that he neveven dreamed a thought in the speeching of human creachies and that he trieded and trieded to think up the words for him just only, O Lady, but we crackered his secret, soon because the rest of the story we moreless founded out like that this one is a kind they call the Jews because of his piece of snorkeling and where he was borned is Drohobycz and that this creachy writed a lot and now he runned away from something and said words in a speeching we doodint understid like a music always the same, I killed your Jew. In that case, I will now kill your Jew, you see, O Lady, we understid it through the full and now we fly back to him to learn more more and more ever so to please you, O Lady—

Please me? Ah! I was thrilled. Night had fallen, and I lay on my belly the way I sometimes do, like a tiny baby girl unique in all the galaxies and solar systems, and you have to look at her from the proper perspective so you can appreciate how cute and small she really is, like a little pearl, and my face was turned to the abyss and the wind caressed my bottom, and there were stars in the sky shining and I smoothed the waves so the light would shine through me bright and clear, and I was beautiful.

So, he invented a language, my man. How marvelous. To talk to himself without being understood by anyone else. Without being able to tell anyone about it later, because there would be no words. Really, where does he get these sublime ideas?

Yes, from the start he fascinated me, though I could never quite understand why he had to submit himself to so many worries and miseries when he could just have enjoyed himself with me, oh yes, in such matters I'm not unlike his mother, Henrietta, whom I now know intimately though we never met, and I'm sure would have gotten along just fine—she also used to tell him sadly, "The thoughts of an old man, Bruno, of an alter kopf, not a child, and may you come through them safely, look what happened to your poor father, Yacob."

And what did happen to him? My wavelings tell strange tales, tales I haven't heard since I first saw the Argonauts aboard their ship holding storytelling contests. According to my wavelings' report, Bruno's father was a sort of escapee, like him, only not in the usual sense of the word, ah . . . where did I write that down?

His father, who well-nigh learned how to fly raising tropical birds in the loft, peacocks and pheasants and condors and giant cocks, his father, whom Bruno called *the fencing master of the imagination, parrying the mighty forces of boredom, a great man, dead and resurrected times without number in myriad shapes, till everyone in the house became accustomed to his frequent demise*—so writes my Bruno—*only the portrait of his long-departed visage grew, as it were, to fill the room he had once occupied, and created the peculiar focal point of his wonderfully clear countenance, the wallpaper repeating here and there a nervous quiver, the arabesques taking on the painful anatomy of his smile* . . .

In the end Bruno's father was transformed into a giant crab. He would enter the room through a slit under the door, embarrassing everyone, till one day he was caught. Just like that: Bruno's mother

could stand it no longer, it seems, and she caught him and boiled him
for dinner, and served him at the table, big and bloated after the cooking,
on a lovely platter, but of course, they didn't eat him, cultured family
that they were, but only set him prominently on the parlor table next
to the musical cigar box, though he escaped from there as well, fancy
that, because neither Bruno nor Yacob was one to surrender when
things looked grim, so after a couple of weeks on the platter, he made
his escape, Bruno's father, leaving one leg flung across the dried tomato
sauce, while he himself, boiled, almost defeated, dragged onward, onward, ever onward, wandering homeless, like his obstinate son, so dear
and earnest, who makes me feel frivolous when he chars me black with
a furrow of despair, like the backwash of a battleship, which in this
case I don't erase but cover with a fine sheet of water as a keepsake,
like the other crumbs he leaves me, because what else can I do . . .

[4]

AND THERE IN THE WATER BRUNO to and fro in the big, slow
cradle of the sea marking water time translated into mist that blows
itself softly over the water in the bright dawn. Bruno afloat on the
waves plunked to the endless flow he learned that water has a smell
you know this water has a smell pulling you on and on lulling you
adrift in the cradle of the sea you learned that you can sail to eternity
infinity because you are drawn by the sinewy motion, suckled by the
quiet flow you float among them drawn through the water and the
immanence of long nights a dim moon an orange moon a shining moon
the itinerant clouds on the night sky you float and pass alone through
Creation the power of fish alone in motion the smell of fish alone
bedazzling the nares before you the gills throbbing to the measure the
chill of the waves nuzzling by you stealing into shore a wavy water-
negative of the image of you shattered into a thousand fragments in
the checkered eye of a rock crab stowed away among the stony hiero-
glyphs inscribed in manifold coral brains flowing onward only the
prickly fins chafed your tender skin in the beginning and the hundreds
of scratches that manifested then and the drops of your blood in the
sea set the shoal aquiver and soon you felt no pain no salt you saw
their shiny backs their glossy green bellies and the throbbing of fins

and the pungent smell and the shrieking vastness gasping for joy and your ears were filled with the roaring and the pulsing and the tumult of the watery fair with cries of higgler gulls and reels of blue furled under you and the coins your thoughts dropping into the sea and slinky money changers bartering in the silent alleyways of sunken cities and floating bazaars hushed and trapped in sheer enormous bubbles and the sea full of whispers and rustlings and echoes and frothy words gently strumming the waves on the harp of the shore water strings running through the beach comb on and on you are pulled and plunged into the streams of potency you pressed your arms to your sides your shoulder blades sprouted wings and oh the bliss of their solemn silence the gravity of their silence the somberness when you wondered is this what death is this bliss recording the beating sea-heart on a colossal cardiograph rolling on forever below and when you were borne to the city pier you drifted together in splay formation into the navy port destroyers there were frigates full of sailors and the smell of diesel fuel fanfares and a young sailor welding a machine gun to the deck shooting red sparks that cascaded into the water fizzling and the sailor suddenly saw the vastness of the shoal and stared and stared but did not did not notice you and for a moment you were afraid for one moment of perfidious self-reproach you were overcome and you floundered in the water howling screaming in fear that diffracted like lightning through the heart of the shoal because the sea is a courier whispering because the sea is a fisherman and behold the billowy waist the mighty shoulders casting a network of nerves that are thick and clear and suddenly there was a dangerous *torag* and you foundered bobbing and gasping you didn't know you never guessed your role in the *torag* and a thousand frightened fishes roundly fusing with your human terror veered suddenly colliding into the ranks approaching the skulls cracking jaws smashing and the *dolgan* unsettled suddenly this is the natural law of maintaining distance this is the natural law of loneliness in the crowd and the water foamed now slashed to snippets swarming with dagger fins and somewhere in the margins he was compelled to the detachable calm of his greatness with the fish and ever so slowly they fell in line from head to tail and for the first time you recognized the *ning*, the string extending from the back of your neck to the bottom of your soul, and you listened in wonder to the steady hum as on and on it drew you lonely in the crowd of the lonely and the silent and you were filled with a strange sudden joy you flipped over on your back then

Bruno sweetly wafted this way and that on the whispering on the
chattering rim of the waves you were buoyed up and you smiled down
at the abyss with the twin folds behind your knees and the gulls cried
out in wonder at the sight of your white belly and your right armpit
became a green jungle till it freed itself and drifted away a silky tangle
of seaweed the water has a smell and you smell it then not the smell a
man on a beach or riverbank would notice the water has a smell that
is unlike any other as the sounds in the sea are unlike any other as the
colors as the thoughts are stolen by nimble higglers the slaves of the
sea the rustling of the waves returning like a kind of echo spiraling in
the tumult of the spuming watery bazaar like an aromatic fair because
the water has a smell Bruno a smell that isn't breathed through the
nostrils not through the nose except perhaps in the homesick season
when inside a fish mind is a smell of water the smell of the sea the river
on a night of fish smells and rocks in the deep and spongy plants in the
dark and the smell of the remains of the big beasts of the sea and the
spittle of oyster lips and the vapor of toothy coral puffed through
the night of savage times and the deep secret smell of the far seafloor
and the aroma of a hundred rivers and the bouquet of the currents and
now even as you waken from your trance in the cradle of the sea to-
and-fro Bruno floating with the wise slow ripples you too come to
know that all the others floating about you have not a quibble or doubt
that the thread of smell is sprayed by a river current far away whence
they hatched into the world so long ago and whither they return to
die never again to breathe the myriad smells of the sea every moment
now they sense only the thread the flickering call of fate of a yearning
come to me what counts is the way come to me and death will sever
you from life come to me you hear the salmon fixing on it with all their
might and Bruno stays among them for weeks and for months he tries
to guess he listens to the murmuring waters the strange smells he smells
continuously he relishes for hours and for days on end he seeks the
whiff of his current the scent of his way and the flickering of his life
and meanwhile the sun browns his back his shoulders turn sinewy and
he learns the taste of plankton and the softness the sponginess not for
a minute does he stop listening because before you didn't know Bruno
what this thing you were looking for was you dimly guessed there was
just the longing that made you plunge into the final journey and suddenly you felt a shock in the middle of the sea you floated past Bornholm
island and the fields kissing the shore with the gleaming white church

you felt such a shock that a curlicue of remembered smell wafted by you crooked your nostril hovered an instant and then a fragile curlicue floated by and you were wide awake and you crossed your senses like swords and sparks of memories shot out of your heart into the water they fizzled it was the familiar smell the beloved smell and you wanted to turn back and search for it but the big *ning* was stretched inside you till it hurt and it bound you and would not let you turn back because salmon go onward onward while death drops in their wake and you almost sobbed with grief what was that smell all of a sudden Bruno what was it maybe the cheap perfume Adela the servant wore or the smell of the great rolls of cloth in your father's magical store or *the smell of cherries shining and brimming with a dark liquor under their skins which Adela used to bring home in late August gleaming drunk with light and warmth* or the smell so cloyingly sweet it made you dizzy of the longed-for book the wind was leafing through, its riddled pages rotting like an overblown rose?

And I, too, am like that. Here on the sandy beach in Narvia, by the quiet sea in the month of July 1981, that same smell I keep encountering in so many unexpected places, when I walk past a bench where old people gather to tell their stories; in the cool damp cave I found near my army base in the Sinai; in my laboratory at the university between the rat cages on especially warm days; between the pages of every copy of *The Street of Crocodiles*; in the secret hollow under Ayala's arm (after she decided not to sleep with me anymore, she had the decency to let me sniff her when necessary), and of course the question is: Could it be that I still carry that smell inside me, that it spurts out of me at certain points? Does my own body produce it to compensate for some deep-seated need? I analyze the ingredients: the clean smell of Grandma Henny's cheeks; the thick smell of animals, fur and sweat; the sour smell of Grandfather Anshel; the sweat of a young boy, not the familiar locker room smell but a ranker smell, evoking embarrassment and disagreeable thoughts of glands more ancient than a boy, secreting—

Sea? Are you sleeping?

Sea?!

She's sleeping. Back in Narvia and here, too. Whenever I start talking to myself, she takes the opportunity to fall asleep, saving her strength for later, when I talk about Bruno. Hell, why do I let that frivolousness, that childish egocentric superficiality of hers, make me so—angry, so infuriated without a way—

Ah, there I go again.

Listen, sea. I don't care if you are asleep.

· The first time we met, Ayala told me about the White Room at the end of one of the subterranean corridors of Yad Vashem. I told her that I had never come across such a room, though I spent a certain amount of time there, and none of the staff had ever mentioned it to me. And Ayala, who even then smiled indulgently at my limitations, explained that it wasn't designed by an architect, Shlomik, or built by a builder, and the staff, it's true, knows nothing about it— "A kind of metaphor, then?" I ventured, and immediately felt stupid, and she, patiently: "Exactly." With each ensuing moment I could see in her eyes the growing conviction that a very grave error had been committed here, that her keen intuition had let her down for once: I was definitely not the man to entrust with such a secret, or any secret, for that matter. This was the night we met, at a lecture about the last days of the Lodz Ghetto, which I had attended out of habit, and Ayala because she never misses lectures or happenings of this sort (her parents are survivors of Bergen-Belsen). She was the one who took the initiative right away, and—that night which turned out to be the first since my marriage that I didn't go home to sleep—I made the discovery that, my many limitations notwithstanding, I had an amazing and quite thrilling power to transform Ayala into an urn, a strawberry, and even, in surpassing moments, a woolly mess of pink cotton candy, the kind they sell at fairs. It likewise turned out that, despite my regrettable limitations, the mere touch of my hands on her taut, warm brown skin could launch a thousand strange shivers that seeped through and tensed her soft, comfortable body like a bow and released us both from our frozen, anxious expectations, when at last from her unplumbed depths came the sharp sound, mournful and high-pitched, like a gull being pierced by an arrow, and presently we could resume our cultured conversation for another spell. We repeated this many times throughout our first night together.

"And this White Room," explained Ayala in one of the lulls, "was squeezed into being. It isn't a room at all, in fact, but a kind of tribute, yes"—she shut her large, delicately rounded eyelids, enraptured with herself— "a tribute from all the books, all the pictures and words and films and facts and numbers about the Holocaust at Yad Vashem to that which must remain forever unresolved, forever beyond our comprehension. And that's the essence of it, Shlomik, isn't it?"

I didn't understand. I looked at her with sad fascination, because it was becoming clear to me that we shared a rare, ill-fated "backward love," you might say, now in its last throes, and as Ayala woke up and discovered how utterly different we were, she was certain to banish me from her magic castle. She knew nothing about me. She had read my first book of poems and thought it "not a bad start." This annoyed me somewhat, because people generally liked the first book even better than my later three, and several critics had praised its "controlled inner tension" and all that, but Ayala said that you could sense in my writing how scared I am of myself and of what I have to say about life in general, and Over There in particular. She asked me to promise to be more daring in future, and when I promised, she told me about the White Room.

I was enchanted with her body, so lithe and free, so self-contained, rolling and rippling with carnal pleasure; I was enchanted with her small apartment, with her tiny bedroom, which was—you might say— illusive. I don't know why I say it was illusive, but it was somehow, I don't know, illusive. I had never gone to bed with a woman so quickly before: two hours and twenty-five minutes from the moment we met (I know that exactly, because I kept looking at my watch wondering what I was going to tell Ruth when I got home). Two hours and twenty-five minutes went by from the moment we left the lecture, distressed by what we'd heard there, until we fell into each other's arms (and I mean literally) with a passion I had never known before. It was only after we cooled down that I remembered I didn't even know her name! I felt like a real Casanova: having sex with a woman before she even told me her name! And at that moment she drew the palm of my hand to her mouth and whispered, "Ayala," which I swear I heard "through my hand." I know it sounds suspicious: I wouldn't believe something like that either, but with Ayala, anything can happen.

From the ceiling in the corner hung cobwebs so thick they looked like tangled balls of hair, and when she explained what it was (she wasn't about to destroy this creation out of self-righteous notions of cleanliness), I wondered what my mother would have to say about that and started to laugh. I felt different with her, and different things were evoked in me. I had never known I could turn a woman into an urn, etc., before. The amazing thing is, though, that with regard to us, I guessed what would happen even before she did, because I knew myself,

I knew I had no hope whatsoever of fitting into her dreams. And a few weeks later I could see that Ayala was beginning to tire of me. Handles still curved out on her body, with the fine fluting, the pouting oval lips of the urn; sounds still issued from her body—I don't know from where exactly—like little chirrups: "Drink me, drink me!" but the undulations were definitely becoming awkward. Zeno's spirit of destruction was upon me even then. And later, all was lost: I was rarely able to conjure the little green leaves around her neck anymore, or transform her skin into a shimmering strawberry-flavored surface of crunchy red grains. She would gaze at me with sorrow and pity in her eyes. Sorrow for us both, and the chance we'd missed. Around that time I had been making frantic attempts to write in a systematic way the story Grandfather Anshel told Herr Neigel, but, of course, the harder I tried, the worse I fared. Ruth knew about Ayala and she suffered terribly. I hated her for not making me choose between them, and for the quiet wisdom that taught her to wait it out. To suffer and wait: not once during those horrid months did she turn on me with hatred or rage. But she was not submissive either, she never let me feel she was degraded. Quite the contrary: I was the sweaty male in rut, sniffing around two females. And all Ruth's strength and wisdom showed in her unpretty face: her movements were slower than ever. She emitted a silent warning: she was extremely powerful; she—like everyone, in fact—was endowed with dangerous powers, hence she had to practice self-control; in order not to injure others, she had to restrain herself and wait: to intimate, not scream; to suggest, not decree.

I hated myself for the suffering I was causing her, yet I was afraid that if I left Ayala I would never be able to write again. And sometimes I think Ayala stayed with me out of some weird sense of duty toward Grandfather Anshel's story, not because she especially cared for *me*. In her eyes I was a coward, a traitor even, and though I had every reason and every opportunity in the world to write the story as it should be written, I lacked the courage and the daring. Ayala does not write, but she does write her life. She told me that first night that the White Room was the "real testing-ground for anyone who wants to write about the Holocaust. Like the riddling Sphinx. And you go there to present yourself willingly before the Sphinx, understand?" I didn't understand, of course. She sighed, rolled her eyes, and explained that for the past forty years people had been writing about the Holocaust and would continue to do so, only they were doomed to failure, because while other tragedies can be translated into the language of reality as we know it, the Holocaust cannot, despite that compulsion to try again and again, to experience, to sting the writer's living flesh with it, "and if you want to be honest with yourself," she said gravely, "you'll have to try the White Room."

I didn't show her what I really thought of her, I wanted her so badly. I thought, How different people are from each other. I understood—long before she did—that she chose me only because she'd never come across anyone like me in her circles: a poet who wrote the poems she'd read yet was utterly sane. Who loved his wife and was generally faithful. No, she doesn't know very much about life or me, I thought at the time, and she prefers to see what she believes rather than believe in what she sees. "Illusive"—that's the word I was looking for. And yet—

"And in this room you find the essence of those days," she said, her eyes still distant, "but the wonderful thing is that there are no ready-made answers there. Nothing is explicit. It's all merely possible. Merely suggested. Merely liable to materialize. Or likely to. And you have to go through everything all over again, by yourself. Without a double or stunt man to play the dangerous parts. And if you don't answer the Sphinx correctly, you'll be eaten up. Or you will leave without having understood. And in my eyes that almost amounts to the same thing."

Oh, Ayala. If I could only write all the stories and ideas she comes up with in a single day, I would have enough material for the rest of my life. Perhaps I would also become a different sort of writer. There is nothing in the White Room. It's empty. But everything that exists beyond its membranous walls, everything that flows out of the corridors of Yad Vashem is projected into it: "By way of, call it inspiration. Yes. I'm not too up on physics, but I know that's what it's like. With each new movement or thought, you create a new compound. Your own formula, made up of gray matter and personality and your own genetic code and personal biography and conscience—along with everything else projected from behind the walls: the facts about mankind. The entire human, animal inventory, fear and cruelty and pity and despair, glory and wisdom, and all the pettiness and love of life, all that halting poetry, Shlomik, and you sit there as if you were inside a giant kaleidoscope, but this time the glass fragments are you, the different parts of you, and light reaches them from beyond the walls—" Her eyes are dreamy. She gets up and, wearing only my shirt, walks around the room, looking brown, fat, conglobated, her hair in a small bun on top of her head, putting on a performance for me, miming, What am I doing here? "And if you happen to think about something, like the victims who collaborated with the Germans, then right away—I mean right away!—all collaborators ever mentioned in books and monographs and documents, all the Quislings and Judenrats of the ghetto, all the miserable scum now frozen in the testimonies beyond the walls, are spliced by a single laser beam that dissects the collaborator that 'you are' inside, like this—whikkk!—the way Eve was cut out of Adam," and she opens her eyes in bewilderment again as if to say, What-am-I-doing-here, and tells me in a clear quiet voice, shockingly sad and sincere, that this is how it must be written, this is the spirit of the book.

But I didn't dare. Even now, after meeting you and Bruno, and after all I've been through, I can't do it. Ayala was right about everything. That childish performance was only a mask for her acute vision, a vision far more penetrating than my own, with her accurate and enlightened sense of the bitterness of life. Once again I knew I was wrong.

Suddenly she wakes up. The name Bruno sends a long shiver through her. A white furrow, shaggy as a horse's mane, is tossed along the fringe of the dark horizon. I'm boring her with my story, but those were my conditions, my petty conditions, and once and for all I'm going to tell her!

And now, Bruno. Did you hear that? I said "Bruno" again. You like this story. I heard it from you the first time in Narvia:

Suddenly, after months of riding the sea with a throbbing heart, half delirious with joy and wonder, a drop of human anguish coagulated inside him and its dark color spread through the waters of the sea.

At first he fought it. He pressed his arms to his sides and flapped with vigor, trying to echo the great *ning* of the shoal, and scrupulously to maintain the *dolgan* between himself and the fish on either side of him. He learned that the shoal that seemed to be borne so easily, actually maneuvered through constant and painstaking effort.

Or was it perhaps the ease-and-at-one-ment of a single body, healthy and harmonious? Bruno had sensed this while they were being attacked by a school of bluefish in Mälmo harbor: he hadn't understood what was going on when his shoal was suddenly split in two and sent flying in opposite directions, leaving an empty space in the center that pulled and paralyzed, and while the surprised bluefish were fighting the suction of the treacherous waters, the salmon came back and closed in fast like two hands clapping. The water pressure propelled the bluefish into the distance, and they beat a retreat to the north with fast slaps of their tails. Bruno was jealous of the salmon. They were whole in their way. He, fragmentary in his. He'd lost the musical flow of the first weeks. He dipped his hot forehead in the waves and let them carry him.

He listened to the sea. He heard the murmur of the waves' caress on the sandy floor—like a constant winnowing of grain. He heard the distant rumbling of piers in a northern harbor as the shoal passed by; a pier doesn't sound like the shore: a pier returns a slightly metallic echo while the shore returns a spongy echo. In this way he learned that in the water he could not hear the sounds directly ahead of him, but only the sounds that came at him sideways or from behind. He knew the rustling of the fins of Yorick and Napoleon—that's what he called his neighbors—quite well, but the ripple of the anonymous fish in front was utterly lost to him. Bruno recognized in this, of course, a mocking and symbolic representation of his own helplessness: his ears were still turned backward; he was still intent on the past. Still thinking about his own life in profane terms, and—what was most disappointing of all to Bruno—still not finding within himself a single sentence he could call his own, which no one could take away and distort.

He could not stop reflecting on his former life. Again and again he rolled the years through his mind like amber beads. His father's shop of wonders; the pleasures of childhood; the fabulous dawning of the Age of Genius; his father's illness; the humiliation of poverty; the sale of their beloved home on Samburska Street; the beginning of the war; the waning of the Age of Genius . . . all enveloped him in sadness, because he realized that human beings can never appreciate the life they have been given, keenly and fervently. When first they receive life, they are not ready to understand the gift, and in the course of time they stop troubling their heads about it. For this reason they fail to sense life until it slowly takes leave of their bodies, and they slowly, steadily decline. It would be a mistake to call this "life." An injustice to call it that: it's death they live with caution and fear as though trying to dig their heels in the ground so they won't slip too fast down a very steep incline. Bruno groaned in the water, and for a moment the shoal was alert.

His appetite had also been impaired. During the morning *gyoya*, when the salmon grazed the rich fields of the sea, or in the evening, as the great *ning* subsided and the sated shoal rested on the water like a giant fan, Bruno would float among the quiet fish gilling to cool themselves off from the day's work, and his spirits flagged. He strained the plankton between his teeth, or plunged below to peck on juicy black seaweed and chew without pleasure, a single thought flashing through him in the abyss: Something has been misappropriated and forgotten. Something has been ruined beyond comprehension.

One morning he raised his head above water and looked at the fish, reflecting sadly that they were stronger than he was. From horizon to horizon the sea was flecked with salmon nearing maturity. Almost everyone except poor Yorick and a few other weaklings were already as big as Bruno himself. Their greenish fins were erect and powerful. They were bold-faced, tough, and without charm, and Bruno asked himself for the thousandth time to what end they had set off on this journey. He rolled over and swam sideways toward the shore like a man. The salmon made way for him indifferently. During the *gyoya* no one heeded the *dolgan*. Bruno searched for Laprik, but could not find him. A strange thought flickered through him briefly that perhaps Laprik didn't even exist. That Laprik was merely the fulfillment of the wishes of half a million salmon for a Laprik to exist. Bruno, however, distinctly remembered the sight of Laprik accepting him into his shoal on the beach in Danzig, and besides, there was something about Laprik and his quiet *ning* which could not have been brought into being by the aspirations of the masses: Bruno did not know how to explain this exactly. There was, in Laprik's *ning*, a sense of leadership through discomfort. Isolationism. Bruno had not for a single moment of the journey felt bitter that someone else was determining their rhythm and direction. In the distance, near a broad rock shelf, Bruno spied the grotesque snout of an old hammerhead shark steadily trailing the shoal and growing fat on its flesh. The salmon had become so accustomed to the shark, he no longer elicited the *orga* drive among them, that fast escape strategy they had put into action against the bluefish in Mälmo. Bruno was depressed. At such times—and here I venture a guess—he must have longed for a pen.

He floated around this way among the grazing salmon, like a bringer of bad news. The sky above was overcast. Clouds were piled so thick and still that sometimes the world seemed to be passing below. Soon the storms of November would commence. At night he felt the sudden contractions of a vague fear along the wake of the shoal. His heart curdled because he had been able to say it clearly to himself: he pitied the salmon for having no protection against their very existence.

So what did you want them to do? Bruno shook himself and swam out to the sidelines, muttering, How did you expect the salmon to find relief from their gritty lives? Publish books and go into business, stage theatricals and organize political parties, feign love and friendship, calculate and pull wires and go to war, play football and write poetry? He rolled over on his back and allowed the little currents of the shoal to cradle him. They are the Journey incarnate, Death with fins stuck on and two slits for gills, and oh, the colorful masquerade of Death! Oh, the gay wizards of its choreography! Bruno blew a small water bubble in a kind of toast: To your health, swift artists of Death, kindly half-drunk servants of the one true evolution—that adjusts Life to their Death so gently, nimbly, and methodically. To your infinitely rich imagination! To the light touch of your fingers, plying needle and scissors to make a thousand beguiling costumes and accessories for everyone at the ball—snouts and fangs and skins and horns, tufts of hair and tails and wings, flippers and armor, spikes, nails and claws, scales and stingers—what a wardrobe! No one need go bare! And who is this? Sound the drum. Ingenious, is it not? Here comes the cleverest guest by far, in a most deceptive costume: Death wearing spectacles and a false beard, with a book under his arm! How gay, how gaudy, how unimaginably—blaaah—

Only you, Bruno, float slowly through the recesses of the teeming hall and along its narrow gullies, borne sadly with the uninvited salmon whom the revelers excluded tactfully in order not to spoil the festive mood; but the salmon, though uninvited, are projected as a cool and constant nightmare on the dimmest screens of their brains; these salmon who pass through the streets of life as a bare, bleached fishbone, never to be fleshed with the solace of illusion and fleeting oblivion, wandering accursed—

O Lord, said Bruno (who had never been religious), to what end do you impel these millions of salmon in endless circles around the world? Why can't you content yourself with a single salmon? A pair of salmon? Why, even human beings, Lord, the cruelest of your animals, have learned the knack of using symbols. We say "God," "man," "suffering," "love," "life," packing the whole experience into one little box. Why can't you do that? Couldn't you forbear as the thoughts run through your prolific mind? Why must your symbols be so intricate and ex-

travagant? Is it because we have become more proficient than you at
divining the pain and suffering in each little box, and prefer to keep
the lid on?

A few weeks later, he received a kind of answer. This is not uncommon
at sea: vital questions often send thick-growing fibers through the earth
and down the crevices of the blackest abyss. An anonymous essence
somewhere is roused from sleep, quickened by the fibers, and plucked
out of its seaweed reverie to rise and float slowly upon the water. And
sometimes hundreds or thousands of years go by before an answer
meets the question that gave it a life and a name, though rarely if ever
will they meet. Growing desperate, they slowly lose their vitality and
sink into the soporific arms of the seaweed. My Bruno used to run into
particles of these sensations on his journey: peels of ideas, cadavers of
audacity, half of them unripe and the other half rotting. This produced
in him only a mild, puzzling anguish. He wasn't afraid of them. The
sealed ocean of his writings was full of their kind.

But he, he of all people, had been granted a reply of sorts. A token.
The questions he asked had not been answered directly, it's true, but
neither had they been entirely disregarded. And I have a gnawing suspicion that a certain someone used her influence in this case. Someone
I know did quite a job of thinking, investigating, and organizing, out
of keeping with her drowsy nature. Someone clearly transcended herself.

Because that afternoon, at the Kattegat pass between Sweden and
Denmark, the shoal came to a halt for no apparent reason. It was a
little early for the evening *gyoya*, and Bruno stirred in confusion from
his drowsy afternoon float. He looked around and saw a quiet, waveless
sea. A light wind—like a rustling theater curtain—disturbed the blue
horizon and made it quiver. The fish finned rhythmically in place,
indifferent to what was going on around them. A flock of cranes flew
by overhead. Bruno finned with his hands and moved his lips as he was
wont to do in moments of stress. A troublesome infection had lately
erupted around the two sores on his chest. It burned more than ever
now. He rubbed the strange lesions and waited expectantly.

And then, a short distance away from the salmon scouts, the sea
parted for a band of dolphins leaping like lightning before the shoal.
Bruno took fright, but the fish around him were unperturbed. The
dolphins, big and beryl-green, now orbited in a wide semicircle, till at
last they turned flank and faced the shoal. There was no bristling of

fins, no bulging of lateral lines. The two shoals surveyed each other. The salmon—motionless, tough, grim, and silent—and the dolphins, corpulent, glossy, and full of life. Bruno wondered whether the dolphins had even the smallest notion of what salmon life is all about. For a moment he felt scruffy before them: not scruffy like a sea-hardy salmon, but like Bruno, the skeletal man, the eternal outcast. Perhaps because he remembered that dolphins are mammals, too.

And then it happened: the dolphins were as though transfused by a different spirit. A big *ning* aligned them suddenly, and pulled them together in a huddle. Then they scattered in a wide circle, and the performance began.

Because that's what it was: as if the dolphins wished to pay homage to the salmon for their thankless voyage, or amuse them in recompense for their meaningless sacrifice. Bruno marveled: the dolphins, beloved of the sea, noble, wise, and proud, had sensed the dreadful desolation they were so adept at keeping beyond the pale of their lives. This called for action of some sort on their part—

The dolphins leaped out of the water and somersaulted gracefully in the air. Two by two, four by four, they crisscrossed each other's wake like flashing green corposants, quickly arranged themselves in one long file, and reared up in the water, galloping on their flexible tail tips, leaving a backwash of shattered waves, chortling as they surrounded Bruno's shoal and tumbled over each other like acrobats.

The salmon watched impassively, finning a little faster than usual. Bruno was all attention. His heart nearly burst in silent strain. Though he didn't understand the meaning of the performance, he knew he had witnessed a pure work of art. The vastness of the sea, the joy of life, compassion and communion and defiance and the knowledge of impotence—all these were here, and the water surrounding him sizzled when it touched his skin. He wanted to go with the dolphins, though he couldn't quite figure out why. Maybe it was because he was a non-human human, and they were non-fish fish. Or maybe it was because, however briefly, he had been able to sense that life was a gift, lawfully his, and worthy of the name. The cranes shrieked so loudly overhead they nearly broke their necks. The vastness of the sea unfurled, blue and beautiful. Light shone out of the rich waves. Bruno watched the dolphins in supplication.

They vanished just as they had appeared. Swallowed up by the waves. Bruno felt the old anguish seeping into him again. The salmon *ning*

grew suddenly slack, and the evening *gyoya* set in. The fish were beginning to forget what they had seen. Forever in the present. Only a
few of them—like little Yorick—stayed in formation a minute longer
to search for something already erased from memory, which had left
them vaguely, fleetingly distraught. What a sorry lot they seemed to
him then, and venting his own self-loathing, Bruno despised them for
their mechanical dullness, for the overearnestness that prevented them
from finding shortcuts, and for their uninspired resignation to fate . . .

Yorick scraped Bruno's rib. Bruno turned and saw the fish's mouth
open-closing energetically. He responded with a similar flourish, but
without enthusiasm. For a moment he hoped the fish was indicating
that he, too, had seen the dolphins and was aware of what had happened,
but Yorick was only expressing his pleasure with the excellent food of
the evening *gyoya*. Napoleon, who swam on his left—a dull, drab fellow—was already giving chase to a passing cloud of tuna roe. Bruno
dove below and swallowed furious mouthfuls of fragrant plankton. He
imagined himself in his rightful place—floating gaily among the happy,
carefree dolphins, living the easy life of those who adapt to the fact that
they can never change anything, and so devote themselves to illusion.

But when the *gyoya* was over, and the shoal was preparing for the
evening lap, Bruno felt strangely elated all of a sudden. The salmon
were finning rhythmically in one enormous column. Every face wore
the same dull, earnest expression that had so disgusted him only a
moment ago. But for the first time since jumping into the sea, Bruno
guessed why he'd chosen the salmon and their journey. For he was a
salmon among men. Even as a dolphin, he would have belonged with
the salmon. Bruno took a breath that almost burst his lungs with ex-
ultant joy: just as a man must learn to love a single flesh-and-blood
woman in order to become, however imperfectly, acquainted with pure
and abstract love, so Bruno had had to become thoroughly salmonized
in order to learn about life. The barest life of all, as the salmon drew
their tangible geometric design over half the globe.

He shut his eyes and shivered with all his might. He was intensely
moved, and forced himself to ignore the stabbing pains from the infection on his chest above the ribs. The pain never left him, and Bruno
scratched furiously, angry with his body for thus betraying him again,
in this rare moment of transcendence.

Together they lingered a moment longer, whispering wordlessly,
emitting impatient, nagging questions and fast, stinging answers, and

Laprik listened to the echoes their bodies returned, and they listened to him listening, till suddenly, inexplicably, the departure bulletin shot like a spark through the *ning*, was instantly registered in their flashing lateral lines, and before they knew it, they were on their way.

[5]

AN ETERNITY AND A HALF, as I live and breathe, he has been with the poor salmon, never stopping and never surrendering, shrinking as they grow; by now some of them are bigger than that man of mine who knows not the meaning of despair, who has endured the tempests of the North Sea, an attack by a school of barracudas (though for the life of me I can't understand what they were doing there on the Bergen shore), and a dreadful season of Icelandic fishermen who nearly halved the shoal; yet on he swims, though his eyes burn and his bitter smile stays fixed in the water, and his chin grows sharper every day, he's all bones, not a hair left on his body, and his skin is turning spongy and puffy from the water. Sometimes when I look at him in the moonlight, it seems he's already succeeded in turning into a fish.

The trouble is he doesn't stop thinking, and these thoughts are a torture both to him and to me because there's nothing I can do for him, I just don't have what he's looking for, though at least I can rest assured "she" doesn't either. It just doesn't exist, except in himself, and I hope he has the strength to keep looking for it, and of course I try to do my best, but how can I help him, weak and frail as I am, and I pick him up and lick him and whisper that I'm not like her—blind, deaf, and dumb like her—I am all eyes and ears and tongues, and I read you, Bruno, through and through, I understand everything and I decipher you, because there's no thought you ever thought, no man you ever met, no wistful feeling or memory or beautiful thing or sorrow that didn't leave its mark somewhere on your sweet body, you only have to know how to read, that's all, and the first and last place you can read, Bruno, is here inside me; don't think I'm making this up (heavens, you know how modest I am), but once, many years ago while I was dozing near Australia, under a ship called *The Beagle*, I suddenly felt the moon disappear, and I woke up and saw the face of a young man leaning over the railing and gazing at me with so much love my heart nearly melted and flooded the coast of New Zealand (in Japan

they call these little excitations of mine *tzunam*), and then this man
said to another man I couldn't see who was standing next to him, You
see, Peter, the sea is the great incubator of history and all existence.
We shall never live long enough to solve the riddles of the sea. And
Peter laughed and said, The moon is affecting you, Charles, and my
young man smiled mysteriously and said, I am not a poet, Peter, only
a student of nature, and it is as a student that I speak to you: on land
we find life at a depth of no more than a league or two, or at an altitude
of a few score miles, but in the sea, Peter? There are deeper abysses
than we can possibly conceive of! Did you know that if that mountain
between Nepal and India, reckoned to be the highest in the world,
were submerged in the abyss off Guam, the water would rise two miles
above it? Forgive me, Bruno, for letting myself boast like this, but I
wanted to show you how really deep I can be, and no one else can read
the marks, the thoughts and passions that life has left on you, because
everything leaves the teeniest scar or wrinkle, all you have to do is look
at old human creatures who have nowhere left to hide the marks all
over their faces, why look at your new friends the salmon—the passage
of time and all their tribulations trace rings on their fins like the rings
on a tree, a small ring for the river months and a big ring for the months
in me, Laprik has his second ring already to mark his second voyage,
and if you'll forgive me for meddling, there was such an ache in my
heart when I found out that the only time you ever really laughed was
the time your father, Yacob, put you across his knees and gave you a
spanking, but of course that was a different kind of laugh, and after
that there was no more laughing, and I think it's a shame, because I
adore laughing, we could have had some good laughs together, you
and I, but you, even when I tickle you "there," you stay hard and
gloomy, and it kind of hurts my feelings, Bruno.

   Please forgive me for going on like this. I simply couldn't resist
acquainting you with all the claptrap I was exposed to in Narvia. That
sly little fool! Amorphous liquid cow! She used her cheapest tricks to
hide the things I needed. I knew she was keeping everything to herself,
including the lost manuscript of *The Messiah*, and to me she threw only
the crumbs: dried shrimp legs, empty shells, castrated quotations from
his books. Ah! Ignorant opportunist, guardian of a treasure she can't
begin to appreciate. How utterly irresponsible of Bruno to leave it in
her hands!

   I was boiling mad at her because I had to return to Israel the following week and I hadn't come up with anything important yet. I spent days on end inside her, talking about him to her almost bestial delight; my skin was peeling off like flowered wallpaper, and still she hadn't agreed to give me any tips. In the evenings I used to join the widow Dombursky in the parlor. She sat there mending the sheets and linens, and squinting at me narrowly while I wrote page after page on the antique sewing machine that served as my table and read the pages over to myself. But I found out that without "her" I can't write. I'm dependent on her, and this was the most humiliating thing.

The following day I didn't dip my toe in from morning till night. I strolled along the sandy beach instead, studying the magnificent lilies growing there, amusing myself with the idea of launching, right here in Narvia, a modest shell collection, and pursuing my interest to the point of some expertise. Later I walked over to the lighthouse and climbed the spiral staircase all the way to the top. I don't like to boast, but I was told in the village that there weren't many tourists with the fortitude to make the dizzying climb to where part of the wall drops into the sea and the stairs practically wind over the water. Later I discovered that to get from the top floor to the small balcony where the light projector is you have to climb a narrow ladder that juts high over the sea. Unfortunately, it was getting late and I had to forgo this thrilling part of my little excursion.

And so I went back to the beach and spent an interminable afternoon sitting in my chair, utterly alone and freezing cold in an easterly wind, glaring at "her," and cursing the ill luck that brought us together.

And the widow grumbles openly now. She thinks I'm crazy, or that I'm an American spy, or both. They're very sensitive around here on account of the demonstrations in the nearby village. And she's also angry with me for leaving the light on so late at night (I'm probably sending coded messages to American bombers), and besides, I think she saw me throw the flowers into the sea yesterday.

I admit it was stupid of me. A cheap bribe. A small bunch of violets I bought from a kid in the village. I figured that since she doesn't have flowers, no scented ones anyway, and a certain woman I know loves violets . . . Well, anyway, last evening on the beach . . . it was strangely thrilling . . . maybe because I suddenly missed her very much. I threw the violets into the sea, one by one, the silly woman, who happens to be pretty bright, if inconsistent and always illusive, she loves you, she loves you not . . . it was partly to forget her that I came here in the first place; I had made up my mind on the subject come what may, and planned my liberation like a military campaign, allotting a certain interim for depression, another for the despair I knew would follow, and finally—a period of convalescence—everything was planned out, but somehow nothing worked . . . what a woman . . . she destroyed my entire life and the life of my angel Ruthy, and gave me this damned unquenchable thirst, this disgust with myself, with my whole life, with my writing. She called me a traitor. Go ahead, write for the timid, she said, throwing me out, and in parting she gave me the book, one last sweet blow, as cruel and demanding as she is, and left me for another man . . . and another . . . men who throw caution to the winds, who ardently allow themselves to be devoured and sacrificed, and in the end are abandoned like me, she leaves us no choice—I did come here to forget.

And I think I fell asleep. Because of the blinding sand and the extremely boring waves "she" slyly rolled my way. I fell asleep and dreamed again about Ayala. About our first meeting after we broke up, when I demanded to see her so I could tell her what Bruno's book had meant to me. She listened in silence, all perfect circles of smooth, bronzy skin, and her black hair in a sexy little bun on top of her head. This was one of the rare occasions when she didn't deride me or make nasty remarks. I sensed that it might be my hour of glory and began to get carried away. But as usual I wound up telling her more than I intended and I felt as if I were on trial. Soon her look of fascination faded. She sighed, went to get her red nail polish, and started painting the toenails of her plump little feet. Casually she asked about Ruthy, and muttered something to the effect that Ruthy was a "real saint" to take me back after all I'd put her through (as if she had nothing to do with it!). As she bent over her toenails her breasts were exposed, and I swore inwardly that I would never humiliate myself by begging her. She refused, of course, when I did. Slyly I brought the subject back to Bruno, and did in fact manage to win some of her softer looks. Moreover, I caused her large spiritual lids to droop. How I love it when she looks like that, more distant and mysterious than ever. She asked how Ruth's treatments were coming along, and I said there were still problems and that I had refused to be examined. But let's not talk about that now, it's Bruno I want to discuss. She slowly raised the shutters of her eyes and smiled her weariest smile, and I was sure that instead of responding to the beautiful things I wanted to tell her about Bruno, she would go off on a tangent about the way I dressed ("So, Ruth's still picking out your shirts"), or my hairstyle, or she would simply unbutton my collar button, saying it choked her just to look at me in the middle of summer; in short, she would try to make me feel like a flea. But all she said in fact was that deep inside she was sure I had contempt (!) for Ruth because she couldn't conceive. This, of course, was sheer nonsense. It's true that to a certain extent I believe everyone is responsible for his own weaknesses, for not possessing the inner strength to fight these weaknesses, whereas I consider myself to be a person who has achieved liberation from a biography thoroughly out of keeping with his private history, education, and even—yes, definitely—his character, and as for the other things Ayala referred to, scientific studies show there is a definite correlation between the patient's will and his prognosis, even in cases of infertility, though to say I have contempt for Ruth is plain stupid, stupid and malicious. Ayala listened patiently, and remarked with sweet innocence, "Weakness means suffering; and suffering means sharing; and sharing means exposure. You are an artist, Shlomik, with a strange, evasive art, and sometimes you really scare me. Because cowards like you are capable of anything, when they sense that their art is in danger."

Suddenly I knew what I had to do in order to win her again with one stunning and ingenious move. On impulse I informed her that I intended to set off in Bruno's footsteps. And again she smiled her tolerant smile, and politely wished me luck. She didn't believe in me, which only confirmed my decision. She painted a round toenail, saying it amazed her the way I unconsciously chose to live two such contrasting ages. "Sometimes you're too old and sometimes too childish. I think you're simply running away from the problems of your true age." Hurt, I answered, "You used to appreciate my complexity." And she: "You have no idea how true that is. I believed in it so much. And in you, too, you know."

I woke up in a panic. It was 6:00 p.m. already. I had been sleeping on the beach for a whole hour. Later on I remembered my dream, which merely recapitulated what happened in reality. Ayala used to say that my dreams were as neat as a bookkeeper's ledgers. This is true enough, except for my nightmares, which are really disgusting—and which I would never divulge to her or anyone else. I woke up irritable and fuzzy on the beach chair, and shuddered in horror: yesterday's

bouquet of violets lay at my feet in a tiny heap . . . and the beach was
strewn with the tiny wet prints of a small and very fast wave . . .

I threw down my towel and sunglasses and nose guard, and ran
straight into her, burning with rage, though at the same time—and I
find this hard to explain—I had the strangest feeling that she was running toward me, too, that we were about to share a moment of unexpected reconciliation, of forgiveness, and perhaps even affection, and
when at the least likely moment I plunged into the water and struck
her with my stomach, and thrashed her with my hands, she only droned,
Don't be a child, Neuman, I have flowers of my own, deep meadows
of beauty and color, and how silly you were to think you could persuade
me, oh no, not like that, though there is something you could give me
to soften me up, only don't be such a miser, just think about him
whenever you're inside me, because you know how hard it is for me
alone . . . a minor health problem, a temporary thing . . . Think about
him for my sake, be inventive, make up a story, think Bruno, say Bruno,
for my sake, dearest, for your sake and mine . . .

Very well. I will tell you. Only you'll be sorry you ever asked.

Now listen.

You mentioned how hard it was for him to laugh, and I'll tell you
about his fears. About the loneliness his character and talent ordained
for him. There was the fear of the bonds of love and friendship, the
fear of the abyss between one minute and the next, and of what he
would discover on the page after it was touched by his magical magnetic
pen, which sucked up the magma of ancient truth, that rose steadily
upward through layers of caution and self-defense—and then he would
stop and scream in fear, because what he had written seemed to come
from someone else, and he began to suspect that he, too, formed the
weak link through which irresistible human longings burst forth into
the world, and then my Bruno stood up and paced around the room,
taunting himself that he was suffering from megalomania, and had lost
the ability to distinguish between his real life and his stories, and that
through a nyedoenga, like him, a shlimazel, only abstract essences of
preposterous errors and blunders—could possibly—

But he knew, and was afraid. And it drove him to cheat at times: he
would pay social calls, write sentimental letters (he almost believed the
sentimentality himself), feign candor, and address acquaintances in the
intimate "thou" form (though he rarely addressed people thus in writ-

ing, perhaps because he couldn't pretend in writing). He agreed to give lectures and occasionally allowed himself to be dragged to parties and fancy balls, where he would smile awkwardly while he let people get him drunk in order not to disappoint them, and even chuckled when they clapped him jovially on the shoulder, wearing an attentive expression on his ironic face, as they explained from experience that to know Despair ("Despair!" they shouted in his ear, clutching their hearts as he never needed to do because he remembered where it was) and "write with authenticity, like a genuine writer," you had to commit a little suicide or at least go insane, and in daily life as well, Pan Schulz, you have to come out of your isolation and feel "the pulse of humanity," the "sorrows of life," so don't be such a hermit. Bruno tried his best to be convinced, he really and truly tried to achieve the commonplace despair they prattled about; he struggled to reach it out of the darkness into which he had sunk, if only to escape the eel-like fear that coiled damply around him whenever he looked at what he had written, or wondered what the future held in store. But my Bruno was too honest for the suicide-insanity routine, and he could not dissolve his loneliness in the crowd because he knew the crowd offered no haven from imminent danger. He would have to keep to himself, sit in his chair, abandoning himself to his razor-keen awareness and the two big searchlights—longing and despair—converging in his head, and to bear the mark of Cain on endless wanderings; and he also knew that nowhere except his simple room, at his simple desk, writing in a schoolboy's notebook, would he be able to feel his body tensing on the rack of an inquisition unequaled in cruelty and pleasure, till his flesh and bones were stretched so flat that every ounce of flesh was infinitely diluted in the dimension of distance and dream, and only then, as a single fluttering membrane, would he be able to feel the beating of the big drum at the foundations, the feverish, despairing embrace of savage tongues and putrefying grammars, with no one left to understand them, and helter-skelter Bruno's pen sketches the impressions this secret world has left upon his parchment body, pasting them onto the palpable and visible, and Bruno's stories, his longings and laments for a banished Eden, are wrenched out of him into a frozen secondhand world of exact science, classified language, and tame clock time; see how he droops at his desk, biting his lip, his chin pointed, writing with the same upsurge of violence, frenzy, and obliviousness he knew inside you throughout the daring voyage. See him use his pen to parry the savage apparitions

which have not yet fully materialized, evoking ages of genius for one
brief moment, taking care never to perforate the thin membrane with
his pen, to keep it all from bursting through, and dissolving away, yes
dissolving: because the world is not yet ready for the life that flickers
beyond Bruno: here life is congealed in human bodies, like molten
lava. And only at the end of his journey did he define and dissect and
compose his lost story, *The Messiah*, capering wildly inside you, and
now that we've reached this particular point purely by chance, I had
better shut up and let you talk about the story, and give me a hint or
two, no more . . .

No, I won't. But I will tell you about Guruk's *torag*.

Guruk? Who's Guruk? I don't want to hear about Guruk! I want to
hear about the Age of Genius! I want to hear about *The Messiah*! Now!
Right now!

Okay! Be silent!

And after a pause:

My, you're obtuse. You've just told me things that are terrible and
true. How do you understand him the way you do? I hate you for
being able to guess like that. I know how you do it, too: you look at
yourself and say the opposite. You—

Enough!

No! I want to speak, because you're merciless, too. You have to say
everything, don't you! You have to know everything! You hurt me to
death. You're so mean and so right about everything! I'll tell you something: While he was inside me I licked him and learned that he was
falling to pieces. Many strange creatures, Neuman, nasty little creatures
swam inside him like fish in a sinking ship . . .

But did he succeed? Did he succeed in the end?

For the life of me I can't understand why of all the people who love
Bruno I had to meet up with you?! Now lie still! You want to hear
about succeeding? I'll tell you about succeeding. Lie down! Stop wriggling! The way you swim, dearest, I bet you can't dance worth a damn,
am I right?

You really enjoy putting me down, don't you?

I was just angry. The things you said . . .

He wasn't right for you.

By all the easterlies! You bastard—

He was only right for himself. Don't be angry. It hurts me as much
as it hurts you. Maybe for different reasons, but it hurts just the same.

Now, please tell me about him. Tell me anything you want. Just tell
me.

Shut up, will you. Shut up and let me think in peace. Guruk's *torag*,
I was saying . . .

[6]

. . . SOMEWHERE NEAR THE SHETLAND ISLANDS the shoal became disquieted.

Bruno was slow in sensing this, because he always found it hard to
tune himself to the *ning* in his sleep (the *ning* had never been easy for
him, Neuman, notwithstanding what you wrote, because he had spent
his entire life away from me deliberately "ignoring" *nings*, for your
information), but just then he flipped over, plunged down, and swallowed much water, and woke up, sputtering and screaming something
ter-ri-ble, splashing with his hands and— Sorry.

I said I was sorry, okay? Look, I'm sorry, Neuman. I got a little
carried away and forgot you were here. It won't happen again. I promise. Yes, you can spit it back, dearest, I know . . . it's very salty . . . and
cold too, isn't it?

Where were we? Oh yes, in the North Sea. And it was night, with
a shattered moon in the water, and Bruno was looking for the lateral
lines belonging to Yorick and Napoleon (another one of your silly ideas,
very cute: Bruno would never dream of naming a fish! Not even Laprik!), and Yorick happened to be where he usually was, seaside, but
Napoleon, who always swam shoreside, had disappeared, and Bruno
was fearful now, yes, I felt his fear flow into my narrowest gulfs; see,
Neuman, after an eternity and a half of traveling between them, he
suddenly felt that his free side had been wrenched out of him, and that
his life was quickly dwindling and flowing back toward the shore,
toward the fish he had traveled with halfway around the world, yet
hardly knew at all!

And at that moment, you hear, at that moment strange currents began
to flow through him, like shocks and burning sensations and shivers
cold and hot, and he wanted so many different things at once, to stay
and to go, to drown and to fly, and his arms and legs began to pull in
opposite directions, he was almost torn apart—don't forget the terrible
infection over his ribs, too, which made him a little feverish and con-

fused all the time—and I suppose it was my fault really, though it's still too early to admit it here, and Bruno turned seaside and saw that the entire shoal was in as much confusion as he was, and that hundreds of thousands of fish were being torn apart and joined together in terror and frenzy, and that their eyes protruded and their lateral lines were shining, can you imagine the sight? And Bruno calmed down. He was about the only one who had the strength to control himself a minute more and listen, and suddenly Bruno realized that the great *ning* had all but vanished, and he shuddered, *Mamma mia*, he shuddered and listened intently, despairingly, imploringly, and only then did he discover in the distance, on the far edge of the shoal, the seaside drumming of Laprik, growing faint.

And before he could sigh with relief that at least Laprik was alive, poor Bruno's body screamed something else to him, something entirely different: a strong new muscle began to stretch and stiffen over the shoal, and Bruno heard many voices and echoes inside that he didn't understand, the beating of a new drum, and he closed his eyes and listened through his pores to this voice coming seaside from the rear, a kind of whisper and contraction and a ter-ri-ble pain—oh, how shall I explain it so you'll understand—like having a Suez or Panama operation, being cut open all the way down without an anaesthetic, and the poor salmon began to writhe and fight, they were sure it was the Icelandic fishermen come back with their nasty nets, the kind with three deep hooks for every square hole, and I swear I saw fish actually bursting—pop!—with fear and strain, and no wonder, when even I, and I've seen things like that before, even I went berserk this time, and I saw that even the distant reefs of the little Shetlands were all effulgent, and it felt as if the whole world were panting and perspiring, and Bruno was irresistibly drawn seaside, and Guruk, Guruk, writhed the frightened eels of the chiaroscuro, and Guruk, Guruk, rustled the sea porcupines with their pointy quills, and suddenly through the darkness, through the sky and through me came a flash, the red light of a new *ning*, and everything was clear.

Because an enormous fish flew forward from the head of the shoal and fell seaside where the water tossed and quivered, and Bruno sensed on his seaside, under his darling shoulder, exactly where this Guruk was boiling in the shoal, and that was also when he saw him for the first time: a huge fish, almost as big as Laprik but younger by a whole voyage, his jaws pried open for combat, and my wavelings awakened at long last from their confusion and ran to him and surrounded him and touched him, and then they ran away from him screaming, Run, run, run for your life, O Lady, this one has a temperature 's unbelievable, you could furnace another Gulf Stream with this one, O Lady, and around him, around this Guruk, the salmon were flipping as if they were on a hot griddle, and overhead flew plovers that opened their orange bills but couldn't make a sound, and giant clams snapped shut so hard a few were crushed to pieces, and Bruno looked at Guruk and saw the exact likeness of the tiny stream in the river Spey in the veins protruding all over Guruk's shiny, muscular body, and I swear I saw it, too—that happens sometimes, especially when you really want it to happen—and the shoal was drawn after Guruk in a kind of swoon, and he was filled with the strength and daring of a killer whale, and leaped out of the water and flew over us, and plunged below and disappeared, and returned from a different direction altogether, and in this way he sewed the shoal to him with a strong, taut string, and his body was as shiny as a new star, and his head was disjointed and pointed the way to the little Shetland Islands nearby, and Bruno felt that he had to get there, he knew that it was the best place in the world to be. And he hated Laprik then for leading them too long by a route that was too long, for torturing them or whatever, and it was so obvious now that you had to hurry, and find shortcuts wherever possible, because life is brief, and you have to fly, you have to soar to these wonderful isles, and never waste a moment, because Guruk is calling everyone—

And the real *torag* was on. Not as sometimes happens during the *gyoya*, when fish fight over food, and not even as happens when two rival shoals collide. No, this *torag* was totally insane. The salmon bit anything that met their teeth, and there were some who even bit themselves, because they believed Guruk wanted it, and I was filled with pieces of fish, with gills and eyes and fins, and fish were flying in the air in an ecstatic dream of leaping up the falls of the river Spey, ye-es, it was fluttering fins and snapping jaws and plopping in the water, and Bruno let out a high-pitched, husky scream. "All together now," he screamed, ah, he was one brawny muscle contracting, and his eyes— you should have seen them—they were bloodshot and bulging like the telescope eyes of the box fish in my blackest depths, and his little snorkle was hard as the armor on a scorpion fish, he couldn't even remember his own name, and he was certain that Guruk was the right name, yes, if he owes me an apology, it's for turning into a blood-filled, hate-filled shell, and was I scared; in my heart I shouted, Bruno, Bruno, but he didn't hear me, he suddenly saw the fish you call Yorick, or whatever, this Yorick who was smaller and weaker than the other fish, I can't understand how he made it as far as he did, and Bruno suddenly glared at him screaming with hatred, grinding his bared teeth and snorting, can you believe it? Because sud-den-ly he despised this Yorick, this disgrace to the pride inflating them all and making them strong and glorious (so they thought), and before I managed to see who or what, he pounced on him with a roar, with an open mouthful of teeth, and luckily a great big wave came along, a cold, extremely salty wave I'd been storing in my deepest cellars, and smacked him in the face, not too hard, of course, because it had orders, and it threw him back, far away from Yorick, and only then did Bruno shake himself as if remembering something, and pushed his eyes back into his head with his two hands, and a fast little waveling was already on its way to me, one you can always count on to bring you the most important news—and if you have an especially delicate mission, like returning a bouquet of violets, for instance, then this is the wave for it—and this was the one that brought me the news that Bruno had calmed down, that his muscles had stopped trembling, and a few minutes later he started to swim a human stroke in Yorick's direction, and he saw the little fish floating in the water like a corpse thinking this was it, his end was near, at Bruno's hand yet, and Bruno swam toward him, and I, still a little worried, was about to release another cold, extremely salty wave from a distance just in case, but there was no need after all, because Bruno stopped in front of Yorick, and started open-closing to show the little fish he no longer had anything to fear, and again his heart was filled with compassion (I want to take this opportunity to apologize to the Shetland Islanders for the sudden flood: at that moment I simply lost control). And so they faced each other, and overhead the sky was full of flying fish whose heads were barely connected to their bodies now, showing the island side, and Bruno dipped his head in and looked with open eyes at a convoy of small electric eels passing very slowly and illuminating the water below with a pale, quiet blue light, and what luck, I think now, what luck that I happened to bring them here just then, and with his head still in the water, Bruno could hear Laprik's voice loud and clear again, and he was calming down and breathing slowly, and the clearest sign that he was himself again was the pain of the infection on both sides, above the ribs, and he finned with his hands shoreside, and Yorick finned with him, and thus, with all hell breaking loose around them, the two began to set up a proper *dolgan*, and moments later other fish also organized, and Bruno saw that the fish you call Napoleon hadn't returned, and there was a different fish in his place swimming shoreside—and do me a favor, don't name that one, you read too many animal stories—and now more fish were returning out of the darkness, some of them looked terrible, their faces were bloody and their jaws were crooked, and they came quietly to a halt there and just finned and calmed themselves down and waited for the big *ning* to organize, sensing that the location of the *ning* inside them had shifted a little, more to one side, it seemed, because nearly a quarter of the shoal was torn out and galloping with Guruk, but maybe this is what made Laprik all the stronger with those that remained. They felt him in the water and in their blood and in every gill and scale, and I listened with them and inhaled so deeply I made a mistake with the ebb tide off the coast of Spain, which I didn't even notice till the shattered moon turned red (she does most of the work, it's true, because I can't be expected to handle everything), but I didn't have the patience to listen to the angry chattering of that albino ninny, because I was so tense on account of my present to Bruno, and believe me, Neuman, if he had so much as raised a finger against Yorick, I never would have given it to him, and you should have seen how little Yorick suddenly forgot the *dolgan*, and swam past Bruno open-closing fast, and Bruno answered Yorick's open-close, but didn't understand what the fish wanted from him because their open-close can mean such a variety of things, salmon language is so meager, go know what they want, but Yorick wouldn't come back to his place, and he stayed in front of Bruno, where he started jumping higher and higher, and he even swam backward when the shoal took off, and only then, when my Bruno suddenly felt himself moving faster in the water than before, did everything become clear to him too, and he rolled over on his back and stared in open-mouthed amazement, and you can imagine how happy I was . . .

So let me in on it, why don't you? I'm not a mind reader like you, and I don't have waveling spies. What did Bruno see?

You don't get it? You really don't? Ha! Okay, I'll tell you. I don't want you to think I'm hiding things. Listen: there, on either side of his ribs waved two perfect little side fins newly sprouted. So help me, it was the best work I've done since I learned to make seaweed: two fins fluttered in the water like sea butterflies, fanning my Bruno with a happiness he'd never known . . . he was so . . . hic! Excuse me . . . so . . . happy . . . I'm so excited . . . excuse me . . . oops!

Late that night she took me back to shore. According to my watch (a waterproof watch I never take off) I had spent three hours safe inside a little water nest in the middle of a sudden squall which hit the region. Yes, she really was excited that evening; over and over she savored the memory of Bruno learning to use his fins and navigate with their help, like a baby learning to crawl. Again he throbbed with life. Only the experience with the dolphins came close to this feeling. Never more was Bruno parted from Yorick, even during the *gyoya*. He always needed him around. She chattered on and on about it. It made her deliriously happy to remember, but also very soft. Her fringe of foam glistened, and again I was just a stranger grateful for a few crumbs. Arms bearer of the great love, chronicler of the lover.

Ah, you're angry again. Disgusted with me for being such a crybaby. I see the poor Tel Aviv fishermen out on the pier: their pails have been empty all evening. You steal the bait on the tips of their rods and tie their hooks together. I know your style. That childish temper. They don't understand, of course. They're amazed and furious. I see them looking at each other in disbelief, hear their curses carried on the wind. Most of them gave up and went home. But those who stayed cast their rods more and more obstinately, as if to provoke you. They search everywhere for the culprit: the moon? The noise of passing planes? Now they're looking at me. They don't know the storm was all my fault . . .

Listen. You still don't know what happened to me that night, the night of the fins—

Back on shore in Narvia, the widow Dombursky awaited me with the village policeman. The policeman was holding a bicycle in his muscular arms, and the widow was turning the pedals to make the lamp shine. They beamed it out at the stormy sea, calling my name in all directions. When I suddenly appeared soaking wet out of the waves, they crossed themselves and began to scream at me for giving them such a fright. I paid them five zloty each, and asked to be left alone. They went away, and I sat down on the rough sand in the cold wind, my head in my hands. I felt hollow and defeated. Now I understood how far I was from real talent and courage. I dressed wearily and dragged myself back to the cottage. The widow served me fish and potatoes, cold by now, and grumbled incessantly. I looked at the fish, and for the first time since my arrival in Narvia, I pushed my plate away. Later on, in the parlor, by the light of a smelly oil lamp (there had been another power failure), I briefly recorded the rest of her story: Before dawn the shoal learned what had happened to those who went with Guruk. While the remaining salmon swam in their sleep with Laprik, they had received a shock, as if their muscles and ligaments were being torn. Beyond the horizon just then, to the east, the drunk, seceding shoal had run amok on the rocky reefs of the Shetland Islands. Bruno's shoal came to a sudden halt, and floated quietly, perceiving with a thousand senses what had happened in the distance. Suddenly they were all seized with convulsions: threads of blood went out to the distant waters. Bruno looked at Yorick out of the corner of his eye. In his heart again he thanked him for being who he was. For suffering his difference like a humpback that kept him from passing through with everyone else.

When day broke, the waves were strewn with thousands of corpses borne south and west. The shoal passed through them. Their smell was fiercer than usual, and the expressions on their faces made them look as if they were in shock. In the distance small fishing boats sailed out from the islands. Bruno felt no grief over the dead. He had to save his grief for Yorick, or the one or two other fish he was somewhat acquainted with in the crowd. He finned vigorously with his new fins. He was as proud as a boy with the beginnings of a mustache. Dimly he felt he had earned them: that for one moment he had been worthy of the life he sought.

[7]

YOU STILL WON'T TALK TO ME. You're ignoring me, but I know you're out here by the pier, listening to my every word. I'm talking to you because I have no one else to talk to. Ruth and Yariv are in Jerusalem, and I need to get away from them, both of them, every few days till I finish straightening myself out. I may never straighten myself out. Things used to seem so clear-cut and predictable to me. I was convinced that with enough information you could always predict how X would behave in situation Y. As a kid I used to be fairly good at predicting things. I was a regular Merlin. But then I grew up and everything went wrong. Everything became unpredictable and extremely dangerous. And there's no way of knowing when to be on your guard: sometimes the treachery comes from inside yourself.

I can't talk to Ayala anymore either. She's living with some musician a few blocks away, and I'm not allowed to show my face there after my crime against humanity—that's what she calls that silly business about little Kazik. The only way I can atone for something like that, she tells me, grimacing with detestation, is to write a completely different story. A story of atonement. And till then—please, don't show your ugly face around here.

And you don't answer. The lights are going out on the new boardwalk now. The chairs are upturned in the restaurants along the beach. Tel Aviv, late 1984. I'm out on the pier. Only three fishermen left. And you're so dark, always in motion. And so alert, I feel you. Before you, the city shudders.

I had a child. Ten months after I returned from Narvia I had a child. Just when Ruth decided to stop the treatments, a miracle occurred. We called him Yariv, a name I always liked. A modern Israeli name. And I tried to be a good father, truly I did, but I knew from the start that I didn't stand a chance. I always figured the parent-children business was rough, but I didn't know just how rough. They either resemble you too much or they're too different. And the burden of all my expectations—that he be like me or, wait a minute, like Ruth, the exact opposite of me, healthy and uncomplicated, clean-living and strong. But what a surprise he turned out to be, not like either of us. And if he did inherit anything from Ruth, it's her bad traits. He's painfully slow, he's too fat, and he has a timid, awkward face. He's totally helpless with other children, like a fat pigeon among sparrows. Only when he's with me does he act stubborn, like a big hero. He wasn't like that in the beginning, but something must have gone wrong. I watch him playing by himself in the corner of the day-care center and I want to scream. I can just see him thirty years from now: a big man, with the slightly hurt expression very fat people often have, standing awkwardly and helplessly among his nursery-school peers. Ruth laughs when I confess these worries. He's going through a difficult stage, she tells me, he's a terrific little boy. Half a year from now you'll hardly recognize him. He'll get used to nursery school and the other children, and even if he stays a lonely little recluse, I'll go on loving him, because he's my type of guy, ha ha. But she too is forced to admit that he has a couple of unpleasant characteristics. He's bad-tempered and demanding and afraid of everything. In the days when I did my writing at home, he used to climb all over me and prevent me from getting a single word down. "Do you know what Daddy's writing?" Ruth would ask—she was busy all day long trying to keep us apart—and he, with exasperating childish egocentricity: "Daddy write Yariv." Cute joke, but I know that's what he really wanted me to do, to sit there typing his glorious name from morning till night. And hearing this, Ruth laughs and says, Try to act like a grownup, Momik. And don't attack him full-force like that. There is a slight age difference between you, you know. And then we have the usual argument: I say it has nothing to do with age, you have to train him for war. I told her this once, before he was born, if I ever had a child, the first thing I would do in the morning would be to slap his face. Just like that. So he'll know there's no justice in this world, only strife. I said this when we first started going together, in high school. In later years, I came to see it was a stupid, childish idea, but when Yariv was born I had the feeling it wasn't so stupid after all. Ruth said, Someday he'll slap you back, how will you feel then? And I said, I'll feel great. I'll know I've prepared my son for life. And she said, But he may not love you for it much. Love, I sneered maliciously, I prefer a living son to a loving son. And she: You're taking revenge on him for what you didn't get at home, Momik. This disgusting remark, which she is forbidden to make under any circumstances, drives me to distraction, because what I did get at home was the wisdom to survive, which is something you don't learn in school, and which can't be described in the polite language of Ruthy's ever-so-enlightened parents who never knew danger, a wisdom that can only be communicated in silence, in suspicious contractions around the eyes and mouth, a thick substance that passes through the umbilical cord and is deciphered slowly over decades of life: Always stand in the middle row. Never reveal more than you have to. Remember things are seldom what they seem. Never be too happy. Don't say "I" so freely. And in general, try to get out of the whole thing safely, with no unnecessary scars. Don't hope for more than this.

Evening. Yariv is asleep already and I go in to look at him. He's lying on his back. I feel shivers up my spine. "You feel it, too?" asks Ruth quietly, and her face fills the room with pleasure. I want to say something nice to her, to make her happy, to show her that I really do care for him, but my throat contracts. "It's a good thing he can sleep through all the noise," I say finally. "He may have to sleep with tanks passing in the streets someday. Or on his feet, trudging through the snow. Or in a crowded cell block maybe, with ten more like him to a bunk. Or on a—" "Stop it," says Ruth, and leaves the room.

I'm always testing him. He's taller and sturdier than most children his age, and that's good, but he's afraid of them. He's afraid of everything. I have to climb the slide because he refuses to move without me. I climb down again and leave him there crying that he's afraid he might fall. Some kindly soul walks over to inform me that he's afraid. I smile, coldly beatific, and tell her that out in the forests children his age were used as sentinels and made to sit guard for hours high in the treetops. She recoils in horror. Let's see her kid when the time comes. The other mothers on the bench stop chattering to stare at me and the little idiot on the ladder. He screams and carries on. I light a cigarette and watch him. If someday we're caught in a bunker with soldiers searching for us, how will I shut the kid up? There won't be any choice, I think. I only hope I can teach him to do the same if I ever get in his way. Come here, you little coward, I say out loud, feigning nonchalance, stubbing my cigarette out on the heel of my shoe, and then I climb up to get him. But when his mouth sticks to my neck and trembles with a mournful sob, I feel the heavy pendulum of childish shame swing from his heart to mine with such force it almost knocks me off the ladder. Forgive me, my child, I say inwardly, forgive everything, be wiser and more patient than I am, because I don't have the strength, they didn't teach me how to love. Be strong enough to tolerate me, love me. And stop crying like a girl, I whisper out loud.

No more tender moments. Ruth knows how to play with him. I want to teach him. To prepare him. To make the most of these precious years when the brain is alert and open. Ruth loves to play with him. She draws him cars and tick-tocks and models for him in clay. When they play, their gentle voices blend together. I teach him to read numbers. She melts when he makes a mistake like "Mommy and Daddy good bye-bye." I too am amused, but I correct him. There's no time for mistakes. He stands up on our bed to follow a fly on the window, and suddenly reaches out, and accidentally catches, and crushes it. Then he looks at his hand in amazement and asks why the fly isn't flying anymore. Ruth, a little tensely, says the fly is sleeping, and looks at me. I tell him the truth. I also go into detail. "You killed it," Yariv repeats after me, tasting the new word in his soft, fresh mouth. In my head I feel a kind of dullness spreading. I ought to be happy now, but there's nothing to be happy about. There's nothing to hope for.

"Make a little effort with him, will you?" she says later at night, her face and mine to the ceiling. "You may be causing long-term damage. That would be a shame." Inwardly I scream: Stop me. Throw me out. Give me an ultimatum. Aloud I say that the story I'm currently working on, the story Grandfather Anshel told Neigel the German, must be having a big impact on me. That and all I've been reading and learning in connection with it. Ruthy knows me well enough not to suggest that I stop writing. She would never say anything like that outright. Ruthy believes that we all possess great powers, powers beyond our control, and we have to be careful not to harm others with our advice or attempts to influence them. She's so mature. Why is it that everything she does feels like hard work to me? We lie in bed talking about the difference between writing a poem and writing a novel. A poem is like a love affair, she says, smiling in the dark, a novel is more like marriage: you stay with your characters long after the initial passion has worn off. It was strange that she said that. It's not like her. I'm the one who says the naughty things around here. For some reason I was scared for a moment. A novel, I say quietly, is like a marriage: two people love each other and hurt each other, because who else is there to hurt? We're both silent. I try to remember whether she locked the bottom lock on the front door. But if I ask her she'll be annoyed. She probably locked it. I'll just have to believe she locked it and stop letting it worry me. Sometimes, I tell her, I want to pack my bags and go live somewhere else. Start all over. Without the past. Just the two of us. "And Yariv," she reminds me, and adds that there's no running away anymore. This is the last haven. Well, I reply, that's a dumb thing to say. There's no such thing as a "last haven." You can't let yourself become so attached to any one place, or any one person. "You'll never find peace, Momik," she says. "It isn't places you fear, it's people." Her voice is soothing, serene, what's got into her all of a sudden? "You're afraid of everybody.

What do you see in us, Momik? What could be worse than what we already know?" And I say, "I don't know. I don't have the strength for any more of these questions." There, I should have asked her if she locked the bottom lock, too. I missed my chance. She usually remembers to lock the bottom lock on the way to bed after she turns off the gas. Wait a minute: did she turn off the gas? And suddenly I'm talking about the Holocaust again. I don't even know how I got back to it. I can get there from anywhere. I'm a regular Holocaust homing pigeon. And for the thousandth time, in a voice that doesn't carry much conviction, I ask, "How can life go on after we've seen what a human being is capable of?" "Some people are able to love," she says (at last a bit impatiently). "Some people reach the opposite conclusion. There are two possible conclusions after the Holocaust, aren't there? And there are people who love and feel compassion and do good without any connection to the Holocaust. Without thinking about it day and night. Because maybe it was a mistake? Why not look at it like that, Shlomik?" "You don't believe that yourself anymore." "Sure. I've been living with you for a few years, and your point of view has rubbed off on me. It's easier to become like you than it is to stay like me. I don't like myself when I start to think like you. I have to fight you." "You know I'm right. Even if you say there are people who think differently and get along fine, you won't console me. I'm one of those unfortunates who see the backstage. And the skull beneath the skin." "And what do you see there? Damn it, what do you see there that's so different from what the rest of us see?! What tidings do you bring?" (She's getting angrier by the minute, and I so seldom succeed in ruffling her.) "I don't bring any tidings. It's the same old thing: people killing each other, only the process is projected decorously in slow motion which is why it isn't so shocking. Everybody killing everybody. The death machine has gone through a few more rounds and slipped into the underground, but I can hear the motor running all the time. I'm getting ready, Ruthy. As you well know." "A little birdy told me." She smiles. "Go on, laugh. Someday we'll all be in the convoys again. Only unlike the rest of you, I will not be shocked or humiliated. And I won't suffer the pains of separation. There's nothing I'll be sorry to leave behind." "It so happens I know something about that, too. It was my husband the poet who wrote *The Object Cycle* everyone raved about. Have you read it?" "I leafed through it." "Yes, my husband never allows me to buy him birthday presents, and he can't stand ceremonies that hint at anything permanent—oh yes, I know the man." "I want to be free of attachments." "And people, Momik?" "Ditto." "Even me and Yariv?" Shut up, dummy. Lie, tell her you want to be free of others, but not her. Because without her, without her faith and innocence, your life has no meaning. "Yes, even you and Yariv. Look, maybe I won't be able to stop missing you, but I'd like to think I'll be strong enough. I'd be disappointed with myself if I couldn't stand the pain." Ruth is silent. And then she says brightly, "If I believed any of this, I would get right up and leave you. But I've been hearing this stuff for almost ten years now, ever since we met, in fact. Sometimes you pull yourself out of it and see things a little differently, but in my opinion, you speak this way out of fear, my darling." "Cut the 'my darling,' okay? We're not starring in some Turkish melodrama, you know." Her white-toothed smile spreads through the darkness. You have to turn the key four times in the bottom lock. I'm pretty sure I only heard two clicks. I feel her smile float through the room. Her mouth is the loveliest feature in her potato-ish face. Her complexion is raw, permanently inflamed around the nostrils and under the eyes. When we were sixteen and first started going together, people used to laugh at us behind our backs. We weren't the best-looking couple in the class, to put it mildly. So I had to get my own nasty digs in. Ruth, however, quietly and wisely, steered us to where only the two of us mattered, not what people said about us. But I still hear an echo of their mockery sometimes. And Ruth says, "I do know you pretty well after all this time. We've been together through thick and thin. I've read your poems, including the ones you didn't publish because you were afraid they would spoil your image as an angry young poet. I've known you since you started shaving. I see you when you're sleeping and laughing and angry and quiet and sad and coming inside me. We've slept together side by side for a million nights like teaspoons. Or knives sometimes. And when you're thirsty at night I bring you water in my mouth. I know the way you like to kiss, and how you hate it when I try to hug you in public. I know a lot about you. Not everything, but a lot. The things I know about you are very important to me. Just as the characters you write about are important to you. Our life, yours and mine—and now with Yariv—is the simple creation I work at every hour of every day. Nothing very big or daring. Or very original either. Millions of women have done it before me, probably a lot better, too. But this is mine, and I live it with all my might and main. No, let me talk now. I saw how happy you were when your affair with Ayala began. I suffered terribly. But in spite of the humiliation and hatred I felt toward you, I sometimes thought (when I managed to collect my thoughts) that someone with your talent for love, even if he tried to bury it, would eventually give himself away. And I was willing to wait. Not because of my Solveg syndrome, as you call it, but out of pure simple egoism, in fact." "And what if another woman pulls out the plum in the end, excuse the expression?" "Well, maybe another woman will pull it out. But only for a little while. I know." "What do you know?" "That we need each other, even if you won't admit it, you immature male chauvinist pig. You really are immature, you know, a real adolescent. We're two such different people, yet we want the same things. Only we have different ways of getting there. We're like two different keys to the same lock. But forgive me for waxing poetic. My husband is the poet around here, and now he's something of a novelist, too." "By the way, did you lock the door?" "The bottom lock, too, you can relax." I say nothing (I forgot to ask about the gas!). Love conquers nothing, I tell her in my heart. Only in fiction do writers compulsively have love conquering in the end. But it isn't like that in real life. A lover coolly leaves the deathbed of his contagious sweetheart. People rarely commit suicide with their dying partners. The mighty, tyrannical stream of life keeps us apart. Carries us forward slowly and selfishly like animals. Love conquers nothing. Ruth nestles closer to me. She caresses me gently, but I'm reserved. I need to talk a little more, all right? "All right." Ruth sighs and smiles. "I should have married that wild Circassian who wanted to buy me for seven camels: he wouldn't need to talk a little more."

"You know, the horrible thing for me about the Holocaust is the way every trace of individuality was obliterated. A person's uniqueness, his thoughts, his past, his characteristics, loves, defects, and secrets— all meant nothing. You were debased to the lowest level of existence. You were nothing but flesh and blood. It drives me mad. That's why I wrote 'Bruno.' " "And Bruno taught you how to fight the obliterators?" "Yes. In a hypothetical way, though Bruno doesn't solve a thing for me in the day-to-day. Bruno is a nice dream. But he's more than that, too. What he revealed to me was very frightening, and I felt a tremendous resistance to it. I can feel it even now, when I get stuck in the story of Wasserman and the German. I feel I have to defend myself against what Bruno showed me. I'm fighting it a little even now." "You're fighting yourself."

"Maybe. Maybe. But when I can't stop. Listen. Don't smile. I can hear you smiling in the dark. I want to be ready next time it happens. Not just so I'll be able to break away with a minimum of pain from others, but so I'll be able to break away from myself. I'd like to be able to erase everything inside that could bring me excruciating pain if it were obliterated or degraded. It's impossible, I know that, but sometimes I plan it step by step. I'll cancel out all my traits, desires and passions, and my talents, too—just think what a superhuman feat that would be: I'll get the Nobel Prize for human physics, huh?" "How horrifying." "No, seriously: I'll simply sink into death without suffering. Without pain or humiliation. And without disappointment. I'll—" "Then you might as well have been dead to begin with. With so many defenses up against people you'll never be able to enjoy them. You'll never know a moment's relief from hatred and suspicion. You'll live by the sword. And the more you continue, the more convinced you'll be that everyone else is like you are, because that's all you'll know. And people who think like you will kill each other without remorse, because there won't be any value left to life or death. Like the land of the dead, Momik." "You're exaggerating as usual. But I might try living there. The alternative isn't always easy for me either." "You mean life here? Ordinary, simple love?" "Simple, yes. Very simple." "Doesn't your writing help? You always say that's what saves you." "No. I'm stuck. Wasserman tricked me. He brought baby Kazik into the story." "Maybe you should take the baby out, then." "No no. If the baby's there, there must be some good reason for its being there. You know how I write. I always feel as if I'm quoting. But this time I don't know. I don't understand what the baby wants from me. It's hard enough with my first baby. Terrible things have been happening to me lately. I'm afraid to talk about them. Sometimes I don't have the strength to go on from one minute to the next. People disgust me. It's not my usual disgust: it's real hatefulness. I don't have the guts to face their lives. I walk down the street and feel powerful forces at work drowning me. Like tears, for instance." "What?" "I look at people's faces, and I know that a tenth of a millimeter down in the tear ducts there are tears." "People don't cry so easily." "But the tears are there. Sometimes, when the bus stops suddenly in the street, I can almost hear the tears rattling. But the crying stays inside. And the pain, too. We're so frighteningly frail. And all our desires, yes, desires that have to be consummated. That's a lot of dangerous baggage for one little body to carry around. How do you face it? Do you understand what I'm saying? Don't answer me. I haven't got the stamina to understand the life of a single human being anymore. If it weren't for the story of Grandfather Anshel, I would go back to my object poems." "As long as you know that I love you very much." "In spite of all this?" I ask her ruefully. "Maybe even because of all this." "And I love you, too. Even though sometimes you drive me crazy with your Jesuit naïveté." "You know very well it isn't naïveté. How could I stay naïve living with you? This is a decision. And besides— you can always punish me: the day the stampede starts and I'm there with my two babies and one on the way, you'll run off all by yourself and I won't be able to say you didn't warn me." "That's a deal," I say. "Did you turn off the gas?" "I think so. Who cares? Now come to me. Admit I won you fair and square tonight." And I turn to her, our faces touching in the dark, but only our faces, slowly, in resignation, like old letters reread, and then I burrow into her with all my might, and for one moment I have peace, I have a home, there is someone I can touch, there is someone I'm not afraid of, and we move together cautiously, conserving tenderness, rising and falling like a long, tired caravan, but when Ruth bites my lip and quivers, I return to a land devoid of love, I see those pictures on the tattered screen of my brain. Mankind. And when I come, I remember to make the right noises, though for the past few weeks I haven't really enjoyed it: it's meaningless. Like spitting.

Life was slowing down. I had turned into a sloughed skin. Even channels previously open to me were closed now and nothing flowed. Around this time I stopped writing the story of Grandfather Anshel and took up another project: collecting material for a young people's encyclopedia of the Holocaust. The first of its kind. To spare our children having to guess or reconstruct it in their nightmares. I had a list of some two hundred main entries already: murderers and victims, the main extermination camps, literary works on the subject written during that period and later. I discovered that filing, writing, and editing the material in this way was helpful.

But I dropped the idea because I couldn't find a backer. I couldn't handle the PR work myself. It annoys me and I start shouting at people, and they ask me to leave. At home, too, I was becoming unbearable, but I couldn't help it. I felt awful. Ruth went to meet Ayala, and they talked for four hours. I guess they decided what's best for me. This was disturbing: neither one would tell me what they had discussed. Was I a child or something? At exactly the same time (why does everything happen synchronously), my mother's sclerosis took a turn for the worse. I refused to drive her to the hospital for those disgusting tests. I couldn't bring myself to go with her. Ruth went. I reminded myself cynically that my mother never took care of Grandfather Anshel either, and that when Papa lay dying, she wouldn't touch him, and now it was her turn. The disease—like a beast of prey—had isolated the weakest animal in the herd, and closed in fast: the rest of the animals ran on, their eyes on the horizon. The way of the world, I told myself, but that wasn't the truth. Actually I was afraid something bad would happen to her. I was afraid of what would happen to me once she was gone. For a few years now I had lost all patience with her. I became annoyed after five minutes' conversation. Everything she said, all her primitive notions and suspicions, drove me crazy. But now that I felt I was losing her, I was filled with anxiety and remorse and a sense of loss and injustice.

The doctors released Mama from the hospital and said everything would be okay, meaning there was nothing they could do. They recommended that she come live with us. This time it was Ruth who put her foot down. She told them things were so bad it was all she could do to take care of me and Yariv. So you admit it, then, I screamed at her, wickedly rejoicing in my own calamity, you admit it's just as I always said: even in families you find nothing but petty opportunism and egotism? Yes, said Ruth serenely, but, Momik, this is a problem money can solve: my father will help out and we can hire a nurse for her. Don't lose your sense of proportion, and do me a favor, admit it isn't the gas chamber every time somebody swears at you at an intersection!

So said my gentle wife.

Hey, you're getting impatient. You're finally starting to react: you snort and spit in all directions. No doubt you think I'm drawing this out interminably, that I'm dwelling on the details out of disgust for the story. You mustn't be so hard on me. But you don't care. I'm sure you don't: you, too, protect yourself from pain. Isn't that why they build breakwaters?

And then one day there was a knock on the door and in walked Ayala. Summery as ever, her hair wild, smelling of sea and sunburn. Ruth met her with a smile, rather tensely. How nice to see you. They touched each other. I went to the bedroom and lay down. My head was splitting. They sat in the kitchen and spoke in whispers. My mother used to whisper in Yiddish with Grandma Henny when she was saying things about Papa. Later I heard Ayala approach and rolled over on my stomach with my eyes closed. "Get up and stop feeling so sorry for yourself," said Ayala. "If you really want to pull yourself out of this, start making an effort. Don't poison the atmosphere. You don't know how good you have it." She spoke casually, with the mild contempt that used to make me double over. "We think you should rent a room somewhere," said Ruth, turning in the doorway. "And you can stay there quietly on your own and write. No excuses. You can't keep torturing everyone around you like this. World War II only lasted six years, yours has been going on for thirty-five. Enough already."

I looked at the two of them, joined in the doorway like the pretty pieces of a mosaic. I found myself wishing they would both come over and get into bed with me. Why not? It happens to other men. What more can one person wish for? Physical contact. There are so many things a man can solve with a woman. Any woman. The important thing is to have a woman under you. Isn't that what women are for? I looked at them standing there, and played around with the mosaic: Ayala's heavy round breasts on Ruth's elongated torso. Not bad. If only it were really possible. Ayala wears those tiny lace bikini panties. Ruth wears the old-fashioned kind. A few years ago I actually thought of asking her to buy the sexy kind, but I knew she'd only give me a dirty look. It would be beneath her to tempt me with her body. That side of our relationship has always been weak: for some reason we were still like two high-school students together. And now I'm afraid it's hopeless. I fixed my lecherous eyes on Ayala. Nothing happened: no urns, no strawberries. I had lost my touch. "Make up your mind," said Ayala. "Now!"

They were right, as usual. Women are always more perceptive. I curled up in bed and thought. I had a rare moment of lucidity. I realized that for most of my life I had been making decisions by a process of elimination. It was kind of warped. I always see perfectly well what I *don't* want, what frightens me and puts me off. And slowly, without noticing it, by a process of elimination, negation, contradiction, and war, someone new was born in me, a stranger I didn't like. And then I understood: I am my own prisoner. How could this have happened to someone as aware as I am, who checks himself every step of the way, and is his own worst critic? How could such an error have occurred? I threw my blanket off. I got up and went to the telephone and dialed, hoping my mother would answer, not the nurse.

My mother answered. "Hello," she said. Only someone who's heard my mother say hello will understand. The fear, the failure to which she resigned herself as the telephone rang. Hello, catastrophe, come to me. I've been waiting so long for you to come. And I don't have the strength to wait anymore. Come, world, be real, beat me, sometimes the blow is easier than the anticipation. Hello.

I listened a few more times to the sound of her hello's becoming ever sharper and more terrified. I remembered how she and Papa used to argue in frightened whispers about who was going to open the door whenever there was a knock (once a year). I listened to her. They were even afraid to be with me. They tried not to hover too long around this fantastic, no doubt illusory, fulfillment of their hopes. Hello, hello, hello, Mama, it's me, the child you yearned to love with all the joy and light in you, the child you kept at a distance so as not to tempt Fate. Hello. I put the receiver down. I told Ruth and Ayala that they were right. I begged them not to leave me. I said I'd do anything to pull myself out of this. The same week I went to Tel Aviv with Ruth and we rented a room for me. A room without a telephone. I wanted to be away from everything. And in Tel Aviv there was always the chance that Ayala would come for the night. I asked for no more than this. She never came, though. It was there that I wrote the sixth and final version of the story Anshel Wasserman told a German named Neigel.

Wait a minute. Here they come. The three fishermen from the edge of the pier. Heavy, mustachioed, waving their fists at me from the distance. Who me? What? I should clear out? What did I do? Bad luck? Me?! They're crazy. Their faces are twisted with rage. I can't understand what they're saying. But I do understand they're angry. There's no mistaking that. But I'm not budging. It's a free country, you know. Hey! Don't you dare touch me, you big idiot! What are you—hellllp!! H—

They rub their hands with satisfaction. They spit at me in the water.

They return triumphantly to their places at the edge of the pier. Surprisingly the water isn't cold. It's much colder outside. I drift this way and that on the soft waves. I'm a clump of seaweed. I wait, afraid. I haven't dared to dip my toes in the sea since my return from Narvia. But what's this? The fishermen are cheering. In the moonlight I see their fishing rods arch. Suddenly—around my waist a smooth viscosity melts and disappears. The sea flares up and settles down to caress and roll the happy waves—

Hi, Neuman.

Hi.

Small world, isn't it?

[8]

WHEN DID IT START? Bruno didn't know. Maybe while he was asleep, or during the luscious *gyoya* to my north, near the Orkney Islands. That's probably where it started, because on their way south to the Scottish coast, the rippling of anticipation had, with gentle firmness, deflected him from his shoreside position in the shoal and propelled him swiftly and silently past Yorick, and past a hundred other fish in his row, till they suddenly let go and left him in an unfamiliar position in the shoal, where he heard the great *ning* pulsing through him vigorously.

For some time he floated mutely, adapting himself to the slow, mighty pulsing and the frightening new sensations which the salmon strangers and his new position in the shoal had given him. He had to try very hard to control the trembling in his fins, and to keep up with the new *dolgan* he hadn't quite mastered yet. Only after a few hours of concentrated swimming did he dare turn his gaze seaside, and there for the first time since jumping into the water in the port of Danzig, he saw Laprik.

Laprik was the biggest salmon Bruno had ever seen in his life. He was about a hundred and twenty centimeters long and weighed no less than Bruno. He had pinkish coloring, a bolder pink than the others', and there was a shiny mark over his right eye. His movements were economical, and at the same time lively and vigorous. On his mandible there was a cicatrix, rough and red, like an exclamation point. Bruno swallowed and swam on. His muscles began to contract. He listened to the *ning* in his ears and in his heart, and experienced it less intensely now, as though it were accompanied by another echo. Swiftly he rode the sea, his thoughts pouring out, and his sense of existence growing sharp as a bone exposed inside a wound. The fish surrounding him suddenly slowed down, and he slowed down with them. Strange currents passed through the shoal. Now they discerned another fish broadcasting the pulsations of a new *ning*. Bruno remembered how Guruk had led a quarter of the shoal to their doom near the Shetland Islands. Panic-stricken, he raised his head out of the water to look for Yorick. The littie thing was nowhere to be seen. He searched in trepidation for the fish that was trying to undermine Laprik's authority. The pulsing wasn't coming from shoreside. And seaside there was only Laprik. What could it mean?

The shoal came to a halt and regrouped in a circle. The fish gilled faster and stared blindly ahead. A small circle, free of fish, now formed around Bruno and Laprik, within which the new *ning* resonated powerfully. Bruno saw thousands of mouths open-closing, and beyond them a myriad of tense green fins. He and Laprik were still side by side, and out of the corner of his eye, Bruno suddenly discerned the salmon's lateral lines in bold relief.

. A sharp fear struck him: the *ning* was issuing out of him. It was he who was challenging Laprik. But what for? He wasn't at all sure he would be able to lead the shoal any better than Laprik, and besides, he didn't want to! What did this have to do with him? He turned to Laprik in bewilderment, as though trying to explain something, and Laprik moved in closer, too. The circle of salmon widened by a hairsbreadth. Bruno listened to his *ning* in amazement: it was a fast, sure pulsation. Not the wild, sickly throbbing Guruk had produced. He dipped his ears in the water and listened long. It was so like Laprik's *ning*—and yet it was his own. His true, unique vibration. He felt grateful to Laprik, because without him he would never have been able to hear himself. This was his most wildly irrational feeling in the split second before the life-and-death struggle began, but it was Laprik after all who had taken him into the shoal and turned him into an artist of life. Why did they have to fight each oth—

Whereupon the water eddied and raged. Like mirror images they stormed at each other. The two skulls crashed, retreated, and crashed again. The other fish's supple body wound around Bruno's chest and waist, and the strong, sharp teeth bit into the flesh of his shoulder. He fell with a groan of pain, repulsing Laprik, and sank down down down, weak and stupefied, till he reached the zone where even light was arrested and the red rays failed. Bruno looked around in horror and saw the wound on his shoulder streaming what appeared to be green blood. His fear saved him. He ricocheted up, trapped Laprik unprepared, and smashed him, with open arms, on both sides of his face. For a moment Laprik stayed his ground, as though nothing had happened, and then he slipped under the water and disappeared. Bruno swam circles around himself in fear, then quickly spiraled down, but couldn't find his adversary. He rose to the surface out of breath and saw black: Laprik was attacking him, heavy as a whale, ramming into his chest. Bruno stopped breathing. His blood throbbed in his temples and filled his eyes. Without thinking, he lurched forward, pounding blindly at the air and water. Never in his life had Bruno struck anyone, and the surge of violence that overwhelmed his very being terrified him. But the fear belonged to Bruno the man, and Bruno the fish choked on blood diluted by water and sucked passion from it. He flew at Laprik over and over, and they wound around each other, slippery and fierce, a jumble of sharp teeth, abrasive side fins, and quiet rage, soundless because Bruno didn't break the silence either, and fought quietly, like a fish. He lost count of the minutes, and time throbbed to the rhythm of their onslaughts and the violent pain of their wounds. Bruno was mutilated: Laprik's bites had opened up big ugly holes in his chest and the sides of his neck, but he could see that the big fish was also slowly deteriorating, that his assaults were becoming lax, that he had become disjointed, cut off from the source of his vitality, and at that moment Bruno drew back. At that moment his eyes cleared and his brain shone with a pearly light: he was fighting Laprik because he could not live in the crowd, not even a crowd that was free of malice, not even to the beat of Laprik's *ning*. But he didn't want to be Death's arms bearer either. Laprik was still floating around him blindly, struggling to hold onto his own *ning*, and spitting out chunks of flesh from Bruno's arm, but Bruno had already retreated. The salmon gave him a wide berth. No, he didn't want to lead them. He didn't want to lead anyone. No one has a right to lead anyone else. And how close he'd come to committing a crime. He quickly drew backward. The power of his *ning* was good for a shoal of one only. The singular, secret body language was his alone. And only thus was it possible for him to say "I" without the tinny resonance of "we." Bruno removed himself from the circle of fish and stopped, breathing heavily, beyond the shoal. The salmon turned and looked at him vacantly. They remained in place this way for a long time. Meanwhile, Laprik had partially recovered. Echoes of his *ning* revived and began to reach Bruno, but they no longer penetrated him. The shoal moved slowly on. It left without him, and for one last moment, Bruno was seized with the old fear. But it was merely force of habit.

The shoal drifted away. In the course of a few hours, hundreds of thousands of fish passed him at a steady float, and he waited motionless. The only one he could distinguish among them was Yorick, but in a little while he ceased to see them as fish and saw them instead as a large complex body, dissociated from himself: his former being. All his possessions passed before his eyes, all his memories and shreds of what used to be. He waited thus for an hour after the last of them had gone, deep in the contemplation and sadness of parting from his former self. From now on, everything he would ever do, think, or create would be his by right. On the distant horizon, the last of the stiff fins could be seen. Very soon they will arrive at the great falls on the river Spey. They will leap up three, four meters against the foaming current, fall back into the water, and leap again and again. Whoever survives the waterfalls arrives exhausted at the little stream where they were born years before. For a few days they will rest, huddled together, dead tired, reduced, tortured to the limit of endurance. Above them, birds of prey will circle. The fish will cast dark shadows on the water. A few days hence they will grow a tough hump and auxiliary teeth, and then there will be bloody battles over females and territory. The survivors will fertilize the roe, and die. Bruno knew: little Yorick would not survive the falls. Laprik would make it, but he would be too exhausted to fight the younger males. In a few hours, the Spey would be filled with the mutilated corpses of salmon. All the cruelty of the journey would suddenly hit them and leave its deadly mark. Birds of prey would peck them clean.

Bruno was all alone. The old shark that tailed the shoal stopped midway. He turned from the multitudes of fish receding in the distance to look at the strange creature who gave off the smell of blood and appeared to be particularly easy prey. He decided to have it both ways. He plunged below the water and disappeared. A fast, narrow course in a beeline to Bruno, who noticed nothing.

Only, at this point, something strange occurred: something difficult to explain, the cause of a great deal of embarrassment among biographers of the sea and the conservative archivists of liquid history: suddenly, without any explanation, the shark was hurled upward like some gigantic bird-fish, and he floundered helplessly in the air, snorting two-part harmony through his grotesque, hammerhead-like snout, and landed far far away, in his usual position, at the tail end of the big shoal.

The sea churned a moment more. Bruno thought he heard a strange sound, like clapping: the small waves around the place where the shark had been hurled in the air heard, to their surprise, a fizzling sound, like an angry and particularly juicy curse, but they preferred not to believe it came from the mouth of their Lady. They rammed into each other in harmless, gay abandon, told their different accounts of the shark-spitting campaign, spoke excitedly about old steamships, about navigation by the flight of birds, about different treatments for seasickness . . . in short, they changed the subject.

Nicely told, Neuman.

I'm trying.

Except for the curse at the end. You know I never talk that way.

It was the shark who cursed!

The shark? He can barely swim, let alone— Right. Now I remember. Hammerhead sharks are known for their foul language.

And after a moment's silence: You're cute, you know. You've changed since then.

Are you ready for the rest of the story?

I guess you haven't changed, after all.

Please?

Go on, feel free. I'm not listening in any case . . . Wait a minute! You forgot! You forgot the main thing!

Huh? What did I forget?

Bruno! The wounds! Remember? Please, please, you have to remem—

Of course. How could I forget. You're right. Listen.

Bruno swam slowly through the waters of the North. She was his from horizon to horizon, and he didn't know it. She pressed down on his sores. Stern-faced fish were at work in her laboratories extracting their own special substances. Waves summoned from the Caspian Sea and Dead Sea, breathless and foaming after seeping out of the abysses of landlocked waters, and passing briskly through the telegraphic currents of subterranean rivers, arrived weary and worn to maim themselves by their Lady's decree in order to produce the rare salts required for instant recovery. Seaweed, drifting in Bruno's path as if by chance, wrapped itself around him briefly, dabbed him with mysterious astringents, and floated on, rejoicing in her joy. There were only two sores left, two narrow sores on the sides of his neck, though in fact they were not sores at all but, rather, openings, or little mouths. Or simply: gills.

Bruno swims on, his head immersed in the water. He no longer needs to breathe the air outside. He gazes down at the abyss: the waves have ground the lenses of his eyes till they are marvelously suited to underwater vision, and objects now appear wavy, their colors breaking and winding to reveal the threads of a thousand subtle hues embroidered there and splitting on the waves, which pluck themselves like a harp made of water strings on the giant cradle marking sea time, and also a hand can leave a print on a wave where it no longer is, where it never was, and maybe a wave will carry the body's image away, and when it returns, carry it back, the outlines of soft pacific objects giving in to the soothing waves to the slumberous sea breathing slippery sleep on the lip of the reef and the pages of dreams the sea will tally the invaders flooding it ebbing and rising among the waves there are always the gulls many more than those below and the new ones seem heavier soaking the heaviness of the sea and diaphanous with beautiful colors fanning this way and that way Bruno swims—

She doesn't answer. The waves are smooth, the water shivers with a tender snort every second or so. I look behind me and see that the pier is already empty. Only one fisherman is left out there, tall and sturdy as a lighthouse, his cigarette flickering in the dark. Carefully, shyly, I slip across her cheek. Soon dawn will catch us and we have to hurry up and tell the end of the story of our meeting on the coast of Narvia. The gift Bruno gave me there. His verdict.

This feeling of elation, Bruno. This swelling of the heart and throbbing at the temples—I'm guessing. I can imagine what you felt as the shoal took off and you remained alone, triumphant. The only man in the vast seas. I envy you, I'm proud of you. Because what more can a mortal do than decide his own destiny? (I can say things like this with such a deep inner conviction that they sound sincere to me.) This is a desperate decision, and your chances of succeeding are slim indeed, but your chances, Bruno, no longer interest you: they belong to other realms. To the realms of the first person plural, where one is weighed on scales: "My Jew for your Jew"; "According to my calculations, I killed only two and a half million," etc. Even the dual was too plural for you, and the truly crucial things had to be said in the singular. So you became a salmon. You stripped yourself of all attachments till you were able to put your finger on the wounded vein through which your life was flowing away. The kernel of bare existence, the hidden force you transformed on your journey into a geometric line the eye can follow and the finger can trace on the map. And you also know what I feel for you, or I would never have gone to Narvia, and racked my brains till I nearly went mad—

And so, in the name of everything that has happened between us these last few days, I demand an immediate answer: I demand a refutation of something I just heard from "her" lips. Words she blurted out against her will, like a burning hiccup from her depths straight to the pen that writes on your behalf. I wrote the words, and read them later in amazement: "Bruno, that sly, fatal enemy of language." And with a malicious laugh she added: "Bruno the Nihilist."

Now I write with a steady pen: Bruno Schulz. Ingenious architect of a singular linguistic experience, the magic of which lies in its fertility, a plethora almost rotting with verbal juices. Bruno who knows how to say everything in ten different ways, each as accurate as the compass needle. A Don Juan of language, conquering with a mad, almost immoral passion, audacious explorer of linguistic geography . . . Could it be that you, Bruno, reached the limits of this world, and ran around like a madman on the beach when you couldn't find a suitable verbal vessel to sail you into the misty horizon? Is it possible that the last shore was the Danzig shore in '42? Answer me frankly. I will not tolerate cleverness. Did you, standing on the edge of the pier, panting with exhaustion and foaming at the mouth, look back at the fantastic topography you had left behind—all the twisted ravines and molten lava quarried with your pen from the walls of a simple schoolchild's notebook—did you laugh triumphantly and with relief for having led us all astray through your intricate labyrinths, slyly destroying the very language of humanity?

You're not answering me. And she is also silent. But it isn't her usual silence: it's a kind of self-control.

I put my pen and notebook down on the beach with a stone on top so they won't fly away in the wind, and I go into the water. I wade in over my head, open my eyes in the stinging saltiness, and try to see you from a different vantage point. In the illusive light. The light of the water.

And now tell me: must I charge you with treachery of a very specific kind? Should I write that the sweet frenzied coupling of your despair with your talent for human language engendered one of the greatest frauds in culture and literature, only no one understands?

I write with my finger in the water: Was it in order to perpetrate this fraud that you fertilized language with your seed, so that it proliferated wildly all double chins, and you multiplied its circulatory systems and gave it seven hearts to pump conflicting bloodstreams, and reduplicated its nervous system till it went crazy with morbid sensitivity?

I stare at the water in amazement: the letters daubed on the waves are still there. I continue to write: And when this elephantine language began to sag under its own weight, did you go even further with your skills, using them like germs to decompose the corpse? I look at the letters in the water and wait to see if she'll erase this suspicious writing. She doesn't. I continue: Would you admit to me, Bruno, that from a painter of language you turned into its bitter caricaturist, and your own no less? And what for? Why did you do that to us?

"Silly questions! He wanted to find an even richer world," she says suddenly, jolting me again, swiftly reading the water and rubbing it out, but not completely, gathering it up in two sheer wavy handkerchiefs, rather, and removing it from sight, then flowing on, a little uncertainly.

"I can't talk to you about Bruno," I say sharply. "You won't listen to a single word of criticism."

"You mean I'm biased," she says, winking with a wave that flashes in the sun. "I couldn't agree with you more, dearest, because I will not deny myself the right to be blindly, totally in love, yes yes," she says, tossing a wavy scarf with silver-blue embroidery and swimming with me close to the shore. "With unconditional love, Neuman, which I'm sure you know a lot about—from books."

She bounces a salty little wave into my mouth.

I swallowed my humiliation in silence. I had important matters to attend to, and only a few hours left with her. The mayor of Narvia was about to leave for Gdansk that night in his ancient motorboat and he had agreed to take me along. The following day I was supposed to be in Warsaw, from there—to fly to Paris, and then home. I was extremely pressed for time, but I didn't want her to notice. I whispered in her ear about the view from the water, the simple architectural style of the church in Narvia, the interesting structure of the cottages . . . She was restless. She was holding something back. I waited patiently. I turned over and doggy-paddled, whistling a little tune, all ears.

Stringy, jellylike tendrils, strangely twisted, and the spittle of shame and anger filled the water. Then a great wave arched under me, reared back—and tossed me high in the air, and there she was, at my side.

"You're right, you're so right. Damn you for the way you hurt me every time. He did want to murder language, it's true. He wanted to make it fulsome, offensively replete with cloying, um—" (She was trying to sneak a quotation in, the cow, and I didn't recognize this one, but I knew she couldn't have made it up. How many hundreds of rare quotations had she hidden in her cellars?)

"Thousands," she corrected me with a malicious smile and continued: "After all, even when Bruno was a little boy he understood this, yes, and he longed not merely for a new world but for a totally new language that would enable him to describe it, because even then, long before he came to me, he guessed . . . he knew, yes . . ."

"Guessed what? Knew what?"

She rolls over and spews a small fountain, circling faster and faster. I look down at the water below, to keep from getting dizzy. "At the ghetto in Drohobycz," she circles me, quoting, "Bruno was employed by an SS officer named Landau, who had an enemy, also an SS man, named Gunther. And one day Gunther shot Bruno, and went to Landau and said, I killed your . . ." and she whirls around, forming a vortex that sucks me in and drains all my thoughts, till I sink helplessly down into the depths, and reflect that the explanation must be that Bruno, sensitive as he was, had guessed everything years before it actually happened. And for that reason, perhaps, he had begun to write, to train himself in the new language and the new grammar. He understood humanity and knew; he heard the rumbling long before anyone else heard it. He had always been the weak link. Yes. He knew that a language that will admit a sentence like "I killed your Jew . . . In that case, I will now kill," etc., a language where such verbal constructs do not turn to poison in the speaker's mouth—is not the language of life, human and moral, but a language infiltrated many ages past by evil traitors, with one intention—to kill.

"But it wasn't only language," she says in passing, and I skid to a halt with the screeching waves that throw me up again on a cold water spout. "It wasn't only language," she whispers again, letting me flounder in the air before letting me down gently a moment later in her generous arms, freckled with sand and aglow in the light of the sun. "It was the whole world Bruno wanted to change, yes, everything based on time-worn rules and traditions, and belonging to the petrified, mechanical systems of the past . . . ah, my Bruno, the nihilist . . ." she gurgles and departs with strange haste, her head held high, leaving two briny furrows behind her.

I lunged after her and caught her by the throat, rasping furiously, "*The Messiah, The Messiah*, you hear! This instant or I'll—" She boggled at this and smiled fearfully, suddenly humbled by my rage. "Oh, all right," she muttered, "but don't think it's because of your silly performance. It's only because I know that you, too, love him, yes," and she opened up a long, narrow abyss below and plunged me into it for an eternity and a half, till I landed in a dim and viscous watery deposit, and then from out of the whirling clouds of primeval dust I wandered dizzily over immense underwater jungles, and galloped along forking trails, on the banks of which grew dense gloomy bushes bearing the withered fruit of barren speculations, and giant ferns of first drafts that flourished halfway and froze, and clustered vines of legendary folk, and I cleared a path through the filmy foliage, so tangled it strangled me, and looking around, I shrieked these are not the important things, this is not yet a "book," the authentic life-size creation, in all its natural depth, precision, and complexity, this is not the inimitable brilliance of the Age of Genius my Bruno envisioned in childhood, one wild spring day a long long time before the world began to warp and die . . .

"Enough!!" she roared, and bared her sharp green reefs at me. "Enough of your meddling and torturing me like this!" And I screamed: "The truth now! Everything 'he' left you! The scorching smell! One irrevocable utterance in his own language, or at least the minutes preceding that brilliant utterance I will never understand. I want the big secret from you now and I won't take anything else!"

And she wails and spits, and pretends to oust me, and tries to scare me with the shadows of sharks she uses her pleated skin to project around me, or rudely breaks wind through the Strait of Gibraltar, but I have nothing left to lose, so I smack her with my hands and feet. "The book," I scream through raging billows. "His final conclusion, the marrow of our existence!" And she sobs and bangs her head against the rocks that crack like eggshells, and combs her body till it hurts with the skeletons of sunken ships, and sticks a long, watery finger down her throat and vomits a shoal of dead fish all over me and fragments of half-digested dinghies, and suddenly she gathers her water crinolines and lifts a thousand petticoats to expose the bareness of lost continents and arid wastelands to the staggered eye of the sun, and for a moment we are all floating in dry air—fishes, shrimps, nets, the wrecks of sailing ships and submarines, shells and pirate swords and bottled messages from survivors who died long ago on desert islands, and a moment later the water bursts through with a mighty groan, covers the sunken continents, stirring the dust of earliest memories, raising a huge green folio before my eyes, that floats solitary in the depths, shimmering with a thousand tiny bubbles in the margins, a troubling, monkish folio, dampening the spirits of the fast-recoiling fish, and I don't know what I'm doing here, floating over it, laughing and crying, and straining my eyes to read the title spelled in thick green seaweed: *The Messiah*.

At Easter time, the end of March or the beginning of April, Shloma, son of Tobias, was released from the prison where he had spent the winter after the skirmishes and imbecilities of summer and autumn. In the year when the things which shall be told herein took place, young Bruno peered out of the window of his house just as Shloma left the barbershop and stood on the threshold of Trinity Square. Bruno beckoned his old friend to come over (*"There's nobody home, Shloma!"*) to view his drawings of the Age of Genius, that void in time at the heart of boredom and habit. In those few, remarkable days, little Bruno, with the help of his paintbrush, successfully broke out of the heavy metal bars imprisoning us, into a torrent of light, a ravishing first bloom—

Bathed, barbered, and scented, the released prisoner Shloma studied the drawings of his excited young friend.

"*One might say,*" said Shloma, after studying them, "*that the world has passed through your hands in order to be reborn. To shed its scales like a marvelous lizard. Ah, do you think,*" he inquired, "*that I would steal and commit a thousand and one follies if this world had not fallen into turpitude and decay? . . . What else can one do in such a world? How not succumb to doubt and flagging spirits when all meaning is locked away, and you knock on the bricks as on a prison wall? Oh, Bruno, you were born too late.*"

"*To you, Shloma,*" said Bruno, "*I can reveal the secrets of these drawings. I always doubted that it was I who drew them. Sometimes they seem like unintentional plagiarisms. Something that was whispered to me, that reached my ear . . . as though a stranger had used my inspiration for purposes unknown, for I confess*"—he added quietly, looking into Shloma's eyes—"*I have discovered the 'real thing' . . .*"

So, in these words, Bruno spoke to me in the Age of Genius, from the book called *Sanitorium under the Sign of the Hourglass.* But what this "real thing" was I never learned, because Shloma son of Tobias, a slave of passion, and a coward and traitor besides, used the opportunity of being alone in the house with little Bruno to steal a coral necklace belonging to Adela the servant girl, as well as her dress and shoes, the patent-leather shoes which so fascinated Bruno ("Do you understand the terrible cynicism of this symbol on a woman's foot, her provocative strutting on dainty heels? How can I leave you under the spell of this symbol? Heaven preserve me if I . . .").

And we all missed the moment.

And I was Shloma son of Tobias.

Again.

For one moment I was released from prison. And I stood "*Bathed, barbered, and scented on the threshold of Trinity Square in Drohobycz, utterly alone before the empty square, the blue sky flowing sunless overhead. This large, clean square lolled in the afternoon like a fish tank, like a new year not yet begun. I stood on the threshold, gray and hidden, not daring to shatter this perfect ball of a day with a decision.*"

Up in the window I noticed a small thin boy, with a triangular-looking skull—a high, broad forehead, and a pointed chin. And at first it seemed to me that he was being reflected from one of the glass panes, but then I recognized Bruno, that wonderful child, always afire with precocious ideas.

He called to me and said, "*We're all alone in the square here, you and I.*" And smiled gloomily, adding, "*How empty the world is. We could divide it up between us and give it a new name . . . Come, come up a minute, and I'll show you my drawings. There's nobody home,* Momik!"

[9]

AS SOON AS I ESCAPED from the gleaming expanse of Trinity Square and entered the dark vestibule of Bruno's house, a crowd quickly filled the square, as if my leaving had been the cue for a tremendous cast of characters to start the play. "See," said Bruno, standing with me at the window, "they're all here."

And it was so: all the townspeople, our acquaintances, all of Bruno's family, his classmates and teachers from the Gymnasium, were there, conspicuous among them his two drawing teachers—Chashunstovsky, the "long fellow," and the diminutive Adolf Arendt, smiling esoterically in all directions. We also saw mad Tuoya: Tuoya who lives in the nettle field and sleeps on a three-legged bed among the rubbish heaps; and there was Uncle Hieronymus: tall, with a hawklike nose and terrifying eyes, who hadn't stepped out of his bedroom since the day he lost his mind; he sat there, grim and furious, growing more fantastically furry by the day, engaged in silent, deadly combat with the powerful lion, earnest as a patriarch, who was concealed behind the palm trees on the tremendous tapestry that covered the wall of the room where he lived with wrinkled Aunt Retitia. Everyone but everyone was there: the neighbors with their children and their dogs, bedecked with ribbons, and a small, noisy crowd of apprentices from the family dry-goods store, Henrietta, who trailed the lovely Adela, fast asleep even as she minced on patent-leather shoes, her lips parted in an errant kiss, her robe loose . . .

"What is this?" I asked Bruno. "What are they all celebrating?"

"The Messiah," the child answered, making a magical sign at the window.

The square glowed brighter, and it was now impossible to look without being blinded. People seemed to be illuminated from within, glowing and dimming in turn, as if connected to a single power source which had not yet been properly adjusted.

And when I looked at Bruno I had no doubt that he was the source of this power: the veins stood out on his precociously broad forehead, like the wires of an overheated oven. For a moment his face burned with a strong red light, then turned pale. But another difference was marked in him, which I could not evaluate at first glance: in the midst of all the glowing and dimming, Bruno was galloping backward and forward in "time" as well: one moment he was a mature man burning with tremendous force, and the next moment, an alert and lively child straining to contain his fullness in the hoops of his frail body, and later—but what's this?—he is regressing further still, to the plumpness of babyhood, the downiness of—

"Bruno!" I cried, "control yourself!"

He looked at me, iridescent and dizzy with changing time, and shrugged his shoulders, smiling as if to say that there was no longer anything he could do about it.

And at that moment the Messiah strode into the square. He came from the direction of Samburska Street, to the left, the narrow street between the church and Bruno's house. He came riding a small gray donkey, dusty with endless wandering. On the threshold of the square they stopped, and the Messiah dismounted. He flashed a look at Bruno, who answered with a small nod of assent. These exchanges were so intimate that even I, standing at Bruno's side, could not make out the face of the Messiah. But I did see him spank his donkey affectionately with an open hand, to send it on its way. And then a strange thing happened: the Messiah himself stepped back and disappeared!

With indescribable disappointment I looked at Bruno, but he smiled, indicating with his eyes that I should watch the square: the donkey mingled with the people, and no one paid any attention to it. Donkeys were a common enough sight in the square. But wherever the donkey wagged its short tail, people froze for a moment, and then shook themselves and continued to walk and chat with their friends. But their strings had been visibly cut: expressions of bewilderment and shame lighted on the faces of those at whom the donkey had wagged its tail. They seemed dumbfounded, as though seeing each other for the first time. They stammered. They appeared to be choking, as if they could not remember how to breathe. And they slowed their pace: everywhere feet tripped and knees buckled. Movements were hesitant, angular. They tried to cry for help, but the only sound they could make was a muffled, throaty animal sound. The little donkey continued at a steady pace. Half the square was already under the spell of its pendulum tail, and the other half did not yet feel anything. On one side there was only silence and slow, confused awakening, and on the other side life went on with loud gaiety. The square looked like a man with half his face paralyzed, the other half exhausting itself with mimicry.

"They're forgetting," Bruno beamed. "They're forgetting!"

"Forgetting what?" I asked anxiously, but I had already begun to guess.

"Everything," answered the boy, sucking his cheeks with emotion. "Everything: the language they spoke, their loves, the passing moment, look!"

Now the square was in the midst of a slow, tame dance. The donkey, whose work was done, left the gleaming tank, tarried for a moment on the threshold, and disappeared down the street between two rows of crowded houses, braying with strange donkey glee.

The braying seemed to be a signal: people returned to life, and I sighed with relief. The square looked like a newborn baby and the braying was its first cry. But before long I stopped rejoicing. I looked and knew I didn't understand what I beheld; the scene taking place before me was sleight-of-hand. But whose hand? And for what purpose?

"Mother and Father," Bruno whispered to me. "Look at my mother and father."

His dead father and his mother. His father with the somber prophet's head, lost in reverie, suddenly shook himself awake and looked at his wife, plumpish Henrietta, or Ponchik, as she was affectionately called. He wanted to say something to her, but like all the others in the square, he couldn't find the words.

"No, not like that," Bruno whispered from afar. "Not in words, because—"

They also felt it. And not only they. Words had become as superfluous as primitive tools down in the square. The mute feelings of Bruno's parents were dangerously condensed, and there was no release. Their faces wore expressions of acute distress, of pleading, of passion, and finally—of terror and loss. They held hands, and for a moment were carried away from the commotion in the square, as together they tried to clear a path for themselves. His mother's breasts heaved with yearning, and their movement outlined the missing rhyme of an old forgotten ballad; in some imperceptible way, dizzy scenes were projected out of his father's mind, the reflections of his troubled soul, together with a sprinkling of pleas for help and pleas for understanding. But this time Henrietta was clearly not able to help. She smiled helplessly and slowly retreated, waving in apology, swallowed by the crowd. At that moment—and I could sense this even from afar—an invisible thread which must have been stretched between them broke with a twang.

"They never did understand each other," mused Bruno sadly, with lowered head. Meanwhile, on the other side of the square, next to the statue of Adam Mickiewicz, happier events were in progress: Edzio, the young cripple, swinging his muscular torso on crutches, finally met Adela face to face. Stout Edzio, whose cruel parents took his crutches away at night, and who dragged himself like a dog every night to Adela's window, to press his deformed face against the pane, and watch the lovely servant girl deep in slumber, sprawling naked and moist for columns of bedbugs, wandering through the wilderness of sleep . . . He saw her, and she, without opening her eyes, saw him. And a small spark passed between them, with a trembling that shook the people all around. And they stood and stared at each other, and for a moment Adela's eyes were opened: a thin white film—like the film over a parrot's eye—was lifted, and light flashed, like a magnesium bulb. She saw his soul, understood the full force of his tragedy. She read the story of his nightly vigil over her dreams and felt the column of bedbugs turn to fingers of desire between her thighs. She contracted with pain and pleasure, and let him kiss her, in his thoughts, for the first time. She blushed deeply all over when she realized he hadn't moved from his place at all, and that her lips had remained parted in a dream, and yet she had been kissed, wildly and passionately kissed, and she would never know such a kiss again . . .

"What's happening there?" I demanded to know. "What are you doing to them, Bruno?"

He looked at me with disappointment. "Don't you see? Don't you understand? The Messiah has come. My Messiah. And they're forgetting. And nothing that used to help in the sad illusion of their former lives can avail them now. They have only what they have here—and that's more than enough," he said, indicating Edzio and Adela, who though standing in the crowd were off by themselves, enveloped by thin fibers of brightness. "They're turning into artists, Shloma, great creators! Great as the stature of man!"

"Artists? All I see here are miserable wretches whose lives are falling apart!"

"Ah, that's only because they haven't understood what's required of them yet, and what they're capable of doing," Bruno reassured me, swimming like a tiny fish through the room, gaily swishing his tail, rolling over on his back and returning to stand beside me. "Creation in the fullest sense of the word. In all its splendor. Oh, Shloma, this is the Age of Genius we've always dreamed of, I in my writing and you in your prison. Very shortly you, too, will come to understand that the thousands of years of existence that preceded this were only drafts, the tentative, early gropings of evolution . . ."

Groups were breaking up below into their various components: families separated in bewilderment with a mild pang of regret, wondering why nothing was holding them together anymore, or whether anything ever had. The two esteemed drawing teachers who were engrossed in a lively conversation about the marvelous poet Jachimowitz stopped talking in the middle of a sentence: their hands still traced complicated arguments in the air, but the furnace that had forged their enthusiasm into words was now extinguished. They stood facing each other, studying their still-darting hands, and then went their different ways without regret, trying with what was left of their old thinking to remember how they used to be able to get so excited about words and frozen rhymes.

"They have no literature." Bruno glowed. "No science, no religion, no tradition, even Edzio and Adela have already forgotten each other . . ."

He was right: the two had drawn apart to opposite sides of the square, and on their faces there was not a sign that they missed each other. "There's no longing for the past," Bruno continued, "only a passion for the future; there are no immortal works; there are no eternal values except for the value of creation itself, which is not a value at all but a biological drive, as powerful as any other; look at them, Shloma—they don't remember anything beyond this moment, only this moment in the world of the square is not a single chime of the church clock; it is, shall we say, a time crystal containing one experience only, which can last a year or an instant, yes, my Shloma"—Bruno continued, and now he looked like a real fish, swimming delightedly across the water-soaked green folio that floated beneath us in the abyss—"these are people without memory, firsthand souls, who in order to continue to exist must re-create language and love and each coming moment anew, and to sew the knots that burst from—"

"But this is so cruel, Bruno, so terribly cruel!" I screamed and gulped water. "You can't do this to people! Not everyone is made of the same— hah—original stuff! Some of us actually need an orderly framework, for law, for continu— Oh, Lord! Look over there!"

Off the square, by the mailbox, where the voracious ants of memory quickly and efficiently unraveled the last fibers of the past from the present moment, stood Bruno's uncle, Hieronymus. It seemed that the man was having a ghastly experience, that the transformations of the new age were putting his frail guess at existence to an impossible test: he trembled and shivered. He perspired and panted. Aunt Retitia looked on despairingly, and didn't dare touch him. Strange lumps protruded from his elegant suit, now here, now there. No one clearly understood what was going on, perhaps not even Uncle himself. He leaned heavily against the mailbox (which was also full of chirping as the various components of the letters and the words and feelings in them were dismantled—the ones that had been sent before the new revolution) and listened with closed eyes and a tortured face to the stormy argument within.

And then it happened, that which our poor language is incapable of documenting but can only report as a dry, pale protocol: suddenly Uncle's agonized body gave off a light explosive sound, and a deep sigh of relief, and he became "two." The long battle between him and the old lion in the tapestry had suddenly ended with an unexpected but mutually beneficial reconciliation, and they succeeded at last in pooling their resources to untie the knot of animosity that had choked them both for years, at the price of a small compromise on Uncle's part, an agreement to make himself a little smaller inside so there would be room for the lion, and they would now both be able to carry on, living the tolerable and perhaps even pleasant life of a couple.

Yes. Clearly they were very well suited to each other. Because their long and violent struggles during which the lion trapped in the tapestry would rear and roar faintly while Uncle barked—had in effect occluded the fierce attraction and desperate desire between these two lonely and imprisoned hearts, too vain to admit as much. And Aunt Retitia, of whom I have always been fond, and whom everyone considered to be a dam of rationality between two stormy lakes of madness, was now exposed in all her fanatical, petty wretchedness, and everyone saw that her existence was only justified as a representation of the old view, "law and order," tranquillity in its most banal sense, and indeed now, with her *raison d'être* gone— Oh, I could no longer look at what was happening to her there, next to the red mailbox, and, oh no, on the ground . . .

"Go ahead and look," said Bruno with mild satisfaction. "She isn't there anymore."

When I refused to raise my eyes, Bruno whispered comfortingly, "People like Aunt Retitia, Shloma, are the secondhand souls I spoke of; they have existence only as secondary vessels, feeding on the creative tension of the bulk of mankind who are doubtless original creators, and their existence is justified only as a constant warning to us all of the terrible dangers in store for us should they disappear . . . Ah, Shloma, from the look on your face it is evident that all this is very frightening to you . . . very strange to you . . . but you see, this is our chance to live anew, with the meaning you and I intend, otherwise we're statues, trapped from birth till death, and we have no hope of being rescued from the rock in which a wise, wise and perhaps not very ingenious, or ingenious but not very merciful, sculptor has carved a bas relief. And the Messiah, Shloma, is the one who calls us to freedom, who releases us from the stone, sends us flying weightless through the square like confetti to re-create our lives with every passing minute and write epics in impetuous rendezvous, because by now it must be as clear to you as it is to me that all other roads lead to failure, to defeat, to prison, to the old culture that contracted elephantiasis . . ."

I was silent. I was furious at his exaggerated self-confidence, and the conceit that made him think everyone thought as he did. Naturally I do not dispute certain of his ideas, but such an extreme revolution has to be carefully weighed and planned, to give it a basis and a system. I threw a look at poor Aunt Retitia and felt nauseated again. Better not look! Such a cruel end might also befall certain others. By the way, I deliberately said "end" and not "death," because it would be hard to describe what happened to the good aunty as "death": beside the red mailbox, on the cobblestones, was a pile of strange debris, like sawdust: this no doubt was the residue of all the adjectives, nouns, and verbs for which Aunty had served as conjunction. A cool, indifferent heap. "As in life," says Bruno, who listens in on all my thoughts. "And in fact she is not dead, Shloma, because she never really was alive, alive in the sense that you and I . . . etc. And of course I'm certain you didn't suspect for a minute that I would do away with anyone in order to bring happiness to others?"

I turned away angrily. The square was shaken again. It seems that some of the terror that marked the beginning of the new age had now been eliminated. As happens when forests burn to ashes, here, too, the forces of life resurged, and the first green shoots began to appear: families broke up, and their transparent threads remained in spools all over the square, while new, transient families appeared, sometimes as single persons, who in this remarkable way found a happiness they had never known with spouse and children. New friendships fused between people we had never imagined to have anything in common: amiable Adolf Arendt, the little drawing master, was deeply involved (quite embarrassingly, to my mind) with crazy Tuoya, and interlocking over their heads like horns were glorious opportunities for flights of fancy; Bruno's father, his dead father, finally realized his former passion and soared like a bird over the square, over the entire city. That is, his feet never left the ground, but it was clear to anyone who wished to believe as much that the man was indeed airborne.

And the marvelous thing about all we beheld is that it took place in total silence and not in words. The square was still trickling with whispers and the acoustic condensation of feeling-vapors, which I cannot convey here because of the lamentable impotence of language. I can only say this: Just as the blind have a highly developed sense of hearing in compensation, so now did these mute essences, nameless and wordless, manifest their most latent expressions, and the people responded immediately with a hitherto unfamiliar instinct to the new stimulus. Rapid mutations in sensory perception took place as well. They were all involved in the new and fascinating effort. "Now do you understand?" asked Bruno quietly. "They are all artists."

Except for Aunt Retitia and a few others, however, the revolution claimed no casualties. People looked happier and livelier than ever before. Their blood bubbled through their veins like wine, and I could hear it singing. They shone from within. Men and women everywhere listened with wonder and pleasure to their own *ning*, and nodded in joy and assent. The fact of their existence had suddenly become a palpable reality to them, just as decay and weakness had seemed to be before. Life itself was pungent, a provocative pleasure. Near the mailbox stood Uncle Hieronymus stroking his mustache with his paw. Men and women were seen embracing with a wonderful passion that did not, however, embarrass their neighbors (though I preferred to look elsewhere).

"But, Bruno," I said in confusion, "here you are, offering us life as the very breath of passionate creation. In such a world would thoughts of murder not be possible?"

The boy raises his flashing black eyes to me. He swims past the folio in the seaweed like a youth strolling through his garden. Small hermit crabs hasten away to nestle in the thickness of the letters, sea anemones beseech him with Madonna arms.

"And let us suppose," says Bruno mellifluously, "that such thoughts did arise, due to some misconception or other: obviously they would never be put into practice even in the individual's mind. He would not be able to understand them, he would not be able to grasp them, Shloma! For him they would be only a vague passing anguish, contrary to the most basic precepts of his life. And not only the thought of murder, my Shloma: any thought bearing the bitter traces of decay and putrefaction, destruction and fear. No one will be able to understand such thoughts, just as in the old world you could never really understand a person coming back to life, or the backward flow of time. Because I am speaking to you about a totally different life, about the coming phase of human evolution . . . Didn't we decide to divide the world between us, Shloma, and give it a new name, or maybe you regret that now and prefer the easy way, gazing at Adela's shiny patent-leather shoes and wishing to return to prison?"

And he raises his eyes imploringly.

I think of various arguments against his futile ideas: for instance, how could law and justice exist in such a world, and how would a developed and systematic science be possible, not to mention politics and international cooperation, armies and police forces, and what about the—

But my thoughts turned gloomy. Why, in fact, it had failed already, it had all been a colossal disappointment, and no force in the world could prevent these things from being used for the vilest ends. And, I asked myself in a rage, were Roosevelt and Churchill the "good"? Against evil we pit our tanks and planes and submarines, and we set up a different evil. I was miserable. I wanted to get out of the sea and go home, to forget that I had ever been here and asked these questions. But I didn't have the strength to lift a finger. They'll only disappoint me again. I dipped my forehead in the water. We can't be doomed to this, can we? Bruno must be wrong. "Tell me please," I ask him, trying vainly to sound lighthearted and stinging. "On what do you base your belief that these bits of confetti in the air will ever want to communicate and create, and what would prevent them from drifting down to the cobblestones, or just hovering in the air unconsciously? Tell me, Bruno!"

"You didn't understand at all," says the child, says the fish sadly, and explains, slowly and with evident disappointment, what I should have grasped long ago. "They're human beings all, and therefore creators. They're doomed to be. They're compelled to be by virtue of their origins—to create their own life, their love and hatred and freedom and poetry; we are all artists, Shlomo, only some of us have forgotten that, and others prefer to ignore it out of some enigmatic fear and there are those who understand it only on their deathbed, while others—like a certain aunty whose name I won't mention out of respect for the disintegrating—don't understand it even then . . ."

"And we? The poets? The musicians and writers?"

"Ah, Shloma, compared to real art, natural art, literature and music are nothing but ephemeral copy work, a superficial interpretative craft, not to say poor plagiarism, lacking in imagination and talent . . ."

"If so," I asked with extreme caution in order to avoid hurting him too much, "what would you say, how could we continue living in our old world, after a certain act we've heard about was committed, an act attributed to a man you don't yet know, or may have forgotten, who shot a Jew to challenge his rival, and said . . ." "I told you already"— Bruno interrupted me, finning excitedly and unwilling to listen to what I had to say—"I've already told you three times that such things are inevitable in a putrefying culture." He swam a few circles around himself, dived down, and floated up to me again, steering with his tail like a lusty sperm. "And now everyone will understand," he said, "that whosoever kills another human being destroys a uniquely idiosyncratic work of art which can never be reconstructed . . . a whole mythology, an infinite Age of Genius . . ."

Suddenly he stopped talking and peered at me suspiciously. Perhaps he wondered whether what I had said pertained to him in some way. His small figure darted back and forth from the exterior of the boy to that of the fish. My eyes were disturbed for a minute by a blinding glare, the shiny scales of a shoe or a passing fish, Adela's shoe or the fold of a gleaming wave sent my way perhaps to distract me, and when I looked again I saw that Bruno was in convulsions, throughout which he was shrinking more and more, not in size, perhaps, but in essence, his existence becoming more airy, more abstract . . .

For an instant he materialized again: half his face, the cleft of his mouth, one eye, and a throbbing gill. With a terrible smile he said, "In our new world, Shloma, even death will belong to man, and when a person wishes to die, he will only have to whisper his body code to his soul, which will know how to dismantle the person's unique existence, the secret of the individual's authentic essence, and there will be no more mass death, Shloma, just as there will be no more mass life!"

"Wait a minute!" I shouted. "Don't leave me! Not after you've infected me with such unendurable passions! You can't leave me now!"

"You could always do what I did," he said. "Come with me, or choose your own way."

"Bruno," I groaned, "I deceived you. I'm weak . . . I'm a prisoner by nature . . . I love my fetters . . . yes, Bruno, humbled and shamefaced I stand before you and confess: I am a traitor and a coward . . . with a pathetic Retitia-like attitude . . . Now you know . . . I wasn't born for the Age of Genius . . . If Adela's shiny shoe were here, I would take my chance and steal it and run away from you, as I did . . . as I always do . . . Help me, stay with me . . . I'm scared, Bruno."

Suddenly he fluttered, floundered, stretched his thin body into palpability, and was drawn backward by a tremendous force, sucked up with a whistle. "Bruno!" I screamed, "wait a minute!" He froze. The world held its breath. The sea turned steely blue. "Bruno," I cried humbly, "forgive me for detaining you at such a moment, but this is very important. Do you by any chance know the story Anshel Wasserman told the German called Neigel?"

Bruno swiveled a gill and shut his eyes with concentration. "It's a fabulous story, oh yes," he said, and his strange face lit up. "Only there's . . . ha! The devil take it! I've forgotten!" And with a smile, as though remembering suddenly, he added, "But of course! That was the essence of his story, Shloma, you forget it and you have to recall it afresh every time!"

"And could someone who never knew it, had never heard it in his life, remember it?"

"Just as a person remembers his name. His destiny. His heart. No, my Shloma, there is no one who doesn't know that story."

His voice faded. His whole body convulsed. I hid my face in my hands. I heard a strange sound, as if something big were being swallowed up by an invisible mouth. A heart-wrenching groan sounded through the sea, and a moment later Bruno was no longer with us.

Despondently I turn to her now, and she doesn't answer. I was frightened. I was really terrified at the thought of her leaving me now,

now of all times, when I need her so much; when I grow weaker and weaker and don't feel like going home and lack the strength to write this story in a language suffering from elephantiasis. Come, I sob weakly, imploringly, Come, I want to cuddle you, to forget myself; so hard and obstinate was Bruno's loneliness that we all became the lost and lonely . . . we sank into a bas relief carved by a cunning but not ingenious sculptor, or perhaps ingenious but certainly not merciful, and we suffer pangs of insatiable hunger, or worse still: we have lost even the passion to satisfy our hunger. Oh, I whisper to her, into her little waves, the folds of her flesh, if our life is only in the ebbing, then anything that helps that ebbing is the hidden collaborator of death, and we ourselves are accomplices to murder. We are responsible murderers, albeit, looking out for our own welfare, polite and anxious, but murderers nonetheless. Under the guise of defending our interests, they are committing a crime against us, a crime against humanity, all those we ourselves appoint to defend us, who strangle our happiness little by little; I mean the authorities, authorities of any kind who inflict the few on the many, or the many on the few, and the judicial system that usually forces compromises between different kinds of justice and religion, based on the imperative of not raising questions, and our complacent morality, and time's obedient flock, the hands of the clock gathering the minutes in like sheep, and the fear and loathing that exist in us, the forceps with which we extract every crumb of closeness and love, and our tyrannical sanity, what are these if not the filthy canal down which we flow supinely to our death, and from time to time we find the miserable consolation of narrow-eyed pity and cautious love, and happiness ltd. and skeptical passion, canned bait, even I understand that man—man in the sense that Bruno and I say man—is capable of greater comfort and joy, of an incomparably richer color scale . . .

"Now you're talking," she says quietly, her eyes a little red, facing the setting sun. "At last you're beginning to understand." And she stretches her waves, sends them out, wide and calm, suddenly full of serene joy. We swim silently toward the small Polish town. The water is suddenly sweet in my mouth. I taste again and discover that I am not mistaken.

"Did he make it to the river?"

"You sensed it."

"And the falls? How did he leap the high falls? How did he swim against the current?"

"The only way he knew."

Silence. And then she asks, "And you? How will you leap the falls?"

"Don't ask me that now."

"You're back to your old self again, hey, Neuman? Starting to forget already?"

"How could you think such a thing! After all I've told you?! For shame!"

But two small water funnels gave the impression that she was faintly smiling, with dimples in her cheeks.

"Strange," she says, smacking her lips. "My little spies tell me that even now you're regretting most of the things you said—ah, what does it matter. It's your life, not mine. If you can call it a life. Too bad. Too bad. For a moment I believed you. For a moment I even . . . I even believed *in* you." Did I detect a note of tenderness in her voice? Was that an affectionate tone I heard? She doesn't answer. She flows off, swimming on her back. The sun caresses her with its last rays. Now she looks like Van Gogh's palette while he painted the wheat fields of the Low Countries. So beautiful, mysterious, and mature among the cloudy scarves over the horizon. Did Bruno recognize her beauty, or was he too involved in himself, in his unceasing efforts? Did he give her little tokens of affection, her man?

She is silent. Thin bluish veins stand out on her brow. A man like Bruno probably didn't notice her or her beauty but, rather, created his own enclosed sea to swim in. And she deserves love. She really does. Perhaps even the love of someone with far smaller claims than Bruno's. A more modest and practical man, not lacking in a certain poetic sensibility, who would be able to distinguish her subtle nuances, a man who is, well, a mere nothing compared to our lofty, transcendental, uncompromising Bruno, but perhaps precisely because he is so involved in the petty details of daily existence because he's such an obvious product of decadent society, and so human, such a man, I say to myself, perhaps he would be able to— "Nu, shut up, will you?" she says, and pounds me, accidentally on purpose, on a sharp rock, which was definitely not there a minute ago. "Now shut up, Neuman," she says again, more gently, and skims my aching rib consolingly. "You'll have a little sore there, like Bruno had. But yours will heal. Your kind heals. What's that? Somebody's calling you!"

"Pan Neuman! Mr. Neuman!" On the beach stands my landlady dressed in black. Waving energetically. It seems the mayor is going to

Gdansk. I have to get out of the water immediately and go with him. And the day after tomorrow I'll be home in Israel. "Home"—how strange and dull the word sounds to me now.

"You're kind of cute, you know that," she continues our interrupted conversation, licking my rib. "But you're not for me. No. Your territory, dearest"—she tarries while the reefs in the distant horizon shine with laughter—"your territory is the shore, yes, you like to wade in sometimes, but you prefer to stick close to 'her,' in case of danger, in case you suddenly feel like running away deep deep inside me. Yes, Neuman, you are a cautious one. I would say definitely a peninsular type. Oh yes."

And I suppress a groan.

"And now"—her voice is forced as she sets the waves dancing before me—"now do me one last favor. Don't be angry at this request of mine, and think of him for my sake, dearest, one last time think of him inside me, think of our Bruno, please, please, a moment from now we'll be separated and there'll be no one to tell me about him like this, about my Bruno, all alone here on the edge of the pier in Danzig, think of him, so I'll be able to think with you, you know: a minor health problem . . . please, please . . ."

Fluttering her long seaweed lashes, flaring her nostrils and quivering. No. She will not get me with her cheap tricks, with her feminine water colors. And I will not think of him. Let her explode. She's not going to lead me around anymore like a dizzy child, like a lover, to the port, to the edge of that pier, the rim of the old world, no!—I'm stronger than she is—no, she won't lead me to the light rain falling on him like tears, and he's so thin without his clothes, he has only his watch left for a moment, a watch that still tells the old time, and he jumps in, bravely and despairingly, come what may, off the tip of the nose of that huge, recumbent hag, lonely as the first pagan who ever rose from totem pole to the unseen God. What a magnificent flight, Bruno, what breadth and vision—

And she, here beside me, explodes with suppressed laughter.

By all the easterlies.

WASSERMAN

WHEN THE THIRD ATTEMPT TO KILL Anshel Wasserman came to
naught, the Germans sent him running to camp headquarters with a
very young officer named Hoppfler at his heels yelling, "*Schnell*." I can
see them now, as they leave the grounds of the lower camp, where the
gas chambers are, and approach the two barbed-wire fences concealed
by hedges between which new arrivals are forced to run naked past a
double file of Ukrainians, who set dogs on them and pound them with
clubs. The inmates call this route the *Schlauch*, or tube, and the Germans
with their peculiar humor call it *Himmelstrasse*—the Heavenly Way.

Anshel Wasserman wears a gown of gorgeous silk, and a large watch
on a chain that bounces against his chest as he runs. He is bowed and
wizened, with a wispy beard and an incipient hump on the back of his
neck. Though I've looked through hundreds of pictures of concentra-
tion-camp prisoners, I never saw anyone dressed like that before. Now
they pass the parade grounds and stop in front of the commander's
barracks. Wasserman is panting. The barracks are a grim-looking
wooden structure, two stories high, with curtained windows. A small
brass sign on the door says CAMP COMMANDER, and another, on
the outer wall, CONSTRUCTION—SCHOENBRUN INC., LEIPZIG,
AND SCHMIDT INC., MÜNSTERMAN. I know countless details of
this sort. What I need, though, are the essentials. Hoppfler says something to the Ukrainian sentry at the door. Now Anshel Wasserman
turns and sees me. It's only a side glance, but I feel reborn: after the
gloom and fog of recent months, his glance is like a clap on the back

that makes all the seemingly unrelated pieces of the mosaic fall neatly into place. Grandfather Anshel recognized me, I sensed him. He was terror-stricken. Behind the door, Camp Commander Obersturmbann-führer Neigel awaited him. Maybe I shouldn't be putting Grandfather through this, I reflected, maybe it was wrong of me to bring him back Over There, but I knew that he was my only chance since he had been there personally and was, I daresay, one of the few who knew the way out again, so having made up my mind to go in, I decided it would be better for me to go in with him.

The door opens and they enter the barracks. And there stands Herr Neigel. Well, well. Not at all as I imagined him over the years—fat and bestial, a butcher with a cruel grin. He is rugged-looking, though: tall and muscular, with a well-developed cranium, visibly balding, despite his close-cropped black hair, with two deep inlets over the forehead. His face is unusually large, his features elongated, with dark patches of stubble where the razor missed. His mouth is small and tense, and there's a kind of aggressive contempt in the corners of his eyes. The overall impression he makes is of a strong man who wishes to avoid attention. In my childhood, Grandfather always called him by his civilian title, Herr Neigel. A certain rapport must have been struck between them at some point, or was it a bargain? And what did Neigel call Grandfather? *Dreck Jude*? No, I don't think so. His face attests a dry pragmatism incompatible with *dreck Jude*. He looks up from his orderly desk, suppressing an ill-humored scowl at this interruption. "Yes, Untersturmführer Hoppfler?" he says, his voice loud and measured. Hoppfler reports a strange case. Neigel quickly interrogates him ("Did you try shooting?" "Yes, Commander." "Did you try the truck?" "Yes, Commander." "And gas, you say you tried gas?" "Yes, Commander, it all began with the gas." "And what about the others? Maybe the gas was defective?" "But no, Commander! The others died as usual. No irregularities, except for him").

Neigel groans at this waste of his time, stands up, smooths his trouser creases, and begins to fiddle absentmindedly with the silver medal on his lapel. Somewhat wearily he asks, "Is this some kind of joke, Untersturmführer Hoppfler?" But when the younger officer launches into a garbled explanation, Neigel dismisses him with a wave of the finger and an order to return a few minutes later after the short examination has been completed, "to remove the body." Neigel watches the young man leave the way people of a certain age watch an ambitious young man who never does anything right.

He draws a gun from his holster. A shiny black toy with a mag— Wait! Oh no! He's going to shoot Grandfather! I turn away. I look at the military placards on the wall behind the desk: THE FÜHRER COMMANDS—WE OBEY, RESPONSIBILITY DOWNWARD, OBE- DIENCE UPWARD. And then Neigel steps forward and puts the gun to Grandfather's temple and I hear myself scream out in fear with Grandfather, and the gun goes off, and Grandfather says inwardly, "It was like a fly buzzing between my ears," and the wooden stag head over the door falls down, nebuch, and one of its horns cracks. "Sholem aleichem, Shleimeleh, how you have changed, though I recognize you all the same. Hush, not a word. Time is running out and we have much to do. We have a story to tell."

This is how he addressed me. Not in his own voice, of course. I wrote "Grandfather says inwardly" because it's more accurate. His voice sounded like the voice I heard under water: like the faint crinkling of a thousand broken shells. Not like speech exactly, more like a steady flux of drab gray verbiage without the vigor of *speech*, yet closely re- sembling *written* language. Grandfather Wasserman spoke to me in the language he wrote, in the words that crumbled out of that torn yellow sheet of an old children's magazine, preserved since the beginning of the century among Grandma Henny's belongings. This was the first time I had ever heard him speak about his story. The story was really his life, and he always had to write it again from the beginning. Once when he was a little discouraged he told me he was rolling the story uphill like Sisyphus. Then he apologized for never having enough time or energy to listen to my story, but as he saw it, all stories were cut from the same cloth, "except that sometimes you have to push the stone uphill, and at other times you yourself are the cumbersome stone."

But now the German is incredulous: he looks from Grandfather to the gun, and twists the old man's head this way and that in search of a bullet hole. Later Neigel asks dryly in fluent Polish (his mother was Polskdeutsch, and, of course, the SS language course), "Are you getting smart with me, farshivy zhid?"

Let me clarify: he mumbled the epithet, scarcely moving his lips, in an effort to hide his discomfiture so conspicuous in the simple contours of his face. And Anshel Wasserman replied, "I do not understand either, sir. This is the fourth time already, and if your honor would be good enough to shoot me again in such a way that I can die, heaven forbid, because the pain is unbearable." Neigel turned a little pale and stepped back, and Anshel Wasserman whined, "Does the commander think I enjoy this?"

The humming I've known since childhood fills the silence: Anshel Wasserman is talking to himself, arguing, writing his story. And now I offer my pen to one whose needs are greater than my own, who has waited these many years for his story to be written. "Nu," he says. "So Esau was beside himself, beside himself, but I spoke the truth. Oh yes, I wanted death, may its bones rot. Why, even this morning, with the gas and the shooting and the truck, I desired it, choleria, and I wish it even now, but what happens? Nu, it seems I have a problem, perhaps I should consult a doctor? Ah well, I suffered, I tell you, and I tried to die. Zalmanson gazed at me wistfully in the gas chambers. He was already on the floor, nebuch, but he managed to give me a little sign, like, What is going on here, Wasserman? And, nu, what could I do? I stooped down and whispered so the others would not hear me—why vex them?—that I was sorry, but this was perhaps a defect from birth, may you never know. Nu, they were writhing and groaning, the dentists I had lived among for three months, and only I, Anshel Wasserman, was left standing like a lulav, and Zalmanson started laughing then, would that I had never heard him, snorting and weeping, such a laugh, till suddenly he died. He was the first to die! And it is important you should know this, Shleimeleh: Shimon Zalmanson the Jew, my only friend, editor of *Little Lights*, the children's magazine, died laughing in the gas chamber, a fitting death for a man like him, who believed that God reveals Himself through humor."

Now we are all three silent. I look at the old man: he looks just as I remember him, only thinner. Bald with brownish-yellowish skin and big, ugly moles, a bulbous nose, the sharp-chinned profile. As I live and breathe, Grandma Henny used to say, you look just like him. What are you talking about, Mama would scold her in Yiddish, examining the only existing portrait of Anshel as a child. Look at the nose on him and look at this one's nose.

The German walks back to his wide desk and stands behind it, deep in contemplation. As he thinks he sucks his cheeks. "No!" he pronounces, pounding the desktop with his fist (Wasserman: "I almost died, heaven forbid!") and again: "No! This is impossible!" And later, frankly angry with Wasserman: "We have an important job to do here and we have never yet failed!" And Grandfather withdraws farther into his gorgeous, enigmatic gown. (Wasserman: "I was ashamed. What do you think? I did not enjoy this at all. Tempting fate is not a thing I enjoy, why make trouble?") By way of encouragement he says to Neigel, "Commander, sir, if you would be good enough to view my little problem statistically perhaps; what, no?" But Neigel is alarmed. "Statistically?"

And Anshel Wasserman, taking alarm at Neigel's alarm. "Oh no! What have I said! Such a fool I am! Ha! Nu, yes, I only had in mind that since your people have a natural inclination for, that is, your fondness for numbers is well known, inclining you to a statistical—nu, I myself have been the recipient of a most excellent number here, and I—ah, what does the likes of me know of such matters? Less than nothing. But common sense, you see, informs me that when you slay millions upon millions of people throughout the world, then is it not possible, heaven forbid, begging your honor's pardon, that statistically speaking, one or two perhaps, yes, perhaps, would be unable? To die, that is."

Neigel leans forward, squinting suspiciously. "Two? You mean there are two of you?"

"No, Commander, heavens! Not two. This was only by way of illustration. Let us suppose two."

And he tries on a wry smile to pacify the German, but it's clear that anything he says will only aggravate the situation. Neigel scrutinizes him a little longer, like a scientist inspecting a new breed, and exhales with annoyance, or wonder, or contempt—curling his upper lip and emitting a humph-like sound.

And then he sits down, his head in his hands, suddenly lost in the room. The military telephone rings and he barks something into the receiver and slams it down. (Wasserman: "This yekke was afraid, Shleimeleh. See what the Good Lord had sent his way! A Jew who cannot die! What if other Jews were to catch on to undying now? And the Führer, the little housepainter from Linz, was bound to fly into a rage when he received a report of the Jew who foiled his grand design, the apple of his eye.")

Wasserman dares to raise his head and peer around. (Wasserman:

"It looked like the room of a very important *Offizier*, with maps and placards and cabinets full of goods, and books by the score, bless me, documents with the picture of the eagle, too, and I rejoiced for Neigel that he had been awarded such a lovely decoration, like a pig's nose ring, on his collar.") And they are both startled by a knock on the door.

Hoppfler steps in. "What do you want?" asks Neigel, weary now and suddenly ashen-faced. Hoppfler looks at Wasserman and nods sympathetically to Neigel. But when Neigel does not respond and appears to be lost in thought, Hoppfler reminds him, "You ordered me to come back for the body, Commander . . ."

Now we see Neigel decide to be angry, for a decision it is: he allows his minute-old anger to simmer. His chest turns into a pressure cooker, and the steam escapes through his shirt collar and spreads over his face, coloring it a bright red. (Wasserman: "Ai, I was familiar with this performance. Every day at five in the afternoon, Neigel would leave his office for a stroll in the garden . . . He was in the habit of attaching himself to one of the work squads just then returning to camp—before, on one pretext or another—is there ever any lack of pretexts?—selecting a prisoner and shooting him on the spot. This brought him the relief he sought. But in order to kill he had first to make himself so angry his face seemed to burst into flames! And then, how effortless it was! Nu, this is how I recognized the performance. And now this young genius Hoppfler was his target, holy lamb, and I saw that he was shocked or perhaps furious, understandably so, that Neigel had shamed him in front of a Jew like me, so while Neigel reprimanded him I looked away and pretended to have suddenly remembered ships at sea.")

Hoppfler walks out in deep humiliation, and Neigel's face instantly loses every trace of anger. It's as though he's peeled it off and thrown it away, which is of course all the more frightening to Anshel Wasserman, who starts to cringe, his collarbone protruding around the hump. Neigel strides angrily across the room. He stops behind Wasserman, and the old man, who has lost him for the moment, swerves frantically around, like a blind chick sensing a stranger approach the nest.

"Your name!" demands Neigel.

"Anshel Wasserman, sir."

"Age?"

"Age? Ah, hmm . . . about sixty years old today."

"To whom do you belong?"

"To Keizler, sir. The lower-camp commander."

"And what is your work there?"

"Well, sir, you see, I used to live among the dentists who extracted the teeth of the dead. Nu, yes, but I myself was not a dentist. Whereas they were."

Neigel stares uncomprehendingly. "You yourself were not?"

Wasserman, with strange humility: "No, I was not, sir."

"So what were you, then, damn you?"

"Me? So what could I be? A *Scheissemeister* I was there, yes. So I was." Neigel recoils and screws up his nose, and Grandfather, speaking softly, "Commander Keizler allows me to bathe once a week, sir. I am even allowed soap and soda, thanks to Keizler, so you needn't worry about unpleasant smells." The German grins sharply. That is, his mouth grins. His eyes remain aloof. "Interesting. A *Scheissemeister* who doesn't know how to die? Here's something I never heard before! Perhaps there is a wonder cure in shit?"

Grandfather Anshel, in other words, was in charge of the latrines in the lower camp. Bella, rest her soul, would have called this "yiches," or prestige.

Neigel has a plan, but he is as yet unsure about it. This is evident from the way he says, "And if—if we were to tie you up to four SS jeeps and send them off in different directions?" and the Jew, sadder but wiser: "I am afraid, sir, you would be left with four of my very inferior type."

"That, of course, is out of the question."

They say this together in Polish. Strangely in earnest. For a moment their eyes meet and Neigel, with a vestige of childish superstition perhaps, touches the cuff of his sleeve, by the SS skull-and-crossbones, which must be how they cast out the evil eye in his native village when two people say the same thing simultaneously. Or maybe he is warding off an even greater danger. I don't know: I know very little about Neigel. It was for Grandfather Anshel's sake that I went into my White Room. I don't have the strength for anything else.

Neigel jots something down in his little black notebook, and Anshel now notices the back of a framed portrait on the German's desk. (Wasserman: "Naturally I tried to guess who the lucky one was—his Polish woman? A loving mother-father? Or perhaps a likeness of the painter from Linz himself? That this Esau had children, nu, I never for a moment imagined such a thing, I assure you.")

Something has to happen now! Neigel will ask, "You say your name is Wasserman? Wasserman!"—leafing through his black notebook, staring at the name—"I know I've seen that name before . . . ach well, you're all named Wasserman . . . Tell me, though, were you ever—no, nonsense." Nonsense, yes, but before the German, his wispy bearded face lights up the room like a drunken moon, an orange moon.

(Wasserman: "When he said this, a smile crept like a cat over my lips. Because I knew what this Esau was thinking. Yes, and I even knew what questions would follow upon my answer, but in truth I never did envision such a thing befalling me here?!") And with unctuous false modesty he answers, "No, sir, we two have never met face to face heh heh, though if the commander would permit me an anecdote of sorts, uhm, I was a Hebrew writer once; that is, the stories I wrote for darling children were rendered into many a European language, including the eloquent German tongue, nu, yes." But then something Neigel cannot hear: "Anshel, Anshel, you vain old fool!" And in reply, compelled to justify himself: Nu, how stupid of me to wish for such a thing though it is true my stories were greatly popular even in Germany! But to wish a murderer for reader? Feh, Anshel! Have you lost your wits? Or are you so vainglorious you allot yourself more than an eighth of an eighth of the pride conceded to scholars of the Bible? And to Neigel Wasserman says miserably, with a terrible thirst that is not so alien to me, "I, sir, my name, that is, the name I signed to my little books, you saw it once perhaps, sir—Scheherazade? Anshel Wasserman-Scheherazade?"

Is that a glimmer in Neigel's eyes? Do they grow round with wonder, wonder too hurriedly quelled? Wasserman and I lean forward a little, as if pulled by a single string.

(Wasserman: "Did he recognize the name? Does he know? Ah, feh! Do not judge me, Shleimeleh, and find me wanting. I thirsted for a look of recognition, saying, 'Ah! Could it be? Are you the one we read and loved so well, whose stories we cut out of magazines for our collections?' Nu, do not deride me; after all, many thousands of children read me in those days. My 'Children of the Heart' was published in a dozen children's magazines throughout the continent of Europe. And only five years ago new editions were still appearing—though not a mite was I paid—and letters from fledgling readers reached me all the way from Prague and even Budapest! And I will tell you a little anecdote, even in the train that brought us here, may it choke on its own steam, in the midst of all the pushing and shoving and hunger and dizziness, a Jew wound his way to me, one neither young nor old, with a red burn covering half his face, and informed me that in his youth he had read my stories. Et! This Jew, poor thing, for ten years he and I had dined in each other's company at the same hour in Feintoch's restaurant on Kreditova Street. I sat here, he sat there. And of course he said not a word to me. But now in the train, nebuch, he began to cry wistfully over my stories, nu, think of it! Of all things to think of at such a time, and nu, I had no more consolation for him . . .")

Neigel leans back and plays with a small ruler. "I understand nothing about literature, *Scheissemeister*." And Wasserman blurts, "Nu, to each his own, your honor." And blanches with fear.

But Neigel does not get up and pound him with his heavy fist. Nor does he call in the Ukrainian sentry and order him to trample this impudent Jew. Neigel merely gazes at him, tracing fat figure eights and sloppy zeroes with his ruler. A small muscle in his right jaw tightens with strange vehemence, after which the ruler begins to trace adamant sevens and resolute fours in the air, Neigel's way, perhaps, of telling the world he is about to make an important decision. Wasserman is still surprised that his impudence has not cost him dearly. (Wasserman: "Perhaps because he was helpless, and saw a kind of hocus-pocus in me that mitigated his murderousness, or perhaps every lion likes a mouse about to tickle his toes, so they can both have a taste of glory; in brief— I had dared and he had smiled, and that was enough for me.") And the German surprises him even more now by asking him to tell a little more about those stories he used to write.

Wasserman blushes from head to toe ("I was unaware that I had enough blood left in me to color a single cheek!"), and it's disconcerting to see him like this. He stares at the floor, locks his fingers together, and chuckles self-deprecatingly. "Ah, well! Et, such folly . . . simple tales for children they were, though children liked them well enough . . . and the critics, too, rejoiced . . . at least some did, that is, in the tales called 'The Children of the Heart' serialized in magazines . . . a chapter a week . . . and the children, of 'The Children of the Heart,' that is, were sons of many nations, there was even one of ours, begging your permission, and two sons of Poland, and one Armenian fellow, and there was also a son of Russia among them, and they fought the powers of darkness, no disrespect intended, sir, on many an adventure! They battled disaster, disease, and deformity, injustice, ignorance, and blight, and once, by way of example, they came to the rescue of a small Armenian fellow, when the Turks attacked his village with blade and sword, at the close of the century, before the great massacre . . . and the little warriors fared thither in their time machine . . . a trick of my own devising, heh heh, and once they saved the Negro people from the Americans of yore who wished to slaughter them, and once they assisted the sage whose name for the moment escapes me, the doctor who waged war on the microbes of hydrophobia, choleria, and one time they lent support to Robin Hood, who fought the rich in the land of Albion, and what else? Oh yes, they also rescued the Red Skins, and flew away with them, to the moon, that is, and even offered succor to your own Ludwig van Beethoven, who was thick-of-hearing, and sundry other follies to regale the hearts of children, to please them with instructive stories about history and famous personages . . . but indirectly, in order not to tire them . . . historical facts, tamed in genial tales . . . nonsense . . . empty prattle, ah well, I liked them . . ."

Neigel listens patiently to this embarrassing outburst of self-adulation. He studies Wasserman narrowly. A faint flush spreads over his cheeks, and when Wasserman finally stops talking, the German continues watching him, as though listening to a distant voice.

Suddenly he shakes himself, coughs with annoyance, passes his hand over his face, and says, "What is this ridiculous costume you're wearing, perhaps you can explain?"

Wasserman is surprised. "This? Et, this costume, sir . . . one of Commander Keizler's pranks . . . he ordered his *Scheissemeister* dressed in glorious raiment, and even went to the trouble of finding me the Yom Kippur attire of a very great rabbi . . . with a fine embroidered hat and eight tassels that he ordered especially for me, only I lost it on my way here, I am afraid . . ." "And the watch?" demands Neigel. "What's the watch for?" "That, too, is a joke of Commander Keizler's, your honor. He thought, and perhaps it is so, that when the prisoners visit the House of Honor, your honor, the work runs slack, therefore like the prophet Samuel, he took me behind the flock and made me, nu, yes, *Scheissemeister*, and hung a timepiece around my neck, and even set a limit, begging your pardon: two minutes and not a second longer did he vouchsafe unto us in his great mercy." And to me he turned with a bitter aside: "Nu, and what do you think happened, Shleimeleh? I quickly developed a terrible case of hemorrhoids! I clench my teeth in agony, I tell you! And afterward—like everyone, the gates were closed unto me and the doors were sealed! Eternal constipation, that is. But at least I had the good fortune to lack a sense of smell . . . nu, a word to the wise . . . though I will never again hear an alarm clock with equanimity."

"Yes," says Neigel, scoffing lightly, "Keizler has flair. Now, he could have been a writer, don't you think?"

Wasserman thinks, a feig, The hell you say, but answers, "Why, yes, indeed, Commander."

And Neigel, at rest: "But I know exactly what you are thinking this very moment, *Scheissemeister*. Inside your small and cowardly heart you're saying, A Nazi could never be a good writer. They don't feel anything. Am I right, Scheherazade?"

Of course he was right. I don't doubt my grandfather's answer for one moment, but I want to arm him with the facts. For instance, in the SS Führerschule at Dachau near Munich, where Neigel was probably trained, there was a sign in the classroom that read: 1. THE MAIN GUIDELINE—PARTY DISCIPLINE! 2. WILL IS THE OVERCOMING OF FEARS AND WEAKNESSES LIKE COMPASSION AND SYMPATHY! 3. LOVE FOR ONE'S NEIGHBOR SHOULD BE RESERVED FOR THE GERMANS OF ADOLF HITLER!

And when I see that Wasserman still hesitates, I send him a compelling answer for Neigel, an answer invented for us by Adolf Hitler himself, in his Berlin speech of '38. "Conscience is the business of the Jew." This sentence was interpreted by Jürgen Stroop, the German commander of Warsaw during the rebellion, as follows: "And thus he freed the Nazis from conscience."

And these words seem to swing Wasserman like a mighty pendulum. "So?" he asks me. "Ai, a heavy load has been placed on us by the housepainter from Linz, may he have a good short year!" But to Neigel he says, "Heaven forbid that I should think such thoughts about you, your honor."

"Coward," cries Neigel, his contempt perhaps not totally unjustified. "You miserable coward. I could respect you if you weren't such a coward." He smiles a short, mocking smile. "And on what, I wonder, did you base your preachings to young readers about pride and courage? Your thoughts are positively screaming!" And the Jew: "Heaven forbid, Commander." ("Naturally I fear him! What did you think, Shleimeleh?

My heart turned black at the sound of his sweet voice! And so big, keinahora, his bones are like iron bars, and I myself—courage is to me what intelligence is to a chazzan. Even when I catch my finger in a cup handle, I sweat streams. And now, nu, go tell Chaimkeh here that my bones are quaking.")

The German, musing: "So here we have a Jew who doesn't know how to die, and who's also a bit of a writer. Perhaps we can even the score with Staukeh now, eh?" And Wasserman: "Pardon, your honor?" Neigel: "Staukeh. My adjutant." Wasserman: "Nu, yes, I know the man. What of him?" And Neigel: "Staukeh is the one who found Scheingold here."

And Wasserman: "Nu, Shleimeleh, my bowels at this moment were tied in knots, because this Scheingold, perhaps you have heard of him, was the leader of some of the finest Warsaw café orchestras. He, too, arrived in a transport some months ago, and had stripped and run naked through the *Schlauch*, past the Ukrainians with their clubs, and had said Shema Yisrael already, and gone in, to the Holy of Holies, that is, when Staukeh found out who and what Scheingold was, nu, and Staukeh took him behind the flock and ordered him to set up a camp orchestra, he even gave him an amber baton, and Scheingold said a prayer of thanks and girded his loins like a man, and established a fine orchestra here! And he also toiled unceasingly to set up a choir of men and women, and introduced pluckers of the fiddle and blowers on the flute, and how fond the sons of Esau are of melody and song, especially when their hands are soiled with blood—they are such subtle souls—and sometimes, on Reich holidays, or the little housepainter's birthday, may the Good Lord send him a new soul already, they would indulge even us with a little music, as beautiful to our ears as the sound of timbrel and psaltery in the Temple of yore! Ah, each concert began with our anthem, the camp anthem, that is, nu . . . ai: 'Work means life/duty and obedience/till someday joy/ta ta ta [I forget!]/Will lead the way . . .' Yes. Nu, and afterward they would play the Polish Army march, 'Mi Fierbsha Brigada,' nu, so, and the concert ended with a song written by one of us to the tune from a film called *The Girl from the Pouszche* . . . ah, like honey!"

And Neigel is still wondering. I see now that there is something peculiar about his face: his nose and chin are strong and determined, impressive at first glance. His compelling eyes are vaguely unsettling.

But then you notice the dead spots in the big face. The long cheeks, for instance, and the very broad forehead. Even the area under the mouth. A wilderness, where not a single distinctive trait has taken root. At this moment the nose and chin are speaking: "Look here, *Scheisse-meister*, I have an idea, something that may help you stay alive here, or even to live better—" But Wasserman, who seems to be cringing inside his gorgeous gown, emits a choking sound: "To be truthful, your honor, I do not wish it."

Neigel is offended. His eyes seem to retreat and harden like lead. "Do you hear what you're saying? I offer you life, more than that—a good life! Here!" To which Wasserman, in a tone of fearful, stubborn apology: "Many thanks, only I cannot. A whim of mine, begging your pardon, not worth the mention, your honor. Begging your pardon."

("Oi, you should have seen the look he gave me, this Esau, like daggers! He has eyes, keinahora! They leave you timorous and ashamed because the seven deadly sins in your heart have been exposed! A look that says, Well, I know who and what people are! And because even you are a human being, you are a criminal with no alternative but to commit crimes, et! I tell you, Shleimeleh, the man knows one thing about mankind, but this bit of knowledge outweighs every science, and with it he takes the measure of the world!")

For just then—and it's high time, too—Neigel will say quietly (his eyes on Wasserman, like a snake transfixing the mouse it is about to swallow): "Is the heart willing?"

And Anshel Wasserman answers, unthinking: "The heart is willing!" And then silence.

("It was as though my entire being had shriveled up and disappeared from sight like paper catching fire, and I felt a sharp stinging, and drooped as if beheaded, heaven forbid. Ai, Shleimeleh, if I live and die seven times, if I tell this story to the unhearing world a thousand times, I will never forget the moment Neigel uttered the secret password of the Children of the Heart.")

And Neigel in the same barely audible whisper: "Come what may?" And the Jew, with a deep, weak sigh: "Come what may."

And why is this so unusual? thinks Wasserman, who is shivering all over, and trying to persuade himself that he is unstirred. "Every meeting between two people is a wonder and a mystery, for even a man and his beloved, even if they are man and wife and have lived in partnership for many years, nu, yes, still, how rarely do they meet, while he and I here—remarkable!" But there is not a drop of blood in his body, and Neigel, too, is very pale. They both look hollow. As if everything inside them has been sucked out and spilled into the veins of a new, transparent embryo made entirely of the supplications and fervor and anxiety of two who briefly glimpsed each other over the trenches.

Neigel's face is sharp. There is a kind of defeat and startling frailty in the great wilderness. He can barely find his voice. He sputters a few times before he can bring himself to tell Wasserman heavily, hoarsely, that back home in Fissan, his village at the foot of the Zugspitze in Bavaria, he used to read the stories of Wasserman-Scheherazade; that he remembers most of the adventures in the series; that when he was eight years old he named his beloved dog Otto after the leader of the Children of the Heart; that he and his brother Heinz—"Were raised you might say on those stories of yours! They were our primers, together with the New Testament, that is!"

Okay, this sounds a bit farfetched, so Neigel will now add, "Of course, we were given other books, too," quickly appending, "Karl May's books, for instance, and others I can't remember offhand. My father wanted to make sure we read. He would have preferred for us to read the New Testament, of course, ah, he had great plans for us, but the pastor persuaded him to let us read your stories too. They appeared in a magazine called *My Native Land!* I can remember exactly how it looked, I even remember how it smelled, I swear. It arrived at the church once a week, and Pastor Knaupf would lend it out to me and Heinz on Sunday. I believe he used to read the magazines too, because once I heard him tell Father that your stories were reminiscent of the Old Testament." His face is redder than ever, with embarrassment perhaps for having let his feelings go to such an extent, but these feelings doubtless issue from inner depths where an SS officer's rules of conduct diminish in influence, and Neigel exclaims, "Listen, Scheherazade, I can see it all! It seems like only yesterday! The town, Pastor Knaupf, who had a telescope and used to gaze at the stars, not to mention some quite different things, they say, and—really! Once my father whittled the Zugspitze in wood! The tavernkeeper in Fissan bought it from him, and it's there in the tavern to this very day; strange, isn't it, my father dead and gone but that piece of wood still there . . . yes, and most of all I remember your stories, I really do remember them, and just to prove it—" (Yes yes! Wasserman and I shout in unison; do it quickly, we beg him silently, prove it now, ply us with names, details, facts. Facts! I rasp, give me facts, Neigel! It's a rickety building we've erected here, a frail fetus of fiction, a weak blue baby that has to be rubbed with devotion, nu, lie to me, Neigel, lie like an expert with charm and grace, because I'm willing to believe you, I'm willing to forget myself and be half deceived, I want to believe that such a thing is possible, so on with it, Herr Neigel, *schnell*!)

And Neigel conjures the ghost of "that boy, their leader, Otto was his name. I named my beloved dog after him. And the blonde, Otto's girlfriend, the one with the braid, what was her name—no, don't tell me—Paula, right?" And Wasserman says, gently, drowsily, "Excellent, Commander, and almost perfectly correct! Only Paula was not Otto's girlfriend, she was—" And Neigel smacks his forehead: "Oh, of course! How silly! Paula was Otto's sister! Now it's coming back to me: the other one was in love with Paula, the one who could make friends with animals and knew how to cure them. Wait a minute—and he could talk to them, too, right? Alfred? Was that his name? No? Wait, no, let me think. Fried was his name! Yes. I remember everything now. Everything. Albert Fried, and he loved Paula, but he never told her. See, Scheherazade? I remember everything! Everything!" And his face gleams with perspiration.

Wasserman—I think I'm beginning to know him now—will have to do something to dampen all the good cheer coming his way. "But, your honor, there were stories about . . . nu . . . how shall I put it . . . the lowliest people . . ." And Neigel cuts him short with a smile: "Yes, I know. Stories about your people, and the Armenians and the Negroes, only don't forget, times were different then. That was—let's see—about thirty years ago? More? Thirty-five? Forty years? Yes. Forty years ago. At the turn of the century. How time flies! I was six years old then. Just learning to read. And for years after, five years, maybe more, I read your stories every week . . . of all things . . ."

Neigel continues to bask in the remembrance of those days. His big head seems to rise and fall with the effort of drawing memories from a deep well. Anyone looking at him now, at this grown man, happy as a child, would discern at once that things truly had been "different then." Only Wasserman, for some reason, quickly strips himself of pride and pleasure ("Nu, Shleimeleh, would you believe it? A regular 'And

Joseph revealed himself to his brothers'! Feh!"), to await the ominous interpretation of this incredible dream.

"And what else can you do, besides pulling gold teeth and running the shittery?" asks Neigel as the first excitement fades. "Nu, well, I can tell stories, your honor. Adventuresome tales, Commander," answers Wasserman in all humility. "We'll take care of that now," says Neigel casually, and Wasserman: "Pardon?!" And the German: "Shut up a minute. I have to think. Yes, yes. Definitely possible. There's only one problem: your number has come up with the group we're finishing. But that can be remedied. A new prisoner will have to do without a number. It won't be much of a problem." And he jots something down in his little black notebook. "Now let's see. What was your profession before the war? Just writing?" "Just writing? Don't you know?" "Know what?" "Nu, well, I have written nothing for the past twenty years . . . The Children of the Heart are no more . . . To earn a living I worked as a proofreader for a small magazine in Warsaw . . . and every so often I edited articles and essays by other writers, or prepared other people's stories for the printer, and other such things . . ." "Cooking!" cheers Neigel suddenly. "You could help my cook. That way you can stay here without a lot of questions." "Begging your pardon. About cooking I know less than nothing. A cup of tea, perhaps, and a boiled egg." ("In all my years of bachelorhood I took my meals at Feintoch's home restaurant, Shleimeleh. Clear noodle soup for a first course, followed by herring with a little shmaltz, and for dessert, nu, what else, heartburn.") But Neigel doesn't give up so easily, and rattles off a list of domestic positions ("Ironing? Mending? Plastering?"), and before long I realize that he is ridiculing Grandfather, and this makes me furious, all the more so when I see Wasserman giving in without a fight. He hides his head between the wings of his protruding shoulder blades and silently tells me that "I always think about my Sarah. My thoughts forever flock to her. And how we used to laugh that I, nebuch, with these two poor arms of mine, mere straws, not arms at all, a travesty of arms, Mephibosheth's legs were stronger than my arms! It was a miracle that I found her, my Sarah, who was also a real baleboosteh, and managed the housework in her father's home, and even knew a thing or two about electricality, and could turn a collar like a master tailor, or repair a shoe like a cobbler, ah, what could she not do!" And Neigel, beginning to despair, vents his anger with a viscious insult ("Not a great record for a man of sixty, Wasserman, who can't even die!"), and then he suddenly remembers another possibility and exclaims, "Gardening!" at which point I interrupt the conversation and answer in Wasserman's stead, much to his amazement, "Gardening! Yes!"

Neigel smiles with satisfaction. He is already spinning a green dream ("Ah, you'll lay out a glorious garden for me around the barracks!"); already settling invisible scores ("Far prettier than Staukeh's, eh?"); already improving and expanding on the original plan ("And you can till a vegetable patch so I won't have to eat the turnips those Polish farm women water with donkey piss"); and I quickly jot down a reminder to myself to find out about gardening for poor Wasserman (Ruthy is good at such things), but Wasserman, my maddeningly unpredictable Anshel Wasserman, says, "The truth is, your honor, that my spirit is not so inclined, not at all so inclined."

Neigel is unperturbed by this refusal. He wants Wasserman, and nothing will prevent him from carrying out his plan. Slyly he brings the conversation back to the safer topic of the Children of the Heart, with a recollection of an episode about a Negro slave rebellion in America, concluding artfully, "Admit it, Scheherazade, you never dreamed you'd find such old admirers among us, did you?"

Here my Wasserman acknowledges Neigel's compliment with a light nod, unique in its synchronistic disclosure of multiple expressions: 1. amiability, 2. sham meekness, 3. feigned self-mockery; and likewise, in combination with a very thin smile—a. an almost dog-like gratitude, b. abject deference, but only superficially, and c. a wretched craving, suppressed with iron jaws, that forges the spasmodic smile.

(Wasserman: "Feh! How certain I had been that I would never again resort to this little pose, and in my old age yet . . .") Neigel continues to drip flattery into Wasserman's ears; he also weaves in a few interesting details about himself, his childhood in Fissan, and his father, but suddenly something strange and totally incomprehensible happens; Ubersturmbannführer Neigel's face grows rigid and serious, as though he had called it to attention, and he makes a rapid, formal declaration, in no way related to anything previously discussed by them. "I have 120 officers and men under my command, Wasserman. And 170,000 persons have arrived here in the transports so far—as of the beginning of this week!" Once again I needed Wasserman ("Did you see? So proudly

Esau spoke his piece, I quickly looked under the table to see if he would click his heels. He did not.") And he explains to me that Neigel had been impelled to make this perplexing declaration out of "a source deeper than the lesson he learned in Reb Himmler's cheder," and that "Nu, such things oftentimes betide me when I chance upon fleshly men of family who read my stories in their tender youth. And strange to say, such men always feel obliged to vaunt their manhood before me, to magnify their accomplishments as princes of Torah scholarship or of the marketplace—in short, to be Moishe Gros! Perhaps they wished to impress me that their latter days had brought no blame to the lessons they gleaned from my stories in childhood. Ineffable are the ways of man, Shleimeleh, and how very schoolboyish they seemed to me, then, boasting before an old teacher in whose presence we all revert to juvenility, and perhaps the same holds true for the writer of children's stories, so when Neigel said such things here, nu, you understand how sweet the melody was to my ears, and yet I refrained from answering a fool in his folly, and merely stammered a kind of 'Nu yes, very likely true,' but he saw he had made a dunderheaded ninny of himself, and he buried his nose between the pages of his black notebook, and there was silence.")

Wasserman takes this opportunity to tell me what little he knows about Neigel and his adjutant, Staukeh, mentioned earlier by Neigel. Neigel's nickname in the camp is "Ox," because of his unusually large head, and because of his outbursts ("You should see him in a rage! Flames shoot out of his mouth, balls of fire!"). His assistant, Obersturmführer Staukeh, is called "Lalakeh," or Dolly, by the prisoners. ("Because of his face, he has the face of an innocent child, the pure-hearted son of the Passover *Haggadah*! But a killer nonetheless, with the bite of a fox and the sting of a scorpion.") Neigel is different from Staukeh in every conceivable way. Staukeh, according to Wasserman, and judging by the written testimony I looked through recently, was a sick sadist for whom "the gates of intelligence were ever open for the devising of new schemes to harrow and torture, and he grabs and guzzles and kills with a pleasure and a passion not of this world." Staukeh was also corrupt, not above a bribe here and there, or getting drunk at the officers' club, and sometimes, "Nu, well, mangling a young doe of a farmer's daughter." No, Neigel is no Staukeh, and Staukeh is no Neigel. "They are different yet they complement each other, like Tweedledum and Tweedledee. Or Pat and Patashon!" Neigel, according to Wasserman, "is all of a piece, felled, as it were, by one swing of the ax. We never saw him inebriated, nor did he ever smile at us. Not even viciously, like Staukeh. Zalmanson liked to call him 'Bellyache,' because he looked as if he had eaten bitter herbs, like someone who has no time for nonsense, only duty. And here I am in the nest of the viper himself, for over an hour now, and he has yet to pluck my beard or strike my mouth, and what is more, I have even seen him smile now and again, he has even told me of himself and of his ancestry. Imagine, Shleimeleh, at first he wanted to murder me, and fired a shot, but he did it according to rule, and I noticed he averted his eyes in order not to see. On the whole, it appears he does not know what to do with me, and this troubles him. Sometimes he looks at me strangely and says 'Humph,' and, Shleimeleh, though I cannot think what this 'humph' might be for, I only hope it is not a 'humph' of sadness, heaven forbid, for I do not wish to make him sad, he too was a child once, after all, and read what he read and liked me a little, and who knows what he endured at the SS Führerschule, for surely no one becomes a murderer without forfeiting happiness, and if I knew how a man like Neigel could be turned into a murderer, perhaps I would try to turn him around and reform him, et! Senile musings, Anshel! You want to change the world in your old age? With a kind of prophetic hindsight? But inside, I feel the worm gnaw, because after everything this arch-murderer Neigel did to me, I spent the last hour with him and saw his face as a boy, and I was beginning to think that these many months in Neigel's camp I was wrong not to count him a human being, with a wife, perhaps, and children, and these musings of mine filled me with amazement, and I put them aside for future consideration, and to Neigel I said that I was distraught to have caused him such inconvenience, and I saw that my words touched his heart, because he gazed upon me like a shaken man. And I confessed to him that it was no small discomfort for me either that the man about to finish me was nu, well, a man with whom I am somewhat acquainted, and to stress my point, I quoted Papa, may he rest in peace, who was a grocer and taught me one must never mix work and sentiment, but instead of being appeased by this, Neigel groaned and stared at me in horror, as though, heaven forbid, I had uttered obscene words."

"Enough!" screams Neigel suddenly. "Enough of this talking! You start work today, Wasserman, you hear? Now shut up a minute!" And Wasserman says, "Work? What work, your honor?" And Neigel: "Trying to be clever again, eh? I've already informed you: you will lay out a flower garden and a vegetable patch. And in the evening after work, after I finish with my meetings and reports, you will come in here and do your duty." "Pardon?!" "You will tell me a story, Wasserman. You know exactly what I'm talking about. A story! Not for children, of course, a special story for me!" "I? Heaven forbid. I am no longer adept at telling stories." "You are no longer adept? Then who is adept? You listen, Scheherazade, I'm giving you a chance to justify your nickname. Tell me a story and stay alive." And Wasserman says, "No, no, I cannot, your honor. You see I never . . . this is the truth . . . moreover . . . I cannot . . . it died . . . the desire . . . the imagination—" And Neigel, tempting him: "You have a great imagination. You always had, you know. That story with the gladiator in Rome, the Children of the Heart come to his rescue, and the little one, Fried, persuades the lion not to eat him, ah! Or when they help Edison just when he's going to give up on the invention of the electric light—who else could have thought of that?" And Anshel Wasserman says gloomily, like a bird plucked clean of every plume of pride, "Anyone, your honor."

I record here word for word what Wasserman disclosed. "Yes, Shlei-meleh, it was not modesty that made me say this to Esau. And to you I will tell even more, because today I am no longer afraid of the literary critics who made my life a misery in the days when I wrote my stories. But they did well to smite me below the belt! What they wrote about me was true: that my cleverness is feeble. That I know only how to plagiarize from other authors, and employ their cleverness. And the sharpest among the critics was a wickedly clever man by the name of Shapira, whose arrow-like pen dubbed me 'the writers' matchmaker,' an epithet that stuck forevermore. Ai, Shleimeleh, is there anything I keep from you? Yes, yes, they were right. I was greatly taken with Jack London, the American, and Jules Verne, the Frenchman, and the young Karl May and Daniel Defoe of Robinson Crusoe and his man Friday, and why deny the part played by H. G. Wells and the time machine I borrowed in friendly fashion? And Franz Hoffman and James Fenimore Cooper and Korczak, from all of them I borrowed something, whether in Polish or Hebrew, and also from translations in the Holy Tongue by Grozovsky and Ben-Yehuda and Sperling and Andres and Kalman

Schulman and the good Taviov, and many others, nu, yes, it was not for want of skillfulness that I did this—in my youth, you know, they say I wrote with penetration! I used to compose poems you see, and some were even published in magazines and created a kind of stir, nu, yes, and it was because of this that Zalmanson the editor looked upon me with favor and took me out of the archives, where I had been bored for five years, and made me an author; only when my writings began to be published, I turned coward and was afraid to give of myself and my milk and blood. My powers of creation ebbed as my villainous powers of imitation flowed. And I do not deny it, Shleimeleh, with so much yearning in me again, the passion of the artist stirring in my bones, I wished to write something else, something all mine, out of the singular spark in the chambers of my heart, to quote Bialik's famous words, a small spark, but all mine, neither borrowed nor stolen . . . and so—I tried. Ten years ago it was . . . oh, the fire that raged in me then! But I was frightened . . . drowning in chaos . . . The story that began with human beings unfolded with ghosts and goblins and other insolent dogs . . . and words of wickedness, lechery, and magic, and loathsome, unearthly laughter, all with a kind of despair which cast my spirits down and left me too weak to crush it into letters . . . Perhaps you will laugh—but I thought constantly about what they would say in the village, my Bolichov, when they read these things, and how it would grieve my mother . . . and in the end, I had not enough strength left me at the age of fifty to set off in this new direction, to go to war, nu, well . . . you understand? I tossed it in the fire . . . of course I regretted that, I have given you but an inkling of my regret . . . Here in the camp, I told Zalmanson about it, too, and he was sorry. He said it was time I wrote something worthy of myself . . . that now that I had been carried off beyond my life, as it were, I should write with daring, with madness . . . ai."

And Neigel continues: "Listen, Wasserman, let me speak plainly. I need some distraction around here. Something to occupy my mind after work." Wasserman, weakly: "Is there no club here for, nu, gentlemen officers?" And Neigel, with a certain pride: "You see before you one German who does not enjoy beer. I'm neither a beer Deutscher nor a wine Deutscher nor a schnapps Deutscher. But I do need to let off a little steam. That's why I've decided that you will sit here with me in the evenings for half an hour, an hour, and tell me a story." And

Wasserman, nearly screaming: "A story about what, Herr Commander?"

"I really haven't the slightest idea," Neigel says with a cold, crafty smile, "but I have no doubt you'll think of something good. I can't tell you what to make up, can I? You see? There are things even I can't order you to do." And the idea seems rather to appeal to him.

Anshel Wasserman, nearly fainting, suggests a compromise ("I will tell your honor the old stories"), which is summarily rejected. In anguish he proposes another compromise, a silly one ("I will tell your honor Wilhelm Auf's Scheherazade stories. Ach, delightful! 'Kalif Chasida' and 'Little Mok,' ai, your honor will be pleased!"), but Neigel dismisses these evasions with a crass-sounding argument ("I want fresh goods, Wasserman"), and for a moment there is silence, and we both think Wasserman is about to accept the offer, only once again he surprises us and declares, "I am grateful for this generous offer, your honor, eppes, what applies to Scheherazade does not apply to me, for the simple reason that the same lovely maiden wished very much to live, which was why she told the sultan her stories, whereas I, on the contrary, wish very much to die, heaven forbid."

Neigel gives him a good, long look. He rubs his chin and repeats his "unique offer" in a quiet, well-modulated voice: "The best you'll get in your situation anywhere in the Reich," and hesitates another moment before tossing another idea into the room: "Every evening, after you tell me more of the story, I am willing to try to kill you. One shot in the head. That will be your reward, understand? Like the other Scheherazade, only exactly the reverse. Every evening I will shoot you, on condition that your story is a good one. Sooner or later it's bound to work, isn't it?" and he leans back in his chair and calmly looks at Wasserman, allowing the feeble author to bow under the weight of the idea, and to tell the truth, I can't help admiring the man's initiative, though Wasserman, with a certain peevishness, is not at all prepared to see the exquisite literary malice of the offer, and he scolds me, "Feh, Shleimeleh, ashes in your mouth, it is a human life he speaks of so complacently, this yekke, wicked Armilus! It is my life and . . ." and he musters his remaining strength to whisper, "And what will happen, your honor, if one night, heaven forbid, my story is not a success?" And Neigel says, "You'll stay alive for one more day," staring boldly at Wasserman. "I want you to know," he adds, "that I'll make sure you won't have any opportunity to do away with yourself along the way. And I can assure you that no officer or soldier in this camp will ever try to kill you. You will be protected here, as in a warm nest." And again he smiles.

And Wasserman sighs, having quickly weighed the situation and concluded that there is no way out, and declares sincerely that "if I must tell a story, sir, in order to die, I am ready and willing."

But "Liar! Wretched liar!" screams somebody inside Wasserman, and the author allows him to continue. ("Say thank you, wretched liar, that no sooner had the word 'story' left Neigel's mouth than it fanned the cold, dying embers of your life. A new story! New ideas, new plots and drafts and your pen dancing on the paper, and sleepless nights of thinking and reflecting and all the subtle pleasures of the soul! And it will be seven times more wonderful after ten fallow years to sit down at a desk, here of all places! Here! In the bowels of hell!"), and Wasserman nods at the German officer and informs him that he is willing to tell him a story, about those Children of the Heart, only not as Neigel remembers them from childhood but as fully adult. And when Neigel fails to understand, Wasserman explains with strange assurance, as though he had long awaited this moment and inwardly rehearsed the words till they were fluent, "The kids grew up to be goats, your honor, as we, too, have, only they aged quicker. This happens in books sometimes, and now they are sixty-five or even seventy years old, may they live to be a hundred and twenty, or to a very ripe old age, at least." And Neigel, concerned by what seems to him an unnecessary complication, asks, "Maybe you could let them stay young all the same?" And Anshel Wasserman with a bitter laugh says, "Nothing in this world stays as young as it used to be. Even babes burst out of their dams already old." And Neigel asks if the Children of the Heart will continue to do the same fantastic things together, and Wasserman promises that the things they do now will be even more fantastic. And Neigel says, "Isn't that, I don't know, a little childish?" And the writer, outraged: "Sir!"

"Don't get so insulted, *Scheissemeister*," says Neigel. "I didn't mean to hurt your feelings." And Wasserman swallows hard and makes the most of this extraordinary apology to inform him with lowered eyes that "the commander will not have a say-so in my story. This I must make clear from the start, otherwise—it is over." And the Nazi officer we know so little about nods his heavy head and says, "Naturally, Scheherazade, naturally. There's a name for that, isn't there? 'Poetic license' you artists call it, right?"

Wasserman studies him anxiously. I, too, am anxious. "Poetic license" doesn't seem to either of us to belong on the intellectual menu of a Nazi officer. He may have been quoting someone. I'll probably know more about him when I get under his skin, as I did so easily with Wasserman. It's my duty, after all. As Ayala said, In the White Room everything comes out of your own self, out of your own guts, victim and murderer, compassion and cruelty . . . soon, then. Meanwhile, I will just have to make do with Neigel reflected in Wasserman's eyes. Very slowly.

"I'll bring you plants and seeds," says Neigel. "Tomorrow you'll start hoeing and clearing. The soil here is hard and stony. It's high time we did something about it." "Yes, your honor." "I'll order petunias. You know petunias? I hope they'll grow here. My wife grows them in the window box." "As you wish, Commander." "And radishes, too, of course. I like radishes. Especially the small red ones, crisp when you crunch them between your teeth, ah!" And while he speaks thus, waxing enthusiastic, Wasserman tries desperately to remember whether radishes grow on bushes or on trees.

"Ai, Shleimeleh, again I reflected how much my Sarah could have helped me with this awesome task. How would I ever be able to write without her wisdom and intelligence? She was such a fountain of knowledge, it was extraordinary. Et, before we met I used to spend days on end in the Lutheran library in Warsaw, looking up facts and details. I am scatterbrained by nature, and have a terrible memory, and compared to me, Zalmanson was as pedantic as the School of Shammai. "Accuracy, my little Wasserman, ac-cu-ra-cy!" he used to repeat in my ears before Sarah's day, underlining with a venomous stroke of the pen, phrases like "the princess's tunic"! "We mean 'the princess's ballgown,' do we not, my little Wasserman? A tunic is a short coat. Does your princess go off to the ball in a tunic? Oy, *mein kleiner* Wasserman, if only you would look at women in the street, if only you would undress them and take their garments off, one by one, you would find better things to write about than princesses and fairies . . ."

"And then my Sarah came along, and my stories were exceedingly enriched. They glittered with a thousand brilliant hues! In a very little while I learned the difference between turquoise and Bordeaux, between linen and cotton, and between Antarctica (which lies by the South Pole) and Alaska (which lies by the north. Or is it the other way around? I forget!), or the difference between various Italian dishes, e.g., spaghetti and macaroni, one of which is a thinner variety, and I learned that elephants sleep on their feet, and that in scientific books the white race is called Caucasian; ai, there was nothing my Sarah did not know, a mind like a cistern that loses not a drop: she furnished and adorned her mind beyond her youthful years! And through her, my writing became more 'earthy,' in the elevated sense of the word, and I remember, Shleimeleh, ah, something insignificant really, but since I thought of it, I will tell you—namely, how filled I was with poetic inspiration when I wrote the words 'Robin Hood in fine array danced the first waltz with the rich and comely Marchioness Elizabeth, and his heart kept time: one, two, three; one, two, three,' ah, like honey!"

Later Neigel informs Wasserman that he will not be returning to Keizler's lower camp anymore, and will reside from now on in the second-floor storeroom of Neigel's barracks, and that Anna, the Polish cook, will prepare one hot meal for him a day. "So you can't say I don't look out for my intelligentsia, *Scheissemeister*!"

I should also describe Neigel showing the writer around his new quarters—a tiny hole in the attic, at the top of a flight of wooden stairs behind the barracks. Wasserman climbs heavily up, opens the small door, and recoils with a grimace of pain. ("Paper. I smelled the smell of paper, reams of paper!"), and he calls down to Neigel and asks permission to use one of the many notebooks in storage there. He also asks for a pen. And when Neigel wonders ("What, you mean to tell me you won't remember the story otherwise?"), Wasserman enacts a scene that must have come out of some gladiator film he saw in Warsaw: descending the rickety stairs as erectly as possible, he pronounces with all the gravity he can muster in a nasal, monotonous voice, "I am an artist, your honor. An artist who polishes every letter a thousand times!" And Neigel mutters, "Of course, of course," so Wasserman returns to the attic and comes back holding a brown notebook with a picture of a big eagle and the legend *Property of the Quartermaster Corps / SS / Eastern Division*. And Neigel, with a gesture at first casual and eventually grand ("Esau felt he was dubbing me thus his knight of the realm of literature"), takes his own pen, a steel Adler, glory of the Hapsburg

Empire, out of his pocket and offers it to Wasserman, as they stand looking into each other's eyes. (Wasserman: "When I held the pen in my hand I knew: I will vanquish him. And if I can prevent him from using me like Scheingold the musician, who fawns all over the officers and wags his tail, and who even turned informer, they say, and slanders his fellow prisoners—but to be truthful, Shleimeleh, I was afraid. A just man knows the heat of the beast within, and though it filled me with loathing, I knew myself to have been a toady, Zalmanson's toady, and I could not stop myself, feh, wretch that I am!")

Neigel looks at the Jew, whose eyes are suddenly shut tight. Though I don't know what he is thinking now, I suppose there is something about this weak old man that is vaguely troubling to the determined Nazi officer. He leans over Wasserman and whispers emphatically, "A story with Otto and Paula, right?" "With Fried and Sergei of the golden hands and Harotian, too." "Harotian? Who's that?" "The little Armenian fellow. A sweet magician, have you forgotten him?" "Oh, right. The boy who played the flute for Beethoven." "That is so. And there will be others, naturally."

"Who?!"

Neigel squints suspiciously, and Wasserman is quick to reassure him, "Boon companions all, your honor, do not forget that a mighty task awaits the Children of the Heart this time, and they need all the help they can find!" "And what task is that, if I may ask?" "How should I know, your honor, the story is barely conceived inside me, though I assure you it will be an unparalleled adventure, else why drag them out of oblivion and raise their ghosts in this manner?"

Neigel reflects for a moment. Perhaps he is feeling a passing anxiety, which he dismisses with a vigorous shrug. Then he orders Wasserman to leave and goes back to business.

Wasserman: "Whereupon I dragged my old bones up the ladder, made a kind of resting place in this my new atelier, and reflected: Ai, what a day! First they take my friends to die in the gas chambers, poor innocents, and then it transpires that I am not fit for death, and then finally this calamity called Neigel befalls me, Neigel with his tempting offers. Feh! I took the notebook in my hands and looked down at it. Anshel, Anshel, I said to myself, here you are about to write a story. And though it will be, to my deep regret, a one-volume edition, why grumble when the sales are guaranteed? And under the wings of the

Nazi eagle, may its feathers molt, I wrote in handsome characters, in
our Holy Tongue: *The Last Adventure of the Children of the Heart*."

[2]

SLOWLY ANSHEL WASSERMAN'S LIFE unfolds before me. He often
mentions his wife, "my Sarah," but never speaks of his daughter, Tirza.
He loved Sarah, but I sometimes wonder whether he wasn't a confirmed
bachelor at heart. He had been forty years old when he married her,
and she twenty-three. Just five years old when Wasserman first published
the stories she loved so well, like other children her age, she continued
to think of them on different occasions till one day, years later, she
happened to see a new edition of "The Children of the Heart" in a
Warsaw magazine. With uncharacteristic audacity she sent the editor
some of her wonderful illustrations for the stories. The drawings floated
around for some time before they reached Zalmanson, and he, calculated
and sly, brought her and Wasserman together, chafing his palms with
pleasure at the flowering of the timid couple's love affair . . .
    And thus, through Wasserman's remarks in passing, I learn something
of his way of life. About how he loved to sit at home wearing an ironed
shirt and tie, even when he was alone. How he indulged himself with
spectacular little treats in the years of his bachelorhood—a ride in a
ricksha on Sunday on grand Marshalkovska Boulevard, a slow and
pleasurable stroll over the Kravedjeh Bridge, and from there through
Saksy Park, with its statues and poplars and plane trees. And when it
grew dark he would go to the cinema for what always seemed to him
a stolen pleasure, a motion picture that touched him to the quick. From
this point of view, Sarah seems to have been the ideal partner: like him,
she was enchanted by the cinema. They were not selective: any picture
would do, as long as it was about people having exciting adventures.
They would sit together in the darkened hall like a couple of open-
mouthed children watching *Frankenstein*, and *King Kong*, and *The
Masked Spy* with Hanka Ordonovna. Wasserman told me with curious
pride that he and his Sarah had seen Greta Garbo in *Queen Christina*
four times, and Marlene Dietrich in *The Blue Angel* three times. They
even liked Westerns and saw every cowboy picture in Warsaw (Wasserman's excuse for this predilection is that he needed to learn about

the cowboy life in case he ever wanted to write about it). The couple had no friends to speak of, and their weekly visits to the cinema were minor celebrations. They delighted in discussing the pictures together, and weeks later Sarah might say something like "How sad that she lacked faith in him," and Wasserman would understand at once what she meant. They also enjoyed the popular Tuesday radio program *Play of the Week*, which brought great works of drama and literature into their lives; they would listen in bed, side by side, their eyes to the ceiling, not touching in the dark, but very close. Another exciting activity they shared was visiting the Warsaw zoo: Wasserman would stand for hours in front of the exotic animals from Burma and India, nodding in wonder. By the way, Sarah had been born on the same day as Tojnika, the baby elephant (so named because Tojnika means "Twelver," and he was the twelfth elephant born in a European zoo), and she was therefore entitled to a free ride on the elephant once a year on her birthday. Wasserman could not help becoming excited about this, for some reason; over and over he asked Sarah to describe those moments now faded from memory. "Like a Queen of India, a Jewish princess of the elephants!" he would murmur in undiminished wonder.

Wasserman rejoiced in his daily routine. I have listened countless times to the descriptions of his fastidious rites, how he would polish his shoes and keep house. Once, he recounted the varied pleasures of his spectacles: the polishing motions large and small, the different ways of taking them off, and the satisfaction of the frames going down behind the ears, or of resting your hand on your eyes and losing yourself in thought. (Perhaps I should explain here that his spectacles had been taken away immediately upon his arrival in the camp.) He would describe his favorite method of boiling an egg as earnestly as he described his work among the dentists. One evening he told me—unconstrainedly—how he used to make "a steaming hot glass of coffee" back in Warsaw, from the moment he put the water in the kettle and set the glass on the spout "to warm it up a little from the hot steam," till he poured the coffee into the glass. I also learned from him that he wore the same pair of shoes for seventeen years and kept them in excellent condition. And when I asked in amazement how, he replied with a smile of modest pride, "I step lightly, Shleimeleh . . ." and he also never had his fill of telling me about the used-book stores on Scweintokshiska Street, where all the dealers knew him and where he never missed an

old edition. In short, we may conclude from the above that Grandfather
Anshel was not a great adventurer. His gambling urge, for instance,
was satisfied by grabbing a number from the sausage seller's basket in
the street. Only twice in his life did he win a free sausage this way, but
he deeply appreciated the two wins and saw them as signs that he was
not a "complete shlimazel."

I watch him hoeing and weeding three furrows in front of Neigel's
barracks, and later bandaging his sore hands with bits of torn sacking,
resigned in pain and silence to the criticisms addressed to him by Neigel
from the window ("Try to make them a little straighter, *Scheissemeister*,
otherwise I'll be the laughingstock of the camp"). Crossly he picks up
hoe and rake, and sets them in place under the wooden ladder. Later
I see him eating, grabbing and gulping (he always ate like that, even
when he came to live with us), and I ignore a small potato he has
pilfered, unnoticed by the surly cook.

When it grows dark, I accompany him to Neigel, who is amazed that
the first chapter is not yet written ("Judging by your other stories, I
would have thought you pulled them out of your sleeve!"), and in
answer Wasserman delivers an impassioned speech about the hardships
of creative endeavor ("One must delve, your honor, one must quarry
from the depths of the soul!"), and the only reason I mention this is
that by the end of the speech, Wasserman is so deeply moved and
persuaded by his own words that he makes Neigel an unexpected and
very generous offer ("And I would also like to consult your honor,
about the stories, that is"), and immediately regrets his hasty words,
too late, however, for Neigel, taken by surprise and smiling broadly,
declares, "But of course, of course! It would be a great honor for me,
Scheherazade!"

Wasserman exploits (with shocking alacrity) Neigel's gratitude, to sit
down on a chair for the first time in his presence and say, "I will discuss
my difficulties with you," in the impertinent second person, though
wonder of wonders, Neigel does not fly into a rage, but merely gets
up to shut the heavy curtains and locks the door, while Wasserman
looks on, a wan preliminary smile taking shape in his heart.

And when Neigel goes round the back to send the cook home,
Wasserman daringly turns the desk photograph around and sees "Frau
Neigel there, Shleimeleh! With two tender babes in her arms! The big
one, Neigel, feature for feature, and the little one a replica of her mother.

And the woman, you ask? Ai, beautiful she was not. Feeble and sickly she was, almost bowed under the weight of a healthy baby. I cannot deny it: I was furious, but I knew not why. Perhaps because my Sarah and I had never been the beau ideals. I have known other Jews less than beautifully formed, et! So it was decreed by the Creator. Nor did old father Mendeleh Mocher Sephorim, who in his writings depicts us in all our uncomeliness, paint us out of the fancies of his heart. Nu, and here I had always thought Chaimkeh, Ivan, and Esau were all finely turned by the Creator's hands. Perhaps it was easier for me to think so—that they are different from ourselves. And now here was this frail little thing! My heart went out to her. Of its own accord, my mouth dripped honeyed words . . . and I asked myself if she knew what her amiable husband was doing here, in this place. Et! Pretty thoughts filled my heart, and she was one of them, she and her two bouncing babes. But were my loved ones frolicking, eating, and drinking and cracking nuts that I should take pity on a daughter of the infidels? Nu, quiet, sha sha."

Neigel returns. They discuss the setting of the story. Neigel in his ignorance suggests, "Write about the moon again, as you did in the story of the Indians." And Wasserman gently reprimands him, explaining the preferability of a familiar setting, where the writer feels more comfortable, because "we will need sundry facts and piquant details to create an atmosphere. Accuracy, Herr Neigel, ac-cu-ra-cy!" he tells him, with a strange note of vengeance.

And to illustrate this he makes clear that if he should decide (!) that the Children of the Heart go to Moscow this time, Neigel would be expected to supply him with many hundreds of facts—what, for instance, men's boots are made of in Russia, and how women wear their hair, and whether there are trams or buses in the streets; but when he goes too far and hints that he may also need maps and photographs, Neigel laughs indignantly ("Tell me, *Scheissemeister*, have you gone mad? They'll arrest me for contacting Communist agents! It's 1943, don't forget! Try to find a more logical location for our story, is that clear?"). And Wasserman hangs his head and chews the dirty, brittle wisps of his beard, but again waxes courageous ("Nu, well, I suddenly remembered that things between Neigel and myself were not so simple, and I must not make myself a doormat here"), and he takes a deep breath and says that this time—and this time only!—he would comply with

Neigel's request, but it would be positively the last time Neigel would be allowed to give orders with regard to the story, and the German hisses at him with a freezing glance, "Stop puffing yourself up, *Scheisse-meister*, and start telling the story!"

And Wasserman says, "Nu, surely you understand now, Shleimeleh, what a critical moment this was! But I took aim and did not miss! I stood up on my two feet and stretched my neck out to Esau uttering these words: 'Come then, slaughter me! Slaughter me now, please, Herr Neigel, but never ask me to betray my art!' "

And Neigel is in fact impressed: his big face expresses amazement and embarrassment, and even confusion. (Wasserman: "Such scenes my mother, may she rest in peace, your great-grandmother, used to make whenever Mr. Lansky, our landlord in Bolichov, may his nose run like the blood he spilled, raised the rent. The more urgent my mother's excuses, the farther she stretched her neck out to him and the louder she wailed 'Butcher!' I used to hide under her apron and want to die of shame. But who was a prophet then to know that one day I, too, would debase myself like that; only, artistic integrity was at stake this time!")

He sits down. Still overly excited, the way he gets when he feels unjustly insulted (I think he enjoys feeling that way), and again he stands up and says in a quaking voice, "Herr Neigel, the important thing here is not myself, Anshel Wasserman-Scheherazade! Who and what am I, after all? Dust and ashes. A mere nothing. I only ask to redress the honor of art, your honor, pure, unadulterated art! Pristine literature! Because here we sit, the two of us, planning a singular experiment. Think of it, a writer is writing a story for a one-man public! And everything concealed in his heart, the anguish in his soul and its illusions, will all be testimony for a single man! Who would have believed it possible?"

This idea immediately wins Neigel over. Perhaps because nothing flatters a tyrant more than control of the mysterious channels of artistic creation. Wasserman senses this, too. "And when we have finished our little experiment, you, Herr Neigel, will hold in your hand the only remaining copy of a story by Scheherazade-Wasserman! And someday, God willing, the war will be over, and you can sit in comfort with your honorable wife and children around the spitting hearth, reading the story aloud to them, and I am certain that she, too, your honorable wife, that is, will appreciate all you endured to fan the embers of creativity even here, in such a place as this, in the midst of a terrible war, nu? What do you say to that?"

The German answers simply that he only hopes Wasserman really means what he says. The more he thinks about "our situation," the more he believes that they should, as far as possible, "behave like civilized people. Yes, civilized people." (Wasserman: "He tastes the words on his tongue as though about to say a blessing over them. Nu, beyond the curtained windows three columns of smoke rose over the camp by night and by day, and I heard the sound of the machine that stirred the corpses, and the big shovel squeaking as it lifted them and took them to the fires. And with all my might and main, I nodded my heavy head in a sign of 'Yes.' ")

"A location," says Wasserman in a barely audible voice, "we need a location for our friends." Silence. The two rest their heads on their hands and think. Wasserman, though he does not yet know the form the story should take, has an idea that the plot will unfold someplace where the war is raging. ("That is, Poland or Russia, or perhaps—even wicked Germany, though I preferred the story in my location, not his, for you understand I had to guide my actions wisely and with a sure hand, because I had hidden motives from the start, and it was not entertainment I was planning for Neigel here, but, in order for my plan to succeed, I had to resort to every weapon that came to hand, and they alas were few, so I faced him almost empty-handed! Only words did I have for slings.")

They continue the search for a location. The story, explains Anshel Wasserman, should take place in a distant, but not too distant, land. ("Perhaps you have remarked, Herr Neigel, that writers like to set their stories on desert islands?" "What good does that do?" "Ah, nu, that turns everything into a great parable!") And it should also take place in the midst of nature, where Albert Fried can show his famous skill with animals ("That was one of the more fantastic elements in my stories"). And they return to their musings: Neigel popping his knuckles, Wasserman tearing at his wispy beard and twisting an imaginary earlock around his finger. Suddenly a smile breaks out over Wasserman's face and he cries, "Lepek! The lepek mine!"

Neigel doesn't know what lepek is, and neither do I. Wasserman's explanation carries so much conviction, though, that I begin to think he's making the whole thing up. Lepek, he says, is a by-product of oil, with a special economic importance for Jews in the area of Borislav, in the Lubov region: oil, as everyone knows, is piped from the drill area to the giant refineries. Only, in many cases the pipes do not fit each other ("One pipe is the size of Chupim and the other the size of Mupim"). Or else they are old and riddled, and sometimes burst and the crude oil, known as lepek, flows over the road. "This no longer happens today," explains Wasserman. "It used to happen many years ago. Thirty or even forty years ago!" When a pipe burst, the Jews, who were the lepek workers, called "lavaks," would hurry over with their barrels and buckets and rags to collect the spilled oil and sell it cheaply to the oil company. According to Wasserman, hundreds of Jewish families eked out a living this way, as had his own brother, Mendel, before he disappeared in Russia: day and night the lavaks hovered, praying the pipes would burst. Wasserman: "I had kept the lepek story in my heart since the days of Mendl's touching letters with their air of hunger, but now I saw its time had come."

He is already leading Neigel through a thick forest near Borislav, and down the lepek mine under a boulevard of pipes from the drilling site outside the city. Thirty years now the mine has stood abandoned, and throughout that time no one needed lepek. But when the war began and oil became expensive—Wasserman weaves his story—a group of people was sent to work the lepek mines.

"And a very special group it was, Herr Neigel. A band of lavaks, Jews and Poles, one Russian and an Armenian and various others, and their leader, Otto, Otto Brig, and Otto's sister, whose name was Paula, watched over them and prepared the meals, and they rarely emerged from the mine for fear of the big Carpathian bears only Fried could tame . . . Yes, Herr Neigel, there they dwell in isolation, and once a week Otto Brig walks to the nearest town to bring in the lepek yield and carry home a bit of food for the mouths of his hungry crew, but with your permission, Herr Neigel, I will need a few extra facts about the place and its inhabitants, and about the mines, too, because in Warsaw there were libraries with books and mountains of learned journals and bibliographies, while here in our camp . . . in short, all I have is you. Perhaps you could take a little trip to Borislav, sir, to feel the atmosphere?"

Neigel, of course, reacts to this with amused laughter ("Do you hear what you're saying, Wasserman? I am running an extermination camp here! The Communists are advancing in the East, and you want me to drop everything and take a trip to Borislav for you?") and I, too, find that Wasserman has gone too far, though he certainly does seem confident. ("Because I have come to understand Neigel's soul, and I know that he is enthralled by the story, and that it is not so simple as it seems. I have also perceived that he is quite eager for the facts and details, and a man like him will not leave the story adrift in a sea of imagination without a cast-iron anchor under the boat, ai, how different he is from my poor Zalmanson, who was also keen on the facts, only for a different reason, because he abominated them! By presenting them in all their paltriness and carrying them to the brink of the absurd, he could sneer at them and rest firmer in his belief that there is no God but the God of laughter, illusion, and confusion, ai, the crooked liar . . . Nu, how did we get to that? Et! Be that as it may, I was setting the bait for Neigel by telling him 'to feel the atmosphere,' which was the very expression used by the Children of the Heart before they set off on their adventures, and I knew that Neigel would bite the hook.")

And here Neigel finally wakes up and asks a most pertinent question ("Tell me, please, who will they fight this time? Bears? Ants? The oil companies?"), a question Wasserman evades ("Who is a prophet to know? The story has not even begun yet"), till the German demands a better answer ("We will not produce any writing against the German Reich of Adolf Hitler, is that clear, Wasserman?"), and the writer: "We will produce anything we wish to write, Herr Neigel! For this is the mettle of our situation, which you were good enough to describe earlier. Think of it, we two share a wonderful secret! And we must never betray our sacred trust! It is a great boon, the privilege of being here, completely free. For me, but also for you! Oy, Herr Neigel," says Wasserman, wagging his head this way and that, "I do not know in what campaign sprouted the medal on your chest—" and Neigel says, "The battle over Lake Ilmen Shemaga. Theodore Eike's Deadman's Skull Brigades!" "Nu, yes, as you say, where was I? Aha! There I am certain you did not need half the courage I require of you now as you help me breathe life into our new story! Will you retreat in fear? Will you prove yourself fainthearted by asking for an idle tale smothered in the dunghills of the petty life with all its anguish and care?" ("I swear to you, Shleimeleh, where I found the courage I do not know. With

Zalmanson, who never asked permission to rob me of my finest sentences, never was I impertinent. Like a sheep I hung my head and smiled at him in silence.") And Neigel, stubbornly: "No no. We will not allow ourselves to be anti-German." And Anshel Wasserman: "Let us allow the story to lead where it will. I cannot decide anything in advance." And Neigel: "Is that how you always write?" Wasserman: "Almost always. Yes." ("But to tell the truth: it was not so. Even my Sarah, my chosen one, used to say in jest that for every shopping list I wrote at least three drafts.")

"Perhaps," says Neigel suddenly, "perhaps I could go through Borislav next week, on my way home on leave. I worked in the region for a few months once, and I have some matters to . . . attend to there. Yes. And also a few people I used to know. Perhaps it's time to pay a little visit." And Wasserman, his expression unchanged, points out that "a small map of the region and the oil wells there would be of great help to us." And he overcomes the temptation to ask the Nazi to investigate the Jewish community of Borislav and find out if if anyone from the old days is still around, and Neigel, a highly efficient officer, writes something in his notebook. ("It was only later, Shleimeleh, that I discovered it was in this book that Esau noted his requirements for extermination gas, as well as the number of bars of gold teeth extracted and the amounts of hair shorn, and though I did not know this at the time, I shivered as the first anchor of my fiction was cast in the firm ground of his life.")

Despite the lateness of the hour, they remain together a little while longer, at Neigel's instigation, it seems. Neigel presses the writer to describe "in a word or two" the old-new members of the band, by way of introduction, he says, to what is to come. "What is to come," he says, but his face expresses "the pleasure to come." And Wasserman consents, and tells him about the thick forest and the deep mine, and about the tunnels in the mine, and in the tunnels— "Humph," observes Neigel, troubled. "Sounds like a partisans' hideout; watch out, Wasserman." And the writer makes no reply, but I feel a burning sensation suddenly running along the umbilical cord that stretches between him and me. An old memory we share leaps briefly into consciousness, and sinks before we are able to grasp it. Wasserman answers the German, but his words are aimed at me: "No, Herr Neigel, that is, not partisans in the ordinary sense of the word but, shall we say—"

Neigel bellows something that sounds like grudging approval. Then he glances at his watch, expresses amazement, and stands up. Wasserman also stands up, facing him. It isn't easy for them to part now. They look like two comrades who, after planning a long journey, are still unsure of themselves and have to draw courage from each other. Neigel switches the big light off, so the only light now comes from his desk lamp. In the dimness where his face cannot be seen he hesitantly asks Wasserman for his opinion of their experiment, and whether he thinks it will be possible to tell a good story. Wasserman confesses that he is worried, but also rather curious. Inwardly he thanks Neigel for bringing his creative passion back to life, "and my most cherished and secret longing."

Neigel unlocks the door that separates the two wings of the barracks. With face averted he suddenly asks why Wasserman has not written anything in all the years since "The Children of the Heart." Wasserman replies, and Neigel says, "I didn't know talent was something you could run out of. Interesting . . . and . . . I just wanted to ask, how did you feel without your writing?" And Wasserman, bluntly: "May you never know, Herr Neigel!"

("Yes, Shleimeleh, I would not wish it on my worst enemy! More dead than alive, heaven forbid, you become your own tombstone. And all the while young children from all over Europe, ours and theirs, were dispatching letters of appreciation and innocent love. They read the stories reprinted in their magazines—not a mite did I ever receive!— and when they proceeded to ask why Scheherazade-Wasserman had not written in all these years, ai . . . I had to grit my teeth and answer them as amiably and affectionately as I could. And as the years went by, nu, well, the way of the world and the way of all flesh . . . In any case, I grew farther and farther from the young man who had written those stories. At first I envied him, as one envies a stranger, because of the happy days he had known, but eventually I began to hate him for not having dared more. And worst of all, my wife. My Sarah. She had met me as the writer Scheherazade, beloved author of 'The Children of the Heart,' not Anshel Wasserman the cranky proofreader, chronic sufferer from flatulence . . . and my Sarah, my soul, you understand, said not a word about it, but in my ears her silence rang, ai, may you never know such evil days and thoughts.")

I escorted him to his attic. There he sat among the piles of paper, crates of steel and wood, and scurrying mice. He put his notebook down and leaned his head against the wall. His eyes were shut. A small, frail man in an absurdly gorgeous gown there in the wretched attic. He was waiting for something, I didn't know what, and I asked him, Grandfather, what are we waiting for? but he was silent, and I asked him, What should we do now? and with eyes still shut he replied, "There is nothing to do now, Shleimeleh. I have noticed that you always want to be doing something. Waiting seems to frighten you. Only now be patient, surrender body and soul, for even if you become frightened and run away, I will not stir this time, because I have nowhere left to run, history is my life, my purpose, it is the mark God left on my flesh, and perhaps you are now beginning to glimpse the hidden side, nu, well, enough said . . ."

The next moment we were no longer alone. The air was all aquiver. My hand began to tremble as though it had a life of its own. My fingers pulled and pressed together. I looked at them in astonishment: they started to pull, but there was nothing there. They didn't stop moving. They groped. They prodded the air to make it flow toward them in a certain pattern, they propelled it wisely, stubbornly, churned it into a thicker substance, and suddenly there was moisture on my fingertips, and I understood that I was drawing the story out of nothingness, the sensations and words and flattened images, embryonic creatures, still wet, blinking in the light with remnants of the nourishing placenta of memory, trying to stand up on their wobbly legs, and tottering like day-old deer, till they were strong enough to stand before me with a measure of confidence, these creatures of Grandfather Anshel's spirit, the ones whose stories I had read and searched for and sensed so ardently, like stocky Otto Brig, always dressed in short, stained blue trousers, Otto whose movements are full and broad and infinitely generous; and now his sister, little Paula Brig, with the thick blond braid and blue, blue eyes, like Otto's eyes; vivacious Paula, who always finds the shortest distance between two points, no-nonsense Paula, who cares for the band firmly and lovingly . . . but there were still others waiting to be born, and the invisible womb contracted, and Grandfather Anshel was panting and his face was red and perspiring, and my fingers pulled out a clear, viscous liquid, and then with a long, hoarse groan of regret, and with a great yank out came Fried, little Albert Fried, silent and introverted, imprisoned in his shyness and anxiety, with barely a hope of ever knowing friendship or affection, though luckily for him, Anshel Wasserman projected him into the company of Otto and Paula, and they accepted him with such ease that he was happy to surrender his suspicions and secrets, which were unimportant and superfluous anyway, and open like a flower to the world. And who else is here? Sergei the Russian, thin and tall, Golden Hands Sergei, who could build any kind of tool or machinery, or sew the leap-in-space boots, or open a little door in the wall to distant worlds, and especially memorable in Grandfather Anshel's story were his experiments with the time machine, and the only humorous episode in "The Children of the Heart" stories is the one in which he threw the whole city into confusion—unintentionally—by turning back its clocks. And Harotian the Armenian is also here, flute in hand, and Grandfather Anshel turns to me, weak and pale, but smiling. "Heed me, Shleimeleh, invoke anyone your heart desires . . ."

"What did you say?"

"Anyone your heart desires!"

And he reaches out a limp hand and indicates the tiny attic filling up with the Children of the Heart. I notice that something is preventing them from feeling each other, it's as though they are inside a bell jar. Yes: they are moving, treading in place, they even look around as though waiting for something, but they are totally isolated. And for some reason I think I've seen them standing like this before, or almost like this anyway, but there were others with them, I couldn't remember who, and Grandfather doesn't help me. He lies on his back, his hands covering his mouth, a strange smile in his eyes, a happy smile of longing. He looks like a very ancient baby. "They are all here before you," says Grandfather gently, as though telling a grandchild the fairy tale he couldn't tell me. "And here you see them as they should be seen, not as I wrote them, but as my Sarah drew them, line for line . . ." Incidentally, only then did I realize that it was not until he had seen her drawings—and that was eighteen years after writing the series—that Wasserman had any idea what his characters looked like. "Her drawings," he confirms with a moony smile, "were to my stories what Harotian's flute was to Beethoven's leaden ears: suddenly the sweet sounds trickled behind the screen of my deafness . . ."

But five were not enough. We both felt this. And even though I didn't know at the time about the traps Wasserman was planning to set for Neigel in order to "send him back to Chelm," it was clear to me that for this war we were going to need many more warriors, partisans of an unfamiliar kind, "partisans," I say, in a special sense, that—

We looked at each other. "We are now alone in the world," said my grandfather. "Just you and I. How empty the world is. We could divide it up between us and give it a new name . . . Come, Shloma son of Tobias, sit with me in this attic, there is no one here but you and me and our friends, enough evasion, Shleimeleh! Hurry and bring in your partisans . . ."

"NO!" I screamed. I was a little frightened. Things had ended badly last time someone invited me to divide the world and name it, and the rest is history. "No, Grandfather, not you!" I screamed out loud, maybe too loud. "Not with you! I had enough of Bruno's utopia! I don't have the strength for great aspirations."

And then my grandfather explained—in his language—that utopias are not for mortals. And that people are like flies, that the stories they are told must be like flypaper. Utopias are gold-covered paper, he said, and flypaper is covered with everything man secretes from his body and his life. Especially the suffering. And our hope is that its measure is the measure of man, and forgiveness.

"And THEY, you really think THEY will be suitable?" I asked with great skepticism. "After all, they're only—"

"They are the best of warriors, in their own way. You know that as well as I. In the first place, you thought of them even before I thought of them. And though they did not appear in my story last time I told it, it will be seven times sweeter to be with them now, as it was then, on our street, in the one war worthy . . ."

And we gave birth to the others as well. Aaron Marcus and Hannah Zeitrin and Ginzburg and Zeidman, our miserable Max and Moritz, and Yedidya Munin, fresh as on the day I led them to the Beast. And they, too, stood as if surrounded by an invisible screen. Hannah was scratching her thighs and groaning. Aaron Marcus's tortured face was still twitching. Nothing had changed: feverish Ginzburg, his skin covered with ugly white scars, and not a tooth left in his mouth, was nodding his head and asking who he was in the same familiar way, while his little friend, Malkiel Zeidman, a doctor of history, they said, who had lost his mind and was now all empty inside, was as usual mimicking everyone around him, this time, by chance, it was Yedidya Munin, and the hands of both were deep in their pockets, as they groped for something with all their might. They were sighing and moaning, filled with life and motion. Wandering Jews who never stirred. We all smiled, but we didn't know why.

"Perhaps you wonder," said Anshel Wasserman at last, "why I am so generously allowing you to mix your own creations into my story? Et! What care I, so long as they are warriors, girded with bravery? You understand that this is not the first time I have spoken about the story. It is possible that even before I told it to Neigel I roamed the world telling it, and that it has given rise by now to a thousand other stories— yours will be the thousand and first—and everyone who ever heard it wished to bring his favorite into the picture, and let me tell you a little secret, even Neigel, when his time came, made a contribution to my story . . . Everyone brought only what he was, a shred of his own life, of his dear ones, his forgotten ones . . . No, Shleimeleh, no matter how many people you bring me, there will always be room for more, only the story itself is always hidden from me, and I have to approach it with my inadequate powers, and in this there is no one to help me, and you know that I, nebuch, was always a coward, and even now I shudder as I transform our friends, with a stroke of my pen, from tailor's dummies to flesh-and-blood heroes, and I know if Zalmanson were here, he would twist his mouth in mockery and say, 'The trouble with you, my little Wasserman'—this is how he used to open all his sermons to me, and someday I should sit down and try to discover where he found those flaws—'is that you are a coward! A coward in life and a coward on paper! Do you perhaps recall how many quarrels we had before I could convince you to leave your boring job in the archives and start writing in earnest? And later, when things turned out well, the trouble I took to persuade you to write a real series?! And how many nights I sat up with you urging you to dare to write children's stories unlike any written by your Hebrew predecessors? You could have taken their straight paved roads and written as they did about young Abraham smashing the idols, and King Solomon, the boy who refused to eat his porridge, until Joab the army chief hid under the table and frightened him with a terrible scream. No! We had enough of those! 'Love of Zion' and 'Youthful Instruction,' and I knew, my little Wasserman, that you would write the way an enlightened writer should. As their writers do! Yes yes (so Zalmanson said to me, would that he were here now), I was not frightened by the accusation I knew they would level at us, and I thought it fitting that at last a Jewish writer would write beautiful adventure tales, thrilling and exciting stories full of love for all mankind, not just the Jews! Nu, Shleimeleh, he so provoked me that I sat down to write my 'Children of the Heart,' and the jealous critics attacked the stories as though they had come upon much booty, and they dipped their pens in gall and slandered me, and complained about my meager talents, and also about my wicked scheme to corrupt the youth of Israel, and they were not content till they had conjured up the amiable Abraham-Mordechai Piurco, one who had written a book called *Faithful Shoots* twenty years before, and had dared collect and copy into the language of the past simple tales of goodness, loyalty, and courage, these not only from our brethren but from the Gentiles as well! And when he wanted to describe a man of character, he did not refer to Father Abraham again but, rather, may I not be mistaken, to an English sea captain named Richardson! Ai, Shleimeleh, these critics became so loathsome to me that if not for Zalmanson, whose hand never stirred from mine, I should not have written the little I wrote. Yet though I wrote, I knew I grieved him by failing to realize his hopes. And in my twenty years of writing 'The Children of the Heart' we argued over every letter and apostrophe, and he would attack my manuscript, brandishing his pen to correct and delete in a fury with a band of bad angels, screaming, 'Murderer! Thief! Plagiarist! Such talent is not lost, it is betrayed! Your talent has been left in the lurch, Wasserman! And would that you were a better thief, so the moist prints you leave in fear and perspiration would remain undetected! But all the characters are made in your own image: and even when you send them off to the most enchanted places, they remain cautious little Wassermans winding their way through your tedious sentences! You write like a Galizianer! Too long-winded! The devil only knows why I go on publishing you, and only he could understand why children are so enamored of your haggard prose! Ach, Wasserman, a little more courage! And a little more humor, too, you're not so dry in real life, you know, and you always raise a smile, however unintentionally, so why be stingy with the spice of irony? Nu, be a clown, my Wasserman, be a wedding entertainer, and something of a liar and an adulterer of words, and write with love, and most of all with madness, otherwise everything is so boring, so flat, so soulless and Godless. Nu, Wasserman, what do you say?' "

[3]

BUT SEVERAL DAYS HAVE TO ELAPSE before the story can be told. First of all, Neigel has other things on his agenda besides listening to a fairy tale about the elderly Children of the Heart. It's true, sometimes in the middle of an important meeting, or when he goes out to supervise the transports arriving on the train, he feels briefly tempted to savor an errant bubble of pleasing memory before attacking his duties once again, yet even without trying too hard to get to know Neigel, I'm sure his work doesn't suffer in the least from these digressions. Anyone who has ever seen him at work (like Staukeh, for instance) will testify with envious regard that Obersturmbannführer Neigel is made of in- destructible stuff; and even after a year and a half of the backbreaking work of running a camp, he is as tough and decisive as ever: relentless in the pursuit of duty, his own and that of his men, a dispassionate murderer, the very ideal delineated by Reichsführer Himmler (who is extremely fond of Neigel!), and now for the past few days, it seems, new strength has been steeling his limbs: you see him everywhere around the camp. It's as if there were ten Neigels, all brimming with energy and initiative and efficiency. He personally executes the two Ukrainian guards caught taking bribes; at the entrance to the gas cham- bers, he cold-bloodedly shoots four women with their children for creating a disturbance and throwing the guards into confusion; every night, the light burns long past midnight, and after that, at 2:00 a.m., he goes out to inspect the guards. Dr. Staukeh has been asked to advise the commander to take something for his insomnia. Staukeh dismisses the rumors of insomnia with a scornful laugh. Staukeh believes (I learned this from the memoirs he dictated to an American journalist visiting the mental institution in Lodz he had been committed to in '46, pending a court decision as to whether he was insane. This he certainly appears to have been, save during rare flashes of lucidity, one of which was the occasion of the interview) that no one anywhere in the Reich better exemplified Himmler's ideal of a German officer than Neigel. "But he was also so boring!" Staukeh groaned. "Such a narrow-

minded, deadly bore! There was no subject you could discuss with him
for more than a few sentences, except maybe the battle at Lake Ilmen
Shemaga and his childhood in Bavaria—Bavaria, where else? Did you
think he came from the Rhineland? Listen, you'd better not print that—
or about the horses, either. But he was a good officer. That yes. A little
unimaginative maybe, but straight and loyal as a dog. And he was
awfully serious, that Neigel. I've been thinking a lot about him at night
lately. It's hard to fall asleep here, because of the noise and the screaming.
Do you hear them? It's enough to drive you crazy . . . [irrelevant passage]
Yes. He was too serious. He took life hard. I just remembered something
else: he would laugh whenever someone told a dirty story, but it was
plain to see he was embarrassed, or that maybe he didn't even get the
joke. No, he wasn't sociable, if you understand my meaning. It's possible
that he had friends in the movement, I don't know, but in our camp
—no one. He never went drinking at the officers' club, and naturally
there was resentment, people said he was arrogant and all that"—Staukeh smiles his weird smile, the ghostly smile of a man who has experienced the indescribable—"but I think he was just shy and had childish,
conservative notions about how a Nazi officer ought to behave, a lot
of them were like that in the SS [irrelevant passage]; he—Neigel, that
is—didn't even know his driver's Christian name for a year and a
half! Only once did I ever see something really fillip him, that was
around the beginning of '42, a night in February or March, after an
officers' meeting, when he asked me to stay, much to my surprise. He
waited for everyone else to leave, and then went to the cupboard for
the bottle of 87 proof he kept for official receptions. He poured out
two glasses and said, 'My son, Karl Heinz, is three today! I promised
him I would celebrate his birthday! To his health!' And he raised his
glass in a stiff toast, and nearly choked on it. He wasn't used to drinking,
you see. I nearly choked laughing, he was so—how shall I put it—
dutiful! Of course, I tried to make the most of the situation by asking
him about his wife and children, etc., but his laconic answers gave me
to understand that our friendly visit was over." Staukeh asks the American journalist to light a cigarette for him and put it between his lips;
he is wearing a straitjacket after three attempts at suicide, a great embarrassment to his doctors, who are unanimous that Staukeh's pathological lack of conscience, and the fact that he has never expressed
remorse over his deeds, make his suicidal tendencies totally inexplicable.

And we also have to wait for Neigel's monthly leave, and his return two days later. Meanwhile, we follow Wasserman at work in his new routine and let him ramble on about a subject which has been greatly preoccupying him of late—the importance of good food for creativity, with endless laments about his digestive problems and agonized guesses about the menu for the next supper and reminiscences of other meals. ("On an evening like this in Warsaw, ai, it seems a hundred years ago to me now, before I started eating at Neigel's, I used to go to Feintoch's, spread my paper out on the checkered oilcloth, red and white always, and old Feintoch would greet me with a smile and call out to the Pole in the kitchen, 'Wasserman!' They used the customer's name instead of a menu . . .") The prospect of a nutritious daily meal after a period of prolonged starvation is naturally very exciting to Wasserman.

Many days later Neigel returns to camp, but does not bestow a single glance on Wasserman hoeing in the garden, and Wasserman is worried that something has gone wrong, but nothing has gone wrong, and at night, when Neigel finishes his work and catches up on the backlog, he calls Wasserman in and with ill-concealed pride hands over three pages torn out of his notebook, with the notes, in large letters, from his visit to the mine.

Wasserman says nothing and begins to read. ("What can I tell you, Shleimeleh, he lacked the inspiration of a fly! His notes had the ring of a military bulletin. Yes yes! In one instance I noticed our Esau had tried a little embellishment, perhaps he wanted to be charming when he wrote: 'Forking tunnels full of strange mystery.' Ah, from a pig's tail one does not a Hasid's shtreimel make!")

"Like honey!" Wasserman lies through his teeth as he finishes reading, and now Neigel lets go and starts to describe, with pride and enthusiasm, his trip to Borislav and his meeting there with an officer of his acquaintance, for whom he concocted a story about the purpose of his visit so the man would agree to take him to the deserted lepek mine, which they finally managed to locate on an old, turn-of-the-century map, and what a yarn he had had to tell to stop his suspicious questions, ah! Neigel recounts this as though boasting about some highly involved and successful military campaign in enemy territory, and Wasserman listens with downcast eyes and says at last, "Excellent, Herr Neigel, it seems the passion of the story burns in you!" and the German smiles broadly, a smile the likes of which I doubt his men have ever seen.

"Listen, Wasserman—there's a beautiful health spa in the area, with mineral springs and even a cinema! And what did I do there? I went to look for a stinking lepek mine!" And Wasserman: "Ai, Herr Neigel, that is what I sensed in you from the very beginning! You have the makings of a real artist!" And Neigel: "Ah, now you're talking nonsense, Wasserman, you know very well I'm not cut out to be a writer, though my wife did always say I wrote beautiful letters." But Wasserman shamelessly repeats some nonsense about the hidden spark in Neigel, and how important it is to free it from the daily grind of work and duty, and Neigel laughs again, dismissing his words, but a certain glow spreads over his cheeks for a moment, and suddenly he waves his hand, whereupon Wasserman and I almost start laughing rudely, because the German has unintentionally made the appropriate gesture conveying (1) a false show of protest; (2) the familiar pleasure of flattery; (3) pretended modesty; (4) and a powerful craving for more! More! (Wasserman: "See, Shleimeleh, my mother, may she rest in peace, was right when she said, Flatter Chaimkeh, and to him it rings true . . .")

"As you know," says Wasserman, when they have both settled down to embark upon the story, "we are underground."

"In the lepek mine," confirms Neigel with a hearty smile.

But Wasserman, averting his eyes, blurts out, "Perhaps yes, and perhaps no. I am not absolutely certain as yet."

At which point Obersturmbannführer Neigel wishes to ascertain whether he has heard the Jew correctly, and when it seems that Wasserman did in fact say, "I am not absolutely certain as yet," he is so furious his lips turn white and he demands to know "what is this circus?!" when only a moment ago they were discussing the mine in Borislav, where they planned the story, not to mention the considerable efforts, "and risks!" Neigel had faced in order to "feel the atmosphere" of Borislav, the stupid lies he had become entangled in, and the good name he had jeopardized, and all for what? "So you can decide on a whim that you don't want the lepek mine?!"

But Wasserman is undaunted. At most, he is thoughtful. He answers Neigel with suspicious ease. He soothes him slyly in his usual way, explaining that this is how it is with creative work—"You build something and challenge it and again build it and challenge it a thousand and one times!" And he confides to Neigel this, his mode of writing: he invents nothing but merely reveals the preexistent story and follows it like a boy chasing a pretty butterfly. "I am only the scribe of the story, Herr Neigel, its obedient servant . . ." And when Neigel at last snarls words of controlled rage and hurt pride, Wasserman goes even further and teaches him a lesson, in which I alone discern the sting of revenge: "Your main problem (!), Herr Neigel, if I may say so, is that you never leave the confines of your own skin! After all, even the powers of imagination need gymnastic exercise, else they wither and die, heaven forbid, like atrophied limbs."

Is Neigel finally going to get up and pound Wasserman with his iron fist? Will he throw Wasserman out of the barracks, back to the lower camp and the loathsome Keizler? Neigel does nothing. He contemplates that which he just heard from Wasserman. He still looks furious, but a different expression steals over his face now, a new expression, difficult to define. ("You, too, noticed, Shleimeleh? You have a scholar's eye! Yes, indeed, for a minute his face took on the look of an apprentice, of a devoted pupil attuned to his master's every word, who in his heart is already plotting to steal the master's wisdom . . .")

"Go on, tell the story," roars Neigel, "I'm listening."

"Well then," says Wasserman, "for now we are underground. Between the caves and tunnels. Can you assist me here, Herr Neigel, and tell me what it smells like in there?"

"Smells like any other mine, I should think. Only it stinks more."

"Please, begging your pardon, that is not sufficient."

"Well, okay—it smells like oil!"

"Is that all?"

"Listen, Wasserman, am I telling the story or are you?"

"I am, sir, with your generous assistance. But I may be in need of your gifts here, you understand, for I have no sense of smell, may you never know, and I am alas unable to write about scents, the prize of every nose, with which my wife used formerly to assist me. Please, Herr Neigel."

"Humph. What? Smells, you say . . . smells? Maybe there were also—" And he shuts his eyes and leans back and tries to remember. "Yes. It seems to me there were also animal smells in there. Maybe rabbits. I'm not sure. That's what I remember."

"Rabbits!" says Wasserman joyously, writing in his notebook. "I like rabbits, Herr Neigel. Listen: 'Rabbits also meet in the mines before their migration to warmer climes. And foxes by the hundreds come to hibernate here.' Nu? Nice, yes? Progress!" and he rubs his hands with satisfaction.

Neigel raises doubts about these zoological particulars, and Wasserman does not hesitate to give him the task of verification. Neigel angrily makes a note.

Wasserman continues reading from his notebook. He tells Neigel about the big hall, the "hall of friendship," the meeting place in the tunnels, adding gallantly, "with its forking tunnels full of strange mystery." Once again I must point out here that Grandfather Anshel's voice is not at all pleasant. It has a monotonous nasal quality, and when he speaks, white saliva foams in the corners of his mouth. Yet all the same, there is a certain elation in his face which makes Neigel want to listen to him. Near-charm wells up in the ugly face of Anshel Wasserman as he describes the hall of friendship built around the giant roots of an old oak tree, and there is a long and wonderful interval when I forget I understand the words and return to that old tune, and feel the passion of a child to understand the story.

The hall of friendship, says Wasserman, is where they meet toward evening, after the day's work is done. They lean against the walls and the roots, chatting pleasantly, or silently content, eating a thick soup cooked by Paula, and in the center of the hall, the flame from a paraffin lamp is dancing ("You should know, Herr Neigel, that we produce the paraffin ourselves from the lepek!"), and if Neigel strains his eyes, he will be able to see his former friends reclining among the shadows. "There is our Otto Brig, beloved leader of the band, and he, as you know, is no youngster anymore, no, he is sixty-eight years old today, and still wears those short trousers, stained with mud and lepek, and smiles his wonderful, luminous smile . . ."

And Neigel, too, sitting before Wasserman, smiles unconsciously ("May I find comfort, Shleimeleh, you saw for yourself—only a second ago his face had fallen like a wild beast's about to pounce, and now he smiles in spite of himself") and for a moment his hard, penetrating eyes reflect a distant gleam of the past, his palms rest limply, and Wasserman looks up and for a twinkling allows himself to savor what he sees, but then once again his face grows tense, with a fast, straight line under the lip, like the lash of a live and painful memory, and he mumbles, "He is very sick, our Otto."

Neigel's eyes darken and his face is suddenly alert. It looks like the face of a destroyer emerging out of the mists at dawn. "What did you say? Sick? Why is he sick?" And Wasserman: "That is how it is, most regrettably. Our Otto, who appears so strong and sound of limb, is sick indeed. He has suffered from falling sickness now for a few years, and lately his condition has deteriorated, and the doctors give him little hope of a cure. And please, begging your pardon, Herr Neigel, I am urgently in need of scientific information about his disease. And now we will proceed. Here with us in the mine is also the lovely and amiable—"

"One moment!" screams Neigel and, forcing himself to be calm, repeats, "One moment! Maybe you can stop being clever for once and give me a straight answer. Why, damn it, does Otto have to start out being sick? What can he do in that condition? Think, Wasserman! Don't ramble without a plan! Without planning and organization nothing is possible, not even a story, Wasserman!"

But it seems Wasserman has no intention of planning and organizing his story. That's how it was many years ago when he insisted on bringing a baby into the story, and even though I was still a child, I knew a baby would ruin the plot; why bring in a baby at the wrong place in an action-packed story dealing mainly with war. I had noticed this tendency in Grandfather Anshel before, this dreamy vagueness, this impressionism. Maybe I'm being too hard on him, but it seems to me that for all his pedantry—and pettiness at times—with regard to material things, in spiritual matters he belongs to that category of people who rely on the existence of a kind of benevolent logic in the world to instantly repair any damage caused by their lack of forethought and organization. And with utter unconcern, bordering on insolence, in fact, Wasserman reiterates his request ("Scientific information about falling sickness"), and Neigel disappoints me somewhat by angrily but obediently jotting down the provocative request. ("Still, I saw through him to the little boy hoping a good fairy would suddenly appear, and for this reason precisely he is willing to let me aggrieve him, because the greater the grief, the greater the pleasure in the happy ending.")

"Other than poor Otto, you will no doubt be happy to hear that all the others are in good health."

"I am truly happy, *Scheissemeister*."

"Except, of course, for those who have died."

"What?" asks Neigel in a quiet voice extruding red-hot wires of rage.

"Ai," says Wasserman sadly, "Paula has died. Our good Paula is no more . . ."

Now Neigel bursts into loud laughter, gushing over with all his contempt for the old Jew. "Paula?! But only a moment ago you said— how did it go?—that she cooked soup for us. That's it! You said hot soup!"

"Hot and thick," Wasserman agrees with him, sadly shaking his head. "What a wonderful memory you have, sir, and your words are very true. Good hot soup our Paula prepared for us, every evening she prepares it, thick as porridge; only, she died. Yes, I am afraid so. How sad it is. She is dead, yet still among us in her way. And not only she. All of us are. Living and dead. And one can no longer discern who among us are the living and who are the dead, ai . . ."

In a fury Neigel says, "Give me a simple story, Wasserman! Give me something straight out of life! My life! Something even a man like me who never went to a university can understand and feel! And don't kill anyone!"

To which Wasserman replies, "What right have you to ask me that, Herr Neigel?"

A long silence ensues. Wasserman's quiet words, said not in anger but in poignant bewilderment, seem to fill the room. Only when the impression fades is Neigel able to speak again. He says he knows exactly what the Jew thinks of him ("It's written all over your forehead"), but if Wasserman wants to go ahead and "keep our bargain or little un-derstanding," he must, even under these conditions, "show some flex-ibility," and Neigel rises from his chair and storms around the room. His large, authoritative face, determined to the point of cruelty, is now stretched to its limits. "The time has come to speak frankly," he says, rhythmically pounding his open palm with his fist. "True, fantastic things were always happening in 'The Children of the Heart,' but in the old stories it was 'cute,' not like modern writing, 'the kind you're trying so hard to imitate,' by writers who are out-and-out misanthropes. That's right! They enjoy confusing us, and what do they give us in return? Nothing! I'm telling you: only grief and disappointment!" And Wasserman refrains from asking him where he learned so much about modern writing. Wasserman feels, as I do, that this speech is just the prelude to more important things. And Neigel is indeed approaching his main point. You can tell by the way he picks up speed now, sucking his cheeks and punching his palm again and again. "That's what they give us, these modern writers, unlike the good old stories I remember fondly to this day, which must say something for them, no?" Of course, he understands nothing about writing, and doesn't pretend to be a judge of "literature," let alone stories he read maybe thirty-five or forty years ago, but Christina, his wife, whom he visited on his last leave in Munich, has a better understanding of literary things. And she has a better memory than he does, too. "Christina doesn't forget, there are people like that," he says gravely, and Wasserman listens attentively. "No, don't get the wrong impression—she isn't educated" (Wasserman: "Esau has his own special way of pronouncing 'educated,' like someone spitting out the rotten half of an apple"). "And she never attended a university either. A simple woman, that is, a normal woman. But with a certain—well, I don't know how to say it—something like a nose, a sense, a sense for what's real and what's phony." Neigel continues to speak, turning away from Wasserman, clearly it is a great effort for him to arrange his thoughts in such an orderly fashion. "She has a healthy instinct, I mean she really does," he repeats, suddenly propelled away from his gray office cabinet toward Wasserman, before whom he stands with a kind of primitive candor or sense of duty compelling him to look directly into the eyes of the Jew and exclaim, "I told her you're here. I spoke about you on my last leave. She remembers the Scheherazade stories from her childhood." And Wasserman sits up and blushes. ("You understand, Shleimeleh, I was all ears, this was no trifling matter, two admirers in one stroke!") "My wife says you were a lousy writer, Wasserman. That your stories were pretty boring, in fact, except for the hocus-pocus stuff with the time machine and flights to the moon, and even that sounded a little too familiar. You hear, Wasserman? My wife says you were just a curio. That's what she called you. A curio who was fortunate enough to find a publisher. I just wanted to tell you."

Neigel is silent. He has the unexpected decency to turn away from Wasserman, now wincing. I regard the pitiable little Jew. I should have made him more talented, more successful.

And Neigel says quietly, his face averted, "But I stood up for you, Wasserman. I defended you for the sake of my happy memories. How do you like that?" Yes, these words pain little Wasserman even more than the previous ones. Suddenly he grasps that Obersturmbannführer

Neigel may be the last person in the world to remember and appreciate his miserable creations. That perhaps simpleminded Neigel, who did not read the venomous criticism leveled against him, regarded Wasserman as Wasserman wished to be regarded. That only with Neigel could Wasserman's most cherished dreams come true.

"And now that you know," says Neigel, "there's something else I'd like to tell you. Not just about your story, but about this experiment." He starts pacing around the room again and speaks into his clenched fist. One could imagine that he was forcing the words out of his mouth. "You know," he says at last, "I've done some thinking about this over the past few days. About me and you, I mean. This is new for me, and I'd like to understand what's happening." And for a moment he stops pacing nervously and stands at his desk, neatly arranging his papers and notebooks. "You despise me," he says, his back to Wasserman. "It's like this: you're a writer and in your eyes I'm a murderer. No, don't speak now! Naturally in the old world you come from, someone like me was considered a murderer. But the world has changed over the past few years. Maybe you've failed to notice, Wasserman. The old world has died and old mankind has died with it. I live in the new world, the future I was promised by the Führer and the Reich. Yes, Scheherazade," he says, lifting the curtain and looking out, "what we took upon ourselves for the Reich is being carried out for reasons you will never be able to grasp. You and your Jew morality, with your notions of justice. I'm not so good at explaining myself. For that we have philosophers who use their noggins. I am paid to carry out their ideas. And I like my job. At officers' school in Braunschweig, I was excused by the Reichsführer himself from our ideology course to attend to the cavalry formations for the commencement exercises. I'm better with horses, you see. Still, something got through my noggin, all the same, and I know that you and I belong to different species. Your kind will cease to exist in two or three years' time, when our plan has been carried through. We'll survive. The strong will survive and they will determine everything," he vociferates at the window, and Wasserman's head nods vigorously on his spindly neck. Neigel turns to him, sees him, and is filled with inexplicable rage. "It will be our country, our air, our idea of justice and what you call morality. We'll be around for a thousand years, and that's only the beginning. If anyone comes along with different ideas, they'll have to fight us. And if we are defeated, it will mean they were right. That's how it is. And in this war you're on the losing side. We're the winners. That's what they'll say in the history books my son will read: that we're the winners."

Wasserman can contain himself no longer. He jumps to his feet, his beard bristling. He looks pretty ridiculous, I must say. His (slightly muddled) answer is that Neigel is "bitterly mistaken." In the first place, there is no such thing as old mankind, so how can you speak of new mankind. "Mankind is always mankind, and it's only mankind's astrologers who change." And he and Neigel are both on the same side, the losing side, only Neigel and his friends are willing to "sell themselves for this ephemeral mess of pottage, the illusion of defeating the weak," whereas, in fact, he, Wasserman, has always known ("The knowledge has been engraved upon my heart and body for thousands of years") that the bottom line of the cryptic ledger—he does not bother to explain who the accountant is—shows him and Neigel both on the losing side.

Neigel smiles wanly. "You have the nerve—or should I say, the idiocy?—to make such a statement here?"

And the Jew replies, "It is here in this place that you are being defeated with every passing minute. And how terrible, Herr Neigel, that you have made me feel more hopeless than I have ever felt before. Yes, perhaps you know that the soul is a wonderful apparatus, and in it are various courses and passages, all of them irreversible, indeed yes." And Neigel: "I don't understand. Please explain." Wasserman squirms, gets entangled in illustrations, and at length explains that "cruelty, indeed, cruelty, for instance, once you learn it, you may find it difficult to wean yourself thereof. Just as once you learn to swim in the river, you never forget how, or so I have been told by those who swim in the river, and about cruelty, or evil, or the doubt in man, nu, a person cannot be cruel by turns, or evil every third time, or suspicious of his fellow man every fourth, as though evil were an object man carried with him, to take out and use when he pleases, or leave in his pocket if he so prefers, and peace be unto you, my soul. No, I am certain that you, too, have witnessed the fact that cruelty, suspicion, and evil infect all of life. Once you open a loophole for them, they infest the soul like mildew."

"Ah, this is a waste of words," says Neigel. "I wouldn't expect you to understand." But his mocking smile looks strangely hollow ("The smile was a slough, I observed!"), so it is difficult to understand his need to pursue this philosophical discussion, which is beginning to bore me. "Are certain passages—I mean—do you think any passages of the, um, soul might be reversible?" "You can easily get rid of grief, of compassion, Herr Neigel, and the love of mankind, the wonderful capacity of fools to believe in mankind, in spite of everything. And the operation will be almost painless." "But can you bring them back again?" asks Neigel, his eyes fixed on Wasserman. "I hope so," Wasserman replies, and to himself, or to me, he says these unintelligible words: "After all, this is my mission, Shleimeleh, for this I am staging my comedy here."

There's no time to absorb this and respond. The plot continues of its own accord. Neigel at this point will be forced to say—in answer to what Wasserman said about love and compassion—what we all expect him to say, namely, the old cliché. "You'd be surprised, Wasserman, but we in the SS, or most of us anyway, are model family men, we love our wives and children—"

"For now," says Wasserman wearily, "for now you love them." ("Oy, how sick I was of Keizler's heartrending professions of love for his wife and their three little cherubs, and the sweet canary in the cage. How thoroughly repulsive it was!") But Neigel, a missionary explaining the principles of the new religion to a savage, is undaunted. "We pledge our love to the Führer, the Reich, and the family. In that order. These three loves sustain us when we carry out our orders." And again the Jew jumps up, waving his hand and screaming in a whiny, broken voice, "Someday—when the order comes—your people will rise up and slaughter their wives and families!" And he cackles convulsively, "The order! The order!"

Neigel regards him with a trace of mockery, but he controls himself, and waits for the outburst to pass. He then explains his position, admitting ("I won't deny it") that the "movement" ideology is harsh and extreme at times, but this, after all, is its only chance to succeed, "unlike other movements and revolutions and ideas that are doomed because they compromise at every step with human weakness!" though he is willing to acknowledge that "there have been cases of nervous collapse among us. It's no secret. I myself was acquainted with an excellent officer who committed suicide because he began to have nightmares about murdering his wife and daughters, of all things. But every war has its deserters and cowards and traitors!" And at this point I am forced to put into his mouth a piece of factual testimony from Himmler's

1943 address in Poznan: "When one hundred or five hundred or a thousand corpses are lying side by side, to continue to be decent human beings anyhow, this—with a few exceptions, the result of human weakness—is what makes us strong."

"And we are all fighting this war, Wasserman," says Neigel in a strained, almost husky voice. "Things are not as simple as they may seem to you inside the camp. Because when we kill mothers and children, we have to be strong, as the Reichsführer said. In our souls, that is. We have to be strong. To make decisions. And no one else can know about it. It's a silent war, fought by each of us. Yes, there are some types, of course, like Staukeh, for instance, who get a sort of sick pleasure out of it. There's that type, too. But a real SS officer isn't supposed to enjoy his work. Did you know that sometimes Himmler himself comes out to watch us when we make the selections, to see whether our feelings show? You didn't know? Well, he does. It's a secret war, I tell you. The winner is one who can walk the line . . . who can understand that the party demands sacrifice. Because we are on the front line here, between two kinds of humanity . . . and we are exposed to certain dangers, and in order to be a good officer, sometimes, as I said, you have to make decisions, like sending a part of this . . . of this machine out on leave," and he places two stiff fingers next to his heart. "Suspend it till the war is over . . . and then you put it back and enjoy the new Reich . . . and I want to tell you something no one else knows, it's all right to tell you, because with you it's different."

And Wasserman stares at him, and understands immediately, as I do, what has been happening here in this "White Room," under the reign of absolute physio-literary laws. Because both of us, Wasserman and myself, have waived the writer's foremost obligation, that of delineating his characters, and because we prefer to dismiss or delay our involvement with Neigel for the time being, he has cleverly and subtly taken advantage of our distaste for him in order to expand the terrain of his personality, the *Lebensraum* of his limited, posterlike existence within us, and to annex more and more character traits, levels of depth, biographical details, and logical considerations, in a word, vitality, which is what now enables him to tell Wasserman that "in the past few months, due to a certain incident of a private nature," he has been fighting that secret war here, and winning it anew each day, and again he says what Wasserman has also been saying in his own way: "These things are not as simple as they seem."

Wasserman sighs and rubs his tired eyes, and answers in a weak, weary voice. Replaceable parts, he says, which can be taken out and put back later, exist only in machines, whereas "the self, Herr Neigel, the soul, the brain and heart, ai, these do not fall into the category of machinery, unless you take a part out and turn it into a machine with your own hands. In that case, it would be very difficult indeed to repair the damage, because to do so you would need a soul, or someone who has a soul to love you." Only, between machines, he continues, love cannot exist. And he who turns himself into a machine will quickly discern that everyone around him is made the same way, and those who are made differently he will not even be able to see, or else he will want to be rid of them. "One can, Herr Neigel, be exceedingly cynical and say that we are all machines, automatons, digesting and reproducing and thinking and speaking, so that even our love for the wife of our bosom, our noble and eternal love, could mayhap, begging your pardon, fit another foot just as well, if, heaven forbid, a disaster befell our darling. And if instead of our child, whom we sometimes love till it chokes our throats, another child had been born to us, we would have loved it just as dearly. In short, the vessels we are equipped with in life, our pots and pans and paraphernalia, are by and large the same, only the world infuses them with its sundry fare, and as such—we are machines and automatons, only there is a trace of something else within us, I know not what to call it, and that is effort. Indeed, the effort we make on behalf of this particular woman, or this particular child, the evanescent spark that flashes between two evanescent creatures like us and no other two, ai, that same exuberance which brings us into each other's sphere I will call 'choice.' And inasmuch as choice is given to us so rarely, we must never relinquish it . . . that is what I wished to say, but everything is becoming so complicated and twisted, nu, well . . . I am not accustomed to making speeches either . . . forgive this mawkishness . . ." And he stops, ablush. They would have gone on arguing for hours, those two. I could see that. They were still worked up. But what interested me now was the story. The story, and the way the writer had succeeded in "infecting Neigel with humanity," clear and simple. But first I had to ask Anshel Wasserman to let me in on that "incident of a private nature" the German had alluded to; only, Wasserman was truly shocked by my request and he categorically refused. ("I cannot rush matters, you understand! After all, we have an obligation to our story, the story as a living, breathing creature, a mysterious, lovely, and delicate creature we must not twist or break to suit our own impetuous whims, lest we bring forth a kind of zhibaleh, or fetus that drops out of its mother in the seventh month, making us murderers, murderers of a living story . . .")

"And now, Herr Neigel," pronounces Anshel Wasserman, "if you wish, I will tell you my story."

Neigel grumbles that he isn't sure he wants to hear it anymore, but he folds his arms and orders Wasserman to begin. The writer opens his notebook. I alone can see that there is only one word written there. One word. Nu nu, I tell myself, I have a feeling Neigel isn't going to be satisfied with the rate of delivery.

"Begging your pardon, I will not read much to you this evening," says Wasserman, and Neigel glances at his watch. "There's not much time left anyway, after all your clever tricks!" he answers angrily, unable to refrain from asking Wasserman again, "Is Paula really dead?" And Wasserman replies, "Of course. Only, she is still among us, as I told you before." "Tell me," asks Neigel caustically, "how do you propose to bring it off? Artistically, that is—how can she be alive and dead at the same time?" And Wasserman answers, "What choice have I, Herr Neigel? Maybe you would understand better if you found yourself, heaven forbid, in my situation. Because when all your dear ones are dead and gone, you are forced to enlist them as they are." "Is that so?" asks Neigel suspiciously, but he says no more. Wasserman coughs self-importantly, and takes a deep breath.

"We worked in the forest" (reads Wasserman from the empty notebook). "The mine was deep and musty, constructed with tunnel after tunnel full of strange mystery, which gave off a smell of mildew and the dung of foxes and rabbits. The tunnels led to the hall of friendship. There we would meet of an evening after the day's work, to converse and enjoy each other's company. Old friends were with us, as well as new companions, recently recruited by our good Otto. The years that have gone by since last we met—fifty years or more!—have greatly changed us, engraved bad tidings upon our faces, and sown the seeds of old age and death in the folds of our skin. But the most important thing of all remains unchanged, with all its charm and vigor, and time, it seems, has no dominion over it, that is, the desire to do good unto those who are in need, and to have compassion on those in need of compassion, to love those who need love. And with us were Otto and

Paula and Albert Fried, ai, Fried had received the honor of a doctor's mortarboard! He, it seems, has aged more than any of us, and 'Golden Hands' Sergei was with us, too, still aloof, always busy, with the same peculiar walk, as though his neck were made of delicate glass, and Harotian, too, is with us, ai, Harotian the Armenian, world-renowned magician and wonder-worker! From Ludwig van Beethoven's loft to the banks of the Ganges in India. The same Harotian who had been miraculously rescued when the Turks fell upon his small village like a cloud of locusts, to slaughter and plunder, oy, Herr Neigel, see his sad visage, see the horrible sights engraved therein! . . ."

Neigel merely hums. Wasserman regards him briefly and continues: "Harotian, no longer a youth, has performed his magic everywhere. He was, it seems, the only member of the band lucky enough to amass a small fortune before the war . . . but when war broke out, it found Harotian in the city of Warsaw, and the gates were closed unto him, and he cursed his evil fate, ai, his magic was of no avail this time, and I will tell you a secret: for some years now Harotian has refrained from his truly wonderful magic, the magic he performed as a youth with the Children of the Heart, and now his tricks are naught but legerdemain, this for reasons of his own about which I will tell you presently. In short, Harotian was detained in Warsaw, in the Jewish ghetto, in other words, and was forced to lend a dissenting shoulder to the building of the wall round and round us, and he stood apart from us and despised us, I believe, but what choice was left him? And for his living Harotian performed his magic tricks in return for a feast at the weddings of the rich, or at the elegant Britannia Club. Our Harotian, you will recall, Herr Neigel, had captivated all his spectators in bygone days. Who could make a piano vanish together with the pianist? Harotian! Who could saw a maiden in half, heaven forbid, inside her bath? Harotian again! There is no summons of magic Harotian failed to answer. But in the ghetto, fortune did not smile upon him. Imagine, we had seen these performances so often we were sick of them. We knew all the folds in his red velvet jacket, and all the hidden pockets in his yellow tie, and the pouch with the double lining and the illusive saw. All these we knew till they tired us. But most fantastic of all was the trick with the vanishing piano, which Harotian refused to perform for us in the ghetto, his reason being that it would be wrong to show a person vanishing into thin air when so many were vanishing around us every day, and they not even pianists. Eppes, we knew it was only an excuse on his part, because to do the trick Harotian needed a stage with a trapdoor, and in the ghetto there was only one such door—in the gallows box at the Paviak, which was our prison."

Neigel, with half-shut eyes, says quietly, "I'm beginning to catch on now. Ah! You're trying to arouse my pity, *Scheissemeister*, is that it? A kind of revenge by way of a story? What sort of childish game are you playing with me here? For your own sake, Wasserman, for your own sake, I hope I'm wrong!"

Wasserman wears a look of astonishment, but says nothing in reply. ("He hit me below the belt, the brute, and did not miss his mark! He must have possessed the spirit of prophecy to understand how 'twould sour a children's writer's heart to be called 'childish'!")

"You keep that up," says Neigel, "and you'll lose your last reader." Wasserman swallows hard and continues: "And with us in the mine were also the most beautiful woman in the world, the enchanting, lovesick Hannah Zeitrin, the admirable Aaron Marcus, a man of daring experiment and despair, and the incomparable Yedidya Munin, one in a generation, slave and master of his body, aficionado of science, a man of vision, flight—"

"Just a minute, please!" Neigel raises a finger like a weary pupil who doesn't understand what Teacher said. "What's this new part? And what do you mean, slave and master of his body and all that, what's going on here?"

"You are not acquainted with him, honorable Herr Neigel. Yes, he is one of the new ones, the outsiders, hee hee, but you may be sure that Mr. Munin well deserves to be counted among our friends. Yes, all his life he has made himself the vessel of his lofty aspirations, with one thought only running through the clefts of his brain. He is the bold and even desperate warrior a man should be."

"But I don't understand what . . . that is—what can he do? All the others are good at something, aren't they?"

"Mr. Munin? Ai, a man of longings, no one ever longed as he . . . a man of flourishing dreams, winged as angels . . ." ("Ai, Shleimeleh, here I took a deep breath and imagined Zalmanson looking down at me from his heaven, the heaven of laughter and madness and falsehood and wonder, and all at once it happened: I was possessed of a new spirit, and my spirit was sweetened with all the juices of the imaginative current that began to flow in me, and for the moment I held my ground

like a tree in a storm, and I was almost uprooted, only now the tur-
bulence of my heart was quelled and I became imbued with a new and
secret joy, and I knew what I must do.") And Anshel Wasserman
continues to explain that the great Mr. Munin is the passionate hero
of unspilled seed, the arch-copulator who has not touched a woman in
many years, the Casanova of vain imaginings.

Neigel laughs a wild, nearly despairing laugh, and slaps his thighs.
I look at Wasserman and pity him. The inner war he's waging seems
pretty transparent to me: on the one hand he has his goal, his "mission,"
and every word of the story is committed to it, and on the other hand
. . . yes, on the other hand, little Wasserman simply wants to tell a
good story, the way he used to, and again see those misty eyes and the
mouth open in a smile of delight; but duty calls . . .

"Very nice, very nice," groans Neigel at last, wiping tears of laughter
from his eyes. "I haven't laughed like that in a long time," he says. "You
surprise me, Scheherazade! Now we have some Jewish pornography in
our story! I guess all the things they say about you in our *Greuelpro-
paganda* are true!"

"Herr Neigel, sir!"—Wasserman raises a hand in protest—"my story
is poor indeed at present. I, too, know that. Perhaps I know it even
better than you, because I glimpse the flaws you yourself are unable to
see, begging your pardon. Only, you understand, in my wretched state
here I am forced to present you with the first, rudimentary draft of the
story. And believe me, it breaks my heart to bring such an inferior
version into the world, but since I have undertaken this task, a man
such as I will not run away; only, I ask you to be merciful and patient,
and entrust my story to the cushions of your compassion and good-
heartedness, as you would a tender babe. I promise you that you will
be amply recompensed in time to come."

"Fine," says Neigel, careful not to start laughing again. "We will
finish here today. I have a little more work to do, if you don't mind.
You may return to your room now and write. We'll continue tomorrow.
I wish you better writing in future. For your sake, Wasserman, I hope
my wife was wrong."

"Pardon," whispers Wasserman. "Perhaps you have forgotten, sir,
my part . . . of the bargain, that is."

"Not today, you don't deserve it today," says Neigel aggressively.
"As you very well know."

("Meaning that before me lay another evening and another day, ai, so many hours of life, and the exhausting work in the garden, of digging furrows, may the earth cover them already! And another three transports will arrive in three trains, and people will run naked through the *Schlauch*, and there will be more smoke, blacker than black, how will I endure it, Shleimeleh? How can a person see this and live?")

"Good night, Herr Neigel."

[4]

"IN THE MONTH OF APRIL of the year 1943, an old man stood at the entrance to a lepek mine in Borislav forest, and with grim determination traced a line in the dirt with his toe. This singular act was the old man's way of challenging life to cross the line and reveal itself. And since there was no law forbidding Jews to draw lines in the dirt, Dr. Albert Fried, who was a Jew, had been doing this with the same grim determination every morning now for three years."

Thus Wasserman reads to Neigel. But as I peek behind him, I see that there is still only one word there, a word I can't make out, in the notebook he reads from so fluently. Now he puts his notebook down and pauses. He's waiting for me. He wants me to help him sketch the figure of the doctor. I still remember Sarah Wasserman's illustrations from the late editions, showing a tall boy, shoulders slightly hunched, with a serious, sensitive face, but now I also have to forget in order to remember him as he is today, and look at the face Wasserman calls "grimly determined," moving his foot again and again in that strong, defiant movement. It seems to me the shoulders should be placed a little higher, in a threatening posture that conveys his defensiveness, and the eyebrows should look a little more ferocious, and be joined over the bridge of the nose . . . A pipe? No, not Fried. But a cane— definitely. The kind he agreed to only after walking became utterly impossible for him without it. The kind he carried with reluctance, with loathing, by way of punishment. Now I have to think: What is it that our Fried calls "life"? Or maybe, after one look at him, I should put it the other way around: What does he not call "life"?

An easy question. The answer flows: Various events in his life, most of the people he's known since childhood, all of his relationships; in short, everything that once seemed almost unbearable and had become totally unbearable since the war began, and which seemed to him only the prelude to what must soon begin, but never soon enough. The old doctor refused to accept the idea that a man could pass his entire lifetime without once being vouchsafed the taste of life. He felt this way because he had a great respect for life and refused to believe in the drafts his own life constantly tried to push into his hands.

"Well spoken," says Wasserman to me, his face aglow. "And now listen: only once did the taciturn doctor reveal his thoughts, in a confidential moment, to Otto. Raising his enormous bear-paw hands in wonder, he called the life he was living 'camouflage.' With that, it seems, he had told all, all he endured till after several months' agony he had come to believe in the wonderful desperate act of illusion performed by his beloved Paula."

"What desperate act?" asks Neigel suspiciously. "Do explain." "Later, later, if you please," Wasserman scolds him. "Soon enough you will know and understand, but now you must listen patiently. Where were we? Ai . . . nu, yes. For three years since the day his Paula left him and went to her grave, the doctor has been drawing a determined line in the dirt with the tip of his shoe. And only Otto Brig, who can see deep into the heart, knows all Fried's secrets and understands what lies at the root of this strange act. But life, Herr Neigel, real life, simple, worthy life, did not hear his cry, and the doctor began to suspect that the silence of his adversary was not so simple as it seemed, or perhaps—that it was a condemnation . . ."

Wasserman is still "reading," but by now he senses that Neigel's silence isn't so simple either. Therefore, he raises his head and meets the contemptuous eyes of the German. "What are you dribbling on about, *Scheissemeister*? Who did you copy all that philosophy from?" (Wasserman: "Ai, if I could, I would have rent him asunder like a fish! But I contained my rage and waited for my Adam's apple to stop bobbing, and spoke to him with shining countenance.") "I did not copy it, Herr Neigel. I wrote it with my heart's blood. Our Fried is about to become the cornerstone of a new story, you see." And Neigel says, "But really! You're not going to fool me like this. You used to write so . . . differently!" "Indeed I did." "I don't like this new style one bit." "Ai, would that you blessed me with your patience, sir." And Neigel, weary, almost whining, says, "I like simple stories!" To which the writer, with a trace of cruelty, replies, "There are no simple stories anymore. And now, be silent and listen, and stop interrupting all the time.

"A greenish eczema had erupted around the doctor's navel one morning, and when he looked in the journal where he used to note his symptoms and diseases, not because he was a hypochondriac by nature, heaven forbid, but due to his simple curiosity about the portents of his demise, he found that both the year before and the year before that, on the anniversary of Paula's death, the same strange vegetation had erupted in the same spot. Two years ago he had described it as a 'light skin rash,' and last year as a 'greenish fungus,' and this year it was 'a moss-like acne.' At first he tried to scrape it off with borax, and later with alcohol, and then finally he tried to pull it off with his fingers, only it was like plucking hair, and he screamed in agony. Just then the quite uncharacteristic thought crossed his mind that perhaps it was not so simple. At the same time he experienced a strange delight, verging on giddiness or perhaps despair, and made a decision not to remove the eczema until evening. For the time being he merely touched it secretly under his shirt, with a kind of private pleasure, as though it had been a perfumed letter smuggled through to him in his prison."

Wasserman inhales deeply, and quietly waits for something. ("Nu, what do you say, Shleimeleh? The old tailor still remembers how to stitch, eh?") But Neigel pays no attention to the subtleties of Wasserman's narrative style and is interested in something entirely different. Were Fried and Paula married? he asks, one finger raised sternly, and Wasserman becomes confused and stammers, "Married? Well—no. That is, they were not married. But they lived together as man and wife. That is how it was. Yes. Now I remember." "In '43? Don't forget she was Polish, and he was one of yours! A little while ago you told me that a story has to be convincing in all its details. Accuracy, you said, remember?" And Wasserman cries, "I remember. And may I again remind you about patience." ("But my earlobes burned with shame, Shleimeleh, and the old fear possessed me that again my absentmindedness would be my stumbling block. For this kind of blunder overtook me from time to time when I was writing 'The Children of the Heart,' and had it not been for Zalmanson checking the details, there might have been, heaven forbid, real catastrophes in my stories, and I will confess another secret to you, Shleimeleh: Harotian's parentage is based on just such an error. But enough of this. Back to our story.")

". . . and now Otto and Fried recline outside the hall of friendship, playing a game of chess by the light of the paraffin lamp." "Like the old days, eh?" roars Neigel, his eyes softening. "Oh yes, Herr Neigel.

And Fried is still winning. Just like the old days." Wasserman describes
how the doctor, Fried, makes another V sign in the long column under
his name on the oily page. Otto's column is empty. Otto—Otto of all
people—was the one who insisted that they keep the score each game,
and the doctor, who guessed the reason for this, pretended these easy
victories afforded him pleasure. Neither of them made mention of the
anniversary of Paula's death, though it was never out of their minds.
But after a while the silence became unbearable, even to two such
taciturn men, and Otto cleared his throat and said quietly that Fried
was torturing himself, that Paula had loved him as he was, that there
was nothing to regret, that they had shared beautiful moments of friendship, and perhaps even love . . . [Wasserman:] "Fried answered not a
word. His face was impervious, and he seemed to have heard nothing,
but unconsciously his hand pushed the black king toward the white
queen, and lingered there before her, a small muscle twitching on his
cheek.

"Then Otto raised his blue eyes to Fried. And this act was known
to have a remarkable influence on the doctor, because Otto and Paula
were brother and sister and Otto's eyes were as blue and clear as Paula's,
and whenever the doctor felt the sadness in his heart about to crush
and destroy him, heaven forbid, he would approach stout Otto and lay
his hand upon his shoulder and gaze into his eyes. Then a small act of
real grace took place: Otto quit his own eyes, nobly absenting himself,
and allowed Fried to commune with his Paula."

"That could happen—I mean, it could, you know," says Neigel. "My
little one, Karl, has the same eyes I do. But exactly. And my wife,
sometimes when she used to—when she misses me, she picks him up
and looks at him in the light . . ." And only now does Neigel recollect
his status and the status of the person he is talking to, and he laughs
awkwardly, jerking his nose, and then with unjustified anger hurries
Wasserman on with the story.

"As the doctor immersed himself in Otto's eyes, he felt his hardness
of heart and bitterness melting, and for a moment all the bad years
slipped away. He was frightened when the time came to pull out of
this enchanted pond." Wasserman sighed deeply and his eyes wandered
in space: "Ai, Herr Neigel, one could say that our story, or any story,
for that matter, comes out of the blueness of Otto's eyes . . ."

Fried was talking to himself. I could hear him. His voice, like Wasserman's, had the gray quality of the written word. He said, "I think of her when I rub my elbows with half a lemon so they won't be rough like tree bark, and I think of her when I brush my teeth to the tune of 'Gertie Had a Fellow,' that's how she taught me, and I think of her when I put a rose in a glass of sugar water to keep it fresh. Paula could stare at a flower for a whole hour. And I never put a flower in water in my life before I lived with her; I didn't know my elbows were rough. I think of her when I spit three times on seeing a spider—it doesn't do any harm, she said—and I think of her when I take my socks off at night and smell them, in homage to her, because Paula was a great sniffer of socks and underwear. I think of her when I deliberately leave the faucets dripping and the lights on to show her, wherever she may be, that I, too, am careless and absentminded, and that I regret having lost my temper with her over such trifles, we quarreled unnecessarily sometimes, and I think of her also—" Fried is silent with embarrassment. Wasserman leans forward, as if to whisper encouragement, Nu, Fried, there is no need to be ashamed, we know each other's kishkes here, but Fried chokes on a prolonged cough and blushes (What is he hiding? What secret has the doctor been keeping all his life?), till little Aaron Marcus, elegant even as a miner, comes to his aid. "And even when you pass wind, dear dear Fried, never be ashamed . . ."

Silence. I take advantage of the interlude to read the lines I hurriedly wrote down. I correct a word here and there, add an explanatory note. (The pace of events!) And I thank God when Neigel, calm and self-assured even now, saves me from my terrible embarrassment and scolds ("I thought you were a cultured man, Wasserman") this terrible old man with a look of amusement. But Wasserman doesn't react. He continues to read, and I can only wait for more of his follies.

"And even when you pass wind, Pan Doctor, says Mr. Marcus, and indeed, Herr Neigel, sir, while Paula was alive Fried discovered a secret law: that whenever he thought he was alone and allowed himself to pass wind modestly, to twitter down under, as it were, Paula would appear out of nowhere, and though Fried wished to bury himself alive, Paula only smiled secretly, and the same intimate happening repeated itself many times each day, as fixed as the laws of heaven, till even now, three years after Paula's death, our beloved doctor passes wind and shuts his eyes, waiting like an innocent child for the sound of her approaching footsteps, ai, and on days when misery and sorrow fill his life, Fried leaves the mine and strolls through the forest alone, tooting and honking, the sounds rolling down through the tunnels like the bitter cry of wild geese . . ."

Neigel can no longer control himself and again he laughs out loud. Who would have believed that this tense and suspicious man had such merry laughter hidden inside him? "Not bad, Wasserman, not bad," he groans. "That's what I call entertainment. It's not at all what I meant when I asked you for a story, but it's getting interesting now, although"—he admits and wipes his eyes and cheeks—"it is a little difficult to think of my childhood heroes as a bunch of old farts." "I hope you will become accustomed to this in time," says Wasserman dryly, disappointment and deep humiliation filling his eyes. ("Nu? Have you ever seen the like of this yekke? Nothing could ever touch his heart, for he sees only the outward manifestation of things! Feh! The way he opened his mouth and bared his ox teeth with a bellow of laughter! And here I am, telling him a story about true love between a man and a woman, a love that overcomes the barriers of time! And about the agony of saying words of love when there is no longer anyone there to tell them to, and no more words to tell . . . and he—ai . . . a bull, I tell you, A bull even if you send him to Yahoupitz returns a bull!"), and Neigel continues, "And I hope, Scheherazade, that we'll soon have more serious action than farting, pardon the expression." And Wasserman: "But of course, your honor! Extremely serious! Yes indeed, 'action,' as you say!" ("And God only knows how I had the audacity to lie like this. Nothing in particular was in my mind at the time, Shleimeleh. And I knew not why my Children of the Heart had banded together again, or against whom they would wage war this time, or how I would infect Neigel with the Chelm disease, as I call it . . . but for the first time in my life I knew I had the chance to succeed as a real writer. And I only hoped I would have the strength to conquer the unknown and to overcome the forgotten and to tell the story as it should be told, from birth to death, and in all my old bones now the new fire burned and filled me with heat and pleasure, till I could hardly contain myself. It was as if an invisible presence on the other side of the page were tugging at my pen and my heart.")

Neigel now stifles a broad yawn. He announces that if Wasserman has finished he is free to go to sleep now, because Neigel has a lot of work before him, adding generously, "That wasn't too bad today for a start." Wasserman gazes deeply into his empty notebook. Over and over he reads the single word written there, and says that if Herr Neigel wishes, they can stop here. It makes no difference to him. For his part, he could go on reading till dawn.

They are about to separate. Something strange is taking place here. I don't understand what Anshel Wasserman is getting at with his grotesque and vulgar story. These vagaries of his are pretty embarrassing. They even make me angry. He's bringing a dimension of low cunning into a story which in my eyes is too momentous to be turned into cheap comedy. But he'll stoop to anything to get what he wants. It's not easy with him sometimes.

And then there's Neigel: I find him strange, too. That doesn't surprise me, because we're so different. And yet, my responsibility as a writer, and my curiosity: Where will Neigel burst forth for me? Is it possible to bridge the gap between us for the sake of art? I wait patiently. "Good night," says Neigel, the character I don't yet know. "Please, begging your pardon," says Wasserman, "if I may remind you, sir, you owe me something." And when Neigel arches an eyebrow in wonder ("I? Owe you?"), the old man calmly replies, "Our contract, your honor."

I do not understand him. Why does he still want the— Neigel, too, is surprised. Even alarmed. His hand touches the revolver in his belt and recoils from it, as if it were boiling hot. And when Wasserman stubbornly refuses to yield ("You promised, sir!"), Neigel takes his gun out of the holster.

It's a medium-sized weapon, of a type I'm not familiar with (could it be an Austrian Steyr?), highly polished. (It must be a Steyr. Or maybe—of course! The Parabellum. How could I have made such a mistake! It's definitely that, the Lüger Parabellum, with an eight-shot barrel—let's see if I can still remember those army quizzes we used to have fun with—9 mm caliber). Neigel shifts his position again and again. He tries steadying his right wrist with his left hand. (Definitely a 9 mm . . . Like a German Mauser, except with the Mauser you can load ten bullets at a time.) The gun traces a couple of tentative circles around Wasserman's temple, where beads of sweat are glistening. ("Through the window I saw the red flame, the eternal light, atop the great smokestack, and also the blue lightning from the torches the guards flashed at the fences. Neigel's hand is steady but tense.") (Naturally I'm talking about the semiautomatic Mauser here, not the au-

tomatic Mauser with a 25 [!]-shot barrel, the kind they say you can
actually feel the bullets shooting through at a fantastic speed.) And
here's one more attempt by Neigel to stop ("Look here, Wasserman,
this is pretty stupid now that we've gotten . . . well . . ."), an attempt
that provokes a theatrical explosion of anger from Wasserman ("In
dreierd, Neigel! You gave me your word, the word of a German officer!"), and Neigel, in a rage: "But that was before, before we started
telling the—" And Wasserman, mercilessly: "You slay thousands every
day, Jews from all over the world pass before you like sheep to the
slaughter, and I have seen you dispose of many with your own hands
without a moment's hesitation, heaven forbid! And what am I asking
of you now? A mere trifle! To do what you always do, only this time
willingly, as a matter of choice. Or are you unable, Herr Neigel? Shoot
me, let fly, nu! Ashes in your eye, a bullet! *Feuer*, Herr Neigel, *feuer*!"

Neigel closes his eyes and fires, emitting a strange sound, a moan or
a strangled groan of fear. Wasserman is still standing safe and sound,
with a peculiar expression on his face, as though listening to something.
("In me, between the ears, flew the familiar buzz.") Behind Wasserman
a windowpane is shattered. Neigel stares at it with trembling hands.
He makes no attempt to hide the trembling. His face is contorted, as
though someone were crushing it from the inside. To me Wasserman
says, "In any case, Shleimeleh, when the shot rang out, an exceptional
message was engraved in my heart: Unto my tale shall a child be born."

Sometimes he tells me a little about his wife, producing a distinct if
incomplete portrait of her. Sarah Ehrlich entered his life when he was
a confirmed bachelor, forty years old. She was the daughter of Moshe-
Marizi Ehrlich, the owner of a small café in Praga, and her mother had
died when Sarah was three years old. Sarah worked in the Schillinger
wig store. Wasserman said he remembered that once, on the eve of a
holiday, when the store was empty of customers, he had walked by and
seen the "thin gray girl" behind the dingy glass playing her recorder
for two of the other salesgirls. He remembered the look of elation
softening her sharp features, the mocking smiles of the two salesgirls,
and the way her black hair fell on her cheek. He wondered how he
could ever have felt such strangeness toward the woman who later gave
birth to their daughter. It seems to me this disappointed him. Anshel
Wasserman, despite his humble, rather dry appearance, was a romantic
at heart. I asked him whether he ever felt the same strangeness after

his marriage, and he was silent. I told him I believe that in marriage one is destined to know the whole gamut of feelings between any two people anywhere. He looked at me in bewilderment. I don't believe he expected such a remark from me.

The best time to get him to talk about his former life is when the trains arrive. Wasserman can hear the train from miles away. Then he starts digging in the garden with renewed industry. He abandons himself completely to the digging. A few minutes later the train sounds one long and two short whistles. This is the signal for the Ukrainian guards from all corners of the camp to take their places on the rooftops and watchtowers overlooking the *Himmelstrasse*. The engine throttles as the train silently enters the station, sliding over the rails with an eerie hush. Then there is a loud screeching of brakes and sparks fly. One can see the eyes peering through the slits in the boards nailed to the windows. Looking out, they see the well-kept grounds of the camp, the benches and occasional flower beds along the handsome boulevard. They see the little signs pointing TO TRAIN STATION, or TO GHETTO, arrow-shaped signs with the figure of a bowed and bespectacled Jew carrying a suitcase ("Zalmanson, may he be healthy, would have said this Jew was the image of me"). Now they're getting off the train, hundreds of them from every car, and the Ukrainians hie them on with shouts and blows. The arrivals are stunned, numbed from standing throughout the long journey here. They are still dressed, but in Wasserman's eyes they are already naked. Though they are alive, he can already see them piled on top of one another. He groans in the dirt. His tears are spent.

He's talking. At times like this he seems almost eager to talk, forthright and uninhibited. He talks fast, frantic to drown out the other noises. Sarah was twenty-three years old when they met. Wasserman: "Nu, what could we do? We were married in four weeks, with Zalmanson for a witness." The chuppa ceremony took place at the home of Zalmanson and his wife, Zilla, who, as may be expected, invited many of their own friends. "Believe me, Shleimeleh, most of the guests were strangers to me. Nu, well, I hardly even knew the bride . . ." But the marriage seems to have turned out well in the main. His forty years of dour loneliness had been shattered the very first time he acknowledged his need for another person. In the eyes of her family, Sarah had been an old maid, and her father never believed she would marry. One flaw he saw in her was her lively intelligence and education. "No one wants to marry a yeshiva bucher!" her father screamed whenever he saw her "ruining her eyes" with her reading. He was a sprightly man, coarse and friendly, who loved his daughter and pitied her. Perhaps it was because he considered her a bad match that he consented to her marrying Wasserman with the hump, who was also—disconcertingly—almost his own age! Wasserman tells me dryly that they spent the honeymoon in Paris, obviously the least suitable place in the world for them. Paris had been chosen for them by the father of the bride. He paid for the wedding trip, in the hope (no doubt) that the City of Light would brighten the blushing, always earnest couple. Wasserman staunchly refuses to discuss that week in Paris. I can imagine how lost and helpless he must have felt sometimes as they wandered the busy boulevards at each other's side. He was angry with himself for being such a clown, for betraying his solitude and the understanding silence between him and his life.

Now families group together, and parents call their children around them. They smooth a child's wrinkled garment, moisten their fingers with spit to groom a stray curl. They are intent on trifles. Wasserman wants to stick his head into the loose earth. Jews, camp inmates from the "blue" group, welcome the new arrivals on the platform. They calm them, smile at them. They have their own reasons for wanting the process to run smoothly and quickly, which is why they help the hoax along. The passengers begin to thaw. The illusory station deceives them. It has everything: a small ticket office, an information booth, signs pointing to the TELEGRAPH OFFICE, RESTROOMS, BIALYSTOK TRAIN, VALKOVISK TRAIN, as well as a list of departure times, a restaurant, and the big, punctual station clock.

Wasserman tugs at my sleeve. He wants me to listen. He has things to tell me. Now. Right now.

After their return from Paris to Warsaw, things started to improve. Sarah was an intelligent woman, and she saw into his heart. She did not bring change into his household. She did not overstress her presence. She sensed the hidden threads of his routine and was careful not to tear them. Summery suppers were served at the table on the tiny veranda; sometimes she played tunes he liked on the recorder. At his bidding she read the books that were important to him (*Errors* by Lilienblum; *Fliegelman* by Numberg; the stories of Sholem Aleichem,

Gordin, Asch, and, of course, Tolstoy and Gorky. And again our own
Peretz, and Mendeleh Mocher Sephorim, of whom he was very fond).
Her small, gay sketches, drawn in very fine pencil, gradually surrounded
him. She accompanied him on a visit to his parents in Bolichov, and
rejoiced with him when he spouted a fountain of memories. From his
old mother she learned to bake rugelach and strudel, and biscuits that
tasted just like hers, till he felt a vague, irrational annoyance with her
for cooking as well as his mother.

At such moments I try to get all the information I can out of him.
I suggest a phrase and wait for his reaction. I already have some idea
about their life together, but occasionally I make a mistake, like the
time I said, innocently enough, "But I was never a good husband to
her, ai, a good husband I was not, Shleimeleh." He was perfectly furious
with me, and only after I appeased him did he correct me. "I was a
good husband to her. I did everything she wanted, I gave her everything
she needed. Only sometimes I was also, eppes, a bit of a miser. In love,
that is," and a moment later, to himself, "Nu yes, yes. But who was a
prophet then to know we would have such a short time together?"

On another occasion he elaborated still further: "But yes. I was a
cheapskate, a miser in love. And I should have been happier and more
forgiving than I was. Happy with her, that is. But I, may I atone for
her little fingernail, even when I wanted to show her my feelings, once
in a great while, all my feelings for her, nu, I would choke with a kind
of swelling in the throat, like the ruffles on a stuffed turkey, which
condemned me to silence and made me turn my loving countenance
away from her. And why? I do not know. Perhaps I feared to show
her how much I needed her. Sometimes it seemed to me that I would
burst, heaven forbid, into a thousand pieces if ever I allowed my love
for her to peep out the width of my little finger."

And I help him with all my heart. "And maybe it was a kind of
childish anger, too, at the humiliation. The silly, imaginary humiliation:
after forty years of self-sufficiency you were now enslaved to her. To
the sound of her voice. To the way she smelled after her bath. To the
way her hand brushed her hair away from her eyes." And Anshel Wasserman, touched by this, reciprocates with a hint, which only I, knowing
him so well, can fully appreciate. "And the flesh, begging your pardon,
how shall I say it, Shleimeleh . . . the body, that is"—and I quickly
rush to his assistance—"and the body, too, the body needs her so much.

Her youthful agility, her flesh taut across her bones with the wild power of life and passion. The disorientation engendered by the new, not quite ripe, wholly imaginary geography of her young breasts, and her waist and belly and thighs, and sometimes, too, Grandfather, after all the words of wisdom, how great is the solace two people bring each other with their bodies . . ." And he: "Even on the way here, may a curse fall upon my head, Shleimeleh, nu, it is a little difficult for me to talk about . . ." I provide him with the words: "And we were crowded together on the train through the night and she clung to me like a fledgling, but I could not enjoy even these last few moments, I was peering around every minute to make sure the child was asleep, that no one was watching these pure, desperate embraces . . ."

And on another occasion Wasserman says, "Today I know that for some people the meaning of life is their work; for others, perhaps, art or love is the root of their soul and the only meaning of their existence. But it seems that I am the shlimazel type, because my Sarah was the very meaning of my existence, but it was only here that I found out. Ai, I think most creatures know how to preserve their souls from such an error. And may you preserve your soul as well, Shleimeleh, because he who is in love with love will always find someone new to love, but I pierced my ear for a single woman. I had no life after her, though I never knew how to love her as she deserved to be loved . . ."

Now the buffet. The arrivals notice the buffet in the simulated station. Everything is there: rolls and cigarettes and little cakes and chocolate balls wrapped in red foil. It's always the children who discover the counter first, and beg their parents to buy them something. Wasserman says, "The display of refreshments beguiles even us. For a moment we all turn into children. To this temptation, even the most suspicious among us succumb. Et! Do you remember, Shleimeleh, that young genius of an officer named Hoppfler who chased me to Neigel's? He is in charge of the buffet. He sells nothing, of course. He is a respectable officer, not a vendor. But he wipes away the soot of the engines and the crematoria each day, and washes the thin glass pane, and replaces the moldy rolls with fresh ones, and folds the colored paper in the crack set up for that purpose. I watch him and wonder: So young and yet so enterprising! How painstakingly he builds the lovely stack of cakes, to make it look more enticing! Happy the eye that beholds his handi-work! He steps back, studies it, and approves. An architect he should be when he grows up. Or a pastry cook. The boy is clearly an artist. A very real and humble artist. Now he will take a damp towel, but not the one he uses to wipe the glass, heaven forbid, and polish the red chocolate balls and the refreshing bottle of seltzer."

Wasserman digs holes in the ground and reckons on his blackened fingers: twenty years they lived together. About seven thousand days. Only seven thousand days. Wasserman: "That makes a thousand Thursdays . . . ai . . . how sad it is . . . and so much spoiled by petty quarrels and my foolish temper . . . I did not know, I could not bear the simple happiness, the guileless joy she tried to give me. I despised the sacrifice she made for me. The sacrifice of her youth and her talent for loving . . . in my mind I confected the delusion that Sarah had married me because of a mistaken ideal . . . her ideal of me as the gifted writer inspired by lofty thoughts, and the war between good and evil, nu yes, she, too, had swallowed my stories in her childhood, and because of them she came to me . . . and that is why, out of spite, I tried constantly to make her see how wrong she was about me. That this Wasserman she took for her husband was nothing but an ugly weakling and a coward, feh! I had to test her, you see, to find out when the breaking point would come and she would finally chide me and hurl disgrace at me, the disgrace of her disappointment . . ."

Yet: "All the same, I had no one else but her, and she, too, it seems, loved me, and we were fond of being together, and talking; that baleboosteh, my Sarah, was very clever, cleverer than I by far . . . and we also enjoyed doing housework together, nu, well, I am not ashamed to admit it . . . Sometimes, in a moment of tenderness, while baking a cake together or taking down the winter clothes and storing the summer clothes away, or scrubbing the floor, sometimes our eyes would suddenly meet, nu, you understand . . . the air, I tell you, the air was charged, and flowed like honey between us . . . Then we looked into each other's eyes, and once we looked, we were compelled to, nu, that is—embrace, begging your pardon. Ai, like bolts of lightning were our kisses then . . ."

About their daughter Wasserman never speaks. Her name was Tirza, and she was born nine years after the marriage. The little I know about her comes from fragments I heard from Grandma Henny when I was five or six years old, and from my mother's faded memories. That is all.

"And I will reveal another secret to you, Shleimeleh," says Wasserman, his face softening. "We used at first to be silent together a great deal—my Sarah and I, that is. She—she was diffident, and I—nu, well, that suited me, for I could find nothing in my life worth telling her about in the evening. Et! a life of utter boredom, I was convinced. And did this life of mine deserve magniloquent phrases? Nu, and then came my lamb, my Sarah, and taught me the usages of connubiality, and showed me in her modest way that every moment brings wonders and no one is without a thread of grace, even a soap bubble shimmers in the sunlight; in short, she edified me, saying, 'Everything, I want to tell you everything, Anshil'—that is how she pronounced my name: Anshil, like a kiss—'everything, and you, too, if you met somebody and spoke with him today, please tell me what he said to you and what you said to him, and about the angle of his hat and how he laughed or sighed,' and she, too, would tell me about the wig shop, and little by little our life together blossomed with trifles, and at length the trifles grew very precious in our eyes, you see, in this way Sarah in her wisdom enlivened my humdrum existence . . ."

Neigel leaves the barracks now. Spruce and polished in his uniform, he walks out past Wasserman, pretending not to see him. He strides toward the platform, signifying that today he will choose fifty new workers for his camp to replace the present squad of blues. Wasserman watches the blues. They are watching Neigel. They know that if he approaches the platform there will be a selection and new workers will replace them. Yet all the same, they continue their work of greeting the arrivals with soothing words. "Oh, Lord," whispers Wasserman. "Do you, Shleimeleh, understand why the blues do not rise up against their captors and barter their lives for the life of at least one of them, when everything is plain for all to see? I will explain the matter to you now . . ." But I'm not interested in hearing his explanation. I have my own ideas on this matter of "sheep to the slaughter."

"And once, about two years after we were married"—Wasserman tears his eyes away from the platform and resumes his story—"I was plunged so deeply in self-pity that my Sarah went to a Hanukkah party at Zalmanson's without me. It was the sort of party I had wearied of, the sort I had always attended for fear of giving offense to Zalmanson, who never noticed me in any case: he always had a new crowd around him to impress, ah, that Zalmanson was a shvitzeh." "Yes, yes," I press him. "We'll hear about Zalmanson another time. Now tell me what happened there." "Do not rush me, Shleimeleh. It is a delicate matter . . . You see, Sarah went alone, as it happened. With tearstained eyes she went . . . and I was dour and let her go without restoring the harmony between us, wretch that I am . . . and at the party"—his voice sounded distant and gravelly—"you see, she let Zalmanson push her into the coat closet and kiss her on the lips. Nu, well, that is what happened. Now you know. I never told a soul . . ."

What? A thing like that, happening to them? In those days?

"And how did you find out about it, Grandfather?" He probably followed her around and tortured her with his suspicions, till she confessed. Or maybe he found a letter from Zalmanson. Or did someone tell tales?

"When she came home she told me everything. She did not ask for mercy and did not lay the blame on him. The rake! She said she saw he needed her, and she could not refuse. He needed her! Ah, the innocent child! How was she to know that Zalmanson was a lecher? Oh yes, the virtuous paterfamilias he seemed, devoted to his wife and three ugly daughters; only, I knew, from his own lips I knew, that any passing skirt was enough to ignite a spark, an all-consuming flame! Pardon."

When she told him, little Wasserman trembled with rage and humiliation. All the noisome creatures of his psyche were let loose. He only wanted to know whether Zalmanson, after "dishonoring" her, had mocked him. Sarah gazed at him in doleful wonder and answered that Zalmanson had said nothing. That it was not a question of dishonor. She had submitted willingly and she would never do it again. Zalmanson knew that too, she said, "He was sad. I would not have believed a man like him could be so sad." (Sarah always used such "gentle" words.) And Wasserman: "Sad, shmad! Like Jesus rose to heaven, like Muhammad soared to the Compassionate One, Zalmanson was sad!" Sarah said that Zalmanson had asked her not to tell Wasserman but that she had decided to tell him anyway, because since nothing really happened, the whole matter was of no importance to her, and she did not want a lie to stand between her and Wasserman. She only asked him never to raise the subject again. And he agreed, I imagine, in his own way. "Indeed, Shleimeleh, for a year after that I made her a little hell of my silence. Nu, that, too, is past, like the proverbial spilled milk! It was a long time before I could imagine the two of them there, in the coat closet, without feeling the blood churn in my veins. A Jew, I tell you, is made of strange stuff . . ."

And meanwhile, Neigel sits in judgment on a folding chair, selecting his workers from among the new arrivals. His face is impassive, utterly blank. Himmler would be proud of him. He fixes his eyes on the people before him and nods left or right. *Links, recht, links, recht.* Wasserman: "And my head, too, choleria, moved with him, left, right . . ."

Neigel selects his new workers. The previous blues are pushed into the station to strip. Neigel returns to his work in the barracks. Wasserman studies the nape of the German's neck. "Do you see? Not a mark there from nodding his head. Not even so much as a wrinkle!" The aged, the young, and the lame are taken to the *Lazarett*, where Staukeh's revolver awaits them. Muffled shots are heard at short intervals. Hoppfler—his face like a wise, responsible child's—pulls the shutters down over the small buffet so the sun won't ruin the merchandise before the next train comes in. Wasserman says goodbye to the chocolate balls for another three hours. Wasserman: "And so it happened that from one end of the universe, a hundred paces away, my child, my darling Tirzaleh, brought her innocent young life, and from the other end came Death, and they met just as her little hand went out to touch the chocolate ball." And sighing deeply he reflects, "it may be that I will never be able to die, heaven forbid, though I taste my death so often, at least three times a day, when the trains come in . . ."

Afterward, when the naked prisoners are running through the Heavenly Way, he bends down and sticks his face into a hole in the flower bed.

And after the run through the Heavenly Way, when the bloody mouths of the dogs are silent once more, Wasserman stands up, sniffs his fingers, and rubs away the damp black soil sticking to them. His body smells strongly of sweat. Wasserman: "Nu, in my mind's eye I see Sarah sniff the armpits of my shirts and wrinkle her nose. My wife, may I not be mistaken, was an unsurpassed sniffer."

[5]

OTTO: "We had been in the forest for a year. I returned from Borislav one night and found, near entrance #1 to the mine, a wee babykin wrapped in a tattered blanket. It lay there without a peep, and looked straight at me with the open eyes of a grown man, and you should have seen our Fried when I walked in and gave him the present. Oho! He peeked at the bundle, and his face slammed shut like a door in the wind. And all he could say was 'What is this? What is this?' like some kind of parrot, though he could see very well what it was, and then he asked, 'Is it alive?' so, naturally I shoved the bundle into his arms and said, 'Have a look, have a look, you are the doctor around here, aren't you?' "

For a moment they looked at each other. The doctor wearily and suspiciously, and Otto with emotion, shifting his weight. Dr. Fried put the baby on the wooden crate they used as a table and went to wash his hands in the basin. His scrubbing movements stirred memories of bygone days when he had had many patients. Fried was a devoted doctor, though he would have been annoyed to hear himself so described. He never admitted to himself that he gave his fellow beings medical treatment out of concern for their well-being. He always preferred to view himself as a fighter of the enemies of mankind. Now he returned, waved his hands in the air to dry them, pulled a corner of the baby's blanket down, and gazed at it. The baby appeared to be quite premature. It was like a tiny fetus, with gray eyes that seemed covered by a thin membrane, and its wrinkly skin made it look as though it had been soaked too long in the tub. Its little red fists swam blindly in the air, and the wee forehead was furrowed with strain. Fried: "What is this! In the middle of the forest! For God's sake, who could have—" And Otto says, "Some poor woman. She probably hoped it would die quickly and painlessly." Fried says, "But the bears might have eaten it, choleria!" And Otto: "You'll help it, eh, Fried?" Fried: "What? Me? What can I do with it in a place like this? You'd do better to put it back where you found it." Wasserman: "Only, unconsciously the old doctor stroked the baby's soft, tender chest with his finger, and drew back with an overwhelming ache in his throat. And when he looked up, he saw that his fingertips were coated with a soft, white, fatty substance. Otto, too, reached out and touched the baby's tummy. Then he sniffed his fingers and tasted them. Otto: 'Like the dust on a butterfly's wing, right?' "

But here suddenly Neigel leans across the desk, and for the first time since Wasserman began reading to him this evening, he speaks: "No, Wasserman, not butterfly dust, that I can tell you from personal experience, if you don't mind." And since Neigel has two children, he is able to explain to Wasserman that babies are sometimes born with a "kind of fatty coating that helps them in some way, I don't remember how exactly anymore." But Anshel Wasserman, making no effort to sound patient ("Ai, how sick I am of his thickheaded pedantry! For one instant I stray to realms of far-flung fancy and he stands aghast. He will just have to become accustomed to the errors in this story"), explains to Neigel that if he, Wasserman, decides that this is butterfly dust, then butterfly dust it is, and Neigel, chided, says more softly, "But there really is a kind of dust on newborn babies." And Wasserman, fiercely: "And with regards to Otto's falling sickness, have you caught anything on your line yet?" And Neigel: "Yes, yes. And don't be impudent. Staukeh told me a couple of things. I don't see what Otto will be able to do if he has an attack out there, though." And he leafs through his notebook and tears out a page in his own handwriting. "By the way, what did you tell him, Staukeh, I mean?" asks Wasserman, and Neigel replies, "Ah, I made up some story about a sick aunt in Fissan. He was actually glad to help. Incidentally, about the rabbits and foxes, you made some glaring errors. Rabbits don't migrate, and foxes don't hibernate. What nonsense! I thought you might be wrong at the time. I happen to know something about rabbits and foxes, but I trusted you more than I trusted myself. I expected writers knew more than other people, and Staukeh was laughing up his sleeve. He laughed in my face when I asked him. Try to be more accurate next time you make a guess."

"The baby is cooing," says Wasserman. "What? What did you say?" "The baby is cooing. We are back in our story now. Where were we?" (Wasserman: "There in Neigel's wastepaper basket I spied a blue, not-at-all-military envelope, and even without my spectacles I could distinguish the small feminine script. Before I knew what I beheld, I felt the sharp bite of my flesh: it was she! The soft writing, and a kind of mist around the envelope, ai, a woman's hand . . .")

Neigel clears his throat. "Your butterfly dust, Scheherazade." And Wasserman says, "Butterfly dust? Not butterfly dust, the learned doctor Albert Fried would answer you, but a fatty coating meant to protect the fetus from the strong waters of the womb." Neigel: "Go to hell, *Scheissemeister*, now you're really—" "Tweet tweet! Cockledoodledoo! Jug jug jug jug! He hears me, Fried!" (cries the good Otto). "The baby hears me!" Fried: "They can hear you all the way to Borislav." Yedidya Munin: "What's this? A baby here?" Fried: "Otto found him. As if we didn't have enough troubles." Munin: "What an ugly little thing!" Otto: "They're all like that when they come out. It'll grow up to be a beauty. It needs milk."

Neigel, who has been waiting in ambush all along, now pounces. "What, here? In the forest?" Wasserman: "Yes, I know we have a problem, from the point of view of dry facts we have a problem. But we have no choice in the matter, and we need this milk. Help us, Herr Neigel."

The German sits bolt upright, as if his commander had just entered the room. He puts on a soldierly expression. Wasserman repeats his request. Neigel drums the glass, leaving moist fingerprints. After a long pause he suggests that perhaps one member of the band, "Otto would be the best, because he wouldn't be in danger," should go into the village to buy milk from the farmers. Wasserman nods enthusiastically and pretends to write this in his notebook, and Neigel relaxes, his face smug and ruddy, till suddenly Wasserman pretends to scratch out the German's words, declaring that "it is too dangerous, alas, because any minute the forest will grow dark, and bears may roam, and gunshots may be heard. It would be better for him not to be there at this time of day." "Gunshots, you say?" "Oh yes. I forgot to tell you about that earlier." "Naturally." For a minute Neigel seals his lips with such determination that his jaws clink and his mouth reaches almost to his nose. But then suddenly, much to his own surprise, it seems, a new idea flickers in his brain, which he announces with barely contained enthusiasm, with the joy of revenge on Wasserman: "Listen! Fried can take the baby to a gazelle! There must be a gazelle somewhere in the forest. I know it. And this gazelle—well, she gave birth not long ago. I suppose I forgot to tell you about it . . . Anyway, she has a lot of milk in her tits, and Fried will convince her to contribute a little for the baby, no?" And the writer, somewhat tensely: "A fine idea, Herr Neigel, excellent. I doff my hat to you, in a manner of speaking, of course!" ("Esau blushed down to his oversized earlobes, and I knew I was in difficulty. I showed him that God had given him a brain with which to think and a heart with which to feel, and already he was using them with typical German efficiency, tfu! I had to gird my broken loins and give him a fight!") "Indeed yes, Herr Neigel, a splendid idea. It came out fully formed from under your tongue, only the trouble is, it is too realistic. That is, too clumsily true to life, too stifled by the crude bonds of verisimilitude. We are both trying to make a small improvement here, to turn a donkey into a galloping steed, so now I will tell you what really happened . . ."

"I'm listening," says Neigel, distinctly annoyed.

"Otto approached Harotian and whispered a secret in his ear. Harotian recoiled with a groan that cleft him in twain! But Otto at last prevailed upon poor Harotian, who for many years had refused to engage in real magic, as distinct from legerdemain or outright deception—because no one refuses Otto. So he asked Otto for a dish, covered it with a sack, then slipped his head and most of his body into the sack, till only his knees peeked out; and he struggled thus over the dish for a long time, emitting sighs and moans, (because with all his heart he detested the magical talents with which I had endowed him in 'The Children of the Heart'); the sack withered about his body, it squirmed and writhed like a stormy sea, and when at last it was becalmed, Harotian stood up and revealed himself, his face as gray as the sack itself, as though he had seen the face of Satan, heaven forbid, and with a trembling hand he passed Otto the dish, now filled to the brim with a steaming white liquid, ai . . ." And Wasserman is silent for a moment. ("How well I remembered the taste of this milk, Shleimeleh, from the happy days when my Sarah, my treasure, nursed our lamb, Tirza . . . et! She, that is . . . you know how women are at such times . . . they have no shame . . . they are mothers . . . she urged me, she begged me to taste, and I refused, of course I refused . . . I was mortified! To you I can tell such things . . . but one time, in an intimate moment . . . I tasted a drop . . .") And here Neigel, Neigel of all people, says quietly, as though to himself: "A warm white liquid, sweet, too." And the Jewish author says tensely, deliberately, like a secret agent verifying the password, "Very sweet. It melts in your mouth." And Neigel: "Yes, and so creamy." And the two men, highly embarrassed, peer into each other's eyes for a moment, then quickly look away.

At their wits' end, they hand the dish of magic mother's milk to Fried, hoping he will disembarrass them, but Fried only withdraws his hand, tense and suspicious, perhaps because of the baby's rude intrusion into his life, or because of the cruel injustice of it—a live, healthy baby in such close proximity to Fried, who for two whole years had been engulfed by a barren passion for a baby. And here, as Wasserman pronounces the word "barren," he notices Neigel's eyes widening just as Zalmanson's had whenever Wasserman said "My wife, Sarah." ("Zalmanson was always suspicious that I knew everything about him and my Sarah, but I made things difficult for him too and said not a word about it. I was silent as a fish and let him stew in his own juice.") Wasserman does not understand the meaning of Neigel's sudden vigilance at the sound of the word. For a moment he amuses himself with the idea that the two children in the photograph are adopted, which would explain their tender age compared to Neigel's forty-five years. But the boy resembles Neigel, and the girl resembles Neigel's wife. So what is it? Wasserman is perplexed. He stops reading and stares into space. All at once, even without a shot in the head, he has an idea, and now he knows or, rather, remembers the cause of Paula's death. Those hints he scattered for himself have now come together and he is more certain than ever that someday "I will have Neigel eating out of the palm of my hand."

Fried goes out to bring a spoon from the nook that serves as kitchen for the band, and from a distance hears Otto announce that the baby has two teeth. From the kitchen he roars in reply that he has heard of such cases before, that babies are sometimes also covered with down at birth, and Otto unties the blanket anxiously and announces: "There's no down! Only butterfly dust, and—Fried! Our babykin is a manchild!" Fried hears this and is overcome with fatigue. He leans against the cooling chest as though it were the shoulder of a friend. He wonders why he does not hear a voice offering him a bargain: his remaining years in exchange for a single day with this child and Paula. And he slowly straightens himself up and clenches his fists. Or could it be that the child is the very sign Fried has awaited for three years? For seventy years? Could it be that life has made an extraordinary concession and deigned at last to answer his plea, his despair, his impertinence, by crossing the line he draws in the dust every morning? And Otto, from a distance, laughing: "Hey, boy! Not on my shirt!"

Afterward, when Fried brings Otto a clean spoon and stands beside him, he edges closer to the tiny head covered with whitish down and sniffs. "Ai," murmurs Wasserman, in a voice full of longing. "And the doctor breathes in the sweet fragrance, unique in all the world." Neigel indicates with a nod that he, too, knows this inimitable smell, and

Wasserman wails: "Like scorching is that smell in his heart. The bandage is torn from an old wound, still oozing blood." And Neigel, after a moment's silence: "Don't look at me like that. I want to tell you something. I know you'll use this against me, but I don't care. When my Karl was born and I came home on leave, I used to go to his crib at night and stand there smelling him. It sent chills up my spine." And Anshel Wasserman says, "I knew it."

The baby drank and drank, then gurgled "Ah" contentedly, and spat up a little milk on the doctor's trousers. Fried screamed, "Call somebody! Report it to the authorities!" Yes, Fried was frightened. He paced the room like a camel, howling with rage. Otto, with awkward cunning, handed Fried the contented baby. Fried threw him an angry look. He knew perfectly well that Otto was trying to tempt him to love life. ("Or, if you prefer, Shleimeleh, to walk him back to Chelm.") The two had been disputing this wordlessly ever since Paula's death. Or perhaps since the first time they met in the distant past of their childhood. Suddenly, with firm resolve, Otto pushed the baby into Fried's arms.

But who is this peeking into the darkened hall, dressed in filthy gabardine, so haggard and worn, her face wrinkled, caked with dirt and strangely blotched, a frumpy blond wig on her head? She peeks into the hall for only a moment and says—she says nothing, because Neigel interrupts and asks, "Please introduce me to our new friend, Wasserman!" And the writer replies, "Gladly, Herr Neigel. She is another new member of our band, and her name is Hannah Zeitrin, the bewitched and lovesick Hannah, the daring, despairing fighter; she is, um, indeed, the most beautiful woman in the world."

And he ignores Neigel's protests ("The most beautiful woman in the—? But you said she was wrinkled!") and again declares that no woman in the world is as beautiful as Hannah Zeitrin, though she is also miserable, it is true, sick with love and longing, and when Hannah hears from Otto that "we have a new baby, Hannah," she flinches and hurries away. These people have their caprices, Herr Neigel, each one, and his pack of woes, as they say, and Hannah cannot yet look at babies. The memories are too fresh, and you will have to understand this, Herr Neigel.

But, scolds Wasserman, while we were heeding Hannah, we nearly missed the main thing! Fried, daring at last to approach the baby, lays a tentative finger on the soft part of the skull, strokes it, and lingers anxiously for a moment above the forehead. Neigel: "The membrane over the hole between the bones? Yes, I know. I never dared touch him there." And soon they are deep in conversation about that spot, the soft spot where (Neigel:) "you can almost feel the brain breathe. There's a pulse there, too, like a heartbeat." And also (Wasserman:) "you can feel the throbbing of life at your fingertips." And Wasserman takes this opportunity to mention a bird he once read about, a tiny bird that lives at the South Pole (or is it the North Pole?), so delicate that if you touch it lightly on the chest, its heart stops beating. "I do not wish to hold such a bird in my hand, Herr Neigel." "Yes," says the German. "It could be irksome."

And the revelation. The doctor lifts the baby up in the air and the tiny hands fly forward. Their movements are still haphazard, uncoordinated. They touch the big bald head and drop down to the trimmed, silver mustache and, suddenly filled with animation, flutter gaily above the two pouchy cheeks and the great red nose, the winepress of tears, becoming more intelligent by the moment as they explore the doctor's garden of life with slow curiosity. Yes, they all held their breath and watched: the tiny fingers rested on his large, pale lips, coaxing a sensuality long dead in them. Magic writing loomed large and quickly faded on the cool wall of Fried's face, and the doctor groaned one of his bitter groans. "Poor child," he said, and Neigel: "It will be difficult for him to start his life this way." And Otto: "Some story." And Fried answered stiffly: "Such things happen."

Fried had made a resolution never to be surprised. He had decided simply to banish surprise. Wasserman: "Unlike Mr. Marcus, who always did his best to adopt fresh feelings, the doctor spent his life trying to reduce his feelings to the bare minimum." But the decision to eschew surprise did not bring the doctor satisfaction or relief. On the contrary, the older he grew and the more wisdom and experience he accumulated, the more difficult it became to stick to his decision.

Now comes the moment when Otto announces that the baby will spend tonight with Fried. "And tomorrow, we'll see." He ignores Fried's alarmed protests, argues wisely that "babykin needs a doctor's care, right?" And together with the other Children of the Heart he leaves the hall, after first advising Fried to make some diapers for the baby out of an old sheet or shirt. The pounding of the mad doctor's heart is almost audible.

They departed, and Fried was left alone with the baby. But not alone: an enormous white butterfly suddenly alighted from one of the thick roots of the oak tree and drifted through the half-darkened hall. The butterfly glided slowly down before Fried's eyes, as though trying to understand him. It studied him so carefully, the doctor felt embarrassed. He noticed, meanwhile, that the butterfly's wings were shaped like a heart, and this brought back an old memory: In the past, whenever Otto wanted to send the Children of the Heart on a rescue mission, he would draw hearts on the trees and fences outside their homes. This was the signal. The butterfly now fluttered over the baby's eyes. It seemed to be blowing the first breath of life upon them, and upon Fried's eyes as well, perhaps. He did not stir as the strange dance continued. Once again the butterfly hovered, traced a circle around the two of them, and flew up and away through the tunnels. The silvery traces of its wings in flight were still visible weeks later on the sooty walls.

Suddenly the doctor noticed that the baby was breathing faster, and that it was wriggling restlessly. A fearful premonition made him peek at the baby's tummy: there were no signs of clotted blood on the navel. In fact, there were no signs of tearing or cutting on the navel: in fact, there was no navel.

Much else took place that night, both in the story and in the barracks, and it is difficult sometimes to distinguish between them. Did Fried examine the baby on an army cot in the office of the commander of the extermination camp and discover that the baby's pulse was very fast indeed, almost ten times faster than a normal baby's? Did the telephone suddenly ring in the hall of friendship with a call from "a very important personage" in Berlin, and moreover, did the speaker from Berlin extol Neigel's recent work in the camp to such an extent that he had recourse to bright musical imagery, comparing "your work and creative power, my dear Neigel," to the operas of Wagner and "the greatest National Socialist composers of our day." And later, when Neigel, blushing with pleasure, signaled to Wasserman to be quiet and guess from the expression on his face what was being said, he asked Reichsführer Himmler to send him everything necessary for the setting up of three more gas chambers ("We must accelerate, Commander, accelerate more and more!"), Himmler promised to give the request his sympathetic consideration, though he couldn't promise anything for now ("No doubt you've heard, my dear Neigel, about certain temporary exigencies in the East"); again he commended the "excellent tempo" of extermination in the camp, hinted something about the rank of Standartenführer soon to be bestowed upon a certain dear somebody, and ended the conversation with a crescendo of compliments, and the crowning touch (by the way, this quotation, too, like the previous one, is borrowed from Himmler's night call to his protégé, Jürgen Stroop, the night of the *Gross Aktion* in the Warsaw Ghetto): "Keep playing like that, Maestro, and our Führer and I will never forget it."

Wasserman, who had listened in fear to the conversation, sat up straight when it was over, denying Neigel his moment of glory and the opportunity to divulge the identity of the distinguished caller. He continued in an anxious stream to recount how Fried, who had been left alone with the baby, scurried from wall to wall in the little hut, abstractedly tweaking the tip of his big red nose and stopping from time to time for a look at the baby, asleep on the couch with his fists clenched, "as though he held the secret of life in his hands."

"Tatatatata!" Neigel iterates smugly. "What do you mean 'couch'? What's this 'little hut' doing here all of a sudden? Did I miss something while I was speaking to Reichsführer Himmler on the phone?" Wasserman coughs, smiles hollowly, and apologizes for "my annoying slackwittedness! I almost forgot to tell you that . . . anyway . . ." In short, he'd moved the story elsewhere.

Neigel, half stewed with the pleasure of the call from Berlin, half frozen with hostility toward Wasserman, explodes with a rage-choked scream to remind him of "the humiliation I underwent for you in Borislav . . . health spas . . . lies . . ." and he is not prepared to listen to the writer's explanation that "such sacrifices are unavoidable in the creative process, pray take no offense, sir . . . It transpires sometimes that a writer will suddenly become aware of a change of course that must occur, and so will wend his way back, or leap into the distance . . ." And Neigel slams the desk with his hand, proclaiming, "We will stop this game here and now." Much to the surprise of both of us, however, he does not send Wasserman back to Keizler in the lower camp but demands to know why "you artists always have to complicate the simplest things, and ruin art!" He then preaches a long and exhausting sermon about the purpose of art, which is, if anyone cares to remember, "to entertain people, to make them feel good, and even to educate them, yes, definitely!" But under no circumstances to "encourage doubt, to make people feel awkward or confused, and to accentuate the negative, the sick, and the perverse!" And after this speech—in which there is a certain obvious element of truth—he sinks down again, in a rage and in a sweat, confused and bitter, but still does not banish Wasserman, signaling him instead to go on with the story! And Wasserman, bewildered, wonders whether this is "the first time in his life that Esau has had use for such deep thoughts about the nature of art, et! I kept this to myself." But he does not succeed in guessing why Neigel is so intent on hearing the rest.

He resumes in a hesitant voice. It seems he has relocated the story in the Zoological Gardens, or zoo, of Warsaw, where he spent such lovely hours with Sarah. Neigel, whose bitterness has sharpened his tongue, guesses scornfully that the writer's purpose is to "take us with *dreck Jude* slyness into a little fable about human beings who turn into animals, eh, Wasserman?" Wasserman denies this, staunchly disagrees with the German that any story which takes place in a zoo must be childish, and introduces his cast of characters in their new location (Fried—veterinary doctor, Otto—zookeeper, Paula—in charge of zoo administration and domestic arrangements for both Otto and Fried). And the rest of the band? "Zoo employees all, of course! The regular workers, you see, were called up when the war began" (Neigel: "Hah!"), he says, and returns us to the doctor, busy taking the baby's rapid pulse. He prolongs his description, in anticipation of Neigel's inevitable question ("What does a veterinary doctor know about babies?"), so he can tell the German the marvelous story of Paula, Fried's life companion, who in 1940 made up her mind to have a baby, yes, she filled the house with longing for a child and sweet resolve and popular notions, like the preferability of breast-feeding over bottle-feeding, and she even embroidered dainty didees with gaily capering figures; indeed, she became the artist of the only child, and made her body over into a battlefield against the tyranny and narrow-mindedness of nature, and with all her tremendous creative force, and despite the fact that certain doctors warned her against it and laughed at her behind her back, she never lost faith in her powers and the justness of her cause, and she lay with Fried at all hours of the night and day. Otto: "I mean we used to catch them at it in every place imaginable; on the elephant's haystack, among the rotten cabbages in the storeroom, and by moonlight in the empty crocodile pool, and even at my house, in my bed! They just got the love bite and couldn't stop!" Fried: "She was the one." Otto: "It was kind of annoying at first, I tell you, Friedy mine, while we're on the subject, because who would have believed that my sister Paula had men on the brain? At the age of nearly seventy? But then, a few weeks later we understood, yes, she'd simply caught the infection from our other resident artists, the new members of our band, and though at first she was as much against them as you were, Fried, she caught the infection and wanted to try out her special talent, nu, and then it stopped being annoying, quite the contrary, wherever the two of you went to you-know-what, it was as if you'd sprinkled holy water and exorcised a ghost, and I knew our zoo was saved." And Wasserman: "Yes indeed, Herr Neigel, it was fortunate for Paula and Fried that they were never caught in the act by your friends the guards in Warsaw, when they posted the strict laws forbidding the holding of Jewish rituals in public, which is precisely what Fried was doing!"

Neigel is silent. He stares at Wasserman and doesn't respond. His lips are parted. Wasserman makes use of this interval to quote Otto pityingly. "Our poor Fried, he's practically exhausted." "Yes, yes," admits Fried. "I was sixty-seven years old at the time, and Paula was two years older," and so for the space of at least two years, day and night, most assiduously ("And with great feeling!"), the two made love. "You nearly broke my record, Pani Fried!" chuckles Mr. Yedidya Munin, exhaling the foul-smelling smoke of a cigarette prepared from the dried turds of zoo animals, his eyes twinkling slyly behind two pairs of glas—

But Neigel shakes himself. He stops Wasserman with a loud bark and a hand raised in negation. "Explanations," he demands, "explanations, Wasserman, this instant!" And slyly Wasserman allows Munin himself to explain what he means by "my record." "What is there to explain here, Mr. Neigel?" (explains Yedidya Munin). "In love as in prayer, in prayer as in love. In the words of Rabbi Leib Melamed of Brody, while praying, imagine a female before you and you will attain the highest rung." And Neigel: "More of your Jewish pornography, *Scheissemeister*?" And Munin: "Heaven forbid, Mr. Neigel, speak not abomination but only purity. Transcendence. And man must worship the Lord, blessed be He, with a fervor drawn from the evil inclination, so said the Magid of Mazeritz, whose own flesh may have taught him the power of the evil inclina—" And Neigel raises his arms, in jest or in despair, revealing two shameful perspiration stains. "Go on like this, *Scheissemeister*, and not even I will listen to you anymore. I have the feeling you've lost control over your characters." And when Wasserman ignores the comment and describes how Fried and Paula made feverish love near the baby elephant's cage, Neigel rubs his red eyes and makes a note in his black notebook. It isn't the first time he's done so this evening, and in fact he does so every evening when Wasserman sits with him, and Wasserman has been planning to look offended and mention it to him. ("Because I am not a musician, you know, playing for diners at a cabaret.") But he forbears and keeps his silence. He paints for Neigel the small, sweet arc of Paula's belly, which had begun to swell of late under her withered flesh. Paula stood before the mirror, smiling her quiet smile, without the faintest trace of humor or irony, a good and simple smile, because she had always believed in this baby and had chosen a name for the child already—Kazik she would call him—and when Neigel interrupts to point out without much hope that Paula is seventy years old, the writer agrees with him wholeheartedly: she is sixty-nine, to be exact, and we, too, he says, all of Otto's artists, all of Otto's fighters, were astonished. And he asks Neigel to imagine how excited they were, how they never ceased talking about little Kazik, and how they all hoped he would change everything, everything. "And someday give us the final proof we had sorely hoped to find when Otto gathered us together for our last adventure," because this Kazik was meant to be the first victory of the band. Otto took Paula to a friend of his, a Dr. Wertzler. Otto: "A fellow you could count on not to talk too much." And the honorable doctor examined Paula and then sent her behind the screen to dress. Otto: "And then he led me by the hand to the window and showed me the darkened city in the curfew, and said, Hard times are coming, Brig, some will be able to hold out and others will not, and he looked at me sourly and whispered, Surely you know what's happening to our poor Paulina, that's what he said, Our poor Paulina." Aaron Marcus: "She smiles happily to herself behind the screen, weighing her swelling breasts in her hands." Otto: "—and he told me that I, as her brother, would have to have a serious talk with her and warn her that at the age of sixty-nine the body is no longer fit for pregnancy, even an imaginary pregnancy, and he said it was my duty to protect her not only from physical injury but also from the disappointment which would be sure to follow, and of course I did no such thing, leaving it to Fried to decide what to do; it was his, after all, this imaginary pregnancy—"

But Fried didn't want to tell Paula what Dr. Wertzler had said, because he'd already begun to understand, and wanted to believe—in direct contrast to his temperament and point of view—that her work of art was bigger than people like Wertzler, and he began to care for her in keeping with her special condition. Wasserman: "He would walk with her of an evening along the Lane of Eternal Youth, and place cool compresses on her forehead when her head hurt, and Otto went to great lengths to find the foods and sweetmeats she fancied on the black market, and once"—Wasserman smiles, remembering—"and once our Paula craved a fresh grapefruit, but go find grapefruits in Warsaw in '41! Superhuman initiative was called for this time, but all the Children of the Heart together could not find a solution, and Paula almost sobbed with the intensity of her craving, ah, who could see this adorable woman without melting—"

"Just a minute," says Neigel dryly. "I'm beginning to understand what you're driving at now. Please write down: Officer Neigel was the one who brought Paula the grapefruit." "From where, if I may be permitted to ask?" asks Wasserman, his clever little eyes smiling gratefully. "The Quartermaster Corps sent me a food package. A big grapefruit, direct from Spain. With greetings from General Franco."

For a moment they are silent. Amused, but also a little disturbed by the thread of excitement suddenly quivering in the room. The invisible grapefruit looms between them and spreads its fragrance. Wasserman cannot understand why Neigel, despite his angry outbursts, will not let the story stop for a single moment, but he wastes no time and continues. Fried: "And at night I put my hand on her belly and felt the baby kicking. Boom! Boom! He kicked like a little Hercules." Silence. And Neigel, swallowing his words: "You have children, too, eh, Wasserman?" Wasserman looks down at his notebook, a white whip lashing his face. ("Esau did not know what coals he was heaping on the tablets of my heart with this question.") "One daughter, your honor," he answers at length. "I ask, because only someone who has children knows this kind of thing." "You have two, you said." "Yes. Karl and Lise. Karl is three and a half. Liselotte is two. They're both war babies." And reflecting briefly: "I rarely have a chance to see them." And Wasserman, with unsteady voice: "You are not a young father, if

I may say so, Herr Neigel." And Neigel, inclined at first to interrupt this "impudent prying," stops himself and, suddenly looking around the room, at Wasserman, at the curtained windows, he rubs his tired, red-rimmed eyes, and says in a dry voice without a trace of aggression: "We couldn't have children for a long time. We tried for over seven years." And Wasserman, in a quiet whisper: "Neither could we, Herr Neigel, eight years we . . . nu, well." And in the heavy silence that envelops them both like a thick scarf Wasserman grits his teeth to hold back a scream. "Nu," he reflects sadly later on, with tired, defeated anger not directed at Neigel, "there is nothing more to say."

"Let us continue, then," Wasserman sighs, the leader of a weary caravan forced to continue its wanderings. "Maybe Paula could have the baby, after all," says Neigel with almost childish innocence, and Wasserman, gently: "Paula will die, I am sorry to say. But Fried will believe in his heart of hearts that the baby discovered in the zoo is Paula's baby." And Neigel: "I understand I have no choice but to accept this." "Indeed. I am sorry to say."

And they return to the story. But now Wasserman tells the story cautiously, walking a thin line. And Neigel too is tense. He no longer offers comments. No longer bullies him. They carry the story between them. Wasserman describes how "Paula's cheeks bloomed with the fire of destruction, how her strong and pretty teeth began to loosen and decay," how her skin became dry and cracked, and only her breasts continued to swell and ache, and the ache unraveled the stringy smile on her lips, an apologetic smile to Fried for the trouble she was causing him, but Marcus: "When our Paula leaned over the toilet bowl in the morning to vomit, and you, Dr. Fried, knelt to support her forehead, the two of you saw your faces reflected in the tiny pool below, two messages detained so long, and you knew, Fried."

And at this point, for no apparent reason, Wasserman slowly closes his notebook with a smile and confesses to Neigel that this evening in Neigel's company reminds him of other evenings, long ago, during his bachelorhood, before *Little Lights* went off to the printer and he would go to Zalmanson's office in fear and trembling to turn in his latest installment, and together they would go over the writing, argue and make peace a hundred times, and toward midnight, when both were exhausted and the room was malodorous with the smoke from Zalmanson's little cigars, for a few moments, "nu, well, there was a pleasant feeling in our bones, you understand, Herr Neigel, as we confabulated about this and that . . . yes, how pleasant it was." ("At such times, Zalmanson spoke truthfully. I would listen to him in silence, he said the deepest, most beautiful things when he wanted to! Without crooked cleverness or bad-natured jokes. About myself I told him nothing. What was there to tell? That the cat had been whining in the courtyard? That there was a leaky faucet in the house? And here, with this big goy, of all people, nu, well, it appears that even Anshel Wasserman can stitch a tale . . .")

"This Zalmanson," asks Neigel casually, "was he a friend of yours?" And Wasserman looks at him in surprise and answers, "Indeed he was." His only friend. And when Neigel does not seem to be in too much of a hurry to get back to the story, Wasserman tells him, hesitantly at first, about Zalmanson, ready to retreat at a moment's notice, but when he sees the expression of amused interest on Neigel's face, he is filled with courage and speaks. This Zalmanson, he says, was always pretending he had just stepped out of the pages of Dostoevsky or Tolstoy, always dropping hints about the other realms where he lived his real life. A very important man, says Wasserman, raising his hand in a gesture of deprecation and mild annoyance: "A Moishe Gros! Never down here with the likes of us, heaven forbid," Wasserman continues angrily. "Here in our world, Zalmanson is merely doing his duty, visiting poor relatives, but there, in his invisible realms, that is, he is among the wheels of heaven and the secret spheres! Oy vay! The anguished soul and its travails! That Zalmanson—feh, why I am getting so angry with him now I do not know, Herr Neigel, for I came to like him a little with the years . . . with his subtle smiles and his vainglory, and such a coxcomb he was, ai!" (Here Wasserman gets carried away and tells an amusing anecdote: When the armband orders were issued in the ghetto, Zalmanson did not go out to buy the band at Shaya Gantz's with everyone else, but sat down instead with his wife, Zilla, who sewed bands for themselves and their three daughters. "Such fancy armbands, a Polish soldier almost shot them, heaven forbid, on charges of inciting to rebellion.") "That Zalmanson . . ." continues Wasserman. "How sick I was of his merciless derision of any poor soul who happened to fit a witticism, nu, the house parties, have I told your honor about the house parties?" "No," answers Neigel. "Ai, the parties at the Zalmansons' . . . all Warsaw was there . . . and the wine flowed like water, and the poor guests were forced to listen to Madame Zilla banging on the piano, and her three daughters torturing their flutes and violin . . . Zalmanson liked to surround himself with people . . . and a womanizer he was, too, begging your pardon . . . To tell you the truth, sir, I was not fond of attending these parties, nor was my wife . . . we felt drab and gray there . . . shy. We knew no one, and no one knew us. They were people of the world, while we, nu, well, we were field mice, no more. And in the end I refused to go, and my wife went alone, just once, and that was enough. And by the way, Zalmanson was a religious man, and very Orthodox in his religion. He had passed through sundry changes of faith in his short life, but in recent years, with the world so topsy-turvy, begging your pardon, he came to believe exclusively in humor. Perhaps I will tell you someday, when the time comes, about his complicated theory, which he argued with the usual crooked acuity. He could find reasons to laugh about anything in the world, and said, 'If I cannot laugh at something, I have not understood it properly.' 'And you,' he said to me, 'are like a man sleeping soundly beside his wife, who fails to see his own ludicrousness when a stranger's toes stick out from under the blanket of their double bed.' I happen to think this example is more tragic than comic, only I do not wish to discuss it further, and will say only that Zalmanson did have certain virtues—he loved his fellow man in his own peculiar way, though he used to say that he hated humanity but loved particular individuals for their merits, a bitter sort of humanitarian, and to look at him, you would say a hooligan. But no, you would be doing him an injustice, Herr Neigel! Because I know that deep inside he was different, and if you told him a secret, you knew he would keep it in his heart forever, and tell no tales; the only trouble was, he would tell people what he thought to their faces, and for this reason he had many enemies, too . . . When I needed a loan once, he opened his hand and asked no questions, and another time when I felt dizzy and fainted and needed a blood transfusion, he came and donated his blood for me . . . Perhaps not the best friend in the world, and yet—I had none other . . . and I—nu, well— he was my friend. But why do I speak of him so much?"

"So you people have them, too; the Zalmanson type, that is?" asks Nei-gel, yawning, drawing his finger casually across his glass-covered desk, and the Jew ("Esau was not bandying words here. Not at all. His ques-tion was of the utmost importance!"): "We have all things, Herr Neigel, all varieties. Bad and good and wise and foolish. Each and every variety."

Again there is silence, and Neigel is probably contemplating something when he glances at his watch and is very surprised to see what time it is. He gets up and stretches his full height and yawns broadly. He says good night to Wasserman, pretending that their agreement has totally slipped his mind. But tonight, thank God, Wasserman himself is in a special mood, which he does not feel like spoiling with an argument. He makes no mention of it, but when they look into each other's eyes, they know they know. Neigel hums, remarks that Wasserman has not yet told him anything about the baby, or what their mission is this time, why the Children of the Heart are involved in all these "artistic things," and besides: "This story is awfully peculiar. I would not have believed myself capable of listening to a story like this." Wasserman smiles and thanks him for his patience.

"Go to sleep now," urges Neigel, and when Wasserman remains standing there another minute, a breeze of goodwill wafts out of Neigel's heart, something forgotten and betrayed over the years, and he finds himself saying, "I have some more work to finish here, and I also want to write a letter home to the little woman." Wasserman is astounded by this candor ("Human beings give each other fine gratuities when they have no objects left to give"). And he is compelled to ask, "Will you mention me in your letter?" And Neigel almost starts to answer, but thinks better of it and replies obliquely, "No, in fact. Go to bed already and don't press your luck, Wasserman."

And then they part for the night.

[6]

MUCH TIME ELAPSED BEFORE the story was resumed. A minor health problem caused the delay. To enter the White Room, a certain amount of forgetfulness and sacrifice is required of one. But again and again the mysterious warning voices were heard: Get out of here. The White Room is too dangerous for you. And the story was postponed. It was pushed aside and frequently forgotten. A collection of documentary material for a children's encyclopedia on the subject of the Holocaust was initiated at this time, but the idea turned out badly. A sense of helplessness and despondency prevailed. The intention here is not to go into details (as most of this has already been explained), but let it be said that Zeno's freezing breath was blowing down a certain neck.

The story froze, together with life itself. Paralyzing questions were posed continuously: Why should anyone expose himself to the dangers of the White Room anyway? And who could tell what would happen to him if he ever decided willingly to sacrifice his well-known aptitude for defending himself against the demands of that fictional White Room, an aptitude acquired through much suffering and effort which proved itself over and over? And why, in fact, was this sacrifice necessary? So that a certain woman, to wit, Ayala, would be satisfied? So that after all the dangerous and backbreaking labor, another book on a familiar topic would grace our bookshelves? Who the hell needs it?

"Indeed, yes," said Grandfather Anshel. "To write another book. Very necessary! Necessary for you, Shleimeleh, and who else is left to give you this story? You know yourself that my story, the one story, can show you the way . . . so please write: A baby will enter the story. He will live his life in it."

No he won't.

Anshel Wasserman is trying to help me. There's no doubt about it: it's the baby. This is the help Wasserman intends to offer. But there's not enough strength left for this baby. There's not enough strength left to create a new life, the old life is a burden as it is; for instance, one night Neigel shot twenty-five Jewish prisoners.

In the middle of September of '43, says a book written by one of the inmates, a prisoner made an escape. He was the first prisoner to escape since Neigel had taken over as commander of the camp. He hid, it seems, in a quarry, in the space between two huge boulders, and the guards didn't notice anything. During the night they dragged all the prisoners out to the parade ground in front of the commander's barracks. It would be reasonable to suppose that Wasserman woke up from a light sleep and peeked fearfully out of a hole in his attic. Down below he saw Obersturmbannführer Neigel walking between the rows of prisoners. Oh, Lord, thought Wasserman then. This is the man who sits with me every night and listens to my story, and tells me about his wife and children, and I have even wrenched a chord of pain and laughter from his heart . . .

Neigel pronounces the verdict. Every tenth prisoner in the row is to be put to death. Twenty-five prisoners in all. Staukeh approaches him and says something in a whisper. Neigel refuses. Staukeh repeats himself and raises a hand in argument. Twenty-five dead are probably not enough to ease his mind. For a moment it looks as though a real fight is going on out there. But Neigel controls himself. Staukeh steps back in place. He looks furious. His thin, gold-rimmed glasses flash angrily in the cold glint of the searchlights. Neigel chooses the victims with a wave of his finger. He squints, reviewing them with utmost care. Some of the prisoners later swore that he made the selection with his eyes shut.

The Ukrainians segregate the condemned men, two of whom faint with fear. They are carried away. Everything happens in silence. Someday the episode will be described in a book: "Silence. The moon shone above, and the searchlights below. Commander Neigel executed the condemned men. He shot them each through the head. After the third shot, he was covered with blood. Then he leaned down and shot the two men lying in a faint. Did they know? And did the others, the living beings standing in line, know?"

With that it ended. Neigel turned and disappeared into his barracks. When he passed outside the attic, Wasserman could see that his face was rigid and his eyes appeared to be closed. Wasserman curled up between the two supply cupboards. He wanted to say something— even to himself—in memory of the dead. But there was nothing really to say. He hadn't known them. And even if he had, quite possibly he would not have had any special feeling for them. It had been like that serving with Zalmanson and the dentists for three months. Wasserman: "Everything that had once been between us was extinguished. There was friendship, but it was different. It would be impossible to describe it in words. We were not fond of each other, nor did we hate each other very much. Perhaps because being here, we were already dead in everyone's eyes, even we began to see ourselves and our friends as dead."

Neigel, meanwhile, is showering in the little stall in his barracks under Wasserman's attic. He howls something, and I am shocked to think he might be singing to himself in the shower. But he isn't singing. He's talking. He's saying something out loud. And even though the water's running, I know exactly what he's saying. He's talking to me. He's reproving me for "negligence." "Isn't it true," he asks contentiously, "that writers are supposed to enter all the way into their characters?"

But I'm not ready. I'm not ready yet to "enter all the way." That is, I needn't tell Neigel that. I can just pretend and let him dictate a few autobiographical details so he won't feel I'm neglecting him. A list of facts, common to thousands of SS officers like him, and that's all.

So: he was born forty-six years ago in Bavaria, in the small village of Fissan at the foot of the Zugspitze. By the age of ten he knew how to lead mountain climbers up the most dangerous paths of the Alps. He had one brother, Heinz, who died in childhood of tuberculosis. His mother, raised in Poland, came to Germany at a relatively late age and married his father just after his army service. She was a milkmaid, and Neigel remembers—while soaping his broad chest—how he used to ride with her in the cart, early in the morning, along the lake. She was, he says, "a good, simple woman. She knew her place." His father, like Neigel, had been a soldier in his youth ("The truth is, though, that the Kaiser's soldiers were mere children compared to us"), and after his release from a long term of service, he became a carpenter in Fissan. As a soldier he had served in East-Africa, and Neigel recalls "the wonderful stories he used to tell about Africa. They seemed to come from a different world." And since Neigel does not descend to particulars, I quote similar disclosures by Rudolf Hoess, commandant of Auschwitz, in his diary (*The Commandant of Auschwitz Testifies*), about the exciting stories his father used to tell him in his childhood: "They described battles with the rebellious children, and told about their customs and way of life and their benighted pagan rites. I listened with fervor and enthusiasm to Father's tales about the blessed civilizing efforts of the missionaries in Africa. For Father they were as great as kings. We wanted to be missionaries too, to explore darkest Africa, deep in the jungle."

And Rudolf Hoess continues to transfuse biographical data into Neigel's transparent veins: "Whenever my father's old friends, the missionaries, visited us, it was always a real treat for me. They were bearded old men . . . I hung on to their every word . . . Sometimes Father would take me with him to visit the holy places of our country. We even went as far as the monks' cells in Switzerland and Lourdes . . . Father hoped I would grow up to be a priest. And I myself was as ardent a believer as any young boy could be."

Again I will have to bore myself with a few quotations from Neigel about his home and upbringing: (1) My parents were strict with us, but it was for our own good. Does Krupp make steel out of butter?

282)

(2) Very early on, we were taught self-reliance. (3) We were expected to show respect to our elders, even the servants in our home. (4) I was expected to obey the wishes of my elders, all my elders, unconditionally.

The countryside where Neigel grew up? Green hills, dark Bohemian forests, barley fields, vineyards, and, looming in the background, the "King," the Zugspitze, the tallest mountain in the fatherland. By the age of seven he had climbed the peak on an expedition with his father. Heinz had decided to stay behind in the village . . .

He reports these things in a dry, matter-of-fact tone. The German language suits him: he cuts the hard consonants and inflects at the end of the sentence, where the verb is. This gives his every utterance, however personal, a peremptory tone.

He wants to talk about horses. Please. In my own way I, too, am close to the subject. In the village they had a horse his mother used for delivering milk. A mangy horse, but Neigel has been "crazy about horses" ever since. And now? He doesn't ride anymore. His body is too stiff, and the wound from Verdun is troublesome, too, but he still knows how "to approach a horse like a master." We discuss this interesting, amusing coincidence, my also liking horses. I've never actually mounted a horse—it doesn't look very comfortable to me somehow—but one summer when I was a boy I worked at a riding stable near the flour mill in Jerusalem for three or four days. I was forced to quit for some silly reason (asthmatic sensitivity to horse manure), but I still remember the warm smell of the beautiful horses, their raddled sinews, the male movement of muscles under the skin; ah, Neigel, I could talk about horses for hours with you, about the sharp smell of the oil they rub on the harnesses, about galloping, about the shiny whips hanging in the stalls, the simple pat of the groom on the horse's neck—I still remember the beautiful poster that hung in the manager's office with pictures of the different breeds, Franconians, Schwabians, Westphalians, Parisians, Hungarians, Polesians and Detmolds and Arabians—truly a man's animal.

"Humph," mutters Neigel in my direction, with a strange expression on his face, changing the subject and declaring rather tactlessly, "I'm not exactly wild, you know. I mean, I never get drunk, and I don't, well, how shall I put it, fool around with women, and in fact—" He hesitates for a moment, and finally admits with a kind of relief, "In fact, I don't have many friends. I don't need them either. In a word, you can't really trust anyone, and I prefer it like this. I find satisfaction in my work, and also with my family, of course. And generally speaking, you could say that, yes, I do enjoy living. I simply enjoy living."

And after these last words, I feel Wasserman's breath on my ear. I turn around and see him wince, as though he's suffered a heavy blow. And much to my surprise, I understand that this agony is due to his complex system of attitudes toward everything the word "living" represents. But Wasserman is not content with this expression of pain, and he turns to me as arbiter or judge or whatever, and demands that until it is proven that Neigel has the "inalienable right" (!) to use this word: "he will not be allowed to abuse it any way he likes." I try therefore to explain to Wasserman that even from a simple technical standpoint I can't prevent a character in my story from using a normal vocabulary to express himself, but Wasserman covers his ears with his wrinkled hands and shakes his head in the negative. I try to be clever with him and ask what he, as a writer, would do in a similar situation, and without a moment's doubt, he says, "Herring. And onions if you like." And when I ask if he would mind explaining, he answers impatiently, "Instead of having him say 'I enjoy living,' from now on Esau will say, 'I enjoy herring,' or even 'I enjoy onions.' This will not impoverish him, and it will certainly be a relief for me."

I turn to Neigel hesitantly, and take his words down: "I find satisfaction in my work, and also with my family, of course. And generally speaking you could say that, yes, I do enjoy onions. I simply enjoy onions. Oh yes."

I squint at the German: he doesn't react. It's as if he never noticed the substitution! How strange. In any case, I see that in contrast to Neigel, Anshel Wasserman lives totally in a world of words, which means, I imagine, that every word he utters or hears has for him a sensual quality which I cannot perceive. Is it possible, then, that the word "supper" is enough to satisfy his hunger? That the word "sore" cuts his flesh? That the word "living" enlivens him? These thoughts, I admit, are a bit over my head. Could it be that Grandfather Anshel became a fugitive from human language in order to protect himself from all the words that cut his flesh?

But Wasserman is unwilling to answer my probings, and instead says furiously that they, the Germans, are "artists of merciful translation," so why not make use of their talent and extract the pain found in certain words? And when I still don't understand what he's talking about, he disgorges one German word after another, which he translates fluently for my benefit: *Abwanderung*, which means "exodus or migration," is the word used to describe mass deportations to the camps; behind the word *Hilfsmittel*, "a device or helpful tool," lurk the gas machines; and what would you say to *Anweiserin*, that lovely maiden who ushers you to your seat in the theater, and in their language becomes the sobriquet for *Kapo* woman? And he throws out more and more examples, till his voice grows hoarse and he whispers furiously, "Poison! A death potion in their language from first to last!"

"Wasserman!" says Neigel, who was left out of the conversation this time (in what could be called a state of suspension). "It's a good thing you're here. I want you to go on with the story." "Now, your honor? But it is past midnight!" "Now!" "But, your honor, everything that happened outside . . . the executions, that is . . . do you feel like hearing a story?" "What do you think?!"

Wasserman glares at him. ("Go thou, Anshel, and play before the king, whose mood is black upon him . . .") It should be noted (I hate it when things like this are left dangling) that somehow we all proceed from Neigel's shower stall to his office. He stretches. From his desk drawer he pulls out a bottle and takes a sip. His cheeks are flushed. I have to report here that contrary to Staukeh's claim (in the interview he gave after the war), Neigel drinks like a pro. Wasserman mutters to himself and, sliding a hand into his gown, gropes for the notebook. He spies another blue envelope in Neigel's wastebasket and glowers. This would be a good time to fill in a few more details about the room, like the little army placards on the walls, and other silly maxims with a hypnotic effect on persons of weak character who hear in them the echoing of a primitive call of the blood, the beating of the great pulse, ten thousand feet marching in step, the smell of sweat at the stadium, the boyhood memory of a ride on Father's rugged shoulders, the jolly concussion of a rifle butt, or the way the spirit soars when the band is playing with ten trumpets and six drums, and every tune is your anthem. And suddenly Wasserman lets out a bitter scream, to drown out a noise I hadn't noticed: "The story, the story must go on!"

"Go on, then," says Neigel, smiling a very thin smile. "Who's stopping you?"

Wasserman breathes and looks at me with a curious expression in his eyes. "There, I have begun," he says quietly.

"When night came, Herr Neigel," he says at last, "the baby would not stop hollering, and his bitter screams drowned out the din of a tank rolling by on a nearby street and the frightening explosions from surrounding houses, where heavy combat was in progress . . ." And again Neigel raises a hand and, in a voice like iron, demands an explanation. Wasserman looks at him and turns to me. ("Ai. I am about to sell Esau the smell without the fish, as they say . . .") He explains to Neigel that the story has moved again, this time to Nalvaky Street in Warsaw, "at the time of our little rebellion against you, begging your pardon."

"Ha!" shouts Neigel in amazement, and stands up, his finger trembling with rage as he points to the Jew. "Still at it, still trying to fight us with your puny weapons?!" And once again we witness his astounding self-control: he forces himself to sit down, and squeezes his fingers around an invisible neck. "I know exactly what you mean to do with this nonsense," explains Neigel in a soft, noxious voice (Wasserman: "Like a sharp razor wrapped in kidskin"). "You, like all people in love with words and talk, think everyone else is as susceptible as you are to their magic power. You really believe you can wage a war with words here, and fight battles with diversions and raids and precision bombings? Don't interrupt me! I'm talking now!" And Neigel stands up again, tugging at his belt and pacing furiously around the room. "You started your story in the forest of Borislav, in that lousy stinking mine, and as soon as you saw I was beginning to understand, when you saw I was getting used to the place, you moved the story away, to the zoo! And you waited till I was comfortable there, off my guard, and—hoopla! You move the story again! A surprise attack on an unexpected front! Warsaw! The rebellion! Ach!! You shuffle your stupid characters around like a general moving battalions. You're waging a guerrilla war with words! Hit and run! Feints and harassments. It's a war of attrition! I wonder where you're going to take me after Warsaw. To Birkenau? To the Führer's bunker in Berlin? Believe me, Wasserman"—he stands very close to the Jew and speaks into his ear—"I despise you and your ridiculous efforts. I pity you. Pity you. If you had a knife in your hand, even a little jackknife, it would be a lot more convincing and effective than the millions of words you're going to chatter here." And he takes a jackknife out of his pocket, snaps it open irritably, and sets it on the table next to Wasserman. "Here you are. What are you going to do with it?" Wasserman is silent. He looks away. Neigel explodes: "Here's the jackknife, Wasserman! A fine, sharp knife. Now I'm going to unload my gun. I'm kneeling on the floor beside you. I can't see you. What are you going to do with it?!" Wasserman is still looking the other way. Neigel waits a minute more, his face to the floor. Then he lumbers to his feet, picks up the jackknife, and shuts it. He looks defeated. "What did you think, Wasserman," he asks quietly, without malice or rancor, "that if you jumped your story around from place to place you would unhinge me? Did you think you could addle my brain that way? Ach, so old and yet so childish, Wasserman, and so stupid, too. We could have done something wonderful here together. Something nobody has ever done before. But you insist on playing your *dreck Jude* games with me, and destroying your last story with your own hands, besides losing the only person in the world willing to take any time out for your silly nonsense, you old curio!" And again he tugs at his belt, for emphasis, and returns heavily to his chair. Wasserman preens his molted plumes, admits to himself that the German is right, and that "Neigel is my scourge." And at the same time, inexplicably, he swells with stiff-necked pride ("Nu, well, though I am almost prostrate on the ground baking a bagel, as they say, meaning, Evil has overtaken me, I knew that Esau had never needed to beat words into such thin threads before, and that the more he did so, the more he would become unraveled"), and partially recovered, if still cautious, he apologizes to Neigel and suggests that "with your permission," he will continue the story now, without trickery, if Herr Neigel would be good enough to forget this little incident and return to the zoo?

Neigel consents. There is no logical explanation for this. He just can't seem to do without the rest of the story, as if he needed it for some purpose. Wasserman denies that he knows the reason. Inwardly he smiles his thin, crooked smile and reiterates that he is duty-bound to retrieve all that is forgotten, and that he has a commitment to the story, which is "like a living, breathing creature. The feet must not come before the head." And he returns to the screaming infant, and to Fried, who carries him in his arms and paces his room, murmuring *na na na* and *lu-li lu-li* in his ears, and also *cheep, cheep, cheep*! But none of this helps to soothe the baby, still screaming into the large and hairy ear of the doctor, who has never experienced such violence before. The screams seemed to unravel the premarked stitches of strained vigilance in his brain and the old hopes that froze so long ago.

No, the baby isn't going to make it.

Our little story will end here.

Because suddenly, without warning, a certain person is paralyzed with fear, utterly paralyzed, as if a cataract had spread to the root of his soul. And again there are reflections, such as: (1) A certain person has no faith left in ideals and/or other persons. (2) Therefore, he can no longer undertake responsibility, or make choices and/or decisions about anything whatsoever. Consequently, all actions, procedures, and relationships entered into by a certain person will be henceforth significantly reduced—together with the pain he may cause or which may be caused him. (3) All is lost. In other words, if a certain person should raise his hopes again, he may expect to be bitterly disappointed. Only, he didn't raise his hopes. Even his legal wife showed her true face under the new conditions and, in league with a certain other woman who had at one time engaged in sexual relations with a certain person, advised him to leave their joint place of cohabitation ("home"; "the nest") until such time as he should "feel better," "work things out," etc. Naturally this was done in the name of "love," "concern," and "understanding."

He was exiled (of his own free will) to another city. A rented attic room (with a separate entrance) housed him for six months. A fog wound through his tortured brain. The pages were blank and white. A certain person no longer belonged to anything, and nothing belonged to a certain person. In the evening, after days of white glare, three cigarettes were smoked under a Persian lilac tree on a quiet side street near his room. A cheek was nicked while shaving. Confusion reigned. Or, at the risk of overfamiliarity, a certain person was confused.

Across the empty pages of the notebook in which the story was to be written, a single word flashed through the sleepless night: BEWARE. But of what was he supposed to beware? And to what end had he built a fortress around himself so adeptly all these years? Mama and Papa never said. They left an order: Beware. So you'll survive. And later, when all the wars are over, there will be time to sit and talk about the full implications of the life you guarded so fiercely. But meanwhile, make do with this. There's nothing more we can tell you now. There are those who regard this word ("Beware") as the word Wasserman read his story from to Neigel. Others suggested that the word was "survive"; but that was not it either, apparently. In the White Room there are efficient ways to investigate such questions: if something is written down on paper, and must be weighed in order to ascertain whether it is true or not, then a certain person is clearly on the wrong track. But if the procedure is such that it is enough for a certain pair of eyes to close in order for consciousness to return and for a clear reflection to appear on the mirror of the inner eye without recourse to rational intervention—herein lies the fulfillment of the capricious, physio-literary demands of the White Room.

Fried lays the screaming baby down on the carpet. He doesn't know what to do. Standing his full height, he feels as if he's seeing his own scaled-down reflection inside a well. For the first time this evening he allows himself to loosen his tie and roll up his sleeves. Otto: "Paula and I had never seen him like this; I mean, so unkempt. A real Zanyedvany. And because the baby's face is turning purple from screaming and holding his breath, the doctor kneels down beside him on the carpet and pries the little mouth open with two fingers, grumbling, "Otto didn't see right. He has four teeth in there." He lays his long, hard palm on the baby's belly and gently massages it, as he sometimes does with baby baboons suffering from gas and shrieking in pain. The child under his hand was, as Marcus said, "like a fresh leaf sprouting from the trunk of a withered tree."

And while Fried was giving this pleasant massage, he suddenly heard . . . Fried: "Nu, how shall I say it, the baby—that is, suddenly I hear . . ." Wasserman: "A mighty gurgle from the baby's bottom, as smooth green beads of excrement squirted onto the carpet." Munin: "You can describe it as beautifully as you like, but it's still shit." Marcus: "The good doctor wrinkled his nose at this foul wind from his guest and ran to get a rag . . ."

Neigel raises his hand. In the past few minutes he has made several notes in his black book. With his left hand waving in the air, he continues to write with the other hand. He wants to know, once and for all, who this mysterious Mr. Marcus is and what he's doing in the story. Wasserman is still evasive. He tells the German that Marcus is an apothecary. That he is extremely musical and, as a pastime, copies scores for the Warsaw Opera Company. He is also very interested in alchemy, but he joined the Children of the Heart by dint of certain experiments which have no bearing on the philosopher's stone. "A human experiment par excellence, Herr Neigel!" declares Wasserman. "An act of self-sacrifice and mortification for the sake of an ideal. More I cannot divulge to you at this time, and I beg you for a little patience."

It should be noted that Fried preferred using a torn sheet for diapers than the diapers Paula had embroidered for the unborn Kazik. He did his best to diaper the baby, who writhed and screamed and kicked till finally— Fried: "*Du yassni choleria!* Right in my nose!" The doctor, in agony and with a bloody lip, let out a furious wail, which scared even him, and then tried to blur the impression of it by dangling the baby, tickling him, batting his big eyelids at him, and finally— Marcus: "Hallelujah, Fried! You sang him a song you remembered from childhood!" Fried: "Little sheep are turning home . . . baa baa baa . . . Skipping over rock and stone . . . baa baa baa, etc." Otto: "But the babykin wouldn't stop screaming, and if you've ever heard Fried sing, you'll know why." And Fried: "I sat next to him on the carpet, feeling very low. I kept telling myself that there was nothing else the poor little fellow could do, and it would be best just to let him go on screaming. And as soon as I thought this, what happened?" Otto: "The babykin started smiling at the doctor!" Fried: "Smiling, hell. He was laughing! He was actually laughing!"

No strength left. No strength for baby or anybody. A certain person has lost the strength to go on. The writing authority, previously mentioned, doesn't have enough vitality left for itself, let alone another living creature, even a literary character. Utter passivity has taken over. In the wake of this, additional considerations have gradually matured, e.g., a new system of living with others (or frying omelettes with them, not to mention peeling onions!) will have to be devised. We will have to go back a few hundred steps and start anew. But this time, we will proceed very slowly, so we won't repeat those ghastly mistakes. It will be necessary to assemble all the most highly intelligent professionals for this vital research, our in-depth analysis of man to help us understand what we have here. We will grind down all that is human, flatten it out, make it so shallow that the various clues will stand out, the combination to the safe. This machine-book will explain once and for all what it was intended for, and how to use it and improve it. What to do in case of breakdown, when it can't correct its own mistakes, and how an outsider can fix it. And now Wasserman is telling the story to Neigel. A Jew who can't die is trying to save the world with the help of the Children of the Heart. And an innocent wish is made—that this innocent effort of Wasserman's might win the faith of a certain person; only, a certain person is unable to believe or find redemption. Yes, man will have to be taken apart limb from limb. And that which is called "life" will have to be vivisected down to its finest fibers, and put under a microscope lens. In order to neutralize scientifically that which can no longer be withstood, like "murder," for instance, or "love," until they are at last deciphered and stopped from causing such "pain" and "anguish." Until they are understood. And till then, everything is suspended: "love" and "mercy" and "morality." And there is no "right" or "not right," "love" or "not love." There is no "choice" and no "freedom." This is an emergency, one fist, four fingers, whereas those are luxuries, suitable for times of "peace," and for people willing to "believe" in "man" and his "kind" "heart" and "moral" "destiny," and in the "purpose" "of" "life" "but" "Wasserman" "brings" "us" "a" "baby" . . . Neigel coughs and calls Wasserman's attention to a mild discrepancy: the baby is rather young to laugh. Wasserman readily acknowledges this. Fried was also surprised. Fried remembered that voluntary, directed smiling begins at the age of, uhm . . . say . . . "Two or three months," Neigel volunteers. "Karl started a little later. He is more serious . . . With Lischen we saw a smile when she was two months old. She's always first at everything. Christina says she was like that as a baby, too." And Wasserman: "Your memory is truly amazing, Herr Neigel. Perhaps you recorded it in a special baby book?" "What? Yes. I mean, Christina, she recorded it in a special baby book. You should have seen it—very nice. Like a children's story. I couldn't write like that. I mean, if we ever have another child, I might give it a try. After all, you and I have tried our hand at more complicated things than that, haven't we, Wasserman?"

"Most assuredly!" answers Wasserman, and the story continues. The doctor, he recounts, decided to find out what caused the unusual smiling and laughter. He conducted a small scientific experiment. He chuckled in a thick, exaggerated voice to make the baby laugh, but the little fellow sensed the trick immediately and grimaced. The doctor smiled despite himself, a real smile this time, and the baby beamed at him. This was so comic that Fried roared with laughter. The baby responded. Marcus: "Primordial smiles searched the baby's body for the happy bolt hole. First his knee tried to smile. Then his elbow essayed it, disclosing a magnificent dimple." Neigel: "Ah . . . why does it have to be on his elbow?" Wasserman: "Would you prefer it elsewhere, Herr Neigel?" Neigel: "Well . . . it's a little silly, I know . . . but would you mind putting it on the right knee instead? Just above the knee? Liselotte has one there. I don't know, I just thought . . ." "But of course, Herr Neigel; you see, it is there already!" "Thank you, Herr Wasserman."

Wasserman shuts his eyes with a long flutter of pain and pleasure. It was the first time in years that a German had called him "Herr."

The baby shook all over as he tried to find the seat of the smile. His face quivered and turned red. His bright hair glistened. Fried: "I started thinking maybe he just needed a burp, so I picked him up and gave him a little pat on the back. Marcus: "And the smile just slid into place. Then, as the baby was gaily opening his mouth, laughing and gurgling with pleasure, Fried glimpsed six white teeth in the pink gums."

Neigel: "Six? You said four."

Death to this baby. Death to everyone. A certain person's powers are utterly drained. There is strength left for one last spasm of resistance to Wasserman. Only when the activity of writing takes place is there any "vitality." In the fingertips. The rest—numb. The written pages in his hand are like a fresh leaf sprouting from a withered tree. But at least this: Wasserman's hidden, malicious intent has been revealed, and all the necessary operational plans to frustrate it have been made. The situation is still under partial control of the writing authority. The situation is as follows: Wasserman is aiming his efforts at a certain person, trying to "provoke" him—using unbelievably cheap tactics to bring him back to "life." But Wasserman will be assailed. Wasserman will be soundly combated!

That night, on a narrow bed in a rented room in a strange city, a dream was dreamed. Neigel was dreamed in the guise of a certain person. Neigel's children were also in the dream, and were encountered without enmity. They were even deemed "sweet." They were cared for gently and with devotion by Neigel (who was a certain person). In the aftermath of the dream, the dreamer awakened with the following thought: A certain person has been dreamed of as a Nazi, and all this evoked was a mild depression, which soon lifted, having nothing much to hang on to. The strange thought occurred that they always say the little Nazi in you (henceforth LNIY) with reference to the wrong things, the obvious things like bestial cruelty, for instance, or racism of one sort or another, and xenophobia, and murderousness. But these are only the superficial symptoms of the disease. The chair at the writing desk in the rented room was oppressed by a certain ambiguous load. A pen was raised in the hand and chewed by the teeth. The rented attic room in which the aforementioned activities took place had a view of the sea. Oh, sea. They always say the LNIY and they're so wrong. They put vigilance to sleep, and pave the way for the next disaster. Yes, such thoughts revolved with astounding clarity. Total wakefulness and an acute understanding of his situation were detected, together with the inability to change what had already been fixed and determined. The broken closet mirror reflected his self. A bird face. Bright red eyes. An ugly shaving cut under ugly stubble. But the real problem, the disease, lies much deeper. And it may be incurable. And it could be that we are all no more than germs. And when here and there the LNIY is signaled, could it be that this is only a sly and cowardly act of blackmail, the goal of which is to reach a general consensus about the things it is convenient and easy to agree upon? That is, to fight whatever can be fought? But what, then, is the proper treatment? Or should we eradicate everything and start all over again? And do we have the strength?

That night things were examined: Could a certain child (who will henceforth be called Yariv) be destroyed by a certain person who also serves as his father? What about a certain person's wife, and what about his mother?

At 0445 hours, a pair of trousers and a gray sweater were donned. The door leading out to the roof was opened. The roof was paced briskly. The feeling of awakening and recovery was experienced by a certain person. Beyond the roof, with its antennas and solar heaters, lay the blue borders of the great water reservoir. At exactly 0449 hours it became a certainty that these were not the right questions to ask, and that the mistakes, it may be ventured, had come with the questions. At this point certain questions which one had been taught to ask by a certain B. Schulz were recollected, and it became regrettably clear that they had been too much feared to be asked. They had always been feared. Now again it was recollected that questions must be asked in a different vein: Not "Would a certain person destroy X, Y, and Z?" but "Would he bring them back to life? Would they be brought back to life by him with every passing moment?" and—this may be the decisive question—"Would a certain person's own self be brought back to life, with the same fervor, passion, and love—by a certain person—with every passing moment?"

And since no answer to this question was found, one peevish last question was posed: Which is the real horror, death or life? Real life, without reservation, life in the sense that—etc. Suddenly a certain person went running back to his desk to write. But his pen refused to write. The ink refused to flow. A certain person received a kick. A cold sweat broke out. His pen was jabbed and banged on the table as though in an attempt to wake somebody under it, beyond it. At last the ink flowed.

Wasserman is still there. He's always there, facing Neigel. He describes the bewildered doctor, too cautious to register the baby in his notebook yet (the same one he has been using a few years now for both zoo animals and employees), because he has no name, and Fried: "It's not my job to give my patients names, is it?"

Thus writes Fried: "Anonymous baby. Brought to me by Otto Brig at 2005 hours on 5/4/43. Wrapped in woolen blanket. No sign of parents. Sex: Male. Length of body: Impossible to measure because of resistance; an estimated 51 cm. Head measurement: Ditto; an estimated 34 cm. Weight: Ditto; an estimated 3 kg. At 2020 Otto Brig saw 2 teeth in the lower jaw. At 2110 I myself (A.F.) saw another two teeth in the upper jaw. Approximately two minutes later another two appeared in the lower jaw. All in all: six teeth." Since the baby did not interrupt the rest of his scientific documentation, Fried returned the favor with extravagant generosity, noting: "2120. The baby is alert, and even smiling." Fried: "And there I was, writing away, paying no attention to him till he moved on the carpet, or fell or something, and I looked and saw—ah! The baby was suddenly lying on his tummy! Poor thing. I turned him over on his back again and watched him, and believe it or not, he flipped over on his tummy again!"

Fried detested any form of fraud or deception, and there was always someone trying to deceive him, poor Fried! He lived with the sense that somebody out there had taken advantage of his momentary carelessness to change the world's scenery from top to bottom. And in furious protest against the lies and decadence engraved on the world, Fried clung to his decency, and gripped it by his fingernails. Marcus: "And the more the world deceived him and opened up its books of legerdemain and deviltry—" Harotian: "And all the suitcases with false bottoms and trapdoors and hidden pockets—" so the doctor buttressed his hate and shame-filled faith with the necessary logic of things, and with the existence in our world of a proper order, lucid and simple, which is bound to be discovered someday, in somebody's life.

Neigel raises a hand. "You're wrong there," he says to Anshel Wasserman. "There's always a logical explanation." Wasserman appears to object. Neigel is willing to elaborate: "Even when something seems unnatural at first, it turns out to have a logical explanation." And Wasserman: "Herr Neigel, the role and mission of logic in our world is to divide things into categories and connect them to each other, in the manner of every winged fowl after its kind. But things in themselves," he says sadly, "things in themselves are totally lacking in logic! And so are people. Yes, indeed. A mixed leaven of passion and fear, ai, a fine world, and what is logic? Only the divider and connector between them. Yes. Logic, for instance, is your wonderful program for transporting trains here from all over Europe. To the slaughter. Logic is the railroad tracks stretching over most of the world, and the cars that never tarry in the station. Logic, Herr Neigel, is the invisible string that binds the hand of the dutiful functionary whose signature authorizes the engine's oil supply for the day, and the engineer who drives it over the tracks, and, if you will, logic is what conjoins the two and prevents them from meeting the corrupt stationmaster, the best of men, who in return for a purseful of mammon, which we shoved through the train window, brought a flaskful of water for my little girl when she fainted. He, too, behaved according to the logic at the root of the situation, only this logic, sir, connects things that are lacking in logic, the coils of cruelty and mercy, human beings, my daughter's life and her death . . ."

Neigel, who has just heard about the death of Wasserman's daughter for the first time, prefers to ignore it. Or maybe he doesn't have the emotional stamina to cope with the information. He looks down with a "humph," that seems to indicate that Wasserman should continue. Wasserman gives him a long look full of pain and bitterness, and then his face takes on an expression as close to hatred as I've ever seen on it. Then he nods to himself and continues.

Marcus: "And in our Fried, honesty and disillusionment were so intertwined that they developed into a permanent spasm of the throat and stomach, and Paula claimed that by this strange form of self-torture Fried was perpetrating no less an injustice than falsehood or fraud." Paula: "But I can't understand why people are always trying to fool my Friedchik. He's so sensible and smart and suspicious of everyone, while me, of all people, such a dupe I'd believe a cat, they leave alone." Harotian: "But you've got to hand it to our doctor, when it came to a choice between logic and the merciful lie, he chose the lie. And hope.

I appreciated that very much, Fried." Fried: "Oh, you! You're the all-time master of camouflage!" Marcus: "Yes, indeed. And with an illogical love, Fried, with a real camouflage-love, you allowed yourself to believe in the child Paula wanted to bear." Fried: "And I suffered. You don't know, any of you, nor will you ever know, how I suffered. I will never let myself suffer that way again as long as I live." Otto: "No, Fried? You won't let yourself?" And Munin: "Hey, you! Enough with the arguments already. The baby has flipped over again!" Fried: "Pshakrev!"

He bent down and turned the baby over roughly on his back, and screamed, "This is how a baby your age is supposed to lie, get it!" and he looked away stern-faced, with arched brows, but the baby, our baby—

"Flipped over again?" asks Neigel. And Wasserman: "Exactly so! And poor Fried—" Neigel: "Screamed in terror, and quickly turned him over on his back again!" "And the baby flipped over again!" "And again! And again!"

With a sudden suspicion the eagle-doctor snatched the baby off the carpet and held him silently up to the light. "The baby, Herr Neigel, laughed contentedly, and in his mouth gleamed, ai—" Neigel: "Wait a minute! Four, six, eight teeth?" Wasserman: "Exactly so!" Neigel: "Listen! I don't know if I'm so crazy about this, but now I'm beginning to get the whiff of a real story!" And he writes a word or two in his notebook.

Fried quickly leafs through the German medical encyclopedia he bought as a student in Berlin fifty years ago. A cloud of dust rises from the pages, and Fried coughs. The peculiar rash which had broken out that morning on his belly itches, but he ignores it. The foundling crawls at his feet, exploring the flowered carpet. The movement of his limbs, clumsy at first, is becoming more coordinated. Fried: "At four months, the first teeth appear . . . at eight months, eight teeth . . . at three months the precocious baby will try to flip over . . . Nu, and I looked down and saw he was trying to sit up, believe it or not, and only a few hours old, two at most, I think, and it said in the encyclopedia: 'At four months the baby will control the cervical muscles well enough to hold its head up. At six months it will sit with a certain effort . . .' "

Fried cursed in alarm, and wiped the steam from his glasses. The baby sat up and examined his chubby toes. For one last minute the doctor could comfort himself that at least his head still drooped.

The baby was hungry and crying again. Fried, with sly logic, thought that if his little guest could sit up by himself, then he had already relinquished the baby-right to be bottle-fed or spoon-fed. Therefore, he poured a little Harotian-type milk into a plastic cup, put it in his hand, and showed him how to drink. Instantly the baby learned.

He finished drinking. The doctor, unthinkingly, asked, "More?" and the baby, imitating the pleasant sound, said, "More?" And Fried, who had locked every portion of his body as a last defense against wonder, said to himself, as if writing in his journal, "Started talking." And he brought a slice of bread from the kitchen, which the baby quickly gobbled down while trying to stand on his feet.

No. Now it can be stated. The LNIY: less dangerous, it seems, than the disease at the very root of our nature which we proliferate with every move. The Nazis merely outlined it and gave it a name, an army, workers, temples, and sacrificial victims. They put it into operation, and in a sense became vulnerable to it. They relaxed their grip and dropped gently in. Because you don't "start" to do evil, you only continue doing it. So says the undaunted Wasserman to me. But in order to fight our nature we need power. And a goal. But how vain are our goals, our ideals. They don't seem worth fighting for. Why fight? To become a human being, as Wasserman says? Is that all? Always to fight for that? And to suffer so much? Therefore, let it stand that: Wasserman is wrong. Humanity protects itself from such barren attempts. Nature is wise, adapting her creatures to the predetermined conditions of life. This is a Darwinist existentialist process: those who can't defend themselves will be wisely discarded. Yes, dear madam, "wisely"!

And now silence fell, a vague disquiet spread, and—how strange— a hand reached out to write the following lines, a sort of anachronistic reactionary concession by a certain person, to his forgotten past, four or five lines intended once and for all to sum up the "Old History," or scrolls to be stored in the archives. And thus it was written: "I had been deeply immersed in 'it' almost from the moment I was born, from the moment I began to despair and relate to people as self-understood, when I stopped trying to invent a special language for them, with new names for every object. And from the moment I stopped being able to say 'I' without hearing a tinny echo of 'we.' And I did something to protect myself from the pain of other people, from other people. And I refused to maim myself: to become lidless and see all."

These are the lines a certain person wrote before his strength ran out. He could "say" these fine words to himself, but he could no longer feel the sweat of life in them. He was finished in this war. This war was finished in him. There was nobody to fight for. For him it was over. He was dead now. He was ready for life.

I stood up and wanted to leave the White Room. There was nothing left to look for. I had forgotten the language spoken there. But I couldn't find the door. That is, I touched the walls, I walked all the way around the room, but there was no door. The walls were smooth. But there had to be a door!

And Anshel Wasserman comes in and faces me. As before. Bowed, hunchbacked. His skin yellow and sagging. He wants to show me the way out. He knows the way. All his life he has been lost in this forest, scattering crumbs of words to help him find the way out. The man from the fairy tales, Anshel Wasserman-Scheherazade.

"Grandfather?"

"Write about the baby, Shleimeleh. Write about his life."

"I want to get out of here. The White Room scares me."

"The whole world is the White Room. Come walk with me."

"I'm afraid."

"So am I. Write about the baby, Shleimeleh."

"No!!!"

I screamed and threw off the soft, warm hand where the story streamed in torrents. I flung myself against the smooth white walls, across the pages of my notebook, at the mirror, at my soul—there was no way out. Everything was blocked.

"Write, then," said Anshel Wasserman patiently, gently. "Sit and write. There is no other way. Because you are like me, your life is the story, and for you there is only the story. Write, then, please."

So be it. The baby. I have to fight against him. Against him, and against his creator. For that I still have a little strength left. Not much, it's true, but anyone who tries to hurt me is going to pay with his life. That is, with his story. Pay attention, Wasserman, your story is now in jeopardy! Even the closeness between us won't make me feel sorry for you, because in war there's no mercy, and I declare war on you and your story.

Fried calculated. It was clear to him by now that every four or five minutes the child developed at the rate of three months in the life of a normal child. In other words, in half an hour the baby would be eighteen months old. Now Fried remembered: it was when the white butterfly flew out of the hall of friendship that the baby began to hyperventilate. In other words, his special time should be reckoned from approximately nine o'clock. ("Approximately??!" The doctor shuddered as he grasped how important every second was now.) Wasserman: "The doctor vigorously scratched the rash that had erupted above his navel that morning. He organized his thoughts: In one hour the tot would be three years of age!" Fried: "Bozhe moi! It can't be! Have to check again!"

And he coolly checked again. His calculation proved correct. Fried bit his finger and tried to remember. Fried: "Wersus? Werblov? What was that name?" Wasserman: "And he leafed through his trusty encyclopedia, past the hundreds of crystallized fragments of destruction and devastation, the plagues and impairments of body and soul, may we never know, and in the end he stopped, out of breath and panting like a dog, under the heading—Fried: " 'Werner, Werner's syndrome. A process of rapid aging . . . beginning at thirty years . . . the deterioration of all systems . . . premature calcification . . . depression . . . rapid agonizing death . . . See under Progeria.' "

Neigel sits up. His face is stern, a little pale. Who would ever have believed he would take the story so personally? Or maybe there's something we don't yet know. "Please, Herr Wasserman. No." He says quietly, "Don't harm the child." But Wasserman, who hears the words as though he heard them before somewhere, a long time ago, continues: "And with every hope laid low, the doctor journeyed to the land of doom he had been referred to by the book. Fried: " 'Progeria. The childhood version of Werner's syndrome (q.v.), process of rapid aging starting at age three . . . only a few cases recorded in medical history . . . development declines by the age of three, and acute symptoms of deterioration, retardation, and depression appear.' "

And Neigel: "*Bitte*, Herr Wasserman, listen to me for just one moment!" And Fried: "Dear God!"

Because the baby was standing up and smiling happily at Fried. Fried was overwhelmed by a wave of pity that instantly sank the iron armada in his heart. Pointing to his chest with a stiff finger, he gruffly said, "Papa." "Papa," said the baby.

Marcus: "Our good Fried felt a stabbing in his chest. He hesitated and then—curse the nasty trick life had played on him—said, You're

Kazik. And the baby repeated his name. Again and again he tasted the new name. "Kazik."

Fried wanted desperately to protect him, to brandish his sword around the helpless young body and ward off the disease. But too late, the disease had already taken hold with all its grotesque power. Neigel shakes his head. Wasserman doesn't stop to look at him. Wasserman is sure that Neigel's objection is based on the fact that the baby has a dimple on his right knee. Neigel pounds the desk and screams, Enough of this warped story, but Wasserman will not yield. He boils. He screams that he can't go on with these interruptions every minute. Now he is so beside himself that he waves his hand at Neigel, and the gesture shocks me, because I remember exactly when I first saw it: more than twenty years ago in my parents' kitchen in Beit Mazmil the time the German tried to interfere, and Grandfather waved his drumstick at him and screamed. But back then I wanted Grandfather to win. "Don't you dare touch that child!" screams Neigel, his face very red, and Wasserman's face is terrible and grim as he chooses his words: "There are things you must not say to me, Herr Neigel. My life is bitter enough without you. And the child will live and die, heaven forbid, according to the story's requirements. It shall be so."

Wasserman is aware that he looks ridiculous when he's angry. He freely admits that "anger is not always becoming." But this time something in him convinces Neigel, who averts his eyes and waits patiently, pen in hand.

Fried breathed deeply. Life had picked up the glove he tossed it every day. There was no other way to interpret it. Only, life had chosen an unexpected battlefield. Through the child's body he would be made to experience sufferings he never knew. Wasserman: "Oy, Fried, you might have guessed this is how life would answer the challenge you drew in the dirt." Fried: "Don't worry about me. Old Fried knows a trick or two." Neigel unexpectedly, clearly contradicting Wasserman: "Hurrah, Fried! In war as in war!" Marcus: "For a minute our Fried was so filled with the lust for war that he almost reared and neighed. But then he realized how meager his chances were and grew sad at heart."

He reviewed his calculations once more, as proof against the second wave of terror which even then was sweeping over him. There had to be some mistake. Perhaps this was not progeria in its acute form. And perhaps the rapid development would soon slow to normal. Yes. Fried reckoned in his head, moving his big bloodless lips. Then he wrote out a list of numbers and studied it. The itch on his stomach was becoming more intense, and he furiously scratched the stupid rash.

One last time he attacked the paper. A moment later he cooled off, looking very pale. Gone was the small hope that life would be merciful, after all, if only because of their long acquaintanceship. Carelessly he sniffed his fingers. Where did this fresh smell of rosemary come from? He gritted his teeth and stared at the page. There, under the bottom line, were two numbers.

Wasserman stops reading. Neigel's eyes are fixed on his lips. Wasserman's eyes are fixed on his empty notebook. For a moment he beams with a wild look of love, like an animal defending its young. And though he is no lion or panther, and more like a rabbit or an angry sheep, the wildness and love in his eyes are undiminished. I could have peeked in his notebook just then and finally seen the word written in his empty notebook, but I was afraid to. Wasserman nodded his head at the word, and inhaled deeply, about to continue.

"One minute, please, Herr Wasserman—let me try to persuade you— you mustn't!" But Fried, obstinately, cruelly ignoring Neigel's plea: "It's like this, if the baby continues to develop at this rate, he'll complete the life cycle of an average man in exactly twenty-four hours. Yes."

Neigel is silent, brimming with bitterness and anger. But even now, he is trapped in the magic of the biological formula "twenty-four hours." He starts to say something and thinks better of it. A few seconds go by. Neigel is calmer. Now I know what I must do. I have no choice. Poor Wasserman. But I, too, have a story writing me, and wherever it leads, I follow. And perhaps my way is the right way.

"This story of yours," says Neigel bitterly, "I can't decide what to make of it." Wasserman, with tremendous relief: "You will approve it by and by, Herr Neigel." And Neigel: "Ach, you're just ruining a good story with all these strange ideas. Twenty-four hours, really!" And Wasserman: "A magnificent twenty-four hours, I assure you!" And then he turns to me and says, "Nu? I have trapped him now— What is it, Shleimeleh? How your face has changed! But—"

The baby toddled across the carpet, his hands held high, his eyes aglow with joy and triumph. When he reached Fried he stopped and looked up at him. "Pa-pa," he said to the weeping doctor. "Pa-pa."

The Complete Encyclopedia of Kazik's Life

FIRST EDITION

READER'S PREFACE:

1. The following pages represent a unique attempt to compile an encyclopedia embracing most of the events in the life of a single individual, as well as his distinctive psychosomatic functions, orientation to his surroundings, desires, dreams, etc. Those normally "resistant" to analysis manifested their unfamiliar aspects and capitulated to the objective demands of an exhaustive study with their first introduction to this rigorous and (seemingly!) secure framework of arbitrary classification. Perhaps it is this very arbitrariness—i.e., the alphabetization of the entries—that transformed various illusive and equivocal figures into wieldy and effective raw material, and helped to reveal the simplicity of basic mechanisms animating all members of the human race.

2. Consequently the following pages will provide the reader with the most comprehensive biography available of Kazik, hero of Anshel Wasserman's story, as told to Obersturmbannführer Neigel, during their stay in a Nazi extermination camp, on Polish soil, in 1943.

3. Since it was not always possible to sever Kazik's biography from the circumstances under which it was recounted, the reader will find that Neigel, Wasserman, and their miscellaneous biographical accretions have left a mark here and there in the pages of this volume. The reader, of course, is free to skip these entries.

4. In an effort to preserve the authenticity of those characters who influenced the life of the subject of our study (Kazik), the monologues and fragmentary conversations of said characters are cited herewith.

Admittedly such a procedure impairs the academic objectivity of the project and "popularizes" it to a certain extent, perhaps unavoidably so at the present time. We shall do our best to amend this in future editions of the encyclopedia.

5. In order to dispense with literary tension wherever possible and to avoid diverting interest from essentials, we shall do our utmost to remove any burden of knowledge likely to create this tension, this extraneous illusion of a purpose, as it were, at the root of things, toward which all "life" is supposed to flow. Accordingly we hasten to report that Kazik died at 1827 hours, twenty-two hours and twenty-two minutes after he was brought to the zoo as a newborn infant. He was sixty-five years old at the time, according to his own chronological frame of reference, that he killed himself. Unquestionably it is the fact that Kazik lived a full life in so short a span which justifies and motivates this modest scientific project, inasmuch as it offers a unique opportunity for a full encyclopedic transcription of one man's life, from birth to death.

6. In view of the aforesaid, the reader should feel free to read the encyclopedia entries in any sequence he chooses, skipping forward and backward at will, though we wish to thank the disciplined reader in advance for taking the king's highway of the Hebrew alphabetical order.

7. The editor's deep sense of commitment to the facts has prompted him to include certain encyclopedia entries shedding light on the attitudes of Anshel Wasserman, some of which bear traces of a powerful struggle between Wasserman and the editorial staff before one side prevailed. Needless to say, the inclusion of these passages in no way signifies an endorsement of opinion on the part of the editorial staff. The wise reader will judge for himself.

And in closing, some personal remarks:

The editorial staff is aware that certain readers are going to be put off. The editorial staff is quite familiar with those malcontents, those unruly heretics for whom nothing is sacred!

For instance, I've got to tell you this, I mean it nearly drove me insane! The first time I revealed my idea to Ayala, you know what she did? She *laughed*. No joke! She laughed in my face. Okay, at first I was pretty upset, but then I realized what was going on: She kept laughing and laughing, not with pleasure but with a look of total absorption and—possibly—fear. She stood there laughing at me, perversely, complacently. Her laugh sounded eerie as it rollicked and rolled and then fluttered away like a flock of colorful birds, like the waves of the sea, like—ah! Now I knew I had to put an end to it, because there's no end to illusion, so I said, coldly and harshly:

EN-CY-CLO-PE-DI-A! And then it happened: Ayala was silent. The old anger flickered in her eyes, and turned to amazement. She recoiled and faded, then shriveled as though struck by lightning; in short, exactly like Bruno's poor Aunt Retitia, by the mailbox in Trinity Square, she disappeared without a trace. The victory of the editorial staff was complete.

אהבה

AHAVA*

LOVE

See under: SEX

אוננות

ONNENUT

MASTURBATION

An activity for the purpose of achieving autoerotic gratification.

1. Kazik took to this practice after the unfortunate episode with HANNAH ZEITRIN [*q.v.*], which occurred at 0630 hours when Kazik—according to his chronological frame of reference—was about twenty-eight and a half years old. Kazik had "touched himself down there," to use Fried's awkward description, before the episode with Mrs. Zeitrin but now he added a dimension of overt enthusiasm and despair. He masturbated relentlessly. The Children of the Heart tried their best to ignore him but to no avail: the tip of his little sex organ discharged fine jets that exploded like firecrackers when they hit the black dome of the sky, and congealed into brilliant animal and human shapes, invariably flawed and sketchy; spermatozoa—full of life and brightness—shot through gloomy space, wiggling their little tails in an infinite stream of birds and fish, toddlers and graybeards, who shone fleetingly, and were swallowed up by the darkness, leaving only a vague sense of anguish in their wake. The members of the band had briefly cherished the hope that Kazik's visions would show them a world more

---

* *The entries follow the order of the Hebrew alphabet.—Tr.*

beautiful, more colorful and vivid than the one they were forced to inhabit, but they soon realized how tainted the visions were with the woes of reality as they knew it. Those visions offered no new departure, no love, but only their generative frenzy, which cooled from moment to moment till nothing remained except the compulsive rubbing, the sense of waste and emptiness, and the enigmatic anguish that instantly vanished. Kazik sensed this, too, of course. Only he couldn't stop. He was humiliated.

2. The masturbatory feats of Yedidya Munin, which became his art: *see under*: MUNIN, YEDIDYA; *also*: HEART, REVIVAL OF THE CHILDREN OF THE

אחריות
ACHRAYUT
RESPONSIBILITY
The sense of duty.

In the heat of an argument between Wasserman and Neigel about whether Neigel's murders in the camp could be considered "crimes," Neigel declared that he was not personally responsible for what happened, that he was only following orders from the "Big Machine," and reinforced this by saying that "the extermination of Jews here will continue even if one person, like myself, should decide to drop out." Wasserman: "But that is precisely the heart of the matter! And what can the matter be likened to, begging your honor's pardon? It can be likened to the sentimental concerns of men and women. For if another man loved your wife, begging your pardon, nu, how shall I put it . . . the human race would continue its course . . . What matters it to me, says Mother Nature, who carries the chain, so long as the big machine of existence keeps running, you see?" Neigel: "Humph. Yes. Of course. Because we have no control over the big things, right?" Wasserman: "Yes, you are right. All is foreseen, and scant indeed is the freedom of action given us!" Neigel: "Then why go on about responsibility all the time, if there's no point to it?" Wasserman: "Perhaps because that is freedom, Herr Neigel. It is the one protest a coward such as I am is free to make." Neigel: "Ach! It's an illusion of protest." Wasserman: "And what choice do we have?"

Also see under: CHOICE

אמנות

OMANUT

ART

The expression of human creativity in the pursuit of aesthetic and functional objectives, in accordance with rules and techniques requiring skill and practice.

Throughout his lifetime, Kazik lived in a creative environment. In fact, the only people he ever knew were the artists collected by OTTO BRIG [q.v.]. Little wonder, then, that he sought in art a creative outlet for his depressions, impulses, and anxieties. First as a PAINTER [q.v.], and later, unwillingly, as a CARICATURIST [q.v.]. He came to see that not even art can promise salvation; that, at best, it augments human aspirations and intensifies longings while never actually fulfilling them, and that, in fact, it is his very freedom that deprives an artist of comforting illusions and brings him closer to acknowledging the limitation of hope.

Also see under: MASTURBATION

אמנים

OMANIM

ARTISTS

Persons who express the creativity of mankind, in the pursuit of aesthetic and functional objectives.

Kazik's sole acquaintances were the artists gathered by OTTO BRIG [q.v.] at the Warsaw Zoo between 1939 and 1943. These were: Paula Brig, Otto's sister, whose art protested the narrowness and cruelty of nature; ILYA GINZBURG [q.v.], seeker of truth; HAROTIAN [q.v.], who waged war on the tyranny of sensory organs; MALKIEL ZEID-MAN [q.v.], artist of the frontiers of personality; AARON MARCUS [see under: FEELINGS], a man dedicated to enlarging the scope of human feeling; YEDIDYA MUNIN [q.v.], the great Orgasman, advocate of human transcendence, seeker of happiness, lover of the immanence of God; Albert Fried [see under: BIOGRAPHY], doctor: at first he resented Otto for collecting "these filthy maniacs" at the zoo instead of a reliable work force. Later, however, when Paula became pregnant with an imaginary child, Fried closed his eyes and allowed himself to believe. He, too, was awarded the title "artist."

Otto calls his artists "fighters," or "partisans," as well.

אקדח

EKDACH

REVOLVER

A lightweight handgun with a short barrel.

1. The weapon used by Neigel upon his return from leave in the bosom of his family in Munich.

2. The weapon used by Paula to kill Caesar the lion during the siege of Warsaw in 1939. The regular zoo employees had been drafted into the army by then, and the zoo itself had been almost destroyed by heavy bombing. Hungry animals roamed the paths, and according to the testimony of Fried's DIARY [*q.v.*], there were a great many cases of depredation. On a single day (10/3/39) some seventy-four animals were killed in one bombing raid, among them a female lion and a female tiger from Rangoon shipped to the zoo only two months before, and two precious Grant zebras. Caesar the lion refused to eat the carcasses of the dead animals. Fried had foreseen this: from the professional literature he knew that lions will eat only monkey carcasses. As it happened, no monkeys had been killed during the bombings. Otto and Fried therefore, decided to kill a monkey a week in order to keep the lion alive. Paula: "But of course I objected, what is this, anyway? Such SWINISHNESS [*q.v.*] in our zoo? Who gave you two the right, I'd like to know, who gave you the right?" According to Fried's diary, Caesar could barely crawl and his ribs protruded sharply. Fried explained to Paula that one lion is worth fifty monkeys, but Paula, being a woman, said, "Even if it's worth a million!" Fried: "Look, there's only one lion and there are seventy monkeys, use your sense, Paula!" And she: "It's a question of life and death, Fried, not a question of logic. Each one of those seventy equals one." And in the end Paula took the zoo revolver, and—Otto: "With love, with deep love, we were there with her, you know, and we witnessed everything"—she shot Caesar the lion and killed him.

אקזמה

ECZEMA

ECZEMA

An inflammatory condition of the skin manifesting in a variety of ways.

The eczema around Fried's navel developed most bizarrely throughout the twenty-two hours of Kazik's existence. In the early-morning hours, when Fried and Kazik and the other artists approached Otto's pavilion [*see under*: LUNATICS, VOYAGE OF THE], the doctor noticed to his great dismay that fresh green, rosemary-scented branches were jutting out of his shirt. For several hours he tried to hide his predicament from the others, but when he finally understood that his body was trying to talk to him, he stopped his painful pruning and allowed the branches to grow unchecked. By evening the doctor was covered all over, and resembled a large, ambulatory bush with bloodshot eyes

בגידה

BEGIDA

BETRAYAL

The sin of breaking trust.

A term Neigel used to describe the plot hatched against him by Wasserman. Neigel used this term more and more often as Wasserman's story progressed, till ultimately he lost all control of himself and cruelly beat Wasserman. According to him, Wasserman's betrayal came very late in the story—"after confusing me like that!"—when the writer had disclosed that this time the Children of the Heart were going to war against the Nazis. And it was indeed a strange war, this war of unarmed dreamers, but in its own peculiar and circuitous way, the war was being waged against him. [*Editorial comment: Regarding Neigel's accusation, Wasserman reflected, "I, too, have noticed of late that Esau uses the word 'betrayal' more and more often, and I remember that Zalmanson once pointed out to me that the most commonly found words in my writings are 'fear' and 'pity.' He confessed a certain predeliction for identifying the favorite words of real writers (not mine, heaven forbid). Every writer, Zalmanson informed me, has a certain pet word he reverts to unconsciously every few pages, the way one keeps touching a sore."*]

בדידות

BEDIDUT

LONELINESS

Aloneness. The condition of being forlorn.

When the Germans entered Warsaw, Otto Brig and Albert Fried decided it would be better for Paula not to live with Fried, the Jew, in his pavilion anymore. And so, after four years with Fried, Paula returned—against her will (she didn't really understand this business

about Jews and non-Jews)—to live with her brother, Otto. That night
Fried lay alone in his bed. Though he had regretted his bachelor days
during his life with Paula, and spent most of their time together in ill-
natured quarrels, he felt unbearably lonely now, like the last man in
the world. He got out of his overlarge bed and went to sit on the stoop
of three stairs in front of the pavilion. He inhaled the scorched air, in
the aftermath of the bombings, and without warning, was deeply struck
by the din of the silent zoo: the swishing, roaring, gurgling, and droning
sounds, the smells of animals, the musty juices bubbling up inside them,
the blood of afterbirths drying slowly on the cubs, the frightening stench
of corpses, milk heavy in mammalian teats, and old Fried, with great
feeling, though as yet self-consciously and cautiously, joined this quiet
chorus, murmuring, "Paula," and then, with a strangled cry, ancient
and terrible, like any man calling out his woman's name, he stood up,
screaming because they had taken her away from him, screaming because this mad war was keeping them apart like a steel cage, screaming
so that—Otto: "Hey, all the peacocks started screeching, and the newly
widowed tiger lamented with him, and the owls and foxes joined in
too, and all that noise woke me up, and for a minute I could have
sworn the animals were rioting against us, against the war, against
everything that was going on at the zoo." Marcus: "And the zoo was
inundated by a thick, desperate sweetness, a cloying sweetness that had
to be purged or there would have been an explosion, heaven forbid!"
In fact, the steel cage bars had begun to shake and bend. Wasserman
reports that tiny parrots swelled up as if with some exotic disease, till
they resembled brightly colored turkeys, or ostriches with their little
cages dangling from their necks like charms. "The zoo," says Wasserman, "respired like a mighty lung." Afterward, the artists concurred
that unless something was done immediately, the unbearable agony
would cause the zoo to pull itself out by the roots and fly up to the
sky. Fortunately, however, Otto grasped what was going on just in
time and woke Paula. (Otto: "You think that was easy? Jesus and Mary,
our Paula sure can sleep!") She listened closely for a moment, understood, and ran out to the cages in her flowered nightgown (Fried: "The
one I hate"), laughing and crying, falling and rising, and shouting from
afar: "I'm coming, Fried, I'm coming," galumphing up the small stairs
and crashing into him with the full force of her clumsy body, then lying
on the balcony with him till Fried forgot to be ashamed.

בדיה

BEDIYA

FICTION

Falsehood. A fabricated story.

Wasserman confessed his "emotional need for fiction" after Neigel had told him, at Wasserman's request, about the first man he killed, an Indian soldier in the British Army whom he shot in combat during World War I. Wasserman was not satisfied with this. He asked Neigel to tell him about the murders that followed, and what he had felt at the time. Neigel reluctantly agreed, but when Wasserman began to interrogate him ("Have you ever asked yourself how you of all people came to be the murderer of this particular person?" "Did you sleep soundly the night after the battle?" etc.), Neigel lost his temper and declared roundly that (1) when he killed, he was only following orders; (2) he never killed for pleasure, though killing did not disgust him either; in any case (3) he couldn't understand what Wasserman wanted with all this *Kwatz mit sauze* (nonsense in sauce). Here Wasserman turned pale and said that he was "obliged, obliged, am I, Herr Neigel, to believe that even you have pangs of conscience and prickings of the heart!" And Neigel: "Why? So I'll be a little more interesting to your pathetic literary mind?!" And Wasserman: "No, Herr Neigel. Not for literary reasons! For my sake. For the sake of my wife and daughter. Yes, it is what I have beheld with mine own eyes, a kind of egoism, begging your pardon, that makes me believe you did not coolly kill us the way you would remove a nail from the wall. Because the soul recoils, your honor, the soul boils with rage! And all my wretched life within me weeps, the little I have gathered in my wretched lifetime, the fears I feared, and my complexities and ignoble passions, the small amount of love I have known, and even, please forgive me, my God-given gifts and abilities, this ugly character of Anshel Wasserman, fortunate we are perhaps that there is not another such to blemish the beauteous world, and yet, that soul is mine . . . my only possession, and how unthinkable that it should be so callously destroyed, you did not even ask our names before killing us, and now, let me amuse myself and seek contrition in you, a single twinge or scruple, let me endow you with the idea of compassion, because I need this little fiction, and then you may do as you wish." Neigel: "Do whatever you want, Wasserman. But don't expect something like this to have any effect on me."

בחירה

BECHIRA

CHOICE

The voluntary selection of one possibility out of many.

In Wasserman's view, the act of choice is the fulfillment of the truly human in man. He expressed this view in the course of an argument with Neigel about the future of little Kazik, who had reached maturity at 0130 hours, upon awakening at the age of eighteen from ADOLESCENT DORMANCY [*q.v.*], and having reentered the flow of time, and demanded that Fried tell him who he was. "Whoever you choose to be," answered the doctor, cautiously adding that he hoped Kazik would choose to be a human being. "Perhaps the worthy doctor can teach me how one chooses to be a human being?" asked Neigel scoffingly. "I always thought one was born so, no?" which sparked off the argument. In Wasserman's opinion, one became a human being as a result of choosing to uphold certain values and precepts. Neigel, on the other hand, argued, "But I did choose!" Wasserman: "Pardon?" Neigel: "I chose to uphold the values of the party, and obey my orders to kill. Does that make me any less of a human being than you are? If a person can do something, that's human, isn't it? What do you and your *dreck Jude* morality have to say about that?" And Wasserman: "Herr Neigel! It should be evident that by 'choice' I mean choosing the higher human values, the purely human values, thus re-creating and redeeming one's self." Neigel, with a stubborn smile: "I chose the other way. I 'chose' to start killing! You can't tell me that isn't choice. Have you any idea how much effort of will goes into a choice like that?" Wasserman: "Ai . . . One does not choose to begin killing, Herr Neigel, but continues to do so, just as one does not begin to hate one's fellow man, or torture him . . . but continues to do so. One must rather make the conscious choice not to kill . . . not to hate . . . This is the root of the difference, I believe . . ."

Also see under: DECISION

ביוגרפיה

BIOGRAPHIA

BIOGRAPHY

A composition describing a life.

In Neigel's opinion, a major flaw in Wasserman's story was his failure to account for the Children of the Heart between the time of their disbanding and their reunion. "Take Fried, for instance," Neigel complained. "I hardly know anything about him! Where's your sense of RESPONSIBILITY [*q.v.*] as a writer, Scheherazade?" And Wasserman, reflecting a moment, read out of his empty notebook: "Our Dr. Fried, oldest child of a physician father and an amateur pianist mother, was born in the year——, but what is the point of these wearisome biographies?! The same chaos in strange and diverse forms takes hold of all the characters, and is oftentimes unworthy of man . . . and so let it be said: For seventy years Dr. Fried has been running between the double file of cudgelers."

[*Editorial comment: A key to understanding Fried's character was offered by Paula, who said, "Some people stretch when they get up in the morning. My Friedchik contracts."*]

בריג, אוטו

BRIG, OTTO

The Polish Catholic leader of the Children of the Heart both times around. An epileptic. Otto is, in Marcus's words, "one in a million." He can do anything. Marcus: "Our Otto, nothing is too difficult for him! Can he run a zoo? you ask. Of course. But he can also draw shadows on the wall with his fingers, or hypnotize a leopard cub by swinging a gold chain; or make wine from apples and jam from corn; or make a coin vanish by rubbing it into his palm; or calm a stray dog with one long whistle; or midwife a frightened giraffe in the midst of a bombing raid so that the calf is born alive; or carve a charming figure out of a potato; or build the kind of kite birds flock to; or play the harmonica . . . As I said, there is nothing of value our Otto can't do. And there's his wonderful laugh, too, his slow, contagious laugh, and though he doesn't speak much, everyone listens. And so generous, yes, Otto has a great big heart. He never studied in a university, and I don't know if he ever read a book from start to finish, but he has a brain in his head, and he always knows the right thing to do." It should be noted that it was Otto who reconvened the band for one last mission [*see under*: HEART, REVIVAL OF THE CHILDREN OF THE], and who first discerned that Kazik needed a wife [*see under*: ZEITRIN, HANNAH].

גוף, האובייקטיביות של ה-

GUF, HAOBYEKTIVIUT SHEL HA

BODY, THE OBJECTIVITY OF THE

As Kazik matured, he came to feel more and more dissociated from his body. Wasserman offers this analogy: Kazik saw his body as the suitcase anonymously thrust into the hand of his soul, as he climbed aboard the ship bound for our world. At first his plaintive soul had hoped someone would come and take the suitcase when the ship arrived at its port of destination, but there was no one waiting at the dock, and his soul could not get rid of the strange suitcase with its thousands of pockets and drawerfuls of unwanted gifts, gifts of suffering to be slowly deciphered throughout one's life, and also, of course, a little gratuitous pleasure. But because the soul cannot master it, even pleasure degrades it, enslaves it, and derides it on its way. Much to his amazement, Kazik discovered that all his life he was fated to drag his left foot, that one eye could barely distinguish shapes and colors, that the older he got the more of those ugly brown spots appeared on the backs of his hands, and the more hair and teeth he lost. He followed these changes as though reading a story about somebody else, but the pain came from within and tortured him: the pain of deterioration, the pain of sepa-ration. Blue varicose veins suddenly covered his left thigh, and he bent down as if to read the map of an unfamiliar region. His eyes watered whenever he came near fresh hay, he got diarrhea from eating cherries and strange rashes after crossing the zoo lawn, and his right eye twitched in moments of emotional stress; all this gradually made his life a misery. As time passed, he was forced to pay more and more attention to the suitcase, which left him with less and less energy for the things that really mattered to him. Then he began to think he had made a big mistake: that perhaps the suitcase was the important thing and the soul was subordinate to it. By this time (around 1330 hours of the following day, when he was fifty-seven years old), Kazik was already so exhausted, and suffering so much physical pain, that he lost interest in finding an answer.

Throughout his life, because he had been given the agonizing ability to perceive the processes of growth and decay simultaneously, Kazik was keenly aware of the misery of his friends, the artists. He saw their futile efforts to hide the defects they had no part in creating; he saw that physical flaws can produce the kind of misery that consumes a person's vitality; that an entire lifetime can go by in a tortuous struggle to condition the person to his defect. He learned that so often when a person says "my fate," he is in fact referring to a hunk of maimed flesh. It was Aaron Marcus the apothecary who suggested that after thousands of years of existence on the face of this earth, man was perhaps the only living creature not yet fully adapted to his body and frequently ashamed of it. And sometimes, the apothecary remarked, it seems that man is naïvely waiting for the next phase of evolution, during which he will separate from his body and become two distinct beings. Wasserman believes that physical defects and suffering (he had them both in abundance) are merely the reins by which God controls man, pulling them ever tighter, to make man remember Him. It should be mentioned that Neigel understood little of what was said regarding man in relation to his body; perfect health was requisite for SS candidates, who could be disqualified because of a single dental filling. The wound Neigel had suffered at Verdun was viewed as a decoration for bravery, not a flaw. With great pride he informed Wasserman that he for one had fully accepted his body, and had never "entertained such twisted thoughts."

גיהינום, הגירוש מן ה-

GEHENOM, HAGERUSH MIN HA

HELL, THE EXPULSION FROM

According to Wasserman, this was one crime the Germans would never be forgiven: "God expelled man from Eden, and you harried him out of hell." Neigel: "Explain!" Wasserman ("Esau has a singular way of saying that word: his face glowers and his eyebrows jump at each other like two billy goats, or like a soldier clicking his heels *Heil!*"): "Nu, well . . . you see, you deprived us of the illusion, the illusion of hell . . . Hell, too, calls for illusion, and some ignorance and secrecy too . . . for only then can hope exist, the hope that things may not be so bad as all that . . . you see, we always pictured hell with boiling lava and pitch bubbling in barrels, until you came along, begging your honor's pardon, and showed us how paltry our pictures were . . ."

גינצבורג, איליה

GINZBURG, ILYA

A street person from the city of Warsaw. The rejected son of a wealthy timber merchant, he never held a steady job. He was wizened, with a pencil-like neck and gangly elbows, and his appearance was thoroughly repulsive: he did not wash, and gobs of filth collected in the corners of his eyes and nostrils. He was also afflicted with an ugly skin infection. The only impressive feature in his crooked black face were his heavy eyebrows, which lent him the appearance of an anguished prophet. Wasserman remembered Ginzburg back from the days when (Wasserman:) "He would wander the streets, chased by gangs of children chanting, 'Ilya, Ilya/The yellow moon is asking/Who are you, Ilya/Who are you, Ilya?/The yellow moon is asking/Ilya Ilya/The white colt is asking/Who are you, Ilya/Who are you, who are you?' " . . . Aaron Marcus claimed that Ilya was not insane, that he was full of heart, "and not so stupid as people may think"—a highly doubtful speculation in view of the fact that when Ginzburg inherited a fortune from a remorse-stricken relation, he turned it down. Marcus the apothecary, held to be an adept in the mysteries of the soul because of his ministrations to the miserable man, described Ginzburg rather picturesquely. Ginzburg, he felt, had refused the money because, in his own way, he was a man of principle who believed it preferable to live one's life without property or family connections. Though this view generally met with skepticism, Marcus nevertheless considered Ginzburg a lamed vavnik [one of the legendary thirty-six just men], or hidden philosopher. Incidentally, it was Marcus, the spiritual apothecary, who affectionately nicknamed Ginzburg "Diogenes," though much to his regret the name stuck to the madman as a taunt. Ginzburg may not have gone as far as the Greek mortifying his body and soul by stripping in winter to embrace a cold bronze statue, but he, too, courted indignity, annoying everyone— always underfoot, always turning up at unsuitable moments, and on his lips—like a monotonous chant—the perennial question: "Who am I? Who am I?" When anyone bothered to answer him, he would merely repeat the question in the same monotonous chant, and when kicked, he would hobble away, his face cast down, his arms spread out in the same inquiring pose. Had it not been for kindly souls like Aaron Marcus, who saw to it that he had an occasional piece of bread, he would have starved to death, but more than Ginzburg needed food, he needed a listening ear, and this he found but seldom. How long, after all, can a person stand there listening to the question "Who am I?" Wasserman said that on a few occasions he decided to listen to Ilya Ginzburg out of pity, but changed his mind. He was ashamed of himself for having given up so easily, not because of the madman's stench, which did not present any real difficulty to Wasserman, who had no sense of smell, but because the monotonous question, always steeped anew in a deep, absurd-seeming despair, made him vaguely uneasy. Aaron Marcus, Ginzburg's chief patron, kept him in food and clothing for a full twenty years, admitted him into his shining apothecary's shop, and listened long hours with laudable patience to Ginzburg's question. Often, when the two were left alone in the shop, and Marcus was busy preparing his medicines (he was the first apothecary in the city of Warsaw to sell natural remedies), Ginzburg would wax silent, and Marcus would speak about his life, hinting painfully at difficulties with Mrs. Marcus (he would not have dared tell anyone but Ginzburg), and it was during one such conversation that he mentioned the fact that Diogenes had lived in a barrel. He never imagined that the madman had understood anything, but the following day Ginzburg quit the park bench where he spent the summer nights and went to sleep in a herring barrel from Hirsch Weinograd's grocery store. Now he really stank unbearably, and Giza, Marcus's shrewish wife, said her husband could go on thinking Ginzburg was a lamed vavnik if he wanted, but he smelled more like a mem-tetnik, one of the forty-nine degrees of impurity. But someone watches over fools, it seems, which may be why, despite his madness and limited intelligence, Ginzburg could survive even the most difficult days in the ghetto. He was never caught by the guards, and twice miraculously escaped an *Aktion*. Eventually, however, his exploits were discovered, and people began to say there was method in his madness. What Ginzburg did was this: Because he stayed in the street at night when no one else was allowed out, he could see members of the various Jewish undergrounds roaming around like shadows. There's no evidence that he understood what they were up to exactly, but something must have sunk in. It would be hard to explain otherwise why on a very cold winter's day early in December of '42, Ginzburg walked into the Paviak, or prison, by the back entrance, directly past the guard, who mistook him for one of the slave laborers. He walked down the moldy corridors, opened doors, and peered in. He had, it would seem, a definite goal. He walked in this reckless and innocent way past all the sentries till he reached a door marked INTERROGATION ROOM. SS interrogator Fritz Orf was just then sitting inside. A handsome young man embittered with boredom, Orf had been posted to Warsaw six months earlier by order of Von Zamern Franknag, chief of police and the SS Warsaw region, who thought an expert interrogator would be more useful to him than a battalion of half-witted Polish soldiers patrolling the streets of the ghetto day and night.

But the Jews captured in the ghetto had nothing of interest to tell Orf, and were ordinarily put to death before the interrogation stage. Orf requested a meeting with Von Zamern and complained to him that he was "rusting away" in Warsaw, where there was no real need for him, in his opinion, but he was only reprimanded by his commander for insolence and ordered to obey without question. So Orf sat dully in the workroom, polishing his tools and reading books. No one had mounted his "ironing board" for six weeks now; not a fingernail had been removed, and the floor was clean of blood. Behind the door, on a hook, hung his shiny black-rubber treatment apron, and Orf was ashamed to look at it. A serious, responsible young man, he would have been incapable of "rusting away" even if he had been idle for ten years. He was a real professional, and proud of it. He found aesthetic pleasure in his work, in the fixed rules of interrogation, in its predictable stages and moments of tension and climax. In other words, Orf viewed his work as ART [*q.v.*]. He never allowed himself to enjoy the suffering of his subject. He knew perfectly well what his fellows in the army and police thought of him and his kind. He could feel their looks of revulsion and fear when he rode the train with them. Even high-ranking officers glanced suspiciously at his black uniform with the white epaulettes. And his own father always found a way to be out of town when Orf came home on leave. So be it. He was strong enough to withstand this covert antagonism. Only a strong man could handle a tough job like his, and somebody had to do it. Orf justified himself by believing he had chosen his special vocation out of a sense of idealism. As the door opened and Diogenes peered in, Orf was deep in Nietzsche's *Will to Power*. In the SS interrogation course, his admired advisor had recommended *Thus Spake Zarathustra*, and Orf, who considered himself an intellectual, was captivated by the wild, deep power of Nietzsche's writing. It should be mentioned that Orf was somewhat disappointed with *The Will to Power*, because of Nietzsche's denial therein of "objective truth." Orf was a firm believer in objective truth, because when you stuck electrodes into a prisoner's sex organ and nipples, he eventually told you things that had an unqualified dimension of truth, subjective truth, perhaps, but torture made everyone alike in the end, which raised the suspicion that a single harrowing voice was screaming out the words.

The really strange thing was that Ilya Ginzburg had reached very similar conclusions. Otherwise he would not have done what he did: like old Diogenes in his day, Ilya Ginzburg braved countless dangers as he wandered with his candle in search of truth, till at last he arrived in the interrogation basement. Orf looked at the filthy Jew standing before him and was filled with revulsion at the sight and smell. He demanded roughly what he was doing there, and Ginzburg stuck his hand into his filthy shirt and pulled out three posters warning the ghetto Jews of mass transports to the "East" for "resettlement." "Not to the East, but to Death!" screamed the posters in Polish. Orf jumped to his feet and circled Ginzburg, covering his nose with a handkerchief. "Suspect everyone!" he had learned in military school. "The innocent-looking ones are the most dangerous!" He made a quick decision. He shut the door behind Ginzburg and beckoned him into the room. Then he locked the door. He had the vague impression that the Jew had wound up here by mistake, but Orf did not want to waste the opportunity. He intended to get out the truth about the people behind the posters. When the interrogation was over, he would send the results to Von Zamern and reinstate himself. He rubbed his hands together quickly like a fly over its food, then turned and put on his black-rubber apron, smoothing it down with the accustomed movements that inspired him with confidence. Surprisingly gentle, he led Ginzburg by the shoulder and sat him down on the interrogation chair. Then he sat facing him across the table, folded his hands, and asked emphatically, "Well then, who are you?"

He was astounded to see the smile of joy and relief spreading across the face of the Jew. "Who am I! Who am I!" Ginzburg nodded in rapture. His gamble had paid off: "they," too, were interested! And in fact, he had heard this about them: that they could uncover the truth even when a person was unwilling or unable to divulge it himself; he had long suspected that every person knows (deep down inside) who he is and why he was born, only, due to some innate flaw, he isn't able to disclose this truth even to himself. Yes, perhaps the others had succeeded, but he, Ginzburg, had not. Perhaps he really was a little backward, as the children chanted, but he, for all his backwardness, had come up with the wonderful idea to present himself before this sympathetic and serious young man, who was obviously eager to help and had already asked him the right question!

"Who are you?" Orf repeated, this time without a smile. The Jew echoed the question with the beaming face of a tourist showing the native that with a little effort they will be able to communicate. Orf sighed and opened his notebook. Inwardly he was a little disappointed, because he was almost certain by now that Ginzburg was a madman: no one in his right mind would come in here smiling like that of his own free will. But Orf wanted to interrogate. For some reason the Jew roused up his old anger at having to rust away here in Warsaw instead of working with the real fighting forces. He was angry with himself: one must not begin an interrogation in anger. An interrogator must always be levelheaded and cool. Orf asked Ginzburg a few more routine questions, for form's sake, and the Jew, who understood that this was only an administrative procedure, did not even bother to reply. Orf had the odd impression that the Jew was trying to make some kind of pact with him in order to get to the point more quickly. He stood up and faced the treatment table. [*Here the editorial staff takes the liberty of skipping the detailed description of what occurred in the room during the ensuing hour and twenty minutes. Suffice it to say, during this period of time the following tools were used: forceps, pincers, matches, rubber hoses, spikes, a candle flame, a hook, a nail, and something they called the "vegetable peeler."*] Ginzburg looks very different now than he did when he walked into the room. But so does Orf: not just because his hands and apron are smeared with blood, or because of the perspiration staining his uniform and streaming down his forehead and blinding him: there is a remarkable expression on his face. Never before had he come across a case of this kind: when he shouted dryly, "Now who are you?!" the subject had shouted back enthusiastically, "Who am I? Who?!" And when he changed the question to "Who sent you here?" Ginzburg screamed with him, "Who sent me here?!" And when Orf became uncontrollably angry and shrieked, "What is your mission?!" the subject had repeated the question with such longing it made the experienced interrogator shudder. Ghastly tortures which had broken even the toughest men till they begged to speak the truth one last time before succumbing to insanity seemed to have no effect whatsoever on Ginzburg. Quite the contrary in fact; Orf was willing to swear that when one of his trusty instruments failed, he saw an expression not unlike disappointment on Ginzburg's swollen face. The room reeked of the sweat, blood, and excrement that had poured out of Ginzburg. Teeth lay scattered on the slippery floor. Orf poured a bucket of water over Ginzburg and waited for him to revive. For a moment he saw himself reflected in the big mirror on the wall, and recoiled. He was tense and frightened. In his heart grew the suspicion that if there was any hidden objective truth in the world, this man was keeping it to himself. There were moments when Orf thought the Jew had come to him in order to help him discover it. And then he experienced a singular feeling of sympathy and COMPASSION [*q.v.*], as if the two of them had conducted a difficult new experiment in this room. Orf went to wash his face with cold water and combed his hair back with his fingers. He coldly reprimanded himself before the mirror for these soft thoughts, turned smartly on his heel, and stepped back to the table. The Jew had already come to and was muttering on the floor. Orf connected the electrodes to his earlobes, nipples, and sex organ. In the SS course they had been jokingly told that it's less of a problem hooking up electric tongs to a Jewish sex organ. Then he tied Ginzburg to the table with two thick leather straps and asked him stiffly who and what he was. Ginzburg did not have the strength to repeat the question, but his eyes expressed the wild longing to know the answer. Orf pressed the electric switch. The magnet worked. Ginzburg was thrown up in the air, and he screamed. Orf closed his eyes and opened them much later. Then he leaned over the subject and asked who he was. Ginzburg's lips were still. Orf put his ear to the thin chest. As from a distance came the beating of the heart. It was weak and slow, and it spoke to Orf and said, "Who am I?" Orf was terrified. A strange noise broke out of him, like a groan. He freed the Jew from the leather straps and poured another bucket of water over him. Then he lit a cigarette and noticed that his fingers were trembling. "He's crazy," he said to himself. "He's plain crazy. He knows nothing." But deep inside he knew that though Ginzburg was crazy, it was untrue that he knew nothing. Orf considered what to do with the Jew. He didn't want to turn him over to the Polish police, who might start asking questions and discover something disgraceful. He decided instead to personally escort Ginzburg out of the building through the back entrance. It was suppertime and chances were that he wouldn't run into anyone on the way. He lifted Ginzburg up and supported him till he could stand on his feet. This took quite a while, and the touch of the Jew was almost unbearable. Ginzburg's pain was so tangible it overflowed into Orf's body. He felt weak and lost. When Ginzburg's legs were steadier, Orf began leading him to the door. He had to hold him up as they walked through the corridor, and he prayed he wouldn't run into anybody. His prayers were not answered, however: someone approached in the corridor, a short, stocky man. They met in the light of the yellow lamp with the wire netting. Praise be to God, thought Orf, the man was a Polish civilian. The corridor was too narrow for all three to pass, and the man made way, taking a good, long look at them, which was enough for him to figure out what had taken place. That is, in retrospect Orf was convinced that one look was enough for the little blue-eyed Pole to figure out what had taken place. The man hurried after them and cleared his throat politely. Orf, supporting Ginzburg's weight, turned to him angrily. The man hurried to say, "Pardon, my name is Otto Brig, and I have a permit here to remove Jewish prisoners." Orf didn't miss his chance. "Take him!" he almost shrieked. "Get him out of here!" But as Orf watched Otto walk away supporting the bleeding wreck by the waist, he sensed with anguish that perhaps he hadn't understood what had happened in the interrogation room at all, that perhaps the terrible Jew had, in some strange and unintelligible way, uttered man's deepest truth.

האלוטיון /

HAROTIAN

Foe of the tyranny of sensory perception. A magician by trade.

Harotian was born in the small Armenian village of Faradian in the last quarter of the nineteenth century. His wonder-working power was discovered quite by chance: The Children of the Heart, who in 1885 flew to Armenia in the time machine to save the town of Faradian from the marauding Turkish Army, had hidden in a cave, surrounded by a battalion of cruel Turks. So ends Chapter 9 of the story. A week later, Wasserman delivered the sequel, Chapter 10, to Zalmanson, wherein the Children of the Heart make a last-minute escape through the back of the cave and are saved. This was Wasserman's usual way of rescuing the band from the predicaments into which he put them. The new chapter was already on its way to the printers, and Zalmanson and Wasserman had a friendly chat in the office before departing each for his home. A short while later, at around midnight, Zalmanson came banging on Wasserman's door, nearly waking the dead with his screams. Wasserman (in neatly pressed striped pajamas, soft slippers, his thin hair tousled, looking highly alarmed) carefully opened the door and absorbed the brunt of Zalmanson's fury: a shocking error had been committed, it seems. At home in bed, Zalmanson had suddenly recalled that in an earlier chapter Wasserman distinctly mentions that Otto inspected the cave and found no second opening! Wasserman shuddered. Zalmanson stood in the doorway wearing a coat over his red silk pajamas, shrieking almost effeminately, "Ac-cu-racy, Wasserman, ac-cu-ra-cy!" They ran back to the editorial office together and stopped the press. Wasserman was frightened and confused. A table was cleared for him next to the machine, and the printers, whose work had stopped, stood watching. He knew he would not be able to write a single word. He needed at least a week to "ripen." The room was full of smoke and the suffocating smell of ink. The printers looked dirty to him, hostile and violent. Zalmanson sat opposite him, drumming nervously on the table. And Wasserman understood exactly how the band felt, trapped inside the cave. He groaned in despair. His spectacles were covered with steam. He knew that only a MIRACLE [*q.v.*] could save him now. And so Harotian came into the series, issuing from the following sentence: " 'Hark,' whispered Otto into the ears of his frightened companions, 'is that the bleating of a babe, or a wee tot of the village?' " Zalmanson pointed out maliciously, though not unjustly, that if Otto could miss the child on his earlier search of the cave, there might have been a hidden tunnel, too, but this was no time for arguments. Moments later, while Turkish sabers flashed at the mouth of the cave, a flight of mysterious white eagles burst forth, bearing the small Armenian boy of magical power high over the heads of the Turks, who prostrated themselves on the ground crying "Allah! Allah!" Chapter 10 was received with such wild acclaim that Zalmanson gave Wasserman a 25 percent pay raise, though the expression on his face deprived Wasserman of any pleasure. After that, Harotian never departed from the Children of the Heart, and joined in all their adventures, performing wondrous feats of magic and trilling melodies on his little flute that "wrenched tears from the eyes of the basest villains." When the Children of the Heart disbanded (their last adventure was written in 1925), Harotian traveled around the world and prospered. He performed with all the

major circuses as a clown and magician, and appeared with Barnum &
Bailey for five years running. He never learned how to read or write,
but his experience with people gave him worldly wisdom. Perhaps this
is why he was willing to perform only the banal side of magic, the
familiar tricks of all magicians, for the public. He learned some fine
magic from the famous clown Grok and from a mad Hungarian magician named Hornak. Again and again Wasserman stressed that there
was no connection between Harotian's natural wonder-working power
and his skill as a circus magician. He put tremendous effort into his
training, but never achieved the kind of perfection his natural abilities
might have given him. He preferred legerdemain and illusion to mystery. He loved his work and devoted most of his time to it, deriving
pleasure from the gaily colored scarves he pulled out of his sleeve,
laughing in wonder each time the seven white doves flew out of his
top hat; never tiring of the delighted cries of children and guileless
adults. He loved to give them pleasure.

But the older and more experienced he grew, the more the smiling
Armenian's joy in life faded. He had always been a loner. He had no
relationships with women to speak of (except for a number of brief
affairs), and his entire family had been wiped out in the massacre of
his native village. He had no past. He had no country. He had no
continuity. He was rich enough to retire from Barnum & Bailey's and
travel around the world for his own pleasure. Whenever he needed
money, he would join a local circus and astound the audiences. But life
began to weigh on him. More and more he felt what the other members
of the band were feeling, scattered through the world: the senselessness
of their existence deprived of the daring adventures of old, the op-
pressive dullness of a life without aim or meaning, in brief, the regrettable absence of a writer to pave this doleful path they had walked for
sixty years or more. Harotian decided he could no longer live this
miserable life. It was at this point that Obersturmbannführer Neigel
interrupted the story and asked why Harotian hadn't used his talents
to transform himself into a happy man. It seems Wasserman had been
eagerly anticipating this question. Harotian, he revealed, detested wonder working, regarding it as an unfair advantage over his fellow man.
The wiser he became, the more he realized that man is trapped in a
dead end and the more he despised his supernatural gifts and the One
who had bestowed them. They were like hush money from the Creator,

His overgenerous alms to one of his beggars; to only one of them. This act of bribery, he felt, had corrupted his human side, the thoroughly unmysterious side.

When war broke out, Harotian the Armenian found himself imprisoned in the Jewish ghetto of Warsaw. By then he was a bitter old man. Otto found him one night in the street walking backward, crying like a lost child, dragging one foot on the sidewalk as he hopped along the street with the other. He explained that his feet were singing a canon, an old Armenian hymn, and invited Otto to listen. Otto: "The truth is, I heard nothing, maybe because I'm not particularly musical, but I understood immediately: Harotian was one of us again." In fact, explained Wasserman, Harotian had discovered a way to become magical again without recourse to his original gifts. This is how he overcame the corrupting influence of the Alms Giver. It all started one evening at the Britannia Club, where Harotian was appearing as magician. His wages were his dinner. After the performance that night, he sat down at a side table and began to devour his food like a hungry dog. He was painfully thin, and his eyes were strangely incandescent. Most of his tricks that evening had fallen flat, and he was jeered off the stage. The audience had seen him performing the same tricks ten times before, and he was too weak tonight to get them right. He felt no resentment toward his jeerers. On the contrary, he blamed himself for having deprived them of their innocent pleasure—the pleasure of simple sleight-of-hand. Again he shivered. Strange. For a few days now his hands had been trembling, especially when he was onstage. He stopped chewing so frantically and looked down: there on his table was a small vase holding a single paper flower. On each table at the Britannia there was a vase with a single brown paper flower. Harotian had not seen a real flower for many months. He wanted the flower to be green. For his eyes only he wanted the flower to be as green as a flower should be. Neigel turned his nose up in protest—green flowers? Wasserman ignored him. Again he stressed that Harotian was careful not to turn the flower green with his magical powers, that he searched instead for other, more ordinary powers within himself. He gazed at the flower. Tears came to his eyes, and his face began to twitch with effort. People were staring at him now and laughing. He paid no attention. He gritted his teeth and stared through his tears till the flowery contours yielded and turned green. The green spread slowly over the petals. Harotian sensed the new locus of his efforts: somewhere in the middle of his head, where—to quote Descartes—body and soul are joined. The old Armenian sat watching the paper flower till closing time. The waiter who cleared his plate dropped a leftover slab of horse meat into his pocket. The proprietor rudely helped him on with his tattered coat and screamed in his ear that he was dismissed: they wouldn't be needing such a terrible magician anymore. Harotian didn't hear him. He picked up the green paper flower and walked out into the night. He walked backward, because he could no longer abide his usual walk, which, he believed, had been inflicted upon him through no preference of his own. It was a rather silly idea, but REBELLION [*q.v.*]—and this was indeed rebellion—begins with a symbol, and Harotian (Wasserman, too) was not afraid of being laughed at. His vision raised him above petty contempt (from people like Neigel). He stopped under a streetlamp and pondered. The lamp gave a sickly, dim yellow light, and Harotian asked himself angrily why he had to see the light exactly as others saw it. This, too, was unbearably humiliating. He touched the crushed paper flower in his pocket, and his Adam's apple bobbed up and down. He fixed his eyes on the lamp and stared at it till he grew dizzy. His eyes were puffy and brimming with tears. A German patrol marched down the next street, and Harotian retreated into a darkened hallway out of which he continued to stare at the lamp. For four hours he stood there motionless. At some point during this strange night his legs gave out and he collapsed on his back, still staring at the lamp. Toward dawn the lamp surrendered. It poured out myriad grains of pollen that gave off the scent of oranges. He sniffed with pleasure. The street was filled with the pungent smell he remembered from his childhood in Armenia. His old head ached, he felt the pounding of heavy hammers but was too elated to notice. The amazing thing was, said Wasserman, that the moment Harotian crossed the frontier of the incredible, everything seemed possible and simple, even logical in its way: he had all five senses at his command, and he felt he was exercising a natural right denied to the rest of mankind. Wasserman likened him to a prisoner who starts to make inspired statues out of the bars of his cell. When Harotian ran his hand over a fence made of wood and steel, he could hear, through his ears (or through his fingers?), strange sounds melodiously weaving in and out. Soon he could "hear" the rough and smooth texture of things without even touching them, and—eventually—their density.

The world suddenly held vast kaleidoscopic treasures. He could imbue different smells with flavors; he could stop the sounds of a girl singing as they floated by, paint them purple with a look, twirl them around like a swarm of fireflies, and let them ring again and fade away. Life teemed with his new gifts. He stopped scavenging for food, and his face grew sharp as a fox's. His clothes were so worn his arms and legs showed through the holes. Passersby nodded at him with COMPASSION [*q.v.*], but he had no need of their compassion. He was happy.

And then one night he suddenly woke up on the pile of rags he used as a bed in the vacant lot, and dragged himself with his remaining strength to the street corner, where he had seen the lamp. A terrifying thought struck him. He stopped by the wall and looked: the lamp was still shining murkily in a small circle. Harotian could not see the light: he could only smell the orange pollen wafting through space. He steadied his wobbly legs and straightened his shoulders, as he always did before the difficult part of a performance. This was the big test: he tried to see the lamplight once more. There was no point to all his work unless he could bring back the old reality of his five senses. For a long time nothing happened, and Harotian broke out in a cold sweat. And then very slowly he saw the murky lamp again, like the searchlight on a rescue ship cutting through the fog. Now he knew that his war had ended in victory: he could "choose" the world he lived in the way one leafed through a giant catalogue. He had almost completely freed himself from the bonds of sensory perception. The color red was his by right, like the smell of soil or the texture of bark, or the sound of a harmonica coming from a window, or the taste of raindrops. He was, as Aaron Marcus said of him, "the resurrector of the obvious. The autodidact of the senses." And he could have been happy, if only things had not gone amiss. "What went amiss?" roared Neigel, who for the last few minutes had been listening with some interest. "The war," Wasserman elucidated. "The war shuffled the deck. Listen and judge for yourself." Harotian's first difficulties began when the old reality he remembered became more and more garbled and contradictory. It, too, seemed to overflow into the realm of imagination. When he walked, the streets seemed emptier than usual. He heard strange talk of people disappearing from the ghetto to a place of no return. Harotian could not believe his ears. He feared that his new talent was deceiving him: human voices were saying outlandish things, altogether inconsistent with the old world he knew: things about sealed chambers with ceilings that emitted a strange ether that killed everyone inside; one man who had escaped from such a place stood on an old fish barrel on a street corner and told passersby about what happens "there." He described the crematoria where hundreds of people were burned by the minute; about doctors conducting experiments and infecting healthy people with cancer; he swore he'd seen people flayed alive so their skin could be used to make lamp shades. He said they had found a way there to make soap out of people. Harotian thought there was something wrong with his hearing, that his mind was mistranslating the sounds people made. But his sense of sight began to worry him too: when the man raised his hand to swear that every word was true, Harotian saw that numbers had been tattooed on his forearm like a greenish numerical rash. Harotian fled, but he couldn't stop seeing what he had failed to see for so long, and the sights were overwhelming: people who had remained behind in the ghetto and starved like him took on strange forms: their skin turned bluish, their nails thickened till they resembled claws. Their bodies swelled and their faces hardened into masks. Harotian saw and could not believe his eyes: women grew thick hair on their faces and bodies. Hair sprouted on people's eyelids, too, and their lashes were so long they looked like the wings of a giant moth. All this was due to hunger; only, Harotian didn't understand. He was isolated, suspicious and frightened. Walking through the darkened ghetto streets, he saw fabled creatures flickering before his eyes: colorful seahorses, tiny and winged; forest elves gleaming in precious light; Cinderellas, witches, unicorns, phoenixes, and Peter Pans hurried past him on the stairway. These, of course, were the phosphorescent pins made and sold by a Jew of the ghetto to help prevent people from bumping into each other on the darkened streets. Harotian knew nothing about it. He sensed vaguely that somewhere out there a greater magician than himself had arisen who, like himself, used the simplest human material, only he was crossbreeding it into something utterly grotesque. Harotian was horrified. He began to leaf feverishly through his enormous catalogue, but he was no longer sure where to find the old, simple reality he remembered. He dragged himself through the empty streets, miraculously preserved from harm. The posters he passed on the walls screamed so shrilly that he shuddered. He was almost suffocated by the stench of humiliation sent his way by a yellow patch rolling in the mire. He began to sob, and a religious chant he remembered from childhood ran through his mind. At that moment he heard the approaching footsteps of the patrol, and with the instinct of a hunted animal, hid in the courtyard; at the head of the patrol marched a short, elderly citizen, one Heinrich Lamberg of Cologne, a perfumer by trade. The Germans had brought him to the ghetto in order to use his highly developed sense of smell for ferreting out the underground hiding places of the Jews, whose faint cooking odors he was able to detect. Harotian knew nothing of this. He saw the little man stride quickly at the head of the patrol, wrinkling his nose this way and that. He stopped before a certain house, sniffed attentively with flared nostrils, and gave a short cry. The patrol burst through the door, and a few minutes later returned with a little family: a father and mother and two small children. They shot them on the spot. The patrol continued to follow the perfumer with the virtuoso nose. Harotian understood that this was a catastrophe: for all his gifts, it had never occurred to him that someone could exercise the sense of smell to hunt other people, and now he knew that he would never find his old world again. His estrangement was complete. He sobbed in terror as he walked backward, one foot on the sidewalk and one on the street. His tears shone purple and phosphorescent, and they tasted cold and metallic. He had burst all his strings. Once again he was little Harotian, hiding in a deserted cave at the far end of the earth. And now, as then, he was rescued by Otto Brig, on his way home late at night from a futile and tiring tour of the Jewish ghetto, to recruit artists who "might suit us," as he put it. Harotian threw his arms around him with relief. Otto, at least, hadn't changed. Even the fifty years since their parting, and all the calamities in the world, could not change someone like Otto. The two embraced silently for a long time and cried without shame. Harotian tasted Otto's tears shyly with his tongue, and wept harder for joy: they were salty, thank God. Just like tears should be. And so Harotian returned to the Children of the Heart. Incidentally, Otto continued to support him, and when things became really difficult, he cried with him, just as he allowed Fried to use his blue eyes to see Paula. Whenever the old world threatened to collapse before the Armenian's eyes, it was enough for him to lick Otto's salty tears awhile. This was not especially difficult for Otto, who always found it easy to cry.

הומור

HUMOR

HUMOR

The disposition or mental faculty that accentuates the ludicrous side of phenomena.

1. According to Shimon Zalmanson, editor of *Little Lights*, humor is not just a disposition or mental faculty but the only true religion. "If you were God, nebuch," he said to Wasserman during a late-night chat at the editorial office, "and you wanted to reveal the potential of creation to your believers, all the coincidences and paradoxes, all the joy and reason, the ambiguity and deception your divine powers spilled out into the world every minute, and if, let us say, you wanted to be worshipped as befitting a deity, that is, without sentimentality and flattering hymns but with a clear and lucid mind instead, what method would you choose, eh?" Zalmanson (who was, incidentally, the errant son of a great rabbi) said humor was the sole means to understand God and His Creation in all its mystery, and to go on worshipping Him in gladness. Zalmanson's God went around showering mankind with little favors of divine will. "No doubt you remember, Anshel, the sight that greeted us at the entrance to the Holy of Holies, the little gas chamber?" Wasserman remembered very well: the Germans had brought the ark curtain from a synagogue in Warsaw and hung it at the entrance to the gas chambers. Embroidered on the curtain were the words "This is the gate of the Lord. The righteous shall enter" and here Zalmanson began to laugh, and died laughing with the realization that even someone like fusty old Wasserman has his funny points. Laughter itself was the spontaneous ritual of his religion. "Every time I laugh," he explained, "my deity, who doesn't exist, of course, knows I cleave to Him, knows I have understood Him profoundly, if only for an instant. Because, my little Wasserman, the good Lord created the world out of nothingness, out of chaos, and He took His blueprint and building materials from that chaos . . . nu, what do you say to that?"

According to Zalmanson, jokes were touchingly primitive offerings to this God. "And what is a joke, after all, but a kind of bastardization: Think of a man standing on a street corner, telling his friend some story he invented just to make him smile! Does he sing him an aria, heaven forbid, or play a tune on the *garmoshka*? No, but a joke he tells him! And sometimes when friends gather, serious, sober people, they tell each other jokes all evening long!" Zalmanson calls jokes "the sham psalters of idol worshippers." Not that he makes light of them, heaven forbid. On the contrary, jokers, he believes, are true visionaries, with an insight into something, "though the means at their disposal are poor, ah, pitiable indeed!" And this because "most people have not the gift of real and penetrating humor, but can only chant their shabby second- and third-hand litanies by rote . . ." Wasserman offers this comment on the subject of Zalmanson's laugh. "His squeaky, effeminate laugh confirms his twisted theory even more: most people laugh in a voice unlike their speaking voices. It would seem that the vocal qualities used for laughter," Wasserman propounds with a shy chuckle, "cannot be used for—how shall I put it—'secular purposes.'"

2. Kazik's humor

Kazik, according to OTTO BRIG [*q.v.*], had his own peculiar sense of humor; in fact, there was a kind of painful irony in the way he experienced simultaneously the processes of growth and decay; and whenever one of the ARTISTS [*q.v.*] talked about their hopes for the distant or even near future, or used words like "chance," "improvement," "victory," "PRAYER" [*q.v.*], "ideal," "faith," etc., or experienced intimacy and communion, or whenever the feeling of STRANGENESS [*q.v.*] shifted briefly to an illusion of cooperation and solace—at such times Kazik emitted short, compulsive bursts of laughter, over which he had absolutely no control, an almost physical reflex as irrepressible as the hissing of a hot skillet under a stream of cold water. This laughter afforded Kazik no pleasure; in fact, he had no idea why he was laughing, and was keenly aware of the artists' reactions of grief and humiliation. The editorial staff agreed to call this quality of Kazik's "humor" only after Otto Brig had done so, most nobly and generously. It should be mentioned that the strange quality disappeared once for a few minutes during Kazik's lifetime when he too became one of the ARTISTS.

Also see under: PAINTER

החלטה

HACHLATA

DECISION

The process of arriving at a conclusion after study and consideration.

Following their debate on the subject of RESPONSIBILITY [*q.v.*] and CHOICE [*q.v.*], Wasserman maintained that Neigel must not rest content with his initial decision, made twenty years ago, upon joining the SS. In order to carry out certain actions in the present, which Wasserman tactfully failed to specify, Neigel had "suspended" his conscience, "sent it away on leave." No. In Wasserman's view, we are all duty-bound to renew the moral validity of our decisions for as long as we act upon them. In other words, "no decision, Herr Neigel, is permanently valid, and if you are a man of honor, which what you say appears to suggest, it is incumbent upon you to reaffirm your decision each day, each time you kill another person in your camp; indeed, sir, you must mold your decision anew with fresh words, in order to hear whether your initial wish, your voice, and your essence resound in those words." To which Neigel, incidentally, replied, "You'd be surprised, Wasserman. That doesn't frighten me one bit. In fact, I like it. I intend to adopt your little idea." Wasserman: "Each and every day, Herr Neigel. And each and every time you shoot your gun and destroy another human being. And twenty-five times when you kill twenty-five prisoners here. Decision after decision. Can you stand it? Can you promise yourself as much, Herr Neigel?" And the German: "I don't understand why you're making such a big fuss about this. I already told you, I'm not worried. It will only reinforce my faith in the Reich and my duty. I'll do my work—in the words of our Führer—*mit Einsatzfreudigkeit*—with pleasure."

Also see under: REBELLION

היטלר, אדולף
HITLER, ADOLF
(1889–1945) German leader, directly responsible for World War II, and—indirectly—for the love affair between Paula and Fried.

Throughout Fried's years as chief veterinarian at the zoo, he was in love, silently and hopelessly—as he had been since the glorious days of the Children of the Heart—with Paula Brig. Paula, who was in charge of zoo administration, kept house for her brother, Otto, and out of the kindness of her heart did not neglect poor lonely Fried either. In 1931, Fried sold his sterile luxury apartment in a wealthy Warsaw neighborhood and went to live at the zoo, in the small hexagonal pavilion next to the reptile menagerie. In the evenings Fried used to walk over to Otto and Paula's pavilion near the zoo gate, where the three would eat supper together, play chess, smoke, and plan the work schedule for the following day. Their lives might have continued like this had it not been for certain events, or had not . . . Otto: "Hitler made Paula so furious with his race laws, I mean Paula, who never took an interest in politics till one day the radio happened to be on and she heard those vicious Nuremberg Laws; it was around noon, she and I were home alone, and she jumped up as if she'd been pinched and said she had to go to town, and 'It's Fried I'm thinking of, he's my concern, the humiliation will break his heart.' And she took her savings out of her piggy bank, the money we'd put by all these years zloty by zloty, muttering, 'Swinishness,' and 'What do they think, those lousy Deutschers, can't they see they're going to hurt somebody?' And off she went, without a goodbye, full of anger and confusion, and she took the tram to the swankiest shops on Potozki Square, where for two hours *clink! clink!* she spent her money like never before!" Paula: "I bought me a beautiful dress made of that stuff we used to call 'koronka,' and a cute little brocade *chapeau, très gai*, with little loops over the forehead and ears, ooh these Paris fashions, and something they call a 'pelisse' trimmed with velvet, and I also bought some underclothes, you should pardon the expression, made of real synthetic English silk! And French soap I bought, and eau de Cologne, sweet-smelling crêpe-de-Chine, and did it cost me, mama droga! And then I came home in the evening and scrubbed away the zoo smells of so many years, and put on my new dress, and the pelisse, and some fingernail polish, and rouge on my cheeks, and I brushed my hair for about an hour to get the tangles out, I had hair down to my waist, sir! The only time I ever cut it was during the typhus epidemic of '22! So anyway, I went down to the flamingo pool, because there were no mirrors anywhere in the zoo, and I saw I was beautiful, a little high-flown maybe, all dressed up like that, but definitely feminine-looking, even though 'aunty' hadn't paid a call in twenty years, and I went back just to say goodbye to Otto, 'cause with him I didn't have to explain anything, he understood right away." Otto: "And off she went on her nuptial journey, past the cages on the Lane of Eternal Youth, with the animals staring after her in a way that made me pray they wouldn't start laughing, but you can count on animals more than you can on certain people, whose names I won't mention, and it was obvious that they knew exactly what was going on." Fried: "Only I, idiot that I am, understood nothing, and when I opened the door for her I was completely mystified by that carnival getup, and all her perfumery—" Wasserman at this point offers the plausible explanation that the doctor felt a little sorry for the elegant lady, who even with all these womanly accoutrements, was not really beautiful: her age showed and her arms and legs were coarse and scratched, but her eyes shone blue. Fried smiled a shy, crooked smile because he didn't quite understand, or dare to hope perhaps that his love had at last been requited and his loneliness would soon end. Wasserman: "Just as sometimes mayhap it troubles us to bid adieu even to the woes and miseries to which we are accustomed, even as a dog becomes accustomed to the fleas on his back." Paula did not allow Fried time to recover his wits. She stood on tiptoe and kissed him hungrily on the mouth. Only Fried's mouth, fearful and well schooled in shameful aridity, recoiled sideways, and he felt her thin, lively smile trembling in the fold of his neck, like a drop of water on rocky soil, till suddenly, without wasting words, they fell upon each other with the passion that had been waiting for so long. Wasserman: "And the old doctor found joy—and with your permission, Herr Neigel, it is only at such moments that we are justified in using the term 'joy'—because all his emotions and deepest stirrings, and even, begging your pardon, his lust, had been stored away for so many years of loneliness, far from the destructive hand of time, and afterward, nu, you understand, they lay nestled together, his left hand under her head, his right shall embrace her, half dead, heaven forbid, from the rapture that almost plucked them out by the roots of their existence." Paula: "And then, silly me, me and my big mouth, I had to tell him all the swinishness I'd heard about on the radio, and at first Fried didn't understand why I was talking about that just now and what the connection was, he never thought of himself as a Jew and me as a Pole, and always said, I am a Pole of the Fried persuasion (that was a saying of his), and when he finally figured out why I mentioned this, Jesus and Mary! he turned white as this wall here, and at first I thought he was angry because of the swinishness, but then I saw it was because I hadn't come to him out of LOVE [q.v.] but for political reasons, as they say, yes, my Friedchik was always getting angry over the wrong things, and I, well sure, I was hurt, because that's no way to treat a lady, and I got up to leave but then—" Fried: "But then, nu, I saw the bloodstain on the sheet, yes, and then, well, the rest is clear enough, I believe."

[*Editorial comment: Of course, Neigel demanded that Wasserman delete all references to the Führer and the Nuremberg Laws. Wasserman refused categorically. A sharp dispute ensued. See under: TRAP.*]

התאבדות

HITABDUT

SUICIDE

The violent act of putting oneself to death.

1. One evening, after Wasserman had finished telling Neigel the daily installment of the Children of the Heart, he requested "my medicine, sir." A certain closeness had grown between them on this particular evening as a result of the story, and Neigel informed Wasserman indignantly that under no circumstances would he agree to shoot him. Neigel had been behaving strangely that evening: he listened to the story intently, chuckled, and even cheered out loud, too loud sometimes, in the right places, enjoyed the exciting descriptions, generously contributed intimate details from his own life, and—in brief—was the ideal audience. It is quite possible that this relaxed mood was enhanced by the new bottle of 87 proof on his desk, only one-third full by now, and it is also possible that a new letter in a blue envelope from Munich was a contributing factor, or there may have been a different reason altogether, like the hints coming in from Berlin to the effect that those concerned had approved Neigel's patriotic request for more gas chamber apparatus, as a result of which thousands of Jews would be arriving in transports the following week by day and by night to fill the original camp quota, because Berlin was satisfied that a man like Neigel would be able to carry the load, and even now they were preparing a "small token" for Neigel's services to the Reich and the Führer. Again, it is possible that Neigel was in fine fettle for all the above reasons, which he did not want to risk by shooting Wasserman in the head. The Jew insisted, however, and a brief dispute followed, in the course of which Neigel's mood was spoiled. His face turned ashen down to the tip of his nose, which was a bibulous bright red. During the quarrel, the German had, in fact, gulped down three glasses of 87 proof, the third of these raised by a no longer steady hand, and his expression of proud disdain was replaced by a veiled look of what one might risk calling horror. All of a sudden he jumped up, drew his gun, and without a word handed it, pointed at himself, to Wasserman. "Here's a gun!" he screamed hoarsely. "Do whatever you want. I'm through. Do whatever you want." He sat down again, swiveled his chair decisively till he was facing Wasserman, and said mysteriously, "I won't even look at you. Aim, pull the trigger. Only please hurry." Wasserman, a Jew who had never held a weapon in his life, did not take advantage of this unique

opportunity. He did not shoot the German in the neck, although Neigel's posture seemed to demand it; nor did he take him hostage to get Reichsführer Himmler into the camp so he could kill him; he did not rush outside and shoot the guards and start a rebellion among the prisoners. None of these simple, obvious ideas occurred to him. For a moment he held the gun to his own temple, but his knees were knocking so hard he nearly collapsed. He did not shoot. He set the gun down on the desk and politely cleared his throat. Only after a moment did Neigel turn around in his chair: he looked dead. He had been holding the blue envelope in his hand all this time. It was crumpled and damp. "You are a coward," he said. "Pity. Pity." But, said Wasserman to himself, the wise will understand that I did not want to shoot him once, and poof! For Neigel I had another fate in mind, and besides, am I, Shleimeleh, a man to spoil a good story in the middle?

2. The suicide of Kazik: *see under*: KAZIK, THE DEATH OF

התבגרות, תרדמת ה־

HITBAGRUT, TARDEMAT HA
ADOLESCENT DORMANCY

Kazik's childhood was marked by his alert, lively, and rather rowdy character [*see under*: CHILDHOOD], which exhausted poor Fried, forever chasing him through the house. And then at 0108 hours, the doctor found a few moments' respite, if not pleasure, when Kazik reached the approximate age of sixteen and a half and suddenly, just as he was dashing through the corridor making those loud noises with his lips Fried called "utterly barbaric," he abandoned the chase abruptly, felt his limbs grow heavy, and—Fried: "Well, I was sure that was that. Kaput." In the dim lamplight the doctor thought he saw a silvery luminescence spread over the boy's body. When he put his glasses on, he discovered fine, semitransparent threads, sticking out all over Kazik. Aaron Marcus supposed these were "physical manifestations of adolescence and related complexes," but Fried insisted, "No, no, he's beginning to rot." Much to his amazement, however, he soon realized that the child was simply "pupating," like an enormous butterfly inside the fibers; that before Fried's very eyes Kazik was under the domination of impervious adolescent glands common to all, and that he would shortly break out of this cocoon as a mature adult. The doctor regretted this, because he had always viewed childhood as a period of special

inspiration—that's how his own childhood seemed to him—as opposed
to adulthood, which doomed one to shameful conformity. Even the
surface characteristics—the toughening of skin and hair, the ossification
of the bones, the increasing sex drive—seemed to him like the bars
around the cell in which the adult imprisons child. But as he watched
the sleeping boy, Fried was filled with wonder, because for the first
time this evening, or maybe in his life, he felt in awe of the mighty
stream of life that held sway in this room, so close to Fried, and it may
also have been the first time Fried had ever been steeped in time—
according to Wasserman—as befitting the stream of "Grandfather
Time," that human flux in which you are assigned to your place "between your parents and your own progeny." And Fried reflected with
astonishment that what he had always believed—that the father gave
life to the child—was basically erroneous; that the father needed the
child to help him out of his prison and remind him of all he had
forgotten. Fried: "Ah, very well, it's true, but the important thing was
that during those moments of sleep my Kazik was beyond time. For
maybe a quarter of an hour he didn't grow at all, and it was also the
only time since he first came to me that I had a moment to think about
what had happened up to now and what was going to happen in the
future, but then he woke up, he woke up fast . . ."

Kazik woke up. He tore at the strange fibers, and they vanished. His
period of adolescent dormancy was over in thirteen minutes, and once
again he waded in the "river of time." He was confused and angry. It
should be mentioned that despite the process of physical maturation
he had now completed, Kazik's head did not yet reach the seat of the
chair. Till the last second of life he remained milky: his diaper wet, his
tummy protruding in front, and his little posterior behind; his face,
however, hardened with the bite of anxiety and confusion, and a wild
and to him unintelligible desire. Kazik: "Am I—who am I—who—
am—I?"

Also see under: CHOICE; GINZBURG, ILYA

זיידמן, מלכיאל
ZEIDMAN, MALKIEL
Biographer. One of the ARTISTS [*q.v.*] Otto collected from the Warsaw
Ghetto in December 1939 [*see under*: HEART, REVIVAL OF THE
CHILDREN OF THE].

A scholar who won a certain reputation with the first two volumes of his biography of Alexander the Great. An elderly, sensitive-looking man, flapping around in a pair of old shoes given to him by Otto, he carried a worn leather briefcase that smelled like rotten fruit containing his current opus: *The Main Circumstances and Events Leading to the Suicide of Laizer Mellinsky, Watchmaker of Kremlitska Street*, a work which, according to Wasserman, "had been destroying him for nine years, his cynosure and his doom." Wasserman tells of an awkward meeting between Zeidman, Fried, and Paula: Once, at three in the morning, the biographer knocked on the door of the couple's pavilion to protest, with all his sensitive, infantile self-assertiveness, what he had overheard the doctor telling Otto that morning, in front of the parrot cage. Malkiel Zeidman had been working nearby when he distinctly heard Fried shout that they couldn't go on running the zoo this way anymore, because Otto was spending all his time in the Jewish ghetto and coming back with these freaks, these lunatics, these primitive barbarians who never lifted a finger to help Fried with the work. Fried: "Nu, well, that's how it is with lunatics, they're so wrapped up in themselves, so incredibly egotistical, they barely even notice each other! All they care about is their 'art,' as Otto calls it, ha! And of course, they do nothing to earn the food Otto gives them here, though admittedly they don't eat much, in fact, hardly anything: Hannah Zeitrin eats only fruit because the sight of meat disgusts her, and Marcus always forgets to eat, and that poor fellow Ginzburg, he doesn't have any teeth left after his interrogation by the Gestapo, but Munin, the maniac, the disgusting barbarian, he gobbles down enough food for all of them put together! Because he needs energy, that's what he always says, the pervert; and the little one, the one who's always frightened, Zeidman, well, he eats nothing but the animal feed in the cage he's in charge of on any particular day, like wheatberries. No, they don't eat much food, it's true, but they don't help us either, and the way they behave, bozhe moi! Like animals! Like animals! Animals behave better!" So the little biographer came around to protest Fried's use of the term "primitive barbarians." He woke the couple up from a sound sleep, and inflicted Fried (who was boiling mad) and Paula (who was dumbfounded) with an exhausting account of his past.

Some time ago, he said, he had decided that his duty both as a biographer and as a man lay in writing the definitive biography of an ordinary human being, one who had never made a name for himself in any public realm or achieved fame. From the moment the idea took root in his mind, he could not stop thinking about it: he was convinced that such a biography would be at least as valuable as the biography of Alexander the Great, which had won him a certain reputation among historians and knowledgeable people. Zeidman: "Ah, two large volumes I wrote about the Macedonian, Pani Fried, and I must say I found him exceedingly interesting at first! Absolutely fascinating! But I finished the second volume in a condition of ennui. You see, this same Alexander who plucked up hills and transplanted nations and sent his armies over half the globe had become in my eyes something of a natural force, like a storm or an earthquake, and he wearied me! Yes, sometimes, while writing about—Alexander—I would find myself thinking, What would he have done to me and my kind if he had encountered us on his way? . . . You understand? I should not have entertained such thoughts . . . I, a man of science, a teacher at the university, but with all that was happening in the world, beyond the ivory tower, that is, I could not shut my eyes. Yes, yes, this Alexander began to frighten me so much that I could not sit down to write the third volume! And to myself I said that out of the life of the Macedonian, a man such as I could never find guidance . . . perhaps one man in a generation, a Hitler type, for instance, could! Of course he could! Tfu! Pardon. But I wanted to write for little people like myself and you, for frightened people like us, I wanted to write. You understand, Pani Fried [*Editorial comment: Zeidman, like several other zoo artists, thinks Fried is a Polish Catholic*], it takes tremendous, even tragic efforts to write the faithful biography of another human being. It is nearly impossible, in fact, ah yes, and the truth is, we know no one. We are utter strangers to each other [*see under*: STRANGENESS]. Every man is a kingdom, a castle with his own God, his own Satan, and a thousand secrets to be discovered over time. We are each endemic, to borrow a term from the learned Pan Fried's field of work, as if in each of us existed a single animal, and the resemblances between us are only illusion, wishful thinking, the fruit of despair and loneliness . . . And though the Macedonian is interesting enough, Laizer Mellinsky the watchmaker is also wonderful! Believe me! (Fried leafed through the torn and dusty pages of Zeidman's research, written in a crabbed and clumsy hand, and read the table of contents in amazement: "The Struggle with Brother Zvi-Hirsch over the Clock, Bequeathed by His Father of Blessed Memory"; "Laizer's Feelings of Nostalgia for the Wallpaper in the Bedroom of His Mother of Blessed Memory"; "The Mildness of Sarah-Beila"; "The Secret Diplomacy of Abraham Pesach [the Lublianer], Who Tried to Restore Peace and Was Found to Be a Troublemaker"; "Laizer's Hopes of Becoming the Partner of His One Friend, Meyerson, in the Textile Business, and the Illness of Sarah-Beila, Which Ate Up His Savings.") "Ah, we are all so very lonely," continued Malkiel Zeidman, addressing Paula, whose eyes were big and round, and who smiled at him as if he were a page flying out of her dream. "And I realized that there is no great difference between the pains I took to get under the skin of Alexander the Great or the skin of the Warsawian . . . because the important thing is to steal across the frontier, and not just that of another but across my own frontier as well, if only to escape myself by slipping away into another! These onion biscuits are delicious, if you don't mind my tasting another . . . hmmm! Simply delicious! Would that I could bestow such a pleasure on . . . As I was saying! There are millions of people everywhere, I said to myself, and we cannot go on knowing no one but ourselves anymore! We have to know others! From the inside! To feel their pulse deep inside ourselves for one swift secret moment. Nu, yes, sometimes we imagine that we know someone or other, my wife I always imagined I knew and understood, but later there were things I discovered . . . ah, you see? I talk, and your eyes are closing, because when the mood is on me, I talk. Nu, of course you understand, I have practiced silence for three years since my Laizer took his own life and left me empty-handed; midway through the song of his wretched life he killed himself, his strength gave out, with me, of course, in his footsteps! Nu, yes, it happened three years ago, when the world was stricken with terror . . . Ah, I forgot to tell you, in those days I had honed my skills to such perfection I could scarcely tell whether I ruled over it or it ruled over me and my desire was unto it . . . You understand, great and subtle powers of sharing fate, of communing with another I had developed in myself during the years I spent following my Laizer every day and every hour. And he, goodly soul that he was, never once protested, never threw me down the stairs! On the contrary, he saw how much I needed him . . . you understand? At around this time I began to slip, yes, I was dismissed from my office at the university as an undesirable scion as early as '35, and my wife ran away with a rogue, may his name be blotted out, and my children, flesh of my flesh, began to be ashamed of me because my toilette was less than fastidious! That's what they said! My own children, whom I thought I knew! Uhm, where was I? And he, Laizer, was intelligent, certainly more so than I am, and while I was endeavoring to know him, he peered into my soul and saw what was there, and for that reason, I suppose, he let me follow him for so long eager to tell me all that befell him, even family matters he confided to my ears, yes, if not for his goodness of heart and the goodness of his poor Sarah-Beila, my work would not have prospered so . . . And people used to chaff him and say he had a shadow, Mupim and Chupim, they called us, Chillik and Billik . . . but Laizer understood, and allowed me to continue, because what did I want?" the little man suddenly bellowed, dramatically waving his fine smooth hands in the air. "Did I want to hurt anyone?! Did I want to make anyone angry?! Ah, everything I did, I did for love. Out of the desire to know the man who dwells 'outside,' who walks beyond my skin. To know, oy, to know! To tear this tenuous envelope of flesh which separates us from one another, and is stronger than steel! Stronger than steel! This has been a torture to me all my life; or it used to be, that is, because now I have vanquished it! I have utterly defeated it! And do not ask me how! Do not ask. Because I do not know myself: something burst in me, something went snap like a shirt button, 'snap' and no more! And I was suddenly able to do as I chose. Do you know when it happened?" (Fried and Paula respond in the negative, gaping at him.) "I will tell you, then, that you, too, may rejoice! It happened one night when Laizer told me about the bookcase in his father's house. Yes, so it was. A polished cabinet with two glass doors where they kept the silver and the cherished books of his father of blessed memory. 'Saronatka' we call these cabinets, madame, which may be decorated with wallpaper or a sweet ribbon with tiny brass tacks, you know? And in this cabinet we stored our silver, and on the bottom shelf there were all sorts of special clothes, like the scarves Mother made for Father when she was a bride, you know, a scarf of woven stuff with a dark-green silk thread braided with leaves and rosebuds, you would have thought it was real!" (Fried looks at Zeidman in wonder, barely listening to what he is saying, as he tries to decide who Zeidman has been reminding him of for the past few moments, whose rounded, charming gestures and soft, forgiving smile.) "Yes, what? What did I say? Pardon! For a moment I forgot myself. So, Laizer told me about the cabinet, and I suddenly felt that I myself was Laizer; a complete Laizer from A to Z, with the knowledge of his every secret and the sorrows of his heart, and that any moment he would raise his hand and press it to his mortified face. I knew everything, but everything! And so for several months I was like him, Laizer, and stuck to him till I could not stop myself—it was no longer a matter of choice! I would imagine that I was Laizer. That I was married to Sarah-Beila . . . and he, saintly man that he was, did not reproach me, let me follow wherever he went, let me sit with him all day long in his little watchmaker's stall and answer people's questions in his stead, ah, for I knew exactly what he wanted to say before he could open his mouth! I never left his side, day or night! And because of this, I too found a rope for myself . . . Life had become a burden to him, you see, and it was even worse after the death of Sarah-Beila, my wife—pardon! his wife—Sarah-Beila, may she rest in peace. They killed her, you understand, she was sick in bed and they came into the house and killed her before our eyes . . . We wept for a week. Before our eyes! Nu, and in the middle of the night Laizer tells me that the time has come! You, he says, are a saint among saints, there is none like you in our world anymore, a lover of mankind such as you, but I can no longer endure it, he tells me, I can no longer endure your kindness, because your kindness is killing me with sorrow and compassion . . . Therefore, I am about to do the deed, and I will ask you to leave me now . . . let me be alone for a while . . . so he spoke to me. He worried lest I should follow his example with the rope, and I left the room, knowing what he wanted to do, and I made a noose for myself, because what was the sense of life without him? Without me, that is? What was left of the old, forgotten Malkiel Zeidman? Nothing! Dust and ashes! But he died, and I, nebuch, was saved. I was cut down from the noose and taken to the asylum and there, nu, injections and bandages and swathing, a plague on all doctors! Tfu! Pardon. And when I was released, that is, when the Germans arrived, may their names be blotted out, and scattered our council of the wise into the streets, inside me all was emptiness and death. I do not know, perhaps it was Laizer's death alive in me that made me feel so hollow, so unresisting; you want me to be a rabbi, I'm a rabbi, I don't complain, what is there to complain about? Life seems more interesting this way, and in any case, I have no choice now, because I trickle into others like water and steal what is inside, but outwardly nothing changes, and even now, at this very moment, woe is me! No! Not now!" (He slaps his right hand with his left.) "At least here, control yourself, wretch! Where were we? Ah yes, these weaknesses overpowered me . . . they brought me down . . . the pores of my skin open like flowers thirsty for sunlight, my bones relax in their sockets, and everything melts and overflows so that the other whose essence cannot resist me is unwittingly, insensibly, sucked in to fill the void . . . A stealthy kind of PLAGIARISM [*q.v.*]; all his contents flow serenely into me, yes, his longings, his secret fears, his passions and pains, the lies he whispers to his soul; ah, Fried, my Friedchik, it would probably drive you mad, you would not believe the hell a person can live through, may you never know, and the devils in him, mama droga, but don't eat any more of those biscuits, Friedchik, because you'll get heartburn again and you won't be able to sleep." "Enough!" Fried screamed, jumping to his feet, and Paula, in amazement: "He sounds exactly like me, doesn't he, Friedchik?" and the hollow biographer apologized and explained, ah well, he had these spells, at times acute, because he was consumed and hollow inside like a haunted house, like a ghostly watch ticking on though the watchmaker, alas, is dead, and someone else has to wind the mechanism . . . or, the old peddler at the zoo gate for example, with his dish of kaposzta, peas and cabbage. "I stand beside him for only a few moments, and he is suddenly inside me, his whole being, the blood humming in his veins and the passion in his heart and the secret of the fatal disease which he hides from his wife and children . . . And when I work near the parrot cage, ah, all at once I feel feathered and colorful and talkative" (Fried makes a frantic mental note to see to it that this little eccentric never works anywhere near the carnivores). "But the strange thing is, Pan Doctor, that the evil-hearted have no sway over me; that is, over my art . . . or rather, the common mean type—yes. But the utterly insensate—no. Never! A kind of barrier exists between us. For instance, I pass 'their' patrols a hundred times, you know who I'm talking about, and nothing happens inside me. Though I'll tell you a secret, I 'like' to pass them, because then, if only for a second, I feel relieved of my tyrannical art, my calamity, and for a little while I am myself again, poor Malkiel Zeidman . . . the utterly insensate, it follows then—no. Murderers—never. And I do not know the reason for this. It will always remain a riddle! But as for the rest—on the contrary, the kindhearted wreak havoc with me . . . I flow into them and they flow into me unchecked! Even here, in our zoological gardens . . . nu, yes, I never stop! Otto was the one who asked me. He said that we who lack physical strength are obliged to do everything we can, and I do as he bids me, because nobody refuses Otto, and that is why I take such pains and lose my soul and steal across every frontier! Indeed, call me a rebel if you will, waving my fist at heaven! Escaping each minute from the most highly guarded prison in the world, and gradually overcoming the barriers set up between man and his fellow man . . . thus increasing in however small measure the love and compassion that exists between people, because, well, we are all so lonely, locked up in our boxes, deaf and dumb and blind all . . . and I, ah, I at least can wander freely . . . contain everyone . . . send a wordless greeting at least . . . I am a hostel of sorts, the mute translator of numerous strange languages, because they can say the words, for instance, 'misery' and 'agony,' 'hope' and 'longing,' ah, but only I know what they mean by them, why you, for example, Pan Doctor, when you say—pain, what Madame Paula means by that is as different as if you both called two different women by the name of mother, yes yes, and only inside me can those blind, deaf pains touch each other . . . only inside me do they acknowledge themselves to each other in all their depth . . . A dictionary I have become, a person-to-person dictionary, but there is no one to read me, because I myself am not able to read, I am only the pages, and the doctor said barbarians, in jest no doubt, but now that I have finally said this, I'll be on my way, yes, I have been wanting to do that for a few moments only . . . Nu, something is holding me back, a kind of bite from the depths of the stomach, no, not because of your wonderful onion biscuits, madame, but because of a kind of gloom, a kind of pregnant rage, dear Lord, what is this, help me, help me, Pani Paula, ha, this pain, do you feel it, too, take it away, take it away from me, it's yours, all yours, not mine . . . please . . ."

And before the startled eyes of Paula and Fried, the biographer collapsed, writhing on the floor—Wasserman: "Panting like a woman in travail!"—struggling with invisible cords that seemed to bind him inside and all around, to pull him in the direction of Paula, toward that which lay beyond her, toward that which she herself did not yet sense, and finally he was hurled in the air, curled like a fetus, and fell out the door he had entered by, with a strange shrill wailing sound, and Fried and Paula looked at each other, and Paula, for the first time, felt the biting in her womb.

זמן

ZMAN

TIME

Rudimentary data of intelligent being, not susceptible to unambiguous definition due to its primacy and indeterminateness. Signifies the cadence and duration of phenomena.

1. Kazik's time

Fried reckoned Kazik's time from 2100 hours the evening of his delivery, when the white butterfly fluttered across the infant's face. With the seventy-two-year life span of the average male as his frame of reference, the doctor computed one moment of Kazik's life per eighteen days of normal human life. One second of Kazik's life thus equaled eight hours of Fried's, one minute and forty seconds, a month. An elapse of ten minutes represented six months for Kazik; one hour, three whole years. Fried was aghast. Worthy of mention perhaps are his two frantic attempts to arrest the galloping of Kazik's time that night: First he extinguished all the lights, hoping—Marcus: "Not because he was stupid, heaven forbid, but because he was desperate"—that the tyranny of time would diminish in the dark. Then shortly before dawn, when Kazik was approximately twenty-one years of age, the doctor immersed him in a cold tub again, in the vain hope that water would decelerate the process. All this, however, only served to intensify the doctor's perception that his own time was dwindling at the same fearful rate; that as soon as time had finished harrowing Kazik, the whole world would begin to deteriorate at the same maniacal speed. Every so often, however, the doctor sensed—it should be stressed—that he was not fighting for Kazik's sake alone.

2. The semblance of time

The semblance of time was revealed to the astonished Fried through an unfortunate incident: Kazik, running through the house with Fried at his heels [*see under*: CHILDHOOD; STRANGENESS], pulled the doily on the bookcase, knocking down a large ceramic bowl with four blue stags painted on it, which Paula had always loved to gaze at dreamily. It broke to pieces on the floor. Fried had reached out impulsively and slapped the boy's face. Kazik let out a piercing sob, and then there was silence. Fried: "Moi bozhe! What have I done?!" Kazik, incidentally, forgot the slap right away, and turned his attention to the broken pottery. He was astonished that something could be destroyed by breakage rather than slow expiration. Fried shut his eyes with heart-rending remorse for having so distressed the doomed, defenseless baby, but there was barely sufficient time even for this, because just then Kazik stepped on a sharp splinter and let out a scream. He screamed more from surprise than pain, and clung fiercely to Fried, who had struck him only a moment before. And Fried screamed with him, because with his own eyes he saw life was streaming out of the child, and knew that Kazik was awakening to pain Fried could neither prevent, suffer in his stead nor bargain away, but when he bent down and hugged the boy, he saw it wasn't blood flowing out of the deep cut in his foot at all but what appeared to be fine, sheer, dustlike particles sprinkling out of his body to the rhythm of his pulse and dissolving in the air, and Fried knew beyond a shadow of a doubt that this was time.

3. Non-time: *see under*: PROMETHEUS

זרות

ZARUT

STRANGENESS

The quality of being strange. A sense of isolation. Distance and difference.

Fried felt it in all its pungency when he was alone with young Kazik [*see under*: CHILDHOOD] in his pavilion. Kazik was a wild and lively child, always into mischief. He broke everything he set his hands on, and made a terrible mess with his daredevil pranks. He grew quickly; that is, never taller or heavier than the fifty-one centimeters and three kilograms Fried had first estimated him to be, but decidedly stouter and stronger. He rocked on his naked legs like a little hooligan in diapers. His albino hair grew long and thick, and Fried was forced to tie it in back to keep it out of his eyes. The doctor—leaning on his cane—chased him around the house, gently pulling him away from the door handles and lifting him out of the sink and toilet bowls through which he tried to escape. Suddenly Fried was angry with himself: "Nu, that I hadn't given him a better EDUCATION [*q.v.*] in these formative years, and that I had been too preoccupied with how I was feeling and with my soul-searching about life and memories of my own childhood, oh yes; I hardly know the child, I know only his aggression, his energy, as I watch him running and falling and picking himself up again, and his tyrannical passion for grabbing the world and stamping on it victoriously, and this frightens me, yes." Or to expand the point: it scared Fried that the child was so powerful and strange, that he didn't know what Kazik thought, or whether Kazik loved him, or considered him instead to be his inevitable and painstaking servant, or whether he would grow up to be like Fried, or perhaps like Paula. He would have preferred him to be like Paula, but there was nothing he could do about it. He wondered whether he should pit himself against the child with all his might and experience in order to prepare him for life, or whether it would be better to lie to him about the world, since the child had so short a life span anyway. He watched Kazik burrowing deeper in the closet and wondered if he would ever be able to get close enough to him. It was like watching your own reflection in the mirror: even if you say "me" a thousand and one times, you never really know what you mean. You are both too near and too far. For the first time, the doctor envied the strange biographical talent of MALKIEL ZEIDMAN [*q.v.*], who could enter his fellow man and feel him from the inside.

The old doctor closed his eyes, shocked with the bitter knowledge that this child was a stranger to him; that he would always remain so. That Fried would always love him more than Kazik loved Fried. And even if he were wonderfully successful and Kazik lived a complete and happy life [*see under*: PRAYER], Fried would suffer the same hunger and grief at his inability simply to "be" Kazik, to overcome the strangeness, the part of himself that was banished forever. And he wondered whether he shouldn't reconsider, whether he shouldn't start defending himself against this disappointed love and the unendurable pain that bound him. And he also knew that there is something in parents— even in the best and most sensitive of parents—that the child must always kill in order to free his way into the light and air, like a sapling struggling against the old trees in the forest. Now, the doctor realized that he and his child had only a very short time together, and that their capacity for understanding, love, and compassion was scant indeed, and as he was staring into space, Kazik emerged from the closet, ran past the bookstand, yanked the doily and brought down the porcelain bowl with the four blue stags, and the bowl was shattered to bits.

Also see under: TIME

חדש, האדם ה-

CHADASH, HAADAM HA

THE NEW MAN

The German prototype delineated by Nazi theoreticians.

The NM is what Obersturmbannführer Neigel contraposed to Wasserman's type in speaking of the "new future" pledged by the Reich and the Führer. At this point, for precision's sake, the NM concept will be enlarged upon: In *Mein Kampf*, Hitler claims that the Nordic race is the bearer of civilization; thus the struggle against the alien, the Jew, the Slav—in short, all inferior races—is a holy struggle. Hans Günther, the official theoretician of the National Socialist Party, on the basis of his study of ten million Germans, delineated the ideal NM: tall, with straight blond hair, an elongated skull, a narrow face, a well-formed chin, a thin nose, fair deep-set eyes, and a whitish-pink complexion. (Neigel, like most Bavarians, had dark hair and dark eyes as well.) Since there were not enough ideal subjects in Germany to ensure the NM's dominance of the Reich for the next thousand years, German leaders began to look for ways of increasing their human resources. A plan was proposed, for example, with regard to the improvement of Bavarian stock, to transplant Norwegians to Bavaria, where by means of crossbreeding and proper diet the local stock would become pure Nordic in only a few generations. This idea was just the beginning of a more far-reaching plan, as Dr. Willibaud Henschel wrote in *Die Hammer*, the official propaganda organ of the National Socialists in Berlin: "Round up a thousand girls, isolate them in a camp, mate them with a hundred thousand strapping young German youths, and then, with a hundred such camps, you will beget a generation of a hundred thousand pure-blooded German children." Or as the Gauleiter of Bavaria, Paul Giesler, reminded the females in the audience during his address to the students of the University of Munich on 2/19/39: National Socialists regard SEX [*q.v.*] solely as a means of procreation, and every woman should bear a child for the good of the fatherland, and "any girl who lacks sufficient charms to find a mate of her own, will be assigned one of my adjutants. I can promise you she won't regret it!" He also stressed Reichsführer Himmler's concern with the problem of increasing the German population and the improvement of the NM. It was Himmler who promised the Führer to populate Germany—by 1980—with a hundred and twenty million Nordic Germans. He made himself the godfather of all children born on October 7, his own birthday. These children were to receive a lamp as a gift from Himmler, and one Deutsche mark and a candle on every subsequent birthday. The first hundred thousand lamps were manufactured by the prisoners at Dachau. As Himmler used to say, "If Frau Anna Magdalena Bach had stopped with the fifth child, Bach would not have come into the world!" Himmler was also extremely interested in folk customs that fostered male offspring, and the results of his "research" were officially circulated in the SS. More than once he complained that SS men were not interested in respectable Nordic girls and preferred plump, short-legged women. Deserving of mention for their part in the attempt to improve the strain are the institutions known as the *Lebensborn*, founded by the SS at Himmler's instigation. *Lebensborn* (meaning "lifestream") is what the maternity homes established by Himmler throughout the Reich were called. These "human breeding farms" served both as orphanages and as brothels, and were intended to breed the new master race according to the racial standards of the Reich. To this end, hundreds of thousands of children classified as "racially valuable" were kidnapped by the Germans and raised on farms for crossbreeding with pure-blooded Germans and each other. The chief director of these institutions was Max Solman (Nazi Party membership number 14528), who joined the SS in 1937. Frau Inge Wirmitz was in charge of resettling the kidnapped children among childless SS families. The SS breeding farms received children hunted in Eastern and Northern Europe. The kidnapping squads were ordered to steal only the most attractive children. Their method was simple: spotting a child in the street who seemed to fill the racial requirements, they tempted the child with sweets, and learned his name and address. The information was then passed on to the kidnapping squads. This method allowed them to kidnap several children from the same family. Unsuitable children were put to death. Parents were usually killed too so the children could be taken without any unnecessary complications. Once kidnapped, the children were subjected to psychological pressure to repress their origins and hate their parents. They were told continually that their parents were sick criminals, that their fathers were drunken murderers and their mothers "sluts who died of tuberculosis and alcoholism." The children were not permitted to speak their mother tongue. They were tortured if they ever dared to mention their origins. The author of a book called *Children of the* SS met a woman in Germany who at age five had been shown the stone casket of an archbishop and told by the SS that her mother was buried inside. After the war her mother found her (she had been in a concentration camp), but the child refused to go back to her. "I saw my mother die once," she explained, "I didn't want to see her die again." The *Lebensborn* organization also dealt in Norwegian, Dutch, and French women pregnant by German soldiers, for Himmler did not want to lose high-quality offspring to other nations. These women were transferred—sometimes against their will—to the institutions in Germany, where they were given appropriate treatment. Children born flawed from the point of view of racial requirements were put to death. Children from orphanages in all occupied countries were kidnapped as well and sent to *Lebensborn* institutions. In Hungary and the Ukraine alone more than fifty thousand children were kidnapped; in Poland, about two hundred thousand. The children were immediately examined for racial traits. Measurements were taken of their skulls, chests, penises (boys), and pelvises (girls), the ostensible intention being to crossbreed them as soon as they reached sexual maturity. The girls were given hormone injections to accelerate the onset of puberty. At the age of fifteen they were to be inseminated by SS men. This is how the *Lebensborn* centers turned into semiofficial brothels for SS men, who made free use of them. Kidnapped children were branded on the neck and arms. Himmler himself supervised the institutions down to the most minute details: there is a cable of congratulations from him—preserved in the archives—to Frau Annie O. (the full name is missing), who in a single week, between the first and seventh of January 1940, yielded 27,870 grams of milk as a wet-nurse at the *Lebensborn*! Himmler likewise encouraged births among unmarried mothers and promised them the economic support of the Reich. He addressed German girls with a request "not to be so scrupulously modest and pure in these times of war," and asked them "to be patient with the demands of our young men going off to fight on the front for the Führer." Today, decades after the war, kidnapped children and their parents from all over Europe are still searching for each other. At the Nuremberg trials in October 1947, those responsible for the *Lebensborn* institutions were found guilty of membership in the SS. No other charges were brought against them.

חופשה

CHUFSHA

LEAVE (military)

An authorized absence from military duty.

Neigel's leave was undoubtedly the turning point in Wasserman's story. On the eve of his departure, Neigel ordered the Jew to continue telling the story of Kazik, who was by then around forty years old. Wasserman refused, for some reason, and insisted that he must now fill in some of the missing details for Neigel, e.g., why the Children of the Heart had banded together again for this last adventure, and whom they were fighting now [*see under*: HEART, REVIVAL OF THE CHILDREN OF THE]. Without this information, he explained, the story "will never be properly cooked." Neigel was furious. He accused Wasserman of BETRAYAL [*q.v.*], but Wasserman refused to tell him any more about Kazik's life. Neigel lost control and gave Wasserman a beating. Later, when he broke down and asked the Jew's forgiveness, his ugly secret was revealed [*see under*: PLAGIARISM].

And so Neigel went away on leave without hearing the rest of Kazik's story. By the time he returned to the camp, in a state of shocked and anxious remorse over what he had done at home, Wasserman, Fried, Otto, and the others had become Neigel's family, his near and dear, his entire world. Neigel—if one may say so—had dissolved into the imagination of Anshel Wasserman.

(ה)חזירויות האלה

(HA) CHAZIRUYOT HAELEH

(THIS) SWINISHNESS

What Paula called the Nuremberg Laws.

Also see under: HITLER, ADOLF

חיים, משמעות ה־

CHAYIM, MASHMAUT HA

LIFE, THE MEANING OF

חיים, שמחת ה-

CHAYIM, SIMCHAT HA

LIFE, THE JOY OF

A unique or prolonged sense of identification with Being.

At 0425 hours, Kazik experienced the joy of life full-force. Twenty-seven years old at the time, he had gone out with Fried to wake Otto and break the news that he was ephemeral. Together they made their way to Otto's pavilion, as one by one the other ARTISTS [q.v.], the living-dead who never shut their eyes, joined them from every corner of the zoo. The zoo was dark and the moon shone brightly, and Kazik saw dusky shadows everywhere that folded gently as he approached; he saw mysterious paths stretching through the darkness into the future; he saw the fresh grass sparkling with dew, the vast night sky strewn with thousands of slowly breathing stars that brushed his face with their veils . . . and though the shrill, metallic sounds of loudspeakers and the rattle of machine-gun fire could be heard in the distance, and the horizon was red because the Germans had set the ghetto on fire, Kazik did not understand this, nor did he want to understand this, or the sadness and despair on the faces of his companions. Because suddenly his heart swelled, till he could barely contain it, and his body was light, full of a bubbly effervescence and the murmurings and cracklings of joy, yes and he began: (1) to tumble over the wet lawn; (2) to hop on one foot and wave his arms; (3) to scream, drunk with happiness because (a) look, here he is! (b) he's alive as can be! (c) and this is where he will stay! The eternal emperor of the moment! Divine singer of his own beating heart! Artist, painter of grass and the night sky! Yes! Alive! Alive! There was no deeper or simpler explanation for it than this! To hell with the sad sounds of trudging behind him! To hell with everything we know about this lousy life and about the inevitable end of KAZIK [see under: KAZIK, THE DEATH OF]!!! And Fried, seeing Kazik's euphoria, was filled with dark dread, because how infinite was the great stream of time in which Fried was only a comma, a brief pause, a caesura in the flow; seventy years ago, Fried had not yet been steeped in time, and soon he would be out of it forever, and he and his world and everything he loved and deemed important would be extinguished then, and he saw the artists walking beside him and reflected, this was what was in store for each and every one of them, they would be erased as fast as footprints in a swamp. There was nothing new to this, and yet it shocked him, because for a moment he could feel how strange and lost and hopeless they all were, and then suddenly, for no particular reason, sensible old Fried was also filled with this feverish, fearful joy, and he spread his arms and stifled a small happy sob, and felt a thousand tiny fragrant rosemary flowers budding all over his body, filled with nectar.

חינוך

CHINUCH

EDUCATION

A process of instruction that forms, changes, or develops the character in a certain direction.

As soon as Fried realized how brief Kazik's allotted time was, he decided to devote himself entirely to his son's education, and to make good use of every moment of childhood while Kazik's brain was still alert and receptive. He led him by the hand—that small architectural wonder!—around the room, bending over to point out objects and call out their names. Fried: "Carpet. Lamp. Table. Chair. Another chair. Another chair . . ." and the child repeated the words and remembered everything. Fried told him frantically about the house full of rooms made of bricks, and about the zoo made up of cages and about the people who come to look at the animals, made up of limbs and organs, but his description immediately seemed to him lacking in truth somehow, not the truth of simple facts but the living truth behind them, and so he stopped and reproached himself. Fried: "Nu, really! What nonsense you're filling his mind with! Don't you see that first you have to tell him the important things!" And he crouched down, holding Kazik firmly by the arms, and lectured him warmly and fluently about the people of the world, and their division into nations and religions and political parties . . . He stopped himself here again and added hesitatingly, "And ideologies," but he could taste the dry, bland flavor of division, and when he named them—Poland, Germany, Christianity, Communism, Britain, Judaism, etc.—he felt as he had felt some fifty years before in the middle of his examination at the faculty of medicine in Berlin, when he was obliged to rattle off, to a full hall, a list of incurable diseases, and again he stopped and reproached himself. Fried: "Nu, really, what nonsense you're talking, first you have to teach him what to be, that is—" But despite his noble intentions, Fried could not hold back slapdash advice, like: Beware of strangers, and doubt your friends, and never tell anyone what you really think, never tell the truth unless there's no choice, someone is bound to use it against you, and don't love anybody too much, not even yourself. He spoke in a fever, in the tone and manner of an irascible father, regurgitating from his soul bitter advice from his own father, after a lifetime of denial; and the more convinced he was of its validity, the more he hated it and wished it proven false, and the more he wanted to speak his mother's silent words of comfort to his son, for he had loved her so much when she and her little Albert would sit down at the piano, and the melody flowed out of their fingers like a kind of mist, till his father scoffed and said, "Who knows, maybe Albert will grow up to be an artist and bohemian," in a tone Fried could not easily forget, and he heard it escape his own lips with a cruel precision—which pained him—when he spoke the selfsame words to Otto, after Otto started bringing his lunatics around to the zoo [see under: HEART, REVIVAL OF THE CHILDREN OF THE]. Yes, Fried had dreamed in childhood of becoming a pianist, till his mother was taken ill, and one day his father walked into Fried's room and announced sternly that Mother had gone away on a long journey. What, for no reason at all, gone away, without saying goodbye? He asked no questions, and tried to forget her as quickly as possible and to hate her for what she had done to him. He began to avoid other children and wandered over the fields near his home. There he met little animals which, he discovered, were not afraid of him. There was no rational explanation for this: even wild rabbits waited patiently for him to touch them gently. Around this time Fried met OTTO BRIG [q.v.] and his sister, Paula, and thus began his happiest days with the Children of the Heart. But these days, too, passed. Fried grew up and became a doctor like his father and grandfather before him. Then World War I began. Fried, drafted as a physician, saw a few battles and witnessed things he had never believed man capable of. Life battered Fried on every hand [see under: BIOGRAPHY], and in revenge he lived it as though it were his booty. And now, as he sat talking to Kazik, he became sadly aware that everything his father and grandfather had told him either explicitly or with a frown of disgust had come true to the letter in his own life, and he wondered whether things might have been different if he had dared to fight courageously for the misty comfort his mother had offered with her gentleness and beauty, with the fragrance of her body as she waved her hand, and only then did he stop talking nonsense to Kazik and begin to speak of the essence: he told him about Paula, trapping the child who squirmed and kicked in his arms, though Fried hardly noticed, he was so busy telling his story. He had never dared speak about it to anyone before, or even think about it; yes, he had never allowed himself to say a single word of love or endearment to Paula. Otto: "But she knew, Fried, I know she knew." And Fried stared ahead, and saw nothing beyond his tears, and he told Kazik about the fierce longing for the smell of her underarms, for the wrinkles around her eyes when she smiled, for that beauty mark, his private property—he was the only one who knew of its existence, not even Paula had ever seen it "there"—and now Fried understood the depth of the loss he had suffered, because he loved Paula more than anything on earth, and loved her wonderful gift for life, her own life, and everything about her, like her way of sitting on a chair, or bandaging a sore, and at times in her presence Fried knew that he, too, was alive, that perhaps there was something in him also deserving of the good life, and Fried spoke to Kazik of this with eyes closed and cheeks burning, and he was deeply grateful, because thanks to this child born to him in his old age, he had begun to straighten out the chaos of his life, and to settle into his own time, the way a seed dry these many years is suddenly blown by the wind and dropped on fertile soil, where it begins to germinate, and Fried spoke, or—in fact—did not speak, but only growled and splattered Kazik's face with words and groans because he sensed the brevity of TIME [*q.v.*], and Kazik almost suffocated under this avalanche that destroyed his quickly dwindling life, and transfused him with experience he would never be able to use, because he wanted to live his own life and make his own mistakes, and Fried opened his eyes and looked at the child with COMPASSION [*q.v.*] and perceived how small and weak and miserable he was, and fell sadly silent. And so they sat hugging each other for a long while. And the doctor knew that at last he was doing something truly important for his son.

חמלה

CHEMLA

MERCY

See under: COMPASSION

חשד

CHASHAD
SUSPICION

An instance of mistrusting something. The supposition of negative phenomena.

While Neigel was away on LEAVE [*q.v.*] in Munich, his adjutant, Sturmbannführer STAUKEH [*q.v.*] beset Wasserman in the garden. Slyly he interrogated him, "Is it true what they say about you, that you can't die?" (Wasserman denied it), and then asked about the Jew's relationship to Neigel. Wasserman: "This Staukeh, may he live a long life far away from me, amen, has a look about him, merciful heavens, as if his eyelashes have been plucked out one at a time! It seems he wanted to make use of me to test the atmosphere and find out whether Neigel and I have become bosom friends, like David and Jonathan in love and affection! Nu, well, even I was not hatched in Chelm, and I pretended to be a perfect simpleton, and told him humbly with lowered gaze that it is not seemly for a *dreck Jude* like me to gossip with an honorable German *Offizier*! He glowered at me then like a scorched pot and walked away. Toward evening he returned, stepping ganderlike this way and that, and again began to question me about things between me and Neigel. (That is, they had begun to suspect something about my officer!) He even removed his black cap and blinded me with his Sahara of a shaven skull shining in the light. No doubt he thought he would put a little fear into me. Only I remained loyal to Neigel. At length he smiled a smile that made me sweat between my teeth, and went his way. He was suspicious of me, which is not important, but it was plain as the midday sun that Herr Neigel was not clear of this Staukeh's suspicions either!"

חתונה

CHATUNA
WEDDING

The celebration of marriage. Nuptials.

When I married Ruthy, Aunt Idka showed up at our wedding with a Band-Aid on her arm. She had covered her number with a Band-Aid because she didn't want to cast a pall on the happy occasion. I felt crushed with grief and compassion for her, for what she must have endured to do a thing like that. All evening I couldn't tear my eyes away from her arm. I felt as if under that clean little Band-Aid lay a deep abyss that was sucking us all in: the hall, the guests, the happy occasion, me. I had to put that in here. Sorry.

טבח, כצאן ל-

TEVACH, KETZON LE

SLAUGHTER, LIKE SHEEP TO THE

Only once did Wasserman wonder why the camp prisoners were so passively resigned to suffering at the hands of their tormentors. Neigel had gone out to choose new workers from the latest transport, and again Wasserman observed the "blues," the Jewish prisoners in charge of meeting the transports on the platform. They saw Neigel approach and knew what this meant for them. All the same, they continued to do what they were doing, just as their predecessors had when Neigel came to choose a new shift of workers two weeks before. Wasserman: "Dear Lord, even when we were being led 'there,' to the gas, that is, with a sole Ukrainian in the lead, we never thought to rise up against him! A decree from heaven! We knew what was in store, for we had lived in the camp these three months and our eyes were not dimmed nor our noses blunted by the smell of smoke, so why, pray, if not a real rebellion, then at least a slap on the Ukrainian's face, may grass grow out of his cheeks, or at least one small stream of spit, a bubble of spit in all of Sodom? No? Ai, shame, I believe, flowed in our veins like a sleeping potion. And when shame is visited upon man, who was created in God's image, it leaves nothing in the world worth rebelling for. Is this an answer, dear Lord? Have your beings betrayed themselves to such an extent that the one punishment they deserve by my own pitiable hand is that I should never again raise a finger to earn the doubtful privilege of being called a 'human being'? Et, fine thoughts, as I delved and hoed in my garden. Only, I had no such thoughts when we were herded into the gas chamber. The same song, I believe, played inside us all, a lullaby tamed with anguish, to the dry, old tempo measured by the great metronome of Grandfather Death, the great jaws clicking in our honor, sucking us up and grinding us, tick tock, tick tock, as we all became part of this death machine, ai, we are not human beings going to our death here, no, but only what remains of them after being so shamed and depleted: the metal skeleton of human character, soulless mechanisms . . . Only these could we offer as a kind of poor, ironic challenge to our killers; indeed yes, we were their reflection, their own cruel likeness, for we were not dying here as Jews but as living mirrors reflecting an image of the world in our endless procession, and we decreed the fate of the world . . . ai, our mass death, our meaningless death, will be reflected forevermore in the arid wilderness of your lives . . ."

Wasserman's words are recorded here in full. And yet, for the sake of balance, I have to ask: Not even a curse? Not even a slap on the face? Really? Like that? Like sheep to the slaughter?

יומן

YOMAN

DIARY

A record of events, activities, thoughts, observations, etc., kept daily or at frequent intervals.

Dr. Fried's diary of the Warsaw zoo is our only available record of the vast changes that took place in the running of the zoo during the early thirties. At first Fried noted only purely professional facts pertaining to the condition and purchase of animals (here, for example, is an excerpt from his diary for 8/3/37: "1. X-ray of the leopard cub, Max—pelvic region and hindquarters. No indication of spinal injury. 2. Pelvic bones intact. Lines of epiphysis indicating deficient calcification in the epiphyseal line of the femur and tibia. Amadea the baboon is urinating blood. That is, estrus has begun . . . Requests for two pairs of Nando-conor birds brought offers from Rabbitsden Garden, England; Boros, Sweden; the de Branfère Zoological Gardens, France; and the Wildlife Company, Redding Center, Hampstead, England"). But when the zoo had been coerced into joining Otto's war and changing its "interests," reports and information about the newly arrived ARTISTS [q.v.] filled the diary instead. So, for instance: "11/2/42: ILYA GINZBURG [q.v.] arrived at the zoo. Physical state: Severely deteriorated. Mortal danger. Physical and emotional trauma resulting from electric shock. All ten fingernails removed . . . sixteen teeth extracted . . . burns around genital area and nipples . . . 2/5/43: MALKIEL ZEIDMAN [q.v.]: Abscesses under the arms like two open wounds that do not respond to treatment. Recommendation: Reassign him immediately, far from the young flamingos, who are just beginning to fledge . . . 9/6/43: RICHTER [q.v.]: His blindness is total now. Both cataracts covered with a white, phosphorescent dust—source unknown. When wiped away, it reappears . . ." etc., etc.

ילדות

YALDUT

CHILDHOOD

The period from infancy to the end of adolescence.

Kazik's childhood lasted six hours, from 2100 hours, when the white butterfly hovered over his face, till approximately 0300, when he woke from ADOLESCENT DORMANCY [*q.v.*]. He was a lively, wild, and curious child. He climbed up on the chairs and tables, and jumped fearlessly down. Every so often the doctor would ask him nicely to stop, but—Fried: "I could sense it was wrong of me to restrict this child who had so little TIME [*q.v.*], and, in fact, his stubbornness even gave me pleasure—I liked the way he picked himself up each time he fell and threw himself back with all his might, with so much courage, so unswervingly, and, if I may boast a little, this courage and confidence was, I believe, the product of the EDUCATION [*q.v.*] I gave him. Yes." Fried also noticed that Kazik used to blink every few moments, as though he were being whisked away somewhere. He hoped this was not a quirk of the disease, and later realized that it was merely Kazik's way of snatching sleep, because one second of Kazik's life corresponded to eight hours in the life of a normal person, and these intervals were the boy's nights, which left him strong and vigorous again, to push chairs all over the room, throw thick books up in the air and tear out their dusty pages, rummage shamelessly through the drawers (Fried: "Touching my most personal things! Where did I get such a child?!"), and to scream with all his might just for the pleasure of screaming and delight in the sound of his own voice. Fried: "And asking questions all the time, why this, and why that, and what and how, little questions and big questions, never waiting for the answer!" Indeed, sounding out the words with their special interrogative inflection is what seemed to stimulate the child most, like a painful spring coiled up inside him in the shape of a question mark that popped out every moment and gave him temporary relief. With the same graphic movements—if one may say so—salmon leap the falls. Otto: "Poor Fried! At first he tried earnestly to answer all Kazik's questions, and sometimes he would run to his books to make sure he had not misled the child." Paula: "This was exactly the kind of thing that made me afraid to ask Fried questions, even the simplest ones, because right away he would start lecturing . . ." At first the doctor was infuriated by the child's superficiality, but he controlled himself and began to wonder about Kazik's compulsive, wormlike way of thinking, because the questions reminded him of the contractions of a certain organism he had seen under the microscope in his student days, the type that completes a single life throb with every contraction and leaps on to the next. Marcus: "And you must admit, dear Fried, that his questions were always interesting and imaginative and full of hope, and far richer than the answers you were able to offer him . . ." Soon after, the old doctor sank into a depression, because the child was so strange to him [see under: STRANGENESS]. Fried: "It lasted only a short while. Really. I managed to get over it right away, and stopped thinking about myself. I thought only of how to make him happy, as every normal child deserves to be."

Also see under: CHILDHOOD DELIGHTS

ילדות, מחלות

YALDUT, MACHALOT

CHILDHOOD DISEASES

Besides his other complaints, Kazik suffered chills and fevers all through the night. He whimpered like a puppy and the doctor's heart melted. Fried surmised that the child was passing through a series of childhood diseases in rapid succession, the inception of the double file of cudgelers [see under: BIOGRAPHY]. Fried could see the arabesques of chicken pox, the strawberry fields of measles, and the scarred moon face of mumps, and so on and so forth, and he kissed the moist little brow and let Kazik drink from a tablespoon, and spent long nights at his bedside—nights which lasted however no more than the twinkling of an eye, though anxiety knows a time of its own, and it was through the sufferings of the child—more than through his joys and smiles— that Fried could feel his strong attachment to Kazik and how much he loved him.

ילדות, מנעמי ה–

YALDUT, MENAAMEI HA

CHILDHOOD DELIGHTS

Even when Kazik was being impossible [see under: CHILDHOOD], the old doctor tried his best to make his life more pleasant. He racked his brains to remember what he had enjoyed as a child, especially the things connected with his father, who was less harsh during Fried's early years, and did more than merely try to prepare him for life. And so, at 2101, when Kazik was about three years and three months old, Fried put on a little shaving lotion and quickly shaved his face, just so Kazik could smell his smoothly pleasant and frightening cheeks; but the doctor was not content with this: he turned the lights out and threw a few silver coins on the floor. Fried: "That really was a little foolish, and I'm ashamed to admit it, but I had reason for doing this. You see, when my father came home from work at night and took off his trousers, the coins would spill out of his pockets and roll on the floor, and I would wait for the jingling sound every night." Marcus: "And our much admired Fried put up a tender and affectionate struggle against his ferocious little cub on the carpet, and very gently pinned his arm behind his back and forced him to surrender according to the family formula." Fried: "I declare my total and unconditional surrender to my father, sir, family physician to the archduke . . ." and then finally he marched the boy on his enormous feet up and down the room singing— Fried: "Shefi malenki/Zamakni ocheh tiuva . . . Sleep my child/Close your sweet eyes . . ." and when Kazik gave a throaty giggle of delight in response, Fried felt he was a real doctor for the first time in his life.

יצירה

YETZIRA

CREATION

The act of creating the world. The formation of something new. The work of the artist.

During the big argument between Wasserman and Neigel [*see under*: TRAP], when the German asked Wasserman to change the story and get rid of those "anti-German parts," Wasserman admitted to the editorial staff that he does not fully understand most of the clues he scatters for himself through various stages of his writing. He swore, in fact, that for a long time he had no idea why the Children of the Heart had banded together again and whom they were going to fight. He only knew, he says, that he had to "risk his life" (he's so melodramatic!) in order to "remember the story from its beginning, a story forever slipping away from memory." Wasserman: "Ai, I do not yet know the story's ending, but now there is a spark in me, a kind of passion that knows before I do . . . a spark that flies from letter to letter and word to word

inside me, and lights up the story like a Hanukkah menorah . . . and
at first I knew not the real art of writing; indeed, the spark did not
exist in me . . . the passion was hidden . . . and now—see! A precious
light! Now I know that even a shlimazel such as I, who performed no
daring deeds nor ever set the world afire, who was not a duke or minister
or intriguer, and never lusted after houris or explored the world; in
short, even a simple Jew like me has the dough to bake a bagel for
Neigel to choke on, heaven forbid. Beware, Neigel, beware! I said to
him in my heart. Beware, for I am a writer!"

And shortly thereafter, when Neigel accused Wasserman of "ruining
the story! I don't understand why you can't write like a human being.
Think of your reader, Wasserman!" the writer replied, a light blush of
pride in his voice, "I am telling the story for no one but myself . . .
Yes, this is the important lesson I have learned here, Herr Neigel, as I
never learned it before in all my days, for now I know that there is no
other way once you have set your heart on creating a work of art. A
work of truth, that is. Yes, so it is: for no one but myself!"

כוח
COACH
FORCE
See under: JUSTICE

לב, תחיית ילדי ה-
LEV, TECHIAT YALDEI HA
HEART, REVIVAL OF THE CHILDREN OF THE
OTTO BRIG [*q.v.*] was responsible for banding the Children of the
Heart together again after fifty years of idleness. The events leading up
to this are unclear at times for lack of proper DOCUMENTATION [*q.v.*],
due to Otto's lamentable and even sinful ignorance of the tremendous
importance of historical records and the chronicling of individual actions. It is nevertheless possible to reconstruct a (hypothetical!) picture
of the days that preceded the band's revival: when the world turned
"topsy-turvy" (Wasserman), Otto began to wander the streets of the
Jewish ghetto looking for workers to replace the drafted zoo employees
who did not return when the fighting was over. Polish patrols checked
Otto's permits and sent him to search among the slave laborers lined
up on Gezibowska Street, where Jewish work brigades were orga-

nized—builders, cobblers, professors, violin teachers, etc.—to clean the streets and latrines of Warsaw. But Otto wasn't just looking for volunteers. He had no intention of forcing anything on anybody. On Carmelitzka Street, by the last linden tree in the ghetto (the Jews were drawn to it like bees to nectar, and gazed with longing at its golden, life-filled flowers), an old Jew explained to him that Jews have an inborn aversion to working with animals, "and it's a little late to change us now." Other Jews recoiled from him without any explanation. They suspected a trap. A man Otto remembered from the old days who used to sell him meat scraps for the zoo (he was a hotel supplier) advised him to go over to Delizhneh Street, to the Paviak, and bribe the man in charge of prisoners to give him volunteers for one day's work. The word "prisoners" moved Otto, for some reason, and he rushed to the prison, feeling more and more oppressed by the sense of doom emanating from everyone in the street. Otto: "Things were really bad, heartrending. All these Jews looking like hunted animals, and I didn't have the strength to run away. Yes. Then I understood that I had to do something. I had to help. Yes, to fight. And on those first days when I looked for workers in the ghetto, I thought to myself, Here, Otto, you'll help these poor people, you'll give them a good meal and treat them like human beings. But a few days later I knew that wouldn't be enough, that a whole lot more had to be done. Because in the store windows on Krakowska and Pashdmishzche and on Yarozolimska Street, too, the Germans had put up giant pictures of the poor Jews made out to be fiendish murderers, with a sign saying THE JEWISH-BOLSHEVIK MENACE, as if we were all idiotic enough to believe such things, and at every intersection they stationed barkers, that's what we used to call them, who read the OKV news all morning and announced the latest victories and blamed Jewish traitors for the fact that ten thousand Polish officers had been taken prisoner in battle with the Russians near Smolensk, and this was such a pack of vicious lies that I said to myself, Otto Brig, I said, fifty years ago you had a lot more gumption, you weren't afraid of anything, there was no corner of the world you couldn't reach when someone needed help—Armenia, the Ganges after the floods, even the moon with the Indians, and what about that old man Beethoven, who lost his hearing, and Galileo, with all his problems, you flew everywhere with the band, and suddenly, as I thought about the band, bozhe shivante! The blood ran through my veins again, like Jesse Owens at the Olympics, vroom! And quietly I said to myself, We have to do something, because who else but the Children of the Heart can save the world when the world starts going crazy, and who else has so much experience on the job, eh? Because if we don't start doing something at a time like this, then I say we're not worth a whole lot more than the paper we're written on, we're nothing but a bunch of pathetic literary characters, weaklings that go wherever you take us. No, Otto Brig! (that's what I said to myself), no no no! We have to do something! We will band together again and fight the most important war of all! And though at the time I didn't know what kind of war it would be yet, I burst out with: 'Is the heart willing?' And I answered, 'The heart is willing!' 'Come what may?' and I answered, 'Come what may!' This had been our rallying cry fifty years ago, and back in those days when I wanted to call the band together for a new mission I would start drawing chalk hearts on all the trees and fences to let everyone know, and now the time had come to draw new hearts, and so, with this in mind, I arrived at the Paviak just when they opened the front gate and kicked out an old Jew who rolled all the way over to me, smiled a calm, nearly toothless smile, and asked me if I had a cigarette for him." (About Otto's first encounter with YEDIDYA MUNIN [*q.v.*].) Fried: "While we're on the subject of those early days, to tell the truth, Otto went through some pretty awful changes. It was hard to look at him. He seemed to be running a high fever. His face glowed. He was always busy and talking to himself, always running. Always. He left me in charge of the zoo while he spent the day combing the ghetto, in and out with his special permits, searching the streets, the jails, the insane asylums, the Juvenile Criminal Institute . . ." Otto: "You probably thought I was a little sick in the head, eh, Fried?" Fried: "I sure did. You should have seen yourself then! And once we woke up in the morning and saw"—Paula: "a huge heart drawn in chalk on the oak tree in our yard." Fried: "And on all the benches in the Lane of Eternal Youth, and on the wrinkled body of the baby elephant." Paula: "Fried was terribly dejected, and so was I, sure. It broke my heart to see our Otto acting so strangely. And the worst part was that he wouldn't tell us what was bothering him. He just kept saying that he intended to fight, and mama droga, was I scared!" Otto: "You probably thought I meant to fight with guns, eh?" Paula: "What else was there to think? Sure that's what I thought! How could I know?

And afterward the zoo started to fill up with this bunch of loonies, it got pretty scary with things going on like that poor woman, the one who had to wander naked at night near the cages of the carnivores [*see under*: ZEITRIN, HANNAH], or the little biograph with the stinky briefcase, who was kind of a cutie, only he kept getting under my skin and becoming more and more like me [*see under*: ZEIDMAN, MAL-KIEL], and even you, begging your pardon, Mr. Marcus [*see under*: FEELINGS], analyzing our emotions and what we felt all day, not to mention that poor thing, the one who had such a strange smell [*see under*: MUNIN, YEDIDYA] you couldn't stand to be anywhere near him!" Fried: "Ach, it was disgusting! I decided to put an end to it, and went up and asked him, as a doctor, of course, what that smell was, and why he walked in that peculiar way, and the old rascal shamelessly dropped his trousers in the middle of the zoo and showed me a kind of cloth pouch with belts and buckles and the devil knows what." Munin: "I have balls like ostrich eggs, Pan Doctor, all because of my ART [*q.v.*], about which Pan Otto has probably told you, and it hurts, sir, but then of course it has to hurt! One must always suffer for art. And we must endure great affliction for the 'Lord's redemption in the twinkling of an eye,' it's always like that with us Jews; for us there are no miraculous shortcuts, our prophets had none either, and just as Hosea the prophet was forced to live his life with, forgive me, a whore, and have three children by her in order to fulfill his divine destiny, his 'art,' so I, your honor, tirelessly rub my little ram's horn, rub it but never blow it! God help me if I blew it! For then all would be lost! All my travail will have been in vain! And if you say to me, Ashes in your mouth, worm, how dare you compare yourself to the prophet Hosea, I will tell you this, that the Baal Shem Tov bequeathed unto us his teaching that the Lord, blessed be He, wants us to worship Him in many ways, sometimes in this way and sometimes in that, and we find in the Cabala that gluttony is but the divine spark in us seeking to couple with the divine spark found in food, meaning that down in the pricker stick, begging your pardon, is that same passion, so even in a lesser one than I, a spark may spark off another spark and cleave to the sparks from on high, ah, oh, may it be . . ." Fried, who understood little but sensed that something disgusting was being alluded to by the foul-smelling old man, stormed off in the middle of his monologue, to Otto's office, where he demanded an explanation. Paula was there, and she agreed with Fried. Otto felt their fury and fear, considered a moment, and decided to disclose his secret. He told them that he intended to fight the Nazis. Fried stifled a groan and told Otto through clenched teeth that if Otto really wanted to fight, let him bring rifles and real fighters and Fried would join up, too. Otto listened and then explained gently that they lacked the power. "You've got to be realistic," said Otto, and Fried stared at him and shook his head in shock and rage and helplessness. Where, he wanted to know, had Otto found this latest zoo bum "fighter" Zeidman, and Otto replied that the Nazis had released all the inmates from the insane asylum on Krochmalna Street, and they were standing naked in the street, shivering in the cold and utterly bewildered, Fried: "Nu, and out of all of them you chose yourself this winner!" Otto, happily: "Right! Ah . . . you laugh. Listen, Fried, a man like that on his own, perhaps not, but three like him, ten like him, might save something. Might make a difference." Fried asked what Zeidman knew how to do, and Otto in grave wonder told them that Zeidman was a biographer who stole across the frontiers that separated people and understood them from the inside. Fried, with loathing: "And maybe he has something to use against the Germans, too?" Otto: "But 'this' is what he has to use against the Germans, don't you see?" And Fried thought about it, and with painful irony said: "You've got to be realistic, hey?" By the way, at this point Neigel ordered Wasserman to refrain from "anti-German propaganda" and to get on with the story. Neigel was about to depart on his forty-eight-hour LEAVE [q.v.] that night to his family in Munich, and he pressed Wasserman to tell him something about Kazik's life. Only, Wasserman stubbornly insisted on telling Neigel about the early days of the Children of the Heart instead. There was no logical reason for this, outside of his desire to annoy the German. And when Neigel asked him to stop his provocations and get on with the story, Wasserman said, "Forbear, Herr Neigel," and promised that if Neigel allowed him to continue weaving the thread of the tale, he would soon tell him about Kazik. Neigel glanced with annoyance at his watch and agreed with an angry nod. Wasserman thanked him. He told the German that a long silence fell upon the three. That Fried and Paula understood for the first time how deeply the war had infiltrated their lives, and how it chilled the subtle intimacy that had been formed between them over the years and made them icy strangers to one another. Wasserman: "This I experienced in my own flesh, Herr

Neigel, when Sarah, my soul, sewed the yellow star on our Tirzaleh's birthday dress . . . ai, the child wept so bitterly! You see, Herr Neigel: the star spoiled her pretty dress . . ." Neigel: "Damn you, Wasserman, I'm losing patience! My driver will be here in half an hour and you're just avoiding the story of Kazik!" [*see under*: TRAP]. Wasserman, who had not yet realized why Neigel wanted so badly to know what happened to Kazik, and why he was so adamant about it, perspired with fear. But he could tell that Neigel's eagerness was a good sign, and that he must not under any circumstances give in now. Consequently, Otto whispered, "Noah's ark." That is, he didn't whisper, he said it with deep reluctance, as though he had decided to yield a small portion of his secret so they would let him keep the more important part. Neigel stared at Wasserman. Fried and Paula stared at Otto. Otto explained to all three: "It's like the Bible story, only the other way around. Here the animals will save the people, you understand? It's so simple, don't you see?" Neigel: "What's simple?" Otto: "We'll band together again and take in new members. We'll need a lot of fighters this time. It won't be easy. That much is clear. And after our victory over this flood, we can go back to normal life, all right?" Fried and Paula looked at him and felt their hearts break. Otto's eyes shone infinitely blue. Fried stood up, pale and exhausted, by the window of their pavilion, just in time to notice the mythological beast outside, its forequarters sheep, its hindquarters man, crossing the path with loathsome bleats and groans. Despairingly, feeling the whole world had gone mad and collapsed on his shoulders, Fried hurried out after the ravished animal. It was only as he ran that he finally grasped Otto's meaning, and was even more distressed. He had no doubt that the age of children's stories was past.

לידה

LEIDA

BIRTH

The act of bringing forth a living creature.

The birth of Paula's imaginary baby. Otto was thinking of it in his pavilion while Kazik, Fried, and the ARTISTS [*q.v.*] were making their way to see him [*see under*: LUNATICS, VOYAGE OF THE]. Otto woke up and lay in bed, thinking about the baby he had brought to Fried a few hours before. He then recalled the night he and Fried took Paula to give birth in Dr. Wertzler's ward at the hospital, which served also as a military hospital. Otto: "And there were women in labor, and ordinary Poles, and German soldiers wounded from their battles with the Jews in the ghetto, and the screams of men and women were exactly alike, and every minute someone else was born and someone else died, it was like some kind of crazy marathon, and Fried came with us, sure he came, even though his permit was only good for the zoo and they could have shot him, but he didn't care about anything, he came, and we stood together and saw our lovely Paulinka lying there in a clean white bed, sweating and smiling." And later the doctors sent them both out, and three hours later Dr. Wertzler called them in again and showed them Paula, and left with a frown—he considered them both responsible for her death—and Fried stepped in and did something Otto would never have believed: he slid his hand gently under the white sheet, and gallantly delivered Paula's imaginary baby, which he put on her still heart, and poor sentimental Otto began to cry, and through his tears saw the birth of the protest against what life does to dreamers, and also—Otto: "Fried's forehead was split by a vertical line, as though grief had cut him open from the inside with a single stroke." And the next morning, after they buried Paula in the zoo graveyard near the bird cages, Otto saw the doctor draw a line in the dirt with the tip of his shoe for the very first time, and it was the same vertical line. Then Otto understood that someone was marking Fried from the inside to identify him later on if need be. Otto saw Fried's fate etched in his face, and this is why he made such an effort to bring him back to life, so that eventually Fried would be able to fight back. Fried himself knew nothing about the new scar on his forehead: there were no mirrors in the zoo, except for those in the PROMETHEUS machine [*q.v.*], which could be used only at one's peril.

מונין, ידידיה

MUNIN, YEDIDYA

To quote Wasserman: "A man of longing more devout than anyone has ever known . . . a man of flourishing dreams, winged as angels . . . champion of unspilled seed, artist of suppressed ejaculation, archcopulator who never knew the touch of woman, Casanova of vain imaginings, Don Juan of illusions . . ."

According to his own (dubious) testimony, Munin, scion of Mazeritz Hasids in Pshemishal ("Vinegar begot of wine," he told Otto the first time they met outside the Paviak), had since earliest childhood been unable to control his powerful urges ("Satan danced in my skillet"), and after a disastrous marriage, he fled to Warsaw, where he tried his hand at a thousand and one ill-defined businesses, failed at them all, and spent his free time and energy on an activity which only someone as magnanimous as Otto could dignify as ART [*q.v.*]. The first time they met, Otto saw before him a tall, bowed, lean old man wearing a filthy tailcoat and a pair of dark sunglasses on top of his regular eyeglasses. The two pairs of glasses were tied together by a yellow rubber band. His short, rather dandyish mustache was also dirty and yellow. He emitted a powerful stench, like the smell of carob fruit. He came flying out of the prison yard, stood up on his feet, and with stoic calm asked Otto for a cigarette. Otto had no cigarettes and suggested that the two of them go buy one together. On the way, Otto noticed his bizarre walk: thighs curving inward as if—Marcus: "To churn the testicles." Otto: "Something like that. And he whispered and giggled to himself all the time, and touched himself all over, and I didn't know how to start talking to him, I thought he was some poor lunatic, and I knew right away we'd be friends, and in the end I dared ask if he worked there, at the Paviak"—Marcus: "Otto and his exquisite manners." Yedidya Munin stopped in amazement and let out an ugly guffaw full of spit and phlegm, and then he stuck a sharp finger in Otto's chest and said, "I am Yedidya Munin. I will multiply your seed like grains of sand, morals charge, your honor." And he proudly hiked his trousers up to his chest and announced clandestinely, "One thousand one hundred and twenty-six as of last night, when they arrested me. They always arrest me at night and release me the next morning." Otto: "I didn't understand what he was talking about, but I had the feeling it might be better not to ask." On Novolipky Street they bought two Maachorkowa cigarettes from a peddler, and found an empty bench on the sidewalk where they sat down to smoke. Otto: "The street was full of people. Crowds of them. But it was also very quiet. If I had wanted to hail a friend up the street, it would have been enough to whisper his name. The gentleman with me puffed energetically, and when he'd smoked the cigarette halfway down, he stubbed it out with two fingers and left it dangling from his upper lip. Only then did I allow myself to start a conversation with him, and I was glad to see he trusted me and wasn't afraid!" Wasserman: "The truth is, Herr Neigel, Mr. Munin was highly suspicious and cautious in those days of informers and whistle-blowers, and it was only when Otto began to converse with him that Munin discarded his suspicions and furtiveness and crudity, yes, and admitted that—Munin: "I had never spoken to anyone like that about . . . my art before, well, who but Otto would even have guessed it was an art? And the truth is that the words flooded out of me there on the bench on Novolipky Street, and I was frightened, it was as if the little Pole had magic powers, tfu tfu tfu!" Otto: "And I fell in love with you there and then! How lucky I was to meet you that morning!" Marcus: "It's no use asking Otto to describe anyone. You might as well ask a lamp what it sees; it will say, Everything looks so bright." Munin showed Otto the map he kept in his pocket in a crumpled brown envelope. The envelope was Munin's most precious secret, and he presented it to Otto with reverence. It was a map of the Jewish ghetto, with strange markings and hundreds of little Stars of David scattered haphazardly along the streets. Otto supposed they marked secret arms caches in the ghetto. Munin talked nonstop, and Otto gazed in wonder at the extinguished cigarette with a life of its own on his upper lip. Suddenly the Jew glanced sideways suspiciously, and whispered into Otto's ear, "They're all dying." And then he slid over to the edge of the bench, locked his mouth shut, and was silent. Otto, it should be noted, understood at once that Munin was not just referring to the Jews in the ghetto. A few moments later Munin slid back to Otto conspiratorially and whispered that he was going away. Munin: "You will see, Pani. And sons of light will fly high. I will take off. The world will hear of it. Not even the Wright brothers dreamed of such a thing. Or the Montgolfier brothers, inventors of the balloon, or even Daedalus and Icarus in the mythology of the Greeks who desecrated our Temple! Now you see, sir, how adept I am in these matters! I did not overlook a single book!" There and then, Otto invited Munin— enchanted with his blend of crudity and erudition—to come work at the zoo. Munin gaped at him in surprise, smiled, and said, "All my life, Pani, I have dreamed of wiping up the caca of a lion." They shook hands, but not till they were about to part did the sensitive Otto dare ask the meaning of the number Munin had mentioned earlier. The Jew looked at him in amazement, even disappointment, because he had been certain that Otto understood right away. Then he began to smile— Otto: "Such a broad smile, it spread over both sides of his face"—and explained simply, "Why, one thousand one hundred and twenty-six emissions, better known as orgasms, of course, what did you suppose?" Otto blushed to the roots of his hair, looked down at his shoes and up at the sky, and finally dared to ask in a whisper if Mr. Munin had slept with so very many women. Munin laughed his foul laugh again, and jeered: "Coitus? Is that so remarkable? The great rabbi, nu, I forget which one . . . aha, yes! Rabbi Dov Ber says in *Gates of the Path* that the passions must be refined and sanctified. And then as from an evil love man's heart will turn to the love of Godliness, so that he will not crave the sparks of forbidden fire but only God, of course. Any school-boy can know women, your honor, whereas I, 'controlled' myself!"

The second encounter with Munin took place when Fried stood despairingly at the window of Otto's pavilion [*see under*: HEART, REVIVAL OF THE CHILDREN OF THE] and saw the peculiar Mi-notaur—half sheep, half man—crossing the path. Fried pursued him, limping furiously on his cane past the crocodile pool, took a secret by-path, and collided head-on with the terrible creature. Munin collected himself and zipped his trousers over the bird-cage lining of cloth and belts and buckles. The big ewe took off with a mournful bleat (Munin: "The bleating of bitter disappointment"), and Fried, spitting hellstone and fire, rose heavily from the grass, raised his hand like an angry prophet, demanding an explanation. In self-defense Munin claimed, "What is there to explain? You have to hurry! Time is running out and there is much to do, Pan Doctor, and there are no women here, except for Mrs. Hannah [*see under*: ZEITRIN], who obviously belongs to God, and Frau Doctor Paula, who belongs to your honor." Fried: "How dare you, hooligan, utter the lady's name?!" Munin: "Forgive me, but I always tell the truth. And now the total is one thousand one hundred and thirty-eight. All recorded! Perhaps the doctor would care to see my receipts? Every deed is registered, you see, and there is also a map. Yes, you can rest assured, Pan Doctor, that Yedidya Munin never betrays his art!" Fried, who had a vague recollection of Otto mentioning some other number, a lower one, almost choked with rage when he thought with revulsion of the old satyr's exploits in his zoo. Fried: "But please explain, why?" Munin: "Why? In order to control myself. What, Pan Otto has told the doctor nothing at all?" "*No!*" "Ah!! And I thought you knew everything, sir! That you were here among us to preside over the faithful execution of our art! So this is why you are so angry! You simply do not know the story, sir!! I will tell you something quite explicit, as we say, we Jews, that is: I will tell you all. Because there is no shame in it. It is all for the sake of heaven. And it is very simple, for I, your honor, weigh approximately sixty kilos, or even a bit less, because there is not much food here, begging your pardon for allowing me to point this out, but—" "What does your weight have to do with what you did to the ewe?!" "Ah yes . . . the ewe . . . a darling creature . . . Listen: you see, each time I . . . nu . . . you are a doctor, sir, and have probably heard many such things, no?" Fried: "*Du yassni choleria*, do you want to drive me mad? What am I supposed to have heard?" "Na na na, that isn't nice, Doctor. More anger, more grief . . . Ha! Ha! A joke, sir . . . And the sperm, your honor surely knows that sperm, a drop of semen is more than a drop of semen . . ." "It is?" "Absolutely so! It, too, contains a divine spark! And the organ, the *smitchick*, all the more. And we find in the compilation of Rabbi Nachman that the whole world was created for the sake of Israel, and even for the lesser ones of Israel, such as I, for instance, and even for the least of organs, and all this so that Israel may be redeemed and build the chariot, and his honor has perhaps heard about the cabalists of Safed in the Land of Israel, who wrote in the *Zohar* that every movement made in the lower spheres sets the higher spheres in motion! And what of the cobbler, even the cobbler, yes, who sews the sole and fastens high to low, then how much more so is it with me!" Fried: "Please, I beg you, stop rubbing yourself when you talk to me. And talk like a human being! What are you doing here in my zoo!!" Munin: "But I already explained to your honor! It, sperm, that is, shoots out of the body with a terrible force! Whewww! And I am not speaking in vague generalities either! No, I, Pani, am familiar with the most learned scientific journals! And I read therein that the force of sperm flying is equal to the piston head on an airplane in the sky! Relatively speaking, of course." Fried: "Of course . . . and what about— Will you stop rubbing!" Munin: "Now I discovered such a thing, and I, sir, am a simple man. The least in Israel. Vinegar begot of wine. Baba Yaga's cat. I have not received much learning in my life. In my father's house—nu, of course, the psalms by heart, and later, here and there, the compilations of the *Moharan*, and a little of the *Zohar*, and someone let me peek at *The Angel Raziel*, and the book of *Transmigrations*; nor did I forswear secular learning often deemed forbidden, treif, yes, in Warsaw, the capital, my eyes were opened to the wonders of creation, and I also read many a scientific journal and looked upon wonders and miracles therein! And in the libraries I sat and read the latest scientific studies! Of Tsiolkovsky has your honor heard? He hasn't heard. Nu, yes. I have heard. This man was the greatest Russian naturalist and scientist. The meekest and humblest of men! And he invented the idea of flight in space through the use of rockets! Nu, admit: a genius, no? Rockets! And I also read, of course, the complete writings of Goddard the American and Obert the German, and out of these hints gleaned—" Fried: "Maybe you would be good enough to explain so that I can finally understand?" Munin: "But I already explained! Why don't you listen instead of watching me down there! I told you that sperm leaves the body with a terrible force, but perhaps, that is—if I saved this force . . . Now do you understand, your honor?" Fried, weakly: "No." Munin: "The doctor is joking, of course, heh heh! Not once, but hundreds of times. Thousands of times, yes yes! And it is known that a man, even the least of men, has many thousands of sperm in his body, numerous as the stars in the sky, as it is written, and if I saved them up and stored them inside, and if once, just once, I let myself go, that is, a kind of let my people go, what a great and mighty people it would be! For this powerful thrust alone could send even a lightweight such as I— sixty kilograms or less on account of, begging your pardon, the food here—in short, it could send me all the way, you see?" Fried: "All the way where?" Munin: "Nu, wherever it takes me . . . and the sons of light will fly high . . ." Fried: "But where? Where will you fly—to God?" Munin: "Who is wise enough to know? If He takes me to Him, I will go. Whither He sends me, I will fly. Perhaps to God, and the important thing is that I will fly high. Above these mortals here called men. It is a mistake. And I know there is a different place for me. Not here. Here not." Fried: "You mean to say you're going to fly up like that? To God?" Munin: "Nu, have you ever seen anyone so stubborn? I have told you a thousand and one times already: He, blessed be He, is contained in every seed. In the soul of every living being." "And you really believe it? That you'll get there, that you'll be able to ascend a single centimeter?" "With all my heart, your honor, like a homing pigeon returning to its master." "But God—is holy! Transcendent and all that, while you—foo! It's too revolting!" Munin: "Only seemingly, your honor! Seemingly indeed it is revolting, but God's glory is everywhere, as they say in the *Zohar*, Munin's commentary—there is no place where God is not, He pervades even that which is called sin, and the sparks that fell from on high are tarnished now and sullied in every kind of corruption, in the drop of semen, too, and we, the children of Israel, are commanded to worship the Holy One, blessed be He, with devotion, in order to bring those sparks back to their rightful place, and even the most terrible sinners will be His support, for who if not He, may His name be praised, tempted the heart of King David to count the people? As it is written in the Book of Samuel: 'God tempted him,' but the Book of Chronicles says, 'Satan!' Does your honor understand? And I, I have the soul of a beast, already in my childhood they called me 'the calf,' but even the bestial soul of someone as lowly as I has its roots in the luminous shell, and can turn from bitter to sweet, and here on this map I write on all the streets of Warsaw, the capital, the word 'luminous,' a kind of system I myself devised, here in this forehead! And they call me calf. Nu, well, why should I be angry, shortly my lot will no longer be with theirs, a different world awaits me, a world of winged beings! Of angels! Do you see? Come closer! Don't be shy! Come closer and look at the map! Here now, everywhere I rubbed but controlled myself I drew a little Star of David, and here, all along Gensha Street and Lubetzky Street I have most of an *L*, and from Nizka and Zamanoff Streets I almost fashioned an entire *U*, but I will fill that out soon on Wellinska Street . . . and the *I* is still faulty. Now do you understand, sir?" Fried: "Bozhe moi! And that's what you do to my sheep! You play with them to control yourself? And for that you think God will take you in?" Munin: "Oh yes, your honor, nu, at long last this Gentile is catching on. With us, with us Jews—" Fried: "Will you stop making up stories! I, too, am a Jew!" Munin: "Your honor is one of ours? One of us? And I never knew! Welcome home! You don't look it, though . . . and Mrs. Paula shares a room with you . . . who would have guessed?! One of ours! Nu, now I can explain wholeheartedly. One of us. Think of that! And so you probably know, sir, that even wicked thoughts, if properly exploited, become a kind of Grandfather Archimedes lever, a kind of eagle organ, an awakening of the soul. You are a little tired. Sit here on the rocks . . . (A Jew he may be, but he thinks like a Gentile) . . . Yes, and now you understand, sir, what I intend to do; from childhood I have had the evil inclination, and I suffered torments, and I was small and pitiful. A little fertel. And

an organ I had, nu, as tiny as the prayer for dew and rain in the little
siddur! But my inclination, ha! Like fire in the bones, my wicked
thoughts disturbed the prayers and mitzvahs, and though my parents
of blessed memory took great pains to find me a wife, the thoughts
would not leave me . . . and my poor wife was very sorry for me, she
was weak and could not satisfy half my desires . . . and in the end I
ran away. I deserted her, a living widow with six chicks, because a voice
said unto me, Go, go, run away, a wanderer you will be in the land;
yes yes, I will not weary you further, Doctor (it's clear he's an ignorant
Jew, a head that never lay tefillin!), and I only hope that my deeds are
deemed worthy by the Holy One, blessed be He, because even the
Holy Ari of Safed said that the Torah has seventy facets, each of which
is revealed in its generation and time, but it has six times more that
number of facets, and every son of Israel has his own secret way of
reading the Torah, as a living body adhering to the holy speech, a secret
way that envelops the roots of the individual soul in the upper spheres,
known to him alone, yes, and each man worships God according to
his way and manner, and I in my way, this is my prayer, I know no
other, and perhaps of me it was written that prayer is the arrow shot
heavenward, and this because it is not the evil inclination I believed it
to be in my youth but a holy angel, as Rabbi Nachman says, as one
who has known God has this evil inclination which must be overcome
and tempered with justice, till it becomes goodness, as the candlelight
shines and the wick that turns to fire is destroyed, so the light of the
Shekhina shines on the godly soul by destroying the bestial soul and
turning it from darkness to light, and from bitter to sweet among the
saintly ones, and do not think, your honor (A Jew! Who would believe
it!), that it is easy to do that which I have taken upon myself! It is not
at all easy! And sometimes so much control could make a person lose
his mind! And there are other dangers, too . . ." Fried: "Dangers?"
Munin: "Dangers, grave dangers indeed! What did you suppose, sir?
Lilith, cursed be her name, dogs me, hoping a drop of sperm will hatch
her some demons, the holy lambs! And every time I put my hand out
to my little shofar she flies out of hell with a whistle, wheeeee! But I,
as you already know, control myself. I bite my cheeks! Any second
. . . but I control myself! And I am not obliged to perform a penance,
as do those wretches who yield to temptation and spill their seed!"
Fried: "Enough! Shut up! My head is splitting from all your talk! How

long have you . . . that is, how many years have you—" Munin: "Controlled myself? More than seven years, your honor, since everything went bad."

מין

MIN

SEX

1. *See under*: LOVE

2. An unusual discussion on the topic took place between Wasserman and Neigel while Dr. Fried was plunged in grief and longing for his Paula, who had died [*see under*: EDUCATION], and Marcus drew the doctor's attention to the "sad and banal contradiction in our nature"; that is, "All the powers of love, all the mighty forces of passion, and at whom do we aim them? At a single soul, a smile, a dimple, a mere cluster of habits and opinions, a whim-filled bag of flesh, it would seem. How wonderful it is, ah, how wonderful: one person loves another person. Nothing more and nothing less." At this point Wasserman put down his notebook and sank in thought. Then he began to tell Neigel things which were not at all relevant to the subject. He quoted Zalmanson, his adulterous friend, who had once confessed that in the streets of Warsaw, especially in springtime, when women walked through town wearing high-heeled shoes and all their finery, he was often seized with a terrible passion. Zalmanson: "At such times I want to ravage the whole world! To flatten it under me! And I walk along, groaning shamelessly, and the women . . . they look at me and smile, the bitches! And I walk among them in the street like a satyr, and at such moments—how strange it is—I feel an enmity, a strange enmity toward them . . ." Wasserman, who listened to Zalmanson's confession with mixed emotions ("The brute had almost raped my wife! And I sit before him in the darkened office, and a smile rises to my lips . . . a smile of agreement, feh!"), asked Zalmanson what he meant exactly by "enmity," and the editor, who had lost his usual stinging arrogance for the moment, said he felt enmity not because of something any particular woman had done to him, heaven forbid, for women had always dealt charitably with him, all of them, and he was a sworn lover of womankind (the editorial staff is prepared to wager that Anshel Wasserman smiled approvingly at this). No, he felt enmity because of what they compelled him to be by their very nature. By his very nature. Because

he, if anybody cared to know, could love anything, everything. Zalmanson: "I could love the whole world and love nothingness with the same passion," in order to learn fresh nuances, the subtleties of falling in love with a flowering lilac tree or a mad flight of butterflies, or the sound of the accordion. Zalmanson's ideas here are a bit vague. One may suppose he felt degraded because of his lust for women, because he was a rebel by nature, and in his warped mind the desire to love them was a limitation. He felt degraded like Aaron Marcus [*see under*: FEELINGS] when he realized that we are all imprisoned by our limiting emotions, and therefore we—Marcus: "have our ears pierced like slaves against the door of the pale world that speaks to us in its one, halting language!" Zalmanson, with a sigh: "Women, they drive me crazy, you know; I adore them, the way they move, the way they smell, their marvelous bodies, yet what are they but the small, monotonous, finite, and limited materialization of the superhuman passion imprinted inside me, inside us all . . . for they are the jail, the narrow channel, the impoverished speech into which I must translate all the abundance in me." Wasserman, with nonexistent strength: "And they, too, women, I suppose, feel the same toward you; that is, toward us." And Zalmanson: "But of course! I'm certain of it! We and they—like prisoners condemned to uninspired exile together on a desert island." And having said this to Neigel, Wasserman was silent, while upon his face played all the human expressions that signal tough decisions are being reached somewhere deep inside, and suddenly, driven by some inscrutable urge, Wasserman told the German something very intimate, which even the editorial staff was embarrassed to hear, let alone Neigel. Wasserman told the German about his sexual embraces with his wife. It is possible that he did so because he had grown accustomed to speaking to Neigel as one speaks to oneself. Or perhaps there was a different reason, totally incomprehensible. In any case, he expressed amazement: "Tell me, Herr Neigel, you are an intelligent man, after all, how is it that with such great love between man and woman, and such passion that consumes the heart and flesh, all you do is stick a little *smitchikel* into a hole and that is that! But only that? The woman's body should divide before you like the Red Sea! A raging Sambation River should flow between you and drown you seven times, and you should rise gray as ashes, your eyes dim, unable to utter a single word for a year to come, having reached the land of love! As if once having seen the face of heaven-knows-what you were saved by a veritable miracle!" Neigel nodded in silent agreement. For a moment he appeared to be distinctly envious of the Jew for his ability to say all this out loud, for having such confidence in another human being. Marcus said, "Do you hear, Rabbi Anshel? I say, about love I say that a man may love anything, anything in the world, but true love, ah, he can feel for only one person." Wasserman: "You yourself, if I am not mistaken, love music very much. And sometimes it even brings you to tears?" "Ah, a great love that, yes. But abstract. And therefore, not a true love. It is lacking, it is too noble and ideal." Fried: "And I prefer to turn your formula around, Mr. Marcus, and say that a man may hate anything, anything in the world, but he can never hate anything as much as he hates another person."

מלכודת

MALKODET

TRAP

Twice during the course of their meetings Neigel claimed Wasserman "led me into a trap." The first time was when Wasserman brought Hitler and the Nuremberg Laws into Fried and Paula's relationship [see under: HITLER, ADOLF; see also, THIS SWINISHNESS], and Neigel demanded that Wasserman remove his provocative anti-German references. It should be noted, too, that Neigel flew into an almost childish rage: he stomped around the room with big, violent steps, pounded the open door of the office cupboard, leaned over his desk, and pressed all ten fingers against it. Wasserman looked away, rebelling inwardly against this censorship. He smiled an embittered smile at Neigel's empty chair and, tugging irritably at his wispy beard, avowed that "the story will lead us whither it will." Neigel insisted, his back to Wasserman and his face to the curtained window, that Wasserman had hidden intentions he wasn't prepared to overlook. He was furious with Wasserman for pretending to have made a purely arbitrary choice to write about the war all of a sudden, "when you know that's not the type of thing you wrote about in the old days! You used to write about American Indians and floods in India and Beethoven and Galileo—a different type of story! With different settings! You never used to write about real things! I already know about our lousy life here! That's what I want to forget when I hear a story! What do you think we have stories for, anyway?" Wasserman, who listened angrily but with great interest, replied into the palms of his hands covering his mouth, "It is always the same war. Always. And my tales are its written history. Indeed." Neigel stamped his foot, as though trying to level the wooden floor, and screamed at the writer to "get rid of those Nuremberg provocations!" He hurled the word "trap" at the crack in the wooden wall before him. Wasserman, of course, did not understand which trap the German was referring to, but as they swelled and contracted in a kind of ludicrous pantomime of rage at the various objects in the room, never for a moment at each other, the Jewish writer felt that Neigel was not referring to the trap he had set for him, the trap of humanity. No, Neigel was not yet thoroughly enough infected with humanity to satisfy Wasserman. Neigel feared something far more immediate and tangible, and Wasserman could not imagine what it was. It made him nervous that the German was suddenly relating to the story with such fateful seriousness, when only a few days before he had told Wasserman that he was deluding himself about the power of words!

The second time Neigel yelled "Trap!" was on the night before his LEAVE [*q.v.*]. The train to Berlin was due to depart from Warsaw at 0600 hours. His driver had made all the necessary arrangements with the car. But Neigel refused to set off before Wasserman told him the rest of the story of Kazik's life. And here Wasserman, with great cunning, insisted on telling the German the story of the revival of the Children of the Heart [*see under*: HEART, REVIVAL OF THE CHILDREN OF THE] instead, and drew it out all night, like Scheherazade in her day. When the story was finally told, Neigel demanded that he keep his promise and give him "just the outline, Scheherazade, it's very important!" of the remainder of Kazik's life. Wasserman refused. He was pale with fear, but he knew he must say no. Neigel felt betrayed. "BETRAYAL!" [*q.v.*] he screamed, pounding his desk, and again demanded to hear the rest of the story. At this point Wasserman suddenly caught on [*see under*: PLAGIARISM] and refused all the more adamantly. He smiled and said that, if Neigel wished, he could tell the rest of the story himself. Neigel glanced at his watch with alarm and proceeded to beat Wasserman. This was the first and last time he struck him. Wasserman: "He grabbed my poor throat and pounded me with his fists, and I uttered not a sound, and made myself small in the hope that my end was near, because like this, at close range and with the hands, they had not yet tried to kill me, they always did it from afar."

But Neigel suddenly collapsed on the floor beside Wasserman, panting and groaning, and then clambered to his feet, washed his face, handed the Jew a towel, and told him to wash himself off. Wasserman: "My *Scheissemeister*'s gown was covered in blood. Teeth jiggled in my mouth, and when I touched them with the tip of my tongue, three fell out on the floor. Oh well. Less money to pay Dr. Blumberg."

מצפון

MAZPUN

CONSCIENCE

When—during the course of their conversation—Neigel said, "Conscience is the invention of the Jews, the Führer himself said so," the Jew at once replied, "Indeed yes, it is a grave RESPONSIBILITY [*q.v.*], and a heavy burden we have never forgotten, never . . . Sometimes we were the last remaining souls on earth who remembered what a conscience is, and we were so lonely, we and it, so forlorn, that one forgot who the inventor was and who the invention . . ." [*Editorial comment: Wasserman's words here should be viewed indulgently, inasmuch as a Jew like him, "doomed" to a lifetime of absolute values of morality and conscience, especially since he had no other kind of weapon at hand, cannot be expected to understand the complexity and multifacetedness of the question of conscience. It should be recalled that for the weak, without any means of defense and the ability to express power, there is only one possible course of action: to react to situations created by others. They are never able to recognize the cruel and common choice between two just courses. The strong have power, and when power demands to be actualized, it creates complex situations in which sometimes a decision must be made between two flawed, alternative approaches to justice, leading of necessity to relative injustice. Oh, the good innocent Wasserman!*]

מרד

MERED

REBELLION

An act of insurrection against authority.

The only rebellion in Neigel's camp took place one morning while Wasserman was out working in the garden. A new transport train had just come in from Warsaw and the arrivals were already running naked through the Heavenly Way, a common enough sight, as it happened

four times a day and twice at night. Only this time something unusual
occurred: A dire-looking youth attacked one of the Ukrainian guards
and grabbed his weapon. He began shooting and screaming as he ran
blindly in Wasserman's direction. His eyes bulged with fear, like the
eyes of a crab. It took the Ukrainians a few seconds to organize and
begin shooting. There was a terrible commotion. The Jews ran helter-
skelter into the line of fire. Hearing the tumult, Neigel peered out of
his barracks, holding the gun Wasserman knew so well. [*Editorial comment: This occurred the day after their conversation about* RESPONSI-
BILITY (*q.v.*), CHOICE (*q.v.*), *and* DECISION (*q.v.*), *and Neigel
promised Wasserman that henceforth he would kill only after reconfirming
his initial decision to do so. Neigel claimed this would only "reconfirm my
faith in the Führer and his work."*] The sequence of events was as follows:
Neigel charged out of the barracks and ran headlong into the young
Jew, armed with a rifle. Neigel struck him and knocked the rifle out of
his hands. Just then, STAUKEH [*q.v.*] was leaving the *Lazarett*, where
the old, the young, and the crippled from the last transport had been
put to death. A ghostly silence filled the Heavenly Way, littered with
the dead and wounded. The young Jew fell to his knees, his head on
the ground, panting like an animal, his skinny rib cage heaving violently.
In terror he discharged a jet of excrement. Neigel aimed his gun. He
did so slowly, because he wanted everyone to see and learn a lesson.
He looked around at the crowd. For an instant his eyes met the eyes
of Wasserman standing nearby. Wasserman's eyes shot sparks. They
called something out to him. They reminded him of something, they
demanded something. Wasserman: "For the span of one second only
did Neigel hesitate. Ask what a second is. All the forests of pens and rivers of ink, etc., will not suffice for the story of this one second. And
therefore, let me say in essence: Neigel shot once, he shot twice, and
he shot ten times. He emptied his gun out on the innocent youth.
And he went on shooting after there was no longer any point. Because
it was not the boy Neigel was so furious with but himself, and perhaps
with me. Because against his will Neigel had kept the promise he made
me. Perhaps if I had not been there at that moment he would have
forgotten; only, my eyes commanded and he obeyed. For a fraction of
a second he hesitated before firing, and everyone saw. Everyone, Staukeh, the Ukrainians, everyone." Then Neigel turned on his heel and
slammed the barracks door behind him. He seemed to be terror-stricken,

like a man whose natural talents leave him suddenly and inexplicably; like a swimmer in the middle of the ocean who forgets his strokes. The Ukrainians wasted no time and began to massacre the Jews who were still alive. Two bullets hit Wasserman as well, but they could not harm him. He sat where he was, with his head between his shoulders, his hump held as high as possible. Ten minutes later, all was still. The blues were sent in to clear away the bodies. That evening Neigel did not ask Wasserman to read to him.

מרכוס אהרון

MARCUS, AARON
See under: FEELINGS

נחות, האדם ה־

NACHUT, HAADAM HA
INFERIOR MAN

A term used by the Nazis to designate non-members of the Master Race.

In order to obtain a marriage permit [*see under*: MARRIAGE PERMIT], an SS member was required to ascertain that his bride was not of the type known as Inf. Man. Neigel showed Wasserman an SS circular on the matter. This document, issued to all SS units, quotes the pamphlet titled *Inf. Man* (published by Nordland, Germany): "Inf. Man has a biological structure similar to that of natural man, with hands and feet, eyes and a mouth, and something resembling a brain. But despite the remarkable human appearance, he is indeed a monstrosity, utterly distinct from man. Woe unto anyone who forgets that resemblance to a human being does not amount to being one."

נישואין, אישור ה־

NISUIN, ISHUR HA
MARRIAGE PERMIT

A document without which no member of the SS was permitted to marry the woman of his choice.

The document came into force in 1932, with the promulgation of the SS Marriage Law. A permit could be dispensed by Reichsführer Himmler alone. Neigel, in telling Wasserman about his marriage, commented that "luckily for us, we were married before '32." "Luckily" for them, because Christina's prolonged barrenness early in the marriage might have held back Neigel's promotion in the "movement." Wasserman did not understand what Neigel was talking about. Neigel explained that in order to obtain a mar. perm., the bride-to-be had to be examined by a doctor and certified for her child-bearing potential. To this end, too, marriage applicants were required to enclose a photograph showing the bride-to-be "naked, or wearing a swimming suit," in the words of the marriage law, so German race experts could study the photograph under a magnifying glass. Wasserman shook his head in shock and sadness. Neigel explained that the experts were particularly anxious to prevent breeding with persons known as INFERIOR [*q.v.*]. The Jew reflected, "Perhaps it is the way of the world: he who considers his fellow man as non-human becomes so himself." Neigel, who was thriving in this atmosphere of candor, said, "In '38 our situation became even more, uhm, complicated. That is, delicate," because that was the year the divorce law came into force, stating that a German male could divorce his wife for not bearing him children. He was even entitled to divorce a woman over forty who had borne him any number of children on grounds of infertility in order to marry a younger woman. Wasserman bitterly: "The Reich needs children, eh?" Neigel: "Exactly! A woman must give children to the Führer and the Reich. This is Himmler's private obsession. He, by the way, left his own wife, Marga. I knew her personally. Then he went to live with his mistress and Marga sent him a letter of congratulations. Can you believe that? She wrote: 'May Hedwig bring you many children!' What do you say to that, Wasserman? Are your people capable of such generosity?" Wasserman ignores the question: "And what did you do, you and your wife, that is, about the divorce law?" Neigel, trying to downplay the importance of what he was saying: "Christina offered to divorce me right away, of course. She didn't want to spoil my chances for promotion." And after a moment's silence: "And the strangest part is, Wasserman, that a few months later Tina was pregnant. Everything worked out fine. Everything. Karl was born four months after the war started, in February 1940, and Liselotte a year ago." Wasserman: "Because she touched your heart." Neigel wants to dismiss this sentimental conjecture with his usual *Kwatz mit sauze* but refrains, and appears to be rather amused with the idea. Silence. Then Wasserman says aloud, "Herr Neigel, once, many years ago, my wife went to a party at Zalmanson's, about whom you have already heard, I believe, and there Zalmanson pushed her into the coat closet and kissed her on the mouth." Neigel looks at Wasserman, at first uncomprehendingly, and then, little by little, the significance seeps into his brain. The information in itself was less important than the fact that Wasserman had confided in him. He understood. (Wasserman: "What dybbuk ever possessed me to make me say this to him? God alone knows. Perhaps being the son of a grocer had taught me that you have to pay for your wares. Yes, I was obliged to recompense him for the secret of his wife and their love with a precious secret of my own. Feh, Anshel! A magpie you became in your old age!")

נכות

NACHUT

DISABILITY

The condition of being disabled by a physical impairment.

According to Wasserman, this is the condition of all beings created in the image of God. He expressed this when Kazik was asking Fried how people feel about their lives, about whether they love living [see under: YOUTH]. Neigel, tired and defeated at the time, protested weakly against "your cruelty, Wasserman," and was prepared to swear that "before I met you I enjoyed my life. I loved living. You understand? I loved getting up in the morning and doing my work! I loved breathing and riding horses and spending time with my wife and the little ones, I loved it!" To which Wasserman replied with a bitter smile, "We are all maimed, Herr Neigel, disabled in flesh and spirit, lame, and blind. And if you look closely, you will discover that in the depths of our hearts, even those of us who call themselves happy feel the same gnawing sadness, the same worm of despair. For how well we know that happiness, transparent as a soap bubble and just as elusive, will be taken away and lost to us forever. Though ours by right and merit, we have been robbed of it by villains unknown. And that is why I say we are all disabled. Amputees of happiness, cripples of joy, paraplegics of significance, Herr Neigel. Only, like a severed limb, the body still longs for it and does its best to remember the warm pulse, and it is this sadness, the sadness of longing for that which has been cut off and lost forever, that grinds our hearts in its mortar, is it not so, Herr Neigel?"

ОЈ

NES

MIRACLE

An extraordinary event from the point of view of causation, significance, and purpose.

1. Wasserman was saved by a miracle. The miracle occurred when he had lost the thread of the story and did not know how to answer a logical question posed by Neigel, for the third time, out of sheer peevishness: How could Paula, a Polish woman, live with Fried, a Jew, in the middle of the war, despite the law? Wasserman could find no adequate explanation for this. Various clever replies came to mind, but he dismissed them one after the other. It seems he could no longer "remember the eternally forgotten story." Just then Neigel felt the need to confess that his wife had suggested a separation a few years before, so her infertility would not prevent his promotion in the SS [*see under*: MARRIAGE PERMIT], and that a new closeness had come into being between them as a result of the external threat to their relationship. Wasserman: "And at that moment I knew exactly what to hatch for him! I told him how Paula had heard about the execrable laws [*see under*: THIS SWINISHNESS] and had gone to Fried's house where she fell to lovemaking so that . . . Perhaps it was a miracle, and perhaps it was due to my own stupidity that the idea had never occurred to me before, and perhaps, nu, everything is possible. And miracles, of course, need luck to make us believe in them, as we used to sing: "The rabbi performed a miracle / I saw him myself. / He climbed the ladder / And fell down dead. / The rabbi performed a miracle / I saw him myself. / He waded in the water / And came out wet . . ."

Also see under: HITLER, ADOLF

2. Two days after the REBELLION [*q.v.*] on the Heavenly Way, after Wasserman had finished telling Neigel the latest installment and before they parted for the night, the Jew demanded his shot. Neigel jumped to his feet. "Absolutely not!" he said. "But you promised! You promised!" screamed Wasserman, and Neigel: "You can forget about that tonight." "Is the word of a German *Offizier* no longer important to you?" asked Wasserman, and Neigel blushed, popped his knuckles, and exclaimed in a fury, "Listen here, Wasserman, you yourself said I have to make a decision each time I shoot, you're the one who put that into my head! And I have made a decision: I will not shoot you! Not now

and not ever! No no no! Is that clear?!" Wasserman, evincing more anger than he really felt: "You promised! You promised! Curse you, Neigel!" And Neigel, his face contorted: "No! Ach! For you it's nothing! You feel nothing when I shoot you! No pain at all! But for me it's different! I know you now! You're not just another Jew for me like the others out there!" He indicated the windows behind the closed curtain. "No, Wasserman. Forget it. I can't do it anymore." And he fell silent, alarmed by what he had just blurted out. Wasserman, trying him to the limit: "You are a German *Offizier*, Herr Neigel, paragon of the Third Reich, and I am the lowest of the low, an *Untermensch*! [*see under*: INFERIOR MAN]. Shoot me, Neigel, for if you do not, I will stop telling you my story!" Neigel screams: "But you can't! You must continue to tell it!" "So? Why do you think I torment myself before you every night? Because I like the color of your eyes?" Neigel, breaking down: "Because you enjoy telling the story! You love it!" "No! Because I wish to die, Neigel! Shylock the Jew demands his pound of flesh! Shoot, Herr Neigel!" Wasserman's shout brought Neigel back to his wits. Or perhaps it had had an immediate effect on that part of him which was trained to obey. He stood up, pale as whitewash, took out his gun, cocked it, and pressed it to Wasserman's temple, where the barrel danced (Wasserman: "Like a wedding entertainer before the bride"). Wasserman harshly told Neigel to control himself and stop trembling that way. Neigel admitted that he could not stop. That nothing like this had ever happened to him before. Anxiously he asked, "And what if I lose you this time?" And Wasserman smiled to himself and demanded almost martially, "Shoot, Neigel! Release a bullet! I am only a Jew, a Jew like all the others!" But it took a few minutes for Neigel's hand to stop trembling, and steadying his gun, he suggested meekly, "Humph, maybe . . . that is—would you mind facing the other way? In the direction of the door, say." Wasserman: "What lies in that direction? The Mecca of murderers?" And Neigel: "No, it's just that . . . anyway, why should I break the window again, right?" Wasserman began to laugh. A moment later Neigel also caught on to the ludicrousness of his excuse and began to laugh with him. It should be stressed: they laughed together. For a brief moment they sensed how well they understood each other. Wasserman once said that man is made of flexible stuff, and he was right: killing seems to be something that can be gotten used to, as can non-dying. And little deals are made with the miracle. When their laughter died down, Wasserman said gently, amiably, "And now, I beg you, shoot me." Neigel closed his eyes and fired. Wasserman: "The buzzing flew from ear to ear, and as it did, I learned what Neigel had been writing as I told the tale. Ai! Neigel dropped the gun and began to laugh again, both because I was still alive, but also because a miracle had occurred: the bullet had hit the doorframe, ricocheted to the window, and shattered the pane. The miracle refused to make a deal."

3. As Kazik's end drew near [*see under*: KAZIK, THE DEATH OF], and the hopes invested in him by the artists seemed about to be disappointed, because the Children of the Heart had not succeeded in their final mission, Neigel and Wasserman spoke in whispers that rang with defeat. They tried to understand the root of the failure. Wasserman supposed that the cause lay in the nature of miracles. "Miracles?" Neigel wondered. "What's all this about miracles?" And Wasserman: "Ah, well, nu, both you and my own Children of the Heart have tried to work a kind of miracle . . . an exaggeration of human nature . . . you in your way and my Children of the Heart in theirs. We were both trying to create a new man . . . and we failed. Everything is lost . . . You, by your actions, have caused . . . nu, you already know what you have caused, and I, by my actions, nu, et, as usual: for once I hoped to tell a beautiful story. A well-wrought story, a moral lesson, a philosopher I tried to be, feh! Old fool that I am! For that, of course, you need talent, gifts of intelligence and heart! Whereas I, what have I produced here these weeks? Only a poor joke. A pitiful jest. A Munin or Zeidman or Hannah Zeitrin . . . Your wife was right, Herr Neigel: I am a curio. Your wife saw through me all along! And I, I wanted miracles here! A man who would fly up to heaven, a woman after the heart of God! A Moses of Warsaw I tried to be! Ai, no, Herr Neigel. There is no hope in miracles, neither in miracles of evil nor miracles of mercy. Out of the leaven of humanity one cannot bake a miracle! One must take it step by step, nebuch, and get along with the barest necessities, yes, by loving and hating what there is, yes, love thy neighbor as thyself and hate thy neighbor as thyself, this is the whole law. And have COM-PASSION [*q.v.*]. Our glory will not come shining through a miracle, Herr Neigel . . ."

נעורים

NEURIM

YOUTH

The time of life between childhood and maturity.

At 0300 Kazik reached the age of eighteen. He had just awakened from his cocoonlike sleep [*see under*: ADOLESCENT DORMANCY] and was once more firmly entrenched in time. A difficult period followed. He was harrowed by tyrannical forces, hurled between shifting moods that left him depleted, depressed, and depraved. Even when he was happy it was a turbulent kind of happiness. Dressed only in a diaper, his body suddenly sprouted hair that made him feel ashamed. His voice turned husky, his face coarse. Fried, who never left his side, heard tiny popping sounds and in the lamplight discerned ugly pimples breaking out all over Kazik's face and bursting with pus. The vital force was bubbling up under the skin. A whitish foglike down appeared on his cheeks. Kazik was suspicious of everyone, including Fried. When the doctor refused to indulge his whims, he would stamp his little foot, looking so fierce and hostile that Fried was quick to comply. Fried: "He's so miserable. He doesn't know what he wants yet. You have to help him through it." At times Fried felt as though he were watching an angry artist painting with both hands, grimacing all the while, and tearing off one page, ready to attack the next. Fried could no longer even cherish the illusion that the child belonged to him. Kazik was at the mercy of nasty thoughts, and disagreeable emotions that appeared on his face and desperately sought the proper outlet. Yet Fried did not for one moment stop loving him, and always looked for reasons to love the boy and forgive him, attributing characteristics, motives, and feelings to him which he grasped at like straws in order to maintain his relationship with the strange boy. In addition to all this, Kazik was blessed with a depressing natural ability: due to his ambivalence toward TIME [*q.v.*], he was able to view simultaneously the processes of growth and decay in every object and person. He saw each plant and animal as the cruel battlefield of a never-ending struggle. This distressed him, and intensified the violence that erupted in him unchecked. And yet, as sometimes happens, out of this jumble of emotions a boy emerged who surprised even the doctor with his strength, determination, and the optimism that flowed out of him like a tonic produced by his own body as a cure for all the pains of adolescence. At around 0330 Kazik's impulsiveness subsided somewhat. A kind of coordination was now observable in his limbs, and a new look appeared in his eyes, curious, confident, clear. The doctor's heart was filled with happiness. Kazik sat at his feet, holding Fried's old hand in his, and asked if what he had told him once, years before in his childhood, was true. Kazik vaguely remembered certain things Fried had told him once about the world beyond the closed pavilion, and about other people [*see under:* EDUCATION]. The doctor's heart sank. Now he was going to lose the child, too. How many separations could one man endure? In a quiet voice he admitted that there was a world out there beyond the pavilion. That there were people there, too. For a moment he detested the boy's smile of delight. Kazik asked what kind of life people lived out there, and the doctor said, "Just life." Then Kazik asked if people love their lives. Fried wanted to lie, but could not. There was something in the boy that made lying seem to him like a revolting waste of time. Kazik listened to Fried's reply [*see under*: DISABILITY] and brooded over it. Then he asked how many people there were outside, and the doctor specified a number that seemed to be closest to the truth. The boy gaped. He didn't understand the number. Then he smiled his painful smile again and said never mind how many there were, one of them was bound to love life, and that he, Kazik, intended to be the one. The doctor asked with emotion how Kazik would define this love of life, and what happiness meant to him. But these questions were too complicated for Kazik, whose ability to think and express himself was regrettably limited. He could only say, "It's something good. Something I want. Something that's there. Let's go get it." And so, forgoing needless preliminaries, the two set off on their way.

Also see under: LUNATICS, VOYAGE OF THE; LIFE, THE JOY OF

סבל

SEVEL

SUFFERING

1. A weight, a burden, an affliction. 2. By analogy: pain, trouble, or distress. Physical or mental anguish.

Wasserman says: The compass or lighthouse, the criterion for every human decision. Wasserman sees sensitivity to suffering and consciousness of it as the highest goal of mankind. Moreover, it is man's protest, and the highest expression of his freedom. The measure of man's humanity, in Wasserman's opinion, is defined by the amount of suffering he succeeds in diminishing or preventing. [*Editorial comment: It is almost superfluous to point out here that Wasserman himself never faced the kind of dilemma wherein, for example, he was forced to "cause" suffering in order to save his own life. At the same time, the editorial staff assumes that his passive, righteous attitude was so deeply ingrained that he would have preferred to be destroyed rather than cause suffering. Arguing with Wasserman about this is like talking to a blind man about a rainbow.*]

–סהרורים, מסע ה–

SAHARURIM, MASA HA

LUNATICS, VOYAGE OF THE

The voyage made by Fried, Kazik, and the other ARTISTS [*q.v.*] from Fried's residence to Otto's pavilion. The voyage began at 0427, when Kazik was twenty-seven. They walked along the boulevard of bird cages, past the mound with Paula's grave, and down the Lane of Eternal Youth. They were a tired bunch, nearing the end of their tether, and Kazik was their last hope. They showed Kazik where each of them lived, or slept, or practiced his art, and explained who they were and what their special talent was. They didn't talk much. Just a few words or gestures (Munin: "For me, gestures were enough"). Marcus: "Because there are some among us who never stop talking to themselves or to others, but when asked an important question, are struck dumb. They are extremely embarrassed. And what were we, after all? Otto Brig's heart people. Wretched partisans living out in the wilderness beyond the human race, how could we hope to triumph alone?" Undoubtedly something of the artists' anguish and despair began to filter through to Kazik's soul. He listened with open mouth to their descriptions of strange and varied wars. He sensed the tremendous effort that went into them. For the first time in his life his sensitive antennae touched human limitation, and he was amazed to discover how close it was to him. The expedition proceeded at an incredibly slow pace (it took thirty-four minutes), because there were certain places where they had to stop to explain something or to answer Kazik's many questions. On this voyage Kazik passed THE SCREAM [*q.v.*], stolen time [*see under*: PROMETHEUS], Paula's grave, the tortured face of GINZBURG [*q.v.*], and other such focal points. Almost two years of Kazik's life went by on the voyage, decisive years in terms of character integration. For a few moments of the voyage, Kazik discovered the world, a time of sublime happiness [*see under*: LIFE, THE JOY OF], but for the most part he experienced a painful awakening to life and what it portends [*see under*: SUFFERING]. Wasserman: "And as we walked behind him, Herr Neigel, as we walked behind him, bowed and weary, a band of dying lunatics, we felt we needed him, we needed him sorely . . . our fate and our war were entwined with his . . . and how cruel it was of us to make demands on so small a youth, but that's war, is it not, and what choice had we?" It was a warm night in early April 1943. The horizon blazed red, and the smell of scorched flesh assailed them from afar. At 1501 hours the band reached Otto's pavilion. He was waiting for them at the door.

סיגריה

CIGARIA

CIGARETTE

A small paper tube filled with tobacco intended for smoking.

When Neigel returned from his final LEAVE [*q.v.*] in Munich, he began to chain-smoke. One night, in a burst of generosity, he offered Wasserman a cigarette. The author, who had never smoked in his life, took one—for the sake of his friend Zalmanson, who missed his little cigars to the bitter end. Wasserman inhaled, therefore, and nearly fainted. Wasserman: "Like a wheel my head was spinning! And who was wise enough to know that a cigarette has such a bite? May it burn!" Again he bravely took a small puff, and threw the cigarette away. "A black year upon him, that Zalmanson! I have to choke for his sake?"

סרגיי, סמיון יפימוביץ

SERGEI, SEMION YAPIMOWITZ

Russian physicist. In his youth, member of the Children of the Heart. After leaving the band, he achieved worldwide fame with his research into the laws of light. An introverted recluse by nature, he preferred to stay in his laboratory with his paraphernalia and calculations than to mingle with people. He had been like this since childhood: golden hands and a closed heart. Wasserman's mixed feelings toward him can be gauged by the fact that in seven out of sixteen tales of the Children of the Heart, he "forgot" to send Sergei along with the rest of the band. Wasserman admitted freely to the editorial staff that there is "something about our good Sergei . . . he seems to understand gears and mechanisms from the 'inside,' as though he were one of them . . . I was never able to put a humorous or tender word into his mouth . . ." Wasserman always had a vague suspicion that Sergei was not really interested in humanitarian missions, and his only contribution was the machinery he constructed for the band's use. Since Sergei himself spoke little and Wasserman was reticent about him, it is not at all clear how Sergei wound up with the band a second time. What is known about him is that during the war he was drafted by the Red Army for his knowledge of the laws of light. He was in one of the Budyonny divisions, which must certainly have been on the southwestern front, where he assisted in the improvement of a range-finding mechanism for long-range artillery. He was captured by the Germans and sent to Berlin, and later to a Russian POW camp before arriving in Warsaw as a worker in a factory that manufactured eyeglasses for the soldiers of the Wehrmacht. The Germans never found out who Sergei was and the extent of his knowledgeability in his field. After this, his story becomes unclear. Toward the end of '43, Otto arrived at the military factory on the outskirts of Warsaw. He spotted Sergei in his prisoner's uniform and recognized him immediately. Sergei did not recognize Otto. He was already in the realm "beyond his life" (Marcus). Otto bribed the man in charge of prisoners (Fried: "Half our monthly budget for the zoo!"), and led Sergei to the zoo. Bathed, dressed, and properly fed, Sergei began to recuperate, although he was never completely himself again. He was sickly-looking and had a strange walk ("Craning his neck, like it was made of glass!") and a body that seemed to have been put together piece by piece out of some sort of delicate material. Timid in the extreme, he used to run into the bushes whenever anyone approached. Otto was the only person he ever exchanged words with, and when he did he always blushed, one eye tearing. A few weeks after his arrival at the zoo, he began to conduct his baseless scientific experiments. But when Otto told him gently about what the other artists were doing at the zoo, his eyes flashed. This is how Otto had always kindled new ideas in Sergei. Otto: "But this time, what can I tell you, this time the fire in him frightened me a little. I don't know why. I thought maybe I'd made a mistake bringing a man like him back to the band. Just because he was one of us once didn't mean he'd never change and become 'different'?" Among the experiments Sergei conducted at the zoo, two are worthy of mention: THE SCREAM system [*q.v.*] and the

parallel mirror system for stealing time [*see under*: PROMETHEUS].
His experiments were generally clumsy and required complicated technical equipment which the zoo was not always able to obtain. Sergei
was unpopular among the ARTISTS [*q.v.*], not just because of his
reclusiveness, but because he was the only one of them who used equipment other than his own body and soul as a weapon, as a battle zone.
This, of course, until his famous last experiment, at which time he disappeared under suspicious circumstances [*see under*: PROMETHEUS].

עינויים
INUYIM
TORTURE
The infliction of intense physical or mental suffering.

Kazik's torture. Looking back when he neared the end of his life,
Kazik discovered that the years had passed with a suffering which was
in essence inexplicable. His desires, his hopes, his strengths, and his
anxieties—in short, most of his personal resources—had been bestowed
on him in such quantity and with such intensity, they seemed to have
been intended for natural phenomena like storms and oceans, rather
than human beings like Kazik, on whom they wreaked their vengeance.
So, for example—Kazik's self-loathing toward the end of his life was
so fierce it might have split the planet from pole to pole, but it could
only turn inward, against Kazik and the ARTISTS [*q.v.*] surrounding
him. It would probably have taken thousands of years to dilute the
instinctual needs and drives his small body had been burdened with,
but without the diluting waters of time he stood no chance of happiness.
His anguish and passion pained and humiliated him and extinguished
any flicker of grace. No demand of his tortured soul, not a single one
of his powerful urges ever sprouted, matured, and declined in its season,
so that Kazik could turn into a real CREATION [*q.v.*], into that which
is called, longingly, the crown of creation. Wasserman: "He was lost,
Herr Neigel, lost from the start . . . Better that he had never been born
. . . What are these few hours we call 'the life of man'? What could he
do with them? How much could he know of himself and his world?
Et! And do you think Old Methuselah in his dying days knew any more
than Kazik at twenty minutes past six o'clock on the evening of that
day?"

Wasserman asked this in a tired, broken voice the last evening he told his story. Kazik was by now very close to the end of his life. So was Obersturmbannführer Neigel, who had returned from leave in Munich [*see under*: CATASTROPHE]. When Neigel heard this description of the torture Kazik underwent, he muttered, "A little more compassion, Herr Wasserman." He leaned his head on his arm, his other arm flung across the desk. Wasserman told him how Kazik had attacked the remainder of life with fury: he demanded to be told by the artists who he was and to what end he had been created. But they had no answers. He was constantly being carried away by various embarrassing compulsions. There was absolutely nothing stable or predictable about him. To the artists, his short life appeared like a medley of impulses and conflicting whims. Wasserman: "His enthusiasms and depressions, ah, a revolting stew!" Not until a few months before his death [*see under*: KAZIK, THE DEATH OF], at around 1823 hours, did he begin to settle down. This may have been due to his physical weakness, or perhaps he was subdued because he grasped the meaninglessness and despair of his life. And then he looked back and was astounded to discover that what had always struck him as an ordinary life, depressing but stable, was, in fact, only a series of clownlike antics. Marcus: "His tastes seem to change from one moment to the next, and, just as quickly, his many and various beliefs and permanent convictions . . ." Sadly he realized that he had, in fact, accumulated no genuine experience, that his entire life may have been nothing but a kind of preparation. Marcus: "That's the thing, dear Kazik: in return for a lifetime of experience, you have to pay with your life . . . It's like, l'havdil, selling your hair to buy a comb." In his final hours he was unbearable. His body began to putrefy while he was still alive. For moments on end he was filled with remorse and love for everyone, which he radiated in burning waves not unlike his attacks of meanness and hate. One minute he clung tenderly to Fried and covered his face with warm kisses, and the next he crouched down and maliciously flung a handful of dust in the doctor's eyes. Wasserman: "And Fried, a broken old demiurge, did not brush himself off but stood motionless, studying the poor little creature whose body and soul were being torn thus to shreds." And the worst of it was their sense of waste, Kazik and the artists': the bitter knowledge, clear beyond a doubt, that very close at hand was the chance they had not been able to find. And it was altogether possible that happiness had joined them at some point and then abandoned them. They felt they had betrayed something, but they didn't know what.

פלגיאט

PLAGIAT

PLAGIARISM

Literary theft.

The crime of Obersturmbannführer Neigel was exposed the eve of his departure on LEAVE [*q.v.*] to Munich through the following sequence of events: Neigel asked Wasserman to tell him the rest of the story of Kazik's life, which had been interrupted at the point when Kazik was about to separate from HANNAH ZEITRIN [*q.v.*] in his thirtieth year. Wasserman—surprisingly—refused, and made the continuation of the story contingent on Neigel's agreeing to listen to the part of the story he had skipped earlier because it was not well enough developed yet. Neigel wanted to know which part of the story he meant, and Wasserman replied that it was the chapter about the REVIVAL OF THE CHILDREN OF THE HEART [*q.v.*]. Neigel looked at his watch: his train to Berlin was leaving at 0600. At 0400 his driver was due to pick him up and take him to the station in Warsaw. He had three whole hours left, and he decided to be generous to Wasserman and let him proceed with the unimportant chapter of the story. Wasserman thanked him and began telling the story. Neigel listened in angry silence to the "anti-German provocations," as he called them. By the way, that evening Wasserman drew his story out interminably, stalling with every literary device at his command. By the time he finished it was 0200, and Neigel vehemently asked the Jew if he had had enough fun now, and if he would please continue the story of Kazik's life. Wasserman tucked his head under his hump and informed Neigel with cautious intrepidity that he refused to continue the story. Neigel could not believe his ears. He stood up and shouted "TRAP!" [*q.v.*] and later threw himself on Wasserman and cruelly beat him. He cooled down after the (initial) bodily contact with Wasserman, however, and went to the little sink in the corner to wash his face. He brought a towel back for Wasserman to clean himself off with, and sat on the floor beside him. He begged him to stop tormenting him, and the battered Jew noted inwardly that the request had been made in a gentle voice, as a plea for a personal favor. "No no, Herr Neigel," he replied. "You will just have to make up another story for her, I am sorry to say." At first Neigel thought he had not understood Wasserman properly, because of his swollen mouth and missing teeth. Then he looked in his eyes and understood. He drooped down to finger the strap of his black boot and asked in a subdued voice, "How did you know? How did you find out?" And Wasserman, taking his time: "I thought a little." Neigel: "Yes. Now you know." Wasserman, who did not yet know as much as he wished to appear to know, tried his luck: "You wrote her the whole story, eh? In the letters you sent her, you copied out my story, is that right?" And Neigel: "The whole story. Yes." Wasserman laughed tensely. "Nu, yes. And . . . tell me . . . does she still think I am a . . . that is, a cur—a joke?" And Neigel: "No no. She says this is the best story you ever wrote. That is . . ." "That is what? What? Tell me, tell me quickly!" "That is . . . humph, you see, of course, that—" "What? What am I supposed to see?" "That Christina doesn't actually know about you. About the two of us, that is. Humph." "Herr Neigel, please, did I not hear from your very own lips that you told her about me on your first leave? You must remember, the time you went to Borislav and the mine? Nu? Well?" "Yes, yes, I told you, but you have to understand, Wasserman"—he chuckled shyly, with downcast eyes, fastening and unfastening his bootstrap, and said or tried to say—"I told her, yes, of course I told her. I told her you were here. She knows exactly what that means, because she was here on a visit once." "She? Here?!" There was a note of disappointment in Wasserman's voice! For some reason he wanted to keep this woman, so fragile and plain, away from here, both for her sake and for his. Neigel nods. Wasserman: "Nu, and so? Does she think that I am, that is, dead?" "Yes. That's it. I'm sorry, Herr Wasserman. But everything became so complicated. It started out as a joke. Well, not a joke exactly, more like a game, I would say. It's too hard to explain. And suddenly I couldn't tell her the truth anymore, you see?" "See what?" (Wasserman: "Nu, now I understood everything, and without a bullet buzzing through my head. You have to point with your finger for a stupid man like me! That beast, Neigel! Obersturmbannführer Neigel! He sent my story to his beloved as though he had written it himself! Oy, an act of villainy unsurpassed on the face of the earth! Oy, I was wroth!") "Listen, Neigel!" screamed Wasserman, "that is plagiarism! The worst crime you could ever commit against me here! Ai." And he beat his chest and writhed on the floor, rasping, "Worse than death! You stole my story, Neigel, you stole my life!" And the German, standing at the cupboard, uncorks a new bottle of 87 proof, swallows without the use of a glass, wipes his mouth, and says, his back to Wasserman, "But I told you I was sorry! How many times do you want to hear it? I'm sorry! I'm sorry! Do you want me to go down on my knees? You have to believe me, I had no choice! Listen—" And he turns to the Jew doubled over on the floor and smiles obsequiously. "You can be proud of yourself, Scheherazade, because thanks to your story we are going to meet, Tina and I. You understand? She wrote to tell me to ask for leave right away and come to her. That's why I'm going tonight. That is—in a little while. She wrote that things have changed. It's been a long time since I heard anything like that from her. And all thanks to you, Scheherazade. Nu, now are you satisfied?"

(Wasserman: "Good Lord! Anshel Wasserman, conjugator of Nazi families! Now I understood. The notes Esau had been taking all along, the hints of difficulties, and that intimate incident he told me about, et! And I sustained his failing marriage!") Neigel raised Wasserman gently by the arms and set him down on the military cot. Wasserman turned away glowering. Neigel turned Wasserman's face around. He searched the Jew's swollen black eyes for a sign of forgiveness (Wasserman: "He leaned over me like Elijah over the son of the Shulamite!"), talking all the while. He reeked of drink, and spoke feverishly about his life with Christina since the war [*see under*: CATASTROPHE]. He said she knew precious little about his work, "and maybe she doesn't want to know either." He reminded Wasserman that from the time of their marriage until the middle of '39 Christina had "her own troubles trying to get pregnant and taking treatments, and I don't have to tell you what else. I think it was enough for her to know I was happy in the SS, that after so many years of odd jobs I finally had steady work in the movement and a good salary, too, and I would come home in the evening, yes, she didn't even join the party, she's a little like your Paula that way—it's funny, you know, I remember now that when I was young I always looked for girls like Paula, the kind with . . . you know what I mean—and Tina doesn't understand politics, no, the things that are going on these days, she doesn't understand . . . Once I stopped her just in time from mailing an admiring letter to a writer you may have heard of, Thomas Mann—I knew the name from our blacklist, can you believe it? In '41 she wanted to send him a letter, and he was in America, the traitor! Or sometimes she would go out wearing a woolen hat and scarf, both *red*! I mean this was late in '41, while we were spitting blood against Voroshilov's divisions in Leningrad! Luckily nobody suspected her, she isn't the talkative type, and she has no friends other than me, we're both loners. And then there was that business with Karl's fingers." "What business, Herr Neigel?" "He broke two fingers on his right hand and she put them in a splint, she's a nurse, you know; she set them in the shape of a 'V,' and for a whole month while I was at the front, I had a little Churchill walking around my house, you see what she does? Or the petunias." "The petunias, Herr Neigel?" "We have window boxes. Tina loves flowers. She can gaze at a single flower for hours at a time . . ." They looked at each other and, without wishing to, smiled. "Yes. Just like her. But after her visit here she began to do even stranger things: she threw out the brown petunias and planted yellow, pink, and red ones so my window boxes in Munich now sprout yellow, pink, and red blooms. She says it's just for color, but I know she's trying to remind me of the Jews and homos and Communists in the camp. That's her revenge, you see? Because when I asked her why, yes, why she had to go out wearing the red hat and scarf, why she was doing this to me, she told me without compunction that she had worn that hat and scarf the first time we went out together, to see a Charlie Chaplin picture. Tina loves comedy, and I love to hear her laugh. Anyway, she wore that Bolshevik getup in '41 because of that night! And she refused to give me her word never to do it again; she said it was getting pretty hard to keep up with the styles these days—and she wasn't talking about dresses, Wasserman—one day you're allowed to wear red and the next day you're not, one day it's all right to like Thomas Mann and the next day it's not, yes, now you know, and she's living alone with the children in Munich in a tiny apartment she rented for herself, and she refuses to talk to me. At most she allows me to visit the children for a few hours on my leave, but with her—nothing. One word about Tina to anyone and it would be all over for her!" Wasserman, derisively: "Why do you not do it, then?" Neigel looks down in silence. Wasserman nods in silence. "She told me," says Neigel at last, "that she's still living with me, but she means somebody else. The man I used to be, the one she wore the red scarf and hat for, and hung a picture of Chaplin in the bedroom for, can you believe it?—Chaplin, after that film he made about the Führer! She hasn't changed her hairstyle in years, and God knows hairstyles have changed since Adolf came to power, and next to her bed she keeps stacks of books I can't imagine how she ever found, by writers whose names I'm not even allowed to pronounce out loud, and when I look at her I feel a kind of shock, Wasserman, because she's frozen her life, yes, even the expression on her face is different from everyone else's. Hers is a slow expression, if you know what I mean. She lives and looks exactly the way she did in 1930 when I joined the movement. My wife is unfaithful to me—with me. What do you say about that?" Wasserman didn't answer. He wondered how flowers can sometimes go on blooming under a blanket of snow. Neigel kept talking. He couldn't seem to stop himself anymore. (Wasserman: "Like an inexperienced drinker dizzy with his first taste of the intoxicating power of words!") "And it isn't like she's a Communist or anything. Not at all. She's a woman, she has no political convictions. She doesn't read the newspaper or understand what's going on, but she's afraid of crowds, and she's afraid of violence, very sensitive, you understand, she's—" He laughed awkwardly, and for a moment appeared so foolish and helpless Wasserman had to wince. "And you brought a woman like that here?" he asked. Neigel: "It was all a mistake. Sheer stupidity. It was supposed to be a surprise, you see, they brought the officers' wives out here for a visit last year before Christmas. We had no idea they were coming, and they arrived just as the latest consignment of Jewish prisoners ran through the *Himmelstrasse*, blue with cold in the snow. Tina fainted before she had a chance to say anything, luckily for me. Two other women fainted, too, though. But after that, you can imagine, it was even more imperative to show them I was tough, so they wouldn't start talking behind my back." He stopped speaking and spread his fingers in a weak, defeated gesture. "You see, Herr Wasserman, never, not even in my letters, did I tell her exactly what my duties here were. I didn't want to bring her into—into all that. Not everyone can take it. And most German civilians don't know anything. It's better that way. All Tina knew was that I had some important post. She didn't know where. And in my letters home, I wrote only . . . love things . . . I write beautiful letters, Herr Wasserman, with a lot of feeling, almost like poetry sometimes. Actually it was Tina who gave me the idea of writing her a story in my letters. A few weeks ago, when I told her you'd arrived here, she started to cry. She cries so easily . . . like Otto . . . She said she was sorry about you. You're the only Jew whose name she knows who was going to die in the camp. That came as a shock to her, I guess. She also said exactly what she thinks of your writing. She's like that, Tina always says exactly what she thinks, that's her problem, there's no nonsense with her, yes, and when I tried to defend you, Herr Wasserman, she said that even the letters I used to write before I became a 'murderer' were better than your stories. And then suddenly I came up with this strange idea: I thought that if I wrote her a story, that is, a bedtime story for Karl, but something more than that, because since Karl is too young to understand it, maybe she would begin to understand—you see?" "See what? For God's sake, Neigel, stop beating about the bush." "Well, it's just that I can . . . that I can be a loyal, obedient party member and still be a human being." And he struck his fists together with sudden excitement. "Yes! That's what she has to realize! That's it!" He sighed, straightened himself up, and smoothed his sweat-stained uniform. Now he looked strong again and full of fighting spirit. "That's exactly what I'm going to tell her!" He glanced at his watch. Only a few moments to go. "Listen, Herr Wasserman," he said raptly, "you don't know the hell I live in. She won't let me touch her. She says I scare her. That there's death on my hands, and other female nonsense . . . She says she'll consider taking me back only if I leave everything here behind! *She'll* consider! Ha! She doesn't even know what she's saying! Like a child she wants the impossible! Me leave everything behind? Now? In the middle of a war? And what will I have left? But she says, 'Remember how much we had to suffer before we could bring Karl into the world? So much pain and SUFFERING [*q.v.*] for the life of one child, one child, while in your camp dozens of people every single day, you . . .' She has no idea how many people I really . . . every day . . ." (Wasserman: "The overgrown Nazi, the crude beast, he sits with me on the floor-boards, hollow as an empty sack, trying to persuade himself, trying to persuade her, begging her, so weak and foolish, so human, that I, nu, well, I am forced to admit, at such times he touched my callused heart.") Neigel: "Don't judge me, Herr Wasserman. Don't despise me. She and the children are more precious to me than anything in the world. I have no friends, I have no kin—" (Wasserman: "And now he's going to sing, 'Have mercy on me, Jews, I have no father and no mother!' ")

"And I'm not the type who makes friends easily. I'm happiest when I'm with her and the children. And maybe you won't believe this, but the kind of thing I have with you here, the way we talk, everything I told you and the story we made up together, that's new for me. No. Here and there in the army, at night sometimes, before a major battle, somebody'll come over and start talking to you, and you tell him things . . . never too much, because you can't trust anyone nowadays, or sometimes it happens on long train journeys . . . but then you never see them again . . . and I couldn't tell them about Tina, because they'd be sure to talk and she'd be taken away from me. But with you, Herr Wasserman, it's different. Yes." Wasserman: "And so you sent her my story, and never gave yourself away?" (It seemed Wasserman was finally grasping the significance of the situation. Perhaps what angered him was that Neigel had deprived him of his day of glory and "vindication" in Christina's eyes. Wasserman: "Dear Lord, if there were any way to kill me, Neigel had surely found it: he robbed me of my story!") Neigel confessed his crime again. He explained: On his return to camp he had written Tina a letter asking permission to send her a story, the final unwritten story of Scheherazade. "A debt of honor to a dead writer," he wrote slyly, with malicious cynicism, but—he said to Wasserman— "my intentions were good. It must be a great compliment to any writer that his stories have such a strong impact on reality, no?" Wasserman thought this over briefly. It was an appealing idea, but he still took care to look furious. Neigel had promised his wife the most beautiful and exciting episode yet, and in the same letter began to describe the aging children and their lives in the lepek mine. Wasserman: "And then I shifted the story!" "Yes. And then you changed it again, if I may remind you, and you drove me crazy, because I was totally dependent on you. But Tina wrote back that she liked the story, that she keeps my letter by her bed, on her stack of favorite books, you know the ones I mean. Yes, Herr Wasserman, this was my first letter from her in over a year with more than three lines about Karl and Lise. In her next letter she wrote something about my imagination, that it might be a source of hope for us both. I remember those words. She probably meant the way I kept changing the location." "What? Possible. Hmm. Yes." "And after that I wrote many more letters. Would you believe it? After you went to sleep, I'd sit in here a few hours more and write her a little about myself, a little about her, and a lot about the Children of the

Heart, which wasn't easy, believe me. I have no experience as a writer, though in Braunschweig we took a three-month course in military correspondence and I came through pretty well. But a story—that's different, and besides, the only books I ever read were Bible tales and the travels of the missionaries my father brought us when we were children, and Karl May, and your stories, of course, and here I was, all of a sudden, sitting down to write a story. No, Herr Wasserman, it wasn't easy! It would have been a lot easier to go out and do my regular work, but I held fast. I made a DECISION [q.v.]! Night after night I sat here and grappled with the story. And what made it all the harder is what I consider to be your main problem [sic!!!]—you have such a disorderly mind. You jump all over the place. It's pretty hard to write a book when you don't know how it ends, isn't it?" "Ah yes, Herr Neigel, I imagine it is." "But you know the ending already. For me it's almost unbearable, because in the midst of all my other problems in the camp, I have to deal with this wild, crazy thing which would probably be dangerously imaginative for someone weaker . . . Listen, you may laugh, but sometimes I couldn't fall asleep trying to imagine how you were going to continue the story [see under: CREATION]. I think that's when I began to feel, well, sort of like a writer." "I believe you did." "And don't forget that it was harder for me than it was for you, because I had to take everything you told me and change it around so that our censors wouldn't understand what was going on, you see? Because they read our letters. Yes, I found an ingenious system, Herr Wasserman. You'll be proud of me." (Wasserman bitterly: "Nu, finally a little naches.") "I wrote it in the form of a children's story, an innocent tale like 'Snow-White.' The facts were as you told them, minus the provocations, of course, but I wrote it in the style of your old stories, and I think I did pretty well, Herr Wasserman, because offhand you would probably say Camp Commander Neigel was amusing himself with a story-letter to his son, but anyone who read between the lines, like my Tina, would understand very well." "Splendid, Herr Neigel. Mr. Lofting also started his career with letters from the front to his son." "Lofting? Who's that?" "Doctor Doolittle." "Never heard of him. I was loyal to you, Herr Wasserman." (Wasserman: "And a lot of good it did me!") Neigel stretched, adjusted his uniform, and took another sip. He had recovered now. He was relieved. He looked calm. He had unburdened himself, and now he could continue as if nothing had happened. He asked Wasserman if he understood now why he couldn't bring a war with the Germans into the story. Wasserman feigned innocence and answered in the negative. Neigel grew furious again. His calm mood was shattered. Wasserman's writing, he explained, was distinctly seditious, and if such a letter were ever intercepted, Neigel would be promptly executed in no time. Wasserman suggested that the German write the story his own way, "now that you are a bona fide writer." This is where Neigel screamed, "BETRAYAL!" [*q.v.*] again. Wasserman, who could not hold back a smile, asked the furious German officer, "Do you really and truly believe that if I tell you the story of Kazik now, your wife will come back to you? This is not a fairy-tale world, you know . . ." And the German explained that it wasn't like that, it wasn't the story itself but the fact that he could tell a story that restored Christina's faith in him. He glanced at his watch and his eyes widened. Only five minutes left. He begged for a hint: "Just a few words, please, please, just the general drift of the story, so I'll have something to tell her when we meet today. You must help me, Herr Wasserman. It's urgent!" And the writer, stubbornly: "You are already in possession of everything you need to make her come back to you." "No! No!" Neigel shook his bull's head with horror. His eyes were bloodshot. "I can't tell her things like that! Not about their war with the Germans, not that!" "But why not? It will not go past the censor, will it?" "No. Listen, I can't say out loud those things you wrote. It would be a breach of my officer's oath, it would be . . . ach!" "And what of your oath as a human being?" demanded Wasserman, his lips pale, and his wispy beard standing on end. "What oath, Wasserman? Who swore any oath?" And the Jew, coolly and forcefully, pronounced the words: "RESPONSIBILITY [*q.v.*]! Your DECISION [*q.v.*]!" And Neigel: "Help me, Herr Wasserman, help me. My life is in your hands now. You, too, have a wife and child somewhere. You must understand me."

Wasserman turned to stone. Neigel's driver knocked on the door, and Neigel yelled for him to wait in the car. Wasserman spoke: "Listen please, Herr Neigel. Two and one-half months ago, seven and sixty days, to be exact, I arrived here unwillingly on the morning train with my wife and daughter. We stepped off on the station platform, and my little girl flew like an arrow to Officer Hoppfler's buffet. Chocolate was her heart's delight, even though Dr. Blumberg had ordained that it was bad for her teeth and that she must abstain." Neigel: "Get to the point,

Wasserman, my driver's waiting." "That is the point, Herr Neigel. The only one. You were standing there with the selfsame gun in your hand. My daughter ran to the buffet and reached for the chocolate. And then, nu, well, it happened, you see . . . you shot her. That is all, Herr Neigel." Neigel turned pale. His face gleamed unnaturally for a moment, as though a magnesium bulb had exploded inside him. He wobbled. He leaned against the cupboard. (Wasserman: "Only then did he begin to fear me. He understood what was in the balance.") Neigel groaned: "And you never said a word?" "What could I say?" The German gripped his knees and pressed them as hard as he could. His lips contracted with pain. Then he looked up. His eyes were red and scared. "Believe me, Wasserman," he said, "I love children." Outside, the engine was running. [*Editorial comment: Up till now the staff has found it difficult to decide* (see under: DECISION) *what kind of car to give Neigel. It was a choice between a black Hork convertible and a massive BMW, pride of Munich's Bayerische Motorenwerken plant. Actually the editorial staff feels inclined to choose* (see under: CHOICE) *a BMW as the epitome of power. The staff has never had the occasion to drive one, but the manufacturer's elegant brochure was enough to intoxicate even a cautious driver like the staff. The description it gives of the car makes you feel the pedal under your foot and the scream of tires as you gallop away on a wild and magnificent beast, and with the manufacturer's full guarantee and responsibility no less! Yes! The staff has therefore selected the BMW!*] Neigel and Wasserman now stood facing each other. Wasserman's beard bristled and his eyes flashed. "Now go home, Herr Neigel, and tell your wife my story. Tell her about Otto and Munin and Zeidman and Ginzburg and Hannah Zeitrin and Paula and Fried and Kazik. Tell her about them all, and about the simple chalk hearts drawn on the trees. And tell her about the only war there is. I think she will understand. Tell her frankly that it is a story for adults, a story for an ancient people, more ancient than any party, church, or state. Tell it well, Herr Neigel, for it is my tale, and I ask you to care for it and nurture it as you would a tender child in your keeping. Many hours lie before you on your journey home to see your wife, and while you are riding in your car and on the train, tell yourself the story over and over, till you know how to make her believe that it is really yours, that you have devised it deep in your heart, till it has the ring of truth, though it fails to conform to fact." Neigel was already at the door with his valise in hand. He turned heavily to Wasserman, with the look of a great lonely beast staring into the hunter's rifle. "And remember, Herr Neigel, there is only one way to tell the story as it should be told." "How?" asked Neigel voicelessly, and Anshel Wasserman, almost inaudibly: "By believing in it."

פרוטה, פילוסופיה ב–

PRUTA, PHILOSOPHIA BE

PENNY PHILOSOPHY

This is what Wasserman called Neigel's ramblings on the last few days before his LEAVE [*q.v.*]. It was surprising and even a little embarrassing to hear Neigel—a simple, uneducated man—suddenly involved in hollow, abstract reflections. Wasserman saw this as one more sign of his coming victory. Neigel frequently referred to the New Age that would follow the current Age of Blood and War. He even ventured to draw a clumsy comparison between his son Karl and the world (!): "When he's ill, the illness seems to be a springboard for a period of growth and development, and Germany, too, will soon experience a new spurt of progress, I am sure." Wasserman: "You mean at present you are ill?" "Perhaps, perhaps. But it's necessary, like a childhood disease. The German character is being tested. We have chosen to fight the germs that are trying to invade our body." "Thank you!" Neigel then became involved in a discussion of nature's hidden motives, and suggested that perhaps mass extermination of a certain human type is the fulfillment of nature's will. "Like the eliminative process, or something like that. It purges itself." He based his hypothesis on an irrelevant argument: "The world is resigned to this. So many people can't be wrong. I remember there were moments when I had some doubts, like five years ago, in November '38, while I took part in the burning of your synagogues and stores. Everything went up in flames. Everything, everything. We went wild, we killed people in the streets for no reason at all, without a trial or anything, without even bothering to cover our tracks. For weeks after that, I remember expecting something to happen, I don't know what, maybe for a hand to reach out of the sky and smack us in the face. But you know what? Not one church, Catholic or Protestant, made a sound. Not one bishop in all of Germany wore the yellow star in protest. We're simple folk, Wasserman, what were we supposed to think? That's why I tell you: It's the will of God and nature. The world is getting ready for the New Age." (Wasserman: "Esau is trying to knot two lockshen. He is split inside. All this prattle sounds like the wailing of a frightened child. Wait a moment, Neigel. You are lost.") And on the subject of the New Age, he told Neigel about "Duvidel, our king, whom God would not allow to build the second temple, because his hands were soiled with blood." Neigel: "Ha! You and your Jewish God!"

פרומתיאוס

PROMETHEUS

1. A figure of Greek mythology. A Titan. When Zeus punished man by confiscating fire, Prometheus stole it from the gods and gave it back to man. 2. What AARON MARCUS [*q.v.*] called the optical system built by Russian physicist SEMION YAPIMOWITZ SERGEI [*q.v.*].

The purpose of this system was never adequately explained. The inventor himself rarely spoke of it, and it is unlikely that anyone at the zoo would have been able to understand him if he had. Sergei said something vague about it to Otto, whose later discussions with Fried and Marcus gave rise to rather strange speculations. In a muddled, general sort of way, the three understood the system to be a means for stealing TIME [*q.v.*] based on a physically inexplicable phenomenon. Sergei's structure consisted of a space surrounded by a ring of 360 slender mirrors (half a meter high each), set up on the lawn in a perfect circle, each mirror reflecting the one facing it, which in turn reflected another mirror, etc. Thus the circle formed a space infinitely intersected by the perpetual "motion" of light. The principle behind this singular "motion," however, is unaccountable. It is almost certain that the inventor himself never really fathomed it from a scientific point of view. In any case, an unfamiliar dimension had clearly been created, which the inventor called "non-time." This non-time had an amazing effect on any object that entered its confines, an effect which Kazik witnessed when the lunatics [*see under*: LUNATICS, VOYAGE OF THE] found the strange mirrors gleaming in the moonlight like icy tombstones. Aaron Marcus tried to explain what the mirrors were for, but Kazik never fully understood. Then the apothecary gave a modest demonstration, a reconstruction of the one presented by the inventor himself more than two years before at the zoo. This same Sergei (Wasserman: "Registrar of the mysterious, amanuensis of the magical!") had plucked a fresh red rose, still covered with dew like the perspiration on a woman's lip. Now Marcus plucked a rose, then carefully set it in front of one of the mirrors, waited an instant for the mirror to catch the reflection, and then quickly drew back. The rose flashed in one mirror after another; it passed from mirror to mirror at tremendous speed, was projected first as a primary reflection, then as a secondary reflection, and then as the eidolon of a reflection, the reflection of an eidolon . . . There was no end to it: red roses of luminosity bisected each other, merged briefly in a red glow, then dimmed and died. The circle teemed with live red roses, and in the process everyone began to see how "the rose itself," that is, not the petals or stem or color or fragrance of any one particular rose but "the rose itself," before it took on form and color and fragrance, glowing and dimming in all the mirrors, burned inside them like a flame and bound them to the moist, red, imperial rose-essence—all this in less than an instant, before the rose returned once more to the first mirror, whence it began the journey to its essence, quivering, blushing, and heaving its petals, then fading away. Only then did the ARTISTS [*q.v.*] breathe again. Aaron Marcus showed Kazik the rose in his hand: it had wilted, its petals dropping off at the slightest touch. The stem, too, crumbled to pieces. The band stared at the mirror in dread. Kazik said, "But-it-was-dead-all-along."

Again they tried to make him understand. They told him that Sergei had tried to steal a few seconds of time to preserve in this glassy prison. Sergei, they guessed, had believed that for some reason a different variety of time, reverse time, collected within the circle of mirrors and extracted the "moisture" of ordinary time. Sergei had once told Otto feverishly that he was trying to eradicate both suffering and joy, "so people won't suffer so much." To make them more like sticks of furniture, like objects. This, apparently, is why he had tried to change the metaphysical status of human beings: to turn them into the only living creatures existing in the dimension of space but not time. One-dimensional beings, whose parts could be painlessly removed, just as one chair parts from another without sadness. A house crumbles without suffering. A torn page does not cry. He hoped this mysterious essence collecting in the circle—this non-time which caused reflected objects to shrivel and dissolve—would eventually be able to extract anything that interfered with one-dimensionality: memory, a sense of past and future, hopes, longings, ideals, experiences of pain and joy; in short, Sergei had tried to start a bizarre sort of revolution: to dethrone time and free all beings from what he once termed its "side effects." In order to succeed, he believed he had to "concentrate" and "improve" the Sergeian time dimension in the system. To this end he sat with his Prometheus for many months and repeated the experiment with roses, fresh apples, mice, pieces of his own flesh, photographs from newspapers and old albums, and notices which Otto had snatched at his peril from the ghetto walls, lists of Jews transported from the Umschlagplatz to die in Treblinka, love poems by Yorik Wilner ("A day hence/we will not meet; a week hence/we will not greet each other; a month hence/we will forget; and a year hence/we will no longer recognize each other; and tonight with a scream on a black river I almost raise the stone from the pit; hear me/save me; hear me/I love you; you hear me/I am too far away"). Sergei had likewise passed objects and bits of information of intimate personal value before the mirrors. Wasserman: "I called them 'unplumbed possessions,' like the big yellow leaf Sarah and I brought back from Paris, or Paula's beauty mark, or the secret I kept in my heart: how Sarah's right eyelid fluttered when we lay in each other's embrace . . . Nu. Herr Neigel, what token of this sort would you bring to our Sergei?" Neigel was taken aback. He coughed, thought, rubbed his cheek. Only two or three weeks before, Neigel would have scoffed at Wasserman's "softness." But times had changed, and now he told him of the time in his boyhood when his father had whittled the Zugspitze. He had worked at it every day for many months, and produced a magnificent piece of art. The night little Neigel lost his first tooth, his father had fastened it to one of the peaks of the wooden Zugspitze, and promised him that this would be an eternal bond between him and the mountain. Four years later, when they climbed the mountain together for the first time, Neigel slipped and almost fell into an abyss. By some miracle his trousers caught on a rock and he was saved. He and his father looked silently into each other's eyes and knew what had saved his life. That moment, the intense look that had passed between him and his father in their loneliness on the mountain peak, is what Neigel would bring to Sergei. The artists were asked to describe such moments on a piece of paper which the eccentric physicist then passed slowly before the mirrors till the words fell off the paper and crumbled lifelessly in a heap.

But Kazik did not understand this explanation either. "Time-time," he said. "What-is-this-time-you-talk-about," he snapped, and they realized that he was no more capable of understanding time than they were of understanding the blood flowing in their veins or the oxygen they breathed. Kazik looked at the artists surrounding him and asked which one of them was Sergei. An embarrassed silence ensued. Aaron Marcus told him gently that one night the scientist had come alone to the mirror system and presented his own body to one of the mirrors. No one knows what became of him, but it is conceivable that all the moisture of time was extracted from his body and soul. Toward dawn Otto had found Sergei's clothes and shoes on the lawn, together with a few broken mirrors. The artists were sure he was dead, but in the months that followed strange rumors began to reach the zoo: Sergei, or someone resembling him, had been spotted on Nizka Street in the northwestern section of the ghetto, leading a Waffen SS unit; then he— or his twin brother—was sighted in the uniform of the Polish police supervising the extermination of Jews in hiding at the Transway plant; then he—or his double—appeared in all the newspapers in photographs of the mass executions; they began to identify him even in pictures taken a few years back while he was still in Russia, only he was always somewhere else again, busy with murder of one variety or another. It seems he had gained control over the backward and forward flow of time, but could only fill a single role. A satisfactory explanation for all this has never been found.

Also see under: KAZIK, THE DEATH OF; THE SCREAM

צדק
ZEDEK
JUSTICE
See under: POWER

ציטרין, חנה
ZEITRIN, HANNAH
The most beautiful woman in the world. Artist of love.

When the band of lunatics [*see under*: LUNATICS, VOYAGE OF THE] reached Otto's pavilion, and Fried, Marcus, Zeidman, and Munin engaged in a lively dispute about the best way to teach Kazik "the principles of life," in Fried's words, and proposed reading aloud to him from the Old and New Testaments, or discoursing on the great philosophies, or playing him the most sublime music (Aaron Marcus recommended Beethoven's *Fidelio*), Otto said quietly, "He needs a woman," and at once suggested that they take the boy to Hannah Zeitrin. Hannah Zeitrin at this hour (0525) was keeping her nightly vigil in the winding lane by the carnivores. Hannah Zeitrin: "During the bombings in Warsaw, I lost my oldest son, Dolek." Wasserman: "And she was indeed the most beautiful woman in the world. And under her wrinkles and heavy kohl and the paint she smeared all over her face, and under the obscene pictures she drew on her body with pieces of charcoal and colored chalk, and the arrows adorning her arms and legs, some in ink she stole from Fried's desk drawer, some etched with a sharp knife that left white scars, arrows even a blind man could follow home, begging your pardon, under all these guises, our Hannah is very beautiful indeed." Hannah: "And my little one, Rochka, they took her just like that in April of '41." Wasserman: "She used to work at Somer's Café, where my Sarah and I went sometimes on special occasions—holidays, birthdays—and Hannah, nu, she smiled at you in a way that made your heart expand. She was friendly to everyone, a real baleboosteh with her tray full of cups, fortunate the eye that beheld her! Ah, like a dancer she moved as she whispered in your ear that the strudel, nebuch, is getting old, but if you wait a little, stingy Somer will finish frying the blintzes for his son's bar mitzvah and sell a few pieces at the café, you can trust him not to give away his hard work for nothing to the greedy guests . . ." Hannah: "And my husband, Yehuda-Efraim, was taken in the *Gross Aktion* of August '42. And I was left alone. Without parents or husband or children. My native village, Dinov, was razed at the beginning of the war. I had nothing left. Nothing. And a month later, just one month, I decided I didn't want to be half alive anymore, and I married Yisrael Lev Barkov. He was the baker at Somer's. He played the accordion and loved to sing Russian songs. Once, two years before, after he lost his wife and two sons, Nechemia and Ben-Zion, he told me that in spite of all that happened to him, this war and the Germans, he still loved life so much he wouldn't mind dying so long as life went on for good and for bad, so long as people like him continued to feel this joy in their hearts. And the lust for life. That's what he said to me, and I wanted him. He had a little girl left, Abigail. She was eight years old. And together we had a son. We called him . . . oh, never mind." Wasserman: "And this baby, too, was killed, in his sister's arms when she came home with him one night from the café, and a Polish sentry shot them both, for his own amusement . . . only a few moments before the curfew, nu well . . . All night long they lay on the pavement, the innocent children, and Hannah and Yisrael Barkov could not come down to get them . . . and that night 'the cup passed over unto her' and she received her punishment, our Hannah . . ." Hannah: "Barkov and I were like hungry animals that night. We gave birth to my son Dolek, and my Rochka, and then Nechemia, and Ben-Zion, and Abigail. And our last child. And Barkov lay with me again and again. And we scratched and bit each other till we bled. And we sweated buckets and drank buckets to have more and more moisture. And my womb was a giant funnel, a cornucopia. Seas and mountains and forests and land. And children flowed out of Barkov and me and filled the streets, and the ghetto, and all of Warsaw. And our passion knew no bounds. And our children were murdered outside. And we made new children. And then we heard shots outside again. So we made more children. And toward dawn we knew we could never stop. And then we felt everything move with us, the bed and the room and the house and the street. Everything rose and fell and writhed and sweated and groaned. And when dawn broke, all the world was with us, all the world was dancing our dance. People and trees and cats and stones. A dance. Even the sleepers did it in their dreams. Dreams. God was giving in. His terrible secret had been found out. That He can create only one thing. That He has doomed us to passion. To love this life. Love this life at any cost. Love without reason. And faith in life. And longing. A lowly craftsman. Deplorable. He stamped us with His only creation, He impressed it on our souls. He set it everywhere, in the trees and in the mountains. In the sea and in the wind. He spat it out of Himself like a curse. He made this world to unload His problems in. His guilt. His disease. And Yisrael Lev tore himself from me. He dragged himself to the window and threw himself out. And then I knew what I had to do. I did not go down to the street. Not the street. I stayed home. In front of the mirror. And I painted and adorned myself. All over. My body. And people came and talked to me. Words. They thought I was sick. They thought I was insane. They understood nothing. Only Otto. As soon as he saw me, Otto understood. I decided to be beautiful. So beautiful I would catch His eye, the hungry eye of God Almighty. His ever-searching eye. So He would see me as He sees the steppes. The jungles. The oceans. The Himalayas. So that He would see me." Otto: "I took her from the women's shelter, where I also went to look for fighters, and I was right. The caretaker told me secretly that before Hannah came to them, she had been wandering the streets for months, raped by Poles and Jews and everybody, but she laughed as if she didn't feel it, and luckily she didn't become pregnant because of anemia and malnutrition. And here in the zoo no one would dream of hurting her, except Mr. Munin, who sneaks up behind her from the bushes to watch, and performs his art in a quiet and inconspicuous way as she wanders naked all night long, in the heat and cold, up and down the paths near the carnivore cages, trying to seduce God, fighting her war with Him, and believe me, this was no easy war." Wasserman: "Ai, sometimes on a sultry evening we could feel Him struggling with Himself up there . . . The curtains of heaven seem to part, and He peeks out between them, shamed and trembling with excitement. Et! The whole universe was filled with His sweat and trembling then, and the blood in our veins burned and flowed, and above the seven firmaments, cloaked in cloudy raiment, we heard Him bang His hoary head against the wall and moan with pain." Marcus: "On nights like these, Mrs. Zeitrin tempts Him with all her charms. She slinks around the zoo, twirling the curls of her blond wig, shamelessly tinkling her feet. Yes, God in His heaven bellows like a bull. Arches like a mighty tomcat. The moon turns red, and the wind forgets to blow. No, the air is still, full of fragrant yellow pollen that befuddles the mind. The animals mate in a frenzy. Old animals reduced to skin and bones fall passionately upon each other. The dry trunks of trees felled in the bombings four years ago burgeon with red and purple flowers. The earth trembles: it flexes underfoot. And then our Hannah, loveliest of women, dances her dance, whirls with eyes shut, with a soft, enchanting smile upon her lips, her body dripping honey that leaves mysterious signs on the earth—love letters of a sort—and wherever she drips, thick bushes of lilac and jasmine grow, and He reads them, half-insane. And not only He, I fear . . ." Munin: "Ha ha! The saint who worships the Lord, blessed be He, with his evil inclination is of a higher order than the saint who worships the Holy One without the evil inclination, so we find in *The Chronicles of Jacob Josef*, and the Magid reinforces this: I created the evil inclination and I created the Torah as its spice, and the gist is the meat and not the spice, och!! On a night like this Mrs. Zeitrin is worth seven nights to me at least!" Marcus: "But by morning it is over. He does not surrender. He fights His inclination and masters it. We awaken exhausted, scattered through the zoo, on the lawn, in the gutter, inside the cages embracing fairy-tale creatures that flee at daybreak, and all around us on the ground are signs of destruction, the teethmarks of God: trees uprooted and split in two, dry twigs from magical, ephemeral spice bushes, rocks exploding under the terrible strain . . . and our Hannah? Nu yes. Mrs. Zeitrin is sound asleep, curled up like an innocent baby on a bale of hay, under a tree, oblivious to Otto, who covers her compassionately with his coat, while she dreams on about tomorrow night's war."

And it was Aaron Marcus—at Otto's request (nobody refuses Otto!)—who took Kazik, by then over twenty-five years old, and led him to the paths of the carnivores. The other ARTISTS [*q.v.*] followed in silence. It was almost daylight. Hannah had just finished her dance, and for one last moment the expression of longing and anticipation spread over her face, fluttered on her eyelids. For one last moment she listened: Would He come today? Aaron Marcus approached, a little embarrassed by the proximity of her gaily screaming nakedness. He touched her arm gently, and she trembled and froze. The little apothecary whispered that she could stop dancing now. He also said, "He has come, Mrs. Zeitrin. He has come for us all," which to some extent was true. Hannah did not open her eyes. She turned to Kazik, her red face framed by the yellow wig like a big sunflower. Kazik was dressed only in a diaper. A tiny man, fifty-one centimeters tall, according to Fried's estimate. Still, she did not open her eyes, but her lips moved and she asked aloud, "Is it He?" And Marcus nodded and she seemed to hear the retort of the light breeze and smiled. From a distance Munin whispered, "Nu—a-shockel, boy, run and thrust!" And Marcus said, "Do you smell him, madame?" And she smiled again as if asleep. The smell of Kazik wafted her way. The fresh, pungent smell of a wild and mighty passion. A passion that cannot be denied. Even Wasserman, lacking a sense of smell, sniffed a subtle something. "And I do not know, Herr Neigel, how Mrs. Zeitrin imagined God would look when He finally came to her, but I am certain that Kazik had the right smell." And Hannah Zeitrin whispered, "Come." A certain difficulty arises in describing what took place between them. The reader is invited to see under LOVE and also under SEX. Of course it is tempting to risk a "poetic" description at this point, such as: "What transpired between the couple seemed to melt all memory, all reason, and the powers of imagination into a single puddle." Nonsense! It would be safe to say that (1) For a moment it seemed the two had known each other all their lives. (2) For a moment they looked like total strangers who reviled their closeness to each other. But there is another detail: a grain of sand flew into Kazik's eye; he bent over and blinked, and when he opened his eyes again, he accidentally looked in the wrong direction. Hannah's eyes were still closed. Hannah and Kazik began to grope. A cloud blew over the moon, and they missed each other in the dark. According to Dr. Fried's calculations, they lost four months of love this way. When the moon came out again, they found each other. Now they had no choice but to strike out with all the anger and senselessness of their parting, and to delude themselves that their meeting again was a miracle; that it was not so arbitrary and dreary as their parting. The inevitable quarrel was loud and venomous and took twenty-seven minutes, which according to Fried's timetable represented a full year and a half. Kazik was suddenly angry that the other members of the band were gaping at Hannah in her nakedness. He ran up, waving his small fists to drive them away. Hannah suddenly laughed with strange delight. This angered and humiliated him. Six minutes. He returned to her, shrugging his shoulders. The passage of time had somewhat diminished his passion. Now he began to see her as she truly was—an ugly old woman. He blamed her for the wear and tear on her body, because there was no one else to blame. His body, too, was no longer as fresh and firm as it had been in his youth, and his misery over this also turned to malice toward her, because he had no one else. He desired her but was afraid she would not be the love his passion had conjured: he understood now that he would never be able to tell her the really important things. That the more he loved her, the more remote she would always be. A stranger. He thought, I am alone. Alone. Had she come to him then and held him in her arms, his faith in LOVE [q.v.] would have been restored, only Hannah, too, was caught up in the same bitter anguish, and inwardly bewailed her own LONELINESS [q.v.]. They had missed the chance to help each other and forgive. Kazik watched her hostilely. Hannah noticed the evil glint in his eye, and she drooped despairingly. Her hands fell to her sides. Her breasts hung long and limp and hollow. For some reason he was stirred, and he approached her and hugged her knees with his little arms. Then she began to sob. She trembled.

Her tears washed over her and erased the obscene pictures she had drawn, the arrows and the paint. Crying had exposed her, and it touched his heart. He vaguely sensed she was crying over him as well, about the love that was taken away before it was given. Hannah Zeitrin sat down on the damp ground, and Kazik stood between her legs and clung to her. At that moment her smell reached his nostrils. She felt it immediately. She stopped crying. The first stripe of dawn was visible in the sky, as if someone had opened a big box to look inside. Wasserman: "And the truth is, Herr Neigel, it would be difficult to describe what took place there between him and her in words . . . these things are better left unsaid . . . and I, I am not yet divested of modesty . . . and all the same I will tell you, because only I am left to tell the tale." And he described how Hannah Zeitrin picked Kazik up in her arms like a baby. She sniffed him like an animal, and closed her eyes with a pleasure both wild and slatternly, but also innocent. Then she took off his wet diaper and cast it far away. Slowly she began to run the little man over her body—Wasserman: "As though she were informing him of every hair and limb and sinew, and we could see clearly now that that which was meant to happen was indeed happening, that is . . . you see . . . in other words, his smitchick became erect as a little lulav, and he began to pant and sweat and turn red, and she, Mrs. Zeitrin, that is, kissed him with the kisses of her mouth on his eyes and lips, and then she kissed him all over his body, even 'there' she kissed him, shamelessly, and never did she open her eyes, she was so deeply in love, in a dream, for then she stood up her full height on the hard ground and set him down on a bale of hay, on her hunger-swollen belly, and Kazik, though he never studied in a cheder, knew what deeds were his to perform . . . Ai, how they were washed with streams of sweat, how they glimmered and shone in the moonlight, and were reflected in the two pairs of glasses worn by Mr. Yedidya Munin, who never stopped fiddling with himself and whispering obscenely, for then the woman spread her legs, ai, Herr Neigel, spread them wide and, with all the strength in her arms, thrust him 'there,' deep inside her." Munin: "Och!!!" Wasserman: "And we could hardly see him anymore, Herr Neigel! Only his tiny toes peeked out, tensing in convulsions, for then she began to give birth to him, in pleasure and travail, I know because I saw her face, which looked blissful and full of longing and subtle beauty, and there below was little Kazik, thrashing around, crashing against the fleshy ramparts of her thighs, till at last we heard a kind of moan. For the first time, Herr Neigel, I realized how great is the anguish in the small sound men and women alike make at such intimate times, moments of carnal joy . . . the moaning of despair, steeped in torment, the groaning of a secret intelligence, ejaculated in a spasm and instantly forgotten . . ." Fried: "And then it happened! That barbarous crime! Ach, the murderer!" Marcus: "Mrs. Zeitrin suddenly pulled out—nobody saw from where, maybe from her blond wig—a small and very sharp instrument, and began stabbing Kazik in the back with all her might, with all her hatred, again and again—" Hannah Zeitrin: "This is for love. And this is for hope. And this is for the joy of life. And this is for renewal. And this is for creation. And this is for the power to forget. And this is for faith. And this is for illusion. And this is for the damned optimism you implanted in us. And this is for—" Harotian: "I was the first to understand, and I jumped on her and pulled the knife out of her hand. She stabbed me here and here. No matter, it wasn't that bad. The important thing is, the little one was all right." Otto: "Poor woman, what have you done?" Malkiel Zeidman: "I! I! I feel myself again! What is happening here?!" Fried: "Kazik, my Kazik." Kazik cried very hard. Little jets of time spurted from his wounds. His back was a fountain. Otto asked Fried to hurry and dress the wounds, "so he won't run out." But by the time Fried tore his shirt off the branches on his body [see under: ECZEMA], the wounds had stopped flowing and were beginning to close. Otto held the little knife Hannah had hidden for many months in her yellow wig. Only then did the artists understand the strong silent woman's daring plot. Otto weighed the knife in his hand. He thought a moment and said, "Take it, Hannah. It's yours, after all." Fried: "Otto, are you mad?!" Otto: "We will not interfere with the work of a real artist, right, Albert?" Fried, stammering and choking: "But . . . choleria! She's dangerous! You saw for yourself!" Otto: "She's dangerous only to Him. And He is not one of us." He handed her the knife, and she, with the look of a suspicious animal, hid it quickly in her wig. The artists turned to leave, sad and devastated. Kazik sobbed a while longer, but he had already forgotten his pain. Yet strangely enough, he did not forget his passion for her. He kept turning around with the desire to go back to her. He gripped his penis and began to masturbate [see under: MASTURBATION]. He did not yet fully comprehend the extent of his loss.

צייר

ZAYAR

PAINTER

An artist who engages in painting.

Kazik's vocation in the years that followed his relationship with HAN-
NAH ZEITRIN [*q.v.*]. This chapter of his life comes strictly from the
imagination of Obersturmbannführer Neigel. There is no doubt that
what occurred during his LEAVE [*q.v.*] in Munich [*see under*: CATAS-
TROPHE] was a determining factor in this. Wasserman's guess is that
after losing both his conviction in his work and "mission," and the love
of his wife, or the hope of ever returning to her, Neigel began to pour
himself through the only narrow channel left open to him—the story.
Wasserman admits he was briefly alarmed by the "strange powers"
emanating from Neigel: "Who was a prophet to know that this pitiful
tale of mine would suddenly become a cornerstone of faith for this
poor goy? Oy, Anshel Wasserman, with your own hands you wrote a
Third Testament for Esau!" The two were sitting in Neigel's room, as
usual, though not quite as usual: Neigel carried the burden of weaving
the story: he spoke and smoked incessantly, and drank. His eyes were
very red, and his face shone with perspiration. His movements were
no longer controlled and measured; even his blinking was rapid and
nervous. He and Wasserman were searching for the ART [*q.v.*] best
suited for Kazik. Something to alleviate the terrible hunger he felt after
his discovery of LOVE [*q.v.*] and his discovery in consequence—and in
the consequence of the VOYAGE OF THE LUNATICS [*q.v.*]—of the
depth of his FEELINGS [*q.v.*], and the powers of grief and joy envel-
oping man. Something to help him, explained Neigel, to help him
recover quickly from the wounds of love and disillusionment. "To help
him change SUFFERING [*q.v.*] into CREATION [*q.v.*]," agreed Wasserman, adding that Kazik was now a little man in full potency who
loudly declared his love of life despite its bitterness. Life still seemed
to stretch ahead, secure and full of happiness and pleasure, for which
he was willing to pay the occasional price of pain. It was now 1030,
and Kazik was forty-seven years old. It was a beautiful clear blue morning, and Kazik's voice resounded. He talked a lot: about his "eternal
love," about his life and hopes for the future. There was something
metallic and forced about the way he tried to convince himself that life
is good and worthy of being lived. This new talkativeness was a bit

irritating, but perhaps it was his way of healing his wounds. Neigel, in any case, did not perceive these little contradictions in Kazik. He listened longingly, eager to believe. Wasserman therefore added a description of how even the old, disillusioned artists were tempted to believe Kazik, of how a wave of ecstasy caused Fried to sprout more fragrant foliage. Neigel nodded agreement. He poured himself another glass from the almost empty bottle. Wasserman waited for him to gulp the drink before admitting that he couldn't decide which métier to choose for Kazik to express his happiness. Neigel, Neigel of all people, was brimful of suggestions. Wasserman: "Esau sparkled with ideas. Not all of them would make a kosher shtreimel, but a new spirit evidently filled him." "A painter!" cried Neigel in a slurred voice, and tried his ideas out: "A silhouette painter? A painter of deserts? Oceans?" In a fever he unbuttoned his shirt. "He was, Herr Wasserman, a painter of the imagination!" Wasserman: "Please explain." And Neigel set his glass down, leaned back, put his feet up on the desk, and folded his hands behind his head. A smile appeared on his face. A smile the likes of which Wasserman had never seen: a smile of resignation to bad news. The smile when all is said and done. He explained to the Jewish writer that Kazik would be a painter who required neither brush nor easel. He would be able to paint without canvas. "Over there, Herr Wasserman, do you see?" Neigel smiled, pointing a finger. "To the east, please, between the bear cage and the leopard cage." ("Ah? What? Has he lost his mind?") "Do you see the woman lying on the path? Do you recognize her?" Wasserman, squinting suspiciously to the east, snarled with repugnance at the sight and smell of Neigel, but then, in a flash, he understood the German, and his eyes grew wide. ("Ai! It has happened! I have succeeded, do you hear me, Shleimeleh? *Shleimeleh?!*") And aloud he answered, "But of course, Herr Neigel, sir! She is the lovely Hannah Zeitrin, is she not? The most beautiful woman in all the world." And Neigel began to describe in a whisper how the sky over Hannah lying on the ground opened up and a cloud was rent by a bolt of lightning, and how Kazik used the power of his imagination to describe God's feet descending, first one and then the other, to stalk the earth, and then God lay with the most beautiful woman in the world, and she, Hannah, was so dizzy with love and passion that she completely forgot her hidden knife. She was attuned solely to His love agony and His need for her. And then Neigel took the astonished Wasserman to the mound near the bird cages, the site of Paula's grave, where she gave birth in joy and travail to her only child, the fetus of the scream, and he lived, and she lived, and Fried's eyes brimmed with love for the woman and the child, and when Neigel pronounced the words LOVE [*q.v.*] and "woman," words which on his lips are redolent with pleading and hopelessness, he began to talk a blue streak, as though he feared time would run out before he could express what had always been, all that he had "suspended," sent away "on a leave of absence," yes. "And now look north, my dear Herr Wasserman, and see Mr. Munin lying with the beautif—" But when Wasserman turned in the direction of Neigel's cloudy bloodshot eyes, he saw that the barracks door was open and on the threshold stood—who knows for how long—Sturmbann-führer STAUKEH [*q.v.*], his head shaven, his black hat in his hand, and the thread of a smile upon his lips. "Continue, please continue," he said gently, stealing into the barracks on cat paws. "Real *Thousand and One Nights* I've been hearing behind the door these few minutes, Herr Neigel." And because he had addressed Neigel by his civilian title and not his military rank, Wasserman bowed his head and joylessly congratulated himself on his victory.

It should also be noted that following the brief exchange between Neigel and Staukeh, surprisingly indifferent on Neigel's part, Staukeh took Neigel's revolver out of his holster and left two bullets in it, one for Neigel and the other for Wasserman. Before turning to leave, he expressed the hope that Neigel would at least do his honor-bound duty. But when the door closed behind Staukeh, Neigel said feverishly, "Let's continue. There's still time. He was a painter of the imagination, our Kazik, wasn't he? Let's continue."

Also see under: CARICATURIST

צעקה

ZEAKA

THE SCREAM

A loud cry of pain or grief, a plea for help, etc.

The Scream is the title of the complicated mechanism of soldered drainpipes erected in the empty pigsty, another experiment conducted by SERGEI [*q.v.*]. A scream was imprisoned in these tin drainpipes in August 1942. It drove most of the zoo inhabitants—who were a little loony to begin with—out of their minds. Marcus: "We couldn't follow the simplest thought to its conclusion in those days! That horrible noise upset our thinking, devoured our ideas! But Otto—ah, Otto—he would never agree to set it free from the maze. Our Otto is extremely zealous concerning the rights of his artists." Otto: "You'll get used to it." And they did, in fact, get used to it. They became so used to it that by and by they stopped hearing it altogether. Or rather, for one last time they noticed its existence, the night old Fried swore he would give meaning to Kazik's life [see under: PRAYER] when Kazik was very young. So very young. For a single moment after Fried had bravely resolved never to despair, the scream mounted till—for an instant—it became a piercing, defiant shriek. Otto, innocently asleep in his pavilion, smiled in a dream and said, "You hear, Fried? That's your scream, I believe. You have just been born." Kazik first encountered the scream during the VOYAGE OF THE LUNATICS [q.v.]. He did not understand what the assemblage of tin was doing in the empty cage, but everyone could see he was strangely agitated. His face twitched. Strong winds seemed to be blasting him. Again he tried to approach the cage—and again he was blasted. He ran away. He stopped and turned back, hesitant, suspicious. Something was evidently paining him. He tugged at Fried's sleeve and demanded an explanation. Aaron Marcus was the one who told him in his gentle way what the system was for. Sergei had used the pig cage (after the pigs had been killed in the bombings) to build this tin network of passages and meanders straight and angular, wavy and spiraling. Otto: "What, half the zoo budget I spent on that scrap tin and aluminum from the junkyards near the Vistula. Sergei said aluminum would work best, because it produces excellent echoes, and it wasn't cheap, believe me, but you don't waste things like that in wartime." Sergei had planned the maze in such a way that not only would the echo inside retain its volume, but after someone had screamed into the tubes, the sound grew louder and louder: it doubled its volume at a fantastic speed, it trebled it, and within a few seconds filled the entire system with screams and scream fragments and scream echoes, a thick, dense acoustic energy, highly charged and oscillating—according to the inventor at least—in the physical no-man's-land between sound and mass. Fried: "The poor screwball. Back home we call his type a 'pickholtz.' What a dolt!" Marcus: "But how intensely he talked to himself about the invention! He used to walk along lecturing himself, and if he happened to spot one of us, he disappeared! Now you see him, now you don't." Otto: "He had one sensitive eye that would fill with tears whenever you looked into it, and he would blush and stammer, poor man." Paula: "At least if we'd had some idea of what happened to him in the fifty years since we disbanded, maybe—who knows?—we might have been able to help him. But—not him. He kept to himself. Acted like a stranger. Like a real fonieh. A Russian. Or maybe, heaven forbid, an enemy?" Otto: "With me sometimes he talked. I don't know why me of all people. He used these scientific terms to explain the complicated phases of his ideas to me." Fried: "The vocal tension of the scream, that's what he was always going on about with poor Otto, and Otto would come to me later and ask what that tension was, but of course I didn't understand any of it either." Marcus: "It was only months after he performed that experiment with the mirrors [*see under*: PROMETHEUS] and disappeared that we began to understand, yes. He dreamed of a tremendous tension developing among the amplified shock waves of echoes multiplied a hundredfold, a thousandfold; nu, what do you think of that?" Sergei would walk around the zoo tracing scream waves refracting into each other with accruing inertia, infinite bifurcations of collisions and intersections smashing against the tin and aluminum walls, and returning thence to explode into little echoes of their own. Fried: "And the tension! Don't forget the vocal tension! Ach! What a pickholtz he was!" Otto: "And what about the hydrogen, have you forgotten? He insisted on introducing hydrogen into his system, because he said echoes run more smoothly in hydrogen . . . That was getting a little dangerous, but I let him do it anyhow." Munin: "And the splitting? All that talk about 'splitting,' I thought the strain might split an egg in there!" Marcus: "Nu yes. Afterward that, too, was clarified. The poor wretch talked about splitting. Yes, splitting the scream into acoustic energy and human anguish." And indeed, judging by the mad inventor's calculation sheets, discovered shortly after he himself had disappeared, Sergei believed the human scream consisted of two separate elements. Since it was impossible to increase the quantity of human anguish in a scream, he decided to concentrate his efforts on the infinite proliferation of its vocal energy. In this way, he hoped to allow that high-powered energy to carry human anguish like a super-engine. He predicted that the splitting would explode the drainpipes, the cage, and the entire zoo. Paula: "Jesus and Mary! All of Warsaw, too! 'This scream will go very far!' he said."

Kazik: "But why?" Marcus: "So that maybe, a thousand or two thousand years from now, someone will hear it out there in one of the distant worlds of a remote galaxy, someone in the universe will hear it and finally take notice, because maybe they have forgotten us . . . maybe they have been a little negligent . . ." Here again it should be noted that though the idea may sound entirely preposterous, it is nevertheless reminiscent of other ideas in human history, such as the view that the giant pyramids of the Mayas in Central America were constructed in order to draw the attention of dwellers in distant worlds. Sergei himself believed implicitly in the future outcome of his venture. Paula was surprised and frightened when he lurched out at her from the bushes one night, waving a pageful of spidery calculations, and begged her pardon in advance for any damage the experiment might inflict on the zoo. Paula: "Nu, and later when it was time for the experiment to start, you can imagine, child, we were all pretty historical ourselves." Kazik: "And-then-what-happened?"

It should be pointed out that Kazik had listened to the story in wide-eyed amazement. Though he understood very little of what was being said, he sensed that the ARTISTS [q.v.] were stifling sighs deep in their bosoms. One could see the vitiated radiance of YOUTH [q.v.] in his eyes. Kazik: "And-then-what-happened-then-what-happened?" Marcus: "Something terrible happened. The worst that could happen. One fine day Pan Professor Sergei finished building his maze, and we gathered around the cage and waited. We were filled with anticipation. This was, dear Kazik, what you might call a prodigy! After all, it wasn't every day somebody's dream came true! And the professor appeared from one of his hiding places, poor man, wearing a jacket—a bit worse for wear, it is true—which I had lent him, and a red rose in his lapel. For a moment he gazed at us with his usual timorous expression. Perhaps he was thinking he deserved a more discriminating audience, for God help us, we did look like derelicts . . ." Sergei stood up, stared into the air with his ears pricked, hoping to hear a fanfare, perhaps, and then shook himself, waved his hand dismissively, impatiently, pulled the metal lid off one of the tubes leading to the maze, and, with a little bow, invited Aaron Marcus to scream into the tube. Marcus was chosen because the learned apothecary had devoted all his energies for some years now to special research [see under: FEELINGS] which involved the classifying, tracing, and mapping of nuances in human feeling and the plotting of the voids in man's feeling atmosphere. Then, three months before the public demonstration of "the scream" was to take place, Sergei had shyly approached Marcus and asked for his assistance. Naturally he didn't tell him anything about the purpose behind the monstrous tin construction in the pig cage, and also refused to reveal any of his physico-mechanical secrets. He wanted one thing only: to make use of Aaron Marcus's monumental feeling skills for his experiment. Marcus: "Nu, yes, there's no need to go into that now; the main thing is that at the inventor's request I managed to locate the subtlest nuance, the purest octave of human anguish, the worst possible anguish, the cry of the naked soul, and to this I added, again at the good Sergei's request, a subtle note of defiance and a light ring of protest, and for weeks I walked around with the nuance resounding in me, rehearsing it, learning it in depth. The feeling was razor-sharp, the essence of the scream." In order to reach that rarefied sound, the artist of feeling had labored like a sculptor, chiseling away at the layers of stone that conceal the figure there. He used his mighty talent to locate and draw out the finest cord, the ultimate string, stretched tautly in all the artists surrounding him. Wasserman: "The string used by every man alive to loose his only arrow. After this, Marcus went into seclusion for several weeks to prepare himself like a musician."

Marcus: "And when the moment came at last, and Professor Sergei removed the stopper from the tube—what excitement, Kazik! How we trembled! I pressed my mouth to the opening—no! My heart I pressed to it! Nu, and then, I screamed."

"What-happened-then-what-happened?" asked Kazik, but Neigel asked with him, and the artists replied in an uproar. Fried: "What happened? It was terrible! My hair stood on end when I heard Marcus scream!" Paula: "A birch tree at the far end of the zoo fell—crash!—as though lightning had struck it! In the morning we found the pulp burned to ashes." Otto: "Rabbits sucked their fetuses back into the womb!" Munin: "And snakes flew out of their holes—pheww!" [*Editorial comment: None of the artists tells here of the anguish and despair they suffered personally on hearing the scream.*] Professor Sergei, any vestige of sanity seemingly shattered by the scream, hurriedly stopped the tube, and with wobbly knees and a trembling voice, he yelled at the artists to run for their lives and find shelter, though there was no shelter! Marcus: "Nu, and my scream started running through the tin maze.

Did I say run? It galloped! Did I say gallop? It flew!" Otto: "I hid behind my pavilion, and from there I could hear it running through the tubes." Marcus: "Crashing with all its might, colliding into its own echoes, screeching, exploding." Paula: "It was scary! My heart dipped down to my undies, pardon." Munin: "Whistling like an evil wind, Lilith flying out of hell! The Angel Rehatiel on wild horses!" Otto: "Everything, but everything began to shake, the cage, the zoo, the world." Wasserman, whispering: "The universe." The animals began to wail. The earth tremors frightened them, and they tucked their heads in and started to scream. Everyone ran and hid. Only the inventor himself, Sergei, remained standing by the screeching, howling drainpipe system, and, raising his hand high in the air, waving it like the conductor of a blind orchestra, with a terrible bitter smile on his face, he screamed, "More! More! Harder! Harder!" Wasserman was silent now and looked down. Neigel slyly enlisted Kazik to ask what happened next. Wasserman and the artists were silent. Kazik: "Why-aren't-you-telling-me-what-happened?" and Fried: "Don't be angry with us, Kazik. It isn't an easy thing to talk about." Marcus: "Indeed yes. What happened, you ask, amiable Kazik? What happened was that—" Paula: "Nothing happened. The scream rolled around in there and wouldn't stop screaming. There was no explosion, no disaster. Nothing at all." Marcus: "We can't even scream properly." Fried: "Yes, child. It's the same scream you hear now." Kazik: "But-I-hear-nothing." Paula: "No wonder. He was born into it, wasn't he?"

קאזיק, מותו של

KAZIK, MOTO SHEL
KAZIK, THE DEATH OF
Occurred at 1827 hours, at the age of sixty-four years and four months, according to Dr. Fried's calculations. Cause of death: SUICIDE [q.v.]. Contributing factor in the death of Obersturmbannführer Neigel.

Kazik's last years were ones of prolonged agony for him and his old friends. Neigel suffered unendurably when he heard this. Wasserman had been telling the story without any appreciable logic or trace of plot, without concern for the sacred unities of time and place. His characters moved constantly between the Warsaw zoo and the extermination camp. This highly regrettable lapse of control over his story seemed to pass unnoticed by Neigel, who never uttered a word of complaint. On the desk before him were his gun and the two bullets left by his adjutant Sturmbannführer STAUKEH [*q.v.*]. Neigel seemed unaware of the gun. All his attention was directed toward Kazik, only a few years before a boy with a passion for life [*see under*: PAINTER], who declared that even a life of suffering was preferable to non-life, and now an embittered old man [*see under*: TORTURE]. His life, as he saw it, was a web of injustice perpetrated against him through no fault of his own. He searched wearily, hatefully, for a way to unload a little of the anguish of his life and the fear of his approaching end. Kazik: "I-feel-bad-I-feel-bad-I-want-you-to-feel-bad-too." Otto, gently: "What do you want to happen to us, child?" And Kazik: "Don't-know-want-you-gone-want-you-in-cages-like-them." Fried: "But they're animals!" And the hideous little old man: "Want-want." Otto looked at him with sorrow, Fried with shock. The ARTISTS [*q.v.*] waited for Otto's verdict. No one had the strength to decide anything. All they asked was that Otto should burst this bad dream like a bubble. Yet they knew they had nothing save the dream. And Otto, calmly: "Help him, HAROTIAN [*q.v.*]." Fried screamed: "But, Otto!" and the director of the zoo: "We brought this child here and taught him things. We have a RESPONSIBILITY [*q.v.*] toward his ART [*q.v.*], and he'll do everything he has to do. That's the custom around here, Fried, as you know." And the doctor: "I'm afraid, Otto." And Otto: "Yes. So am I. Harotian, help him, please!" Harotian wanted to refuse, but in Otto's blue eyes was a look that barred refusal. And so Harotian was forced to do what he hated most of all, and with the help of the magic power Wasserman had endowed him with fifty years before in a small cave in his native village, he erected a big net cage around Otto Brig's artists. Neigel listened and groaned. He wanted to ask for something, for MERCY [*q.v.*] on the artists, but Wasserman would not be stopped: the story surged out of him. (Wasserman: "I will not deny that the story, with its unhappy ending, gushed out of me like a fountain, whereas to invent a pleasant happy ending for the Children of the Heart I would have had to spit blood, heaven forbid! A thousand agonies I endured in my time to contrive a lot of 'sounding brass and tinkling cymbals' and now, et, flowing like water! Terrible, frightening words danced on my tongue like seventy-seven little witches, enticing me: Come on, be bad, tell more, harden your heart like a stone, for you are only telling the truth, after all, ai, indeed so. A thousand and one times I lived and died before I learned that every horror is but a caricature of what we are already accustomed to, an exaggeration of the known and familiar . . . feh!") Kazik circled the cage a few times and looked at the artists imprisoned inside it. Then he walked away and disappeared in the zoo. Wasserman presented a rather tedious, childish description at this point of the things Kazik did in the zoo—of the wild animals he set free, of cases of cruel depredation that followed, of baby Tojnika staggering like a drunkard, his young tusks dripping red and a piece of deer flesh in his mouth . . . in brief: Wasserman was carried away, milking the situation for more than it was worth. Out of all this verbiage a single passage stands out in which he describes the zoo an hour later, when the wild animals were satiated and a viable balance of sorts had been restored: lively monkeys clustered around the artists' cage, chattering. Several of them removed the bars on the cage and stared in curiously. The rhinos began to munch the roses Paula had tended all her life. Two old elephants, Tojnika's parents, waddled by, fretfully measuring the ground with their trunks before setting their feet down. And the zoo with its empty cages, animals, and artists locked together, and the elderly baby scurrying hither and thither in the evening mist, seemed under the first stars like the stopover of an ancient caravan, wandering accursed from place to place, presenting the created world with the fantasies of its creator: people, dreams, animals, sky, tentative first drafts of a more successful creation; or else like a case of PLAGIARISM [q.v.] committed out of longing, strangled but—doubtless—inept, painfully slipshod, a colossal effort doomed to perpetual failure, banished forever to the universal junkyard, that gigantic amusement park of ideas and hopes that rust and fall apart and turn up again and again in the service of a new generation of children. And now Kazik reappeared out of the mist as a bowed old man, trailing ruffles of albino hair, farting incontinently, a real wreck. Wasserman looked at Fried, who was looking at Kazik. The doctor blamed himself for everything. He had spent so little time in the company of the child—he still called him the child—yet even in so brief a time he had managed to transmit the seeds of ruin. Fried: "Maybe not in what I said to him, and maybe not in what I did for him, because I tried so hard, but—" Marcus: "But the heaviest legacies of all are wordlessly transmitted, my good Albert. Those legacies beyond time . . . take less than a minute to transmit . . ." Munin: "God in heaven! Look at his face! It's all bloody!" Fried: "He's been wounded." Wasserman: "He has devoured prey." And Kazik: "You-there-don't be there." Otto gently: "But where do you want us to go, Kazik?" And Kazik: "Don't-be-there-maybe-I-eat-you," and Otto: "No. I fear not." And old Kazik: "I-ate-this-little-thing-with-long-ears-not-good-oh-no." He collapsed on the ground by the cage groaning loudly. Kazik: "I-feel-bad-I-feel-bad-why-oh-why?" Wasserman: "What could we tell him, Herr Neigel? The forces of life and death were cruelly raging in his little body. Kazik banged his head against the fence and wept bitterly. Then he trudged this way and that, waving his hands, screeching, passing wind, defecating, urinating, pleading, ai, he found no rest." Suddenly Kazik stood still. His eyes were red and dim, and he panted like a dog. "Want-to-be-with-you," he said. Everyone looked at Otto. Otto nodded and Harotian tore an opening in the fence, a tiny opening that disappeared as soon as Kazik entered. The aged boy limped haltingly and stood among them. They gathered around him, giant demons, stone idols gnawed with sadness and disillusionment, silently watching the little creature they had dreamed, had fabricated out of their despair. At this point Wasserman paused, and Neigel asked how all this had come to be. "Where did we fail?" he asked, and Wasserman answered him gravely [*see under*: MIRACLE 3]. Kazik stood motionless and broke down all at once, as though his strength had given out. Feebly, voicelessly, he told them again that he felt bad, and asked them to suffer, too. This was the last thing on his mind, which was rapidly losing its grip on everything else. (Munin chuckled bitterly: "He's sharing all he has with us. A Communist maybe?") Growing more and more decrepit before their eyes, he chanted, "Bad-you-feel-bad," and Otto, Otto who was seemingly obliged to pursue this revolting experiment to the bitter end, as though swallowing the last drop of medication against the disease of his faith in man, even now Otto hid nothing: "We feel bad about many things, Kazik. Many things. For instance, we feel bad when we get old and sick." Zeidman, quietly: "And when we're beaten and starved." Marcus: "And humiliated." Hannah Zeitrin: "And when our hopes are taken away. And when they're restored." Harotian: "And when we're deprived of our illusions." Fried: "And when we're alone and when we're together." Paula: "And when we're killed." Wasserman: "Or when we stay alive." Marcus: "And we feel bad when we do evil." Zeidman: "And we're so fragile." Munin: "Yes, it's true. One little toothache and life is not worth living." Fried: "If someone we love dies, we are never really happy again." Marcus: "Our happiness depends on such perfection . . ." "*Bitte*, Herr Wasserman," asked Neigel suddenly, taking Wasserman's hand (Wasserman: "There was no death in his hand. It was a human hand. Five warm fingers, moist with fear, perhaps. Fingers which have touched tears, the tears of the child he was, and the mouth of a baby, and even, indeed yes, the thighs of a woman"). "It is not a miracle we need," whispered Wasserman, his face close to Neigel's, "but the touch of a living person, to gaze at the blue of his eyes and taste the salt of his tears." And Neigel, whose face was by then distorted, every muscle dancing in convulsive effort, begged Wasserman not to let the Children of the Heart die. Not to let Kazik kill them. Wasserman, smiling wearily: "They will not die. You know them better than that by now, do you not? They are all made of the same imperishable stuff. They are artists, Herr Neigel. Partisans . . ." Neigel nodded slowly. His eyes were glazed and distant. "Tell me about him. About his death, Scheherazade. Quickly."

Wasserman described how Kazik collapsed on the ground. He could no longer bear his life. He asked Otto to help him see the world in which he had lived. The untasted life beyond the fence. At a nod from Otto, Harotian tore an opening in the cage bars. Instead of the zoo, the opening revealed a view of Neigel's camp. [*Editorial comment: No wonder. The camp had always been waiting there.*] Kazik saw the high, gloomy watchtowers and the electrified barbed-wire fences, and the train station which leads nowhere but to death. And he smelled the smell of human flesh burned by human beings, heard the screaming and snorting of a prisoner hanged all night long by his feet, and the tortured groans of one Obersturmbannführer Neigel, who was imprisoned with him. Wasserman told him—his voice utterly monotonous—how in his first days at work cremating bodies in the camp, his overseers had found that women burn best, especially fat women, so they instructed the gravediggers to put fat women at the bottom of the pile. This saves a lot of fuel, Wasserman explained. Kazik's eyes grew wide. A tear burst through so fiercely that it made his eye bleed. He muttered something, and Fried leaned over to hear him better. Then the doctor stood up with a look of horror. "He wants to die, Otto. Now. His strength is gone." Fried looked at his watch: according to his calculations, Kazik had another two hours and thirty-three minutes to complete his life cycle. But it seemed that even this brief span was more than he could bear. Fried implored him, "Wait a little, Kazik. It's only a short while. Wait. Maybe you'll get stronger. Maybe you'll pull through. It's just a phase. Please." He felt the banality of his words and the wretched lie in them, and was silent. Otto shook his head. "If he wants to die, Albert," he said slowly, "we'll help." Fried covered his face with his hands and made a strange sound. The artists turned away. Then Fried bent over and lifted Kazik in his arms. The little body emitted the stench of rotting. Crooked yellow teeth dropped out of his mouth with every movement. Fried, his body's foliage smelling like fresh rosemary, carried Kazik in his arms to the big lawn. Two tear-stained eyes gleamed briefly out of the thick bush. The old doctor bent over and gently laid Kazik inside the circle of mirrors [*see under*: PROMETHEUS] erected by the Russian physicist SERGEI [*q.v.*]. The doctor seemed intent on going in after him, but Otto sensed this in time and dragged him out by the sleeve. Fried turned to him and said angrily, "Let me go, let me go! We're the guilty ones!" But Otto held on tightly, till the doctor calmed down. Kazik was left alone. Then a small storm broke out among the mirrors. Kazik expanded and contracted. He was sucked into time and belched forth again: he was finding it difficult indeed to be digested by vanishing existence. His image flashed and faded from mirror to mirror. The infinite possibilities of his fate were reflected there. Later Otto was willing to swear that some of the side mirrors had created a kind of underground—fast variations of indescribable beauty. But the major movement of reflection caught only his deterioration and demise. A few of the mirrors cracked and shattered with the overwhelming effort. Perhaps they, too, had a limited capacity for containing the dark matter of mankind. The artists stood motionless and watched. Approaching death had roused the same feeling in most of them: it was the right thing. And all of life is a free ticket, but in the end we are returned against our will to the domain of some invisible force, grave and inevitable, which collects its rightful debt, without MERCY [*q.v.*] or solace. To all of them, suddenly life, their own lives, seemed wrong and dreary and senseless [*see under*: LIFE, THE MEANING OF], and even those who weren't religious felt a sudden awe of God, while unfamiliar thoughts of sins committed and punishments deserved ran through their minds. Only Aaron Marcus thought sadly that perhaps death was as arbitrary and inexplicable as life itself. And now, as soon as the old boy disappeared for the last time, the 360 mirrors collapsed in quick succession, like wilted flower petals hit by a gust of wind.

Wasserman: "Yes, Shleimeleh, this is what I told him in the late hours of that fateful night. And when I had finished, dawn was opening its eyes. A few minutes later, Neigel left me. When he shot the bullet into his head, I walked out of the room, because a man has a right to die in privacy. And then the shot reverberated, and I heard the barracks door open quietly, and Staukeh coughed politely and stepped in."

קטסטרופה
CATASTROPHE
CATASTROPHE

A sudden disaster. Unforeseeable tribulation.

What Neigel called that which transpired during his final LEAVE [*q.v.*] in Munich with his family. He departed on a forty-eight-hour leave but returned a day later. Wasserman: "I was working in my lovely garden, enjoying the first sprouts—I never realized I had the talents of a tiller of the soil—when suddenly Neigel returned, his face the face of disaster. It looked as if death had climbed in through the windows. I saw him, and my heart turned to stone, this silly, Chelm-like fancy in my mind: His wife, I thought to myself, did not like my tale, and she threw him out! Ai, at that moment I was like an author with a rejected manuscript . . . Dear God, I said softly, it is true what they say, that when you bury a shlimazel the spade breaks! Ai, I sobbed, anything, dear God, but not this, because what have I besides the story in this life?"

The story of this miserable "leave" only became known to Wasserman two days later, until which time Neigel avoided him. He stayed in the barracks all day, and toward evening, when Wasserman came in, Neigel went out to make his rounds of the camp and vent his anger on the guards. They did not meet the second day, either. Wasserman heard furious screaming from the barracks throughout the day as staff officers went in and out with scowling faces. And then, on the second day, at 2300, when Wasserman was already resting on his sack in the attic and Neigel below had just finished giving hell to a young officer requesting special leave, Wasserman heard Neigel call his name. Wasserman: "I was filled with dread! My knees began to knock!" Wasserman hurried down the ladder ("Young Samuel never ran so promptly to Eli the

Priest!") and stood before Neigel. The officer's face was ashen, and according to Wasserman, he looked "like the living marker of his own grave." Neigel instructed him to sit down, cleared his throat, and said harshly: "There is no more story, *Scheissemeister*! Not for Christina!" And when Wasserman remained silent, Neigel explained in the same tone, "She's left me. For good."

The Jew's eyes opened wide in amazement. A question he didn't dare to ask darted through them. Neigel answered it: "No. Not because of another man. Because of me. I told you already. Because of what I was." And suddenly the mask of toughness cracks, his face contorts in pain, in disbelief, and he screams from the depths of his wounded soul, "Ach, Wasserman, everything's kaput!"

Wasserman, with gentleness, not lacking in a certain tension: "Did she discover your lie?" Neigel: "You could say so, yes." Wasserman, like a playwright whose drama has been ruined by poor acting, burst out in anger: "You should have tried harder, Herr Neigel! I asked you distinctly to love my story and care for it as though it were your own child! Ai, Neigel, you slayed me . . ." He wrung his hands in despair; he rolled his eyes heavenward and pulled at his beard. He was beside himself with grief. The thread that bound him to life seemed suddenly to have snapped. He looked feeble all of a sudden, and as imaginary as his characters. Inwardly he blamed his negligible talents, but he blamed Neigel as well: he suspected him of allowing German sentimentality to "saturate every letter." "No!" he roared suddenly, like a wounded animal, "a story like this must not become sentimental, Herr Neigel! You should have prevented that! It is a story of preposterous characters, about their agonies and their absurd and futile efforts . . . why oh why must you exaggerate so?" The German stared at him for a moment, then waved his hand weakly. "No, you don't understand. I told her your story as it should be told. Exactly as it should be told." "So? Then where did you go wrong?" "That's where," answered Neigel, the echo of a bitter chuckle rising to his lips. "Imagine it, Wasserman, imagine me taking the morning train from Warsaw to Berlin. A first-class carriage, me and three other SS brass hats . . . and two Polish government officials. We sit together for a couple of hours, smoking, talking about work, about the Führer, about the war, and here I am, talking to them, and talking to myself inside all the time. Going over what you told me: Fried, Paula, and little Kazik, and the hearts drawn on the trees, and that raving beauty who belongs to God, exactly the way you told me [*see under*: PLAGIARISM]. I even came up with my own lunatic to add to the story [*see under*: RICHTER]. Ah, you piece of *dreck*, you sly piece of *dreck*, she left me. A terrible thing has happened. I made a mistake. But I had no choice. It just happened. There was no way to stop it. What kind of people are we, Wasserman?" Wasserman, disgusted with this whining and carrying on, cut Neigel short with cruel impatience: "Am I to understand, Herr Neigel, that you no longer require my story?" Silence. And then Neigel raised his defeated eyes and said, "You . . . son of a bitch. You know very well I need the story. What else have I got, tell me." (Wasserman: "Ai! Now my cheeks burned like fire. How his compliment made me blush, the first time a German swore at me like a human being. Now I was no longer '*dreck*' or '*dreck Jude*' in that German tone of disgust, but a 'son of a bitch,' in the language of human beings! Ah, well, nu, it was as if he had pinned a medal on my chest! I was even prouder than I was the first time he called me Herr Wasserman!") Then Neigel began to tell the story of his arrival in Berlin, where he attended a boring meeting, and from there—straight to Munich. His train pulled in at 1700, and Christina was waiting for him at the station. For the first time since the separation she had come to meet him, and she even let him kiss her. (Neigel: "A woman's mouth, Wasserman. You know, I starved here for a year. One whole year without touching a woman, Polish, Jewish, one of ours, or otherwise. And believe me, I had plenty of opportunities, but I remained faithful to her, yes," he screamed bitterly, and pounded his chest with a fist that could stun a bull. "Here, with you, lives a man in the shackles of a faithful husband! Faithful I tell you!") Christina suggested that they walk home, past the Wittelsbach fountains, and Neigel agreed. They walked through the bombed streets, past the big recruiting posters of the Wehrmacht, past young invalids wandering the streets with lackluster eyes, and they talked about the almost-new dress Tina had bought at the clearance sale of a factory that went bankrupt, and about a dream Tina had dreamed, and about Marlene Dietrich, and about— Neigel: "It was strange, because we didn't talk about the war at all. Nothing. All the ruins, and those poor invalids, it was like some strange mistake, an illusion. Everything else was a mistake, only she and I were real. We were life. And I listened to her. As always, she was talkative, and I loved to listen. And it was even nicer this time, because with her talking I forgot everything I didn't want to remember." Wasserman: "Like me, Herr Neigel?" Neigel smiled crookedly again. "You won't believe me, Wasserman, but I didn't forget you. While Tina talked I thought to myself sometimes, This I'll remember to tell him. So he'll see what Tina is like. Yes. You've become a kind of habit with me, Wasserman, damn it." (Wasserman: "Some friend!!") Then, on their way past the Hofgarten (Neigel: "That's where she and I . . . nu, the first time, many years ago"), they gave in to fatigue and took the #55 bus home. Neigel: "And there the children were waiting for me at the neighbor's, and both of them climbed all over me, Liselotte saying words like 'Pappi,' 'Karl,' 'Mutti,' and Karl telling me about his kindergarten, and asking what I brought him, and Tina told them to shut their eyes, and pushed the presents she had bought for them into my hands, and I gave Karl a wooden car and Lise a doll that opens and shuts her eyes and says 'Mutti,' and then Tina whispered, Let's go home, she said 'home' and glanced at me sideways, blushing, she always blushes, and we went home, very excited." There's no need for a full description of the meeting here. Most of it will be familiar enough: supper was simple but festive. Neigel had brought real blood sausage his driver found for him on the black market in Warsaw, and Tina got a little tipsy on a quarter of a glass of the wine they had opened on their wedding day in '28 which they drank only on very special occasions. Then they sent the children to bed. Tina went to do the dishes, and Neigel to wash up. When he finished, he took off his clothes, got into bed, and waited for her. (Wasserman: "To tell the truth, he embarrassed me! Into his bed he takes me! Here I was, like MALKIEL ZEIDMAN [*q.v.*], sticking my nose into the marriage bed!") Neigel looked at Wasserman, and said with a hesitant, apologetic smile, "And don't think I was always a big Don Juan, Wasserman, because I wasn't. The truth is, Christina was my first. There, now you know something even she doesn't know. I liked to let her think I had a lot of women before her, you see . . ." Wasserman mustered his strength to answer him with a feeble smile. (Wasserman: "Nu, well, et! My Sarah, too, my treasure . . . nu yes, she, too, did not know, and I dropped boastful hints from time to time, sparks of bravado . . . I was vague and omitted the details . . . Ai, how full the world is of wretches like me.") Later Tina came and sat on the edge of the bed, and rubbed a sweet-smelling cream on her hands, and Neigel swallowed her simple movements with his eyes, and Tina said,

If you don't mind, let's talk a little first, because I think we have a lot to say to each other, and Neigel, though he was "burning down there, really burning with . . . nu, you know, Wasserman," said, "Anything, anything you want." Because, he said, he understood that women are sometimes inhibited after an outburst of, well, passion. "And my Tina, though she was born in Bavaria, in matters like that has a 'Rhinish' personality, gentle and refined and very slow." Neigel listened to her tell all she had endured these past months, never speaking. She ran her finger over the sheet, very close to his body, and she unburdened herself. She told him about the shock she suffered that day in December when she visited his camp, and how she began to be afraid of him. "She was really afraid, Wasserman, and she hated me. And even our Karl, who looks so much like me, she sometimes, at certain moments, found it hard to love him as before, and she said she was sure I was doing it only because I believed it was my duty, and that I probably hated it, because at heart you're different, that's what she said, and of course I wanted to tell her about Otto's band then, and I also wanted to change the subject, because it wasn't easy to listen to her saying those things, but Tina held her finger to my mouth and said, Let me talk, I've been waiting a long time for this." And she told him that months before she had decided to divorce him, and after some debating, had gone to her parents in Augsburg and informed them of her decision, and "they disowned her, Wasserman, can you believe it? They told her to leave the house. Her father runs a laundry there and works for the army, and her mother belongs to the Augsburg Women's League, and when she told them, she saw how frightened they were. Yes, it was plain fear, as though she had a contagious disease. They simply threw her out of the house so she wouldn't infect them, and told her she was hurting a war hero and sabotaging the war effort . . . These were the best excuses they could come up with on the spur of the moment, and her mother ran after her in the street in her robe and whispered that she was no daughter of theirs, that they didn't want to see her or the children anymore, imagine, a woman with two small children, all alone, with no one to help. I always did everything at home, yes, I'm not ashamed of it. I liked to work around the house. And now everything fell on her shoulders. And you have to understand, she isn't a lousy Communist or anything and she knows nothing about politics," explains Neigel in alarm, his fingers twisting, "and she had nothing to hold on to, no religion or party, no slogans, not even a good friend to talk to; that's how she was, all alone, very quiet, she wouldn't have any part of the general excitement, this woman is stronger than any of us, I tell you."

And then Christina began to speak of his letters, his recent letters from the camp. She told him how she lay in bed at night after putting the children to sleep and read them, laughing under the sheets. "Do you understand what this means for me, Wasserman? I never made her laugh before, the best I could do was to take her to a Charlie Chaplin picture, and now she says, I read and I was moved, and I laughed and I cried, and I knew you weren't a murderer." She caressed his face (Wasserman: "Dear God, her delicate, fragile hand on that face") and said words of MERCY [*q.v.*] and LOVE [*q.v.*]; My love, she said, I know you're fighting a war inside, you who were always so gentle, only I know how gentle you really are, and how tender and loving you can be, and she began to cry, and tears flowed over her cheeks. A man like you, she said to him, who entered HELL [*q.v.*] and emerged victorious, and she didn't wipe her eyes but gazed at him through the tears, and he felt she was baptizing him a second time. Neigel: "The truth is that not everything she said was true, because in fact she knows nothing about me, about what happened during the first war, and later in the movement, and here, too, yes, because I didn't really come out of hell, no, I'm still in it pretty deep, with the stench of smoke and gas and with Staukeh after my butt for a long time now, and those idiot Ukrainians, and the trains coming and going all the time, at night, too, and you can't shut your eyes with all the noise here, and I can't tell anymore whether I'm running this camp or whether I'm a prisoner here, but when she talked to me through her tears, I forgot everything, I forgot the work and the Reich, and I was calm and quiet inside, and I wanted to believe that I had finished my war and that it was possible to erase everything and start things afresh—" Wasserman: "And while she spoke, Neigel forgot his hunger for her and embraced her mercifully like a tender chick, oy, how she clung to him, how calm her graceless face, when he began to answer her, to answer the only way he knew, with the only story he could tell her, about himself he could not say a word without feeling like a liar, he could not utter a single 'I' without protesting inside, and therefore he told her about Otto and his blue eyes and salt tears, and how some people came to look into his eyes and taste his tears, and he told her about Dr. Fried and his peculiar floral rash, and about poor Ilya Ginzburg, who wanted the truth . . . and he narrated my story in a quiet, simple voice, thoroughly civilian, and his Tina listened, her eyes misty, with the well-known look of a woman who is ready." Neigel: "And then I wanted her so badly I couldn't control myself anymore, but she put her hand in mine and said, A minute more, please. Let me look at you and remember you like this, yes. This is how you used to be. I think you've come back, Kurt. Welcome home. And suddenly she started to smile, and bent down to me, and I smelled her, and almost screamed, and she put her mouth to my ear and started to sing slowly, in a whisper, with a kind of smile, 'If we knew / What Adolf would do / When he ruled at the Brandenburg Gate,' and it only took me a second to understand that this wasn't a love song at all, that she was singing me a provocative-imperialist-Bolshevik-Communist-Jewish song from the early years, before they realized how much power he had, and my wife was singing this to me in bed! In my ear! I froze. I couldn't move. And she sensed it. She could always sense things. She stopped singing and froze alongside me. Her face was in my neck, and she didn't move. And for a moment we didn't dare breathe, because we knew what would happen when we moved. And we clung to the moment, and then she sat up and saw my face and was alarmed, and put her hand over her mouth, and in a weak voice, like a little girl's, she asked, 'You really do intend to stop it, Kurt, don't you? That's all over with for both of us, isn't it? You've come back, Kurt, haven't you come back?' And I felt it suddenly exploding inside me, everything, the war and my work, and all the confusion I've been feeling lately, and mostly—the fear, yes, the fear of what Tina wants from me, of what she dared to ask, what does she think, what does she understand anyway, what do I have besides my work and the movement, and what am I worth today without my job here . . . it would be the death sentence, sabotaging the war effort! It would be simple desertion and treachery, and this is what she was asking of me! And Tina understood what was going through my mind, and she stood up, and her face was full of fear, ach, Wasserman, her face showed the kind of fear I see around me all day here, that frightened *dreck Jude* expression which makes me want to vomit, the same expression you came in with the first time, and my own wife does this to me! And I don't know what happened, I went berserk, the fear in her face seemed like a provocation to me, like a curse, and her disappointment in me and the scorn I began to notice in her eyes, and you have to remember how hungry I was for a woman, and then I saw the blood in my eyes, everything turned red, I was suddenly on top of her, and I tore her robe off and, listen—I never felt such passion and hatred for a woman in my life, I was merciless, what a catastrophe, I went up and down on her like a hammer, and I screamed, I screamed in her ear the whole time, Spy! I screamed, Judas Iscariot! Bolshevik! Knife in the back of the Reich! I don't know why those words came out of my mouth all of a sudden, there was blood in my mouth, blood from her mouth, and her frozen face was under me, she didn't try to struggle, she just lay there like a little girl, with open eyes, looking at me blankly, and then I finished and got dressed right away, daggers in my heart because I hadn't wanted it to be like this, everything was ruined and I wanted to make amends, and I wanted her forgiveness, she has no one but me and the children, damn this war to hell, how did it get into our lives and our beds, but it was clear to me that it was all over. Some things are irreversible, you know, and I took my suitcase and walked out of the room, and I didn't have the nerve to go look at Karl and Lise, I had the feeling I wasn't allowed to see them anymore, that I might spoil something just by looking at them, and I left without a word, I walked through the Hauptbannhof, and waited all night on a bench for the first train, and when a soldier walked past and saluted and said Heil, I almost vomited—tell me more, Wasserman."

"Pardon?" Wasserman shook himself. The transition was too abrupt. But it seems Neigel had run out of patience—and maybe time—for the smooth transitions of a cultured conversation. "Tell me more, Wasserman," he whispered eagerly, his eyes ablaze. "More about Kazik, and about the woman Otto found for him [*see under*: ZEITRIN, HANNAH], and about the good life in store, and be careful, Wasserman, pay attention to everything he says and does, make him a human being, don't make him stupid, and don't let him do stupid things. Yes, make him Otto's most successful artist, only don't stop talking, Wasserman, because there's a terrible noise here and a terrible stench, and when I breathe, my breath smells of smoke, and when the train whistle blows in the station, I want to get up and run away, and I want the sentinels at the gate to shoot me; there were people here today and I yelled at them till I stopped hearing the whistle, but now I'm alone, don't leave

me alone tonight, tell me the story, you and the story are all I have,
what a catastrophe."

קריקטוריסט

CARICATURIST

CARICATURIST

One who draws caricatures.

The profession Wasserman chose for Kazik after STAUKEH [*q.v.*]
invaded the barracks and "suggested" that Neigel choose an honorable
death. Staukeh went outside to wait for the shot, but Neigel was in no
hurry to kill himself: it would not have occurred to him to do so before
Wasserman had finished the story. Wasserman could not believe his
ears, but Neigel, in a voice both pleading and anxious, reminded him
where the story had been interrupted. "Kazik was a painter. He helped
the other artists realize their dreams. He always found the good in
everyone. He was happy." "Miserable," Wasserman corrected him
gravely. "He was extremely miserable." Neigel looked at him suspiciously, blinking madly. "But he must be happy, Herr Wasserman!"
"Must?" "He must! He must!" whispered Neigel, smiling obsequiously,
desperately, indicating the door by which Staukeh had left. "A last
favor, Herr Wasserman, Kazik was happy. His life, though brief, had
meaning, right? *Bitte*, Herr Wasserman." (Wasserman: "I looked at this
wreck of a man. I cannot deny that I did not hate him. The moment
he shot Tirzaleh before my eyes, my hatred died. My fury, my fear, my
loathing, even my love grew dim. Only words remained, empty, broken
words, and in their shells I nest like the last bird, a fugitive of a great
disaster. A holocaust. Three months of life, the sloughed skin of an
empty body. Extracting gold teeth from the dead, marking time in the
shithouse. Like the living dead . . .") "Listen, Herr Neigel, I have no
desire to hurt you, but the truth must be told: Kazik was miserable.
He was sullen and ill-tempered, and he had no one to comfort him.
None of the paintings he painted from his fertile imagination brought
him relief. And more bitter yet, the other artists found it no easier,
because from the moment each of them observed how he became the
dream of his art, and how he subdued his fate of suffering, a different
verdict erupted from within, more terrible than its predecessor, like an
open wound threatening to swallow him; ai, Kazik exposed us in our
nakedness, and he could not stop, and whenever his glance rested on

one of us, he saw before him a miserable monstrosity with dreams and passions like thick horns upon his brow . . . how the gaze of the aged boy mercilessly drank up the dark moisture of our souls! With what contempt he drew out our ideas and favorite words and the meager wisdom we had gathered so arduously over the years . . . feh, all the boats that took us to the edge of the horizon so our eyes could behold new, forbidden horizons, yes, indeed so, our Kazik became a cruel caricaturist . . . in a rage he drew the artists, he drew them without affection. And they, poor wretches, beheld themselves in his eyes and saw themselves as ugly tools, and tears flowed from every eye, tears of grief . . .

"And now," continues Wasserman, "as they wept, a kind of MIR-ACLE [*q.v.*] took place, and, as I recall, Herr Neigel, it was the little apothecary, Aaron Marcus, who tried to comfort us then, and told us about the ugly Princess Maria from Tolstoy's *War and Peace*, who became beautiful only when she cried, like a Japanese lantern which loses its charm when the candle goes out but shines forth in all its beauty when the candle is lit again. You see, Herr Neigel, poor Kazik could no longer understand these fine things. Ugliness filled his eyes . . . he no longer knew how to forgive . . . he became estranged from life, like poor Midas: whatsoever he touched sparkled with the gleam of malice. Yes, Herr Neigel, Kazik was miserable: miserable, miserable, miserable."

רגשות

REGASHOT

FEELINGS

A subjective inner experience.

In an attempt to learn more about this experience, Aaron Marcus, the apothecary of Warsaw, conducted various experiments, the results of which, needless to say, are equally subjective and rule out the pos-sibility of drawing objective general conclusions.

An autodidact who had taught himself six languages (including Ar-abic and Spanish), Aaron Marcus was a music lover and copied scores for the Warsaw Opera House in his spare time. He also engaged—within bounds—in the study of alchemy. Out of the group of people Otto brought to the zoo beginning in 1940, Aaron Marcus was un-doubtedly the most highly educated, as well as the most congenial. A

widower, the father of one child (Hezkel, Bella's husband), for forty-
five years he had been married to an embittered shrew whose grumbling
wizened her into strange proportions. He adored her, though, and
rarely spoke ill of her, while she constantly mocked his ineptness in
money matters, disparaged his impractical scholarliness, and conspired
against the alchemical equipment he accumulated in the apothecary
shop. Marcus, born in a small town in Galicia, was the first apothecary
in Warsaw to make and sell natural remedies (he himself was a vegetarian
for reasons of conscience). He was a sensitive man, refined in appearance
and fastidiously dressed. Before the war he always wore a carnation in
his lapel. (There was a little clip sewn into the lapel which held a few
drops of water for the flower.) After his wife's death in 1930, he sold
his shop and moved to a small apartment in the Zoliboz quarter. He
gave his alchemical equipment away (charts, lists, "Mary's crucible" for
the preparation of sulfur water, or "divine water," as it was called by
the alchemists) to a Rosicrucian friend. At this time—and his personal
motives for this are unknown—the retired apothecary began to conduct
exhaustive experiments in the realm of human feelings. He commenced
by drafting a chart of all known human feelings, breaking them down
into categories, sifting out the synonymous feelings, dividing the list
into feelings of the "mind" and feelings of the "heart," "primary feelings"
and "secondary feelings," and then began to scrutinize himself and a
few of his close friends with the aim of isolating the most "active"
feelings in the human psyche. Wasserman: "Would you have imagined
it possible, Herr Neigel, that we human beings, the crown of creation,
make use of only twenty or thirty feelings in our entire life span? And
in a regular and intensive way—ten or fifteen at most?" Neigel: "For
me that's plenty. I wish I had even fewer feelings. Listen, our instructors
at military school were right: feelings are a civilian luxury. For softies.
Two or three feelings would definitely be enough for me right now."
Wasserman: "For you, perhaps. But our Aaron Marcus rebelled against
this hard-and-fast impoverishment . . . he longed to clear a way for
himself into unknown territories, the abracadabra realms we feel inside
which nobody dares to touch; oy, Herr Neigel, can you imagine what
a shock it would be to our foundations if Marcus had succeeded in
publishing his discovery of a single human feeling? A new one? Can
you imagine how many great unnamed and formless things we would
instantly discover within ourselves to fill the new vessel and become a

vital part of ourselves? What a primeval revolution! This with only one feeling, but just think— Two? Three?" "Hitler invented one," answers Neigel, and explains, "Hitler gave us something new. Joy. Yes. The real joy of strength. I myself used to feel it, not so long ago. Before you began to poison me. Real joy, Wasserman, without any phony qualms of CONSCIENCE [*q.v.*], without regret, the joy of hating, yes, Wasserman, the joy of hating whomever you're supposed to hate. These are things nobody before him ever dared to say out loud." Wasserman: "Hmm, Herr Neigel, that is true, certainly. Only, you are wrong about one thing: do not say he 'invented' it but, rather, 'exposed' or 'bared' it. And look what it gave rise to. A boundless energy took on a name and an ideology, armaments and armies and laws and legislation, and a new fictitious history all its own! Only I must tell you, Herr Neigel, I suspect that if the little apothecary had discovered such a feeling, he would have kept it locked in his heart. Even so, in his own modest way, his achievements were truly remarkable."

Aaron Marcus, a quiet, peaceful man (Wasserman: "Whose very heart was perhaps the philosopher's stone he searched for all his life to change base metal into gold"), became a dangerous and determined fighter when he declared open war on the limitations of human feeling. It was clear to him from the start that the fault lay in language: that people were trained to feel only what they could name. That if they ever experienced a powerful new feeling, they would not know what to do with it and would either repress it or wrongfully assign it to an already familiar feeling with a designation of its own. And in this way—through laziness and negligence and fear as well, perhaps, they would deprive it of its original significance. Marcus: "And its beckoning call, its demands. Its subtleties of pleasure and its dangers." And since he was also a linguist, he knew that people who speak only one language are unfamiliar with certain nuances of feeling well known to speakers of other languages. [*Editorial comment: By way of explanation, the relatively new Hebrew word "frustration" provides an example. This word did not appear in the Hebrew vocabulary till the mid-seventies, and in fact, before it was absorbed into the language, people who spoke only Hebrew were never "frustrated." They may have been "angry" or "disappointed," or they may have experienced a sense of turmoil in certain situations, but the acute feeling of frustration itself was unknown to them until the word for it was translated from the English language.*] The learned apothecary of Warsaw also claimed that due to our severely limited linguistic capabilities, we are forced every minute to "make do" with one feeling, or two at most—blended into a single pulpy word. As he saw it, it was as if "we were talking to each other and to ourselves in a monosyllabic language, a language of thin, flat, deceptive words, dumb guardians of a great treasure, a treasure teeming with tens and maybe hundreds of unnamed feelings, half-anonymous sensations, primeval impulses, sorrows, and delirious pleasures." Neigel, with a groan: "Let it stay like that. It's better like that." And Marcus: "No, no, dear amiable Herr Neigel, that is evasion, and perhaps even—cowardice, pardon me for saying so. For we have a RESPONSIBILITY [*q.v.*]!" The apothecary's actual experiments in the realm of feeling began as early as 1933. Wasserman ascertains: "On January 30 of the year 1933 of their calendar." He began by researching sadness. According to Wasserman, Marcus's notes from those days testify to the kind of sacrifice that was required of him. At first he believed he would be able to carry out his research at certain specified times. He still conceived of it as a curious hobby. But he quickly came to understand that the only way to do it was to live it. Wasserman: "To see this optimistic man grow more and more despondent; ai, ai, his soft, pleasant face in those days resembled a horse sinking slowly in the swamp. He saddened himself to death, if one may say such a thing, in order to explore the dark cave from the inside, to open channels clogged with disuse and give them new names." Accordingly, Marcus began to develop his "Sentimo," a new language of feeling, "full of goodwill, if a little primitive," to quote Wasserman. It was an admixture of letters and numerals and secret codes, unintelligible to all but the apothecary. Wasserman: "Ai, Herr Neigel, how well I remember his difficult days on the journey to sadness, his descent into fear between 1935 and 1938, and the eleven months he spent submerged in every shade of humiliation, from November 1938 until September 1939, during which time he conducted additional experiments, much as a writer embarking upon a great novel will jot down little bastards of the pen, professional scourings, ai, this same frightening descent into the pit of helplessness, nu well, and the time he risked his life dropping into the abyss of revulsion, where he found—who would have believed it?—no less than seventeen shades of feeling between revulsion and disgust."

The direction of the apothecary's research began to change, it seems, around February of 1940, when OTTO BRIG [*q.v.*] met him for the first time in the streets of the ghetto, licking the boots of two Waffen SS men. Otto remembers that. Otto: "He smiled, I tell you, under their very noses, as happy as if he'd just stolen a peach from the priest's garden! So I knew, of course, that he was for us!" Otto paid much money to release him from the two SS men who had humiliated him, and took him to the zoo. On the way there, Marcus explained the essence of his experiments to Otto, and the meaning of his beatific smile while being so abused became clear now as well. "There's no time," he told Otto. "And I want to enjoy myself in the few remaining months, and so, now—happiness." Wasserman supposed that in those gloomy days in the ghetto Aaron Marcus had wandered the streets, and using only his psychic powers managed to "balance the scales of suffering and happiness, because unless they are balanced, we are lost." It should be noted, however, that the apothecary was exposed to a great many dangers in the course of his experiments. Wasserman: "Like his tremulous, hasty journey into the feeling of compassion, nu well, and his almost irresponsible self-abandon there, Marcus my friend! And hope, yes, particularly in those times he wanted to explore hope . . . What terrible sufferings he endured! But he was not put off and made his way, step by step, through the hostile jungle of our sentimental life. Armed with the sense of introspection, a sense which became as fine as a butterfly's antenna and as sharp as a razor, Marcus cleared the way, separated the dense undergrowth into trunks, branches, twigs, fibers, and filaments, and gave them names, like the first man in the Garden of Eden, and I swear to you, Herr Neigel, I will never understand how he kept his sanity! His face, always fine and soft, the face of a tranquil baby, aged so! At first it darkened like a cauldron, and then it brightened again, and we saw what had happened: every experiment, it seems, every psychic immersion had left its mark on him, a trace, a scar. Ai, the fate of the lonely artist who has no one to share the dangers with, you understand; all alone, he was compelled to try out each new shade of sentiment before he would consider himself entitled to enter it on his list and give it a name." Marcus: "With great excitement I note the following: Between 'anxiety' and 'terror' I have discovered and classified by name another six shades of feeling, more or less acute, all of them definitely 'primary.'" Marcus's experiments did not end here: his daring brought him to the stage where he had no choice but to go further still. There was no turning back, nor did he even consider turning back. Wasserman: "He understood that he must now conduct deeper experiments, ever crueler, of a kind I shudder to recall even now, Herr Neigel, with seven shades of disgust, for he now began to devote his sacred time to breeding . . ." Aaron Marcus began to crossbreed feelings hitherto considered alien and even inimical to each other. The man who privately called himself "an astronomer of feeling," with modest conceit, attempted, for example, to breed anxiety with hope, or melancholy with longing; in this, it seems, he sought a way to implant every unpleasant, harmful, and destructive feeling with a seed of transcendence, of redemption. The most fascinating hybrid of all, in Wasserman's opinion, was the one the apothecary created in Otto's zoo, a combination of malicious pleasure and SUFFERING [*q.v.*]. Wasserman: "And now our Marcus worked in a frenzy . . . He wanted to modify malice, assuage it, touch it with wise, sweet, suffering microbes—who is wise enough to know the heart of an artist?" "Humph." "Ai, you should have seen him in those days, Herr Neigel, we were worried lest he should burst, heaven forbid, and be torn asunder, like that salamander called a chameleon they put on a colored carpet . . . like a singer, trying to sing two parts at once . . . but he was saved by the skin of his teeth and emerged always like a lion to record the secrets in his notebook. Can you imagine our zoo without Marcus? Who else could have screamed THE SCREAM [*q.v.*]?"

רחמים

RACHAMIM

MERCY

See under: COMPASSION

ריכטר

RICHTER

An all-but-anonymous Jewish boy, distinguished among the ARTISTS [*q.v.*] as Obersturmbannführer Neigel's contribution to the story. Richter's story was recounted to Wasserman during the urgent hours of the night that Neigel committed suicide [*see under*: KAZIK, THE DEATH OF] and can be described as lamentably lacking in suitable artistic treatment. The circumstances behind the story are as follows: Neigel, frightened and desperate, informs Wasserman that he has "something" for him, something he thought about on the train to Berlin, on his way home. The Jewish writer pricks up his ears. "On the train," says Neigel, "on the train I thought about it. Somebody new. For Otto, for the zoo, what do you think?" "At your command," answers Wasserman. Outside, in the distance, STAUKEH's [*q.v.*] melodious whistle can be heard, as he paces up and down waiting for the shots. He is running out of patience now, but he will not go in until Neigel shoots himself. "What do you think?" Neigel implores again. "He's a boy, let's say around twenty years old. And—you hear?—he extinguished the sun. Yes! The sun! So give me a name for him, Herr Wasserman, a good Jewish name, and speak a little louder, I can't hear you all of a sudden. What did you say? Richter? Fine. Let it be Richter, then. Write that down. I want it down in writing. He has to be in this story, and remember, he's mine. If you ever tell anyone the story again, say I made him up, all right? What are you asking? I can't hear you. The whistle's blowing again. The night train has arrived. What can he do? Oh-ho!!" laughs Neigel too loudly, "oh-ho!! The things that boy can do! Write it down, Scheherazade, write it down word for word. He came from one of your ghettos—Lodz, for instance—and he saw things there. There was an *Aktion*, you know what an *Aktion* is, Herr Wasserman? An *Aktion* is—never mind. Forget it. You needn't know. Go on living in your fairy-tale world, yes, because an *Aktion* is by no means something pleasant or easy, it's—" And he whistles through his teeth, perhaps to illustrate the unpleasantness of an *Aktion*, or perhaps to drown out the Ukrainians whistling on the platform. "—And he saw things there, and he started looking into the sun, yes! Directly into the sun that witnesses everything and never does anything, never extinguishes itself or burns the world. And he looked directly at the light—this is what I made up on the train to Berlin. The idea came to me as I was leaving the barracks; at first it was cruel, like your artists, men to the right, women to the left! Children and old people to the *Lazarett*, where you will be given a little injection by Dr. Staukeh, an injection against the typhus epidemic now rampant in the East, and he looks directly into the sun, and his eyes burn, and all the time he cries and his lids swell and fill with pus, but he promised, he swore to do it, strip! Everyone strip! Don't be ashamed! You have exactly what your neighbor has! And a few days later the sun began to yield to him, really, maybe they didn't notice it at the Berlin observatory, but what a difference it made. The sun began to withdraw, now out! *Schnell!* For delousing! These were Richter's hardest days, because suddenly he was afraid—run, *dreck Jude*, run—afraid of the injustice of taking the sun away, but he was a real artist, and so he continued to look into it directly, until it went out—the first fifty march, into the chamber! Silence! This is only for delousing! And it was utterly, utterly dark," groans Neigel, rolling his maniacal red eyes, flapping his arms and asking Wasserman what he thought of his contribution to the story. "Wonderful," answered the Jew. "Now you continue from here," said Neigel, and Wasserman turned the page of his empty notebook and was about to read from it when suddenly he heard Dr. Fried telling Otto that the "contribution," Richter, does not really suit the original concept of the Children of the Heart, it lacks depth, and is, in fact, pretty raw. And then Wasserman heard Otto quietly and resolutely answer the doctor that he accepts young Richter into his zoo mostly out of MERCY [*q.v.*]. Because— Otto: "Even when we seek the greatest and purest humanitarian motives, Albert, we must never for a single moment forget to have mercy, because otherwise we're no better than 'they' are, may their names be blotted out."

שטאוקה

STAUKEH

Sturmbannführer Siegfried Staukeh, born in Düsseldorf. Neigel's adjutant. The medical consensus shortly before he succeeded in committing suicide was that Staukeh had a pathological, sadistic personality. According to his doctors, he was an extremely intelligent man, thoroughly lacking in CONSCIENCE [*q.v.*], and they could find no reason for what they called his "extraordinary suicidal bent": there is no scientific explanation why such a cruel man, a merciless killer in his last days at the camp, should shortly thereafter change into a terrified wreck. The sequence of events that led to Staukeh's promotion to the position of commander of the extermination camp was as follows: For ten months he was Neigel's adjutant, and from the very first moment, he directed all his efforts at replacing the "dumb Bavarian," to use his words. Only, it seemed that his intrigues were unsuccessful: Neigel performed his job to perfection, and it is well known that Reichsführer Himmler himself strongly favored him. This was the situation until

September of 1943, when Neigel set Wasserman up in his barracks as House Jew. Staukeh saw this amiss, and even told Neigel that "House Jews" don't live in their master's quarters," but Neigel dismissed him in a rage. Later, a little here, a little there, the signs increased: at first Staukeh was surprised (he was considered well educated because he was a doctor) to hear certain peculiar questions from his commander. This began with a strange interrogation about diseases. Neigel said something about a sick old aunt of his, but Staukeh knew at once that Neigel was lying. ("People like him don't lie very well. You can spot the arteries swelling on their foreheads right away. They know only the truth. That's why they're so boring"—Staukeh in a newspaper interview in 1946.) Later Neigel's driver told him about the mysterious trip to the Borislav region, a trip Neigel had kept secret. Staukeh made some phone calls, located the officer who accompanied Neigel around Borislav, and heard some astounding things from him about his commander. It seems Neigel had become a collector of an archaic product known as lepek and was spreading strange rumors about opening an oil well in the vicinity of his camp, as an additional hard-labor installation for the prisoners. Staukeh raised an eyebrow and whistled a tune from *The Gypsy Baron*. That same day Neigel summoned him to his barracks and asked him, by the by, several questions about migratory foxes and hibernating rabbits, laughing awkwardly. "It's for my little one, for Karl. Suddenly he's interested in these things." And finally, there was that humiliating episode with the *dreck Jude* who grabbed a rifle and started shooting the guards on the Heavenly Way. Everyone saw it, Neigel's soft, hesitating manner of responding [*see under*: REBELLION]. Staukeh began to listen more attentively to strange rumors among the Ukrainian sentinels about Neigel's unusual relations with his House Jew after working hours. Dagusa, the Ukrainian guard posted outside the commander's barracks, revealed—under the influence of a single bottle of schnapps—that he heard laughter and other sounds "like a bedtime story, you understand, Commander," coming out of the barracks. And around this time everyone began to notice Neigel's deterioration. His appearance became more and more unkempt, he was prone to stormy moods, had furious bouts with his officers, and severely punished German enlisted men over trifles; in short, Staukeh kept his eyes open. On the day Neigel departed on LEAVE [*q.v.*] to Munich, a special emissary arrived at the camp, asking to speak with the "utmost discretion" to

Staukeh. The emissary was an elderly Standartenführer from Censorship, who spread out photographs of seven letters in the unmistakable handwriting of the commander of the camp. Staukeh read and almost burst out laughing: who would have believed a poet lurked in that thick block of meat, Neigel? Staukeh read about the band of old lunatics, about hearts drawn on trees, about a man who tried to cross the frontiers between people and translate their love, and about another one, who tried to breed new feelings. All this was ridiculous, so silly and absurd that Staukeh was able to convince the censor that it was not the secret writing of a spy but the childish scribblings of an officer "whose nerves are a little strained." Staukeh asked the man not to take measures, because it might damage camp morale, which had been low in any case since "the commander began having his attacks." When the censor left, Staukeh hurried to Neigel's barracks, and met the little *dreck Jude*, as anticipated, working in the garden. (Staukeh: "Working? It was more like sabotage, what he was doing to the merciful Polish soil!") He tried to interrogate him slyly about his relationship with Neigel, but the no-less-sly Jew evaded his questions. This convinced Staukeh that some "very unholy alliance" had been formed between the two [*see under*: SUSPICION]. Staukeh was finally rewarded the night he burst into the barracks in the middle of Neigel's description of Kazik's imaginary paintings [*see under*: PAINTER]. Staukeh unloaded Neigel's gun (he offered no resistance) and left him two bullets: one for himself and one for the Jew. Then he went to wait outside. He had to wait a long time, too long for his taste—almost a whole hour—before he heard the shot. And only one shot. That was strange. He took out his gun and went into the barracks. Neigel lay dead on the floor. Staukeh began to search feverishly for the Jew. He was afraid Wasserman had shot Neigel and was now armed and hiding in the other room. Wasserman entered from the kitchen and looked at Neigel lying there. Staukeh approached Wasserman and shot him in the head. (Wasserman: "Nu, well, I hoped that now at least I would die. Because what did I have left to live for now? Staukeh, ringworm on his bald head, held his pearl-handled gun . . . A dandy is our Staukeh. And he did not shut his eyes when he fired the bullet at my head as poor Neigel had always done. Into me he looked. I felt the buzzing in my head and suddenly remembered that Staukeh likes music. There was even a gramophone in his room, and he could whistle entire operas from memory. Feh! Why should I remember that? But because I remembered, I kept the matter in my heart.") On the military map, behind Wasserman's head, there was a big ugly hole. Staukeh stared at it in amazement. Then he looked at Wasserman, turned his head this way and that with his strong fingers in search of the bullet hole. At length he said, "So it's true what they say about you? Hoppfler said you don't know how to die, and everyone laughed at him. So it's true." Wasserman: "To my regret, it is indeed true." Staukeh laughed, with obvious embarrassment. "Very well, then," he said at last. "And what's the name of this extraordinary phenomenon?"

The writer wished to reply but suddenly remembered something else the buzzing had whispered to him. For a moment his eyes grew wide with astonishment, but though he was unwilling, the spell was stronger than he was, and he replied like one possessed: "Anshel Wasserman, Commander, but I was once called Scheherazade." Staukeh furrowed his brow. "Schere-? Damn it, where do I know your name from, Wasserman?" Wasserman underwent a small series of mysterious convulsions. A fierce war seemed to be raging inside him. He was arguing with someone. He protested. He screamed: "Enough! I have no strength! Not again! And why music all of a sudden? What does music have to do with—and how will I tell a new story? A new story all over again?" But the invisible partner in the controversy was by far the stronger, and the old Jew, in his gorgeous gown, drooped listlessly and answered, "Rimsky-Korsakov, sir, is the one who wrote the fine musical composition by the name of *Scheherazade*, but if I may be so presumptuous, that is, yes, I used to write musical riddles for the children's radio program in Berlin . . . perhaps you remember? Every Wednesday afternoon? I am he." And he fell silent, alarmed by the words that had escaped his mouth, signaling to the representative of the editorial staff that he does not understand what's going on, or why he has to tell these lies. But the representative looked the other way at Staukeh, Sturmbannführer Staukeh, whose face suddenly turned red, and a spark shot through his eyes like a firecracker, and a deeper breath than usual filled his lungs; in short, Staukeh was excited. But very soon he managed to subdue his excitement. Very soon the old expression of venomous scorn covered his face. "The writer of musical riddles, you say? Perhaps sometime when I'm very bored you can come tire me out with that nonsense. I, too, know a little about music. But listen: you're moving into my place. You'll be my House Jew. My gardener, Scheherazade. My petunias have been looking quite miserable lately." Wasserman, defeated, with infinite weariness: "And radishes, too, you shall have, Commander."

תיעוד

TIUD

DOCUMENTATION

A system facilitating the storage and identification of various types of information.

"No," said Ayala, "that won't help you, you'll fail. This whole encyclopedia business is utterly worthless. It doesn't explain anything. Look at it: you know what it reminds me of? A mass grave. That's what it reminds me of. A grave with limbs sticking out in every direction. All disjointed. But not only that, Shlomik. It's also a documentation of your crimes against humanity. And now that you've gotten this far, I hope you see that you've failed, that your whole encyclopedia is not enough to fully encompass a single day or even a single moment of human life. And now, if you want me to forgive you, if you want to save yourself so that at least part of this disaster will be canceled and forgotten, write me a new story. A good story. A beautiful story. Yes, yes, I know your limitations: I don't expect a happy ending from you. But promise me that at least you'll write 'with MERCY [q.v.], with LOVE [q.v.]! Not *See under: Love*, Shlomik! Go love! Love!"

תפילה

TEFILLA

PRAYER

A universal religious phenomenon, a silent or vocalized appeal to the Divinity.

Fried said his prayer at 2205, an hour after Otto brought Kazik to him the first time. The boy, who was then six, had just fallen asleep, exhausted, apparently, from his feverish activity. Fried, also tired, sat down beside him on the carpet. Fried: "Bozhe moi, he's six already. I wasted so much time before I realized what was going on." And inwardly he made a DECISION [q.v.] to fight. For the first time in his adult life he made up his mind to fight. And it may seem a strange thing to say about the doctor, who was always so belligerent, but it was not so: Wasserman testifies that all his life the doctor had been waiting for some decisive battle, some act he could throw himself into with all his might and main, which would yield some sort of meaning to his hitherto purposeless life. This was the reason, incidentally, why the doctor had been such an easy and indifferent victim in every struggle or conflict he had ever encountered. There was nothing he considered worth fighting over. There was nothing he could point to decisively as bad or good. All men's deeds seemed to him—in the final analysis—totally insignificant. Even when they were aimed against him, he couldn't find enough outrage inside himself to protest. This is why he had earned the reputation of an arrogant misanthrope. He knew he wasn't really like that, but he realized too late that he had lost the opportunity to avenge his empty years. The realization came when Paula moved in with him. The doctor discovered, much to his alarm, that all his life had been a BIOGRAPHY [*q.v.*] he could not even consider his own. It was the fruit of a prolonged mistake and weary negligence. So when the child Kazik was brought to him, after his first moments of hesitation, the doctor knew that he must fight, that this was his last chance. And he swore he would give the child asleep beside him the best of lives, and be the best of fathers, and the best of friends. That he would give the child what he had been deprived of. Otto, who was sleeping in his bed just then, smiled to himself: "I knew you would fight, Albert." And Marcus: "This was a most important moment, dear Fried, the moment you chose between observing and acting. Between force of habit and creativity." Fried: "I will fight. A life full of meaning [*see under*: LIFE, THE MEANING OF] is what I will give him. Few people achieve this in a longer life span than his!" And now, when Fried finished uttering these words, the ARTISTS [*q.v.*] throughout the zoo heard THE SCREAM [*q.v.*] trapped in the tin maze mounting for a long and unforgettable moment, and then turning into a short, piercing scream. Wasserman: "Perhaps it was shock, or perhaps compassion, or maybe it was a grotesque and vindictive burst of laughter, who knows?" But Otto in his bed whispered, "Did you hear that, Albert? That was your scream. You have just been born." Fried: "And little Kazik lay on his back, his hair sticking up in soft, bright tufts, and his face, ach, there was so much curiosity and courage there, and I prayed I would have the strength to make it through this night and tomorrow." And he looked at the child with mercy, in which there was already love, and blades of pain and pleasure tilled the clods of his old heart, and again, despite himself, despite his decisions and everything he knew about this world and the people in it and this life which is no life at all, again he sprouted fresh new buds of hope. He prayed. Marcus: "To be able to leave the passion for life intact on the boy's face, together with his wonderful confidence, as he lies on his back, open to everything, believing in everything." Fried: "And that I won't poison him with the hatred in me." Marcus: "And with everything I know." Otto: "That I'll let him grow up manly and brave and willing to believe." Fried: "And please don't let him be like me. Let him be like Paula." And Wasserman raised his eyes to Neigel and said, "All of us prayed for one thing: that he might end his life knowing nothing of war. Do you understand, Herr Neigel? We asked so little: for a man to live in this world from birth to death and know nothing of war."

July 1983–December 1984